ROUGHED

GOLD HOCKEY 10-12

ELISE FABER

ROUGHED
BY ELISE FABER
Newsletter sign-up

This is a work of fiction. Names, places, characters, and events are fictitious in every regard. Any similarities to actual events and persons, living or dead, are purely coincidental. Any trademarks, service marks, product names, or named features are assumed to be the property of their respective owners, and are used only for reference. There is no implied endorsement if any of these terms are used. Except for review purposes, the reproduction of this book in whole or part, electronically or mechanically, constitutes a copyright violation.

Charging

Gold Hockey #10

Gold Hockey Series

Gold Cast of Characters

Heroes and Heroines:

Brit Plantain (Blocked) — first female goalie in the NHL, loves boy bands

Stefan Barie (Blocked) — captain of the Gold

Sara Jetty (Backhand) — artist and figure skater

Mike Stewart (Backhand) —defenseman for the Gold, romance guru

Blane Hart (Boarding) — center for the Gold, number 22

Mandy Shallows (Boarding) — trainer and physical therapist

Max Montgomery (Benched) — defensemen for the Gold, giant nerd

Angelica Shallows (Benched) — engineer at RoboTech, also a giant nerd

Blue Anderson (Breakaway) — top forward in the league and for the Gold

Anna Hayes (Breakaway) — Max's former nanny, no relation to Kevin Hayes

Rebecca Stravokraus (Breakout) — Gold publicist, makes killer brownies, known at PR-Rebecca

Kevin Hayes (Breakout) — forward for the Gold, no relation to Anna Hayes

Rebecca Hallbright (Checked) — nutritionist for the Gold, plethora of delicious vegan recipes, known as Nutrionist-Rebecca

Gabe Carter (Checked) — doctor, head trainer for the Gold

Calle Stevens (Coasting) — assistant coach for the Gold, former national team member

Coop Armstrong (Coasting) — talented forward on the Gold, addicted to historical romance audiobooks

Mia Caldwell (Centered) — 5th degree black belt, brings the snark

Liam Williamson (Centered) — Gold forward finding his love for the game, charming and pushy in equal measures

Charlotte Harris (Charging) — new Gold GM, hates losing and the game Chubby Bunny

Logan Walker (Charging) — defensemen for the Gold, skills include: cockiness and being able to buy presents that make Charlotte squirm

Devon Scott (Block & Tackle) — former player, current owner Prestige Media group

Becca Scott (Block & Tackle) — Devon's assistant

Additional Characters:

Bernard — head coach

Richie — equipment manager

Dan Plantain — Brit's brother

Diane Barie — Stefan's mom

Pierre Barie — Stefan's dad, owner of the Gold

Spence — former goalie, married to Monique, daughter Mirabel

Monique — married to Spence, former model

Mirabel — daughter of Spence and Monique

Mitch — Sara's boss
Allison and Sean — Blane's parents
Pascal — Devon Scott's security lead
Roger Shallows — Mandy's dad
Grant and Megan — Devon's parents

ONE

CHARLOTTE

"**D**amn," she muttered, sitting down at her computer and slipping off her heels.

They'd lost.

Her first year as General Manager, and she hadn't been able to get the job done.

She made a show of checking her emails, of sending a few notes to their big sponsors and to the board, thanking them for their support of the team and for a good season, but in reality, all she could think was that she'd lost.

Fuck, she hated losing.

Had hated it from the first time she'd lost the Chubby Bunny contest when she'd been a Daisy at Girl Scout camp.

She *still* hated it.

Hell, she'd picked a career whose main focus was building an organization that could win as much as possible, *that's* how much she hated losing.

What she hated even more?

Being the only female GM in the league and losing in the second round of the playoffs.

God, was it too much to ask for the Cup, just one more time?

Probably.

She sighed. The Gold had won the previous season, and again two years before that. Two championships in four years was still a hell of a record.

It just . . . wasn't *her* record.

"Fuck," she muttered, shutting down her computer. She'd left the locker room long ago, after thanking the players for their hard work, letting them know she was so proud of them. It would take some time for the sting of the loss to fade, but they were a good group. They would be fine. After seeing to the team, she had stopped to see the training staff and the support team, reiterating their importance to the organization. Then she'd stayed in her office, the door open for hours, open and available for anyone who had needed a quick word.

And there had been a lot of them.

But that was her job. To keep all the moving pieces moving, to make sure no balls were dropped. To ensure that everyone felt valued and supported, even during the tough times.

Though emotionally taxing, she loved her job, even on nights like tonight.

Still, she was tired, and the revolving door of players and staff had trickled off. The arena had grown quiet, its halls empty.

Time to go.

Sighing, she shoved her feet back into her heels. Since that was basically akin to torture after wearing them all day, she was not thrilled when the knock came at the door, but she still called, "Come in," while continuing to pack her bag.

If only she'd known who was on the other side.

Unfortunately, her superpowers didn't extend to X-ray vision and seeing through walls—which meant when the man

opened the door and pushed inside her office, Charlotte didn't have the chance to gird her loins.

Like she'd been doing all season.

Because—also unfortunately—she'd made the decision early on in her tenure to bring Logan Walker to the Gold. He was ferociously talented at defense. Big and strong and fast, he'd made an excellent replacement for Stefan Barie this season.

He was also her ex.

And just being in the same room with him had her body remembering *exactly* why he'd become her ex.

Cocky smile.

Sexy body.

Flaming chemistry.

But not ready to settle down.

As one might expect, take a young Charlotte Harris, add in one cocky, sexy, scorching Logan Walker, and the result had been a broken heart.

Not just broken. Shattered.

The pieces scattered to the four corners of the earth.

In case anyone was wondering, young intern meets rookie hockey player did not make for a happy ending.

But that was fine. It was *better*. She'd gotten tougher and stronger, and she'd promised herself that she would never let anyone in that deeply again, never allow herself to be as vulnerable.

"I knew you'd be like this," he said. And fuck if that gruff voice didn't send a shiver down her spine.

She ignored him, continued packing her computer bag. He'd get to the point, or he wouldn't, and she'd keep doing what she did best. Putting her head down and charging forward.

"Always hate losing."

His voice was closer now, but she still didn't look up, even though the spicy scent of his aftershave was drifting through the air, tickling her nose, making her fingers clench on her bag.

No.

Ignoring him and his sexy body, his sexy voice, his sexy scent, she packed a bunch of shit she didn't need, all so she didn't have to look at him.

She reached for a pad of sticky notes—

Warm, calloused hands on hers.

"You don't need a sixth pad," he said, that voice curling over her shoulders, sending heat between her thighs.

She jerked away. "You don't know *what* I need," she snapped.

A sigh. A hip resting on her desk. "Why did you pick me up, Char?"

Charlotte swallowed, zipped her bag closed—*with* the sixth pad of sticky notes, thank her very much—and forced herself to meet his gaze. "You were the best man for the position. We needed solid D. You brought it."

Green eyes, such a rich emerald they almost looked black, locked on hers. "That's it?"

"That's it." She picked up her bag. "I'm tired, so I'm sure you're doubly so." She started to round the desk but stopped, knowing she needed to be professional. Not only was she the first female GM, but she'd set a standard for herself when she'd joined the organization. "You played well this season and especially during the playoffs."

A nod. "Thanks."

That confused her. Before, his cocky would have taken over. Today, he seemed . . . modest? Come to think of it, she hadn't seen a lot of cocky this season, at least not when it came to his game play. But it had been eight years since they'd been alone in a room together, she supposed things had to have changed.

Not that it mattered.

Things had changed on her front, too.

She wasn't the naïve little girl anymore.

She was strong and powerful and had a whole lot of people depending on her.

"If you'll excuse me." Charlotte pointed to the door. "We should be going."

"Your feet hurt."

Her brows drew together. "What?"

Logan nodded at her feet, clad in a lovely pair of heels that, while beautiful, were also the equivalent of bear traps—and if that wasn't the perfect metaphor for the man in front of her, she didn't know what was.

"Those heels hurt you." His head tilted to the side. "Why do you wear them?"

She scoffed. "None of your fucking business, Walker."

A smile—slow and hot and sliding like silk over her breasts, her stomach, between her legs. "I knew you'd say that."

"I—"

He held up a box she hadn't noticed, pushed it into her hands when she stepped back. "Open it," he said, voice dropping and joining that silk of his smile to dip between her legs. "If you think you can handle it."

And then he was gone, the door closing behind him, leaving her with a heavy ass bag packed with who knew what, aching feet, and a box in her hands.

A box given on a challenge.

A box he knew she'd open.

Because Charlotte Harris didn't give in or back down. She liked that even less than she liked losing.

So, she opened the lid.

And instantly knew she was in trouble.

Two

CHARLOTTE

Slippers. The fucking man had given her slippers.

Lavender and fuzzy with embroidered stars and moons all over.

"Fucking hell," she muttered, and for one second, she was right back there. Lying in the bed of the pickup truck that had been his first purchase when he'd made it to the big leagues, her head pillowed on his shoulder, his body surrounding her, warming her more effectively than the blankets above and below them.

Dark skies all around. The crisp air of late fall and early winter.

When he'd still been interested in her.

Before she'd slept with him and he'd moved on to the next woman whom he'd cuddled close.

In those few glorious months, they'd spent so much time together.

She'd been an intern moving up the ranks, handpicked by the GM to learn the different facets of the team.

He'd been the new rookie, not knowing the guys well, a bit of an outcast on an established team where most of the other players had wives and families.

And she'd traveled with the team.

It was unusual for an intern, but her position, and the reason she'd gotten involved with the organization in the first place, made a lot of things about her first paying gig after college unusual.

But all that unusualness meant that she'd spent a lot of time with the players.

A lot of time with Logan.

With Logan sneaking down corridors and kissing in empty rooms.

With Logan slipping into her hotel room so they could order room service and watch bad TV.

With Logan in the back of his truck, staring up at the stars—

Her finger brushed one of the embroidered stars. It was made of sparkly gold thread, tucked neatly near a crescent moon, and it brought those memories that had once been so safely stowed away to the forefront of her mind.

Painful longing. Such painful longing after he'd broken things off.

Because, God, she had *loved* Logan.

She used to wish—

"No," she hissed, shoving the slippers back into the box and slamming on the lid. Char picked up her bag and slung it over her shoulder, teetering for a second before regaining her balance. It had been a long day—cough, a long *year*—so she was ready to go back to her house and not wear a suit or heels.

For at least a weekend.

Because although there would be a short break, pretty soon, the meetings would start up again. Scouts would need to be sent out, positions would need to be filled as the normal turnover from support staff and players occurred—different job offers taking her staff, contract issues changing the roster. There would be endless marketing meetings about the direction of the team, its social media and public image, practice facilities and all the issues that came from having to coordinate what the team needed in two separate spaces, planning ahead for travel, checking in with the analytics crew, making sure the team stayed on budget.

Luckily, she had plenty of people under her.

Luckily, she'd interned in most of those departments and knew some of the pitfalls.

But it was a big job.

And she enjoyed every part. Loved that she could put her degrees—bachelor's in business, master's in sports management—to good use. Loved that she'd been able to make her way from intern all the way up to GM through perseverance, hard work, and sheer dint of character.

The team might not have won, but she'd achieved something special this year.

And just like that Chubby Bunny contest, she was going to come back for a second chance, only the next time she'd win the whole damned thing.

Purse in her other hand. Jacket over her arm.

She almost left the box, but in the end, she picked it up, started walking to the door. It was as she struggled, arms thoroughly full, to turn the knob that she realized what she was doing.

Carrying the box when her hands were already full.

Letting Logan into her head.

Allowing him to make her feel things she didn't want to.

"Ugh."

Despite that, she didn't put the box down. Because she wasn't going to lose to anything, not even gravity, dammit. No fucking way. She got that freaking knob turned and the door opened and made her way down the hall on aching feet.

But the heels stayed on, and the slippers stayed in that damn box . . . at least until she saw the trash can.

Then both the box *and* the slippers went *kerplunk*.

The *thunk* as they hit the bottom of the plastic was beyond satisfying.

Char smiled, feeling better already. Then she hiked her bag higher and turned the corner to head out to her car, her mind on a long, hot bath, on comfy pajamas, and a large glass of rum punch. Though . . . if she knew then what happened to those slippers after she'd gone, she wouldn't have been nearly as sanguine.

It wasn't until later that she understood her downfall had been born the moment she'd allowed Logan Walker into her office that night.

Logan *Fucking* Walker.

His specialty was devastating her life.

THREE

LOGAN FUCKING WALKER

He sighed as Char turned the corner after dumping his gift in the trash.

It wasn't unexpected.

But he hated the idea of her walking around in those torture contraptions, hated with a fucking passion the thought of *anything* hurting her.

Of course, that overlooked the fact that *he'd* hurt her.

"Fuck," he muttered, walking over to the trash can and retrieving the slightly battered box. Thankfully, it had been the sole thing in this receptacle, the Gold staff being scarily efficient at their jobs.

And that included the newest addition of Char.

GM.

Fuck, he'd been so excited to hear the news over the previous summer. So damned proud of her. They'd met during their lowly rookie/new intern years, and to see her climb high, to fulfill the dream she'd once talked about had filled Logan with a pride he knew he had no right to feel.

Because he'd broken any connection between them.

Not just broke but utterly decimated it. Threw it down the fucking garbage disposal and flipped the switch.

Shredded the tie connecting them in order to set her free.

But he was done letting her fly.

They weren't what they once were—untried, in an insecure position. They had long-term contracts, money in the bank, credibility in the league.

And they were part of the Gold.

Relationships ran rampant through the ranks.

Coach and player. Trainer and player. *Player* and player—though in fairness, Stefan Barie, the former captain of the team, had retired a full year before.

So, what difference did one more relationship mean?

And GM and player didn't sound so unusual amongst the mix.

It would probably be unexpected at this one. Which member of the Gold would manage to tame the seemingly untouchable Charlotte Harris? Or just as likely, when would the impervious Charlotte Harris drink the water and steal the heart of one of her players?

Hell, there was probably an ongoing bet on both of those scenarios right at this moment.

The only difference was that Logan had already touched her, had already wriggled his way into her heart.

He'd just had to break it in the process of letting her go.

What was the saying? *If you love someone, let them go?*

Well, he'd done that, and it fucking sucked. Worse was when his life had lived out the second part of the saying. The *if they don't come back, you never had them* part. Because he'd made sure Char would never come back, made sure she was firmly pointed on the trail to fulfill her own dreams.

Fun times.

Sighing, he tucked the box under his arm, forced himself to

focus on the present. He wished he'd handled Char a different way, wished he'd been gentler, had coaxed her down the path she needed to be on.

But he hadn't.

And yes, he was fully aware that he sounded like an overbearing ass.

But the Char he'd fallen for eight years before wasn't the Char of today. She'd been soft, with stars in her eyes that were covered by rose-colored glasses, and . . . she would have done anything for him.

Logan had seen what happened when a woman gave up everything for the man she loved.

He'd lived it.

Going on almost thirty-five years of resentment (of course, he'd only been alive to bear witness to twenty-nine of them; his older sister was lucky enough to have been involved in thirty-four of them, his older brother just thirty-one). But as an adult, Logan understood a little better. His mom had left a promising career to move across the country, to marry a man she loved, to pop out several kids, and all that time, she'd gotten little to no appreciation.

His father certainly hadn't provided it, nor bred it into his kids.

He'd been of the dinner-on-the-table, wife's-job-is-the-housework sect, and for his mom, who'd been the regional manager of a national chain of banks, that hadn't gone over well.

Of course, it wasn't like his parents had talked about their problems.

That would have been too easy.

Instead, they'd set about making each other and everyone around them miserable.

Fun.

His childhood had been a blast.

At least he'd had hockey. As far as escapes went, that was one of the best.

He slipped out of the rink, moved across the parking lot in a quick clip, then got in and set the box in the passenger's seat as he considered his next move. Breaking up with Char had been a necessity as had been pushing her away so forcefully that she wouldn't try to get back together with him.

But years had gone by.

The present was different than the past.

And it had taken him all of one glance of eight-years-older Charlotte to know that his feelings for her were the same.

He loved her.

He didn't want to hurt her.

He didn't want to compromise her dreams.

So, he'd watched and waited. Planned and puzzled it out. Then *he* drank the Gold Kool-Aid, realized they had the skeleton of other successful relationships in the organization to model theirs after, and he'd decided that he was going to win the girl.

Well, win the *woman*.

For the second time.

Though really, who was counting?

FOUR

CHAR

Her bath was drawn.

The candles were lit.

It was after two in the morning, and she hadn't gone to bed yet.

But such was the nature of hockey, of being a GM. Games started in the evening, they went late, and there were always things to be done afterward.

When she'd originally come to the Gold, she'd made it a point to be the last one in the arena, the last one at the practice facility, but that wasn't always a realistic life strategy for her, especially on game days.

Most other days, she did end up locking down the place.

But on game days, the arena belonged to the players.

She stayed until the final buzzer rang, ran down her post-game checklist, and then got out of the way.

Micromanaging was not her style.

Char liked to have systems in place that could run efficiently without her, capable people at the helm. She'd learned this from her mentor, Luc, the GM for the Baltimore Breakers. The man was a former player and a great manager, who'd double-dared her into an internship with that team after they'd had a debate over management styles in a coffee shop of all places.

She didn't even remember how it started.

Just that they'd both been standing in an obscenely long line, at an obscenely early hour, and he'd mouthed off about the incompetent staff.

She'd whipped around, terse rebuke on her tongue about it being a management issue, as they clearly hadn't enough baristas on that shift.

And they'd had an argument in the middle of the shop, the people in line behind them bypassing them, the line eventually disappearing altogether.

Until he'd sighed and raised his hands palm out, saying, "I know when I've been bested."

"Damn right," she'd said smugly, turning for the counter.

"But I'm right about *this*," he'd said, coming up after she'd told the barista the drink she wanted, giving his own order, and paying for both drinks before she could protest. "Come and work with me. I need someone like you to pick fights with me."

Char hadn't agreed then and there.

But she had eventually accepted the job offer.

And learned so freaking much.

She hadn't even been a sports fan before then, let alone knew the difference between a blue line and a red line or what constituted boarding. But she loved learning new things, loved handling all the moving pieces, loved jumping into dealing with a crisis. It hadn't taken long to fall for the game, to give her heart over to the passion and speed, the amazing skills of the huge players so graceful on a quarter-inch-thick piece of steel.

The game and community had been a Cupid's arrow.

Then she'd seen Logan.

And fallen in love all over again.

Stupid, stupid girl.

Well, at least she hadn't quit her internship. That had been her first instinct after Logan had been traded.

He'd ended things before jumping a plane to L.A., and the next week, minutes after she'd walked out of Luc's office, offering her resignation letter—one he'd refused to accept— she'd seen the tabloid pictures.

Logan cuddled up to an actress.

Logan hauling said actress into his lap as he'd kissed her in the middle of a club, one big hand on her waist, the other in her hair.

Char had torn up the letter then and there.

But she hadn't been able to shore up her heart.

That had been torn out of her chest, thrown onto a crowded L.A. freeway during rush hour, run over again and again and *again*. Because she'd known the feel of Logan's mouth, of his hand gripping her waist, of his fingers tangling in her hair.

She'd been acutely aware of what she had lost.

Also, she'd been acutely aware of what she had almost lost. Her career, her livelihood, her pride in her work.

All almost thrown away for a man.

And as the years went by, as she saw him appear in the tabloids over and over again, each time with a different woman on his arm, Char had let go of the kernel of hope in her heart.

The one that she'd been holding on to that said Logan had broken things off because, while she loved her job, she'd loved him more. That he'd known she would have followed him to the ends of the earth and back and didn't want her to sacrifice her life's dream for his.

She'd held on to that kernel, that hope, that desperation for him to come waltzing back to Baltimore for longer than she cared to admit, even to herself.

Then she'd finally let it go.

And she'd soared.

Three years as an intern—the final two because she'd gone back to school to get her master's in sports management. After she'd spent a year as Luc's executive assistant, she'd taken on the official role as an assistant GM. And that was what she'd done for three years, where she'd been happy and content, knowing that Luc was grooming her to take over his role.

In fact, when Pierre Barie had initially offered her the GM position at the Gold, she'd turned him down.

Her team was a known quantity, and she'd worked her ass *off* for seven years, getting to know every facet and system, building a family, working under Luc and loving every minute of the challenge.

She'd gone to her mentor and told him about the offer, thinking they'd share a laugh about Barie trying to poach her.

But Luc had encouraged her to go.

To take the job.

God, she'd been so freaking hurt at first. Thankfully, she'd gotten good at containing her emotions, listening to the facts, carefully crafting her side of the argument . . . so she'd let him say his spiel and had just waited to take a turn to convince him that *he* was the wrong one.

Except, he hadn't been.

So, off she'd gone.

To the opposite coast, to beautiful California, land of the ocean fog and unpredictable earthquakes. And the Gold.

Who had a fucking incredible system in place.

A family. A great support staff. A roster that was on point—albeit lacking a strong, established defensive leader after Stefan Barie's retirement.

Great bones but lacking a bit of hands-on managing.

Pierre Barie was Stefan's dad and had stepped in after the previous board and GM had been involved in a few too many scandals. He'd taken a distanced approach to the team, in part because Stefan was the captain and his son, and the conflict of interest was acute. But also because Pierre wasn't a hockey lifer. He had other more lucrative businesses that took up his time, and the Gold were clearly doing fine.

But Stefan's retirement meant that Pierre was reevaluating his investment.

And his time spent on something that was no longer benefitting his son.

Not that there had been favoritism, but Pierre had flat-out told her he wouldn't have bought the team if his son hadn't been playing, wouldn't have spent so much time digging the organization out of the fucking mess it had landed in if Stefan wasn't playing.

Now, he wasn't going to do anything to jeopardize Brit, Stefan's wife and the current Gold goalie, or her career—especially not when doing so would fuck up his relationship with his son.

How did Char know this?

Because he'd told her. And because she was good at her job and had investigated the shit out of the Gold before accepting Pierre's offer.

No longer dumb.

No longer letting a man make her decisions for her.

When Luc had made the argument for her to go, she'd researched and spoken to her contacts in the league. She'd looked into Pierre's other businesses, even into the tabloids that seemed to love the Gold and their plethora of happily ever afters that evolved from within the organization.

Something that was typically a no-no at best, or at least a conflict of interest, or, at its worst, a symptom of an unhealthy power dynamic between the women in the organization and the players.

Except . . . it had taken her exactly one evening of researching to realize that those men would crawl over broken glass for their women.

And that Pierre had been very careful in the writing of contracts, as well as encouraging those in relationships to document everything through HR.

Kosher.

Smart.

She'd wrinkled her nose at that, wanting the ammunition to tell Luc he'd been wrong, that the Gold job wasn't a good bet.

Instead, she'd ended up with a bigger salary offer and a house south of San Francisco.

"An empty house," she whispered, closing her laptop with a sigh.

Enough with the emails, enough with the reminiscing.

She needed to plan for next year.

She grabbed her glass, the open bottle of rum punch. So, it was nearly empty. This was a no-judgment zone. If she wanted to drink her two thousand calories, then she would damn well drink those calories. And if she wanted to have more than those calories, then she'd have more than those calories—

Char blinked, cutting off the rambling in her mind. That was a lot of calorie talk. A lot of rambling calorie talk that gave her a clue into the other reason she was blinking.

The booze.

Too much after too long of a day. Too much on a mostly empty stomach. She'd been so nervous, it had been impossible to eat.

And now she was doing her best to pickle her liver.

"Probably enough, Char," she whispered, heading for the kitchen and stowing the bottle away—after refilling her glass just once more because . . . they'd been eliminated from the playoffs, because Logan had brought her slippers, because she remembered all too much.

She pushed the fridge closed, took her glass and her tired self in the direction of the bathroom.

Her phone rang.

Two in the morning.

And her phone was buzzing on the counter.

Which meant it was either an emergency or her mother.

Char knew which without even thinking about it. She reached for her cell and answered the call. "Hi, Mom," she said.

"Hi, baby," her mom replied. "I'm sorry about the game."

She grunted. "It's fine."

Her mom laughed, way too chipper for five in the morning Baltimore time. "Definitely not fine, but you'll get them next season. Oh, your dad wants to talk to you. Let me put you on speakerphone."

There was some fumbling then her dad came on the line. "You did a fabulous job, honey. Sometimes things just don't fall into place."

They were trying to make her feel better, but she was slightly buzzed.

And had just lost the biggest game of her life.

And Logan had given her slippers.

Slippers!

"Yeah," she managed.

"You sure you're all right?" her mom asked.

"I'm fine."

Silence.

"Do you think you'll make it home to visit soon?"

"Umm . . ." she waffled. She wanted to visit, missed the time spent with her family, but part of her had felt a bit left out over the last few years. Her brother and sister were always together or hanging with her parents, and she was on the opposite coast, no longer fully party to all of the inside jokes and funny anecdotes. "I—"

"Will and Amelia want to see you. We thought we could all have a family dinner, maybe do a day trip or go somewhere for a weekend."

"I'll look at my calendar," she said. "See how soon I can free up some time."

"But the season's over," her mom protested.

"Isla," her dad warned.

And guilt. *That* punctuated the buzz. "I'll come home soon," she promised. "I just don't know exactly when. I have to wrap up some things here."

A beat. "Okay," her mom said. "We love you, honey, and are so proud of you."

"Thank you," Char whispered. "I love you, too. Can I call you back in a few days? I was just heading to bed."

Her mom's voice gentled. "Of course. Get some sleep, baby."

"Don't work too hard," her dad added.

She said goodbye and hung up, missing her family and what their relationship had been like several years ago. She wanted that closeness back but didn't know how to get there, probably because she didn't understand exactly what had changed.

Was it the move?

Her job?

Or just her? Maybe there was something wrong with her inside.

"Ugh, Char," she muttered, plunking her cell onto the counter and glancing up at the ceiling. She took a long, slow breath. "It's late. You're slightly buzzed and disappointed and a terrible loser. That's *it.*"

Feeling marginally better, she reached for her phone.

The doorbell rang.

Her eyes flicked to her smartwatch, saw it was nearing three.

"What the fuck?"

She snatched her cell, shifted so she had eyes on the hall leading to the front door, and, feeling suddenly stone-cold sober, pulled up the app on her phone that controlled the cameras on the porch.

As usual, it seemed to take forever to load.

Then when it finally did, all the air left her lungs.

The bell went again, and Logan stared right into the camera, somehow seeming to be able to see her right through the technology. The night vision made his eyes seem black, but she knew those deep pools of emerald would be able to look right through flesh and bone and see the vulnerable woman she was beneath.

Walls. Good God, she needed all of them.

Needed them quickly.

Her fingers spasmed on her cell and thank fuck, but a wave of anger washed over her. "He threw you aside like garbage," she whispered. "Like you didn't mean a damned thing and then went on to spend the last eight years fucking everything in sight." A deep breath released slowly. "And he's just a player."

That was it.

Calm washed over her, and she glanced down. She was still in her suit. She'd sobered up, all signs of calorie talk gone.

And one of her players was on her porch.

She had an open-door policy, had told them they could show up at any hour, for any reason, had made sure her address was readily available.

But they rarely needed to see her here.

And Logan had, for obvious reasons, never come.

The bell went again.

He was here now, and she had to deal with this. Put the past to bed once and for all. Simple as that.

Char turned off the kitchen light, hit the switch in the hall, filling the space with a soft, yellow glow, and pocketed her cell as she strode to the front door. One quick flick had the lock open. Another had the knob turned. The last had the heavy wooden panel tugged open.

He stood there, all casual for all it was three in the morning, his legs spread loosely, his thumbs in his pockets, but his gaze arrowed to hers, froze her in place.

Her chin came up, and she spoke through the pounding of her pulse.

"What can I do for you?"

He kissed her.

One second he was two feet away, the next his mouth was on hers, his lips soft and yet demanding, his tongue sliding in to dance with hers when she gasped. It was hot and searing, but it was a reminder—of how they used to be, of *what* they used to be.

And as she was still grasping that—and the fact that she was kissing him back, that her hands were gripping his shoulders and pulling him closer when she should be pushing him away—he broke the contact, cupped her cheek for a split second, then stepped back and shoved a box into her hands.

"You forgot those," he said.

A nudge had her back into the house, teetering on wobbly legs.

This time, it wasn't from the booze.

Oh no, this time, it was all Logan Walker.

The door closed, his voice came muffled through the wood. "Lock up."

She dropped the box on the floor, slammed the bolt home, and stormed off to the kitchen.

She didn't bother with the glass, just grabbed the whole damned bottle of rum.

Logan *Fucking* Walker.

FIVE

LOGAN

He sat in his car for long minutes, watching the light show taking place inside Char's house.

Off and then on. Rinse. Repeat. And repeat some more.

First, in the front of the house. Then in the hall he'd glimpsed before Char had slammed the front door in his face. Next, upstairs in what he assumed was her bedroom. This educated guess was based on the two large windows with only a faint outline of light peeking around the edges of what he assumed were blackout shades, considering the large number of late nights and necessary sleeping in after games. Then those rectangles of light disappeared before another square, this time not just a border, but a full one, albeit slightly softened through frosted glass in what he would bet his slapshot on was her bathroom.

Because Char and her baths.

When they'd been together before, she'd taken more baths

than showers, bringing a glass of rum and a book and soaking until she resembled a prune.

Bubbles clinging to deep russet skin. Strawberry and bourbon scented body wash. Hot water sluicing over his body when he gave in to the temptation of sliding in behind her. The tub would always overflow, and neither of them ever gave a damn.

Fuck, he'd done so many loads of sopping wet towels.

Grinning, he waited in his car, watching that window like a pathetic version of Romeo, sitting there when he should, without doubt, be sitting in his apartment, drowning his disappointment in losing the Cup with a beer.

Instead, he sat in the dark and plotted.

He was twenty-nine years old.

He had a five-year, multimillion-dollar contract with the Gold. A contract that had a trade approval clause, one that had been written very effectively by Devon Scott of Prestige Media Group and ensured that if he didn't approve the trade, he would be paid out his contract.

In the professional sports world, he had it all.

In the having-some-semblance-of-a-personal-life world, he had nothing.

Which sounded completely melodramatic; he knew that. Logan had his family, and he was one of the lucky ones with decent parents who lived their own lives and didn't butt into his, and a pair of siblings he got along with extremely well.

Mostly because they had all survived their parents' volatile relationship.

His mom and dad were kind and caring to the people around them, had been wonderful, supportive parents in many ways; he couldn't deny that.

But . . . they weren't great with each other.

Communication was lacking. His mom harbored understandable resentment about being the one forced to leave the job she loved, to put everything on hold for her family, her kids, all for little to no thanks and zero chance of reentry into her former business circles once the kids were old enough for her to go back to work.

Plus, it was tough to hold a consistent position when a woman had a husband who traveled frequently, who didn't leave his office early *ever*—not for doctors' appointments or school plays or hockey practices.

He'd pick up slack on the weekends by spending all day with Logan at the rink or taking Cecily to her volleyball tournaments, but he'd missed a lot.

And as far as he knew, they'd never sat down and discussed the disparity, talked through what they both wanted and made compromises. He didn't know whose fault that was—if one or the other of them had attempted or rebuffed—but he had watched the resentment grow over the years.

Grow large enough that he knew he couldn't risk doing that to Char.

Or any other woman for that matter. Which was why he was twenty-nine and, aside from the whirlwind of him and Charlotte, had never been in a serious relationship.

Never.

He'd slept around a bit, but those days were long gone, and frankly had been long gone for years. First, he'd been so excited to have anyone of the opposite sex somewhat interested in him. Then, he'd been trying to forget Char. *Then* he'd realized there was no forgetting Char, not when she was quietly and persistently making her way through the ranks of management, making her mark on a sport that was still male dominated. Not when her rise had become less quiet, more noticeable to the press.

Along with everyone she dated.

Athletes—but not hockey players.

Two movie stars—one that had been on the A-list circuit.

A governor.

And Logan had scoured the news, her social media, the gossip sheets for any and all details of who Char had been seeing because . . . he'd been jealous as hell.

Because even though he'd blown up their relationship, felt he'd had to in order to secure both their futures, he'd never gotten over Char.

He knew he'd done the right thing.

But in many ways, missing Char was the gift that kept on giving.

That was going to change. He was done scouring the gossip columns for news of Char's love life. He was done trying to lose himself in work—and definitely done with losing himself in women who could never live up to her.

And . . . he was way fucking done with spending almost every day in the same building, the same plane, the same room as her and not being able to show her how much he cared.

The only problem was how to get back through to Char.

She was different now.

Harder. Tougher. Nearly impossible to read.

Logan had some insights because they'd once been so close, but when he'd signed with the Gold, he'd hardly recognized her. Not because she'd aged or physically changed, but because she had walls of steel and rebar four-feet thick that surrounded her.

Not cold.

Just . . . separate.

So, he'd watched and waited, plotted and planned, and . . . frankly, he had no fucking clue how to win Charlotte back. He hadn't known when he signed. He didn't know after nine months of working with her.

Hell, the only thing he *did* know was that he'd been lost.

And the only thing that made him feel found was Char.

The light in the bathroom flicked off, the one in her

bedroom came back on a moment later, but it only stayed on for a few minutes. Then the house went dark and stayed dark.

In bed. She'd be asleep soon.

He'd always been jealous of that, of her ability to slip into sleep the moment her head hit the pillow. Logan was awake. Char was out.

Logan was alone.

Char was . . . alone, too.

She worked into the wee hours. She was always at the rink, always preparing for the next game, the next battle. Meetings with different members of the organization from sun up to sun down, never missing a game or a road trip.

Beyond committed.

But just as alone as him.

Well, Logan was tired of being alone, and he was betting that Char was, too. That bet was risky, might cost him his job, his career.

But he'd seen the slice of lonely in Char's expression.

And he was going to make it disappear.

Six

Char

Stop pouting and go back to the drawing board.

She glared at her cell, and by default, the message from Luc. Sighing, she pushed out of bed and stumbled to the bathroom, eyes bleary but fingers working in tandem.

I'm not pouting. And I don't need a drawing board. I just need to tweak the one I already have.

Mint toothpaste was on her tongue when her phone buzzed again.

That's the spirit.

A beat.

So, who are you going to let go that I can pick up?

Spitting out the foam and rinsing, she glared at her cell for the second time in as many minutes.

Stop trying to piss me off.

A buzz.

Sometimes that's the only way to get through to you.

She grinned.

You're just saying that as someone who benefitted from pissing me off.

His response came a second later.

Damn right.

Char sent a rolling eyes emoji.

Also, before I let you go. I'm proud of you, kid. I know you didn't win, but you did really good.

Maybe it was Luc or Logan or talking with her parents. Maybe it was the loss or just being so close to something she'd worked so hard on but missing out at the last moment. Maybe it was just realizing that her life wasn't quite as great as she'd been pretending.

She presumably had it all. Parents who were happily married. Siblings she adored. A good friend and a great mentor in Luc. A job that fulfilled her.

And yet . . . there was a hole inside her.

One that had once been easy to ignore but now was growing, a sinkhole gaining speed as it pulled her slowly in.

Her phone vibrated again.

Accept the compliment gracefully.

She snorted.

Just like you accepted being knocked out of the first round of the playoffs gracefully?

A buzz.

Exactly.

Char chuckled and shook her head, remembering how it had taken her a solid fifteen minutes to talk him down from the edge.

Luc?

Yeah?

Thanks.

Anytime. Come home to Baltimore at some point soon so we can have a beer.

Two conversations. Two requests to head East. Even putting aside missing her family and the work she'd had to do before she left, she knew her trip would have to come sooner rather than later. Either that, or she'd be hosting her family and Luc before long.

And her house was not big enough for the Harris family *and* her former mentor, whose personality filled up all available space, Luc.

Planning on it, already.

Plan faster.

Another grin.

You're not my boss anymore.

Remind me why I allowed that to happen again?

Char giggled as she turned on the shower.

Because you love me.

That I do, kid. That I do. Talk soon.

After typing out a goodbye, she stepped into the shower and let the water sluice over her. Maybe she was imagining that hole. She could just be tired and worn out from the season, understandably on an emotional edge.

Right?

Her eyes drifted to the slippers Logan had bought for her. Sometime in her rum-fueled buzz earlier that morning, she'd gone back for the box and brought it upstairs. Now the offending cube of cardboard sat just to the side of the sink and was taunting her.

A sliver of longing wove through her. She could open the box, open *herself* up—

Fuck.

No, she wasn't imagining it.

———

"How are you doing?" she asked Liam when he paused on the threshold of the office.

She'd gone to the arena, purposely leaving her door open in case anyone wanted to talk. Most of the consoling had happened the night before, and the back offices were mostly empty today, except for a few players trickling in and cleaning out their lockers in preparation for summer.

"Bummed," he said. "But looking forward to next season."

"I feel you," she told him. "The team is lucky to have you. That tear of points you had at the end of the series almost snagged us the win."

"Almost." He made a face.

She patted his arm. "We'll get them next season."

"That we will." A nod. "Anyway, I just wanted to stop by because Mia wanted me to let you know that she's running a self-defense clinic this weekend." He shrugged. "She does one every couple of months for free for the women who work for the Gold and I wasn't sure if you knew about it." Liam extended a flier. "The info is there if it's something you're interested in and available."

Char gripped the paper, that strange longing feeling filling her again. Pride and warmth in his voice when he spoke of Mia. Love in his eyes. Her heart squeezed. "Thanks, Liam. I'll try to make it."

He grinned. "I'm the dummy that night, so if you have some beef with me about my gameplay, now would be the time to knock me onto my ass."

"Don't get that ass injured," she teased. "I paid a pretty penny for it."

They both laughed and then spent a few more minutes discussing Liam's summer plans before his phone buzzed. He glanced at the screen. "Mia," he said. "Reminding me that I need to talk to you about the class."

"Well, that mission's accomplished."

"Exactly." He shook her hand. "Thanks again for a great season. I've enjoyed playing for you."

After that they said their goodbyes, and Char returned to her desk, carefully tucking the flyer where she'd remember to check the dates, and then she did her best to clear her decks for the moment.

A knock had her glancing up.

"Mandy," she said, "how are you doing?"

One of their most talented trainers for the Gold, Mandy was married to Blane, their veteran defenseman. She was also heavily pregnant.

"I'm great. Fat and exhausted, but great." She leaned against the doorjamb. "I wanted to invite you to my last-hurrah-before-I-push-out-a-kid dinner next week." She lifted her hands. "It's not a baby shower—I don't need gifts. I just need some adult conversation before it's all breastfeeding and dirty diapers."

"I thought Blane was on dirty diaper duty."

Mandy grinned. "I can neither confirm nor deny that statement."

"Certainly not when it would take away one of the pillars supporting your last hurrah dinner."

A wink. "Exactly."

Char's desk phone started ringing. "Thank you for the invite. I'm going home to visit my parents in Baltimore, but I'll try to make it."

"Great! Brit says I'm required to tell you that I won't cook or bake anything."

"I'll look forward to hearing that story at the party, I mean, dinner," she said as the phone kept ringing. Mandy waved her goodbye as Char snagged the receiver, disappearing down the hall, and it took Char a few seconds to realize that the longing was back. This time it was intertwined with warmth.

Liam and his invite.

Mandy and the pseudo-baby shower.

The Gold were a family, and they were doing their best to include her. They'd done it all season, she realized, offered up the invites and stopped by to visit and chat. But she hadn't recognized the gestures for what they were, not when she'd been obsessing over every aspect of the team and season.

Some GM, she was.

But even as she answered her phone, she knew this realization was less about her ability to do her job and more about her tendency to keep people at a distance.

Something to ponder.

Something to consider if she had the courage to change.

Because . . . Logan.

SEVEN

LOGAN

"Cheers, man," Blue said, tapping his glass against Logan's.

They were all sharing a pitcher of beer, Logan excluded. He'd stuck with water for the impromptu meal Blue, Coop, and Kevin had invited him to join in.

Lunch overlooking the water before Blue and Anna, his wife, took off for a much-needed vacation. The young parents were looking forward to some time together, especially as Anna had been earning her degree.

Their son, Aiden, would be staying with Max and his son, Brayden.

"I really hope Aiden sleeps for them," Blue was saying. He'd been talking about the recent transition from crib to bed and how he and Anna had failed to stick with the change a few times before. Now their three-year-old was older and more stubborn . . . and much better at opening doorknobs.

Logan grinned and sipped his water.

"Why are you hoping for sleep?" Coop asked. "Don't you

want them to feel the lack of sleep pain?" Coop being a newer dad himself. His daughter was almost one and firmly entrenched in babyhood.

"I *want* them to watch him again, so I have some chance of sweeping my wife off on vacation again."

Kevin met Logan's eyes and they shared a look.

That look saying *Good Thinking.*

Coop got on the same wavelength, too, extending his fist for a bump before picking up the menu. They spent the next few minutes choosing food and ordering then talking about anything but hockey.

They'd all lived and breathed it, now they wanted to talk about family vacations and being lazy on a beach.

His cell vibrated in his pocket.

He glanced at the message and stifled a sigh.

Your mother is impossible.

Logan shoved it into his pocket, but the buzz that came a minute later was to be expected.

Your father says that I should quit my job and spend all day cooking and cleaning. Well, I did that enough while you three were growing up! No more!

Kevin scooped up a bite of pasta. "And then Rebecca—"

Logan typed out a message to each of them.

It said basically the same thing. Or a variation of it, anyway.

I'll talk to him.

I'll talk to her.

Thirty-five years and they still couldn't hash out their own arguments.

"You good?" Coop asked.

Logan shoved down the knot in his gut, focused on this time with friends. "I'm good. Family stuff."

"—then Rebecca said, 'I'll never make brownies for you again,'" Kevin finished.

They all sucked in a breath.

PR-Rebecca's brownies were legendary.

"What'd you do?" Blue asked.

"I said I'd go rake the leaves."

"At midnight?" Logan asked, having obliquely followed the conversation, about a "damn" tree Kevin had insisted on keeping when they'd moved into their new house, and the noise the deer living in the woods around them made while crunching through the leaves it dropped.

"Yup." He shrugged. "In my underwear, with a flashlight clenched in my teeth."

They all busted out laughing.

"Hey! Those brownies are the best thing I've ever had in my mouth," Kevin said. "You know you'd do the same."

"Never in doubt, man," Blue said. "Never. In. Doubt."

"How long did you rake before she took pity on you?" Coop asked, displaying the insight that made him such a great player on the ice.

"Maybe ten minutes," Kevin replied, grinning.

"Damn," Coop said. "She must really love you."

"Don't know what she sees in you," Logan teased.

"Hey!" Kevin tossed a napkin at him.

"I don't know," Blue said. "Log has a point."

They started laughing again, chuckling through the waitress dropping off their food and refilling glasses.

"Assholes," Kevin muttered, though he was laughing, too. He picked up his fork and narrowed his eyes at Logan. "You're the only single one here. What's the worst thing you've ever done that's pissed off a significant other?"

Logan froze, gut twisting again as he scrambled for an answer.

Scrambled to say anything other than he broke her heart.

EIGHT

CHAR

She was wearing those fucking slippers when the doorbell rang.

Char knew it had been stupid to put them on, but she'd crawled out of bed that morning and had seen the box. Then she . . . well, once the lid had been opened, her fingers stroking across the soft-as-silk liner, she hadn't been able to stop herself from slipping them on.

Glorious.

Like walking on clouds.

Either that or she'd spent way too much fucking time of late in heels.

Probably both.

But now she was in her rattiest pajamas, with the slippers on her feet, her hair pulled up into a haphazard bun, and in no way prepared to be answering the door.

She was a woman in an industry dominated by men.

She was a *black* woman in an industry dominated by white men.

In too many ways she was the sole representation of her gender, her race, oftentimes both, but she'd long ago accepted that fact, accepted that she needed to always be perfect.

A hole in her black graphic tee emblazoned with "This shirt is the color of my soul"—a hole that showed off a fair amount of side boob, was nowhere near perfect.

Neither were lavender and fuzzy slippers.

And her cause was certainly not helped with the embroidered stars and moons.

The bell went off again.

She weighed her options and decided to ignore whoever was at the door, whether it was a salesman trying to sell her pest control or a player who came needing counsel. The season was over. Char could give herself one day off, for God's sake.

Plus, she reminded herself, as guilt crept in because she was the one who'd created the whole open-door policy at her house for players and staff in the first place, if it were a serious problem, they'd call her. Everyone had her number. So, if it was important, her cell would ring, and she'd deal with it.

For now, she was going to make herself breakfast—*er*, lunch.

Except . . . maybe she should check the camera?

Just to be sure.

"No, Char," she growled. "Take this day."

Nodding to herself, she pushed off the stool where she'd been checking her emails, because her inbox didn't take a day off, even if she was planning on doing so, and headed to her fridge.

The doorbell didn't ring again, so she was safe from that disruption, at least. But as she surveyed the contents of her refrigerator, Char knew another was headed her way. She'd either need to put on suitable clothing—read: not a T-shirt with a near-guaranteed nip slip—or order in. The choice took her all of two seconds.

Order in.

After closing the fridge door with her hip, she moved back to the kitchen island and her stool where she did most of her work, even though she had a perfectly nice office.

But the truth was that she never felt comfortable in that room of mahogany wood, with the big desk she'd felt obliged to fill the space with.

Maybe she'd redo it over the break.

Go with white walls. A glass-topped desk. Pale blue accents. Maybe a soft, cushy chair she could curl up in.

Yeah, that would be nice.

It would give her the same vibes as her kitchen—soothing and flowy. Though, she knew the real likelihood of her feeling comfortable in her office, even post-remodel would be unlikely. Or maybe not unlikely so much as she knew she would always be drawn to the kitchen.

Because it was the center of the house.

Where she'd sat with whatever mix of her family was around, siblings, aunts and uncles, her sassy grandmother, all talking over one another and teasing incessantly as they'd cooked dinner. What some would have called the proverbial Girl's Zone, had been thoroughly invaded, her dad crossing battle lines when he'd cooked his special chicken or pasta or red velvet cake recipe, or when Char's mom had been watching the Super Bowl but her father couldn't have cared less about the big game.

On those instances, her dad had made snacks while her mom had yelled at the TV.

But on Oscars Night?

The roles had been reversed.

Fluid lines of quote-unquote gender responsibilities. Both taking turns, and both recognizing when something was important to the other so they could support and care for each other.

Perfection.

That was her parents. They were still married after thirty-seven years and still sickeningly happy.

Char couldn't be jealous or resentful. Not when they'd given her a childhood filled with so much laughter and love, not when she had learned so much from them.

But when she'd learned so much, had so much, it was hard to picture a relationship that wasn't *everything* they'd had, and Char had enough insight into herself to know that she couldn't ever settle for anything less than what her parents had.

And enough to know that she may never find it.

Anywho, she digressed.

This wasn't the time to think of her love life—or lack thereof lately—nor the time to remember with painful clarity that the one time in her life she'd felt some semblance of peace and happiness that mirrored her parents' own was when she'd been with Logan. This was time to regroup, recharge.

To prepare for next season.

Nodding to herself, she reached for her cell.

But as she unlocked it, opened the app to DoorDash in some lunch from *Molly's*, a flicker out of the corner of her gaze drew her focus.

She spun, and a shriek caught in the back of her throat.

Char clamped a hand to her chest, heart racing. "Motherfucker," she snapped at the man—*the man!*—who was leaning casually against the opening that led into her kitchen. "What the hell are you doing in my house?"

Logan shrugged, a tiny smile curving the edges of his mouth.

She lifted her brows. "A shrug," she said. "*That's* your response?"

"You didn't answer the door." Another fucking shrug. "The back slider was unlocked."

Patience. She was striving for it. Striving and not finding it. "There was a reason I didn't answer the door," she growled.

"Oh?" Affecting innocence. "There was?"

She stomped her foot.

Which was the complete wrong move because it drew his focus . . . to her feet.

To those fucking slippers.

Char braced herself, waited for him to comment on the fact she was wearing the gift she'd deliberately thrown in the trash two nights before. Instead, his lips curved farther as his gaze slid upward, gliding over her flannel rainbow-printed pajamas, then higher still to her T-shirt. Stopping there. Pausing to take in the saying screened on the front, and maybe it was just her, or maybe the man just never missed a detail, because she felt the hot weight of his stare settle on the hole.

The hole. The *hole*.

Lurching, she reached for a hoodie lying crumpled on the counter next to her laptop and slid it on, zipping it to her chin.

Which she lifted and paired with the order, "Get out."

The man crossed his ankles, made himself more comfortable against the wall. "What happened to your *open-door* policy?"

She resisted the urge to find another hoodie to put on, or better yet, one of her business suits. Royal blue with a crisp white shirt. No pencil skirts for her. They just made her five-foot-two frame seem even smaller. She was wide-leg trousers and fitted jackets. Starched, collared shirts with neat rows of buttons. Classic, put-together.

Not hole-riddled rainbow pajamas.

But . . . she was also a professional, and this was her job.

"What did you need, Logan?" she asked. "Is there an issue with someone on staff? A concern about your contract?" His face didn't change, except . . . she thought she detected a glimmer of pain in his emerald eyes, prompting her to ask, "Your family? Are your folks okay?"

He pushed off the wall, walked toward her. "They're fine."

"Good." She held her ground as he closed the distance between them, as he came close enough for her to smell the spicy, masculine scent. It took precisely one second for her to be back in the bed of his truck, his body pressed to hers, the cool nip of the evening air on her skin. He was so fucking handsome it took her breath away.

And he'd broken her.

A fact that was very hard to remember when he was so close, when he was brushing back a loose curl of her hair that had escaped her slipshod efforts at a bun, and when that simple touch felt incredible.

She stepped back.

Tactical retreat. A necessary retreat, because as hard as she'd made her heart, as effectively as she'd been able to keep the men she'd dated safely away from the inner sanctum of her emotions, *this* man had always been able to waltz right through those barriers.

"You asked what I needed," he said, taking a step toward her, making her retreat all but ineffective.

Char glued her feet in place, held her ground.

She would only retreat so far.

Which Logan seemed to know because his smile grew, because he took another step closer.

"What do you need?" she asked.

Closer again. Logan moved until his boots brushed against the toes of the slippers, until his scent surrounded her again, until she could feel the heat of his body wafting through the thin layers of her clothing.

Scorching emerald eyes.

A calloused palm smoothing back her hair.

The man who'd always been her weakness coming so, so close.

He lowered his hand, the back of his knuckles brushing her temple, trailing over her cheek, down her throat.

She shivered.

"You."

The word was laced with heat and made her gaze dart to his, where she felt her pulse speed for a second time in as many minutes, her heart thumping against her lungs. Need had darkened those emerald eyes, a need she recognized from their time together, a need her body felt acutely.

Her nipples went hard. Her mouth watered. Her thighs trembled.

Her pussy throbbed.

God, had she ever wanted another man as she always wanted Logan?

"No," she said, not sure if she was answering herself or telling him to back off. Not sure if she could honestly say she did want him to back off.

Either way, Logan retreated, stepping away from her, walking with loose-limbed grace over to where he'd been standing when she'd first noticed him in her kitchen and stooping to pick up two canvas tote bags.

"What are you doing?" she asked when he headed over to her fridge.

"Putting these away."

These presumably being the groceries he was stocking her refrigerator with. Milk. Eggs. Several blocks of cheese. A jar of jelly. Mayonnaise, mustard, ketchup. A bag of apples, a container of spinach, a loaf of bread. He closed the door, went back over and retrieved two more bags. Rice. Bananas. Bread. Cereal.

And more.

Charlotte finally got over her shock, started toward him.

Logan was just stashing the box of cereal in her sadly empty pantry when she reached him.

"What the fuck are you doing, Logan?" she snapped, grabbing the box from the shelf and shoving it against his chest. "I don't need groceries." He glanced down at her, and she didn't need to be a mind reader to hear his thoughts. Or frankly, the single thought that was present in his expression. *You don't need groceries?* One look at the empty fridge, the scarce pantry would disabuse that notion.

But what she'd really meant was that she didn't need groceries from him.

She didn't need anything from this man.

Logan put the box of cereal on the shelf, well, on a higher shelf, one she wouldn't be able to reach without a stool, and Char knew the move was deliberate, same as his stacking several cans of soup and other nonperishables on that same shelf. Presumably out of reach, but she'd been short her whole damned life. She had plenty of stools.

In fact, she reached for the one propped in the corner of the pantry.

She'd shove those cans of soup so far up his—

"I'm trying to feed you," he said, snagging the stool from her grip and shoving it into the opposite corner.

She'd have to go through him in order to reach it. Ugh. Fine. She had another stool in the hall closet. She'd go grab that and—

"Don't be difficult."

Char's feet skidded to a stop and she halted mid-turn to rotate and face him, fury erupting through her. "Difficult?" she asked, almost tripping over the word she was so fucking pissed. "*Difficult?*"

He didn't know *anything* about difficult—or rather, anything about how difficult *she* could be.

She'd honed those skills over the years.

She could show him precisely how *difficult* she could be.

She *would* show him—

He bent—a long way down since he was a foot taller than her, and a foot was a long fucking way when she was just wearing slippers instead of spiked heels. He was going to kiss her. *Fuck*, she wanted him to, wanted his lips on hers, his tongue in her mouth, his large hands stroking and cupping and pulling her flush against all of his hard.

Her lips parted.

Her body drifted forward.

He scooped her up and carried her from the pantry.

"What are you doing?"

Logan set her on the counter. Not the one with her laptop, but instead the one that was adjacent to the stove. He placed a hand on her belly when she would have hopped down. "Stay."

"Stay?" she asked, incredulous. "*Stay?*"

His lips curved. "You repeat yourself around me a lot."

"Maybe that's because you *don't listen*," she gritted out.

"Nope." He kept his hand on her belly, the heat drifting through her skin, sinking down, warming her from the inside out. "That's not it."

"That's not—"

Now, he kissed her.

One brief touch of his mouth to hers.

She lifted her hands, every thought in her brain encouraging her to shove him away. Instead, her limbs seemed to take on a mind of their own, her arms wrapping around his shoulders, her legs around his waist.

And she kissed him back.

He groaned against her lips, the rough, masculine sound vibrating through her, tightening her nipples, making her pussy clench with longing.

God, it had been so good between them.

The best.

He rested a hand on her arm, wrapped his fingers around her wrist, tried to tug her off him. But she didn't want to let go of Logan, not when he was kissing her, not when desire was pooling in her center, need coiling through her body.

She wanted more kissing. More touching.

It was her day off. She could—

He set her away from him, chest rising and falling rapidly. "You," he growled, "are dangerous."

Char's lips parted, a protest on the tip of her tongue.

Logan kissed her again, swallowing that protest as effectively as Brit swallowed up the puck in the goal crease. Brit. *Brit.* Hockey. The Gold. Her job. The fact the man who was kissing her within an inch of her life worked for her.

Oh, God.

Oh, God.

She shoved at his chest. Not lightly, but rather desperately. Desperate with a tinge of panic.

Hell, who was she kidding?

It was *all* panic.

She couldn't do this. She. Couldn't. Do. This.

Logan pulled back, crouching a little to meet her eyes, but for as strong as Char considered herself, for all that she had giant brass balls when it came to work, she couldn't find the strength in this instant to force her gaze to his.

He saw too much.

He meant too much.

She didn't want that to be the case, but she also wasn't a liar. Not to the world, not to the people who worked for her, and certainly not to herself.

"Don't panic," he said.

"I'm not." Her throat had to work hard to swallow said panic she wasn't having.

He grinned, cupped her cheek. "Welcome back."

Narrowing her eyes, she pointed to the door. "Don't let it hit you on the ass on your way out."

The bastard kept grinning, even as he stepped back.

But not toward the door.

Or at least not toward the door she wanted him to exit through. Instead, he moved around her and opened the fridge, grabbing the eggs and one of the blocks of cheese.

"What are you doing?"

He carried the supplies to the counter, pulled out a pan from the drawer beneath her stove. "Making you breakfast."

It was said so matter-of-factly that it took her a minute to process.

"What?"

He opened cabinets until he apparently found what he wanted, pausing to pull out a medium-sized bowl. Then he began opening more drawers, stopping when he'd located a cheese grater. "Breakfast," he said with a smirk. "That's the meal you usually consume in the morning."

"It's not the morning."

Realizing she was still sitting on the counter, she went to jump down.

Logan appeared in front of her before she barely shifted more than an inch, his palm on her tummy again, the heat making her pulse pound.

He could pound something else—

Get. A. Grip.

"Stay," he said, for the second time.

And for the umpteenth time since he'd appeared in her kitchen, Char got her hackles up.

"Stay. *Stay?*"

"On repeat, Starlight," he said, pressing a kiss to her temple after freezing her in place with the old nickname. His lips moved to the spot behind her ear, touching the sensitive skin there, sending a shiver down her spine. "Don't you know I love how those chocolate eyes look when they're sparking with fire?"

She'd begun to melt, to lean into him.

Then his words processed.

"You have some fucking nerve."

A cocky grin. "Newsflash, baby, I also like it when you yell at me."

Sighing, she shoved at his chest. He backed up all of six inches, so when she slipped off the counter, the front of her brushed the front of him. Her braless, pantyless front, rubbed all along his hard, *hard* front.

She'd had a plan or at least a purpose for getting off the counter.

But hell if she could remember it.

Not when her nipples were acting extra perky from the sensation of rubbing against his yummy chest. Not when he was so close, so big, so strong, so . . . fucking tempting.

Tempting.

He'd been tempting before. So fucking tempting just before he shattered her heart. So tempting before she'd nearly given up everything for him.

Enough.

Just enough.

"Leave," she said, no hint of soft, of heat in her tone now. She slipped between the counter and his body, ignoring the way her body reacted to his this time, ignoring that draw as she strode out of the kitchen.

Ice in her tone.

In her veins.

Desire muted by reality.

This man had broken her. She wasn't going to let that happen again.

"You'd better be gone by the time I come back down."

She hurried up the stairs.

Not a retreat.

It was, quite simply, the only survival mechanism she had at her disposal.

NINE

LOGAN

H e was creeping on Char through her windows again, only this time he'd upped the ante by remaining in her back yard.

He'd just plated the omelet, had been intending on washing the pan, but then he'd heard her footsteps at the top of the stairs, so he'd only been able to fill it with water then scoot out the back door.

He'd pushed her enough today.

Now, he needed to feed the beast.

Grinning to himself, he kept his gaze on the kitchen, on the plate with the steaming hot omelet. She'd come down and see it, smell the deliciousness of that cheese, her mouth watering.

Or maybe that was just him.

Because he was starving.

"Focus," he muttered, waiting for her to appear. He had a plan. Fill her belly, keep her thinking of him—

"You're fucking unbelievable, you know that?"

Logan jumped like a cat that had seen a cucumber.

That was, multiple feet and scrabbling through the air.

And thanks to Max and his copious amount of YouTube scrolling for bringing that particular viral video to his attention.

But that wasn't the point.

The important part of the situation was that Charlotte was standing in the open door, her arms crossed, smirk teasing up the edges of that luscious mouth.

Fuck, she was beautiful.

"Not so funny when you're on the receiving end, is it?"

He snorted. "You know you can't say shit like that around me, Starlight."

Her brows drew together. "What—" She halted her question after the one word, shaking her head and sighing. "*Really?*"

Logan shrugged. "You've been around plenty of locker rooms. What do you think?"

Brown eyes on his, holding him in place.

Then she sighed again, turned back for the door.

She disappeared inside.

He should go. Really, she'd told him to leave. He'd pushed. He'd kissed and touched and gotten under her skin. If his whole end goal was to win the girl—excuse him, the *woman*, because Char would like him calling her a girl about as much as she had liked him telling her to stay—then he should leave her to her day off.

Slow and steady.

Rebuild her trust in him.

She popped her head out of the opening. "Are you coming or what?"

Coming how exactly? he thought before he firmly shook his head. Not the point. "Coming where?" he asked out loud, and that was also not the point, especially when the talk of coming how and where had him thinking of *what* he wanted to be doing when he came.

Namely, Char.

"Inside," she said.

That had him blinking. "You told me to go."

She smiled—the huge, wide grin that was tinged with mischief and was one of the main reasons the press loved to photograph her. Charlotte was gorgeous any time of the day or night, beautiful inside and out, but when she smiled, Logan swore the Earth stopped revolving around the sun.

Instead, it spun around this woman.

"Did you *see* the size of that omelet you left on my plate?"

He walked toward her. "It's a perfectly respectable-sized omelet."

"For a behemoth such as yourself," she said, still smiling, though it was softer now. "Come inside, Log. Let's figure this out. We need to work together, not be at odds."

He followed her in, ignoring the whole *come inside* thing.

"We have been working together, Starlight," he said, closing and locking the door behind him. "That's not exactly at odds."

"It hasn't exactly been comfortable," she pointed out.

No, it hadn't.

Because he'd been longing for this woman, dreaming about her, wishing things had turned out differently, even while knowing he still wouldn't have changed how he'd ended their relationship. He'd known what he would be missing back then, just as he knew now.

"I want us to be able to be friends."

Logan stopped.

The urge to bust out laughing was strong, so strong, in fact, that his mirth nearly burst free.

Thankfully, he managed to pause, to breathe.

Because friends.

Friends hung out together. Friends ate and hugged and touched and spent time at each other's places. Friends was slow and steady. Friends gave him a chance to convince this woman to trust him.

"Yeah?" he asked, studying her closely now.

She crossed her arms, lifted her chin. "Yes. Friends."

He hesitated. Because he knew that while friends gave him an in, it also gave Char an out. She could use it to keep her distance more easily. Friends may spend time together, but they also didn't kiss, didn't hold or caress one another like he wanted to touch this woman who held his heart in the palm of her hand.

She gave him a look he recognized.

One that told him he could accept her offer, or . . . that he could go fuck himself.

Since he'd prefer to fuck *her*, Logan said the only thing he could. "I'd love to be friends with you, Starlight."

Her brows drew together. "No kissing?"

He considered that. "Does on the cheek count?"

She sighed. "Logan."

Lifting his hands in surrender, he said, "No kissing." And so, maybe he'd crossed his toes inside his boots before he headed over to the plate he'd made for her.

"Promise?"

"Mmm-hmm," he said, opening the drawer to pull out a second fork.

"Logan," she said on another sigh.

More toe-crossing. "I promise." He brought the plate over, closing her laptop and shoving it to the side before setting a fork on either side of it.

"You're a fucking liar," she grumbled, sitting on the stool and picking up a utensil.

"How do you figure?" he asked innocently.

"Because I know you and your tricks," she said, nodding at the empty stool. "Your little toes are probably crossed right in those boots of yours."

"What about yours?" he asked, not admitting to anything. "How are they feeling in your slippers?"

Her breath caught.

He took the opportunity to scoop up a bite of omelet and offer it to her.

She allowed her mouth to open, for him to slide the fork inside. She closed her lips around the tines, chewed and swallowed.

Then moaned.

And he was back to thinking about coming.

"This is delicious," she said.

He scooped up another bite, brought it to her mouth. "Good," he said, feeding her again. "Because it's the single thing I know how to cook."

She was mid-chew, her eyes having slid closed, but at his admission, they flew open. "Logan," she said. "Please, tell me you're joking. You cannot almost be thirty and the only thing you know how to cook is an omelet."

He shrugged. "It's food."

Char paused then shook her head. "That's it?" she asked. "*It's food* is the only explanation you're going to give me?"

"I'm really good at ordering salads on DoorDash?" he said, and yes, it was more of a question than a statement.

She huffed out a breath.

"Will you teach me?"

Brown eyes warmed as they held his gaze. "You want *me* to teach *you?*" She chuckled. "I think you'd be better off watching a cooking show. My parents didn't pass many of their foodie skills to me, no matter how hard I try." A shrug tinged with self-consciousness. "And much to their chagrin."

He fed her another bite. "I seem to remember some very delicious cookies," he said.

Maybe it wasn't wise to remind her of the past, of their time together, not when it had ended so explosively. But . . . he wanted her to remember the good times, wanted to build them up, to peel away the veneer that buried them.

She studied him closely.

"I seem to remember that I baked three batches in order to get a dozen decent cookies."

He couldn't hold back his grin. "You did?"

"I did." Char made a face. "I don't even quite know how I managed to get twelve good ones. My apartment smelled like charred sugar for weeks."

"That's why you stayed over?" he teased. "To get away from the smell?"

Her lips twitched. "I traded burnt cookies for hockey funk. I don't know which was worse."

Another bite. "I'll have you know that I haven't had hockey funk in years."

"How many years?" she asked after she'd finished chewing. "One? Two? Because I've smelled that locker room after games, and let me tell you, it's certainly not peaches and cream."

He had a sudden image of a ripe peach, juice dripping down its skin, sliding over lush curves. He wanted to taste the sweetness, to lick and kiss until the stickiness was gone, until it was just his tongue tracing every inch of her, until he was just tasting the woman beneath. Just Charlotte.

The image and its subsequent longing was why it took him too long to reply.

"I figured you'd be immune to it by now."

She shuddered. "I don't think anyone can ever get immune to hockey funk." A chuckle. "That sounds like a bad genre of music."

He laughed and she joined in, but after a few minutes they both stopped, a sudden seriousness entering their conversation. "Fuck, Char," he whispered. "I didn't want to hurt you. I—"

"I know," she said. "We were too young. We needed the distance so we could both grow." A nod, her expression turning rueful. "I-I just wanted to impress you so badly, and I loved you so fucking much."

I loved you.

Past tense.

That shouldn't hurt. That was the bed he'd made up, the same one he'd rested in for over eight years.

But it still did.

But . . . this wasn't just about him and his decisions, his regrets, his love for this woman that had never *ever* waned.

This was about Char and the pain he'd caused. He set down the fork, reached over and covered her hand with his. "You did impress me, Starlight. Probably more than you can ever know."

Her eyes skittered away, and she picked up her own fork, scooped up a bite, and fed herself, all while not looking at him.

"I didn't want to break up with you," he said.

She sniffed, spine going ramrod straight. "It's okay, Logan, you don't have to feed me a line of bullshit. We were both in our early twenties—an intern and a rookie—it was always a recipe for disaster."

"No."

"And if Luc had found out?" she asked, naming the GM that had taken her under his wing, the one who he'd gone to for a trade when it became clear that for as strong and smart as Char was, she would have given up everything for him. "We would have been in serious deep shit," she said and scooped up a bite. "It was just as well you were the smart one and ended us before things got bad."

Logan could deal with a lot of things.

Eight years apart from the woman he loved, watching her love other people, live her life and fulfill her dream, unable to be at her side.

Having her hate him because he'd broken her heart.

Ending a relationship that had meant more to him than his own career.

Those were all things he'd knowingly shouldered, things he'd been able to cope with.

Because Char had been happy and working for her dream.

Maybe not right at first. They'd both been wounded deeply. But she'd gotten over him. Moved on.

Because Logan had drawn the line at watching her love for him die a slow, incremental death, seeing it rot by inches, until nothing was left, not even fond memories.

"I don't know how smart it was," he told her, picking up his fork again since it seemed as though she'd taken up the task of feeding herself, "but I'm so proud of you." Her eyes flew to his, and he couldn't resist brushing his fingers over the shell of her ear, along her jaw, down her throat. Her skin like silk. "You've done so much, Starlight," he said. "Accomplished all you hoped. So yeah, proud doesn't even begin to describe it, not when it's been a privilege to watch you thrive."

"Logan."

He shoved a bite into his mouth before he admitted to the privilege of loving her.

"Can't you see that you've done great things, too?"

He snorted. "I won the Cup with L.A., and yeah, that was incredible. I shot some commercials, secured some endorsements." A shrug. "But none of that is extraordinary. You, baby. You broke barriers. You dreamed big dreams and managed to hold on tight to them."

She nibbled the corner of her mouth. "I don't feel like I did much. I mean, I'm proud of myself, of course, but I only did what lots of other people have done. Keep my head down and work hard, and I had several lucky breaks."

"Maybe," he said. "But Luc saw your value, and you chose to leap. And you didn't squander your chance." Brown eyes met his and though they were still warm, Logan detected a trace of discomfort in their depths. "I'm guessing this is where you tell me that you've had enough talking about you and your greatness?"

She snorted. "I'm confident that you've fawned over me long enough."

He waggled his brows. "So, is this where you fawn over *me?*"

Another snort. "I think you've had far too many people fawn over you." She nudged the plate toward him. "Finish it off, behemoth. I've had my fill."

Since she'd eaten more than half of the omelet and he'd barely had a few bites, Logan took Char at her word, though not before admitting, "My family is good at making sure I don't take all the fawning seriously."

Her expression gentled. "How is your family?"

"Great. Cecily is married now."

"No!"

"Yeah." He grinned. "And much to my parents' disappointment, she has no plans of settling down further. She and her new husband sacrificed a wedding and an expensive honeymoon in favor of an elopement in Vegas and six months of backpacking around the world."

"That sounds like Cecily."

His sister was an adventurer, a woman who always kept the world on its toes, so it certainly wasn't a surprise that she'd forgone the white dress and big shindig, even though his mother had been desperate for a chance to throw a big party.

"We all flew out and watched her take her vows in front of Elvis."

Char grinned. "When in Vegas."

"Exactly," he said. "And then my new brother-in-law plied my mom with many a strawberry daiquiri and an all-expense-paid trip to Neiman Marcus to soothe her disappointment."

"Smart," Char said. "What did she get?"

Logan scooped up some omelet. "I think the better question might be, what *didn't* she get?"

Charlotte laughed.

The sound was the warm breeze on a summer day, the gentle swoosh of a lake's waves in the evening twilight, a thick coat when the cold was seeping through his clothing. It was beautiful and comforting and meant so much.

But what meant more was Char squeezing his hand, sharing in his happiness over his sister and mother.

What meant more was her letting him in—even just as friends, even just the smallest bit.

What meant *everything* was the absence of hatred in her eyes.

TEN

Logan had taken her booting him from her house with good humor.

And he didn't even reappear at her back door or teleport himself into her kitchen.

But though he'd gone, she couldn't deny that his presence was still heavy in the air. His spicy scent, the two forks in the sink —dishes that were only there because she'd had to argue with him about doing them in the first place.

Sighing, she finished drying the pan, stuck it back in the drawer, and then set about loading the dishwasher with everything else.

What the fuck was she doing?

Her eyes went to the plate she was stowing in the bottom rack of the dishwasher. She wasn't a moron, didn't take shit from anyone, least of all herself.

The *what the fuck* didn't have a thing to do with dishes.

It was directed to herself, to her interactions with the man who'd broken her, the man she'd just invited into her house for breakfast.

"Idiot," she hissed.

And yet, she couldn't deny that she felt more settled right then, after sharing a meal and some conversation with Logan than she had in years. In . . . eight years.

"Why Logan?" she asked, closing the dishwasher and avoiding the temptation of her laptop. She was going to take the day off, dammit. She could deal with whatever crises were hurtling toward her tomorrow.

The trouble was that Char didn't have a ton of hobbies.

She lived and breathed work.

She took baths and drank rum to unwind.

And returned emails and looked at stat sheets and negotiated contracts. That was her happy place, and one she'd gladly spent the majority of her time in. But the season was over. The team had lost—fucking hell—but there wouldn't be much left for her to do until draft day came around.

There might even be weeks and weeks without much for her to do.

The thought made her shudder.

It also made her reach for her bottle of rum.

So, she'd just had breakfast. It was nearly two in the afternoon, and she was *taking the day off*. Pouring a fingerful, she stowed the bottle away then carried her glass out into her small back yard.

She lived in one of those typical California suburbs, large houses on small lots, all cloistered together, all with tiny slivers of a back yard.

Char wasn't much for nature, didn't like to go hiking or stick her toes in the sand—though there was plenty of both of those things within driving distance. She much preferred her bubble baths, her books, and bingeing on shows and movies.

Or cuddling in the back of a pickup truck with plenty of blankets and a sexy hockey player to keep her warm.

So, the small yard didn't bother her.

Especially when she didn't have too many plants in it to worry about killing.

She'd hired a gardener soon after moving in, along with a landscaper to redesign the yard to be drought tolerant, but cozy. The effect was a green and colorful space filled with native trees and bushes, with very few flowers. An umbrella shaded the deck. A lounger with a bright floral cushion was positioned beneath it to get just the right amount of afternoon sun, and she crossed over to that chair and set her drink on the table.

It only took a few more steps to retrieve a blanket from the storage box, and while she considered returning inside for her E-reader, Char ultimately decided she was too lazy.

She wanted to sit and drink and enjoy the sunshine.

Soon it would be summer, and the fog would cling to the hillside, the sun only peeking out on days that were uncomfortably hot.

She much preferred the cool late spring days.

Yet, none of this thinking about weather or loving her back yard got her any closer to the reason why she'd invited Logan into her house.

For all intents and purposes, she should hate him.

But . . . she couldn't.

Then she'd stopped at the top of the stairs, had seen him hurry for the back door, smelled that he'd cooked something delicious for her, and part of the ice around her heart had simply melted. And that ice had melted more when she descended a few more steps and had seen him looking through the back windows, longing on his face.

Longing that resonated deeply.

Loneliness she could never get rid of.

A well of emptiness that had been inside her from the moment Logan had left her.

Fucking hell.

She lifted the glass to her lips, took a long swallow. "You're getting soft, Harris," she muttered. "You live for the business, for the team. Nothing more."

And . . . she still couldn't lie to herself.

The bottom line was that Char wasn't as content as she liked to pretend. Something was missing, and she had the sneaking suspicion that the something missing was a some*one* missing.

"Damn," she muttered, shaking her head at herself. "You're a mess, girlfriend."

Yeah, she was.

But she also wasn't going to let it ruin her afternoon.

So, instead of moping, she shoved the heavy feelings away, stopped the arguing and recriminations, and just *sat* in the sunshine, watching the clouds float by. A moment of still and quiet when her life had been the opposite of late.

She wasn't about to upend her life for a man.

Not even one as tempting as Logan.

ELEVEN

LOGAN

He'd left Char's house determined and with a glimmer of hope that he could salvage things between them.

And he'd driven over the brown hills, through the twisting road, all the way to the ocean. Not the warm water of the Caribbean or Florida, nor the white sand beaches. This one was filled with substrate of an ordinary brown and had a severe drop-off halfway down.

But beyond that drop-off was a gorgeous stretch of flat beach.

He could drop to the sun-warmed ground, sink his toes and fingers into the shifting sand, and just be.

The crash of the waves.

The blue sky punctuated with curls of fog.

The . . . ringing of his cell phone.

He silenced it, collapsed back onto the sand and stared up at the sky. For all of two seconds. Because then his phone began to ring again.

With a sigh, he extracted it from his pocket.

One glance at the screen had him sighing again.

"Hi, Mom," he said, after swiping a finger to answer the call and putting his cell up to his ear.

"Hi, honey," she said. "I'm sorry about the game."

"Thanks, Mom," he told her. "There will be more games."

"Still sucks."

She chuckled and he grinned.

"You trying to revamp my high school years?" Logan had complained to her about losing too many times to remember, and her response had always been *there will be more games*. His response had always been *still sucks*.

"I've decided to reverse the rules," she said.

"Oh how the tables have turned."

"Exactly." A beat. "I'm sorry we didn't make it out for the game."

"It's fine, Mom," he said. "Things happen."

"No," she said. "Your *father* happened. He didn't like that you paid for the tickets and wouldn't use them, and then there were no flights and—" She broke off. "I'm sorry," she murmured. "I shouldn't complain about him. He's your father. I just . . . God, sometimes he drives me . . ."

Logan closed his eyes and waited until she got it out of her system.

This was a fine skill he'd honed over many years—the whole waiting-until-one-of-his-parents-had-finished-complaining-about-the-other ability. He'd perfected the proper moment to hmm and ha, the right time to chime in with a sympathetic noise.

Finally, she wound down, and he said, "I'll be home in a few weeks. We'll spend a lot of time together, get our fill."

"I love you, baby," she said. "I'm looking forward to that. Did you have your flight scheduled yet?"

"I love you, too." He sat up. "And I haven't booked it yet. I have a few things to wrap up here first. But I'll let you know the dates soon."

"Okay, because you know I'm working at the skilled nursing home now."

"I know," he said. "If my visit conflicts with your job, that's on me. Your clients count on you, and you know I would never hold you working against you."

Right sentiment.

Wrong thing to say.

Case in point—

"Your father feels differently," she grumbled. "He got so mad when I wasn't home to cook dinner. But did it ever occur to him that *he* could cook dinner?"

No. Logan could confidently say that it wouldn't have occurred to his father.

"You know you could talk to him—"

"Talk!" she cried. "He won't listen—shoot, honey. I'm sorry, I'm doing it again. I won't complain about your father anymore. I—"

"Oh, hey, you know what? My other line is ringing," he said. "I need to get that. I'll call you soon, okay?"

"Okay, honey. Love you. Bye!"

She hung up, and Logan, his other line *not* ringing, but also an effective skill he'd honed in order to get his mom off the phone, collapsed back into the sand again and sighed.

Talking.

God, he wished his parents would do more of it with each other than with him.

His phone buzzed, and he knew without looking who it would be.

"Hi, Dad," he said, after answering the call.

"Your mother—"

Logan sank back down onto the sand, stifling a sigh, and

waiting for a moment where he could get a word in edgewise so he could get off the phone.

But that moment was long in coming.

Eventually, however, he managed to end the call, to sit back and try to unknot his twisted gut. He would never tell his mom this, but part of him had been relieved when she'd told him they wouldn't be able to make it out to the final game. He hadn't needed to wade through the bitter comments and underlying passive aggressiveness.

His phone vibrated, and he would be lying if he said he didn't glance at the screen through half-closed lids.

Relief poured through him.

It was a text. Just a simple text from his sister.

I just got the one-two punch of voicemails from our parents complaining about each other. You okay?

He made a face.

Just peachy.

A buzz.

Sure, you are. Ignore the calls. Your life would be infinitely better.

He was starting to understand his sister's point of view in this aspect.

I'm thinking you're right.

Her response came through a minute later.

Of course, I am. Sorry about the game.

It's fine, Cec. How's backpacking?

Another vibration.

Nice deflecting. But I am sorry you lost. Also, Austria is beautiful, Spain is amazing, and I wish I could travel for the rest of my life.

Logan's heart squeezed.

I'm glad you're happy.

Me, too. But, Log, what about you being happy?

This was a text conversation. She shouldn't be able to be so insightful with just letters and cell phone screens.

I love you, sis. Now go back to your regularly scheduled program of honeymooning and having the time of your life.

He could picture her sighing, but her message didn't push—or not much anyway.

Love you, too, little bro. Also, you deserve to find your happy.

Yeah, he was working on that.

For now, that happy was listening to the waves and feeling the sun on his skin.

Later, he hoped it would be because Char had found it in her heart to give him another chance.

TWELVE

CHAR

The sun had just begun its descent, the temperature began to drop, and she'd finished her glass, was pondering either a refill or an early bath and an evening spent in bed with her book, when she heard the ringing peels of her doorbell. "Good grief," she muttered, not moving but keeping her eyes trained on the side of the house, half-expecting Logan to appear from around the corner.

When he didn't, Char wasn't disappointed.

She wasn't.

Don't look at her like that.

"Don't look at who?" she muttered, standing up. "Yourself?"

Maybe. But also . . . look she *was* disappointed. Stupidly or not, there was something about Logan that drew her, even after all these years.

Hence *friends*.

Except, now she was wondering if she'd just signed her own death warrant by pushing Logan to be friends. She'd wanted to categorize him in that way in order to keep her heart safe, but the truth was that her heart had never been safe from him. He'd always been able to wriggle in and make himself at home.

It was why the rest of her relationships hadn't ever worked out.

She'd loved him. She'd thought they had that special magic of her parents—caring for each other, seeing all the flaws and good things, but loving each other more because of them. Instead . . . he'd gotten in, implanted himself, and left.

"And now he's back," she murmured.

Or perhaps more accurately, he'd decided to waltz back into her personal life, not content to stay solely in her business world.

"So, shove him back into his lane."

Char froze, the protest already welling up in her throat.

"That's your answer, dumb ass."

"I happen to like your ass." A beat, as she gasped and turned to face the man who she'd apparently conjured up just by thinking of him. "Don't talk down to it," Logan said, lips quirking, pretty green eyes dancing. He had a flush of pink on the tops of his cheekbones, as though his olive skin had been out in the sun for just a little too long.

She plunked her hands on her hips. "Is there a reason you keep breaking into my back yard?"

He shrugged. "Is there a reason you don't answer your doorbell, except at three A.M.?"

She would not be amused.

She would not smile.

But damned if the man wasn't right.

The only time she'd answered her door for him was the one occasion she should have been most wary. Though, in fairness, she'd gotten considerably *more* wary after the man standing a few feet away from her had shown up on her front porch.

"I was comfortable," she said. "And I figured that anyone important would call or text."

"And what if someone important *did* call *and* text?"

She lifted her brows. "Did you?"

An unrepentant grin. "No."

She sighed and shook her head. "What are you doing back here?"

"Don't friends hang out?"

"Friends usually have boundaries, and they don't hang out every minute."

Guileless green eyes on hers. "Is that so?" He nodded to her house. "Why don't you teach me more of these mysterious friend rules?"

Char pressed her lips together, fighting once more against the urge to smile. "Why are you really here, Log?"

His chest rose and fell on a large exhale. He took a step closer, gaze serious now. "Do you really want to know?" he asked, moving closer still, until he was near enough for her to see the streaks of brown hidden in the depths of his emerald eyes.

Did she want to know?

It took her less time than it should have to admit, "Yes." She did.

Fingers down her cheek, a soft touch smoothing back her hair. "There's no one else I want to spend time with," he said.

Her breath caught.

Then she frowned.

"No one?"

Logan snorted, the puff of air disturbing the curl he'd just tucked away. "Why do you sound so incredulous?"

"Really?"

Lips close and yet so far. Temptation mere millimeters away. She wanted. *God* how she wanted.

No.

Char stepped back, paced away. "I'm mean, come on, really? You're confused that I sound incredulous?" She spun around, met his stare, and found it clouded with what was definitely confusion. "You've decided to flip the script on something I thought I knew for eight years, Logan. I was hurt. Devastated. And you were in the tabloids with an actress." She sucked in a breath. "Then I didn't hear from you, didn't see you anywhere except on the ice, not even when you were playing in my building." Another breath, this one a struggle against that old, jagged pain. "Then you agree to sign with the Gold, and I spent the first half of the season expecting something. An explanation. Derision. For you to make a pass."

"Char—"

She turned away again, continued her pacing. "Instead, I get the consummate professional. A leader on the ice. An asset off. The perfect fit."

Heat at her spine.

She didn't turn around, couldn't bear to look into his eyes.

"Then the season's over," she said when he didn't speak. "And you show up with a present, with groceries. You tell me you want me. But I haven't seen one fucking bit of that *want* for eight years." Char's hand shook as she absently went to push back her hair, but then Logan was in front of her, doing it for her, his hand lingering as it cupped the side of her throat.

And fuck, his touch was everything.

Her body was alive. Her nerves fired with pulses of pleasure. Need burned hot through her center.

"I had to wait until the season was over," he said, carefully wrapping his arms around her.

"Log—"

"Friends hug," he said, moving slowly enough that she could stop him, could step back or push him away. But all of those depended on her having one ounce of self-control when it came to this man.

And—case in point as her body pressed flush to his, as her arms wrapped around his waist, as she inhaled that spicy scent directly into her lungs—she had none.

Not with Logan.

Never with Logan.

Gorgeous, handsome Logan. Sweet, caring Logan. Heart-breaking, shattering—

His palms slid up and down her back, a slow and steady rhythm that calmed and made her yearn more than ever. "I had to wait until the job was done, Starlight," he said.

"Why?"

"Because I will never get between you and your dream."

One sentence that undid her.

One sentence that broke her heart all over again.

That made anger and hurt and terror and *so fucking much* hurt well up inside her. She pushed against his chest, shoving hard enough to make him stumble back a step. "You already did," she said, eyes burning with tears she would not let fall. "You shoved yourself into my dream and then casually set it aflame. Then you danced on the ashes before they had even cooled."

"Char—"

"No," she said, throwing her hands up. "Don't push me on this, Logan. When I said friends, I didn't mean that as an avenue to something else. I meant fucking *friends*, and that was it."

"Star—"

"Either take it or leave it," she said, leaving the blanket, abandoning the glass, and shoving past him to move toward the slider. "Because the one thing I know for certain is that when you ended us eight years ago, you ended everything—our future, our present, our possibilities."

She yanked open the door, slammed—and locked it —behind her.

Then, heart aching, eyes stinging, throat clogged with tears, she went upstairs to take a fucking bath.

THIRTEEN

LOGAN

He'd fucked up.

And he hadn't even had the opportunity to give Char the *why* of why he'd ended things between them.

He'd known he shouldn't have gone back to her house.

It hadn't been in his plans to see her again, the ones made in the dark much earlier that morning, but after he'd gone to the beach, after the phone calls and sitting on the sand, counting the minutes that passed by, he hadn't been able to stop himself. Hadn't been able to find his patience when all he wanted to do was go back to her place and kiss and touch, coax and love his way back into her heart. As the waves had crested on the shore, their ever-pounding rhythm had wound him tighter and tighter.

Until the ocean was no longer calming.

Until he'd been unable to sit still.

Still, Logan had planned on driving back to his place, to work out until oblivion found him.

Then he'd seen the exit for Char's house.

And he hadn't been able to resist.

Just as he hadn't been able to resist going into her back yard when she hadn't answered the doorbell.

Stupid.

So fucking stupid.

But she'd been beautiful in her cut-off jeans, her legs on display, the curves of her ass tempting him even from ten feet away. She'd smiled when she'd first seen him, the impact of that initial reaction filling him with so much fucking joy that he'd blown it.

He should have led with *I deliberately broke up with you, in a way that ensured you'd move on, so you didn't give up your life for me.*

Or perhaps, *I still love you and I've never stopped.*

Or better yet, *I'm so fucking sorry and I'm getting on my knees—even the bad one that sometimes still aches from ACL surgery—to beg you to give me just one more chance.*

He hadn't said any of those things.

Instead, he'd given a half-explanation that only hurt her further.

Fucking hell.

"Shit," he muttered, jabbing at the button on his garage door opener to close the heavy metal panel after he'd put his car into park. He turned off the ignition, slammed out of the door, kicking it shut with enough force that he'd probably dinged it.

Or broken his toe.

Well, what did he need his toes for?

Hockey was done for the moment.

He was alone.

He was . . . fucking moping.

Sighing, he dropped his chin to his chest, inhaled deeply, and tried to quell the anger. All season, all *fucking* season he'd been striving for patience, slowly trying to prove to her—hell, to *himself*—that he deserved another chance, so when he'd finally pulled the trigger, he'd found it nearly impossible to go slow.

If that wasn't a fucking pattern in his life, Logan didn't know what was.

Slow down, you'll crack your head open! his mom had regularly bellowed when he'd barreled down the road on hand-me-down rollerblades.

Slow down with the puck, you'll make fewer mistakes had been his travel coach's favorite mantra.

Slow down. Think. from Luc before he'd asked for the trade.

Even this season, Calle, the assistant coach in charge of offense had told him to move *slower and more deliberately* when funneling the puck up to his forwards on the board.

Slow down.

So easy in retrospect, so fucking difficult in the moment.

He'd always wanted everything as quickly as possible. First place in every tournament he played growing up, first on the ice during travel hockey, first game in the NHL, first goal, first full-season league. First . . . woman he'd loved.

Speed had been great for his career—granted, he was able to temper it.

Which he had.

He'd made it an asset instead of a detriment.

But speed wasn't great necessarily when it came to relationships, not when it meant first love had turned into first heartbreak in the span of several months. And speed really wasn't fucking great when he was trying to show the woman he'd never stopped loving that she could trust him to take care with her.

Fucking barreling right through on those rollerblades again.

Another sigh had him lifting his chin.

He punched the alarm code and pushed into the house, closing and locking the door behind him. It wasn't that he was obsessed with safety or saw a threat behind every corner, but he'd lived in big cities for years now.

This wasn't the small town he'd grown up in, nor the small suburbia Char had spent her last years in.

This was San Francisco, and that meant there were some inherent dangers.

So, locking her doors was definitely an item he planned to address on his plan to take care of her, but it had been shuffled down a few spots because . . . well, first he needed to figure out how to get her to not kick him out of her house.

Or back yard.

Or maybe, he should just start with getting her to talk to him.

He crossed to his fridge on another sigh, knowing that the contents were much sparser than what he'd filled Char's with that morning but happy that at least she had food to eat for dinner while she was probably plotting ways to happily dismember him.

Or dull his skate blades so he'd eat it on the ice—

No. She wouldn't mess with the team.

She'd just mentally voodoo doll him in ways that wouldn't affect his play. His cock twitched, and not in a good way because he knew that *she* knew that he didn't need his dick to play hockey.

That would be the first to go.

Cupping himself and shuddering, he acknowledged his ridiculousness then moved on to more important things than his cock.

Dinner.

He had a mind to eat dessert, but since that wouldn't be happening for the foreseeable future, he focused on food by pulling out the fixings for a salad—spinach, crumbled tofu, quinoa, precut slivers of pepper—and ate with the deliberate focus of fueling his body rather than taste. Not that it tasted bad, but it wasn't a giant steak and a loaded baked potato, and strictly speaking, he didn't need to continue Nutritionist Rebecca's meal plan, but he was going to. He'd never felt better, but more than that, it had been really fucking difficult to transition into her plan. It wasn't like he wanted to eat junk food all summer, but he also really liked to indulge in his food and beer and didn't want a repeat the struggle of cutting out extra carbs and sugar and meat.

He couldn't even do cheat days.

No self-control.

Diet plan day in and out. Limiting the animal products—odd omelet with organic cheese aside. The blueprint for his diet was to predominantly focus on plant-based proteins, to avoid processed foods and refined sugars, and not often indulging in his prescheduled Cheat Days that Rebecca built into the plan.

Because . . . circling back to not having any self-control. To moving too fast and—

His phone buzzed.

Frowning, he put down the fork, wondering who would be texting and why. The season was over, the Cup awarded to someone else. The guys would be returning to their families and, in some cases, to their own countries. They had two months off before team activities would be scheduled, and even then, the time commitment would be light until the season ramped up.

Most guys had their own rest and training schedule. Healing up, securing some ice time, hanging with their families, fishing—there was a lot of fishing.

Not Logan's cup of tea.

But he did have a cabin in the woods. It backed up to a river some *could* fish in. He just preferred to watch the water flow by, to hang out and do nothing, to be with no one.

Well, he wanted to be with *some*one.

She just—rightfully—wanted to light his dick on fire.

Cool.

His phone buzzed again, reminding him of the message, and he picked up his cell, glanced at the screen.

Then immediately shook his head and sighed.

Because Brit had fired up the team's group text chain.

His phone vibrated rapid fire in his hand, moving almost faster than he could as he unlocked the screen and began to scroll up through the newest messages to ferret out what the hell had gotten the boys—and girl—so worked up.

Brit had sent:

Housewarming party at Kevin and Rebecca's house tonight.

This Rebecca wasn't Nutritionist Rebecca, but rather PR Rebecca, and while she hadn't used PR in front of this Rebecca's name, Logan knew which one she was talking about based on the spouse.

Kevin—forward on the Gold—with PR Rebecca.

Gabe—head trainer—with Nutritionist Rebecca.

See what he meant about the Gold being a family? There were so many crisscrossing relationships that his head had practically spun when he'd come to the team and had been trying to keep track of them all.

That tactic he'd given up on.

Eventually, he'd just gone along for the ride, and pretty soon he'd grown to understand the various dynamics.

Which was why he kept reading.

Max: Last minute much?

Brit: As if any of us losers have anything better to do.

Coop: I resent that term.

*Blane: Even if it fits? *rolling eyes emoji**

Brit: I'm declaring this an honorary Cheat Day.

Max: I'll bring the pizza. Players only, or everyone?

Kevin: Everyone is invited. We've got the food covered. Molly's is delivering.

Blue: Cool. I'll bring an IPA.

Brit: I've got the shitty beer covered.

Liam: We know you do. I'll bring something good to make up for Brit's bad taste.

The messages went on, escalating the teasing for several minutes before everyone began to sign off and gather up kids who were around or good beer that would be too refined for what Brit had termed her college-aged palate. Logan squeezed in a reply, saying he'd be there, too.

Because, what else did he have to do?

Sit around and think about how he'd blown it with Char?

Pack his shit and drive up to the Sierras and hide out in his tiny cabin?

He'd save that for next week.

Rolling his eyes at himself, Logan washed his plate then headed upstairs to change into party clothes.

And yes, he knew full-well that if one of his teammates heard him refer to what he was wearing as party clothes that he'd be served up a heaping pile of shit-giving with no end in sight.

But . . . that was also why he was going to the impromptu gathering.

Because they gave him shit. Because he'd give it back—to Brit and her beer, to Max and his nerdiness, to Blane and his inability to father boys, despite really wanting to. His wife,

Mandy, also a trainer for the team, was pregnant with another girl, and so his future of pink hair bows was secure. Though Brit had bought little Madeline skates for her first birthday, so there was certain to be plenty of hockey in the girl's future.

Plus, with women like Brit and Charlotte in her circle, not to mention the fact that much of the staff and management were female, Madeline had no shortage of role models to look up to.

Hockey was for everyone.

Not just a slogan for the league any longer, it had been wholeheartedly embraced by the Gold organization.

More than words.

Actions.

And—

He froze in the middle of buttoning a fresh pair of jeans as the puzzle pieces in his mind settled into perfect arrangement. He'd given Char some words, knew she deserved more, but . . . more than anything he might *say*, she needed actions.

Show her.

Not tell her.

He'd taken a creative writing class in college, a long torturous semester where he'd felt completely over his head, but one in which the instructor said one thing on repeat.

Stop telling and start showing.

Words didn't mean shit if they weren't paired with actions.

Then add in his tendency to move too fast and . . . well, disaster was the first word that came to mind.

He'd given Char a thoughtful present, he'd done a little groveling, and just because she'd let him kiss and touch her, had offered up friendship, he'd assumed—

Fuck. He was an ass.

Because he'd stopped by her house that evening thinking that he just needed to wear her down a little more, that by Char extending the hand of friendship, she'd then given him the greenlight and it was only a matter of time before he would worm his way back into her heart.

But the truth was that *nothing* was guaranteed.

Least of all her accepting or forgiving him or even coming to an understanding of why he'd done what he'd done.

He needed to show her what she meant to him.

He needed to prove he was worth her taking a chance on him again.

Because he'd helped build those walls around her heart, had effectively handed her the bricks, the mortar. Maybe he didn't regret the decision he made, knew it had to be done, but also . . . fuck, he'd been so young, so stupid.

So fast.

Always moving too fast.

He caught a glimpse of his reflection in the mirror, saw the war within himself—the knowledge of what he needed to do fighting against his instincts to barrel in and get her back.

But there was only one outcome in that scenario that resulted in winning back Char's trust.

So, Logan knew exactly what he had to do.

He needed to slow *way* down.

In fact, he thought he was going to slow down so much that he'd be late to the party.

FOURTEEN

CHAR

She didn't normally get to sit around with the team like this.

No barriers.

No necessary professional distance.

Just some adults and kids hanging out, eating way too many baked goods from Molly's—something even Nutritionist Rebecca couldn't get too mad about, considering the season was over.

Well, that and the fact that someone had bought Rebecca's favorites—a gluten and sugar-free pastry filled with eco-friendly chocolate.

Char personally thought it tasted like sand.

But she had dutifully taken the bite Rebecca had offered, and clearly the nutritionist liked it, so she kept her opinions to herself.

Plus, she was too busy filling her stomach with Triple-Chocolate Orgasm cookies to be focused on much else. Brit had plunked a bottle of dark lager into her hand and told her to prepare to have her mind blown.

She had *something* blown.

Stifling a snort because that might have been funny if she'd had *something* to blow or if *someone* had blown her—which, side note, was maybe not possible, or perhaps more accurately, wasn't something she particularly wanted. Lips and teeth and a tongue, yeah that was more her speed—

Logan walked into the room, head bent slightly as Max stood next to him, chatting his ear off.

Probably about the latest fantasy show that had taken Netflix by storm.

God, he looked good. He was tall and lean, with a thick black beard that she wanted to feel against her skin, especially if he paired it with his teeth and lips and tongue. Because . . . God, they'd been good together. After they'd broken up, she'd never had sex with one iota of the intensity as it had been with Logan. Their chemistry had been off the charts.

And based on the kiss the other morning, it was still that way.

As though he knew she was staring at him, he turned his head and those gorgeous emerald eyes met hers.

Even from across the room, she felt the intensity, felt what he wanted to do to her. Char's breath caught and she shifted, an ache between her legs, heat dripping down her spine like honey.

Eight years and she still wanted him like it was the first time.

She knew she should look away.

But she was held captive.

"Is your tongue having an orgasm?"

No, but something else is desperate to have one.

Brit dropped onto the cushion next to her to punctuate that question, or maybe the thought—fuck, she hoped it had remained just a thought.

"What?"

"I've seen the way you look at—"

Char inhaled, fear gripping her when she realized how transparent she'd been by staring at Logan, by basically eye-fucking him from across the room when she was supposed to be a fucking professional.

And because the world was the way it was—read: a cruel motherfucker—Brit got a full glimpse of Char nearly choking on her last bite of orgasm—she meant *cookie*.

Cookie, dammit.

Not sex.

Brit patted her on the back. "Easy," she said. "Sorry, I didn't mean to startle you."

"All"—*cough*—"good"—*cough*—"it's"—*cough*—"my fault."

Char inhaled, this time managing to not choke on her cookie, and then took a long sip of beer. "I'm fine," she said when she'd finished. "I should have been paying closer attention instead of woolgathering."

Brit's blue eyes locked onto hers and Char had to resist the urge to fidget.

"I've never"—Char braced herself for Brit to call her out, to say something like *I've never seen a GM who wants to fuck one of his players*—"heard someone use the term *woolgathering* in actual conversation before."

Char snorted, gaze darting to the side. Logan had moved farther in the room but hadn't come over to her, wasn't even looking at her, even though she'd just nearly choked to death giving that double chocolate orgasm cookie a blowjob. "Oh, no, don't give me that nonsense. It's not *that* uncommon."

"You sure you weren't born in 1950?"

Char smacked her lightly on the arm.

"Goaltender abuse!" Brit joked. "I need that shoulder." She grinned. "And so do you."

"Maybe my plan is to devalue the price of you and that shoulder."

Brit froze for a heartbeat before a grin broke out on her face. "You're devious, and I, for one, love it."

"Because I want to injure you so I can pay less when I renew your contract?"

"Yup." Brit took a sip of her beer. "Well, that and the fact that you've got a sense of humor and don't take yourself too seriously."

Char shrugged. "It's part of the job, part of the needle we women find ourselves having to constantly thread. We can be tough, but not too tough. We can be outspoken, but only so long as we don't hurt some man's feelings. We can assert ourselves, but only so far, otherwise we're a bitch."

Brit's eyes went sad. "Are you feeling that way here? With us?"

Shit.

"God, no." She reached over and squeezed Brit's hand. "This organization is incredible, and I think that's not only because of the focus on gender and racial equity but also because of the men here. We've got allies, not barriers." Straightening, she smiled at the goaltender, who was older than her, but also seemed very young in many ways. Maybe it was the fact Brit was a goalie and goalies were weird, or maybe it was just that Brit was young at heart and had an innocence to her that no one had managed to dim. "I was thrilled to be offered the job, and my experience has been incredible. It's just all the rest of it—the media, the blogs, the nasty headlines. You've been there, done that."

Brit made a face. "Yeah, I know a bit about how rough the media circus can be." She leaned back. "My advice is to avoid looking at the sports blogs. It's a brutal world of misogyny. Hell, they're still saying I'm a publicity stunt, and I've won the fucking Cup. Twice."

"You're my first choice in goalie, any day of the week," Char told her, and she meant it. Brit was smaller than male goalies, but she was beyond talented and a critical part of the Gold roster.

"Yes!" Brit fist-pumped.

"What?" Char asked.

"My contract offer just went up."

Char lifted her gaze to the ceiling and sighed, her eyes flicking to the side when she felt Logan come closer. But the man was apparently engrossed in his conversation with Max, and he didn't once look at her. Shaking herself, she forced herself to pay attention to Brit. "Didn't my invite tonight come with the promise that we were forgetting I'm technically everyone in this room's boss?"

When the other woman had texted and invited her to the team party, Char had been conflicted—and not just because Logan would come (though he'd just shown up, so if he really wanted her and her *friendship*, wouldn't he have arrived earlier?). Instead, she'd struggled with the urge to refuse on principle, because she should keep distance between herself and the rest of the world.

But how could she keep her distance and also encourage the organization to be a family?

Families didn't keep their distance.

Or good ones didn't.

Brit shrugged, teased lightly, "You're the one who brought up contracts." But she didn't belabor the point. Instead, she changed the subject.

To one that Char was trying and failing to ignore.

"Did you need to discuss something with Logan?"

"What?" Char tore her gaze away from the beautiful man who made her thighs clench together and her pussy ache.

"Logan. Did you need me to get him for you?"

Yes. Yes, she did. She wanted Brit to go over there and bring Logan to her, to offer him up like some sexual gift where there would be no consequences for her heart or her job.

But there were always consequences.

"No." She blinked, dispelling the memory of how good Logan had been at giving her orgasms and how much better he might be with eight more years of practice. Char turned to the woman next to her and lifted a brow. "Why do you ask?"

"Because you look like you either want to fuck or kill him."

What had Char been thinking about this woman being innocent? Because clearly Brit wasn't, or at least she saw too fucking much.

"You're wrong."

Brit patted her shoulder, shook her head slightly. "Why does it sound like you're trying to convince yourself?"

Because she was?

Char tipped her beer bottle and took a long swallow, buying time, but also rocked to the core. If Brit noticed, then who else would?

Would Logan?

And if he *did* realize how much she wanted him and he pushed or began pursuing her in earnest, how in the fuck was she going to be able to resist him?

She wouldn't be able to.

Her pulse sped, heart thudding in her chest. Maybe it was because she was the boss and trying to interject some distance between herself and this woman who saw too much. Or maybe because the thought of Logan recognizing too much and realizing she had no defense against him, made her panic. Either way, Char knew in that moment that coming to the party had been a horrible idea.

She had to go, and she had to go now.

"You know what—" She started to stand.

Brit dropped her hand to Char's wrist. "I was like you."

Saw too much. Brit saw too much.

Char forced a smile. "We women in a men's world have to stick together."

"That's not—" Brit stood, dropped her voice. "Look, I know I'm overstepping"—a chagrined smile—"but that's my M.O., so I'm just going to say it. I almost let the best thing in my life go because I was too scared to step outside myself, because I was too worried what the world would think." A light squeeze of those fingers. "Logan is a good guy. He—"

"He broke my heart."

It just slipped out.

The admission was critically embarrassing. Char should be way over a young love gone wrong, some hurt feelings from nearly a decade before.

But the door had been pushed open, and she remembered.

How hopeful she'd been.

How much it had hurt when he'd gone.

Her eyes burned, and it took her a moment to realize that Brit hadn't said anything back. She turned to Brit, words tumbling out. "It was a long time ago, way before either of us were here—" A sharp shake of her head. "It doesn't matter anymore. He is a good man, and I wish him a good future. I just—"

"I understand," Brit said softly, after Char struggled to find out exactly what she *just*.

Just what?

Couldn't? Shouldn't? Was too scared to? Was too furious to?

Take her pick.

They all fit her churning emotions.

"I shouldn't have said anything. I'm sorry."

Pulse still pounding, cheeks scorching hot, Char knew she had to keep it together. She reached over and gave Brit a quick hug. "No," she murmured. "Thank you for caring." She pulled back. "But I think I've had enough tonight."

Brit nodded then glanced over Char's shoulder, eyes widening. "He's coming this way. Do you want me to run interference?"

"No." What Char *wanted* to do was to turn around and run into Logan's arms, to pretend nothing bad had happened between them, and to trust him like she once had. That he was her other half, that he was a good man who would treat her like her dad did her mother.

But that trust was gone.

"I have to do this."

"You don't," Brit whispered. "You really don't." Respect in her pale blue eyes. "But I get why you feel like you have to." She stepped back and scooped up her beer from the side table, voice raising in volume and chipperness. "Well, I'll just go grab another one of my crappy beers."

Then she was gone.

And Logan was at Char's back.

FIFTEEN

LOGAN

She turned slowly to face him, and the weariness in her eyes killed him.

But . . . actions.

Show not tell.

He shoved down how much that hurt him and extended the bottle of water he'd grabbed for her after watching her almost choke to death while talking to Brit. He'd wanted to storm over, to cradle her in her arms, but he'd promised to show, promised friendship, promised to go slow.

So, he'd extracted himself from Max's inane conversation about whether druids was the proper term for some magical being in the show he was currently bingeing then had made his way to the cooler.

Now, he struggled to contain his body's reaction when her fingers brushed his.

"What's this?" she asked when the damp exterior of the bottle met her skin.

Which got him thinking about damp things he *shouldn't* be

thinking of, especially when he was trying to firmly friend zone himself.

"I'm guessing your throat hurts," he said, then mentally kicked himself.

Throat. Damp. Next he'd be discussing how *hard* things were.

And speaking of which—

Focus.

"You were coughing," he said lamely. "I figured you might need something to drink."

Her gaze moved from the bottle up to his, those chocolate depths indecipherable as they held his stare for long moments. Then she dropped her eyes back to the beer bottle she already held.

"O-oh, I-I—" he stammered. "I'll—"

"Thanks, Log." She took the water from him and he had a difficult time looking away from the slender fingers, their nails tipped in pale pink polish. Somehow, it suited her, though it made part of him crave how she'd used to sport all sorts of shades.

Bright green and red for Christmas.

A plethora of autumn tints when the leaves began changing.

Team colors when they'd been on a winning streak.

Now they were pretty but subdued.

He'd done that.

Or maybe it had been a combination that he'd kicked off, but that life and professionalism had required.

Or maybe he shouldn't be thinking about her fucking nail polish when he had so much to make up for.

"Did you get some food?"

She glanced up at him, brows drawn together, and Logan was so twisted up by his longing for this woman that it took him far too long to connect the pieces. Fucking hell, of course she got some food. She'd just been choking on it.

He'd brought her the water bottle *because* of it.

Good grief.

Logan closed his eyes, clenched his jaw. He needed to stop fucking this up. The stakes were too high and—

Fingers on his hand. "Are you okay?"

He swallowed, cleared his throat. "I'm fine. I—"

Fuck.

He what? Had thought himself into such a circle that he was absolutely terrified in this moment of saying or doing the wrong thing. All he could think was *show not tell, slow down, actions not words* on repeat through his brain.

And funny story, that made it incredibly difficult to think of anything reasonable to say, to do.

"Log—"

Get a grip.

"Char, I—"

"*I'm pregnant!*"

The room went absolutely silent, everyone turning to PR Rebecca.

"What?" Brit asked into the quiet. "I thought you couldn't have—" She broke off, shook her head. "Oh, my God! Rebecca, are you serious?"

The slender brunette nodded, and it was the first time that Logan had ever seen her appear the least bit uncertain. "It was a surprise," she said, teeth nibbling into her bottom lip as she glanced up at Kevin.

Logan's teammate's face was soft, gentler than he'd ever seen. "A great surprise," he said, brushing a tear that escaped Rebecca's eye.

Someone sniffed.

The sound seemed to propel everyone into motion.

Mandy, heavily pregnant with Blane's second daughter, rushed over to Rebecca, hugging her as tightly as her belly would allow. "Honey! I'm so happy for you. That's amazing!"

Brit was only a step behind. "Congratulations! I'm thrilled for you both."

Sara—a quiet brunette and former international figure skating champion, who was married to Max Stewart, a defenseman who'd retired from the Gold last season at the same time as Stefan, their former captain—joined the huddle, followed by Max's and Blue's wives, Angie and Anna, respectively. Nutritionist Rebecca was there a heartbeat later, her soft voice nearly inaudible. Soon everyone was talking, excitement filling the room.

Logan didn't know the whole story, but he could pick up enough to understand that Rebecca being pregnant was happy, amazing news.

"I should—" Char's fingers were still on his arm, and he briefly covered them with his own when she jumped and blinked. "I'll just go congratulate Kevin and Rebecca."

Her lips parted. A breath shuddered out.

"Char?"

"Yes?" she said and visibly shook herself. "You're right. We should go offer our congratulations."

She tugged, making to extract his hand, and instinctively, his own hand tightened, not wanting to break the contact, not wanting to let her go. That mantra was ramping up again, spinning through his mind. *Slow, show. Words, trust. Actions—*

He forced his fingers to open, to release her.

Another shuddering breath.

And he remembered the other thing he'd grabbed for her. He extended the napkin-wrapped cookie, the same variety she'd nearly offed herself on. "Here," he said, pushing it into her now free hand. "It was the last one."

She peeled back the corner, glanced between the cookie and him. "I—"

He allowed himself the smallest bit of contact. "Just enjoy it, Starlight."

Then he stepped back, turned away, and forced himself to walk away from the woman he loved.

It made every nerve in his body burn with regret.

But he kept walking anyway.

He'd done it once for her own good, had crawled away from her inch by inch in order to save her dream.

Today, what propelled him was the knowledge that if he did it correctly this time around, then perhaps he would manage to save both of their hopes for the future.

SIXTEEN

CHAR

He'd walked away.

He'd shoved a cookie in her hand and just strode away.

Well, a cookie *and* a water bottle, but still.

He'd just gone.

A beat of annoyance trailed her confusion, but before she could work up any ill-will, she focused back on her surroundings, on what had just been announced. She was new to the team and didn't understand everything that had gone into Rebecca's announcement, but Char knew enough to get that it was a huge deal.

Even without everyone else's reactions, seeing Rebecca with tears in her eyes, her typical shark-like and calculating expression softened with love as she stared at her husband, Kevin, would have told Char enough.

This was life-changing news for the Gold's often cynical publicist.

This wasn't a shot staged to garner likes or positive press.

This wasn't a setup in order to frame the announcement in the best possible light.

This was . . . Rebecca wanting her family around when she made the announcement.

And fuck if that didn't bring tears to Char's own eyes.

Eyes that dropped to the cookie in her hand and had her remembering that she'd once hoped to have kids with Logan, then that she'd once hoped to have them with someone, anyone. But life had changed that. *She* had changed that.

Unwilling to open up, to open the gate to the walls surrounding her heart.

It was easy to put blame on Logan for crushing that dream.

But the truth was that she'd crushed it just as effectively over the last eight years by avoiding any real connections with the men she dated.

The moment—and she meant the *moment*—they wanted to get serious, Char had bolted.

To get too close was dangerous.

Plus, she was the first black woman, the first *any* woman in the assistant GM position. Then the first in the GM role itself. That was too important to slow down.

So clearly, she couldn't open up fully.

Work was important.

Work was *more* important.

And if the men in her life weren't satisfied with the piece-meal bits and morsels she tossed their way, then the door was there and they could walk right through it.

She needed to keep her head down and keep pressing forward.

Because . . . she'd prove everyone wrong.

She, a black female, could do it all, and fuck anyone who told her differently. That made her a BAMF and badass mother-fuckers didn't take names. They kicked asses and demanded people get out of her way.

Barriers? What barriers?

Resistance? She'd wear it down.

Walls? Well, she sure as hell had built thick-assed ones herself.

But . . . what did any of it mean?

Her family was proud of her, no doubt. *She* was proud of her, proud of how relentless she'd been in pursuing what had once seemed like a far-fetched reality and doing it in a way that didn't crush the people beneath her.

Oh, she'd fought like hell for her dream, but she'd never been battling enemies or the people who said she couldn't do it.

She'd been battling herself.

She was *that* enemy. Her biggest enemy.

Because in thinking she had to close off everything around her, she hadn't really been living her full dream.

She'd merely been ticking off boxes.

Intern. Check.

Master's. Check.

Assistant GM. Check.

GM. Check.

Alone? Also check.

Too scared to let anyone really in? Too terrified of being hurt again that she'd let her childhood and college friends wane under the guise of too much work? Check. Check.

And as she stood, separate from these people who'd built an amazing family, one she'd been taking credit for all season, thinking it was she who'd put the final pieces together, *she* who'd made it special, Char realized that she was the least important part. These people trusted each other; they loved without fear.

It was plain as day to see.

Coop cupping Calle's cheek and pressing a kiss to their daughter's head.

Stefan lacing an arm around Brit's waist and pulling her back against his chest so that someone else would get a chance with Rebecca.

Liam, his arm around Mia's shoulders, enthusiastically congratulating Kevin.

Gabe stroking Nutritionist Rebecca's back, lightly reassuring her when she seemed overwhelmed by the noise and women surrounding her.

Kevin never letting go of PR Rebecca's hand.

Blue holding his and Anna's daughter while Anna pressed a kiss to the publicist's cheek.

Blane steadying Mandy when she teetered off-balance with her large belly.

Sara smiling over at Mike, her hand on her stomach hinting at a secret, her gaze saying they wouldn't share with the room at large and take away from Rebecca and Kevin's news.

Angie crouching beside Max's son, Brayden, clearly relaying the news because the little boy smiled hugely then wove his way through the women to hug Rebecca.

Love.

It was in this room. It was clear as day.

And the absence of it in Char's heart, in her life was just as clear.

Fuck, how that hurt.

Her eyes met Logan's.

And fuck how *that* hurt.

Her breath caught. Her heart felt like it had been tossed into a blender. Her insides churned and roiled and . . . she felt like she might be sick.

She stumbled back a step, nearly colliding with the coffee table before catching herself. She couldn't do this. She couldn't be here. It hurt so fucking much, and she didn't want that hurt filling the room, dampening the joy.

Char needed to go.

The back of her throat burning with bile, she sidestepped the crowd and got the fuck out of the house.

Later, she'd make up an excuse for leaving, congratulate them properly.

She'd send a gift or flowers or—her fingers crumpled the double-chocolate orgasm in her hand—*cookies*.

Tonight . . .

Tonight, she just needed to go.

Seventeen

Logan

Not following after Charlotte went against every single one of his instincts.

But slow, steady, patience—

He caught a glimpse of her through the window of the front door, saw her stop on the porch, her chin falling forward and her shoulders shuddering.

Fuck slow and steady.

She was hurting, and he wasn't just going to stand there like a moron, watching her suffer.

He slipped away from the conversation, not that anyone was paying him much attention. They were all too thrilled for Rebecca and Kevin, and he was happy for them, too. He just . . .

His heart was on that porch, hurting and alone.

He grabbed his jacket from the table by the door and went outside, dropping it onto Char's shoulders. It had been warm earlier, but night had fallen, become enshrouded with fog and a chill. The thin sweater she was wearing could hardly protect her.

"Log—"

Sad brown eyes on his, damp with tears.

He bundled her close to his side and walked her around to the side of the house. Then he did something that was probably inappropriate, but something that he couldn't stop himself from doing.

He hugged her.

Just pulled her against his chest, rested his chin on her head, and wrapped his arms around her.

Char didn't go stiff.

Instead, she melted, sank against him, turning her head so her cheek was against his chest, her shuddering breaths soaking through his T-shirt.

Logan held her, knowing that this strong, capable, *wonderful* woman leaning on him for a few minutes was a gift, perhaps the greatest of his life. He rubbed slow circles up and down her spine, took long, slow breaths, hoping that her breathing would steady to match his.

And when it eventually did, when the barest hint of stiffness entered her frame, he released her.

Wide, damp brown eyes on his, but there were no tear tracks on her cheeks, no pain in her expression. There was plenty of confusion, he could easily see in the moon's glow, but the hurt was banked, and for that, he was beyond thankful.

"Why?"

He touched her cheek. "You were hurting," he whispered. "I hate it when you hurt."

Weariness crept in. Her lips pressed flat. "You didn't then."

"Char, sweetheart," he whispered. "I'm sorry."

"Why, Log? Why did you break my heart?"

Quiet words, but the pain had floated in on the coattails of weary, and though he hated the sight of it with a passion, didn't want to say or do anything to increase that emotion, or to push her farther from him, Logan knew that the time was now. He had to tell her why he'd done what he'd done. He needed her to know.

"I asked to be traded."

Her eyes went wide. *"What?"*

"Back then," he said, "I knew we were moving too fast, too quickly. I knew that you were going to give more than me, going to give up too much, and I knew I couldn't let you put your dreams on hold for me." He held her gaze. "So, I went to Luc and told him that we were together, but that I knew it wasn't the best for you . . . and I asked him for a trade."

More hurt. More fury.

More . . . understanding.

"I could never fathom why he took that hit on the trade. You were a rising star, and who we got in return couldn't compare."

"Coleman did well for the team."

A beat, then, "But he wasn't you."

Logan sucked in a breath, although he didn't have the opportunity to form that air into words because she went on. "And furthermore, who made you the person who got to decide what was best for me? Huh?" She poked a finger into his chest, the small bite of her nail poking into him the tiniest pinprick of pain. But it was enough to remind him he was here, telling Char the truth of what happened after all this time, and that if he bungled it, then he might be able to muster all of the *slow down, patience, move steadily* bullshit in the world, but he'd never get her back.

Logan opened his mouth, readying the list of reasons why, all of the logical motivations he'd had for making sure that Char got to live out her dreams.

But none of that came out.

Instead, he said, "*I* made that decision, and it was the right one, the *only* one to be made."

Her brows lifted. "That's it?"

And dumbass that he was, he said, "That's it."

EIGHTEEN

CHAR

The man had lost his fucking mind.

And maybe so had she, because she jabbed her finger into his chest, repeated, "That's why? *That's why? That's. Why?*" When he nodded, she scoffed and started to turn away, disgust in her every pore. What in the fuck was wrong with him?

He covered her hand, held it against his chest.

"That's not what—"

She turned back just in time to see him break off with a firm shake of his head.

"I'm— I didn't want us to turn into my parents, Starlight," he said.

That stopped her, brows drawn together. Their parents still being married after many decades when everyone in their circle seemed to be the product of divorce was something that had connected them, something that had brought them closer. Family dinners and events, holidays spent with each other, celebrating and teasing and loving each other in a way the rest of the world might not understand.

Except . . . she still talked to her family, still loved and saw them as often as possible, but she didn't have what the people inside Rebecca's house had.

She didn't have *that* type of family.

Because she'd pulled back, erected walls.

Because of the man in front of her, she thought, fury boiling within her. Up and up, bubbling to the top of the pot, threatening to cascade over the top and scald everything around her.

Just in time, logic prevailed.

Because this man might have hurt her, but *she* was the one who'd pulled back from everything else.

At first, because she didn't want to keep hurting. Instead, she had wanted to get lost in something that wasn't Logan.

Then because it was safer to be the deserted island in the middle of the ocean.

Crystal clear, blue water surrounding her on all sides, isolated, untouched—except perhaps from a visit from a passing ship or flock of birds or—

Logan shifted, dropping her hand and pacing away from her, thrusting his fingers into his hair and mussing the locks. He groaned. "This isn't—" Another shake of his head as he spun back toward her, all of that long, lean gorgeousness stalking toward her. "This isn't how I wanted to explain it." He ground his teeth together, glanced up at the dark sky, and she watched his shoulders flex as he inhaled and exhaled deeply.

She was wrong.

She might be that isolated island in the middle of the ocean.

But it wasn't just birds or ships visiting.

It was a hurricane.

And his name was Logan.

He stopped in front of her, green eyes nearly black in the evening's light, chest rising and falling rapidly. He was so much bigger than her, stronger physically in a way that made part of her question whether she had any hope in hell of keeping him at bay, or if perhaps, she didn't want to keep him at bay, and instead launch herself into his arms and ask him to keep her safe from the winds threatening to tear her to shreds.

Stay insulated and safe?

Or hop into the churning waves for what might possibly be the best surf of her life?

Char didn't surf.

But she wasn't an idiot. She was in the eye of the storm, Logan was there, he was troubled, and clearly more had happened behind the scenes of their breakup than she understood.

So, waves or not, she wanted to know.

She snagged his hand when he paced close enough, weaving their fingers together and tugging him to a halt. "Start at the beginning."

Startled emerald eyes on hers, a chiseled jaw clenching. "This goes way back," he said. "I—" He thrust his free hand through his hair, mussing it further, making Char's fingers itch with the need to fix it. "It's a long story."

"We lost the big game. The season's over. No meetings, no practices, no media." She shrugged. "Just tell me everything, Log, because seriously, what else have we got to do that could possibly be more important than this?"

His gaze held hers, even as his fingers convulsed. "Nothing," he murmured. "Nothing is more important than this, than you."

She couldn't deny that his words, the way he looked at her, the firm grip of his hand around hers . . . she had absolutely no hope of denying that they soothed a ragged tear in her heart, that they made her feel as though she could take her first full breath in years.

Perhaps since the moment he'd gone.

"My parents are unhappy."

Char blinked. That was pretty much the last thing she'd imagined him saying. He'd panicked because his feelings were too big or they'd moved too fast or they were too young or—

Except, she'd known it was more than that, hadn't she?

That was why it had hurt so much when he broke things off.

Because one moment they'd had absolutely everything—love, companionship, passion, friendship—and the next it had been snatched away, torn asunder by the person she'd trusted most in the world.

"Okay," she said softly, when it seemed like he was struggling with how to go on.

Green eyes on hers. "I know we talked about our families a lot when we were together, how our parents were still married, how cool it was that we got along with our siblings—"

She inhaled quickly. Had something happened with his family, with his brother and sister?

No. She'd *know*.

If something serious had gone down during the season, she would have known. Although, if it had happened before—

"But your parents actually like each other," he said, stopping the panicked spiral in her mind. "Mine . . . well, I guess tolerate one another would be the most apt word, but the reality is that they've been together so long, I think it's simply a case of convenience, as in, it's more convenient for them to stay together than to separate."

"I'm sorry," she whispered.

He made a face. "I'm not telling you this for sympathy or because I'm still hung up on the fact that things always have been tense between them. That's just life and the way it was."

Logan paused again, and she found herself stepping closer, reaching up to cup his cheek. "So, why *are* you telling me?"

"Right." He took a breath. "Okay, so—"

A burst of noise around the front of the house had them

both freezing in place. She waited for the sounds to quiet, for the players and kids to depart, but they seemed to be congregating on the porch, talking over each other. Voices were lifted in excitement, a baby was screaming, a young male voice was singing the last pop song a cappella—and not particularly on key.

"I—" Logan broke off on a wince as the volume rose.

And even though they were around the corner, Char could barely hear herself think, let alone focus on what Logan was trying to tell her, and it seemed as though the noise was making something hard for him to verbalize even more difficult.

Instinct took over.

"Come on," she said, tugging him through a row of trees and away from the cacophony. The yard wasn't fenced, and they were able to slip out the side of the property and onto the long driveway that led down to the main road. Her car was parked just a little ways down. "Did you drive?"

"Yes," he said. "I'm parked almost near the bottom."

A nod, the plan forming in her head. "I'll drop you at your car," she said. "Then you can meet me at my place."

"Char," he said, expression tentative. "I'm not trying to manipulate you or—"

"I know."

"And you still want me to go back to your place—" He halted, free hand coming up to cup her cheek. "As friends?"

She hesitated then admitted what should have been the truth in her heart from the beginning. Being just friends was impossible. She could be his boss—and only his boss—or she could be . . . more.

"No."

It was the barest whisper, but she knew that he'd heard because his fingers convulsed around hers, his breath hitched, and his body came very close.

She'd had his mouth on hers less than forty-eight hours before.

Recently enough that she knew exactly what she was missing, so much so that she nearly turned around and claimed it for herself, because he was a fucking incredible kisser.

But . . . passion wasn't their problem.

She owed herself the opportunity for closure, and maybe she also owed him the chance to explain himself.

Reaching forward, she grabbed onto the handle and tugged open the driver's side door, the locks automatically disengaging as she did so. Fancy—or at least that was what her mom had deemed the system when she'd come to visit a few months ago, and Char couldn't exactly blame her. There had been plenty of food on the table growing up. They'd had power and electricity and a place to live. But there hadn't been brand new cars or expensive vacations or electronics for Christmas.

So, locks opening at the touch of her hand *was* fancy.

She sat down, started to close the door, but Logan caught it. "Wh—"

He reached over her and buckled her belt, tracing his thumb lightly over her cheekbone as he began to straighten. Her breath caught, her pulse thundered. His mouth . . . *God*, it was right there.

He backed up, softly closed her door, and rounded the hood, eyes on hers the entire way.

It would have been an impressive display of peripheral vision if she hadn't seen him carry the puck up the ice hundreds of times without ever looking down, and anyway, her thoughts weren't much on hockey, not when he was opening the door and sliding into the passenger's seat.

His spiced scent filled the interior of her car, washing over her in waves.

Or maybe that was her attraction to him. Or maybe it was the waves of his scent and her attraction to him, and also her yearning . . . for an explanation, for a family like the one inside Rebecca's house, for one person to love her more than anything else in the world.

He pressed the button to start the ignition, and because she'd instinctively rested her foot on the brake, the engine fired up.

More fancy.

More—

"Less thinking, Starlight," he whispered, those emerald depths unfathomable. "More driving."

Her breath shuddered out. She moved her gaze to the windshield.

There was a part of her that wanted to continue to delay, that worried this big explanation and long story of Logan's wouldn't be enough. That she wouldn't be able to forgive him. *Ever.*

And she liked this respite.

This cautious bond between a man who knew her in a way no one else in the world did.

She liked how he looked at her—like she'd hung the moon and stars they'd so often loved to stare at while bundled up in the back of his pickup. She loved how he touched her, made her feel desirable and vulnerable and strong, all at the same time. And she really loved how he listened to everything she said, that he didn't discount or dismiss, that he listened, but that he didn't just give in. Maybe sometimes he pushed back, and even though that could sometimes irritate her, she respected that he challenged her.

He paid attention. He wasn't scared off by walls.

He'd . . . brought her slippers and groceries and cooked for her and—

She didn't want to lose that.

She'd had it all for one day, and she didn't want it to disappear.

Her pulse pounded, her hands tightened on the steering wheel. Fear sat heavy in her gut, and yearning for a family like the team's inside had a thick thread forming in her heart. She longed for Logan. Knew deep down that his explanation made sense. If she was able to forgive him—and she couldn't deny that a part of her already wanted to—then this *thing* with Logan, whatever the *thing* would become, might have the potential to destroy. It could devastate her career, ruin her reputation, and . . . have her serving her heart up to him on a golden platter.

With fresh herbs.

Or maybe herb butter. Heart with herb butter. Now *that* was a disgusting thought. Char bit back a shudder.

Thankfully, it was disgusting enough that she was able to get out of her head, to check for other cars, and to pull out on the driveway.

Part of her expected Logan to say something.

Instead, they rode in silence for the twenty seconds it took to get down to his car. Probably, she should have had him walk, but Char didn't calculate distance or time into her plan. It was a series of steps.

Get to car.

Get Logan to car.

Get to house.

Get explanation.

Get heart *un*broken. Hopefully. Shit. *Shit.* Was she really hoping that? Did she want all of those things? The heart? The spice? The potential of something big with this man?

The logical part of her brain screamed at her, *No. No! No fucking way.*

But her heart said something else.

War. Down to the very marrow of her bones. It was terrifying. A huge swathe of emotions and memories that threatened to bear down on her. Maybe a few days ago she would have bunkered down into her proverbial cellar, would have braced herself until the tornado passed her by, would have rebuilt the walls, cleaned up the devastation.

Then she would have moved on.

Today, she had seen something wonderful, something she wanted enough to not wish to hide in the basement and lock herself away. She wanted . . . more.

More than what she had in her life currently.

She wanted love and emotions and those fucking tornados, even if they might break her. So, while the thought of swinging that cellar door open was absolutely terrifying, Charlotte Harris had never, *ever* been a coward.

She pushed and battled and never gave up.

Today would *not* be the day she stopped being brave.

Nineteen

He tried to get his head on straight as he drove, attempted to put his thoughts together in an orderly manner, but Logan didn't make much headway.

His heart was pounding.

His gut was tied into knots.

His will was resolute.

He needed to stop the buildup, to lay out the facts, to get it over with.

"Would have been better if you'd started the conversation in a private place so you wouldn't get interrupted, dipshit," he muttered.

Yeah, well there was that. Which highlighted his whole problem with patience and taking things slow. But . . . Char hadn't turned away from him, even though he'd been traveling forward solely by left and right turns, hardly making sense as he'd taken her down a tangent.

Not a tangent so much as an aside. A necessary aside in order to give her context.

She turned into her driveway, waiting as the garage door slid open. Logan pulled up to the curb, throwing his car into park and getting out. He made it to her as she was just getting out, his jacket still around her shoulders, her purse in her hand.

He held the door for her, closed it after she'd slipped out.

"This way," she told him, hitting the button to close the garage door then leading him into her kitchen and setting her purse on the counter. It was only a quick pitstop because she turned for the slider she'd left unlocked yesterday—and he was glad to see this time it was locked as she flicked open the bolt—and walked onto the back porch.

He followed her out, watched as she completed a ritual he thought she must have done a hundred times before—moving toward the outdoor heater and turning it on, grabbing a thick blanket from a box tucked next to a planter, draping it over the back of one of her loungers.

She'd just started to sit down when her eyes flicked to his, and his heart swelled when she moved back to the chest and snagged another blanket, draping it over the other chair.

Then she settled in, her frame almost dwarfed by his jacket, and doubly so by the thick fleece covering that she pulled up to her chin.

Considering that Logan was almost sweating from the heater itself, he simply snagged the blanket off the lounger and held it close. The fabric was soft, though not as soft as her skin, but it smelled like Char, sweet with the barest hint of spice—as though she'd been bathing in rosewater and then decided to eat something with chilis.

And he was making no sense in his head, pontificating mentally about roses and chilis and still not explaining.

Enough.

"Four months isn't enough time to know a person," he said.

She sucked in a breath. "You're right," she whispered. "Of

course, you're right." Soft words, pained words. Fuck, he'd hurt her again without even meaning to.

Logan set the blanket aside and moved toward Char, settling next to her. "I was so absolutely in love with you that I didn't want to bring in any of the bad stuff, and I deliberately hid it."

Her chin came up. "I didn't need you to do that."

"I didn't do it for you," he admitted. "I did it for me because your family is so great that I didn't want to pollute that with the drama of mine."

"I've met your family—"

"I know," he said. "You met my parents when they were on their best behavior—you as an employee of the organization paying my salary—but that was just it, they were on their best behavior."

"Your sister—"

"My siblings aren't like my parents. We all survived that tension, the always present underlying resentment, and we're closer for it." He shook his head. "But, while my parents are lovely people in many ways, how they treated each other made it really hard going growing up."

"What did they do to each other?"

Logan shoved a hand through his hair and gave her the quick and dirty version. "My mom quit her job and always resented it. My dad didn't understand how hard it was for her to give up her career, to live only for her kids and husband. He wanted his needs met and made sure they were. She was content with playing martyr as hers weren't." He sighed. "Add in a dash of shitty communication skills and plenty of silent treatment on both sides, and you have a lovely thirty-year marriage that is still going strong."

Silence.

Then she shifted on the chair, her shoulder coming to rest against his. "And you saw me as your mom?"

Logan's eyes slid closed. "Yes. No. *Yes*," he admitted. "Partly, but more I saw me as my dad. I had the demanding career with the potential moves that would uproot everything. I had a wonderful woman, who was willing to give it all up and not look back." He peeled open his eyes, turned so he could rest his palm on Char's cheek. "I didn't want you to give up your dreams for me. I had to let you go so you could achieve them for yourself."

Her chest rose and fell on a long, slow inhale and exhale, but she didn't say anything. But because she also didn't push him away, he kept going. "You'd said it in passing at first, mentioned that you would just move with me if I got traded, but then as the rumors swirled and the deadline approached, do you remember what you did?"

She leaned back, expression clearing. "I think it was something along the lines of not wanting the internship in the first place, so obviously, I would quit and become a WAG." Her eyes flashed, but he couldn't decipher if it was because she was mad at him or herself.

The woman he knew today wouldn't give everything up for a man.

The girl she'd been back then might have.

And that had terrified him enough that he'd taken matters into his own hands.

"So, I went to Luc and asked him for that trade," he said, remembering how the GM hadn't wanted to let him go, that he'd pushed back hard until Logan had to admit what was going on with Char, and the only reason he'd been able to get the trade at all was because Luc loved her like a daughter and felt the same way as Logan.

Neither of them wanted any barriers between Char and her dreams.

The big dreams. The ones she'd whispered to him in the dark of night, the stars in the winter sky overhead their only illumination. To go back to school, to work her way up the ranks, to run an organization on her own.

How in the fuck could she have done that trailing around as he made his way through his own career?

The answer was that she wouldn't have been able to.

So, he'd made the decision for them.

Break their hearts now—and do it in one forceful movement rather than the slow, incremental crack after crack he'd witnessed in his mom.

"Luc knew," she whispered.

"Yeah," he said. "I told him."

Her breath caught, even as clarity danced across her face.

Luc had been absolutely livid. The players weren't supposed to fraternize with the staff, and most especially with the interns, but he'd been able to put that anger aside for Char's own good.

She glared. "So, you two worked together to facilitate the trade, all without talking to me, totally presuming to know everything."

"I did say I take after my dad," he said, attempting a light joke. "Also, this just in, I was a fucking idiot at twenty-one."

"Yeah, you were," she said, gaze dropping to her hands, another breath sliding her shoulders up and down. Then it came back up, locked onto his. "I was an idiot, too." He breathed out a sigh of relief, but then pain crowded back in. "I was immature. I wouldn't have been content just following you around forever, even though I do want to have a family of my own someday."

Logan's heart skipped a beat at the thought of Char's kids. They'd be smart as hell and gorgeous and—

"However," she said, interrupting his thoughts. "You say you did this all for my own good, but what about the girl?"

Logan winced. "What girl?"

A shake of her head. "Nice try, but you know exactly what girl I'm talking about."

He did.

Unfortunately.

"After we broke up, I heard you'd gone to Luc and said you

were going to quit anyway," he admitted quietly. The GM had called him, said he needed to find a way to end things permanently with Char so she didn't come after Logan and so she could move on with her life because Luc wasn't losing his best player *and* his best employee. "So, I did what I had to do."

Her brows came up, those chocolate eyes flashed with sparks. "By *doing* someone else days after you'd been inside me?"

"No!" he said. "Absolutely fucking not. I didn't sleep with her. I kissed her once, made sure it got caught on camera—by paparazzi she called herself, by the way," he added when Char's lips parted again. The woman was now a successful actress, but back then she'd been up and coming and had seized any opportunity to make the press. "And, for all that the photographs looked passionate, there wasn't anything pleasant about the kiss. It was acting on both our sides."

"Was there tongue?"

He frowned. "What?"

She shot him a droll look. "You say it was acting, that it was a fake kiss. Well, movie kisses don't have tongue."

Having followed that, somehow, he tugged a strand of her hair. "No, there wasn't any tongue," he said. "From the little I remember of it—and it was about as pleasant as making out with my pillow—I think my dick actually curled up into my body."

"Log!"

"Nor did I enjoy having her that close," he said. "It was like trying to cuddle a garbage bag filled with hangers." Hard when she should have been soft like Char. Add in that she smelled wrong and that he had been longing for a completely different woman. "And more importantly, she wasn't you, Starlight. She wasn't the woman who owned my heart, the one I wanted but had forced myself to let go because I couldn't be the one to stifle her dreams."

Her lips parted.

But he had one more thing to say.

"I regret every single day that I had to hurt you." He cupped her jaw, held her gaze. "But I will *never* regret letting you go. What you've accomplished, the strength and skill you've shown over the years has made me so fucking proud of you." He brushed his thumb over her cheek, capturing the single tear that dripped down her cheek. "And I've never stopped loving you, even though I had to do it from far away.

"Logan." It was a shuddering sound, one that rattled her frame.

Then she was up on her feet, pushing away from him, pacing to the other side of the deck and staring up at the sky.

He'd just poured out his heart.

And she'd walked away.

The silence settled around them, heavy and stifling and . . . unbroken.

She didn't say a single word.

TWENTY

CHAR

Twinkling lights in the sky.

Cool air.

The man sitting five feet away.

Eight years, and she felt like she was right back in the past. The cool air surrounding them, the quiet of the night all around, the stars overhead. She'd been transported back in time, the only things missing were Logan's arms around her, the steady thrum of his pulse beneath her ear, his scent in her nose.

He'd told her why.

He'd given her the explanation she wanted, and if she were being entirely truthful with herself, it was also the explanation she was hoping for.

He hadn't wanted to leave her. He hadn't moved right on to someone else. He . . . still loved her.

But—

Char sucked in a breath.

But what?

But . . . did the explanation make any bit of difference? He'd still hurt her, he'd broken her, made her question everything in her heart and mind.

She released the breath, blinked up at the sky, and admitted the truth, if only to herself.

Yes, the explanation made a difference. It made a *big* difference.

It was only—

Char was still scared. She yearned for a family, and if she were being honest, a part of her had never stopped loving Logan either, even when she'd been hurt and heartbroken. But—

Fuck.

All of these *but*s.

She wasn't a woman who second-guessed herself frequently. She used her brain, thought through the pros and cons, weighed those options, and then she made a decision. And stuck with it.

Still, to get confirmation that Logan had been trying to protect her changed the way their breakup was framed in her mind. He wasn't an asshole trying to hold tightly to his bachelor days. He was a man trying to protect the woman he'd loved so she could go out and live her life.

It was the news she wanted to hear.

But—another fucking *but*—it also sliced her to the core.

Because he hadn't discussed it with her. He'd thought he'd known the best course of action, and he'd executed it without once coming and explaining why. Though, and this was part of the reason for all the *but*s, she was now thirty years old. She was stubborn as hell. But her thirty years had garnered her some clarity, some understanding that the world, that people and their emotions didn't work in black and white or right and wrong.

She'd also had thirty years to understand that she could be a stubborn pain in the ass, and that it was very likely that if Logan had told her his worries when she'd been a headstrong twenty-two-year-old, then she would have done her level best to prove them wrong . . . even to her own detriment.

So, had he made the right call?

Another inhale and exhale. Another long, slow breath to center her mind.

Yes. Conservatively, she could say that much.

But did it still hurt? Yes. And did she still hate that he hadn't talked to her about it? *Yes.* And did she *really* fucking hate that he'd seen fit to end any hope of reconciliation by orchestrating a media stunt that had stomped on her already shattered heart? Hell *fucking* yes, she did.

Then add in that Luc had known about their relationship, that he'd conspired with Logan to separate them, and Char's heart felt both healed and a little bruised.

Their intentions had been good.

But they'd still been making decisions about her life without her.

And she couldn't deny that hurt, especially when so many years had passed and neither of them had ever discussed it with her.

Even as she made a mental note to call Luc this week—she needed to hear his side from himself, to ask him why he'd never talked to her about it, especially when she'd clearly been so distraught in the days and weeks after the trade. Of course, she hadn't talked to *him* about it either. She'd gone to him and put in her resignation but wouldn't tell him why, and by the time he'd told her he wouldn't accept it, Logan had been on the gossip sites and she'd wanted something, *anything* to throw herself into.

To work so hard until she forgot.

She *had* worked.

Long and intently and, in many ways, she *had* forgotten— the effect Logan had on her, how her heart always seemed more open when he was around, how he looked at her as though she held the secrets to the universe, and how he touched her like she was a fragile treasure that had to be treated oh so carefully.

"I think that's what hurt the most."

Char was so lost in her own head that she didn't realize she spoke aloud until Logan's voice came from just behind her. "What hurt the most, Starlight?"

She jumped then turned to face him. "That I had pinned all of these hopes and dreams on a relationship with you, one that was gone in an instant." Heart aching, she admitted, "But now what hurts the most is that you thought you knew better about my life than I did. That Luc never mentioned it to me." She sighed heavily. "That I almost gave up *everything* for a boy."

He wasn't a boy now—all long, lean lines and a sparse beard.

He was a man—one who'd grown into his height, who was strong and fierce and . . . whose thick, full beard she wanted to feel between her thighs.

Attraction wasn't the issue.

Rather, she felt as though her weaknesses had been exposed to the sunlight, and she was ashamed and embarrassed. Not to have loved him, but because she was supposed to be strong, and at the end of it all, she'd been a pale approximation of herself.

"I understand why you did it," she said. "And I forgive you for it."

His breath shuddered out, relief flooding his expression.

"But I don't know if I can forgive myself."

"I—" He stopped, studied her closely. "I'm not sure what you mean, Starlight."

"It's just—" Char sighed and slipped between him and the railing, pacing away from him again. "All my life, I've been this strong, powerful woman. Confident in myself, seeing what I wanted and unerringly going after that. And . . . I almost gave up *everything* for a months' long relationship that was unlikely to have survived our Stupid Years."

Logan made a sound that sounded suspiciously like a chuckle, and she whirled around.

"I'm serious!" she exclaimed. "I just don't know how I could have thought I was making the right choice by giving up everything I was working for. It makes—" She cringed, unable to verbalize it.

"It makes you doubt the person you were inside."

Shocked, because that was exactly how she felt, she turned and gaped at him. "How—?"

A sad smile curved the corners of his mouth. "Because that's exactly how I've felt every single day since I left."

"Oh."

One syllable.

A worthless one, at that.

And yet, she couldn't think of anything else to say.

Then she thought of the *only* thing she could say. Because she didn't want to send Logan away. He was in her heart, had always been, would always be. So, maybe she needed to reflect on their relationship and subsequent breakup, needed to have a nice long think about what had happened, what had been kept from her, and how it would apply to the person she thought she was today.

Maybe those doubts would coalesce into clarity.

Maybe they would destroy the strong, infallible person she thought she was.

But she knew that she was too raw inside to search for those answers tonight, not after the stark longing at the party, not after having confirmation that hers and Logan's relationship hadn't ended as she'd once suspected.

Tonight, she wanted to forget. Not about what might be, nor about the past, or well, not *all* of it anyway. She wanted to erase everything that had happened from the time Logan had been traded all the way until he'd shown up at her office two days before.

She wanted to go back and to move forward.

She wanted warm arms and cool evening air and stars overhead.

Which was why she said that one thing aloud. "Come here."

No hesitation from Logan. Not a heartbeat or a moment to breathe. One second he was five feet away from her and in the next, the toes of his shoes were brushing against hers.

She shuddered and melted and . . . leaned into him.

And when those warm arms found her, when they wrapped around her like they used to, Char knew that everything had altered even as absolutely nothing had changed.

TWENTY-ONE

LOGAN

His back was on fire. His shoulder ached.

The entire right side of his body was asleep.

But he wasn't going to move a muscle.

Char was cuddled up next to him, not gone to the world, but awake and close and allowing him to hold her as she watched the moon and the constellations shift across the sky overhead.

She smelled like roses and spice. Her curvy body fit perfectly against his, as they'd somehow managed to squeeze themselves onto one of the loungers on her deck.

The woman he'd loved for nearly a decade was in his arms.

So, no, he wasn't moving, not one millimeter.

"Do you remember the first time we met?" she asked. Her voice was hushed, even though it wasn't particularly late, but there was something about being outside after dark, the world muted around them, that gave him the same urge to talk quietly as well, to pretend that nothing else existed except the two of them.

"Yeah, Starlight, I do." He smiled. "You told me I smelled."

She snorted. "Well, what else could I have done? I was assaulted from the stench of all those male bodies." A shudder flowed through her, but he didn't mind that it was at his expense, not when the movement brought her closer, all those curves vibrating against him.

"There's a reason we shower," he said.

"That's true," she said. "But it was also a combination of not having the right protocols in place."

"What do you mean?"

"The equipment manager had left. Do you remember that?" she asked, leaning back slightly. Instinctively, he tightened his arms, and he caught the edge of her smile as she rested her head back onto his chest.

He stroked a hand down her hair. "He went to rehab."

"Yeah. He struggled with pain killers after a car accident." She sighed. "He came back toward the end of the season and still works for Luc now, but while he was gone his second in command didn't feel comfortable bringing issues up with management."

"And one of those issues being *our* smelly asses?"

She snorted. "The issue being that the industrial washing machine wasn't working, and so they were trying to handle things by hand."

"By hand?"

There are a lot of players on an NHL team and loads of equipment. Sets for practice, sets for games, extras in case they were damaged. Hell, he knew more than a handful of players who had multiple pairs of skates and gloves just for one game— because they preferred them to be completely dry for each period they were on the ice.

He was a little less picky, though he was finicky about his sticks and the tape and wax he used, as well as his edges—how his skates were sharpened. Oh, and his gloves. He'd been known to take advantage of the dryers in between shifts. And he supposed he really preferred that his laces be waxed and was always sneaking out the earpieces on his helmet, and his visor . . . he preferred that—

Okay, he was a picky mofo.

But the job was his life, and he liked things a certain way.

"Yup," she said, "by hand. Crazy, right?" She shook her head, the riotous brown curls bouncing across his chest. "Not only was it a waste of time and not effective. It was actually a health hazard." He frowned, opened his mouth to ask how, but she nuzzled against his throat, her arm tightening over his middle, and added, "Hockey players get hit with pucks and sticks and punch each other until they bleed."

He snorted. "We're dumbasses."

"Sometimes," she admitted, making him laugh. "But aside from the occasional idiocy, the blood-stained equipment was the real concern. We can't have someone getting a staph infection or worse."

Logan stopped, once again amazed by this woman. "I never would have considered that in a million years," he said, running his fingers over her cheek. "That's why they pay you the big bucks."

She snorted.

"Or the medium bucks," he amended, knowing that his contract was significantly bigger than hers.

"I'm quite satisfied with my medium bucks," she said. "I'm not putting my body on the line like you guys, and truthfully, I only found out about the biohazard issue after I made it my mission to tackle the smell issue."

"You got the industrial washer fixed."

A statement, not a question. Because he knew she wouldn't have stopped until she had sorted it out.

"I got them new washers, sanitation equipment, and an ozone cleaner."

He laughed. "That's why we started smelling so fresh?"

"Damn right," she said. "Couldn't have my nose burning every time I was within three feet of a player."

"Did it burn near me?"

"Fuck, yes, it did." She shifted, crossing her arms over his chest and resting her chin on them. "You were the worst!"

"You wound me," he groaned, tugging on a strand of her hair.

"You know you were."

He smirked. "I do know that. Because you told me. Do you remember that part?"

Chagrin danced on the edges of her expression, and if it had been fully light, he might have seen the barest pink appear on her cheekbones. "I do," she said then bit her lip, her voice softening. "Because it was also the first time I touched you."

"You pushed my hair off my forehead," he said, remembering the feel of her fingers. Such an innocent touch and, "I got hard in my cup."

Her lip popped free, and she gasped. "You didn't!"

"I did," he admitted. "And nearly unmanned myself in the process."

Char giggled and shifted, one leg sliding over the top of his thighs.

Heat arrowed toward his cock, and he placed his hand lightly on the small of her back, resisting the urge to grip both of her hips and seat her more firmly over him. Her breath caught at the contact . . . and truthfully, he was already hard. Again. Just like he had been all those years before.

Which she felt.

That wasn't like before, or at least not how it had been during their first meeting. She'd felt it many times over the months that followed, but that first night, she'd lurched back, her chin lifting even as she'd curled her hand into a fist at her side. He'd seen that glimpse of pink then, made obvious by the bright fluorescent lights overhead, even though he'd been the one to lean close, to bend enough so she could reach him when she'd extended her hand.

Drawn. Bewitched.

Even then.

"I told you to take a shower," she said, rolling her eyes at herself. "I was so upset that I'd touched you, that I'd dared crossed the line between management and player, that I said you smelled."

He snorted. "I didn't take it personally."

"I did." She made a face. "Both the attraction and the insults. Neither were professional." White teeth nibbling into a lush bottom lip. "But I only gave into one."

"Yup." His lips twitched. "The insults."

"Rude!"

"Yup," he said. "You are."

She gasped in outrage, those lips parting, tempting him, and Logan found he couldn't resist any longer. Levering up as he banded his arm around her waist, he kissed her.

And she kissed *him*. Fuck, but she kissed him, gripping his shoulders, her fingernails sharp spikes of pleasure through the fabric of his shirt. She leaned into him, legs straddling his hips, and her pelvis came in contact with his, the heat of her pressing tightly to his cock.

Fuck.

Heat.

Need.

Desire.

It filled every cell in his body, made red haze in on the edges of his vision, had his fingers clenching on her hips, had him parting his lips, tongue darting out to dance with hers.

Nothing was like kissing Char.

Not hoisting the Cup, not scoring a game-winning goal, not getting drafted in the first place. Not holding his nephew for the first time, or how proud his dad had been when he'd scored his first goal.

Char was *everything*.

"Come in the house," she murmured when they broke apart for air. "Come to my bed. Come kiss me and hold me and *touch* me." Her fingers brushed his lips, traced the outline when he might have protested. Because they'd made big progress that night, and he didn't want to fuck it up. "And then when you've done that for long enough, I want you to come inside me."

TWENTY-TWO

CHAR

She was bordering on brazen.

Which was a characteristic she considered commonplace in her business life but not so much in the bedroom.

Of course, she knew what she wanted, wasn't afraid to ask for it.

But she really enjoyed being able to sit back and not have to be in charge of something, to give and take without considering every angle, to shut off her brain and just *enjoy* herself.

Like she wanted to do with Logan.

"Starlight," he murmured, his tone beyond gentle, and she knew he was trying to be so careful with her, to not hurt her. "I don't think—"

"That's the point," she said, trying to push off him then stopping and glaring when he wouldn't let her go. "Log, *that's* the point, isn't it? Both of us have spent *too* long thinking and considering—me, wondering what I did wrong to make you leave me. You, worrying that we would turn out like your parents. But it's gotten us nowhere. Except, hurt and heartbroken and apart." She sucked in a breath, released it slowly. "I've had a lot of realizations tonight. I've realized I miss my family and hate that I've focused so much on barricading myself in work that I've lost some of our closeness. I hate that!"

"Char—"

"And I hate that I only just now realized that I'm thirty-fucking-years-old and the only thing I want, perhaps more than my job, is my own family—kids and a husband who loves me and—"

He cupped her cheek.

"And I *really* hate that I didn't see through what you were doing, that I internalized it and made you go to a man who I trusted as much as my own father to trick me into making the right decision." A hot tear slid down her cheek, burning a trail from the corner of her eye to her jaw. Annoyed, she brushed it away, shoved hard enough against his hold that he let her go. "And I really hate—"

Her words cut off.

Because she'd wanted to finish that with *you*.

But she couldn't.

She *couldn't* hate this man. Try as she might, she couldn't hate him or what he'd done or even how he'd gone about it.

Sure, she could wish things had gone differently, but also, she knew if the situation were reversed, she would have done something very similar. She wouldn't have let Logan risk his dream for her.

Not ever.

"*That's* why," he whispered, trailing his fingers over her cheek, across her jaw, up to lightly stroke the spot behind her ear. "Because you need some time, sweetheart. To think about us, to sort things out in your head. I'm here to talk through what's going on with your family. I'm here. I really fucking hope to maybe be that person you can build your own family with some-day, but"—he inhaled sharply, released the breath slowly—"I'm also the man who hurt you, who broke your heart, and you need time to process why."

Her heart was pounding.

Anger was a sharp ache in her throat.

Pent-up need a coiled snake in her center.

But . . . he was right.

She needed to allow herself this moment, to not bury every-thing as she'd done for the last years. Feel. She needed to feel and think and come to terms with all that happened.

Sighing, she rested her forehead against his chest.

"As much as I hate to admit it," she muttered. "You're right."

His laughter—slightly strained—and the hard planes of his body—hard everywhere, heh—relaxed her enough that she could think again. Or at least not feel as though she were going to be swallowed by her emotions.

She glanced up, enjoying the feel of his fingers stroking through her hair, his body pressed to hers, his scent surrounding her.

"Will you at least kiss me before you go?"

A wicked smile, fingers tightening slightly in her hair.

And then he did as she asked, kissing her until her pulse pounded in her veins, until her lips were swollen, until her body was a tangled knot of need.

Eventually, they broke apart, his gaze holding hers, and the need in those beautiful green eyes took her already jagged breath away.

As did his words.

"I plan on kissing you goodnight every day for the rest of my life."

———

It was early East Coast time.

Which meant it was *really* freaking early California time.

But Char had woken just as the sun was beginning to lighten the brown-topped hills in the distance, the summer's heat already turning the green grass dry and brittle. Soon enough fire season would be upon them, smoke choking the air, blocking out the sky, making it impossible for her to see the stars she liked to glance upon with a glass of wine in her hand.

Often, she snuck away for a week or two, recharging at a spa, spending time at a beachfront hotel while doing nothing more than sticking her toes in the sand, or occasionally in the ocean. Last year, she'd skipped the break completely, having spent those weeks dealing with the move and getting her ducks in a row for the season.

She'd swung by her family's house for a weekend, kissed her mom and dad, sat around the kitchen table listening to them cook and bicker in equal measures. But it hadn't been long before she'd felt the vise tighten around her chest, and she'd slipped out, losing herself to emails and work.

She'd left early the next day, had come to San Francisco, and all but lived in her office.

At the time, she'd chalked it up to nerves about her new position, to needing to assure herself that absolutely everything she could control was in order. But now she wondered if seeing her parents so in love and happy and in tune had made her shut down.

And then bolt.

Ugh.

More pondering to do, more thinking to complete.

But for now, she needed to slay the demon that was circling in her mind. Or at least try to cage it and glare it into submission.

Which was why she was back on her deck, a coffee in hand and staring at the lightening sky.

"Just do it already," she muttered.

She hit the button on her phone's screen then put her cell up to her ear.

Ring-ring.

Ring-ring.

Ring—

"Lottie!" Luc's voice boomed loudly through the speaker. "I was wondering when you'd get a moment to call. How are you? Terrorized any underlings lately?"

God, one call, and she was back in that arena.

Shaking her head, biting back a smile, because seriously this man was like an older brother and father and friend, all in one package. "I was doing better before you decided to use *that* name."

He laughed, and she could imagine him leaning back in his office chair, plunking his feet onto his desk.

"Plus, I don't terrorize anyone."

"Call it unintentional terrorizing then," he said. "You're so damned good at what you do, it's almost impossible to live up to your example."

Her breath caught, an unfamiliar ache sliding through her stomach.

"My mom said that once."

Silence.

The feet would be leaving the desk now, dropping back onto the floor, his brows drawn together. "What's that now?"

"She said the reason I'm single is that I'm so focused on being perfect that I can't accept the imperfections and failings of those around me."

He sucked in a breath, the noise rattling through the speaker.

"That's bullshit."

Char blinked. "What?"

"You know I love you, Lottie girl," he said. "So, I'm not

going to mince words. I've waited this entire season for him to make a fucking move, to make things right, but he hasn't, and so now I'm going to do what I should have."

"Do what?" she asked, fingers clenching on her cell.

"You're single for two reasons, and *only* two." His voice was sharp, demanding she pay attention. "One, because you're hung up on Logan Walker and your relationship with him overshadowed every other romantic one you've had since, and two, because none of those dumbasses you've dated since Logan had the balls to drag you down the aisle."

"You—"

"Yes, I knew," he interrupted before she got more than that one word out. "Yes, I also knew what I helped you two give up. Did I hate every fucking minute of it? Yes. Did I still think it was the right thing for both of you? Yes."

Char closed her eyes, was silent as his words washed over her.

Luc sighed. "Look, Lottie," he said, voice gentling. "I know that you were hurt badly by how things went down between you and Logan, and I fucking hated him for getting involved with you in the first place. Hell, I hated you a little bit for wanting to drop everything and take away my best employee." He paused. "Then I realized that you weren't two people looking for a quick fuck, but instead you two were just dumbasses in love at the wrong time in the wrong place, and I hoped you'd eventually find your way back to each other."

"Luc."

"Then when you picked Logan up before the season—which was a bold, fucking move that I'm still pissed you were able to pull off without me—I figured you two would work things out. Would realize this is a different time and place and social climate and get back to remembering that you were two dumbasses in love once." A beat. "Then be able to find your way back there."

"I—"

"And since that seems to not be the case," he said, talking over her, "and since I taught you all you need to know about being a stubborn ass, I figured I might as well give you the shove off the cliff you so obviously need."

That was the thing about her former boss.

He liked to talk.

A lot.

He was never short for words, and while most of the time she could filter through the bullshit and arrow in on the important details, this morning they were talking about her life and her job and—

She sighed.

Her heart.

They were talking about her bruised, damaged, pieced-together heart.

"And—"

"Shut up, Luc," she said, interrupting him for the first time in this conversation. "And let me talk."

Silence. For all of ten seconds. Then, "So talk."

"Logan already told me."

A longer blip of silence. "And you didn't get back together?"

It was impossible to miss the disappointment in his tone. It was also impossible to sum up all she was feeling for Logan, considering it was so fresh in her head. "He just told me last night."

"Waited till the season was over," Luc said, tone approving. "That's a good man. Didn't get between you and your job, even though it had to be killing him."

"What do you mean?"

"He's seen you nearly every day for nine months, Lottie. And he couldn't touch or hold you. The man was thrown into close contact with the woman he's crazy about and didn't want to risk fucking up the good thing she had going." He chuckled. "No wonder he played the best season of his career."

She couldn't deny that Logan had absolutely killed it at the blue line throughout the year.

"He came to me the night we lost," she admitted. "With fucking slippers."

Luc burst out laughing. "Oh man, that slick fucker pays attention. How often did I tell you that you were going to end up with a bum back if you kept wearing those death contraptions, but no, you've got to keep clomping around the arena in them—"

"First, I do *not* clomp. Second, I need them in order to be somewhat the same size as the rest of you giants," she muttered. "I was tired of looking up everyone's nose all the time."

More laughter, but she joined in this time.

Before long, though, she sobered. "Why'd you do it, Luc? Why did you keep me in the dark? Why did you lie? I thought we—" She sighed. "I thought we meant more to each other than that."

"I'm sorry I hurt you," he said, sounding more serious than she'd ever heard him. "I hope you know that."

"I—uh—did you not think I could handle it? Handle being on the same team if we broke up?"

"No, honey," he told her. "No, it wasn't that at all. I thought you were young and needed space to think, needed to figure out what you wanted in your head and heart without anyone else influencing you."

"Except . . . you influenced me."

He inhaled, released it slowly. "Fuck, I never thought about it like that. Shit, Lottie, I—"

She squeezed her eyes shut. "Part of me is really hurt you and Logan had this whole plan about my life without bothering to include me in it. Another part of me understands. Still another is pissed at myself for considering giving up my life for Logan, for thinking that his dreams were bigger and more important than mine." She swallowed hard. "And a final part, one I just realized last night when someone I know announced she was pregnant, is furious for not recognizing that in making my life *only* about my dream after Logan left, I missed out on my family, on making a family of my own."

Char blinked like a madwoman. It was too fucking early in the morning for tears, too early to be a blubbering mess with her former boss, her sort of brother, father, friend.

And it was a good thing that she did all that blinking because when he spoke a few moments later, his words made her eyes sting.

"It's not too late," he said. "Not too late for you, and not too late for you *and* Logan."

She sniffed, and since they were talking about all of the serious shit that morning, she told him the other thing that was bothering her, the deep-seated worry she held because she liked Logan so damned much. "What if I get like before? What if I want to give up everything so I can have a family with Logan?"

"Why are those things mutually exclusive?" he countered. "Why can't you have your family *and* your dream?"

"I—" She stopped, blinked. Because, of course, it was the logical thought, but also . . . "It's not that simple," she said.

"Isn't it?" he replied. "You have a demanding career, but so do plenty of people. You like someone that might put you in a complicated position, but the Gold, as an organization, has weathered that particular storm enough times over that I know there are certain HR and personnel protocols in place. You're in the public eye, but so are plenty of other people."

He was right, the bastard.

"If it's so easy," she grumbled, "why aren't you in a steady relationship?"

"This isn't about me and my almost forty-year-old ass. This is about you and Logan and how the man loved you enough to set you free or some other sappy bullshit."

Her lips curved into a smile. "For all that you accuse him of propagating sappy bullshit, you're the one that helped protect me."

"Meh."

So like him to dismiss his role in anything. Just exactly as he handled his career, never taking credit, even where it was due. It was always the guys, the team, the organization.

She'd modeled herself after him, and often did the same, *felt* the same.

But she knew he'd done more in this case than he'd accept.

He and Logan had risked her hurt and anger to try and do right by her. They'd loved her and protected her, and so maybe she didn't approve of everything they'd done, and yeah, she wished they'd handled it differently, but Char was old enough to know that the tough decisions were rarely ever black and white.

"I can't wait until you find a woman who throws your whole life into disarray, until everything you thought you knew is turned upside down." Like Logan did for her. Like she was starting to recognize was something she craved.

"That's not going to happen," Luc said after a beat. "Hashtag bachelor for life."

Except . . . there was something in his tone that made her pause, made her wonder why there was sad on the edges of his voice. She'd known him for nearly a decade, and she had never seen the same woman on his arm more than a handful of times. A few dates, a few months, but never any longer.

Like her.

And she'd always figured he was like her in that way, that things had ended with the women in his life because he was married to his job and didn't have room for more.

Still, considering she'd just realized that her relationships hadn't failed solely because her career kept her too busy, but also because she'd been hurt and had encased herself in a protective shell that only Logan seemed to be able to penetrate, she figured that Luc might have something happening behind that casual, cavalier shield of his.

"You never got close?"

Silence.

Then, "Yeah, I got close. Once, I got pretty damned close."

Pain in that sentence, so much pain that she'd unwittingly churned up. Damn. She went to apologize, paused. Because Luc was like her, but harder, and he'd shown her a little chink in his armor. He wouldn't want her to poke at it, to draw attention to it.

He'd want to move on and make it about something else.

So, she deliberately lightened her tone and said, "Well, I can't wait until you fall for someone, so I can watch you spew sappy bullshit over her."

"Spew. Such a lovely word." He snorted. "Also, why can't you wait?"

"Because I'm both a nosy bastard and I can't wait to make fun of you."

"Nice," he said. "And here I am, protecting you, being nice. I would never be so mean as to make fun of you."

"Should I circle us back to you saying I was a lovestruck asshole?"

"That's fact," he said. "Also, technically, I said you were a dumbass in love."

She resisted the urge to laugh. Just barely. Instead, saying, "One who needs a man to drag me down the aisle?"

"Man, woman, identifies as neither, or both, or at some other point on that scale, I don't care. But the truth is that you do need someone to drag your ass down that aisle."

"I'm not that—"

"You were burned. You need to know someone won't cut at the first sign of trouble. You need proof that your relationship has staying power. That's not bad or wrong or fucked up," he said. "But with this, you need to not be scared, to realize that the only place you ever really felt safe was Logan's arms."

He was right.

In so many ways.

She'd never needed to have her guard up with Logan. He'd always seen right into her heart, straight down to all of the hidden pieces of her soul. Just as she'd seen the same in his heart, his soul.

That trust had been broken.

But for a very specific reason.

So, the question she needed to ask herself now was whether she had the courage to put it all aside and to move forward.

Because this conversation had answered the other question —whether she wanted to move forward.

She *wanted*. Oh, how she wanted.

"Now's the time for courage, Lottie girl."

If she'd been looking for a sign from the universe that moving forward with Logan was the right decision, then one could certainly consider Luc speaking the same words aloud she had circling in her mind as one.

Was she looking for one?

Yes. No. Maybe.

Yes.

"Yeah, Luc, I think you're right."

"Of course, I am, Lottie Dottie."

She sighed. "You know, you're the only one I've ever let call me Lottie—in any form—right?"

"That's because I'm special."

"It's because you're *something*," she muttered.

He laughed. She laughed.

And then because they had eight years of knowing each other under their belts, of that father/daughter, brother/sister, friend relationship, they didn't need further discussion to move on to talking about something that wasn't sappy bullshit.

And because they both loved their jobs, they moved on to hockey.

As if there were anything else.

Twenty-Three

LOGAN

He'd gone slow.

He'd had patience.

And . . . now he had blue balls.

But he'd followed his own advice, and now there was a woman standing on his doorstep for a change. A brown bakery bag in one hand, a bottle of liquor in the other.

His lips curved, and he leaned back against the doorjamb. "What's happening, Starlight?"

She lifted her chin and brushed by him into his house.

Grinning, he closed the door, turned to follow her, only to see that she had stopped all of three feet inside his place. He froze, and maybe he was succumbing to his inner pig, but damn, what a view that was.

Her hair was swept up into a mass of curls. Her skin gleamed in the morning light, set off by the pale blue of her dress—a simple thing that tied at her nape, left the rest of her back exposed. His mouth watered, nearly as much as his fingers itched to touch, because the sweep of that dress, how it teased the tops of her thighs, thighs he wanted to be in between and, fuck, thighs he wanted to stroke, to kiss, to *lick*.

"This is so cliché."

"Me wanting to go down on you?" he asked, slipping his arms around her waist from behind and pressing his front to her back.

Her breathing hitched, hips canting to brush his—

Yes, he was hard.

Hence . . . blue balls.

Char spun in his arms, lifting hers up and resting her hands on his shoulders. She had those fucking tall heels on again, red ones this time that matched her fire engine colored lipstick.

And he wanted to kiss her.

But she was there, and patience seemed to be working, and he needed to keep chugging along, to not fuck this up—

"Logan!" she exclaimed.

"What?" he asked, going for innocent.

Not that it worked, because she glared up at him. "You can't say things like that."

"Why not?"

"Because I'm trying very hard not to jump your bones."

He stilled, held her gaze. "Well, I'm trying very hard to be good," he murmured. "And you talking about bones"—he drew her a little closer, trying to resist the urge to grind his cock against her—"isn't helping my control."

Fingers on his jaw, a smirk on that sexy red-covered mouth. "Yeah?"

"Vixen," he muttered, turning her and cuddling her against his side, keeping that dangerous, tempting body near, while still attempting to maintain his control. Having her curves pressed to him wasn't great for said control, but it was better than finding any excuse to rub his cock against her. Or better yet to lift up the hem of that dress and—

"I thought I was your Starlight?" she asked.

"Yes, to Starlight," he said, leading her farther into the house. "You've been my guide over the years, my beacon to find my way back to you, to show you—"

He broke off, voice definitely wet, even though he was a big, tough hockey player. Yes, he knew he'd ultimately done the right thing in letting her go, but it had hurt, and part of him worried that he would never find a way to make it up to her, to get her back, to have the opportunity to prove exactly how much she meant to him.

"You've showed me, Log," she murmured, then nudged him lightly. "Sure took your damned time doing it though."

"I had to wait," he said. "You needed that time."

She had, even though it had been painful. Even though, for a time, he'd tried to find happiness without her, same as she seemed to be finding it without him. But no woman had ever come close, and it wasn't fair to them to keep dragging something along that only resulted in hurt feelings and damaged hearts—theirs, not his.

And that wasn't his ego talking.

Because his heart had been damaged long before.

By knowing what he'd given up, what he was missing. He'd known it was special and important and way more than a youthful crush or first love.

It was forever love.

That he'd needed to send to slaughter.

Dramatic much? Probably. But in many ways, that was the best description. He'd sliced away a part of each of them, hoping that one day the pieces might be able to come back together. Maybe not in the same fashion as they'd once been, but in something that had the potential to be more, to be . . . *them*.

She inhaled. "Yeah, I think I needed that time too." Brown eyes on his. "For the record, I really fucking hated it."

He grinned, the painful memories of those years apart slipping away. "For the record, I did, too." Logan turned and drew her into the kitchen. "So, if you weren't talking about your glorious puss—*oof!*" He broke off when she smacked him, and he found he didn't have the strength to resist that glorious mouth any longer. Not when it was lush and red and so damned close.

Not when her eyes flashed at him, but her lips tipped up at the edges.

Not when a shuddering breath slipped from them.

And so, he pressed his lips to hers.

She nipped at his tongue when it slid into her mouth, but then she was kissing him back, her tongue tangling with his, her hands kneading at his shoulders. He slid his palm down, tugged her flush against him, cupping that ass he'd dreamed about for years, the same one he'd stroked himself to over and over that season, seeing her parade around in her heels and slacks.

For the record, he knew she'd kick his ass if she caught wind of him thinking she'd been doing any parading.

He also knew she'd been working her ass off.

It was just his inner pig that enjoyed pretending she was strutting around, the same one that imagined bending her over her desk and—

His fingers brushed bare skin.

Fuck. He hadn't realized he'd been lifting her skirt, hadn't even realized he'd lifted *her* up onto the counter and stepped between her legs.

Patience.

He pulled back.

Hot brown eyes on him, swollen mouth, smeared lipstick, rapid breaths mixing.

"You haven't forgotten how to kiss," she teased, stroking a hand down his T-shirt, making him wish he was wearing a suit of armor, only so he wouldn't be tempted to keep sliding her dress up, to keep touching.

"What were you talking about?" he asked, voice like gravel.

"What?" She pushed her hair out of her face then reached over and rubbed at his mouth, her thumb coming away stained red. "That lipstick is ridiculously expensive."

Logan nipped at her thumb. "Then don't wear it," he said. "Because I really enjoy kissing it off your mouth."

She huffed.

"I promise I'll buy you a new tube once I finish kissing off the first one."

One brow lifted. "You don't know how expensive it is."

"If it means kissing you?" A shrug. "I don't care."

Her lips tipped up, making him want to kiss her all over again, but he resisted because . . . patience.

Fuck, that was going to become his new favorite four-letter word.

Or eight-letter, rather.

Regardless, he got back to the point at hand, which was having a civil conversation with this woman that didn't end with their clothes in a pile on the floor or his mouth on her pussy.

Why? his inner pouty man moaned. *You'd make it good.*

He would. That was irrefutable.

But he needed to make everything else good, too.

Which is why he focused and asked, "When you walked in, you said this was so cliché. What's cliché?"

Her eyes danced, and she waved a hand around his kitchen. "Isn't it obvious?" she asked. "This bachelor pad on steroids. It's the most cliché thing I've ever laid eyes on."

He stared at the kitchen. It was a little spartan, he supposed, but he'd already established his lack of cooking ability. The family room was across the hall, and he had a nice leather couch, a big TV, even some throw pillows his mom had made him buy the last time his parents had been in town.

That had sparked a fight in the middle of Target—his dad saying his mom needed to butt out of Logan's life, and his mom declaring she was "just trying to make sure our son is comfortable. Shouldn't I make sure he's comfortable?"

In the end, Logan had bought eight freaking pillows—which had cost him three hundred dollars *(three hundred!)*—but his mom had been happy, and then after he'd shoved the pillows in the trunk of his SUV, he'd driven them to a local brewery, thus making his dad happy.

Oh, so fun.

His parents were the best.

But aside from the throw pillows, the space was organized, clean, and a pretty decent combination of dark wood, black leather, and stainless steel.

Oh.

Now he got what she meant.

Char dressed nice, did her hair and makeup, but she wasn't what he'd consider high maintenance or a girly-girl. She did what she needed to look professional, and outside of work, she dressed in a way that made her happy.

Her home was like that.

Just as clean and organized as his.

But it bridged the gap between professional and happy, between stark and warm.

She had trinkets on her shelves, brightly patterned kitchen towels draped by the sink, pictures on the walls, throw pillows *and* blankets on her couch. She had all the things, that when put together, made an actual home.

His place was just that.

A place to sleep. A place to watch TV. A place to eat.

There wasn't warmth or happiness or joy.

Joy? For fuck's sake.

He knew he was gone for Char, had been gone for her for years, knew he'd played the sacrificing hero, but fuck, he was also a man.

One who'd played his hand and lived by it.

One who'd seen his opening and made his move.

So what if he didn't have trinkets on his shelves?

And this was a conversation he probably didn't need to be having with himself in this moment, not with the woman he loved at his place, a bag of treats—please dear Lord let it be treats in that bag—in her hand, a sexy dress on her body, and her lipstick smeared across his face.

Frankly, he was finding himself hard-pressed to give a fuck about trinkets or bachelor pads on steroids.

"I'll have you know," he said, "that I have throw pillows. A bachelor pad doesn't have throw pillows."

She snorted. "Is that the rule? Throw pillows mean that you've got a real home?"

"I'm a real boy," he joked, *a la* Pinocchio.

Char giggled, and it made him feel about a hundred feet tall. "Here, you goof," she said, thrusting the bag at him. "I've brought your favorite Cheat Day snack."

"But I don't do Cheat Days anymore."

"The season's over." A beatific smile. "I think you can take a few Cheat Days."

All of his earlier promises and rules about sticking with the diet plan for the foreseeable future flew out the window. Because come hell or high water, he'd find a way back to the plan if it meant that Char would show up with that pretty smile and pride in her eyes. He'd just . . . tie himself to the bike to work off the extra calories.

There. Plan sorted.

He shrugged. "Depends."

Her eyebrows lifted. "On what?"

"On what's in the bag."

Her face fell. "Oh."

Stepping closer, he cupped her cheek. Not smart for his control, but the urge to get close to her, to comfort, was impossible to ignore. "What did I say?"

Instead of answering, she handed him the bag. "Apple cinnamon muffin."

His stomach rumbled, the diet plan all but forgotten now. "From Molly's?"

A smirk. "As if I'd get it from anywhere else?" She nudged him back and unfolded the top of the bag, pulled out a muffin.

Spice and sweet filled the air, and his stomach rumbled again.

Char laughed. "Okay, clearly, you're withering away." She broke off a piece of the top and held it up to his lips. "Eat this."

"You first," he said. "I'm sure you're hung—"

She shoved it into his mouth.

He glared, but it wasn't like he was going to spit out the deliciousness, not with the bite melting on his tongue, cinnamon and apples filling his taste buds. But he *was* going to share.

Snagging the muffin, he broke off a piece then put it up to her lips, trying not to moan when her tongue brushed his finger as she ate the bite.

"Again," she said after chewing for several moments, "you need to work on your bite size, sir. I am a tiny woman with a tiny mouth. I need appropriate-sized bites."

"I notice you didn't say tiny bites."

"I'm not an idiot," she said, grabbing his wrist and nibbling at the muffin. "This *is* from Molly's."

He took a bite, and yeah, he supposed when he compared it to what Char had eaten, one might term it a behemoth. But he was six-four, two hundred and sixteen pounds. He had a big body that needed a lot of fuel.

Behemoth bites were a given.

Didn't mean he couldn't share.

He raised the muffin up to Char's mouth, and they spent the next few minutes devouring the treat, along with two others— one more apple cinnamon and a blueberry—before they spoke again.

"Did you eat an appropriate amount of muffin?" he asked after they'd finished and he'd shoved the wrappers back into the bag.

"Yup."

"Good."

She brushed at his chin, met his eyes when he looked at her in question. "Crumb," she said by way of explanation.

"You thirsty?" he asked, not wanting to step away from her but knowing that the longer he stood between her thighs, the less likely he was to practice his patience plan. "I've got water and orange juice. I can make some coffee or—"

"Just a glass of water would be great."

He stepped back, and she shifted as though she'd slide from the counter, but the move dislodged one of those sexy fucking heels—death traps though they were—and it hit the tile floor with a clatter.

Not thinking, he bent and scooped it up.

Then straightened and nearly bit his tongue.

Because of where he was.

Where he was.

Bare legs, a glimpse of naked thigh. The scent of her lotion in his nose, rose and something tropical wafting up, trailing over him, and musk. She wanted him, and he could smell it.

Fucking hell.

He slipped on her heel, straightened farther, not burying his face where he was desperate to, not lifting her skirt and sliding his fingers through damp heat—

"You could," she murmured. "You could just lift up my skirt and—"

His cock went rock-hard.

His eyes flew to hers . . . and saw that, yes, there was desire there, but it was tempered by the shadows of the past, dimmed by pain.

So, yeah, he *could*, but also, no, he couldn't.

Not if he wanted Char to feel like the most important woman in the universe to him. Not if he wanted to be able to look himself in the mirror and not feel like the worst scumbag on the planet.

He could, however, press his mouth to hers, he could kiss her and hold her tight and put everything he was feeling into that simple embrace.

Then he could step back and help her off the counter.

He could take her hand.

He could ask, "Are those heels for walking?"

And he could feel a hundred feet tall when she rolled her eyes and snorted, even as her body drifted close, and she said, "Yes, Log. They're made for walking."

Twenty-Four

Char

"You know, when you asked if these shoes were for walking," she said, glancing out at the forested trail in front of them, "this isn't exactly what I had in mind."

He'd helped her down from the counter in his kitchen, brushing the fronts of their bodies in one languorous slide, making every nerve in her being prickle and fire and fill with desire.

She'd offered up spending a lazy day bingeing on *Great British Bake-Off*, selling it as him learning how to cook something by proxy.

But he'd seen through her.

Or at least, he'd read that while she'd shown up, while she'd come to terms with a lot of what had happened between them, there was still a part of her that was nervous.

She wanted him and was terrified of what would happen if they went for it.

Physically *and* emotionally.

She loved kissing him, loved touching and how he held her.

She loved joking and talking and laughing with him—as they'd done for much of the drive up into the mountains south of San Francisco, twining their way toward Santa Cruz, but turning off before they made it into the sleepy beach town, instead climbing up and up until they'd made their way into Big Basin.

Logan threw his SUV into park and reached into the back seat. He came up with a box that was almost the same size as the one he'd presented her in her office a few days before and plunked it into her lap.

Then he reached back again and came up with a sweatshirt.

"Open it, " he said when she didn't immediately tear the lid off.

"I'm not a puppet," she muttered. "Give a woman a second to process a man who doesn't take appropriate-sized bites and who keeps dropping packages in her lap."

He dropped the sweatshirt on top of the box. "How about sweatshirts *and* boxes?"

A huff. "Really?"

"Really." But he pushed the sweatshirt out of the way and took the lid off for her. "I'd intended on giving these to you in the not-so-distant future, but now seems apropos."

Char had taken one look at the box and frozen.

Now, as she processed the shoes inside, she felt her throat burn, her eyes sting. Silly, romantic, *lovely* man.

"I haven't worn Converse in years," she whispered. "Not since . . ."

She trailed off, heart hurting even though she was happy deep inside.

"I coaxed you into going hiking with me the last time," he finished, running his fingers over the shell of her ear. "I know it's not your favorite, not by a long-shot, but I do think there's something beautiful that you'll really like." He smiled and pointed to a paved path disappearing among the arboreal giants. "And it's not far up the trail."

They'd parked in a lot tucked past the main entrance, and as she'd gotten her ass up at an insane hour, and then had gone over to Logan's at a very impolite hour—so impolite that her mom would have been pissed she'd rung the bell so early—the lot was empty aside from their car. But it was the weekend and it was summer in Northern California. The lot wouldn't be empty for long.

Soon there would be other—she shuddered—hikers and dogs on leashes and families with cute little kids who were either having the best day of their life or their worst.

Her heart pulsed.

She wanted that, and she could admit it—if only to herself, only in her own brain—that she'd always dreamed of having *that* —kids and dogs and tantrums and day trips—only with one person.

This man.

And perhaps that was why she'd focused on work so intently, had tucked that desire down so deeply.

When Logan had gone, she'd buried that longing.

But now that he was back, now that she knew the full story, the craving had made a reappearance.

Either that, or her biological clock was ticking.

She snorted.

"Don't trust me?" he asked innocently, and she narrowed her eyes. Because it was *too* innocent, the scamp.

"When you look at me like that?" She shook her head. "That's a no."

He grinned, unrepentant. "I was going for earnest."

"You succeeded in serial killer."

Laughter filled the interior of the car, bubbling in her veins, making her lips turn up in humor, and then her laughter join in.

"Fuck, I like you, Starlight."

Her breath caught, those emerald eyes holding him captive

for long moments until she remembered her suspicions and asked, "What are you going to show me?"

"Something special."

She wrinkled her nose. "Special how?"

He sighed.

She smiled, took his hand, and squeezed lightly to let him know she was teasing. "No bears?"

"No bears," he said then shrugged. "Just on the very rare occasion, a mountain lion."

"What?"

His face sobered. "I'm kidding."

"Are you really kidding, or are you just trying to get me out of this car so I can see whatever it is you want to show me?"

"One of those." He tugged a curl lightly, asked before she could press him further, "So, what say you? Will you swap the heels for sneakers and a short, paved path?"

"Do you have a sweatshirt for yourself?" she asked, knowing it would be cold in these hills, especially with the marine layer still visible overhead. Later, the whole area would warm up, a sunny day forecasted, but for now, she snagged the snuggly cotton covering from him and tugged it over her head. The box slid, but she grabbed it as she toed off her heels, plucking the shoes out and thinking that this was probably a bad idea without—

"Socks," came his voice, paired with his hand in front of her face, holding out a brand-new pair.

They were patterned with brightly-colored curly lines—

Or not, she realized with a grin.

Because those curly lines actually formed a hidden pattern of cursive f-bombs.

She grinned up at him. "You didn't forget my favorite curse word."

He cupped her cheek. "I didn't forget *anything*."

"Log," she murmured, her freaking eyes stinging again. "You've got to stop being so sweet."

He snagged the socks from her and tugged off the label and hook at the top, handing them back to her one at a time. She pulled them on, shoved her feet into the pale blue converse that matched exactly the pair she'd worn with him a lifetime before.

The size was perfect.

Not that she'd expected anything less after he'd surprised her with the slippers and the treats and the cooking and—

He was thoughtful.

Very thoughtful.

If this worked, she needed to make sure she was thoughtful right back.

Her heart pulsed and her eyes went stingy again, but as she tied the shoelaces and rolled up the sleeves of the sweatshirt, she blinked any extra moisture away.

"You didn't answer me about the sweatshirt," she said, when she'd finished.

"I've got another in the trunk."

"Good." A nod as she pushed open the door. "Let's go."

She stepped out and felt her breath hitch. Even a non-nature girl like herself could appreciate the sheer size of the trees. Huge redwoods towering over her. A cool dampness to the air that made her shiver. The smell of the earth, a preternatural sort of quiet.

The soft *pop* of Logan's door opening broke that silence, and she watched as he moved around to the back of his SUV and opened the hatch.

A minute later, he had a sweatshirt pulled over his head, the trunk closed, and was walking toward her.

"Okay?" he asked, gaze flicking toward her bare legs. "Not too cold?"

"It's not far, right?"

"Right," he confirmed.

"Then, no," she said. "I'm fine, so long as you promise to cuddle me close when it gets too chilly."

He grinned. "And now you know my nefarious plan."

Char rolled her eyes but didn't protest when Logan laced their fingers together and led her down the path. "Should I be happy that you didn't pair that with a *muhaha*?"

He bopped her on the nose. "Too far, Starlight, too far."

She shook her head, rested it on his shoulder so he wouldn't see her smiling, and walked with him. The trail curved to the right just past the tree line, and she had the immediate feeling of being both dwarfed in size and feeling perfectly sheltered and protected. There were large gaps between the giant trunks, these ancient trees needing plenty of space to grow, but they were so tall, their branches overhead so vast and intertwined that she felt like she'd been transported to another planet.

That was, of course, if she ignored the paved path beneath her sneakers.

In her mind, alien planets didn't have asphalt trails.

Although, it did show that, once again, Logan knew her.

This wasn't a difficult uphill trek, nor a dusty and rocky terrain to traverse. This was flat. This was beautiful. This was . . . short.

Because barely fifteen minutes later, he tugged her to the right, and she found herself in a circular grove of trees.

Of *charred* trees.

She gasped, hand coming to her throat.

"The fires last summer came through here."

She spun in a circle, taking in what remained and what had been destroyed by those rapidly moving flames. And God . . . there was black, so much black.

So much beauty reduced to ash.

"I see that," she said, sad for no other reason than it hurt a part of her deep inside to see what had been lost last summer. Fires were part of California, or at least that was what she'd been told by those she knew who had grown up here, but there was no doubt that the fires had grown in intensity and frequency over time.

That, paired with an increasing population, soaring house prices, years of drought, meant that property and businesses and lives were in ever-magnifying danger.

And places like this one burned.

"This is so sad," she whispered, eyeing the circle, of which only a few trees appeared to have survived. Many others had fallen to the ground, the path of blackened trunks a searing visual amongst the rest of the green forest.

"I didn't bring you here to be sad," he said gently, wrapping an arm around her shoulders and hugging her to his side.

"Well, it is sad," she said. "I remember the news stories. I remember how so many people lost so much, and these trees—God, this clearing must have been absolutely majestic."

He nodded. "It was."

At her questioning look, he smiled. "I found quite a bit of time to explore during my time in L.A." A shrug. "And I discovered that I much preferred this northern part of California to the plastic and fakeness of Hollywood."

"So, it wasn't hard for you to come to San Francisco."

He shook his head. "Though, full disclosure, I would have moved to Siberia to play for your team, Starlight. Not only because of this"—he held her tighter, brushed his lips over hers—"but also because you're very talented and smart, and any player would be lucky to be a part of your organization."

Her heart stuttered, and feeling oddly shy, she found herself dropping her forehead to his chest, not moving when he rested his palm on her nape. "Thank you for saying that."

"I mean it."

"Well, thank you for meaning it," she whispered.

"Anytime, sweetheart."

They stayed like that for a minute before Logan slid his hand down her spine and wrapped it around her hip. "Come this way," he murmured, guiding her over to the far side of the clearing.

A huge, absolutely *huge* tree had fallen over, black charring its side.

She could barely process the breadth of its size, a car could drive on it with plenty of room on either side, and . . . it had collapsed. The strong, seemingly impenetrable giant had been felled by flames.

"Look," he said, pointing and drawing her gaze to what she'd missed on first glance.

She'd been obsessed with what had been, mourning what *might* have been if the flames hadn't torn through this forest, and in focusing on the might have beens and the had beens, she'd nearly overlooked the beauty of the now.

Because, yes, that tree had broken into pieces when it had fallen. Yes, it was less majestic on the ground than it was compared to its brethren growing into the sky. Yes, it might have gone on living and growing and becoming even more breathtaking if only the fire hadn't come.

But . . . fire had come.

But . . . it wasn't less beautiful just because it had been knocked down, because it had collapsed.

And it didn't lose its value.

Because in the ruins of that wonderful fallen giant was new life.

"Did you know that some of these Redwoods need fire in order for their cones to open, for their seeds to be exposed, and ultimately for new trees to grow?"

Carefully, she reached out and ran her fingers over the rough bark coating the trunk in one spot, the ashy, charcoal directly next to it, and then, finally, over the delicate green blades of what would someday—if the conditions were right—be a new giant redwood.

"I didn't know that." She sniffed. "You're making my eyes burn again, dammit."

Logan chuckled and wrapped his arms around her. "We're like these trees, Starlight. We burned hot and bright and furiously. And then . . . we fell."

Another sniff. "I'm not missing the symbolism, baby."

He was grinning. She couldn't see it, not with her head plastered against his chest, the steady thrum of his heart under her ear, but she could feel it nonetheless. "Then you also didn't miss that we have that potential, too. That we can make something beautiful and alive out of the ashes of our past."

Char closed her eyes and let his words, this place wash over her.

They could do that. But, more importantly, she *wanted* to do that. With Logan. She wanted the beauty. She wanted the future. She wanted *him*.

Which was why she held him tight and said, "I didn't miss that either."

TWENTY-FIVE

LOGAN

The next week, he strolled up the front walk of Char's house, confident this time that he wouldn't have to sneak in the back.

They had plans.

They'd spent the weekend together, Char surprising him by taking his hand and leading him on a longer hike in Big Basin. Not far, since neither of them were dressed properly for an all-day adventure—no water, no sunscreen, no—in her case—pants and she wasn't a really outdoorsy person, but they had walked for a little while, stumbling upon a small waterfall that had taken his breath away.

They stood and watched the stream spilling over the outcroppings of rock, covering the bright green moss in mist.

Then they'd driven up to the city, those heels had been slipped on her feet, covering the midnight blue nail polish on toes so adorable Logan was considering developing a foot fetish, and they'd spent the rest of the day together. Eating more food that was definitely not on Rebecca's diet plan then had gone back to her house and watched a movie.

More lingering kisses.

More caressing fingers.

More . . . blue balls.

But it was worth it, because fuck, but he never felt more settled than when he was with Char, as though he could just be himself, just not worry about anything, just . . . *be*.

Thus was the power of his Starlight.

Then Sunday, they'd driven down to Carmel and had picnicked on the beach, the ocean breeze coating her lips with salt when he'd been unable to stop himself from kissing her.

Monday through Thursday, he'd cooled his heels, plotting his next moves because Char had needed to work. Several staff members had requested meetings, and then she'd been looped into a Zoom conference with some of the other GMs. After that, she had been drowning in emails—her words, but based on how hard she worked, he didn't doubt the truth.

So, instead of going to her office and indulging in his bending-her-over-her-desk fantasy, he'd left her to her work and instead had lunch delivered.

And dinner.

Because she was clearing the decks, wanting to go home for a week and visit her family, but she had also promised to go up to his cabin with him. He'd coaxed her into going on a few river walks with him—or rather, had promised her several hours of undisturbed reading in his hot tub if she agreed to the odd walk.

Thankfully, she hadn't asked about bears.

Because Tahoe wasn't known for being particularly bear-free.

Last night, he'd delivered dinner himself when he might have kind-of-sort-of-accidentally driven by and seen her bent over her computer through the windows in her kitchen.

Of course, he *would* have peeked in through her back door,

except he'd also gone to the hardware store and bought a lock for her gate that week.

A padlock with letters to form a word or combination that could be used to open it.

He'd chosen *stars*, for obvious reasons.

And when he'd texted her the picture with instructions on how to open it, he'd received a tart reply to *Stop being pushy*. Which had been followed by another text that said simply, *Thank you*, and was paired with a trio of red hearts.

Which made *his* heart squeeze, sap that he was.

Emojis and a thank you. A tart reply, but not holding his need to take care of her against him.

Regardless, the lock meant that any sneaking in would be difficult, so he'd gone to the front door, rang the bell, and kissed the surprised smile off her face, before thrusting the bag of food in her hand.

But when he went to turn away, she'd surprised *him* by snagging his hand and tugging him inside.

She'd shared the food—okay, so maybe he'd brought enough to share, hoping for the invite in—then had coaxed him onto the couch to binge watch some dumbass reality show.

He hadn't bothered to follow the plotline. Instead, he'd followed her—with his eyes, tracking every shake of her head and smile and eye roll. With his ears, committing her laughter to memory. With his nose, soaking in the floral spice. With his mouth, tasting the chocolate cake and coffee they'd had for dessert on her tongue.

And, later, when she fell asleep, with his touch, stroking a finger down the soft silk of her cheek as he'd tucked her into bed.

It had been the best night of his life in years.

Because of Char.

Smiling because he got to see her again tonight, that he might be able to kiss her, and maybe, if she was wearing a dress again, get to kiss her other places and—

His cock twitched.

"Come on, man," he muttered, climbing the three steps that led up to her door. "Focus."

Keep the charm going, the patience in mind. Go slow. Go steady.

With that thought, he pushed everything sexual out of his mind and rang the bell. Footsteps echoed through the door, not loud, and perhaps a sound he might not have ever noticed if he hadn't been so obsessed with all things Char.

But he did hear the pad of her feet.

Just as he heard the lock *click* open.

The door was pulled wide, and . . . his heart thumped, *hard*.

Warm brown eyes, a welcoming smile on lips he wanted to kiss, a dress that had his cock twitching all over again. "Hey," she murmured.

"Hey," he said, too entranced to say anything else.

And . . . silence as they stared at each other.

Him because he couldn't believe he was here, that they were trying this again, that he got another chance with her.

Her because . . . hell, he couldn't begin to read her mind.

All he knew was that she was letting him into her life, and he wasn't going to squander the chance.

"You look beautiful," he said, shaking himself from his Char-stupor.

She grinned, stepped back, smoothing her hands over the amethyst dress. It had a bunch of crisscrossing straps forming a pattern over her chest, making him want to nudge those thin bands out of his way and bury his face between her breasts. The hem was short, flirting at mid-thigh, and she wore another pair of spiked heels—these were black with interlaced bands that matched her dress. "You don't look too bad yourself."

They had reservations at a nice steakhouse nearby that she'd raved about—another meal that would be ruining his diet.

Although, he'd eaten fairly well that week, so that was good enough for him at this point.

Salads for breakfast and lunch to get those greens in. Counteract all the unhealthy dinners they were consuming.

She closed the door, touched the corner of his mouth. "Why are you smiling?"

He nipped at her fingertips. "I was thinking if I ate like we have been during the season, that Nutritionist Rebecca would have my ass."

Char grinned. "She would at that." A bump of her shoulder against his. "Let me just grab my coat and we can go." He followed her to the small closet, helped her slip on her jacket.

"It's a crime to cover up this dress," he said, smoothing a hand down her back.

"You like it?" she asked, glancing over her shoulder at him.

He pressed a kiss to the side of her neck. "*Like* is too bland a word."

A trace of wicked in those eyes. "You should see what's under it."

Groaning—because, blue balls—he skimmed his fingers under the edge of her dress. "When are you going to show me?"

Hot eyes on his, white teeth biting into a bottom lip. "Tonight."

One word, but a wealth of meaning. Not just desire or need. Not just something physical. More.

So much more.

The fear had gone, taken anger with it. And hope and affection had replaced them.

"Mmm," he murmured and pressed a kiss to her lips. "I like tonight."

Heat trailing across her expression, her hands coming to rest on his shoulders, to grip tightly as she moved close. "Or we can skip dinner, and I can show you now."

Fucking hell.

He hadn't had this many erections since he'd been a teenager.

And, just like when he was sixteen, he couldn't do anything about them. At the moment, anyway.

"Come on, Trouble," he said, taking her hand and leading her out the front door. "You know you want that loaded baked potato you were waxing poetic about earlier this week."

She groaned and rubbed her stomach. "Cheese. Sour cream. Bacon. Butter. Green onions. Yes, to all."

"Sounds delicious," he said and opened the passenger door for her, buckling her seat belt. "No lipstick tonight?" He'd seen all shades of red and pink over the last year, but he hadn't often seen her lips naked of color, and especially not when she was going out somewhere.

"Nope," she said with a soft *pop* at the end.

Fingers over her cheek, along her jaw, to the corner of that smiling mouth. "Why?"

"Because then I wouldn't be able to do this."

She laid a kiss on him that should have blown his head off.

As it was, it had him thinking about other things blowing, and then not thinking much further than that. Her arms wove around his shoulders, and she pulled him close, nipping at his bottom lip, slipping her tongue past his lips to tangle with his.

Long and deep and wet, she kissed him until his lungs burned.

"That's why," she whispered, her words bursts of damp heat on his mouth.

"I vote for no lipstick ever," he said, voice sounding like he'd swallowed a flamethrower. His hands—one on the console, the other on the seat by her hip, convulsed, wanting to unbuckle her seat belt and carry her back into the house.

But then he wouldn't be taking care of her.

Reluctantly, he pulled back, ducking out of the passenger's side, and starting to close the door.

Her voice chased him as it slammed shut.

"You must really want that baked potato."

He burst out laughing, love for this woman burning down into his soul.

Char was it for him. It was simple as that. Funny, sexy, smart as hell, she was in a whole different league from him, but he'd already given her up once, and there was absolutely no way he was going to lose her again.

No fucking way.

Twenty-Six

CHAR

The baked potato was glorious.

The way Logan was eye-fucking her was even more so.

"Dessert?" the waiter asked, coming over to the table.

Log opened his mouth, and she knew he was going to indulge her in a slice of that mountain-tall chocolate cake or a cherry-topped slice of cheesecake. But she'd reached her limit on indulging.

At least in food. And in talking, as she'd dominated the conversation.

"No, thank you," she said, shaking her head at Logan when he would have pushed. "I'm full." She wanted something else. "Did you want something?"

He shook his head, and the waiter left.

"Log?" she asked. "We can just go."

Hot green eyes on hers.

Her lungs froze, her pussy throbbed, and she actually

reached for her purse, ready to throw a wad of cash on the table when he asked, "Tell me more about the meeting with Pierre."

"Logan," she warned. She'd already blabbered about her day. Now, she wanted to go.

"We have to wait for the bill anyway," he said, reaching across the table and taking her hand. "Give me all the gory details of the Pierre talk."

"Gory meaning budget talk?" she asked, instead of calling him out. The stubborn glint in his expression was obvious, and she knew he was going to insist she answer, even without dessert.

He shuddered. "Well, obviously." A grin. "Though, feel free to skip to the interesting parts."

Char mock-sighed then smiling, she answered him, telling him about the minor changes the Gold's owner, Pierre Barie, wanted to make for next season. But when she tried to turn the topic back to them leaving the restaurant so she could act on those molten emerald eyes, he asked her about another meeting.

Her lips pursed, but she quickly outlined that interaction. However, when she went again to turn the focus to Logan, he dodged and pointed it back at her, asking another question about one of the Gold's vendors who'd been giving her a hard time and ensuring she'd gotten to say all of what she wanted to say.

She would have to be careful with this one. To make sure he didn't keep giving to the detriment of his own needs.

Because all meal long, he'd been attentive, listening to her rant about her meetings—yes, she loved her job, but, also yes, people were still idiots in a multitude of ways. She'd managed to coax him into sharing what had kept him busy—spoiling her with meals, taking care of her gate that he kept barging through, spending one morning hanging out with Coop and his baby girl while Calle had a spa day. He'd talked about his plans to go home and visit his family during the same week she went to see hers, but aside from deciding to go to the movies the following night—in which Logan again had indulged her by letting her pick the film—she had done more than her fair share of speaking.

Not that he seemed to mind.

And truthfully, she'd been tempted to choose the rom-com that just released when they'd discussed movies. Instead, she'd gone for action.

He'd watched her show about marrying at first sight without groaning. He'd not uttered a single complaint when she'd picked the historical romance movie earlier that week. Nor that drama the next day.

Accommodating, taking care of her, making sure her needs were met.

Well, she could do some of that in return, and he'd mentioned in passing wanting to see the action flick about a senior citizen assassin—not the premise intended, Char knew, but seriously, why did male action stars always get the cool jobs, even when they were old enough to sign up for the AARP? The female actors just got cast as cranky old ladies and—

Not the point.

The real reason she'd chosen it was because Logan wanted to see it.

And cracks about male action stars aside, she was fully aware that she'd definitely consumed worse movies and TV shows (her recent obsession with reality television a prime example). But, further than that, she could do something for him simply because he deserved it, simply because she wanted to treat him kindly, simply because she wanted to make him happy.

That was how real relationships worked, even though she hadn't spent too much time in one, as of late.

Unless she considered her job to be her boyfriend.

If so, he'd been very demanding and only minimally fulfilling.

Lie. Her job was very fulfilling.

It just wasn't great at giving her orgasms.

Heh.

Anyway, Logan had been very good at giving orgasms, and she wanted to explore how good he was at giving them now. Tonight. Five hours ago. Last week. That night he'd kissed her in her kitchen.

Shifting in her seat, her sensitized thighs rubbing together, she was very aware that she wanted to give some back.

Tonight.

Now.

Five hours ago.

Last week.

He reached across the table and cupped her jaw. "Why are you smiling?"

Char turned her head, pressed a kiss to his palm, and told him the truth. "I'm smiling because I like being with you."

Emerald eyes turning molten, slightly rough fingertips on her cheek. "I I—"

The waiter deposited the bill. He tried to do it slyly, tried to slip it onto the table silently, but it bumped into her wine glass, breaking the moment and drawing her focus.

"Sorry," the college-aged male murmured, slipping away almost as silently as he had arrived.

"I guess I should stop staring adoringly at you." Logan picked up the check.

She shook her head. "Nope. I like it when you stare at me adoringly."

"Yeah?"

"Yup." She snagged the bill from his fingers.

He snatched it back. "Not a chance, Starlight."

"We should split it."

His gaze fixed hers in place. "Are we dating?"

The change in conversation made her frown, mind spinning

to understand. "Um, yes?" She felt a sudden thread of uncertainty. "I mean, I *thought* so. I—is this not a—"

"This is a date, Starlight."

"Then why—?"

"I want to date you and be your boyfriend, your lover, *more*," he said, his voice quiet but no less intense for the lack of volume. "Don't insult me by not letting me take care of you."

Uncertainty disappeared, was replaced with *aw* and also annoyance.

"And taking care of me involves paying for things?"

"Yes," he said simply, but when she would have opened her mouth to argue, he added, "When I ask you on a date, I pay. End of story."

She thought of snatching the bill from him and shoving it along with her credit card at the waiter. Instead, she let him throw some cash on the table then take her hand after he'd stood, allowed him to hold it as they walked out of the restaurant.

This was an argument she wanted to have in private.

"And when I invite you out to dinner?" she asked after they'd buckled—well, after he'd buckled them both, something she'd allowed because she felt squishy inside when he did it and liked him close enough to smell his shampoo, his deodorant, to feel the heat from his body—

Focus.

He hit the button to turn on the engine. "Then I pay."

She'd been momentarily lost in LaLa Land, remembering his fingers trailing over her cheek as he'd straightened.

As thus, it took her a moment to process his answer.

"What?" she snapped. "Absolutely not."

"I'm the man. I pay."

"Logan Walker, as I live and breathe, you did *not* just say that."

He shrugged. "What are you going to do about it?"

Her anger spiked, and she went to tell him *exactly* what she was going to do about it, starting with her spiked heel ending up in a very particular location.

Then she saw the edge of his mouth.

It was curved up.

The fucker was playing with her.

She mentally shifted, about to tell him that he'd be out of her life so fast . . . but the words stoppered in her throat.

He was teasing her, just teasing, and she didn't want him to stop teasing or to worry about what he said around her. She could take a joke and dish one back, just as she knew he could take her teasing in that same vein.

But . . . more she didn't want him out of her life, and instinctively, she knew that joking in that way would hurt him.

Probably, because it would hurt her just as much to say it.

So instead, she shrugged and said, "I'll just go down on you until I convince you otherwise."

A blue word.

A curse that blistered even her used-to-profanity ears.

Then the car slid over onto the shoulder, the transmission shifted into park, and suddenly a six-foot, two-hundred-pound alpha athlete was crowding her back into her seat. "And if I say I'd go down on you to convince *you* otherwise?"

She lifted her chin, drifted closer. "Then I'd say we both win."

Hot breath on her cheek, her jaw, her ear. A rough voice whispering, "I think you're right."

And then he kissed her.

TWENTY-SEVEN

LOGAN

The knock came on the door well after the windows had fogged up, long minutes after he'd tugged Char into his lap and kissed and kissed and *kissed* her.

"Fuck," he muttered, wincing against the beam of a flashlight.

Bright lights shone from behind, making what they were doing, and where both of their hands were very obvious to the officer outside the window. Logan smoothed Char's dress down, plunked her into the passenger's seat.

"What—?" she asked, eyes glazed.

"Hang on, Starlight." He pushed the button to roll down the window. "Hello, officer," he said through the window, feeling her stiffen next to him, her soft gasp barely reaching his ears.

Dark hair, deep brown eyes, a smile teasing the corners of his mouth. "Sorry to . . . *interrupt*, but you can't park here."

"Apologies," he said, trying desperately to not think of the fact that his dick was all but poking a hole in his slacks. "We'll head home now."

A nod, before the policeman disappeared back into the night.

Logan watched him get into the patrol car, sucked in a breath, and turned to the woman sitting next to him. "Buckle up."

She did so, and then he drove on.

"I'll have you know that's the politest conversation I've ever had with a police officer," she muttered.

Heart hurting for her, he reached over and squeezed her thigh. "I'm sorry you've had to deal with that bullshit. There shouldn't be a different standard for our interactions with them."

"*Log.*"

His eyes cut to hers before turning back to the road. "What?"

"I like you." A beat. "So much."

More heart action, only this time it was alternating between squeezing and filling up like a balloon. Hurt and hope, who knew they were so closely intertwined?

"I like you, too, Starlight," he murmured, even though it was so much more than just *like*. He loved and adored her. His heart beat steadier when she was near, his skin settled when he held her hand. But . . . he was continuing with slow and steady and patient. And no one in their right mind would declare their love while still rebuilding their partner's trust in them.

Go slow.

On that train of thought, he slowly lifted his hand from her thigh, deliberately gripped the steering wheel. Then because his cock was still threatening to poke a hole in his slacks, he made a joke. "I can say, however, this was the first interaction with the police where I've been sporting a boner like a teenager."

Silence.

Shit.

He turned to look at her, about to apologize.

But then he saw her face, saw that the corner of her mouth was upturned. "How does one sport a boner like a teenager?"

"Namely by frequency and a lack of fulfillment."

She burst out laughing.

He joined in, even though it was at his expense.

"Come on," she said, once she'd gained control of herself. "Don't tell me you ever had difficulty with girls. I saw you as a twenty-one-year-old, and you had swagger even then."

"That swagger didn't accompany me in high school. I can assure you of that," he muttered. "I hadn't grown into my body, despite my poor attempts at weightlifting. And worse, I had acne."

"Aw, poor baby."

"Somehow your tone doesn't sound sympathetic," he grumbled.

"Well, clearly the awkward stage didn't last long, based on the young man I knew then," she said. "The *older* man I know today."

"Now, you're just being mean," he muttered, turning onto her street. "Cecily likes to remind me that, at thirty, the end of my career, and thus my life, is near."

Char giggled. "I did always like how Cecily teased you."

He pulled into her driveway and tapped her on the nose. "Only because you took notes so you could tease me better."

Another giggle, this one paired with her fingers tracing over his brow. "Only because *I* love seeing you glower at me." She leaned over the console, those straps shifting enough to allow him to look right down her dress. And just like that, he had the teenage boy problem again. Her lips quirked. "Like what you see?" she asked, leaning a little farther toward him, making his hands itch to pull her onto his lap again.

But they were in the driveway of her house.

Much more comfortable surfaces awaited them inside.

"Come on, Trouble," he said, pushing open his door. "Let's go in, and I'll show you exactly how much I like what I see."

He slipped out, closed his door, had just made it to her side of the SUV when hers opened and he got a glimpse of the sexiest pair of legs he'd ever seen.

Click. One high heel on the ground. *Click.* The other.

They weren't inside the house, didn't have any more privacy than they'd had on the side of the road, but Logan didn't care.

He kissed her again.

Lips and teeth and tongue. A lush, softly curved body against his.

Tart and spicy with hints of roses, of sweet.

Char.

All Char.

She wrapped her arms around him, jumped slightly to wrap her legs around his waist, and fuck, it would be so easy to unzip, to push home—

Patience.

A wrenching thought from the sliver of control still present in his brain. It scorched down his spine, burned through his arms, his fingertips, his thighs, his feet. His fingers clenched tighter, arms banding around her. His feet and thighs got into gear, moving them to the front door.

Char broke away when they were there, tearing her mouth from his and turning in his hold in order to punch in the code she had on the keypad.

The lock opened with a *whir.*

He shoved through the door, slammed it behind them, locked it again.

And . . .

Then he paused.

Her fingers wove into his hair, grabbed tight. "Don't you

dare ask if I'm sure, Logan Walker." She nipped at his jaw. "I wanted you since the moment I first laid eyes on you."

He started walking toward the stairs, stopped. "You've wanted me for nine months?" he asked, angling his head so he could kiss her temple.

"Nine years," she said. "Since the moment you walked into that arena, I've wanted you. Maybe it's been eight years since we've seen each other, eight years apart, but I will never *ever* forget the way my heart thumped when I first saw you."

"You were standing next to Luc," he said, remembering how earnest she'd been. "You used to carry this giant messenger bag with notebooks, and you had a clipboard in your hand." He nuzzled her throat. "No heels then."

"I didn't mind being shorter then," she admitted. "Not when I was still trying to find my place."

"Didn't take you long."

She grinned. "No, it didn't. And I quickly became addicted to heels."

"You mean foot massages," he accused, remembering all the times she'd come to his hotel room or they'd snuck out in his old truck and he'd rubbed her feet. Hmm. Maybe there *was* something to his quote-unquote foot fetish, or at least when it came to Char's feet.

Her smile didn't dim. In fact, it grew. "Accurate," she said. "You do give excellent foot massages."

He started climbing the stairs. "Want one now?"

"No."

He lifted a brow.

"I'd much rather you massage other places."

He grinned this time. "Yeah?" he asked. "*What* places?"

Narrowed eyes, another nip, this time on his chin. "You think you're so funny, don't you?"

"Funny looking, maybe," he quipped, making it to the top of the stairs and turning to the right. Her bedroom, as he'd discovered earlier that week when he'd tucked her into bed, was the second door on the right. The first was a small closet, and the only door on the left was a home office, one that he thought would be lovely and bright during the day, but also one that he didn't think fit Char at all.

Probably why she always worked in her kitchen.

That was more like her.

Warmth and beauty in the small details. Not grand and over the top. Not that she wasn't outright gorgeous, couldn't glam it up—like she'd done tonight—but rather that her beauty came from the strength inside her. It radiated through the way she carried herself, how she spoke, the expressions on her face.

No one would ever look at her and not think she was completely capable.

But he didn't just see capable.

He saw Char.

Smart and beautiful, but also vulnerable and a little lonely. This was the woman who gasped in outrage on that fiancé show when one of the men was betrayed and laughed when the stars argued about the proper way to grocery shop. This was the woman who'd argued with him about paying the bill, had demanded to share equally or pull her own weight. This was the woman who'd shared the dinner he bought for her, regardless of his refusal. This was the woman who stayed at the arena and spoke with every single player or staff member after they'd lost that game. She'd stayed until consolations were made, until reassurances were given.

This was the woman who'd looked at him with tears in her eyes when he'd broken her heart by leaving.

This was the woman who'd turned that broken heart into something powerful.

This was the woman he loved.

"Where did you go?"

Quiet words pulling him from his mind, soft fingers on his

jaw, a warm gaze on his. Logan blinked, realized he'd paused a foot inside her bedroom.

"I'm here," he murmured, shoving the past down and striding over to the bed.

Fingers in his hair again, clenching tight. "That's not what I asked."

Stern words, a commanding tone, and fuck, maybe he was a sick asshole, but he liked that bossy tone, liked it a whole lot. Didn't mean he was going to voice the bullshit in his brain though. "It's nothing," he said and bent to kiss her.

She kissed him back, lips soft, tongue a sleek dart. But then she used her grip on his head to break the contact, to glare up at him. "Nice try," she said. "Now, tell me."

He could either argue, or he could tell her the truth.

And as much as he enjoyed riling her up, he also didn't want to ruin the night with a fight, so he set her on the edge of the bed, sat next to her, then he met her stare and told her the heavy truth sitting on his mind and heart.

"I have so many regrets."

TWENTY-EIGHT

CHAR

Heavy words.

Perhaps she should have been upset the moment had waned, that Logan wasn't tearing her clothes off and attacking her, joining her in her quest for mutual orgasms.

But he was hurting.

And she didn't like it when her people hurt.

And . . . he'd made their time together thus far so much about her. Her needs, her desires. Her, her, *her*. Well, this would only work between them if it started being about him, too. Before, she'd made it only about him. Now, he threatened to do the same only for her.

And that couldn't work.

Long term, they couldn't forget completely about themselves and focus solely on the other person. Both were important, of course, but equally as important was understanding that they were two separate people with two separate hearts and minds and, frankly, with two different sets of needs.

They had to both be equally present.

She might have been grappling with being left out of the decision, with knowing that she would have certainly made a decision she regretted if Logan hadn't intervened. But though Log had said he hadn't regretted his decision, he had to be grappling with being the one who'd hurt her, of spending the last years knowing she thought the worst of him and not being in a position to change her mind.

Old pain. Baggage.

And beneath that, love and affection.

Because even when she'd hated Logan, she'd loved him.

So many other relationships, so many men, so many disappointing, unfulfilling boyfriends. Because of her and the walls she'd erected between herself and the world, more than anything they'd done.

Char knew it had been the same for him.

Never quite being able to fill that empty space inside, always searching for something but not being able to pinpoint what was missing.

Except . . . he'd known what he'd been missing.

Because they'd been great together. Real in a sea of what could be filled with fake hangers-on. True love in a world of first, fallible love.

They'd gone eight years without it.

"Come here," she whispered.

"Char," he began, thrusting a hand through his hair, eyes pained. "I didn't want to do this, to ruin our night. I made the call. I was the one who decided to end things."

"It was the right call," she said, feeling that deep in her soul. "You know that."

A nod. "But . . ." He trailed off, fingers yanking at his hair again.

"What, baby?" she pressed. "But what?"

"I don't want to drop this at your feet."

She took his hand. "Then whose feet will you drop it at?"

He stilled.

She put her hand over his heart, cuddled up to his side. "If we're going to be together, then you *have* to bring it to me. I have to feel needed in that way, have to know you can talk to me about anything, that you'll turn to me when you have problems."

His eyes flicked to hers, held for a long moment. Then he exhaled and said, "I know I made the right call, but I don't know if I can ever forgive myself for hurting you."

Her heart squeezed, her nails dug lightly into his chest. "You *have* to."

A jaw clenching tight, and pain in those emerald eyes. "Why?"

"Because I have."

The truth hit her with the strength of a bullet penetrating skin, quick and piercing, taking breath, followed by a trail of burning agony. She *had* forgiven him, but neither of them had finished mourning what they had lost.

And perhaps, neither of them had completely forgiven themselves.

His breath caught, his jaw relaxing, his eyes widening. "Starlight—"

She clambered into his lap, cupped both of his cheeks in her palms. He needed to understand this.

"I forgive you," she said fiercely. "*I* forgive you."

"Sweetheart." It was a single rough word, one that was paired with his arms wrapping tightly around her, with him burying his face against her curls, with him holding her close for a long, long time.

Eventually, he leaned back, and his emerald eyes collided with hers again. "I love you," he murmured, making her heart thud hard in her chest. "I'm sorry I hurt you, *so* sorry—"

"Enough," she whispered, hands dropping to his shoulders. "Just enough."

A shuddering breath, his arms still around her, still holding her close. "I never stopped, you know? Never stopped loving you."

Her lungs stretched on an inhale, as she held the air deep inside before slowly releasing it. She wanted to give him the words back, her feelings so bright and heady and *big*, but she also knew that she wasn't quite there yet. Yes, she'd forgiven him. Yes, she was ready to move on. But, no, she wasn't quite ready to admit aloud all that was in her heart.

"I know, baby," she said.

His face warmed, and she relaxed, realizing that he wasn't expecting the words just because he'd said them.

Of course, he wouldn't expect that.

Logan wouldn't *ever* demand from her in that way. He'd push her to fulfill her dreams, demand she take care of herself—or let him take care of her, anyway. But he wouldn't ever put pressure on her to bare her heart before she was ready. He might be impulsive and hard-headed and pushy, but he had shown her he would tread lightly and treat kindly.

Which was why, when he just held her, hand shifting to slide up and down her back, she murmured, "Come here."

Amusement danced across his face, his eyes going to the centimeters that separated them. "I *am* here."

"Well, come closer," she grumbled, pressing a kiss to his mouth.

The moment their lips touched, he exploded into a fury of motion.

One hand wove into her hair, his other gripped her hip, tugging her flush against him. He nipped at her bottom lip then slid his tongue inside her mouth, stroking along hers, demanding she meet his intensity. She did. No hesitation . . . and approximately ten seconds later found her back on the mattress, all of Logan's hard, hot gloriousness perched over her.

She reached for the hem of his shirt, wanting—no, *needing*

to get her hands on him, needing the steely planes of him beneath her palms.

"Skin," she gasped when he nipped at her jaw, nibbled at her earlobe, laved his tongue down her throat. "I need—" He leaned back, calloused fingers tracing the pattern of the thin straps criss-crossing her breasts. She'd loved how the dress made her feel earlier, how sexy she'd felt with the silk caressing her skin, the strips of fabric hiding but also emphasizing her cleavage. In all honesty, she'd imagined Logan doing exactly what he was doing at that moment.

What she hadn't anticipated was how incredible those little teases of sensation would be.

She wanted the dress out of the way.

She wanted his hands on her.

She wanted *skin.*

He sat back, tugging her up into a seated position. "Skin," he growled, grabbing her hands, which had somehow found their way into his hair, and bringing them to the top button on his dress shirt. "Yes."

Not needing to be told twice, she began working on those tiny discs, slipping one after another through their holes, parting the fabric and revealing golden skin as he kissed his way over her jaw, back behind her ear. His fingers caressed her throat, slipped down to cup one breast through the silk of her dress.

"Mmm," she moaned, her desire ramping to a fever pitch, making her move.

She jerked forward, pressed her mouth to his chest. Fuck, he tasted good. Salty and spicy and driving her to keep tasting him, to continue tracing the hard planes with her tongue, her lips.

A groan that had her thighs attempting to clench together, moisture pooling, but the powerful slack-covered legs between her own prevented the movement.

Logan didn't miss it, however.

He nudged her back, slid his palms down her sides, and

gripped the purple silk hem with his fingers. Seeing her dress crumpled in those big hands, so close to where she was desperate for him to touch, sent a wave of heat over her. Head to toe cloaked in desire, nerve endings on fire, fingertips tingling, pussy aching. She wanted her dress off, started to reach for the zipper under her arm, ready to yank it down.

Warm hands covering hers.

"I've got it."

She froze, breath shuddering out when he dipped a finger beneath the fabric, grasped the tag and began to tug it down.

It moved . . . all of four inches.

And she was kicking herself six ways to Sunday.

Because this wasn't one of those easy-on, easy-off dresses.

This was a twist and contort and curse and wiggle dress.

Which Logan seemed to process, at least in some small manner, when his eyes flicked from the open zipper up and down her body.

Then he shrugged, slipped a hand in the opening.

"Oh fuck," she whispered when that rough hand cupped her breast. Arching back, her hips canting up.

"Oh fuck," he groaned, "you're not wearing a bra."

She managed to peel open her lids long enough to see his eyes burning into her, a liquid emerald she could feel down to the marrow of her bones. Then he brushed his thumb over her nipple, and she lost the battle, tossing her head back, arching against him as he rolled that sensitive bud between his fingers, sending piercing bolts of pleasure through her.

He managed to coax and tease her other breast, her other nipple, but slid his hand out when a low tearing sound filled the air.

"Shit, sorry."

Her eyes slid open, and she shook her head. "It's fine." Yes, that was a rasp, her voice so husky with pleasure that she hardly recognized it.

He tugged up at the hem, only succeeded in getting it stuck just above her hips. "How do you get this torture device off?"

"With a fair amount of cursing."

A sharp grin. A quick movement that launched him off her. Another that had her on her feet, wavering from the sudden elevation change. "What—?"

He tugged at the hem again, bunching the dress beneath her arms, just above her breasts.

"Up," he ordered.

She lifted her arms. He tugged it up and over her head.

But the fabric stalled at her elbows when he groaned, bent his head to suck a nipple deep, and Char's legs threatened to buckle under the waves of pleasure. "I—" Warm hands on her breasts, massaging the flesh, his mouth switching sides.

This time she *did* wobble, her knees bending, her body collapsing against his.

He clutched her close, whipping off the dress, tossing it who-knew-where. The next instant she was on the bed, and he was sliding down until he was kneeling between her legs, using those big hands to spread her thighs wide.

A deep inhale, a groan. "Fuck, I've missed this. Missed you."

Hot breath on her skin, his tongue tracing higher and higher, and then . . . his mouth was on her.

Fuck. *She'd* missed this.

The way he devoured her like she was his last meal and he was going to make damn sure it counted. How his strong tongue pressed firmly and deliberately, always knowing the exact spot that made her moan. How—

"Holy hell," she gasped when he pulled out a trick with his tongue she didn't remember him knowing before.

He glanced up at her and grinned. "Should I write and thank the editors of the *Cosmo* blog?" he asked lightly before a curl of jealousy could spiral up and ruin the moment.

She shouldn't be jealous, not when they'd both dated plenty of other people.

But she wanted all his sex secrets and tricks to be about her, to be learned with her. Ridiculous. She knew it. She understood that. So, she was just going to accept the burst of jealousy and move on—

A sharp nip to her thigh.

"Stop thinking," he grumbled.

And then he did the tongue thing again.

And then she forgot about being jealous, forgot about absolutely everything except for Logan's mouth and tongue and fingers and the desire swirling within her.

It tightened.

Had her spine stiffening, moans pouring from her lips.

Heat billowed outward, incinerating her from the inside out.

Her fingers clenched on the sheets.

He pressed the flat of his tongue to her clit, slipped a finger inside, and reached a hand up to cup her breast, pinching her nipple.

One stroke. Two. And . . . she exploded.

TWENTY-NINE

LOGAN

S he still had her heels on.

They were pressed into his back, sharp bites against over-sensitized skin.

Her eyes were heavy, her lips turned up at the edges. "God, I've missed that," she whispered.

He chuckled, kissed her thigh, and gently dislodged her legs before crawling up her body and taking her into his arms. Fuck, it felt incredible to be able to hold her, even if his cock was threatening to break in half.

The bedroom lights were on, gilding her in golden light. Which meant he didn't miss her frown when he'd gathered her close.

"What are you doing?" she asked.

Fingers in her hair, sweet scent in his nose, warm, lush curves against him. "Holding you."

"I see that."

He waited.

She pushed up on an elbow, glared down at him. "The problem here is that that's *all* you're doing."

"Starlight." Yes, he wanted her. *Of course,* he wanted her. But this was all fairly new, and she needed time, and patience was working so far. "We should pause here. I don't want you to have regrets."

"Regrets?" An annoyed jerk of her head that shook her curls. "*Regrets?*"

"Char—"

"You say you love me," she snapped, poking him in the chest. "You say you've never stopped."

"That's true."

"So, why would I have regrets?" she asked, tossing up her hands. "I'm trying to be with a man who cares about me, who says I own his heart. Why wouldn't I want to—" She stopped. "Or is it you? Do you have regrets? About this *now?* Am I pushing you—?"

"*No.*" He reached up, hauled her down against his chest. "God, no, sweetheart. I just—"

Words cutting off, he shook his head.

How did he begin to explain everything in his mind, his heart? The constant war between his instinct to push, to consume, to devour, and the need to do right by her. The way the past and present were all tangled. How he felt he knew her deep down, even though they'd spent all those years apart.

Tonight, it was as though they'd picked up right from where they'd left off. As if nothing had happened and he'd never hurt her.

It felt . . . like perfection.

And that terrified him because perfection never lasted.

"You're scared."

His eyes flew to hers, mouth falling open. If magic were real, he would have thought she'd cherry-picked the thought from his mind. But it wasn't the paranormal that had Char seeing into his soul, Logan knew. It was just Char.

She knew him like no one else.

"And the stakes feel really high, especially after all this time."

Breath catching, he nodded.

"But the thing is, neither of us can promise the other everything. The world gets in the way. Bad things happen, and nothing is ever really certain." The ghost of a smile. "Why do I feel like I just stated every single cliché saying about things ending?"

Amused instead of terrified and all the more thankful for this woman, he tugged one of her curls. "You squeezed quite a few in there."

Her fingers were gentle on his cheek. "But do you understand why I said them?" she asked. "I want to be with you. If I'm being completely honest, no other man has ever compared. Ugh" —a shake of her head, her eyes narrowing when he felt smug creep into his expression—"don't get cocky now."

He grinned. "You trying to throw softballs my way?"

"I'm *trying* to make you understand that it feels like my heart was on pause for all these years, and now we've hit play."

"*Starlight,*" he murmured.

"We've jabbed the button, the movie's going, and . . . I don't want to stop, Log. I want to see where things go. I want to be with you—in every way."

"Is this you telling me to buck up and stop being scared?" he asked.

Soft brown eyes. "I can say it in those words if you need me to."

He thrust a hand through his hair. "I know I rush into things. I know I push," he said. "I'm just . . . I know it's a lot, that *I'm* a lot, and I'm trying to give you space and time to process everything."

"And if I needed that time, I'd tell you." A nip to his bottom lip before she gripped his chin tightly between thumb and fore-finger. "And also, I don't want you to be anyone but you. I like you just as you are. I can handle your pushiness, can easily shove you back if I need to. But"—her hand slid down, smoothed over his bare chest—"I trust you to take care of me, Logan." A shrug. "Plus, if you don't, I'll just steal your skates and dull the edges."

Laughter bubbled up in him. "Devious."

Pride in her gaze. "As needed." A beat. "Let's just focus on now, on building something that's good for both of us."

"God, I love you."

Her shoulders rose and fell on a long inhale, her lips parting. Then she laid back on the mattress, spread her legs and lifted her arms toward him. "Then come here and love *me*."

Which was when Logan forgot about patience and slow and steady.

He shoved the tangled knot of fear aside and just went for it.

His mouth met hers before his next heartbeat, his tongue slipping inside her mouth, coaxing hers out to play. One hand stroked down her side, shaping the heavy globe of her breasts, the slightly rounded plane of her stomach . . . lower.

Her waist, one hip. Her thigh and in between.

She was all liquid heat and swollen folds, and when his thumb brushed her clit, she groaned, hips canting up.

But just as he was touching her, she was all over him.

Her palms running over his chest, nails dragging over his nipples. He hissed out a breath, pleasure shooting down his spine, his cock hardening, throbbing in his slacks, reminding him that while Char was very, very naked—gloriously naked—he had too many damned clothes on.

Thankfully, she seemed to have the same thought.

Her fingers flicked open the button on his jeans, tugged down the zipper.

Before his next breath, those nimble digits slipped beneath the waistband of his boxer briefs and gripped him tightly.

No hesitation. No delay.

Just wrapped her hand around him and began pumping.

Red hazing the edges of his vision, he thrust into that tight grip, lost in how good it felt for her to be touching him. His nerves were on fire, and he felt himself growing in her hand, getting impossibly harder.

Once. Twice. Okay . . . maybe five or ten more.

But then he had to tug her fingers free or else this reunion would be a lot less fulfilling for both of them.

Her mouth pulled into a pout, but she let go, reaching over her head to pull out a condom from the nightstand when he pushed out of bed and stepped out of his pants. "Thanks, Starlight," he murmured, taking it and infinitely glad he didn't have to search through his wallet for the condom he'd stashed there earlier that evening—slow and steady plan, or not, it paid to be prepared.

"What put that gleam in your eyes?" she whispered.

"Only that I'm glad to use your condom because I plan on using mine later," he said, tearing open the wrapper and rolling it on.

Laughter and a shake of her head. Then she crooked her finger at him, placed her lips to his ear. "I have a whole box," she murmured, the heat of her words sending waves of need through him. "How fast do you think we can use them?"

Those waves of desire spiked into a tsunami, tearing through him as images ripped through his mind. Him on top. Her playing cowboy. From behind. Against the wall. In a chair. On the kitchen counter and the lounger on the back deck and the hood of his car—

"Fast," he growled, running his teeth over her throat, tracing the fluttering point of her pulse with his tongue. His hands were shaking. His mind had stopped thinking about the past and the future.

He'd focused on now.

On her beautiful breasts and how they felt in his mouth.

On the way she moaned when he sucked her nipples deep.

The gasp as he nibbled the spot just below her bottom rib.

The slight burn of pain when she tried to grip his hair and pull him up. But he was on the edge. He knew he wouldn't last long. So, he was going to whip out every last skill he possessed in order to have her riding that edge along with him.

He tasted her again, avoiding the sensitive bud of nerves, licking and stroking her, watching her breaths come more rapidly, feeling the sting of her grip in his hair— only this time it was pushing him more firmly against her pussy instead of tugging him off.

"Log," she groaned, hips bucking against his mouth, seeking more purchase. "That's—" Her head thrashed on the pillow. "I—"

He released her.

"What—?" Eyes flashing open, she glared. "I—"

"I've got you, Starlight," he murmured, wiping his chin on his arm and rising over her, positioning himself between her thighs.

This time, he didn't stop and confirm if she was one hundred percent absolutely sure. He didn't strive for patience, grip tight to ironclad control. Instead, he braced himself over her and let their bodies meld together.

Heaven and hell all at once.

Tight, wet heat. A soft, feminine body surrounding him.

"Now," she whispered. "Please move, baby."

He couldn't resist her, couldn't deny her *anything*.

A slow slide out. A gentle push in until he bottomed out. Feeling her muscles tightening, wrapping around his cock had him groaning and moving faster.

Thankfully, she was with him.

And fuck but she was beautiful.

Perspiration making her skin gleam, her hair a riot of curls in brown and orange and red, all spread out on her pillow. Her breasts bounced with each thrust, tempting him until he found himself unable to stop from bending down and sucking one nipple into his mouth.

Abs burning, back contorted like a pipe cleaner under a toddler's watchful eye, he kept thrusting, continued moving.

There weren't those moments of learning each other, of trying to find a rhythm.

They'd already done that eight years ago.

Tonight was solely about coming together again, about bringing his woman as much pleasure as possible. He had plans for that box of condoms in her nightstand drawer, nearly a decade of need and fantasies and *wanting* this woman.

But . . . she had plans for *him*.

Plans that unhinged his thoughts of bringing her to the edge so many times it would take the barest touch to catapult her over.

"Fuck!" he groaned.

Her legs had wrapped tightly around him as she did something with her hips that had any hope of drawing this out disappearing like so much smoke. Heat coiled at the base of his spine, every muscle in his body locking tight, and he was suddenly very dangerously at the very edge he wanted to dance with her on.

"More, baby," she said. "I need more."

Fuck slow. He gave her more. He gave her everything.

Teasing her breasts with his free hand as he pounded into her. He slanted his mouth across hers, kissing her in time to his thrusts, ratcheting his own need and desire to dangerous levels, until he was the one at risk of flying over.

But then she stiffened beneath him, mouth torn from his, her legs clenching on his hips, her hands finding their way to his hair again.

They pulled the strands. Hard.

He kept moving.

She groaned, thrust against him.

He didn't stop, just angled himself so he could go deeper, harder, faster.

"Logan!"

And then she was convulsing around him. Not a moment too soon, either, because his own orgasm was upon him, flaring out from his cock, burning through him from head to toe, until he was sucked down into oblivion as they moved and moved and *moved* against each other, wringing every last drop of pleasure from their bodies.

Afterward, he collapsed to the side, unable to hold himself up, finding it impossible to give her any pretty words.

All he could do was hold her tight, press a kiss to the top of her head, and wait for his heart to stop thundering.

Her arms came around him, holding him just as tightly.

And there were no words from her either, just a slowly descending pulse, just gentle fingers tracing circles on his spine, just a head on his chest and warm breath on his skin.

But it was enough.

Because he was here, with Char.

Because they had this moment when he'd hardly dared to hope they would ever get here again.

But they *were* there. Together, they'd found a way back.

So, when sleep came up to embrace him in blackness, he welcomed it with open arms.

THIRTY

CHAR

Fingers in her hair.

Not her own.

Smiling, she watched the hulking hockey player carefully smooth oil into the ends of her hair. It had been a bear that morning, since she'd been too limp last night to bother wrapping her curly locks in the silk scarf she usually wore.

Rookie mistake that.

Her mom had taught her better. She *knew* better.

But they'd dozed off for a little while then Logan had woken her in the most delicious fashion.

The man had the best tongue.

And she hadn't been thinking much about proper hair care when she'd all but passed out.

Four orgasms the night before.

That must be a record.

Or she was pent up. Or . . . that was just *them*.

"Sorry I messed up your hair," he said, pressing a kiss to the side of her neck.

"No, you're not," she teased. "And neither am I." She turned in his arms. "Next time, I just need to summon up enough energy to tame this"—a toss of her head—"wild beast."

"I love your hair." He pushed back the curls she'd spent far too long detangling that morning. "It's the color of fall."

"It can't decide if it wants to be brunette or black," she said with a roll of her eyes. "With a dash of red and gold in there, just to be difficult."

"It's beautiful."

A shrug. "It's me. Plus, I like the hint of my great grand-mother. She was a redhead. Did you know that?"

He lifted her up, plunked her on the counter. "No."

"I've only seen black and white pictures of her, but she and my great grandpa lived in England—she was a relocated Scot, and he was a freed slave."

"How did they meet?" he asked, stroking his hand up and down her back.

"Apparently, he saved her from an out of control horse, and she yelled at him for putting himself in danger." She chuckled. "I suppose that might be where some of the women in my family got their fire."

"An ill-tempered redhead." Amusement in his emerald eyes. "That fits."

She punched him lightly. "Rude?"

"What about your parents?" he asked. "How did they meet?"

"In London. My dad was studying abroad. My mom was out celebrating a girlfriend's engagement." Her lips curved. "He tried to buy her a drink, and she sent it back." A beat. "Along with the next three."

Laughter rippled through him. "I'm guessing he eventually won her over?"

"She went over to yell at him, to tell him to stop wasting his money because she was *not* interested in wasting her time with a man, thank her very much." Char giggled. "Six months later, she was getting her master's at the same college he was attending. They graduated at the same time, were married a year later, and two years after that, Will came along."

"He's five years older than you, right?"

She nodded. "Yup. He's a professor at the college my parents attended, and Amelia just landed her dream job teaching kindergarten."

Her parents were professors, too—her father teaching at a local community college and her mother tenured at a state school not far from home. The teacher gene was strong in her family, though it had clearly skipped right over her.

"Did you ever think about teaching?"

Shivering, since she was still wrapped in just a towel after their shower, and the warmth of the steam had disappeared during their talk, she went to reach for her robe, which was hanging on a hook near the door just to the side of the sink he'd plunked her on top of. But before her fingers grazed the fluffy fabric, Logan was already dropping it around her shoulders.

"You're cold," he murmured, cinching it across her waist. "Sorry, Starlight."

"I'm not complaining." She leaned up to kiss his jaw. "I like talking about this stuff with you. It reminds me of lying in the back of your truck jabbering about nothing." Another kiss. "And for the record, I think despite earning my undergrad degree in business, I would have ended up getting my teaching credentials and in a classroom, anyway." One more kiss. "But then Luc picked me up in that coffee shop and shoved me into the business of hockey."

He helped her down. "I bet your parents were shocked."

"Their scholarly daughter, from a family full of scholars, diving headfirst into sports management?" A grin as she nodded. "Yes."

"Is this where your mom made a fuss about you going into football instead?"

Char laughed, touched that he remembered her mom's obsession with the sport. "Yes," she said. "Although football isn't really a scholarly pastime, is it? So, I really only had her to blame."

"How'd it go when you told her that?"

She lifted a brow. "Do I look like I want to get my ass kicked?"

Laughing, he scooped her up, carrying her through the door and back into the bedroom, plunking them both down onto the mattress. "Your parents love you," he said, holding her close. "There would be minimal ass-kicking."

"Probably." She rested her head on his chest. "But yes, they do."

"What's that in your tone?"

She frowned, sat up. "What?"

"There's sad in your tone, Starlight."

"No, there's not."

"Char."

Rolling her shoulders, she said, "I was thinking about how she's found a new respect of the crazy sport of strapping precariously thin blades to one's feet and adding sticks and regular fights."

"No, you weren't."

"Log—" She paused, considered the thread of emotion weaving through her. "Yes, I am sad. Part of me continues to wonder and worry what I missed out on."

"Because you walled yourself off."

A sigh. A nod.

"Because of me."

She froze then admitted the truth. "Yes."

Pain washed over his face, darkened his emerald eyes to

nearly black. He sat up, and an instant later, his arms were around her. She felt rather than saw his hands clench into fists.

Then she told him the rest of it.

"But also because of me, baby. I—" She struggled for a minute, trying to put to words what was in her head. "I've always felt a bit distant, as though I were slightly on the outside, struggling to find where I fit in. With my family, with my friends, with my relationships, as though there was this inner wall I was just too scared to let down." She sighed. "And they respected that barrier, never pushed fully through."

"But I barreled through like a bull in the china shop?"

"No," she whispered. "I let them down with you. You didn't have to push or shove your way into my heart. It was just like you were always there."

A sharp inhale. A clenched jaw. "Starlight—"

Fuck. She was hurting him, and that wasn't what she wanted. "I didn't need the walls with you then," she said. "And I don't need them now. I think that's why it's so easy to be with you, why I missed our closeness so much when you'd gone. I can just be with you, Log. I've never found that with anyone else."

"Char—"

The emotion in the broken off statement had her gaze flying to his, seeing the deep emotion and dampness at the edges.

And she *knew*.

The truth that had always been. The truth that would always be.

This man owned her heart.

He always would.

The terror from before disappeared. She didn't need more time. She just needed . . . Logan.

"I love you," she whispered.

He froze, his body gone ramrod stiff. "What?"

"I love you," she said, placing her hand over his heart, feeling the organ thundering beneath her palm. "Truthfully, I don't think I ever stopped loving you. Even when I tried to hide behind my walls, to pretend to be untouched, you were always there, always *in* me."

"I—" A sharp shake of his head. "I—you *can't*, Char. I need to prove that I—"

"I don't need you to prove anything, baby." When it seemed as though he'd protest, she captured his cheeks between her palms. "I just need you to be *you*—to spend time with me, to let me bitch about my job, and for you to complain about all the lousy parts of yours. I want us to spend time in the kitchen trying to figure out how to cook something more complicated than omelets and to show you all the gloriousness of my myriad reality shows."

"Sweetheart." He swallowed hard.

She kept her hands in place, pressed a firm kiss to his lips. "I don't want us to go back, I want us to move forward. I want us to find what we can be *now*."

His palm dropped her cheek. "I want that, too."

"Good."

He brushed the back of his knuckles down her throat. "You love me?"

Nuzzling into him, safe in the circle of his arms, she said, "You had me at the slippers."

Laughter burst out of him, shaking the bed, vibrating through her. Then his arms tightened, and he lay back onto the bed, hauling her on top of him. "Let's stay in our pajamas and play hooky for the rest of the day. You can show me those reality shows, and I'll make you my world-famous omelet."

Delight trailed through her.

But she didn't miss the tension just hinting at the edges of his expression. Part of him still worried she'd turn away from him. Or maybe he thought he deserved to be punished, that regardless of his words and convictions of having done the right thing that he needed to be put through the wringer.

She was done with that nonsense.

But words weren't going to do it in this case.

He needed to be shown that she'd put the past behind her, had forgiven him, was truly ready to move forward. Just as her heart needed the time to keep learning all the small things about this wonderful man.

Because he'd spent the last *season* showing her that he was good and kind and stable, a great teammate, a proper addition to the organization.

And he'd spent the last weeks showing her he was the type of man who cared and paid attention.

The lock on her gate.

Meals when she worked through lunch.

Breakfast and strong arms and dessert he didn't want but was willing to make time for in case she did.

Reality shows and hair oil.

Omelets.

Those celestial slippers.

Showing love rather than just giving her words.

So really, how could she have *not* fallen in love with the man?

Which is why she leaned down to kiss him, putting every bit of what she felt into that touch. It was heat and sleek darts of tongue. It was lips pressed tight and fingers digging into her hips. It was desire and pleasure and . . . this man.

His hips thrust up against hers, his erection an iron brand of heat. The towel he wore and the robe covering her body were the thinnest barriers.

She wanted him.

But she wanted to put his heart at ease even more.

Pulling back, she smiled down at him, reached for the TV remote on the nightstand. "Okay, now get ready to have your mind blown while I bring you the gloriousness of Britain's bouncers—*ah!*"

He tumbled her over, his towel coming loose. "How about I show you some of *my* gloriousness first?"

Affection for this man swelled within her, right along with desire as he untied her robe and spread his slightly roughened hands on her. "I—*ah*—" Her breath hitched when he cupped one breast. "I'm fine with that."

A laughing kiss.

Gentle palms skating over her body.

Joy in her heart.

Char wrapped her arms tightly around him, met him caress for caress, touch for touch, stroke for stroke, and let him love her with the same intent focus she then turned onto him.

Because . . . *together*.

That was the only way forward.

———

"I'm not entirely sure about this," Char said.

"Oh, come on," Brit coaxed. "You're fine."

She was not fine, decidedly *not* fine. She was wearing ice skates in someone's insane idea of a good time.

Sharp metal blades instead of heels. What had she been thinking?

"I've seen those death traps you call shoes," Sara Jetty, Brit's good friend and wife of former Gold player, Mike Stewart said.

As she skated by.

Gracefully.

Not at all like a wobbly deer, a la Char.

"Easy for you to say," she muttered. The other woman had scored a gold medal in figure skating in her younger years. That kind of skill didn't exactly disappear. "Why did I think this was a good idea?"

"It's for charity!" PR-Rebecca shouted.

Shouted because she was on the bench. Pregnancy gave her an out.

Hmm.

Maybe Char could lie and—

"Don't even think about it," Calle said, swooping up next to Char and taking her arm.

The single reason she didn't end up on her ass was because Calle had a solid grip on her, and Char's assistant coach had spent *her* younger years playing for the national team.

Once again, she circled back to: how in the fuck had she allowed this to happen?

But just as she was working up a really big panic, a gaggle of giggling girls swarmed the ice, circling Brit and Calle and Sara.

"Remember," Calle said, releasing Char's arm as the swarm took her away. "Bend your knees and fall forward if you're going to crash—that's where all the padding is."

"Fall forward," Char said, skating tentatively forward. She'd had a few lessons from the guys over the years, but she wasn't what anyone would call skilled.

And that was before she'd been dressed in the bulky hockey gear.

"Knees bent," she whispered, adjusting her helmet and nearly eating shit.

Her eyes went to the stands, and she saw Logan was signing autographs, along with Mike, Coop, Blane, and Stefan. They weren't there for any other reason except to watch their significant others play some hockey with girls from the local teams. The Gold hosted many of these events during the year, drumming up excitement for the sport, especially among those who might otherwise miss out on hockey's awesomeness.

Mandy was on the bench with Rebecca, armed with the pseudo-baby shower gift Char had bought for her—a fancy first aid kit on wheels and emblazoned with snarky statements. She was prepared for any spills. Though, in reality, Char was likely to be the only one in need of its contents.

The girls were skilled enough to skate circles around her, even the younger ones, who were just six or seven.

But Char wasn't the major draw.

She'd been roped in to relieve PR-Rebecca after her pregnancy announcement, but Char would have accepted the request to participate anyway. Empowering girls aside, this was her putting her money where her mouth was when it came to making that family in the Gold.

"Knees bent," she whispered again, tearing her eyes away from Logan and his adoring fans, trying to ignore the way her heart pitter-pattered when she saw him talking to a tiny little girl.

Aw.

Shit!

She almost ate it, remembering at the last minute to bend her knees. "Good grief, Harris," she muttered. "Focus."

"I can help you!"

Char smiled at the girl. "Yes, please."

Without missing a beat, the girl helped Char hold her stick properly and was teaching her how to propel herself across the ice within minutes.

"Hey, Calle," she called, coming close to the coach. "I think you're out of a job!"

Calle grinned, and she ran a passing drill practically with her eyes closed. "I'm fine with that." She blew a kiss to the man who held her heart, who smiled at her and made it clear she held his just as tightly. "I'll just go off and make more babies with Coop then find another team to coach."

"Rude," Char teased.

"Coach us!" one of the girls shouted.

"Yes, Calle! Come to our team."

Another grin from the statuesque blonde. She winked at Char. "Looks like I have plenty of job offers." She passed off another puck. "Sorry, girls. I'll be with the Gold for at least a few more years."

"Boo!" the collective shouted.

But it was short-lived because Calle stopped messing around and got into Coach Mode. A trill of her whistle called them to attention.

Another had the girls separating into different stations.

Then all the moving parts got moving—the girls completed a series of different drills, overseen by far better skaters than Char, though she did her best, and her cheeks actually hurt from smiling.

Full disclosure, her knees hurt from falling, too.

But not as much as her ass did from the one time she'd landed on it.

Calle's advice had been solid.

The hour on the ice ended with a short kids vs. adults game, and the only goal the adults scored was Char's.

On Brit in net.

Her goalie tipped up her helmet and shook her head, eyes narrowed.

The girls cheered.

The men at the glass cracked up.

Calle gave her shit. Sara, graceful, lovely Sara who definitely didn't score on her own goalie, patted her on the arm consolingly and whispered, "She'll get over it."

Brit didn't look like she'd get over it anytime soon.

"I don't think she'll get over it."

Calle giggled. "She'll get over it during Mia's self-defense class."

Remembering Liam talking about being the test dummy getting laid out on his ass, Char murmured, "I think I'll be busy that night."

Sara's tinkling laugh filled the air.

Calle put the puck on her stick. "Make it worth your while at least."

"Char," Brit warned.

"Screw it," Char said and shot the puck hard in Brit's direction. So hard she ended up wiping out and having everyone laugh at her before she declared, "Attack!" and pointed at Brit.

Dozens of pucks began flying in Brit's direction, chaos ensuing. Teasing and laughing echoing across the rink.

She glanced at the boys, saw they were laughing, too.

She looked toward the bench, saw Mandy and Rebecca bent in half as they roared with laughter.

But that was okay. Char would take the crap.

Because teasing and hilarity, because competitive spirit and consoling looks and spending time together. Because . . . family.

And Char was becoming part of the Gold's.

Thirty-One

Logan

Oh, the joys of family time.

So. Much. Fun.

Which meant he was wondering again why he'd come home.

Despite his intentions to visit his folks when Char went home to her family, he'd almost blown off the trip, nearly caving to the desire to hide in his cabin and hold on to the bubble of nirvana he and his Starlight had created over the last week.

A weekend spent in bed, watching bad TV and ordering in groceries. They'd trolled the web, had picked several recipes they'd been convinced they could master.

Then they'd nearly set the kitchen on fire because he'd gotten distracted.

By the tiny shorts Char had slipped into that were masquerading as pajamas.

Luckily, she'd surfaced from the haze of desire that had kept Logan in its clutches, realizing they'd turned the bread in the oven into charcoal and the pasta and sauce on the stove into briquettes.

He'd gone out on Monday while she was at work and had bought her a brand-new set of pots and pans.

The other ones had made it as far as the trash.

They'd spent one more night together, not attempting to cook, not watching bad TV shows. Instead, Char had picked him up at his house and coaxed him into her car and driven him to the coast.

Heart swelling because his non-nature woman had taken time out of her busy day to research something for him, he'd kissed her long and deep.

She'd taken him there, just because he would love it.

A narrow slice of land.

A steep staircase winding down and down and *down*.

Moonlight and stars overhead, immune even to the light pollution of the city to the north.

And a blanket spread out over sand. His woman cuddled to his side.

They'd sprawled on that blanket, talking well into the night about nothing and everything, and then he'd taken her home to his house and loved her until the sun came up.

After which he'd handed her the silk scarf to tie around her hair. He'd bought it after the incident with her curls, when she'd been too exhausted to put it on. And after seeing her fight with her hair the next morning, watching her wince as she attempted to put it to rights, he'd promised himself she wouldn't ever go without one again.

He wouldn't do anything to cause her hurt. Not if he could help it.

And in this case, he *could* help it. He now had a stash of her favorite brand of wraps and had watched numerous YouTube videos to learn how to put it on.

If she didn't have one, he now had plenty.

If she was too tired, he would do it.

She hadn't complained about the lack of sleep, even though she'd had to get up in just a few hours in order to make her flight to the East Coast. She'd just shared his bed, cuddled against him, and then fallen asleep in his arms.

Then she'd gone.

And the next day he'd gone, too.

His parents lived in Wisconsin, on a large swathe of property that held a fishing hole for his father—a top priority and must-have that his dad had *needed,* and his mother despised on principle—and a craft room filled with wall-to-wall shelving that his mom had insisted on having custom made that his dad refused to pay for with *his* hard-earned money.

The last had been a major point of contention between his parents over their lives, and one, frankly, he'd lost a lot of respect for his dad over.

His mom might not have worked in an office, but she'd given her job up for them, managed Logan and Cecily and Josh's school and extracurriculars, had cooked and cleaned and *been there.* She'd lived her life for them for many years, and the comments about money had increased tenfold when his mom had gone back to school for her degree without consulting his dad.

Now she worked at the local nursing home, part-time as a receptionist and part-time as the activities coordinator.

His dad, on the other hand, had retired and found himself at loose ends.

Hence, the fishing hole.

But Logan could see he was trying.

He'd spent a lot of time in the garden, particularly concentrating on those spots outside the window of the craft room, trying to make it look lush and green so she would have something pretty to look at. And he made himself lunch when Logan's mother was at *that* job, instead of asking her to—a point that he'd lost any ground on by declaring it far and wide.

But he wasn't going to win any gold stars for his behavior, not when he seemed incapable of understanding how he was hurting Logan's mom.

And on that track, it wasn't like his mom was going to get any either. She just bottled it up, played the martyr, and held on to that anger.

Anger and cluelessness weren't a pretty combination in a thirty-seven-year marriage. Which was how Logan had found himself the referee more and more over the years, how interfering and placating had become his typical standard of dealing with his mom and dad's arguments.

In this case, he'd ensured the fishing hole and the bugs it was drawing toward the house were taken care of—what his mother objected to but seemed unable to give voice to, at least when that person was her husband. Then Logan had hired a custom cabinetmaker to make the craft room everything his mom had hoped it would be. He'd footed the bill because he could afford it, and his mom deserved to have something nice.

But he wished he didn't have to.

Not paying. *That* he was fine with.

It was all the rest of it that had become unbearable. The phone calls and aggravation. The fights and placating. But . . . he'd also learned here was no point in arguing with them or attempting to have them hash out their own issues.

That time had long passed.

In his teenage years, they'd stopped trying to put a happy face on their relationship. Logan wasn't sure if pretending had gotten too difficult or if they just figured he was old enough to deal, but one day the veil had lifted, and he'd seen exactly what was between them.

Tension and resentment.

And then he'd looked back and seen all the other times that

had bled through. The sharp comments and hard looks. The anger, the coldness, the distance.

Not healthy. Not fulfilling.

Not *anything* like he had with Char.

But putting the woman he loved aside for the moment, Logan knew if he didn't step into situations like the Craft Room, he had to listen to complaints from both sides, and life was too damned short to deal with that.

His father exalting all the points of how his mother was controlling and demanding. His mother citing every instance over the course of their relationship of how his father didn't care about her feelings.

No, it wasn't healthy to step in.

He knew that.

Still, he also knew that, at this moment in time, stepping in was making his life less drama filled.

So, peacemaker for the moment.

Until he figured out how to get them to see what they were doing was alienating their children. Hell, John had moved miles away. Cecily was in another country. The only thing that had them all returning home at regular intervals was that they were all aware their mom and dad had been excellent parents.

Once.

Now, they were a burden.

One that Logan wished he hadn't decided to shoulder.

He leaned against the doorframe that led into the kitchen, watching his mom aggressively knead a giant pile of dough. She was making cinnamon rolls, both because they were Logan's favorite, but also for the seniors at the center. She had a shift later, and his father was unhappy she hadn't taken the time off to be with Logan.

"They don't need you," his dad was grumbling. "They got on just fine without you for all these years."

"I promised I would be there," she said. "So, I will be there."

It's four hours, and then I'll be home. Lacy has already promised to cover for me on Friday."

"She—"

"*Can't* cover for me today, as I told you this morning *and* told Logan when he called to tell us he was coming two days ago," she snapped, punching hard enough into the dough that Log wondered if the rolls would be as hard as rocks or the best ever. Did violence count in kneading? Because if so, she'd be getting the gold star.

"They—"

Enough.

"It's fine, Mom," he interrupted, crossing over to her and hugging her from behind. He kissed the top of her head, met his dad's eyes, silently telling him to let this go. "My visit is last minute. I can't expect you guys to drop everything."

His father's glare intensified, and Logan prepared himself for his next peacemaking operation.

Read: torture.

"Plus, that will give us time to go fishing."

His dad's face lit up.

His mom stiffened in his arms, knowing that he hated fishing. But as much as he disliked the tension between his parents, he did enjoy spending time with them one-on-one.

He could throw his bobber in the water, pretend to care about fish for an hour or two, especially if it meant he got a glimpse of how his dad used to be.

"I'll go get the gear ready."

Sighing, after his dad left, his mom nudged him back. "You shouldn't keep doing that, you know."

"Doing what?"

She touched his cheek, sadness in her eyes. "I can handle him."

"I know you can." He covered her hand with his. "But you need to *actually* talk to him, Mom. Not just snip and complain."

"I haven't been doing very well, have I?" She winced when he didn't respond, turned back to the rolls, and he felt guilt slide through him. "I'm sorry, Logie Bear. This hasn't been fair to you. I'll do better."

Dammit.

He didn't want her feeling bad.

He didn't want his mom to hurt any more than he wanted Char to.

She was his *mom*. She'd baked cakes and driven to the rink at God knew what hour. She'd held his hand when he broke his arm, flew out and took care of him when he had knee surgery.

He just wanted his parents to get along.

Unfortunately, he wasn't sure how to go about that.

So, instead of belaboring the point, instead of advising as he'd done for far too long, to just sit down with his dad and *talk*, Logan leaned next to his mom on the counter and asked, "Will you teach me how to cook something later?"

Green eyes that mirrored his own widening. "You? Cook?"

"Just one meal. Something a novice like me can accomplish, but something delicious."

Eyes now narrowing. "It's a woman."

He grinned. "It's a woman."

She smiled, wide enough that he felt its impact in his solar plexus. "Oh, Logie Bear, I'm so happy for you," she said, setting down the dough and hugging him tight. "Will you tell me about her?"

"Do I still get to be your taste-tester?"

"Cheeky boy." She kissed his cheek, opened the cookie jar in front of her, and pulled out a chocolate chip cookie the size of his head.

Not on the diet plan.

But his mom was smiling, and he was going to get to talk about his favorite thing in the world—Char.

He could work with that.

By the time the cinnamon rolls were in the oven, he'd confessed all, had planned out a meal his mom was confident he could execute, *and* eaten two more chocolate chip cookies.

Definitely not on the meal plan.

But definitely better than the day had begun.

Of course, he still had to survive fishing.

———

"Hey, Starlight," he said, answering his cell as he pushed out the front door and stepped onto the porch.

"What's wrong?"

He blinked, realized that his parents and their bickering were bleeding over into his interactions with Char, and quickly shoved the dark emotions down. Never would he allow that to happen again. Never would he let his baggage affect what he and Char were building.

Not fucking ever.

"I'm fine," he told her, leaning against the waist-high railing and staring out at the lake. His dad was putzing around at the shed near the pond, would no doubt be waving him down in a couple of minutes.

But for now, he had his woman on the phone, and he wasn't going to waste a moment.

They'd only had one quick chat, her letting him know she'd arrived safely at her parents' house, and then exchanged a few texts. He'd missed her, even though they'd only been apart for two days, but hadn't wanted to intrude on her family time.

She needed this time.

"You're not fine," she accused.

The urge to disagree with her, to push her back and pretend all was good was strong.

Except . . . that wasn't what he wanted to build. That wasn't what Char needed, and she'd been explicit about that fact. He couldn't be the only one who protected and took care. He needed to be open and let her in and not presume to know the best course of action.

Which was why he shoved down the urge to continue with the I'm-Fine-Everything-Is-Fine path and admitted, "My parents are getting to me."

"You—"

She cut herself off, and he got the impression she'd been about to yell at him for not telling her the truth.

Then her voice softened. "Shit, I'm sorry, Log."

"It's nothing more than I expected," he said. "It's just . . ."

"What you expected."

"Yeah." He made a face. "That."

"Is there anything I can do?"

Heart pulsing, he forced himself to not ask her to come up, to rescue him. Even putting aside his urge to be the rescuer, he wasn't going to take her away from her family. "Just call me every once in a while, Starlight," he said. "I've got plenty of experience dealing with them. Plus, I'll be home and in my cabin soon enough."

Silence, and he braced himself, wondering if she'd want more than that.

He'd give it, of course. He loved her, would flay himself to the bone if need be. But just admitting that he was upset felt like he'd given into the bullshit that his parents created.

Drama. Resentment.

God, he just wanted to have a visit where he could sit in a room with them and enjoy himself. No placating. No refereeing.

Just being.

Like it was when he was with Char.

But that wasn't going to happen, and he needed to learn to deal if he was going to keep visiting. To not allow his parents and their drama to derail him, to smother him in their bullshit.

He wanted to be a mountain undergoing an avalanche, its

snow sliding off in one large sheet, revealing the steady and unbreakable granite beneath. He wanted to be untouched and unmarred. To be able to love the woman in his heart without baggage.

Ah. Hopes and wishes . . . and then reality.

So, he braced himself and waited for more questions.

"I learned how to make a meal you might like," she murmured, instead of interrogating him. "Barbeque chicken with spicy rice and a bean salad. It's low calorie, tasty, and I nearly cut my thumb off last night when I tried to help my dad cook it."

Now he struggled for words, love for this woman in every cell, wanting to find a way to tell her exactly how much that meant to him.

But he didn't want to weigh down the moment. Instead, he asked lightly, "Is it still attached?"

She didn't miss a beat. "The chicken or the thumb?"

He laughed out loud. "Starlight," he warned.

"It's barely a scratch," she said then her voice went serious. "But . . . thank you, Log. For talking to me. For letting me in."

"I—"

"I know everyone thinks I'm the open book because I'm good at pretending I have my shit together and don't hold back in the media or negotiations," she murmured. "But just like you could see through that mask, I can see through yours, baby."

His pulse raced. "Char."

"I see you underneath all that smooth, carefree charm—"

Throat tightening, he went for a joke. "You think I'm charming?"

A chuckle. "Case in point, right there. But yes, honey, I do. You're very charming—so charming that people don't realize you're hurting inside." She paused. "You're allowed to wish things are different."

Heart pounding, he sucked in a breath. "If only wishes could turn into reality," he said lightly.

A long beat of quiet. "I know you do."

Another breath, releasing the hurt of the morning, the strain since he'd arrived the night before. His jaw ached from clenching it. His shoulders were riddled with knots.

But he was on the phone with Char.

And that was enough.

"I really am okay, Starlight," he said and took the next step, letting her in a little deeper, done with pretending he was an island and nothing affected him—not the tide or a hurricane or an invasive species. "I just . . . sometimes I forget how bad it is. The tension between them is unbearable, and I seem to always want to default back to placating everyone. It just never really works."

"They need to grow up and leave you out of it." Sharp words now, but not directed at him, even though he clearly owned some of that burden by always interceding.

Still, the words were true.

His parents did need to grow up, did need to leave him out of it.

And . . . he needed to not let himself get drawn in.

"Unfortunately, you can't make people grow up," she said, voice gentle. "And they're your parents. You love them, want to see them happy."

"I'm starting to think they're at their happiest when they're the most miserable."

A beat as she considered that. "Somehow that makes sense."

"Logan!" his dad shouted from down by the pond. "Let's go!"

A soft giggle in his ear. "It sounds like you're being summoned."

"Fishing," he muttered.

Another giggle. "I thought you hated fishing."

Hate was too gentle a word. He despised it. But . . . it was time with his dad. Hopefully, *peaceful* time. And the plus was that the yelling would probably scare the fish away, so he'd be unlikely to deal with actually catching a fish. "I do."

"Fuck, I love you," she said.

"Sweet," he murmured.

"What?"

"I'd almost forgotten how damned sweet you are," he said. "Thank you for giving me that."

"I think I'd give you just about anything, Log." A beat. "Because I know you'll give me the same back."

"I love you," he told her.

"Show it to me on the ice next season," she teased then hesitated. "I should let you go."

"Yeah."

Except, he didn't want to hang up.

"I don't want to go," he admitted.

"I don't want to let you go."

"*Logan!*"

"Fuck," he muttered.

Laughter in his ear. "I'll talk to you later. Text me a picture of all the fish you catch."

"That's just mean."

Her voice gentled. "Bye, honey."

"Bye, Starlight."

He hung up, pocketed his phone, and made his way down to the pond.

Fuck.

Now he had to catch a goddamned fish.

———

Fishing was proceeding as expected.

Which basically meant it was proceeding in silence.

They'd picked up their rods, walked to the end of the small pier he'd helped his dad assemble the previous summer. All metal and floating plastic barrels, it was meant for a much larger lake.

But it floated, got them into the middle, and his dad was happy.

Easy enough.

Log had plunked his ass into a rickety chair that didn't look like it had a hope in hell of supporting him and cast his line out into the water after baiting it and tying on a weight and lure.

No small talk.

Nothing biting.

Just sitting in silence as he figured out what had to change.

Funny how he'd spent years living in this exact scenario, but it wasn't until this visit that it felt absolutely stifling. Like his skin was too small. As though he couldn't breathe.

Because of Char.

Because it was so easy with her.

Because he would do anything to make her happy.

His parents, his dad in particular, didn't seem to give a damn either way. He sighed, reeled his line in, cast again.

And maybe sighed again. But, fuck, it just didn't make any sense. How could his dad not care that his mom was unhappy? Why didn't his mom make her wishes known and stand up for herself?

Why did they stay together when they were so fucking miserable?

Another sigh, this one stifled because he was trying to find a conversational topic that wasn't his parents and could bring about some enjoyment.

"What's got your panties in a bunch?" his dad asked.

Suddenly, Logan didn't give a *fuck* about enjoyment.

Suddenly, *he* was the resentful one. Furious that he'd allowed himself to be drawn into this battle between him and his parents.

"You," he said on an exhale. "You and Mom have me all twisted up inside."

A grunt, his dad's eyes on the lake, but no more words or inquiries. Just the requisite question and going back to his own fucking bubble.

"The fighting has taken a toll on everyone," he said, forcing himself to be calm. "I don't know why you and Mom can't just sit down and sort it out. Why you have to bicker and argue all the time. It makes it really not fun to be around you."

His dad reeled in the line, cast again.

But he didn't say *anything*.

And Logan's temper flared. "You don't give a fuck, do you?"

Steady green eyes finally came to his. "Give a fuck about what?"

"That this tension between you and Mom is driving me away, pushing Cecily and Josh away. That you both are fucking miserable and make everyone around you miserable, too."

Silence.

Logan gripped the fishing rod, the fiberglass handle making a cracking sound that had him loosening his fingers and striving for patience. "It's gotten to the point where I don't even want to come home."

A shrug. "Then don't."

He closed his eyes, breathed deeply. "Why are you doing this?"

Maybe it was something more. Dementia or a sudden hormone imbalance that had caused the change. But . . . it wasn't a sudden change, was it? This had been brewing for years, growing progressively worse as the roots of whatever darkness between his parents festered.

"I'm not doing anything," his dad muttered. "Aside from trying to fish."

"And fight with Mom about stupid shit."

"What's between your mother and I isn't any business of yours."

Except, they'd *made* it his business. Over and over and *over* again. Logan reeled in his fishing line, secured the hook, and dropped the rod on the dock. "Do you really believe your own bullshit?" he asked, turning toward his dad.

Who slowly faced him and whose only response was a raised eyebrow.

And Logan lost his shit.

Look, he knew he was impulsive, had to regularly force himself for patience. But that patience wasn't often needed for his temper. He dealt with pain in the ass forwards on the ice, pushing his buttons, slashing his calves with their sticks, cup-checking on an occasional basis—occasional because while he was slow to anger, once he got to that point, it was an implosion of spectacular proportions.

Last time he'd lost it on the ice, he'd ended up kicked out of a game when some fucker had taken a cheap shot at Brit.

Today, it was this fucking stranger in front of him.

This wasn't his dad, wasn't the person he'd respected and had fun with, who'd coached his hockey team and taught him how to ride a bike. This person was a miserable bastard who seemed to be completely lacking in empathy.

"You call me to bitch about her," Logan said. "She calls to bitch about you. I find myself completely stuck in the middle."

"You've got your own life to live." A shrug. "Stop complaining and go out and live it."

Yeah, that was exactly the same conclusion he'd come to.

Because it had taken these last couple of weeks with Char to recognize exactly how fucked up this tangle he'd allowed himself to be ensnared in with his parents was.

And he was done.

"I don't know when you turned from the dad whose

opinion I respected more than any other person's to this angry asshole in front of me—"

His dad's fishing rod *clinked* down into the holder. "How dare you call—"

Logan jumped to his feet. "*That's* the only thing that gets a rise out of you? Me calling you an asshole? I don't know what the fuck happened to you, but you're not the man I grew up wanting to emulate, not by a fucking long shot."

"Then go, Log. Go live your fancy life. Go be with your fancy friends and see how happy that makes you."

He sighed. "That's just it, Dad. I don't give a shit about my *fancy* life or friends." The ones he'd made this season he didn't count in that number, but he didn't bother to explain the distinction between them to his father, not when there were so many other important things to tackle. "I haven't been happy. And that's not because of you and Mom," he added, when his dad started to protest. "It was because of me. Because I gave up the woman I loved so she would have a chance at her dream. But now I have her back, and I cannot for the life of me understand how you wouldn't do everything in your power to make the woman *you* love happy."

He shoved a hand through his hair. "Why argue over the craft room or the job or the trip she wants to take to Finland? Even if you don't give a shit about how she stores her fabrics or her dream to see the northern lights or the job, don't you see how working makes her happy, along with piecing together a quilt? Don't you want her dreams to be realized?" Logan waited for his dad to reply, and when he didn't, Log sighed and figured why not say the rest of it? "She gave up her career for yours and didn't complain once. She moved away from her family and support system to advance your career. She gave, Dad, so why couldn't you give back?"

And still . . . nothing.

Beyond fucking done, Logan turned away, started down the dock.

"I would have given her everything," his dad said, and Logan spun back, saw his dad walking toward him. "If she hadn't fallen in love with my best friend."

THIRTY-TWO

CHAR

The smell of peach pie filled the kitchen, and she was sitting full sandwich-style between her sister, Amelia, and her brother, Will.

And having a pile of shit heaped onto her.

Shit of the teasing, sibling variety.

God, it was good to be home.

Her brother and sister had spent most of the last two days at her parents' house, and she was so thankful for her family and their inability to hold the fact that she'd been beyond distant over the last few years against her.

Even when she'd been too wrapped up in work to appreciate them, they'd still reached out, and being here with them, finally being aware of how she'd felt and acted over the years—closed down and separate and probably a bit cold—made her realize how much she'd been missing out on.

Amelia bumped her shoulder against Char's. "You look happy, Char-Char. I'd thought we'd be consoling a defeated barrier-breaker who'd been denied her ultimate prize."

"I was considering holding a Chubby Bunny contest, just so Lo-Lo can win something."

She narrowed her eyes even as her lips quirked. "I may be defeated in my search for the Cup, but I'll never lose another Chubby Bunny contest."

A bag of marshmallows landed on the counter in front of her. "Prove it."

She glanced up to see her dad grinning at them, a laughing expression softening the planes of his face.

And that was how she found herself defending her title of Chubby Bunny champion.

"Twenty-three!" she exclaimed—or rather attempted to exclaim.

She moved to the trash can, spat out the clump of gelatin and sugar in a very unladylike gesture—sometimes sacrifices to beauty and elegance had to be made—and turned back to her siblings, who had stopped at ten and fourteen respectively.

Will shook his head at their mom, who had come in mid-competition. "Isn't the middle child supposed to be the peacemaker?"

"Not our Charlotte," her mom said, kissing their father on the cheek. "She's fire and steel and determination."

"Makes all the rest of us look bad," Amelia grumbled, her eyes sparkling with humor as she wrapped her arm around Char's waist. "Always got to excel at everything."

Will snorted, since Amelia had recently returned for her master's degree and had just finished explaining how excited she was that her bid for a spot on a new committee to develop curriculum with the school district had been accepted. Not that Will was one to talk—earlier he'd shared that his research paper was going to be published in a well-known scientific journal. He'd also just been tenured at the University, not an easy feat in this day and age of adjunct professors.

"My little gig of playing with athletes can't compare with

corralling elementary school students"—she squeezed Amelia's hand—"or, for that matter, college students"—a nod at her brother—"I just get to be the face of a group of people who are more family than workplace." She picked up the bag of marshmallows, began rolling down the plastic.

When silence greeted her, she looked up into the surprised faces of her siblings and parents.

"What?" she asked.

Her mom's eyes were damp. "I'm so glad you're back," she whispered. "I've missed you, honey."

Char blinked, opening her mouth to say she'd always been there.

But that would have been a lie.

She hadn't been there, hadn't been present, and her family had clearly seen that, even if they hadn't called her on it.

"What's his name?" her grandmother asked. Char had almost forgotten she was there, sitting on her usual stool pulled up to the island, silently playing solitaire as they'd all caused chaos in the kitchen while her father cooked dinner.

The room fell quiet.

"What?" she asked, though she had a sneaking suspicion she knew the *him* her grandma was referencing.

"Or her," her grandmother pressed.

Char attempted to play dumb. "Him or her who?"

Steady brown eyes fixing her in place. "The one who brought you back."

She wanted to say she'd brought *herself* back, but that would be a lie. And not only would her family call her on that lie, but she knew they wouldn't stop pestering her until she admitted the truth.

But that was what family did.

What she'd failed to appreciate until she'd seen it with the Gold.

They were nosy and when it came to the important things,

they didn't cut each other slack. They pushed and expected more and dammit, they made it known that they wanted to be privy to all the little details.

Because they mattered.

Because *she* mattered.

Which was how she came to spill the whole story of Logan and her relationship to her entire family. Their clandestine start, the breakup, his present of slippers and lunches and cooking for her. How he'd fixed her gate and filled her fridge with groceries. How he took care of her in a hundred small ways—ways she'd never begun to think of and ways that touched deeply.

And how—most importantly—she wanted to take care of him right back.

"I thought that he'd broken something inside me, that he'd taken away my ability to love a man in that way," she finished, "but the truth was that no other man has ever understood me like Logan. I'm with him, and a part of my soul just relaxes. I don't have to worry about being Char the GM or Char the role model for black women or Char the kickass businesswoman who doesn't get pushed around." Her eyes stung, voice dropping to a whisper. "I can just be Starlight."

Amelia sniffed. "Char-Char, you really love him."

Char made a face. "I do." A beat as the room filled with laughter. "As much as I hate that it ruins my tough as nails exterior."

Will tugged her back against him. "I still want to kick his ass for hurting you."

"He was trying to help me," she argued. "But"—her lips curved—"I already threatened him with dull skate blades if he presumed to make a decision about me without me again."

"That's my girl." Her dad kissed the top of her head. "You sure about him? It makes the work situation tricky, and I know you love your job."

Char was already nodding, lips parting, when her mother

spoke.

"Meh," her mom said. "Those Gold players have made the news for far bigger scandals than this. I bet it'll barely make a blip on the radar."

That was to be determined, Char knew, but she wasn't going to give Logan up regardless of the press or that they both were important to the Gold. "Plus, the HR department with the team is well-versed with this type of relationship."

"And it can't be any more of a conflict than Pierre Barie being the GM for the team his son played on."

"Or his son's wife. Or my coach Calle dating my player Coop."

"It's like a soap opera," Amelia said on a giggle.

"They're a family," Char said. "They're messy and inter-twined, friendships and lovers and business all tangled together, but . . . beneath all that is love." She smiled. "And I'm happy to be just beginning to find my place in all of that messy."

"With Loooogan," Will teased.

"Shut up, you," she muttered, smacking him lightly across the chest. "But yes. With Logan."

"I'm happy for you, baby," her mom said, "but make sure he knows that he needs to get his ass here in order to pass inspection."

"Exactly," her grandmother said.

Char laughed. "I'll pass that along."

The timer went off, and even though they were all grownups, each of them still moved to do their assigned job. Her dad headed to the oven. Amelia sprang to her feet, Char joining her. It was time for Amelia to set the table, for Char to gather drinks and condiments. Will would be on dishes, her mother on lighting the candles her dad required for ambiance.

And her grandma . . . well, her only job was getting her tush to the table and sitting down.

Perks came with age.

As they moved, the conversation turned to other things. To Amelia's rundown of her class and how she was going to miss them in the fall. To the underfunded educational district she taught in. To Char's mind sparking with an idea of how to get her players involved with San Franciscan schools and her whole family helping her refine and perfect the notion.

For the first time in years, she didn't feel distant.

And she knew that was because Logan had filled her up, given her the strength to look into her heart, and helped her recognize what she was missing.

She'd done the hard work.

But he'd had her back.

As she ate some of her father's delicious cooking, she thought back to the phone call, to the way Logan's voice had gone sad, the pain radiating through the airwaves, and she promised herself she would have his back in return.

They'd both spent too long alone.

Now was the time for them to move forward.

Together.

———

But by the next evening, she wasn't sure if together was what Logan wanted.

She'd called.

She'd texted.

She'd called again.

She'd even sent an email.

"Maybe I should send a carrier pigeon," she muttered.

"What's that, honey?" her mom asked, glancing up from the thick book in French she was reading quote, "just for fun."

She made a face, shoved her phone in her pocket. "Nothing," she said, half to convince herself and half to focus on the time with her family. She only had a couple more days with them before she needed to get back to the Bay Area. She wanted to enjoy this time in Baltimore.

"She said she wanted to send a carrier pigeon," her dad chimed in.

"A carrier pigeon?" The book hit her mom's lap. "Why?"

"Mom—"

"No," her mom snapped, and the sharp tone was so different from what she usually used that Char blinked and stopped talking. "Tell me," she demanded.

"I can't get ahold of Logan."

"Was everything you told me about him bullshit?"

Another blink, Char's mouth opening and closing like a guppy. "Um, no?"

"Is that a question or an answer?" More stern.

More blinking, but enough that Char finally pulled herself together. "An answer, Mom. He's always been available, or at the very least, called me back as soon as he could."

"How long has it been since you talked to him?"

"Yesterday morning."

"That's not so long—"

Her dad shut up when her mom's sharp gaze transferred to him.

"You told me this man adores you," she said. "So, is that part bullshit, or is something else going on?"

That was what she was worried about. He'd been upset and now not to hear from him after he'd been so careful to rebuild her trust in him. But at the same time, she didn't want to make something out of nothing. Maybe he was just busy. She certainly hadn't been glued to her phone. Or maybe he dropped his phone in the lake while he was fishing and couldn't call her—

"Char."

She nibbled at her lip. "It's weird to hear you curse."

A sigh. "Charlotte."

"Damn," she muttered. "I haven't heard that tone from you

in about fifteen years."

"I haven't had much cause to use it with you, honey. Tell me why I'm feeling the need to now."

"I don't want to make this a big deal, to start letting our relationship dominate my every waking thought. What if it becomes more important than everything else, and I suddenly—" She cut herself off.

"Suddenly want to quit your job and become Suzy Homemaker."

Char sighed. "Yeah." A pause. "Not that there's anything wrong with that. I think it's amazing that you stayed home with us when we were little, am so thankful that grandma was there, too. I just worry that there's something inside me that will make me forget everything important."

"Maybe what you think is important isn't really."

Soft words that had her spinning toward her dad.

"Your job can't love you back, baby. It can fulfill you in many ways, but it can't fill that hole inside your heart."

No, it couldn't.

"And," her mom said. "You're my smart, talented, lovely, stubborn daughter. You're not one to repeat your mistakes."

There was that.

"What if I decide that work is less important than Logan?" she asked.

"Isn't that how it should be with the man you love?" her mom asked, gaze full of warmth when it met her father's.

The question was both terrifying and also . . . right.

Because would it be the end of the world if her priorities were something *other* than work, if they shifted to the family she hoped to build with the man who held her heart?

No.

That seemed to be the only way forward.

Logan hadn't hesitated to put her first over the last weeks.

Now, it was her turn.

THIRTY-THREE

LOGAN

To say the last twenty-four hours had been tense was the understatement of the century.

The bombshell revelation.

Him walking away from his father, totally unbelieving.

And then his mom coming home from work, taking one look at his face, her face falling, words tumbling from her lips.

"He told you."

Then she'd begun crying, and he'd gone through a spectrum of emotions—disbelief, fury, horror, sadness, disappointment—before he'd crossed through the kitchen and taken her in his arms.

Tears.

God, he'd never seen her cry like that.

Wrenching sobs that shuddered through her, dripping down her cheeks, soaking into his shirt.

So much pain.

Her knees had eventually given way, and he'd picked her up, carried her to the couch and held her.

Such a strange experience, holding the woman who'd cared for him his whole life, who'd kissed his hurts and comforted him when he'd had a bad dream. Seeing her so broken, the tearing sobs coursing through her when the most he'd ever seen was her upset at a movie or book, a few tears here or there.

She hadn't even cried this hard when Logan's grandmother had died.

And all the while his father hadn't come in.

Through the night, when eventually the tears stopped coming.

All through the next morning, when his mom had finally fallen asleep and Logan had covered her up on the couch.

Through the rest of the day, even when Log had gone out to search for him.

Gone.

The fishing poles stowed away and his truck not on the property.

Now Logan was on the porch, his mom having retired to her bedroom and a long bath, and him trying to figure out what to do.

He had no details, wasn't sure he wanted any more, frankly.

In fact, he just wanted to GTFO and lock himself up in his cabin, or maybe track down Char's parents' address in Baltimore and pretend this whole damned thing hadn't happened.

He'd thought he had it all figured out.

His mom was upset about her job, resentful of years spent living her life for everyone else. She could be encouraged to speak up and advocate for her needs and things would improve. On the flip side, his dad was being an ass for the most part but could be forced to see that he needed to change and treat her differently. They both just needed to sit down and hash it out, to figure out their differences and stay together, or to decide the chasm between them was too large and to divorce.

But now . . . what?

This revelation about his mom had changed *everything*.

Or had it?

Fuck. He didn't know.

What he did know was that he wanted to talk to Char. He missed her, *fuck* he missed her. But did he want to lay this burden on her shoulders?

I need you to need me.

The memory of her words sat heavy on his heart.

He didn't want to burden her, and yet, how could he not?

He wasn't that solitary mountain in the middle of nowhere. He was a man who missed the woman he loved and had all he'd thought he knew shredded to pieces.

His mom a cheater?

What in the actual fuck?

His finger lifted, readying to press the button to call her—

The door creaked open, drawing his gaze to the front of the house, to his mom wrapped snuggly in a robe. "Hey," she croaked. "Come inside, I made dinner."

And because he loved her, he pushed off the railing and went into the house, waiting patiently while she served up bowls of a hearty soup, all the while noticing that the table had been set for three, even though his dad wasn't there.

How long had it been like this?

How long had he missed what was really going on?

"Middle school," she murmured.

His eyes flew from the bowl of soup up to hers.

"You were in middle school when it happened. I was . . . stupid. I was feeling unappreciated and lonely, and what I did was unforgivable." She set the spoon down. "I—I probably shouldn't have told your father, should have just ended things and moved on, but as time went on, I couldn't hide it any longer."

"Mom."

"I'll not tell you anything further, as that is something

between your father and I, but you need to know I was in the wrong. He was nothing but faithful, and I'm the one wh-who betrayed—" A deep breath. "I betrayed our vows."

Her gaze drifted to the table.

"Why stay, Mom?"

"I love your father," she said. "It's a twisted, wrong love now, but I-I keep hoping that I can make it up to him, that if I just keep moving forward, we'll be able to make each other happy again."

"That's a lot of years, Mom."

"Yeah," she whispered. "I think recently I've realized that probably won't happen."

"That's why you're working?"

"I do love being there, but yes, I need to be able to support myself."

"I—"

"Don't you dare, Logan," she said. "I've relied on you in a way that I shouldn't have for too many years, and I am so sorry for that." Her chin came up. "But damn if I'll keep doing it."

"Mom," he began.

"Eat your stew, Logie Bear," she murmured. "Then we'll give you some cooking lessons. You only need a few solid recipes, and pretty soon you'll have swept your Charlotte off her feet."

Her tone was familiar, one that told him he wouldn't get any further by pushing her.

He reached across the table, squeezed her hand.

"I love you, Mom."

Her eyes misted again, but she just blinked rapidly, told him she loved him too, and then they dug into the stew.

THIRTY-FOUR

CHAR

She'd been concerned she had the wrong place, but then she'd nearly mowed down a man who was the spitting image of Logan, only a few decades older.

"Shit!" She slammed on the brakes, skidding to a stop far too close for comfort.

Her hand clamped over her heart, and she took a deep breath, making sure to set the rental car in park. "Go to Wisconsin, they said," she muttered. "It will be fun, they said."

Okay, no one had promised her fun.

But she also hadn't planned on running over Logan's father.

Knock. Knock.

Char jumped, gaze flying to the window.

The man indicated she should roll down the pane of glass. It was nearly one in the morning, the area surrounding Logan's parents' house was pitch black—though light blazed from the windows of the home itself—and she suddenly wondered if coming here was a really bad idea.

"Are you lost?" the voice echoed through the glass.

He even sounded like Logan. She hadn't recognized that when she'd met them at Parents' Day, probably because she'd been too closed down at that point to process anything about Logan, least of which were the similarities between him and his father.

Taking a breath, she shut off the ignition, grabbed her purse, and opened the door.

"John," she said, forcing her voice to be steady as she extended her hand.

He was silent, and from the little she could see of his face, there was no recognition there.

"It's Charlotte Harris," she said. "From the Gold."

A flash of white as his eyes widened. "You're here for Logan."

In more ways than he could probably anticipate, but all she said was, "Yes."

"Come on, then."

He led her toward the house, extracting a set of keys as he jogged up the steps and then unlocked the door.

What they walked into was . . .

Unexpected.

Logan and his mom were in the kitchen, the radio blasting with oldies, both wearing aprons, both . . . covered head-to-toe with flour and collapsed on the floor laughing hysterically.

Her heart pulsed with equal parts relief and worry.

She'd flown up here expecting something tragic had happened.

Instead, he was having the time of his life.

Anger bubbled up, furious words filling the back of her throat, threatening to explode into the space.

But Logan's dad beat her to it.

"What the fuck is going on here?" he bellowed.

Two sets of eyes flew up in shock, going first to John then to Charlotte.

Logan scrambled to his feet, closed the distance between them. "Starlight, I—are you all right?" he asked, gripping her arms lightly. "Why are you here?"

The radio switched off.

She glanced between him and his parents. "I thought something was wrong," she whispered. "I thought . . ." Her voice went even quieter. "I thought you needed me."

His hands convulsed. "Starlight," he rasped, and she saw the pain now. It clouded at the edges of his vision, hung to his frame.

"What happened?" she asked, cupping his jaw.

"It's—"

"You *have* to be fucking kidding me," his dad yelled, and they both jumped, stares darting in his direction. "Your son finds out that you fucked around on me, and you two are *baking?*"

Char's lungs froze.

Logan went stiff, spun to face him fully. "Don't, Dad," he said. "Don't say something you're going to regret."

Hostile green eyes in their direction. "You heard me when I said she fucked my best friend, right? And yet, here you are, taking her side." Furious words. "Did she lie? Did she tell you she didn't—"

Logan opened his mouth.

"No."

The word was fierce enough to have all of them looking at Logan's mom, Hallie. "I didn't lie, John. I cheated on you. It was a horrible mistake. I promised to never do it again." She shook her head. "I've spent a long time trying to make up for it, but I see now nothing I do will ever make it right."

Char's eyes darted to Logan, and she saw the pain intensify there, knew this wasn't an old hurt. This was new and fresh and why he'd been out of touch.

She leaned against his side, wrapped one arm around his, and held him tight.

"So," Hallie continued. "I can only offer two choices. One, we go to therapy. We stop ignoring this giant elephant in the room and try to work through it. Two, we divorce. I'll move out, leave you to your life. I'll explain to Cecily and Josh that it's my fault, and we both do our best to repair the damage our unhappiness over the years has done to our kids." She sucked in a breath. "I was too scared to leave before. Too worried about ruining what we once had, terrified to hurt our kids." She looked at Logan. "But I see now by not doing anything, by not taking ownership of what I've done, that I've hurt them more than divorce ever could."

Char wanted to retreat, realizing too late that she shouldn't be hearing this, but when she actually went to step back and out of this conversation, Logan wrapped his arms around her shoulder and whispered, "Please, Starlight."

As if she could deny him anything.

She stayed.

Stayed still and silent and on tenterhooks.

Until she saw the fury replace the shock on John's face.

"Don't," Char blurted before she could stop herself. "Don't say it. Go to therapy."

That fury turned in her direction, but Char had always had courage. She didn't let it fail her now. "You obviously love her, even though part of you hates what's she did. Otherwise you wouldn't have stayed. Otherwise you wouldn't be so mad now." She swallowed. "Don't give up on that love. Just . . . try. For yourself, for the woman you love, and if for nothing else, then try for your kids. They deserve to have parents who are happy."

A long moment of taut silence.

"I think you should be careful who you give advice to, little girl," he said coldly.

"John!" Hallie exclaimed.

"Dad," Logan warned.

Char didn't flinch. She was well-used to dealing with big personalities, didn't shy away from cranky men.

She could handle Logan's dad.

Of that she was sure.

"You either find the balls to do this," she said. "Or you'll regret it for the rest of your miserable life. And it will be a miserable life. If Hallie is half the person Logan is, you'll hate being without her, even though she did something terrible."

Green eyes narrowed. "You—"

"Not a word, Dad," Logan growled. He shifted, snagged Char's hand and tugged her down the hall, not stopping until they were at the end of it and through a door.

It slammed shut, and she found herself spun and pressed to the plank of wood a moment letter.

Another set of furious green eyes met hers.

And suddenly, she had the feeling that she might have seriously fucked up.

Thirty-Five

Logan

His heart was pounding.
Fury was in every cell.
He bent close.

"You were magnificent."

Char's mouth fell open, breath shuddering out to coat his lips, and Logan gave in to the urge that had gripped him from the moment she'd stepped into the situation. He pressed his body to hers and kissed her with every bit of love he felt for her.

Only when his lungs were screaming did he pull away.

"Thank you," he whispered, so fucking touched that she'd stood up for him. "Thank you for saying that—"

Fuck, his voice cracked, and his eyes were burning.

But, damn, he could barely comprehend how much that had meant to him. First, she'd come to him, even though he hadn't asked. Then she'd stayed by his side. Then she'd intervened . . . for him.

With barely any context, wading into an emotional minefield of a situation.

"I love you," he said. "Starlight—"

His voice broke again, but it was okay. Because this time, she wrapped her arms around him and kissed *him*. This time, she held him close and grounded until he felt steadiness return.

This time . . . he wasn't alone.

The rock sitting on his heart was gone. He wasn't facing the world by himself.

He had Char.

And that made all the difference in the world.

"I think I didn't make a very good impression on your parents," she murmured when they broke apart a second time.

He'd just reached up to cup her cheek, and her words had him bursting into laughter. "I don't give a shit what my parents think of you," he told her. "You made a fucking incredible impression on me, sweetheart. You're here. You had my back. That means *everything*."

He froze.

"Wait. Why are you here? Your family—"

"Reminded me that sometimes the most important person in your life is the one who keeps your heart safe."

"Char."

"I love you, baby."

He tugged her close, held her tight, and for a long time they just stayed in place, arms around each other. Then Char nodded, and he remembered exactly how late it was. One smooth move had her in his arms. The next had him walking toward the bed, sitting her on the edge, and tugging off her shoes.

"Log—"

"Let me take care of you now, okay?" The need was strong.

She frowned. "This isn't some tit-for-tat I take care of you, you take care of me thing."

"I know," he said. "But you're here, and I've missed you, and you've just pulled some superwoman wonderfulness that has taken me almost thirty years to get the guts up to consider saying." He ran the backs of his fingers over her cheek. "And twenty-nine years in, I hadn't even gotten my head wrapped around verbalizing it. But you . . . you swept in there and took that weight off my shoulders."

"Log."

"Thank you."

"It was probably overstepping."

"Then consider yourself warned that I might overstep one day for you."

Her eyes narrowed. "Not for breaking up."

A grin curved the corners of his mouth. "No, Starlight, not for breaking up. Not ever again."

"Okay," she said, nodding regally. "Then I'll allow you to take care of me." He started to straighten, but she laced her fingers into his hair and held him close. "But you be forewarned that I'll be taking care of you right back, Log."

"I can live with that."

"Good."

"Good," he repeated, pressing a firm kiss to her mouth before standing up and heading to his luggage. She probably had things in her car, but honestly, he wasn't up for traversing the gauntlet of his parents anymore that night—or morning, anyway.

He just wanted to be with Char.

After tugging out a T-shirt and one of the spare scarfs he'd tossed in when his imagination had taken him to Baltimore instead of Wisconsin, he crossed back over to find her glancing down at her clothes.

Logan winced at the state of her shirt and pants.

Streaks of flour marred the black slacks and a dribble of chocolate was streaked across her right breast—well, the turquoise fabric covering that glorious right breast. Because if it had been on her skin, he might have been tempted to clean it off with his tongue. Cliché, yes, but this woman did it for him. He wasn't ashamed, but he was also completely aware that she was tired, had traveled to him, and then waded through some emotion B.S.

Which was why he kept his tongue to himself and helped her undress . . . and then *re*dress.

Or at least, helped her tug on his T-shirt, handed over the scarf for her to tie up her hair, and resisted the urge to trace every inch of her beautiful skin with said tongue.

A minute later, he'd stripped out of everything except his boxer briefs.

A moment after that, the light overhead was off, and he was in bed next to her, pulling her into his arms, tugging the covers up and over them both.

"How did *your* family visit go?" he asked lightly.

Tinkling laughter coated his skin.

Then she told him about the Chubby Bunny contest and her sister gaining a position on a committee she was excited about. She told him about her brother's paper getting published and her dad's peach pie.

She told him about her mom's advice to follow her heart.

"For the record," she said, cuddling into his chest. "She's summoned you to Baltimore at the earliest convenience, and if that convenience doesn't meet her convenience, expect a visit to San Francisco."

He grinned. That wasn't an order he had the least bit of issue following. "I guess I'd better brush up on my Chubby Bunny skills."

A kiss to his throat. "I won't give up my Chubby Bunny title easily."

"Prepare to go down," he teased, pressing a kiss to the top of her head. Movement on his chest that had him glancing down in question. The room was dark, though his eyes had adjusted enough to see the outline of her body. "What are you doing?" he asked when the movement continued.

"I'm waggling my brows," she said. "You said prepare to go down"—a nip to his pectoral—"don't give me that look."

"It's pitch black, what look could I possibly be giving you?"

"The Char-is-cray-cray look," she said, snuggling closer. "I was making a joke." A beat. "And don't tell me it's a bad joke, I know that already."

He snorted. "I love you, Starlight."

"Well, *I* love you, Moonlight."

His chest vibrated with laughter. "What is that?"

"My attempt at a nickname. I have to up my game beyond *baby* and honey."

"Moonlight isn't going to cut it." He ran his hand up and down her back.

"Cupcake?"

"Nope."

"Comet?"

Another snort. "No way."

"Candlelight?"

"Are you sticking with the letter C?"

"Not intentionally." She yawned. "Speedy?"

"Are you trying to insult me?"

Her chuckle slid over his skin. "No," she said, "and you're right. Speedy definitely won't work. How about Lamb Chop?"

"Starlight," he growled.

"I love you," she whispered. "Thank you for needing me, for inviting me into your life. And thank you for giving me these last eight years." She pressed her palm onto his chest. "I feel so lucky to have had the opportunity and a man who'd give up everything for me."

He covered her hand with his own, throat tight. "I want to have all the fancy, romantic words, sweetheart, but none of them come remotely close to being good enough. Just know you're in my blood, my soul. You're burned into my DNA, the marrow of my bones." He held her tightly, stroked a hand down her spine. "You're my heart, Starlight."

"You did fine with the romantic words, baby."

"I like baby," he murmured, and yawned, the last twenty-four hours plus catching up with him.

"I like *you*," she said softly before ordering, "Now sleep."

He let his eyes slide closed on another order he didn't mind following, happy in the knowledge that these were probably the first of many orders from the Harris women in his life and not giving a damn in the least.

Starlight had filled him from the inside out.

———

A week later, after he and Char had flown back to California, after they'd woken up to find the house empty, his mother at work, his father who knew where, Logan got a text.

The first two words made his heart sink.

Your mother . . .

Fuck.

He hadn't heard a word from his parents since that blow-up, and now it appeared that nothing had changed.

Tossing the phone onto the counter in disgust, he went back to meal prepping.

Char was going to a self-defense class that night, but the next day they were finally going up to his cabin. He was endeavoring to pull together enough palatable food that she would want to come back.

"Hey, baby."

Arms wrapped around him from behind, lush breasts pressing to his spine, sending heat arrowing to his groin.

"Hi, Starlight."

"You're slaving away in the kitchen while I go to work?" She pressed a kiss to his back. "Just as it should be."

He spun and took her in his arms. "Just for that, more river walks for you."

"Oh, the horror," she teased. "I have to spend time with the man I love."

"In nature," he said. "You have to spend time in nature with the man you love."

A shrug. "I'm starting to see that *some* nature is okay."

"Oh?"

"I like the big . . ." Her lips curved. "Trees."

He snorted, nuzzled a kiss to her throat . . . just as his phone buzzed again.

"Oh, that's your cell," Char said, slipping out of his arms. "Let me grab it for you."

"I—"

But she'd already picked it up, her eyes widening when she caught a glimpse of the screen.

"Log—"

"It's okay," he said, turning back to the food. "I can't control them. They'll make their own decisions." But his gut had sunk at those words, at the notion that nothing would ever change.

Nothing except him.

Because he wasn't going to be drawn in again.

"Baby."

"I'm fine, Starlight."

"*Baby.*"

The urgency in her tone had him spinning back around. "What?"

"Look."

"I don't need—"

She stepped close and shoved the phone in his face. "Look."

Your mother found a therapist. We're going next week.

The second message was the buzz that Char had heard, and it said, quite simply:

I'm sorry.

His lungs froze just as another message came through. This one was from his mother, and the words made the organs unstick, his heart squeeze hard. Because it didn't start with *Your father is.*

Instead, it read,

I love you. I'm sorry. I'll do better.

"Progress," Char murmured.

"Yes," he said, slipping an arm around her shoulders. "Honestly, I'm a little shocked they've decided to go to therapy."

"I'm not."

He lifted a brow.

"They love you."

He lifted the other.

"You're worth someone making the effort, Logan," she said. "They can see they're hurting you, and both know it needs to stop." Her fingers traced his jaw. "But more than that, I think—I *hope* they're finally understanding that their relationship is worth just as much." She kissed him. "Otherwise, what's the point?"

"The more important point is that I love you."

Her lips curved. "Yeah?"

He kissed her. "Yeah."

"Good"—she nodded at the food laid out on the counter—"then get back to cooking, wench."

Logan burst out laughing, and because he couldn't resist, he kissed the woman who held his heart again, kissed the mischief off her lips, swallowed her giggles, tasted the love on her tongue.

And then he got back into the kitchen while she went to work.

As one did.

Epilogue

Part One

Char, Three Months Later

She closed her laptop in disgust and glared over at her family, who were gathered around the island in her kitchen.

Which had never smelled so good.

Definitely not when she and Logan had begun expanding their cooking repertoire. Speaking of which, they were up to three whole recipes they could consistently make without threatening her smoke detectors.

But that wasn't what had her filled with disgust.

"That blog post is absolutely ridiculous." The sports blog had sounded more gossip site than real sports news reporting—detailing every moment of their "romantic night out" and how besotted she and Logan were.

Yes, they'd actually used the word *besotted*.

Ugh.

Will poked her in the arm when she fell silent, pondering her ability to learn some hacking skills in order to take the drivel down. "You upset because the title is *BAMF Harris tags Walker*?"

She shuddered. "No, I don't mind being called a badass mf-er," she said, slanting a look at her grandmother, who was apparently enthralled by her solitaire game.

But Char knew from personal experience that her grandma had big ears.

"Then what, Starlight?" Logan asked, running his fingers down her arm.

"They're saying I tagged you, but *you're* the one who came after me."

"I had to," he said. "I know my stubborn Harris women—"

"Hey!" Amelia and her mom said at once, though both of their faces softened when Logan turned his charming smile on them.

Double ugh.

Mostly because that charming smile worked on her, too.

She glanced back at Logan, wrinkled her nose, and . . . pressed a kiss to his mouth. "I love you," she murmured against his lips, "even if you're a pain in my ass."

He just grinned and then went back to the counter where her mom had set him to shucking corn for the vegetable salad he was learning how to make. God, he was pretty, especially all ready for the season, his diet plan locked in and his body . . . her thighs clenched because there were definite perks to him getting into tip-top shape.

Six-packs and strong thighs. Hip bones and biceps she wanted to lick like a popsicle.

She was drooling over him so intently that she didn't realize the room had gone quiet at first.

Not until her grandmother said, "Well, are you going to open it or not?"

Blinking, she tore her gaze from Log and glanced over at her grandma. "Open what?"

Amelia nudged her, nodded at the counter. "Char-Char."

A box.

There was a box in front of her. A box with a card that had her name on the envelope. A name that was written in Logan's handwriting.

She looked at him, but he was still deliberately shucking corn.

So, she reached for the envelope.

Will groaned. "Why? Open the big box in front of you!"

Char smiled even though her heart was pounding. "This is my box, and I say I'm going to open the envelope first." She tore open the flap, lips curving at the short note.

For keeping you on even footing during the season.

-L

Amelia snagged it from her before she'd barely processed the words, passing it to Will and then her dad. Char hardly noticed.

Because she was working on the box.

Slitting open one side.

Tearing the paper off.

Opening the white cardboard lid.

Her mom whistled long and low.

Char was feeling the same upon looking at the contents of the box. Sexy, red heels with just the faintest hint of glitter in their fabric, small twinkling stars that both took her breath away and threatened to have her heart pounding out of her chest.

Her eyes flew to Logan's, and he winked.

"Love you, Starlight."

Another nudge from Amelia, and annoyed at her for intruding on the moment, she glared at her sister. "What?"

"There's another box," Amelia said.

Her heart went well beyond pounding. Now, it was stampeding in her chest, threatening to burst free.

Because there was another box.

A small box.

Her fingers shook as she reached for it, but Logan beat her to the punch, snagging it from where it had been nestled between the gorgeous heels and opening it as he knelt in front of her.

It sparkled.

Just like his eyes.

"What do you say, Starlight?" he asked softly. "Will you keep me around even though I currently hold the Chubby Bunny championship title?"

"Because you cheated!" she exclaimed, jumping up.

He stood and caught her around the waist, lips twitching. "We'll have a rematch," he promised, "so long as you answer the question."

"I didn't hear a question."

Lips on her cheek, near her ear. "Technically, there were two in that. But not the most important one." He straightened, cupped her jaw. "I love you to the stars and back, and you're in my heart until it stops beating." Soft fingers on her cheek, wiping a tear she hadn't realized had fallen. "Will you marry me?"

"Will you admit you cheated at Chubby Bun—"

"Char!" her family yelled in unison.

She threw her arms around Logan's neck and kissed him until her lungs burned. "Yes, baby," she whispered when they pulled away. "I'll marry you."

"Thank God for that," her grandma said.

The room filled with laughter. Love and laughter and happiness that was *all* tangled up. It was complicated and messy and reported about on sports blogs . . . and Char couldn't care less.

Because she was building her family.

CAGED

GOLD HOCKEY #11

ONE

DANI

Shy.

She was painfully shy.

Great with tech. Horrible with people.

But that was okay because her job *was* tech. As a video coach for the Gold, her livelihood depended on how well she could interact with the tech surrounding her at any given time—tech that currently consisted of multiple monitors on her office wall, a desktop, a laptop, and a trio of tablets. She actually had a dozen tablets at her disposal, but the rest were currently being used by the coaching staff.

The Gold had just finished their third game of the season, and though she wouldn't say her job got lighter as the season progressed, this time, in particular, was dizzying.

There were new players to get up to speed.

Changes to the system that needed to be addressed.

Specific plays the coaches wanted highlighted.

And she was down her assistant—who was out with the stomach flu—and an intern—who'd lied on his resumé, couldn't actually isolate and/or edit video, and hated everything to do with the game of hockey.

Video. Coach.

Both of those were important—okay, both were *critical* to her job.

She needed to understand the game, needed to be able to anticipate what the players and coaching staff would need, *and* she needed to be able to move fast to isolate, tag, and make that content available, both during and after each of the eighty-two regular-season games, not to mention any additional playoff games the team might be lucky enough to participate in.

So, an intern with no interest in the sport was useless.

And an assistant coach, who was confined at home with the stomach plague, was similarly not helpful for the fingertip tap dance she had to conduct during a normal game. It meant she'd played double-duty for the contest, watching eight feeds at once, layering alternate angles together of different parts of the matchup—zone entries, injuries, penalties, or power plays—in addition to being prepared to advise the bench coaches on whether or not to challenge a particular goal.

In a word, by the time she was finishing up her end of the game process—superimposing stats pulled by the NHL onto the various video clips and making them accessible to players and coaches alike—Dani was exhausted.

But, crying over spilled milk and all that.

She didn't have time for exhaustion or crying or . . . well, not much except to be staring lovingly into her screens, her fingers caressing the keyboards and tablets . . . and yes, she realized that her referring to staring lovingly and caressing anything tech-related meant that she'd probably been single far too long.

Not that single was an uncommon adjective to describe Dani Eastbrooke.

It was usually included, right along with quiet, shy, and painfully awkward.

"Stop," she whispered. She was who she was, and she didn't have time for reminiscing or self-flagellation, not when she had enough work for three people and only one person to do it.

A ping came across her cell.

Glancing down, she saw it was a request—or technically, *three* more requests, and . . . see? No time to think about her pathetically empty life.

On that pleasant thought, she straightened her shoulders and rolled out her neck, focusing on the screen in front of her as she began transferring the video.

Then turned and focused on the next one, repeating the process.

Once the third was complete, she gathered the tablets, pushed out of her chair, and hurried into the hall.

"Oof!" She skidded to a stop, warm hands gripping her shoulders, steadying her.

Unfortunately, she'd hurried without looking.

Unfortunately, because the tablets she'd been holding tumbled from her grip, hitting the ground with a sickening *crunch*. Yes, they had protective covers. No, she didn't normally launch them at concrete floors.

Also *unfortunately,* because she had crashed into a giant muscled mass of sweaty man. He was tall and blond and too fucking pretty for her mental well-being, especially with gentle gray eyes sliding to hers, with the warmth of his large hands soaking through the fabric of her shirt.

A sliver of heat slid through her stomach.

Oh, *no.*

That would not do.

Tearing her eyes away, she dropped to her knees and picked up the first tablet she could reach, running her finger over the screen and checking for damage.

"Do you stroke everything so carefully?"

Desire coated her spine in honey, filled her throat with cotton.

She glanced up, saw that he'd crouched next to her, and in an instant, was lost again in his eyes, the pale gray of the sky hinting at a thunderstorm.

Storm.

Well, *that* was fitting, considering the storm that had awakened inside her the first time she'd seen this man. God, she could still remember how every cell in her body had stood up and taken notice, and that had just been the result of viewing him through her monitor, just after he'd joined the team. Tall and big and yet somehow still graceful, even despite the beard and the tattoo peeking out of the collar of his jersey. From the first moment she'd laid eyes on Ethan, he'd reminded her of a giant grizzly bear, something any smart human had to fight the urge to not cuddle with.

Fluffy, but would tear a woman to shreds with those razor-sharp claws.

"Dani?"

"No," she said simply and reached for the next tablet, doing a visual scan this time instead of any *stroking*. When it looked okay, she thrust it at him, at Ethan Rogers, at the sexiest man she'd ever laid eyes on. "Here. This is the one Calle wanted you to have."

"No stroking?" he said, almost lazily, taking the tablet from her with a slow brush of his fingers against hers.

More heat—sparking up her arms, sliding down her torso, pooling in her stomach.

Her words stoppered up in the back of her throat.

She simply shook her head in response.

"Dani?" he asked; the heat tempered, curiosity in its place. He was still crouching next to her, the smell of spice and male filling the air. Probably, the strong scent should have been off-putting. Instead, it was tempting, drawing her in like catnip, but she couldn't look up at him, not even when he stayed still, stayed near, clearly waiting for her to speak or meet his gaze.

One rough finger brushed the back of her hand.

Sparks.

Gasping, her eyes flew up, collided with his gaze. Her heart absolutely pounded, but other than that single touch, he didn't make any other moves to close the distance between them.

"Dani?" he asked again.

"Yeah?" she whispered.

"Why don't you like me?"

Her jaw dropped open. Why didn't *she* like *him?* Dani drooled after Ethan on a regular basis. She had dreams about him, had named her favorite vibrator after him.

See? Good with tech.

With people—including the gorgeous man all of two feet away? Horrible.

But what *could* she say? It wasn't like she was going to share the name of her vibrator. Hell, she might as well be honest, she wasn't going to share *anything*. This is what she did.

She got shy. She got quiet. She came off as a royal bitch.

"Y-you're fine," she finally managed, reaching for the last tablet, intending to find a way to bolt, to end her misery, and GTFO.

But he stood when she did, those gray irises dancing with mirth. "Fine?"

"I—uh—" Her cheeks burned, and worse, she felt tears prickle at the backs of her eyes.

Ugh. She hated that she did this, too.

Pushing past him, she tried to bolt.

"Hey," he said, catching her arm. "*Hey,*" he said again, releasing her when she yanked fiercely at his grip. "I'm just teasing."

She shrugged, stepped away, cheeks hot, eyes still stinging, her throat tight, her lips and mouth and tongue barely able to form words. "Right," she managed after a painfully long time.

"Dani?" Another gentle question, and God, she liked the way he said her name, soft with a bit of a rasp, more grizzly vibes, more urges to cuddle.

Her shoulders tensed.

A soft chuckle.

Ethan was close enough that she would swear she could feel that small laugh skate over her skin. "I actually came to find you."

She gaped, heart pounding.

He'd come to find *her?* That just didn't compute.

"Me?"

He nodded.

She lost her words again. Because seriously, what universe was she currently living in?

"I wanted to ask you a question—"

Ah.

Her heart skittered to a stop, resignation sailing through her as she realized what was going down. This was how all of these types of conversations began. People like Ethan sought her out, not because they wanted to have a conversation or hang, but because they needed help with their TV or laptop or cell phone.

Ethan, she guessed, would need laptop help.

He looked like he could handle a cell or a television.

And no, don't ask her how she knew what he needed help with, okay?

She'd been through this rodeo many a time before. Dani's tech guru-ness was a gift that had been bestowed upon her at birth . . . okay, *fine*, it had been honed by many lonely preteen and teenage years.

"I can fix your computer," she said, trying to pretend that she wasn't miserable at the prospect, that she didn't want someone to come to her for once for some other reason.

It was a *good* thing they didn't. Really. It was.

She wouldn't know what to do with them if they did.

Except, over the last few months, she had to wonder if she was selling herself short, if perhaps she'd sat back on her shy laurels for too long, used them as an excuse to keep people at a distance.

A snort bubbled up in her throat.

Or course she did.

That was her M.O. Always had been, always would be.

"What?" Ethan asked. "My computer isn't . . ." He trailed off, and with her brows drawing together, she considered if perhaps her guru skills were out of practice. She hadn't been hit up *too* often since she'd joined the Gold.

"Then you need help with your phone?" she asked.

He frowned, shook his head. "No."

She tilted her head to the side, curiosity overshadowing her shyness for a moment, feeling herself intractably pulled into those gray eyes. "Your TV?"

"No, Dani," he said on a husky laugh, and she ignored the prickles of desire trailing over her skin.

"Oh." She swallowed. "Okay then." She turned away.

"Are you seeing anyone?"

Slowly, she spun back, eyes wide.

"That was my question," he said, when she stared at him in shock. "Dani?" he asked, when she just continued staring at him mutely. "Did I break you?"

A slow shake of her head.

He stepped a little closer, just near enough that she could feel the heat from his body. "No to the breaking you part, or no to the seeing anyone piece?" he murmured.

"The seeing anyone thing," she somehow managed to whisper, despite the fact that the question from a man like him to a woman like her was absolutely one hundred percent unfathomable.

Circling back to sad and single and—

He smiled.

And she actually felt her brain cells collide and fizzle into smoke. That smile was dangerous, could without a doubt, turn her stupid. *Really* stupid.

"Good," he murmured.

Swallowing hard, she nodded, cheeks on fire, and turned away again. "Right, I'll just—"

"Will you go out with me?"

Her fingers went limp. The tablets hit the ground.

This time, the *crunch* sounded much more ominous.

Or maybe that was just her heart.

Two

He winced when the tablets hit the floor again and bent over to scoop them up.

Shit.

One corner was cracked, but Ethan supposed that wasn't the first nor would it be the last time something like that had happened. Still, he'd offer to pay for it. He didn't like the idea of the team having to eat the cost for something he'd caused.

The other was unscathed.

Dani, however, appeared to be *very* scathed. Her mouth gaped, and he could swear there was pink warming the brown tones of her umber-colored skin, making him wonder what exactly had brought on the blush.

Was it that she was embarrassed he'd asked and felt uncomfortable?

That made a sick pit open up in his stomach.

"I—I—" She shook her head. "I—"

"It's okay," he said quickly, stepping back. "No hard feelings."

Deep brown brows drew down. "H-hard feelings?"

"You're not interested." He took another step back, *all* the hard feelings ruminating through him, but unwilling to let them escape, to taint their workplace. He wanted her, but he wasn't that guy. Wouldn't ever be. "I promise, I won't bring it up again."

Her mouth opened and closed, words stuttering out. "I—I—"

"It's fine," he said quickly. "You want me to bring these to the guys?"

"I—"

Another few feet away. "I'll just—"

"Will you stop interrupting me?" she snapped.

He blinked.

Her chin lifted and for a moment, he was frozen in place by her eyes. They were brown—he'd known that from the glimpses she'd given him before—but what he *hadn't* known was that they weren't *just* brown. Shades of russet and amber, speckles of gold, streaks of ebony. No, those uniquely gorgeous irises couldn't simply be categorized as brown. They were . . . spectacular and entrancing and—

Dani kept talking, drawing him out of his head.

"I'm shy," she said. "But I'm not stupid. I can tell someone when I'm uncomfortable or if I don't want something."

Hope bloomed through him.

"Does that mean you *want* to go out with me?"

Her eyes widened, her mouth opening and closing. "I —um—I—"

This time he didn't interrupt, just waited for her to get her thoughts together, her words to catch up, and all the while the prospect of being able to take out this woman he'd admired for so long lingered in the back of his mind.

"I don't think that's a good idea," she whispered. "I need to get these to Max and Coop."

Bleak.

That was the only word to describe what he felt at the moment. But he'd meant it when he'd promised himself that if she didn't return his interest, he wouldn't press this, that he'd just go back to pretending he wasn't attracted to her.

"Okay," he said, holding up the tablets. "I'll take these to the locker room."

She nodded.

"For the record, I never thought you were stupid," he said, "and I don't mind the shy." With that, he turned and made his way down the hall, cursing himself six ways to Sunday as he moved. He should have played it so much cooler, should have won Dani over before springing a date on her. He should—

"Fuck," he whispered on a sigh.

Because he *had* been trying to win her over these last months, finding reasons to be in her presence—e.g. tonight volunteering to grab tablets she was going to deliver, asking for extra tape, casually joining the conversations when she was with Brit or Mandy, testing the waters when she was with people she was comfortable with.

And he'd thought he'd made progress with trying to get her to talk and loosen up.

So today, tonight, he'd hoped for her to let him in just an inch.

Too fast.

Fucking hell.

Ethan knew that most of the guys on the team thought that Dani was a little cold. But most of the guys were idiots. Okay, *that* wasn't true, not even in the least. The San Francisco Gold were the NHL's newest team—though that would soon change with several more expansion teams entering the mix next season —and they were one of the best franchises to play for. He'd been around for the last win of the Stanley Cup and for last season's heartbreaking loss. Before that, he'd bounced around the league, playing a few seasons with different teams. But nothing had ever stuck. Or maybe, the roster hadn't gelled like the Gold's did.

Or perhaps . . . it was because the Gold were more like a family than a business.

Which should sound ridiculous because it *was* a business, and hockey was his job.

But somehow, it *wasn't* ridiculous.

The men and women on the team were a family. Without qualification. As obvious as a crosscheck to his opponent's numbers would get him sent to the box. It was just . . . fact.

What was also fact?

That even now, well after the game, the locker room would still be full of the guys and Brit shooting the shit, hanging around because they actually liked each other.

A rare feat indeed.

Laughing to himself as he strode through the door, handing the tablets to Max and Coop, he thought back on his first game with the team. God, it had been such a weird feeling, as though he'd ended up in an alternate reality.

There wasn't the least bit of hazing or him needing to earn his spot. They'd included him, given him the benefit of the doubt, and right away, he'd felt like he had a place.

They'd invited him to dinner after the match.

They'd actually included him in the conversation from the get-go—as well as giving him an assigned day on manning the radio. The latter was something everyone took turns with, and though the guys had some overlap in taste, it was something of a rite of passage to get your pregame playlist poked at.

Today's *post*game playlist was Brit's choice, which meant that as he finished getting undressed and headed to the showers, he was serenaded by various boy bands with syrupy lyrics and poppy soundtracks.

The songs were fucking catchy, he'd give Brit that.

But he much preferred his classic rock pre or postgame.

He wondered what kind of music Dani listened to, though he supposed he wouldn't be in a position to find out.

"What's going on in that big, juicy brain of yours?" Max asked, when Ethan sat back down in his stall and began pulling his clothes on.

Big, juicy brain was the team's favorite way to refer to him.

A guy works on getting one master's degree, and suddenly he was everyone's favorite nerd.

But seriously, what else was there to do when a man was on the road for half a season and drinking and partying got really old? Plus, his parents were professors, had always teased each other about being career students. It would have been a surprise if he didn't follow in their footsteps, at least a little bit. "What are you talking about?" he muttered.

"You look all mopey," Max said, bending and tying his shoes.

Ethan scowled but didn't otherwise comment as he yanked on his underwear and slacks, began buttoning his shirt.

"You've got a little frown in between your brows. Angie would say you're being all scowly."

"Did you just do air quotes?"

A shrug. "They're endearing."

"No," Ethan said. "They're really not."

"So, does the mope have to do with a certain brunette who won't give you the time of day?"

Ethan's eyes shot up, a critical error that had him giving away his hand before he'd been ready to. This was why he was shit at poker, and he knew he was fucked when Max's eyes sharpened. He was one of the worst gossips on the team, perhaps only eclipsed by Brit.

Though, Coop was honing his skills.

Pretty soon, they'd have three Musketeers to contend with.

Ethan shoved his shoes on. "I don't know what you're talking about."

"Hmm," Max said, leaning back in his stall and crossing his

arms behind his head, "and here I thought you'd be better at lying."

Ethan laughed. "You saw me last poker night. How could you possibly think that?"

Max smirked. "True." A beat. "So, win Dani over yet?"

He froze. Fucking motherfucker was such an asshole . . . and too damned inquisitive for anyone's good. "Don't you have to get home to your family?" he grumbled.

"Not right at the moment."

Great. He sighed, slipped into his jacket, then risked a look out of the corner of his eye.

Max was still staring at him.

"What?" he asked again. "I'm not talking about Dani."

"Ah. No progress. You okay?"

"I'm fine." He shrugged. "It's . . . not fine, but I'm not going to pursue something she doesn't want. I'm not an asshole."

"No, you're not. I'm sorry it didn't work out." His face went serious. "I could—"

"No. Thanks, though, man."

Max nodded, was surprisingly quiet as they went through the remaining motions of getting ready to go.

"So, aside from the lack of progress with the unnamed brunette tech guru, I also detect a dash of sad. Did you fail a pop quiz or something?"

"No, I most certainly did not," he said.

"You're getting straight As, aren't you?"

"My GPA is beside the point." He grinned. "Also, so what if I am?"

Max slugged him. "Brawn. Brains. It's not fair, man. Look at *this*"—he held up his arm, pointed to his bicep, which was respectable in the hockey realm where lean strength was valued over grizzly bear status like Ethan had—"it's puny in comparison."

"You have tree trunks like this," Ethan said, holding up his own arm, "and you'd crush Angie. She's tiny."

"Maybe."

"Speaking of Angie, I heard she was pregnant again. Congrats."

Max smiled. "Thanks, man."

"Is Brayden excited to be a big brother again?" he asked.

"He's a teenager," Max said. "He's not excited about much, unless it's some new TikTok trend." A sigh. "But he didn't sulk off to his room"—Max smiled—"and he stopped after school today to pick up Angie's favorite milkshake from the Dairy, so really, even though he is a teenager, he isn't *too* bad of one."

"Brayden's a good kid."

Max shook his head, still smiling. "Yeah, he is."

Brit walked up, waved a hand in his direction. "What's going on with this face?"

Ethan sighed, waited for Max to dish.

Surprisingly, he didn't, just silently watched Brit as she studied him with laser focus.

"I failed that pop quiz you were teasing me about earlier," he said.

A blip of quiet, Brit's expression stern. "So, you're not going to tell me why you're scowly and moody?"

No fucking way. But he didn't say that, just lifted a brow and waited.

Silence.

Max stood up, clapped Ethan on the shoulder. "See ya." And then the fucker walked off, leaving him in Brit's clutches.

"Spill," she ordered. "Tell me how I can help."

And *that* right there was why the nosiness was tolerable, even welcome, though significantly less so when it was directed at him. Because Brit and everyone else on this team actually gave a shit. They wanted to know every detail, yes, but it wasn't to ridicule and scorn. It was because they wanted everyone to be happy.

"Want to be my study buddy?"

Brit's eyes narrowed. "Sure, you failed that quiz, Eth." She pointed two fingers at herself then at Ethan. "Watching you."

Max poked his head back into the conversation. "And you know the gossip train is, too." He lifted a fist, raised it up and down. "*Choo-choo!*"

"You guys are hilarious," Ethan muttered.

"Damn right, we are." And with that, Max walked out of the locker room, waving goodbye to the rest of the team, most of whom were in various states of their postgame routine or getting ready to follow him out.

Brit gave him one narrowed look then turned and hit the showers.

Ethan sighed. He still had the video to watch—and wounds to lick— but he could do both of those from the space of his own house.

He'd bring the tablet back tomorrow.

Slipping his wallet into his pocket, the tablet into his backpack, which he then shrugged on, Ethan found himself drawn into a conversation with Blane, and while he liked his teammate, a whole hell of a lot, he really wanted to go home, have a beer— since it was close enough to his cheat day tomorrow that he didn't have to worry about Nutritionist Rebecca giving him a hard time about veering off his specially designed diet plan. He was typically a firm believer in the what-she-didn't-know-didn't-hurt her approach to dealing with nutritionists, but the team had bought into Rebecca's plans long ago and truthfully, even though the diet was a bit restrictive, especially for his meat-loving heart, he'd never felt or played better. So, it hadn't taken him long to get on board.

Especially, when she'd worked in those cheat days *and* he could have a beer and burger every once in a while.

"Eth?"

He turned, saw that Brit was back, staring at him, her long, blond hair slicked back after her shower. "What's up?"

She crossed to him, voice quiet when she said, "You know that play wasn't on you, right?" Her nose wrinkled in a way that was decidedly cute and definitely not in the typical tough hockey player realm—but that was Brit, a constant in juxtapositions.

It didn't take much to understand what play she was referring to, especially because it *was* his fault. He'd misjudged an angle, the player from the other team had gotten by him, and he hadn't made it back in time. They'd scored, and it *had* been on him.

"I mean," she said softly. "Shit happens, and it's on everybody, not just one person."

Still, it was easier to let her think that he was upset about the play instead of his failed wooing techniques with Dani.

"Nice try." He bumped her shoulder with his when she sat beside him. "You know damned well it was my fuck up, but"— here he sighed and told the truth, and conveniently, it applied to both the play and the shit with Dani—"I can't do anything about it, so I'm going to go home, have a couple of hours' early cheat day, and I'm going to wallow in my ineptitude. And then tomorrow," he added quickly, when her expression turned concerned. "I'll be over it, and all will be good."

Her eyes narrowed. "You promise?"

"Yes, Mom," he teased lightly.

"So not funny," she said.

"Why?" he asked.

A roll of her eyes. "Stefan wants a baby. He's 'willing to wait' as long as I want," she said. "But he also said that he wouldn't mind if I didn't take such a long contract next time so that he's not a grandpa by the time we have our first."

He sat back in his stall, brows lifting. Now *this* was interesting.

"I mean," she whispered, "I *want* kids. It's just that I don't know if I want them when I'm away so much, but I'm not ready to stop playing, and getting pregnant would mean . . ."

She kept talking, and he'd been part of the team long enough to find this particular bit of gossip fascinating—especially when she was freely offering it up. Though he supposed she didn't have much to hide after she'd fallen in love with and married the former captain of the team *and* spent the majority of her time poking her nose in other people's business. However, that notwithstanding, Brit was great with kids, even if it was obvious that a woman couldn't be pregnant with men shooting pucks at her a hundred miles per hour, not to mention the collisions she took sometimes.

Kids would have to wait until after she retired.

Unless . . .

"You could always adopt," he said.

Her brows lifted, her lips freezing in the middle of describing what Stefan would look like as a grandpa. "I could adopt?" she mouthed.

He nodded.

"Holy shit," she whispered. "Stefan and I could *adopt*."

Ethan patted her on the shoulder. "You'd both be great parents." He'd met Stefan, who'd retired from the team a few seasons back, enough times over the last couple of years to know the other man fairly well. He was a good guy, treated Brit like the goddess she was, and he'd never seemed to hold her successful career against her, even though he was no longer playing.

In fact, Stefan had a reserved seat at the Gold Mine, directly behind Brit's net.

Not the best position for viewing the game.

But perfect for watching his wife kill it, as she did on most nights.

"I—" she whispered. "You think so?"

"Yes, I do." With that, he patted her shoulder again and

decided to take advantage of her befuddlement by calling out his goodbyes and hightailing it out of the locker room.

Babies.

They shouldn't be the obvious conversational topic for big, tough hockey players, but they were common subjects of banter in the Gold's locker room because the kids were folded right into the rest of the team. They were family, too, along with the coaches, with the equipment managers and trainers and support staff. Wives and girlfriends, too. Brothers and sisters, moms and dads.

All were commonly seen.

And the team played the better for it.

It was just . . . today, he was missing that he didn't have more to add to the group. Sure, his parents came to some games, but they were busy, they had their own lives, and those lives didn't revolve around his any longer.

Which was fine.

He was a thirty-year-old man, not a child who needed a ride to early-morning practices and away games.

Not anymore, anyway.

Smiling as he walked to his car thinking of what his mom would say if he called her and teasingly asked her to drive him to the rink, he didn't see the flurry of silken brown hair, the lush, curvy body.

Not until it was too late.

And for the second time in one night, he collided with the woman he'd been dreaming about for months.

THREE

DANI

The universe hated her.

That was the only explanation she had for why she was plastered against Ethan's chest for a second time that evening.

He smelled good, all spicy and male, his hair still damp from the shower.

It was funny, though, for as long as his beard was—a bushy gathering on his jaw—his hair was neatly trimmed, as it always was.

"Are you growing it out?" she blurted, still in his arms, her fingers lifting to trace the bristles, finding they were softer than she expected. Also, such an inappropriate thing to do, paired with an unsuitable question for a workplace, where she liked to at least pretend she was professional, even though she spent many of her waking—and sleeping—hours fantasizing about this man. Dani could also add that it was remarkably tactless to be stroking his jaw, since she'd just turned the man down when he'd asked her out.

So, no.

She shouldn't be looking at his beard, let alone commenting on it.

Or thinking how it might feel between her thighs.

His hands had been resting on her shoulders again, the warmth seeping through her team jacket, making her nerves skip and fire with need, but her words had him lifting one, resting it against hers on his jaw and rubbing lightly.

She heard the bristling sound—*no,* she actually felt it, and not just on her palm. The slight rasp skated over her middle, both dipping down and shooting up, her nipples hardening against the fabric of her bra, her legs quivering.

"Not intentionally," he said, voice husky, his gray eyes the color of clouds readying to drop buckets full of rain. "My trimmer broke, and I just got lazy with the upkeep."

"Oh," she whispered after a moment, after realizing she was just standing there.

Just staring at him.

Plastered against his chest, her palm on his cheek.

Ugh.

She yanked out of his hold, pulse thrumming, moisture pooling, and hating herself for turning him down, even though she knew it had been the only thing she could do. "I-I should go."

He nodded, the movement making a flash of tattooed skin appear, just the swirling edge that crept up the left side of his neck. She'd seen that tattoo in the flesh before, when she'd gone into the locker room as he'd been coming out of the shower. Some nudity was a workplace hazard. The guys did their best, but after games they had to shower and change, and if she ventured in, she caught an occasional glimpse of butt or penis, no matter how quick and judicious they were with towels. And, at least when it came to Ethan, those glimpses were usually tucked into her fantasies and paired with her vibrator—because side note: hockey players had the best butts. For the others, they were met with her cheeks growing hot and Dani quickly looking away. Chests and arms, abs and back weren't so bad. She'd almost become desensitized to them, considering the way some of the guys went around without their shirts.

Not *Ethan's* back though. Or his butt. Or his dick. Or his—

Right. She was ridiculously attracted to *all* of his parts, from his mouth down to his strong calves. But back to his . . . well, his *back*. She'd actually felt her heart stop when she'd first seen it—okay, so maybe not *stop*, but it had certainly skipped a beat, hiccupped against her ribs.

Because the tattoos covering his back were beautiful.

Colorful swirls and lines coming together in something that was a cross between flames and floral that combined to form an Irezumi-inspired look. A term she only knew because she'd gone looking after she'd seen them, had researched for hours online until she'd discovered what they looked like.

She wanted to trace them with her tongue, her fingers, her lips.

Had imagined doing that more times than she could count.

"Yeah," he said, and it took her more than a few moments to realize that he'd said it in response to her telling him she should go.

Which meant that instead of continuing to stare at him like a freak, getting lost in those storm-cloud eyes, she *should go*.

Nodding, her embarrassment at a critical level now, she spun away.

And felt him walk beside her, his long stride eating up her much shorter one. She wasn't a small woman by any means, nearly five-ten and a solid size twelve, but he was so big that she felt tiny in comparison.

"What are you doing now?" he asked.

Dani missed a step, nearly faceplanted on the concrete floor.

Ethan, bless him, didn't acknowledge the klutziness, other

than to steady her again with one of those big hands—which really just made it even harder to focus on her steps and to not just melt into a puddle on the floor.

"Dani?" he said after a few more moments.

His hand was still wrapped around her bicep, and she found that it was hard to concentrate on anything except the contact.

And that was the only reason she could come up with later for why the conversation went as it did.

"Yeah?" she asked.

"What are you doing now?"

"Um?" She nibbled on her bottom lip. "You mean aside from driving home?"

The ghost of a smile. "*After* you get home," he said. His thumb was on the inside of her arm, tracing lightly up and down, a coil of heat tightening in her abdomen.

Her mouth open and closed. Open and closed.

And then for some really freaking stupid reason, she blurted, "Bath, wine, cold pizza, and bingeing *Bridgerton* for about the fiftieth time on *Netflix.*"

Silence.

His feet slid to a stop, sliding *her* to a stop.

Lightning in those stormy eyes, that thumb pausing, pressing a little tighter. His lips parted and he was close, closer than she'd realized, his hot breath brushing over the skin on her forehead, her cheek . . . her mouth.

Oh God.

Was he going to kiss her?

She wanted that. She *didn't* want that. No, she *needed* his lips on hers.

A door slammed in the distance and she jumped, skittering back, his hand slipping free. Her heart squeezed, and she could feel her pulse thrumming through her veins, thudding against the delicate skin at the base of her throat.

"What's *Bridgerton*?" he asked softly, starting to walk again.

She gaped up at him, frozen in place.

He turned back, lightly snagged her arm again, tugging her forward, and he laughed quietly—a rough chuckle sliding through the air, teasing her skin like velvet and lace running over the surface. That husky laugh joined the imagery of his beard to mentally rub against her thighs.

"What's *Bridgerton?*" he asked again.

"A show," she managed to get out.

"What kind of show?"

The *best* kind of show—strong heroines, gorgeous, tortured heroes, pretty dresses, gossip, and drama . . . and there was that duke. Yum. Because that duke was just . . . her cheeks went hot. "Um . . ."

He bent, nearly running into her for the third time that evening, then his face softened, his eyes danced. "Ah."

She swallowed. "*Ah,* what?"

Ethan straightened, but not before she saw the smile on his lips. "It's a sexy show."

Her lips parted, words stoppered up in the back of her throat.

Yes, it *was* a sexy show, an unapologetic romance that was wonderful to get lost in because was it too much for a woman to want a man to burn for her? No.

But also, *probably*, at least when it came to her.

Sighing, shoving down that sad thought, she knew she'd take her fictional duke any day of the week.

Ethan bent, his mouth very close to her ear. "Want to have a watch party?"

Her throat seized, and she found herself coughing, choking on her own spit. *Ah.* That was another reason she didn't have her fictional duke. Duchesses didn't go around choking on their own saliva.

Ethan's hand slipped from her arm, sliding up her shoulder,

drifting to her back, the warm expanse of it running up and down her spine.

"I take it," he said when she'd finally stopped coughing, "that's a no?"

"Uh-huh," she wheezed, turning right at the intersection in the hall and breathing a little easier when she saw the exit to the arena was just ahead. Just a few more steps and she could make her escape from this conversation in which she kept embarrassing herself, get back to her condo, and to her bath, cold pizza, and bottle of wine.

Lucky for her, she didn't have to be on the team's diet plan.

She could self-medicate and ply herself with all the carbs she wanted.

So take that, sexy hockey players with the amazing bodies. She might not have a six-pack—*ha!*—but at least she could eat her delicious crust topped with cheese and sauce and all sorts of other yumminess.

"Dani?"

She jumped, her brain having been locked on the leftovers of her Hawaiian pizza that was currently sitting on the top shelf of her fridge. She could almost taste it—the creamy cheese, the sweet of the pineapple, the saltiness of the ham—and . . . that was not pertinent to this conversation.

"Yeah?" she said.

"Are you scared of me?"

The grizzly bear of a man was touching her, walking close to her, his scent surrounding her, his body towering over hers by a good six inches. He was stronger and outweighed her, and he was certainly way more gorgeous than her—and that wasn't on a hate-herself-vein. That was just pure irrefutable fact. Ethan's cheekbones were sharp, his eyes unique and intoxicating, his lips kissable, and his body . . . well, that was *also* kissable.

Very, *very* kissable.

He made her want to do things that weren't smart.

Very, very *not* smart.

So yeah, he scared her. He fucking terrified her.

A finger brushing along the tip of her nose.

"Yeah," he whispered. "You're scared of me."

"I—"

But what could she do? Argue and deny it? She wasn't a good liar, and she had the feeling that Ethan would see through her anyway.

"Here," he said, in such a gentle way that she immediately felt her spine bristle.

Shy, not fragile.

Quiet, not stupid.

Taciturn, not a bitch.

And what was the point in going down that road again, either in her mind or in this conversation? He wouldn't understand. No one ever did, and it wasn't like she was willing to blab her sad sob story out there.

Or that she had a worse sad sob story than anyone else.

She'd been quiet, not one of the cool, outgoing, beautiful or funny kids. So, she'd gotten her turn as fodder for bullies. It had sucked, but it had sucked for plenty of other kids at her school, and none of them had become this nearly silent, closed down mess of a human that she was.

She was hiding from her life.

Because it was easier and safer and . . . *safer*. That. If she hid, she wasn't vulnerable and could just continue living in her happy little bubble. Could continue to get lost in her numerous video feeds, her computers, her fanciful duke, her cold pizza, and just leave it at that.

"Dani?"

Tone still careful, but marginally so, and the spikes on her spine settled down as she blinked. She realized that Ethan was holding the door for her, and she was just standing there like a freaking traffic pole, staring off into space while he was waiting for her to go out.

Ugh.

Why did he have to be nice?

She wanted to be annoyed but couldn't deny that the chivalrous gesture was a nice one.

Yes, she could open her own doors.

Yes, it was nice when someone—no matter where they fell on the scale of gender—held one open for her.

"Thanks," she whispered.

She walked out. He trailed her, the door clanging closed behind him, and silence fell as they strode across the parking lot. Her car—a small electric sedan that went approximately fifty miles per hour at top speed—was parked on the far end, well away from the players' vehicles, but he still just sauntered along next to her.

"So, what kind of pizza are you eating cold?"

"Why are you here?" she whispered.

Silence.

Tense, painful silence.

It was a sentiment that she'd intended on keeping in her head. It was a sentiment that was probably unforgivably rude, given he'd been nothing but nice and they worked together.

Except for the fact that he asked you out! her inner schoolgirl said. *You don't want to make him mad and then he'll turn on you, he'll turn everyone on you.*

But this wasn't high school.

She didn't have to deal with asshole teenagers.

The team was a family, and even if it was just a family she existed on at the barest fringes—because she wasn't capable of more than that—she was still a part of that family.

They hadn't turned on her.

Yet, her inner cynic said.

He fell quiet at her question. "Do you want me to leave?" he asked, after a moment.

Her car was just a few feet away, and she wouldn't even have to take out her keys. She could just yank at the handle, start her up, and then GTFO.

But the careful way he spoke to her made something inside Dani snap.

People always, *always* treated her like she was weak, like a sharp word might make her cower. So yes, she may be shy and quiet in equal measures, but she *wasn't* fragile. She wasn't breakable.

That had been proven over and over.

So that careful, don't-startle-the-frightened-beast-in-front-of-him tone made her lose her shit.

As in *lose* her shit.

She whirled on him, her backpack jumping off her spine and dropping like a pair of ineffective wings. But she hardly noticed the heavy contents. She was too busy being pissed.

"I am *not* a piece of china to be treated with care," she snapped, poking her finger into his chest. "I am not delicate or fragile or breakable." Each adjective was paired with a poke to his chest—that yummy chest, and the fact that she noticed its yumminess in any form or fashion even while pissed made her even more furious. "I'm quiet." She shook her head. "Yes, some-times I'm really fucking awkward and shy, but I'm not some crystal vase you have to worry about shattering, and furthermore—"

He captured her finger, held it in that big warm hand. "First," he said, his voice silken. "Yes, you deserve to be treated with care." Thunderclouds in his eyes. "You're a good human being, so you *always* deserve to be treated with care."

Her breath caught.

"Second, I like you shy," he said. "I like you quiet. I like you however the fuck you want to be. So what if you're not crossing verbal swords in the locker room with Max? You're smart as hell, you're funny, even if that sense of humor isn't as loud as other people's."

More breath-catching, more words stuck in the back of her throat. More—

"Third." His voice was velvet again, brushing along her exposed skin and making her shiver. "Third," he said, "is the most important one."

"Why?" she whispered, when he didn't expound on that final reason.

His fingers slipped from hers, shifted up to encircle her wrist, brushing along the sensitive skin on the inside of it and tracing more of those delicate patterns that threatened to melt her into a puddle of goo. Well . . . of that *and* curiosity.

"It's the most important because . . ."

She leaned forward slightly, anxious to hear the answer.

"Another time."

He dropped her hand, and she was despising the loss of that warmth when he stepped around her, opened her car door. Was gaping at his response when he bent—giving her a glorious view of his slacks tightening over that fine ass—to set her backpack in the passenger's seat.

He straightened, brushed the backs of his knuckles over her cheek.

Then he nudged her toward her car. "Goodnight, Dani," he murmured.

She blinked, lips parting, but . . . he was gone.

And she was left wondering—and cursing her curiosity—about reason number three.

FOUR

ETHAN

He'd slept like shit the night before.

Mostly because he'd been dreaming about Dani naked in her bathtub, a glass of wine in one hand, a slice of pizza in the other . . . and also, he'd dreamed about Dani *naked*.

Glorious and naked and *naked*.

Which explained the reason for his cock threatening to crack in half that morning.

He had a great imagination.

Some might even say it was stellar.

Because he could picture every curve, imagine how soft her skin would feel when he kissed his way across it. He'd bet it would be even softer than that on the inside of her wrist, and *that* had felt like silk beneath his rough-ass fingers.

However, none of his imaginings were helping his control.

Or making his morning wood go away.

Groaning as he got out of bed and ignoring the jut of his erection against the fabric of his boxer briefs, he shuffled into the bathroom and turned on the shower, then set about brushing and flossing and getting ready for the day.

It was pretty early by hockey standards—with last night's match start time of seven-thirty, three-plus hours of game play, press, cooldown and stretching routines, and then a shower, it meant that he hadn't left the arena until after midnight. Then he'd come home, reviewed the video, had his beer, and watched the first three episodes of that *Bridgerton* show. He could see why Dani liked it, had felt the urge to keep watching, even after his post-game adrenaline high had begun to fade.

But he had shit to do today, so eventually he'd forced himself to turn off the TV, pried the remote out of his hand, and had gone to bed.

Where he'd slept like shit.

Because he'd been imagining stripping Dani out of one of those prissy dresses from the show and kissing every inch of her glorious body.

After setting his toothbrush on the counter with a sigh, his erection seeming to have no desire to go away, he stripped off his underwear and stepped into the shower. Shampoo, soap, warm water on sore muscles.

A cock that ached for the beautiful, shy woman he'd dreamed about for years now.

It was fucking frustrating.

Not because she'd turned him down when he'd asked her out.

But rather, it was fucking painful that he'd purposely been ignoring his attraction all this time, and then for a few days while he'd worked up the courage to ask her, for a few moments as he'd seen her come out of her office, for *one* conversation when he'd thought that maybe . . . just maybe they might be able to have something that wasn't only work-related.

But that wasn't to be.

"Enough," he muttered. He just needed to ignore his dick,

get on with his day, and do his best to forget about one Dani Eastbrooke. Laughter bubbled in his chest, only it wasn't because the situation was funny. Quite the opposite, actually. His laughter was a product of incredulity because he'd spent two years thinking about her, dreaming of her, and to think that he could just ignore the attraction that had been brewing and growing for all that time, especially now that he'd gotten a glimpse of that fire beneath the cool shield she kept in place between herself and the rest of the world, was ludicrous.

Groaning, he dropped his head to the tiles, felt the cool material against his skin, though it did nothing to tame the need burning within him.

Then he gave in to the inevitable and wrapped his hand around his still-hard cock . . . and stroked, pretending it was *her* hand, that *her* naked body was under the stream, touching him, coming close, her breasts pressing against him, her lips on his—

And he came, her name on his lips.

Fuck, but he was in deep.

Chest heaving, he let the water flow over him, sliding along his back until he started to feel guilty for contributing to the California drought and knew he needed to get on with his day. He cranked the shower off, snagged a towel, and wrapped it around his waist, glad his cock was flaccid but feeling the slightest bit dirty for jerking off to thoughts of a woman who wasn't attracted to him. Then he pushed down the creeper feeling, promised he wouldn't do it again, got dressed, and headed out to get his shit done.

———

The first order of business was the library.

Maybe not the most logical place for a six-foot-five, two-hundred-and-twenty-three-pound professional hockey player, but it was one of *his* places.

Ever since he'd been a little kid, it had been his main happy place.

Tagging along with his parents, disappearing into the children's section while they browsed for research books or just novels to read for fun. He still remembered the feeling of getting his first library card, how excited he'd been to have the power to check his books out, all on his own.

Today, he was filled with marginally less excitement.

He was heading in to pick up some books he had on hold for one of his classes this semester. With hockey as a full-time job and the team's travel schedule intense, he usually only managed two classes a semester. Which meant he was on the four-year plan for his master's, but that wasn't the worst thing in the world. It was the only way he was able to do both of the things he loved—hockey and learning new things.

Plus, he was on his last semester.

If he didn't fuck up, he was going to have his master's in psychology by the end of the year.

What he'd do with it, he didn't know yet.

But he'd have it, and since earning his master's had always been a goal of his—one that had sometimes been at odds with his career, with away games and playoffs and travel—he would be happy just to have the degree to shove in a drawer somewhere.

Then he'd do . . . *something.*

Maybe get a dog, although that would be tough since he was away for half the year. If he wasn't single, if he had a partner like some of the other guys, he could rely on that girlfriend or wife to be on dog duty. Though, he supposed if he really wanted a pup, he could figure it out with a pet sitter or boarding or doggy daycare. But he'd never actually pulled the trigger because it just had never seemed fair to the pooch if he was constantly leaving and coming back. And dogs aside, it was hard to even find someone to date when he was currently hung up on a woman who traveled with the team, a woman he saw nearly every day who made every cell in his body stand up and take notice.

Dani with her beautiful brown skin, those amber and russet eyes, with lips and curves he wanted to kiss—

His cock twitched.

And he forced himself to stop, his hand on the handle of the door leading into the library.

One deep breath, Dani out of his mind.

Another to open the door and go inside.

Immediately, the smell of books wafted forward, drifting toward him, filling his nose and settling that itchy feeling inside him.

The vaulted ceiling overhead was covered in translucent glass, each of the panels surrounded by green metal. The walls were a pale, institutional brown, the carpet industrial and a quite unpleasant combination of tan and forest green, but the book-cases in the distance took the majority of his focus, row after row after row of bottled—or papered, he supposed—knowledge.

He wanted to explore.

But he had more things to do today than just browse through books, as sad as that thought was.

Averting his eyes from the temptation of all those books, Ethan headed to the hold desk and waited in line. A few minutes later, and with a swipe of his library card, he had received his stack of reference materials.

And out he went, thinking about the next item on his list.

Grocery store to pick up Nutritionist Rebecca approved food, the hardware store to pick up some samples of the new floor he was going to have installed. He'd bought it, now that he'd gotten the first long-term contract of his career—six years— and knew he'd be able to settle down in one place.

Plus, the Bay Area wasn't a bad place to live, even once his stint in the league was done.

Whether he'd retire after the next contract (most likely), stay with the Gold, or move onto another team wouldn't be decided anytime soon, but he was just happy to have found a team that he truly gelled with, even if he would never be good enough to be on that top line.

Power plays and penalty kills were his specialty, and between them and with his position as left wing on the third line, he got enough ice time to not hate what he was doing, and to appreciate that offer of six years of stability.

That was a lot more than other players.

Including a lot more than he'd had in the past.

Studying the books in his hands, leafing through the medical journal on the top of the stack, he went to push out the front door of the library when he saw her.

Her.

As always, his heart pattered, squeezing tight, and his fingers went all tingly.

She had a stack of books balanced in one arm, was paging through another . . . as she strode right for him.

He opened his mouth to speak, remembered the tablets, and thought better of it, shifting instead to be in a position to catch, and then snagging her arm. Her head flew up, and he saw that she was wearing turquoise-framed glasses, her hair wrapped up into a loose bun on top of her head, her lips painted a bright pink.

The books tumbled free, but since he was ready, he caught them, pressing the stack between one hand and his side.

"Ethan?" she said.

"In the flesh," he said then winced because *in the flesh?* Who the fuck said *that?* But he was struggling here, he'd never seen Dani in something that wasn't jeans or sweats paired with a Gold pullover or fleece.

This however, was different.

Different as in *incredible.*

Her sundress was giving him all sorts of Bridgerton vibes,

even though it wasn't remotely of the era. Rather, he just had all sorts of thoughts about tossing the hem up and losing himself in what was underneath. The fabric was white with large blue and turquoise flowers creeping up from the hem, its hem hitting right at knee level and giving him a view of slender calves, and when his gaze dropped lower, it stuck on pale blue sandals crisscrossing over toes that were painted bright pink.

Fuck, the woman even had beautiful toes.

"Wh-what are you doing here?" she asked.

Since the books were unstable—and not because it would extend this interaction with her—he shifted the stack, tucking them under one arm. "Same as you, I suspect."

Her eyes met his, drifted down in what felt like a physical caress, halting on the stack of research materials he held under his other arm. "You read?"

"I have been known to do so," he said, lips twitching. "Occasionally."

Her teeth found her bottom lip, pressed into that plump, kissable mouth. "I . . . um . . . I didn't mean that like it sounded."

"I know." And he did know that.

Her eyes held his. "I'm sorry."

"Nothing to be sorry for." He started to nudge open the door with his hip, but she slipped past him, held the metal and glass panel wide so he could pass through. "I'm just teasing," he said once they were outside in the courtyard filled with bronze statues of people reading, trees interspaced, their leaves just beginning to change color for the fall, yellows and greens mixing with an occasional orange and red.

They continued walking, this time on the path winding its way to the parking lot. "What did you pick up?"

"Some research material."

She frowned.

"I'm finishing up my degree," he told her, surprised she

didn't know, considering the team teased him about it frequently.

"Oh, your bachelor's?" she asked, and he sensed the air around her relax for the first time. His heart thudded. Maybe she was warming up to him. "That's really cool. I know sometimes it's hard for you guys to finish school when you get drafted young."

Ethan spied her car and started walking toward it. "No, actually," he told her. "I was a late bloomer as far as hockey went, so I finished my bachelor's degree before I ended up playing in the league." Which was a good thing. He'd needed those extra years to build his skills, in addition to the additional time to earn his undergraduate studies.

She froze, sandals making a scraping sound on the pavement.

"A master's then?" she asked, brows raised. Her shoulders rose, and though he could only see the side of one cheek, since she was now deliberately looking down at the ground, he knew that she was embarrassed again.

"Yes," he said gently.

Brown eyes sparked when her gaze jerked up to his, and he was reminded again that she didn't like that tone. He couldn't help it, though. There was something about her that made him ache to soothe whatever hurts were inside her, to draw her close and cuddle her tight.

And not in a sexual way.

Though, that was there. That was always there.

He just wanted to keep her safe and then spend the rest of the time making love to her. Also, this just in, he was embracing that feeling from the shower earlier.

He wanted her.

She was here.

He was in deep.

That was just . . . fact.

"I'm a weird one who can't stop going to school." He

laughed, mostly so that his cock wouldn't get any harder and he'd embarrass himself.

"No, seriously," she said. "That's awesome. What are you studying?"

"Psychology." A shrug. "Mostly because I want to be able to use my powers to ask all the girls to lie on my couch."

He froze, mortification clawing up his throat, stealing his words. Who in the fuck would say something like that?

Maybe some dumbass frat boy.

But not a grown-ass man, who was trying to somehow win over a woman who wasn't interested.

She reacted exactly as he'd expected, given he'd said something incredibly gross and creepy, and in the simplest of terms, the precise wrong thing to say to anyone, most of all a woman he liked. "Wow, that's really . . . *something*," she said, striding past him, those bare legs gleaming in the sun, the hem swishing back and forth along the backs of her thighs.

"Dani, wait," he said, catching up to her. "I'm sorry, that was . . ." He trailed off, made a face. "I just really fucking like you, and for some reason, I seem determined to put my foot into my mouth every time I open it."

Her eyes studied his.

"I'm sorry," he repeated. "I really didn't mean that thing about the couch. I don't even know what I'm doing." He shoved a hand through his hair. "And the degree is just some piece of paper, some goal I've been working toward. I don't even know what I'm going to do with it, aside from shoving it in some drawer somewhere."

She stilled, those pretty eyes continuing to hold his. Then one corner of her mouth twitched. "It's a good goal, all things considered."

"What's one of yours?"

A flicker of an emotion he couldn't decipher sliding across her face. "I'm boring," she said. "My life consists of testing the latest editing software, pretending to attempt to clear off my TBR, even knowing that'll never actually happen, and eating leftover pizza as much as possible."

God, he wanted to know everything about her. "Is leftover pizza like this Bridgerton thing?"

Her brows drew together. "What do you mean?"

"I watched like three episodes last night." He grinned. "I know what you like."

She spun toward the lot. "No," she said. "You really don't. Not if you haven't seen episodes six, seven, and eight."

Okay, now this was getting interesting.

"What's in six, seven, and eight?"

A flick of her eyes toward his, then back toward the cars. "Leftover pizza is better than regular pizza because the flavors have a chance to meld, and then when you pull it out from the fridge and chow down on it, those flavors just explode on your tongue." She moaned. "I buy it for the week and have it for dinner cold every night. It's the best."

Cock twitching as he cataloged that moan away for probable shower time later and attempting (and failing) to ignore the whole exploding on the tongue thing, he needed to revisit the ordering pizza for the week, only to store it in the fridge.

"You don't eat it hot?"

She shook her head. "Nope. Put it straight into the fridge and wait until the next day to eat it."

"Wow," he said. "You either have incredible self-control or you're—"

"Incredibly weird?" Her brows flicked, and he got the sense that amusement was tangling with a sliver of old pain. Then she shrugged, and her lips twitched. "Or maybe it's just both, and I should embrace it." With that, she took off across the parking lot, calling over her shoulder. "I'll see you at the rink."

He waited a moment to see if she'd realize she only held the one book she'd been leafing through, that he had her huge pile of

—he glanced down, studied the spines—cozy mysteries, thrillers, and romances, but she just kept walking and after a moment, he trailed after her.

She was whispering something under her breath when he caught up, something he couldn't distinguish, but also something he really didn't like the tone of.

"That's why the guys call me Big, Juicy Brain sometimes," he blurted.

Dani nearly jumped out of those sexy, strappy sandals, clasping a hand to her chest and squeezing it tightly. "Will you stop doing *that?*"

"Doing what?"

She plunked her hands on her hips, glared up at him, and Ethan had the distinct thought that when she got mad, she forgot to worry about being shy, forgot about all those things that had her whispering disparagingly to herself. "Sneaking up on me," she snapped.

And yup.

Had definitely forgotten about shy, at least for the moment.

Also, yup, he really, really liked it when she forgot to be shy.

"Just saying"—his lips twitched—"I didn't think nearly barreling you down counted as sneaking up on you."

"Ugh."

Sparks in those brown eyes, and hell if that didn't make joy coil up inside him.

She turned away again.

He followed. Again.

She spun back to face him. "What?" she snapped. "What do you want? Why are you bugging me in my happy place when all I want to do is enjoy my day?" Her eyes narrowed. "With peace and quiet." They narrowed further. "Peace and quiet that doesn't involve certain annoying hockey players."

"How about certain hockey players with your books?"

He tilted his head down, lifted the stack of paperbacks he held under one arm.

"*Ugh.*" She reached for them.

He held onto them, stepping back out of reach. "This is your happy place?"

She froze again. Then shook her head, turned away, and sighed. "You're not going to give those back, are you?"

"Of course, I am."

A glance over her shoulder, and he finally registered something other than sleek bare legs. The turquoise sweater she was wearing was fucking adorable, especially when paired with those glasses and sandals. He was so used to seeing her in casual clothes —sweats, T-shirts, hoodies—that he'd always pictured her in something similar. To see her so girly gave him another intriguing insight. Well, that along with her choice of reading material—which as he glanced over the titles again, he could approve strongly of, even the trio of historical romances that he assumed were inspired by her recent foray into *Bridgerton.*

"What do you mean, of course you are?"

"I mean," he said, "that I'll give them back after I walk you to your car."

Her eyes narrowed.

He nodded over her head. "Let me rephrase," he said. "I've been walking you to your car, and now it's less than ten more feet, sweetheart," he said, "and then you can get rid of me."

More narrowing, more sparks.

And so much less shy.

Months ago, Ethan had already slid down the slippery slope of being infatuated with this woman, but that fire beneath the surface, the sass she was—rightfully—throwing his way . . . well, he was no longer gripping at the hillside, trying to crawl back up. He was plummeting right down into the crevice below and not giving a damn in the least.

He was happy to keep falling.

She twisted to face him again, the fabric of her skirt brushing his bare knees, exposed to the warm fall air by a pair of cargo shorts. But he wasn't thinking of his fashion choices when she stepped close, her chin lifting. "I'm *not* your sweetheart."

"But you *could* be," he murmured.

Her breath escaped on a long, slow exhale. He smelled mint and coffee in the air, was fascinated by the bright pink color of her lips. Had she intended to match her toes? Did she always wear dresses and cute little sandals? Why didn't she ever wear glasses at work? What other lipstick colors did she have? Would she let him kiss all the colors off?

"Ethan," she whispered.

And he would have had to have been inhuman to not love the way his name sounded on her tongue. Maybe that put another tally in the creeper-pervert category, but he was who he was, and the slightly husky tone of her voice as she said his name was the most intense aphrodisiac he'd ever heard.

"Ten feet, love," he said—not gently, not at all, not this time. He didn't want more sparks, more fire—at least not for the next ten feet. Instead, he wanted just a little more time with her. So, his tone was coaxing with a dash of fucking hope.

Because she'd already shot back that fire, forgot to be shy with him, so perhaps getting her to agree to go on a date with him wasn't such a lost cause. But he needed a mix of fire and coax to see if he couldn't weasel his way in with one date. Plus, if he got one—and this wasn't him being an asshole, or not trying to be anyway—he'd bet on being able to convince her to give him more than one.

He could be charming. He was smart, had a decent body, could occasionally be funny.

If she gave him one date, then he had a good chance of securing more than that.

So, fewer flames and more persuading now.

An unpleasant thought welled up within him, because unless, of course, she wasn't attracted to him.

Which would certainly put a damper on his whole plan to win her over.

But he could ponder that later.

In this moment, he needed to take a page out of Billy Madison's book and *get on with the chlorophyll.*

"Ten feet," he cajoled.

She sighed, turned again, and flounced toward her car, that fabric brushing his legs, a silken bite that had him blurting, "Are you not attracted to me?"

Still.

Dani went absolutely still.

And if he were one to congratulate himself on his skills, then he could say that he possessed a unique ability to make this woman freeze in place. As far as life skills went, it wasn't the greatest, but he supposed he needed to take his victories where he could.

She struggled to ignore him.

She shot back fire.

Now, to get that date.

This time when she spun to face him, shock was written into every line of her face—from her jaw to her lips to a little furrow that he wanted to kiss that had appeared between her brows.

"You're asking *me* if I'm attracted to you," she said slowly.

He nodded. "Yup. That's the crux of it."

Laughter filled the air, dancing over his skin, freezing him in place, making him the one playing statue. That clear, hearty sound was fucking glorious, and he wanted to make her laugh again and again.

Of course, he'd prefer if she wasn't laughing at *him.*

But he'd learned over the years to take his victories where he could.

And seeing that amusement in her eyes, hearing her delight, *that* was a fucking victory.

"You . . ." She bent at the waist, the book resting on her hip as she gasped out the laughing words. "Me . . . *Attracted* . . ." More hilarity.

Okay, as time went on, this was less joyful.

"Dani," he warned.

She looked up. "You think *I'm* not attracted to you. To *you*," she repeated. "*To you!*"

Yup, less joyful and more irritating.

"Yes, sweetheart," he muttered. "I think I made myself clear, don't you?"

"No." She tossed up her hands, strode to her car again. "Nothing about this makes sense." Her words came in a flurry. "You at the library. You asking me out. You thinking that you're not the absolute most gorgeous man in all the universe, so freaking beautiful and sexy that I've fucking fantasized about you for *years*. I mean, your tattoos, your butt, your *abs—*"

She clamped a hand over her mouth.

Meanwhile, he was processing.

Processing.

Beautiful and sexy and gorgeous and . . . *fantasized?*

About him?

"Oh, my God," she moaned, the words muffled through her hand. She dropped it. "Please, tell me I'm in a horrible dream, that I didn't actually just say that out loud."

He couldn't bite back the smile. "Fortunately, for me, no, we're not in a dream."

She pinched herself on the arm. "*Ouch!*"

Ethan took a step toward her, wanting to grab her hand, to stop her from hurting herself again, but his arms were full of books. "What'd you do that for?" he muttered.

She moaned again, one hand coming to her forehead, the

other still clenching the novel at her hip. "Not a dream. Not a dream. Oh *God*, not a dream."

"Dani?"

Shaking her head, she whirled around and went directly to her car, yanked at the handle and started to climb inside.

He hotfooted it over to her, managing to slip into the opening before she could slam the door shut. The metal panel collided with his hip. "Didn't you want your books?" he asked when she didn't look at him, just slammed the door against his hip once more.

A sigh, her body going still.

Then she released the door.

He crouched. "I like your dress."

"Books, please," she said, twisting to hold out her arms, though her eyes were deliberately away from his.

Ethan separated his from the stack then handed hers over.

"Dani?" he asked again.

She spent an inordinate amount of time stacking them on her passenger's seat.

He waited, had the feeling that he would wait for however long this woman needed. Of course, the alternative was that she run him over or barrel through the parking lot with her driver's door open.

Though, he supposed, given the weight of the glare she tossed his way, neither of those options was out of the realm of possibility.

"You're attracted to me?" He set his books on the roof of the car.

She groaned, plunked her head against the steering wheel. "Why?" she moaned, banging it enough times that he finally reached out and captured her shoulders. "Why, God," she moaned, her eyes sliding closed, "are we still having this conversation?"

He held on to her. Waited.

She peeled back her eyelids, glared at him again. "Did the whole drooling over your abs and tattoo thing not clue you in?"

A smile tugged at his lips.

Another groan.

"What?" he asked, brows drawn together.

"That." She waved a hand at his face.

"*What?*" he asked again.

"*That*," she muttered. "That smile peeking out at me like it's the best freaking gift I've received all day. It's just a smile. I shouldn't like a freaking *smile* so much."

"But you do?"

Her eyes sparked, and she sighed heavily. "Do you have an ego problem or something? You need someone to constantly be building it up?"

A shrug. "Better than it being constantly pricked."

She sighed again, then said, "Why are you tormenting me?"

"Because I have questions."

Another glare. "Well, *I* have errands."

His lips twitched. "Me, too."

She waited.

"What errands do you have?" he asked.

A muscle pulsed in her jaw, just beneath the edge of the bone, at the top of that kissable expanse of neck. He could almost feel the tremble against his mouth, wanted to dart his tongue out to taste the flicker.

"Dani?" he prompted.

Her fingers clenched on the steering wheel. "Grocery shopping."

"What else?"

Her shoulders crept up. "Nothing."

"Sweetheart?"

"Not your—"

"Sweetheart," he interrupted. "Right. Sorry."

Her lips pressed flat.

"So, what else?"

There was that pink again.

"What?" he pressed.

"I should go."

Okay, now his curiosity was seriously peaked. But he was seeing that this woman was stubborn, that she wouldn't give in easy. Which, of course, made her all the more interesting, especially considering this was the longest conversation they'd ever had. "What are you buying?"

Her brows drew down, another V forming.

"At the grocery store," he said, anticipating her query. "What are you picking up? More cold pizza?"

He watched her throat work as she swallowed. But then her chin lifted, her tone growing clipped. "Food, Ethan," she muttered. "I'm buying food that isn't pizza."

"Me, too," he said. "I'm going to the store to buy food, too."

This was definitely not a charming exchange, this definitely bordered on inane and nonsensical, and yet . . . he was having a fucking ball.

"And then what?" he asked. "After the food, you're going . . ."

Silence. Long and drawn out and . . .

That chin lifted again, the amber in her eyes flared with fire. "And," she snapped, "now we're circling back to why are we even having this conversation?" Her eyes were on his, not disappearing over his shoulder or sliding down to her hands. Just fierce brown eyes holding his . . . and he fucking *wanted* her.

Bad.

"I don't know," he admitted.

Other than the fact he was in deep . . . and loving every minute of it.

"So, you'll be going?" she asked, the question so expectant that a curl of wickedness coiled through his abdomen, slipping in alongside the need and affection. She might as well have asked, *"So you'll be coming inside me?"* for how his body reacted.

He liked her like this—her expression arched, her eyes on his, that shyness slipping away so he could see the fierce woman inside.

He rose to his feet. "You're right."

That froze her again, the plump, kissable pillow of her bottom lip separating from the top, a flash of bright white teeth as she scrambled to comprehend his sudden agreement.

As tempting as it was to lean in, to taste that mouth, he gave into wicked.

Well, wicked that wasn't having him take liberties in the parking lot of a public library.

Smiling, he stepped out of the opening between the door and car, snagged his books, crossed around the front, picked up *her* books, and crammed himself into the passenger's seat of the tiny sedan.

FIVE

DANI

The *click* his seat belt startled her out of her shock.

"What—"

Ethan spun toward her, and for a moment, she thought he might tug her into his arms, yank her across the console, and kiss the shit out of her.

She would have liked that, too.

Not that she would have admitted it.

Because even though this man was beyond gorgeous, even though she burned for him, she dreamed and fantasized and touched herself pretending he was hers, that wouldn't ever be.

He would destroy her.

It was as simple as that.

Despite that, she still wanted him to kiss her, still wanted to feel his body against hers, his hands on her skin, his cock thrusting deep. Throat going dry, her fingers actually cramping with the urge to touch because the thought of him inside her was intoxicating and dangerous when this man was so close—

close enough that her pussy throbbed, that her nerves were on fire, that—

He didn't kiss her.

He just set the stack of books on the back seat and faced forward again. Then calmly asked, "Would you like me to drive instead?"

"Wh-what?"

His hand came down on top of hers, squeezing lightly where it rested on the steering wheel. "Are you okay?"

Such an absurd question, she thought.

Of course, she wasn't okay.

She was nowhere even near it, and how *could* she be when this man was so close, the spicy scent of him filling her car. She could smell the mint of his toothpaste on his breath, and it mixed with the tang of pine, the faintly biting, briny notes of the ocean. His smell made her want to move closer, to forget about *him* tugging her over the console and instead, to climb over it herself, to straddle his hips and—

"Whatcha thinking?" he asked, his fingers squeezing hers lightly.

And that little convulsion, the warm, rough hand engulfing hers . . . well, it had the last of her filter dissipating like so much smoke.

Which was the only reason she could account for later for why she just straight up blurted, "How much I want to fuck you."

The air in the car went taut.

"*What* did you say?"

She was horrified, slowly dying inside, that death agonizing, a painful millimeter-by-millimeter creep until she had to physically stop herself from yanking open the door and running screaming through the parking lot.

It was *her* car, for God's sake!

"You should go," she whispered.

He didn't move, except to squeeze her hand again, to unwind it from the steering wheel and bring it across the console.

"Eth—"

Her palm suddenly made contact with a hard cock . . . with *his* cock. Her fingers involuntary clenched, and he groaned.

"Dani?" he gritted.

"Yeah?" she breathed, her hand starting to move.

"I want to fuck you, too."

Her throat seized. "I'm seeing that," she forced out.

"But," he said, gently peeling her hand away and lifting it to his mouth. The bristles of his beard tickled her palm, his tongue a hot brand. "I'd like to get to know you a little better first, okay?"

She was feeling a little dazed, and her words were equally as stupefied. "By grocery shopping?"

"Yup." He smiled.

Her brain short-circuited. The sun was shining through the window, gilding his skin, bringing out a lighter blond, almost red undertone in his hair. His teeth were bright white, though she knew that the one, two right of center, was fake. He'd been hit in the mouth with a stick during the playoffs last season, and even through the mouth guard he wore, his tooth had been knocked out. Instead of doing what any sane person who'd just lost a tooth would have done, he'd played the remainder of the game *and* the double-overtime periods (during which he'd also scored the game-winning goal, NBD). But anyway, by the time a dentist had been able to get a look at him, it had been too late to save the tooth.

So, a fake one.

Which was a mental tangent she shouldn't be going down right at this moment, with Ethan in her car, smiling at her, saying that he wanted to go grocery shopping with her of all things.

But the things she *should* be doing didn't always factor in with what her mouth did.

Case in point, that instant.

"Did it hurt?" she asked.

His smile drifted away slowly, like a cloud floating across the sky, the wind morphing its shape, flattening it on one corner, dragging it up on the other . . . and then she blinked. Or maybe like when she'd been a kid staring up at the clouds, finding creatures and telling stories in the white wisps trailing over the cerulean blue, the sun got into her eyes, making her squint, and all of a sudden, the story was gone, the smile flattened.

But the potential of a new saga could be found in its place.

Fingers on her cheek. The lightest brush of his thumb across her cheek.

"Grocery shopping?" he murmured.

Her lips curved. "Your tooth."

That pulled his hand from her skin, his pointer finger tapping the fake tooth. "Yeah," he said. "It really fucking hurt."

Dani raised her brows, surprise a tiny bolt of lightning zigzagging across her spine. "It did?"

His smile returned, and she found herself searching the lines, the bristles of hair surrounding it, the pink lips, the flash of white teeth for a different story . . . and found it, she supposed. She'd expected a macho reply, something about it not hurting because he was a big, tough hockey player who could take pucks to the body, sticks to the face, checks into the boards, and regardless of blood or bruises or teeth falling out, he got right back up, hopped straight onto the ice for his next shift.

"Yeah, it did," he said, his gray eyes flickering with amusement.

"Oh."

Silence. Then a light tap to her temple. "It looks like you have more questions in that big, juicy brain of yours."

Nope.

The questions had all flitted away to subspace, twinkling along with the stars, pretty, but impossible to grab on to.

"That's your nickname."

His smile was a physical gut punch. "You pay attention."

Mutely, she shook her head.

"No?"

"You just talk a lot."

He froze, and then his laughter filled the car, filled her, made her unstick or perhaps become somehow even more entranced, because she was absolutely rapt by everything this man did—the way his throat worked as he chuckled, his big, scarred hands clenching on his thighs, that mouth tempting as it curved.

More silence. Another brush of his thumb on her cheek. "Should we get on with the painful adventure known as grocery shopping?"

"You don't have bags," she said.

To his credit, he didn't misunderstand about the local law that charged for using anything that wasn't a reusable bag in stores, instead he just shrugged. "I'll buy some."

Her lips parted as she mentally searched for a way to get him out of her car. Mostly because she wanted him so much, and that made him dangerous for her sanity and the well-being of her very jaded heart. "That seems very wasteful."

"Unless you have some I can borrow?"

She didn't. She'd brought the precise number of bags she would need for her weekly trip for junk food with the odd vegetable thrown in. Probably, she could lose a few pounds if she ate more of the latter and less of the former, but she didn't care.

Once upon a time she *had* cared, and that had been disastrous for her mental health.

Now, she ate her fucking Oreos and didn't give a damn if her jeans weren't a size zero.

Instead of getting into her whole woman-hear-her-roar situation, Dani just simply said, "No."

For some reason, that made his lips twitch.

"Why don't you have any?" she felt obliged to ask.

A shrug. "I was going to walk home for them."

Her mouth formed the word *walk*, but even though the sound didn't cross her lips, he still saw or heard it or maybe the man who made her nipples tingle, her thighs quiver, maybe he just had fucking superpowers.

That seemed the more likely scenario when he said, "I live around the corner."

"Oh," she whispered.

"Want to come home with me, so I can grab some and not be *wasteful?*"

She swallowed. Hard. Hated that she felt like she was trapped inside a washing machine, being jerked this way and that during the conversation, not able to feel like she was in the least bit of control, not even for a moment.

She knew she could kick him out, could continue to feel stuck and whirling every time she had a conversation with him. Or—

Or she could just embrace this conversation, the time with a man who was funny and a little pushy and who'd also saved her books from hitting the ground. She could accept that out-of-control feeling and just live for *one* fucking moment.

By grocery shopping.

Yup.

Even when she was pushing her boundaries, she was living a huge, exciting life.

Paper or plastic.

The proverbial question.

Six

He could freely admit that he was shocked she'd said yes.

Completely and utterly shocked.

But instead of wasting his opportunity, he used his hockey player skills to think quick on his feet and give her directions to his place.

It was a little over a mile, tucked on the edge of town, up against a creek. With neighbors on just one side, it afforded him the quiet and privacy he craved, but it wasn't so far from the small downtown area that he couldn't walk to the restaurants and shops a few streets over.

For him, it was the perfect fit.

Also, because he was south of the city, real estate prices weren't so bad, and for a player who'd been shuffled around quite a few teams before he'd found his fit (thus contract offerings hadn't been filled with outrageous professional athlete money), less expensive housing prices were right in his wheelhouse.

She pulled into the driveway, completing the short trip in a way that was much what he would have expected—competent, careful, with no extraneous movements.

He waited until she put the car in park, until she'd gotten out, before he grabbed his books, popped the door, and led the way up to his front porch, watching her as she took in his little house. It was a neat Craftsman two-story home, sitting on a decent-sized lot. The front yard was small with a tiny patch of grass and some planters on one side of the driveway, a curved path leading up to the door. The back yard was nice, though. Good sized and shaded, plus as a bonus, the previous owners had left behind their hot tub.

Immediately, thoughts of coaxing her into that steaming water, her curvy body clad in a skimpy swimsuit, had him distracted and way too ahead of himself.

But that was him with Dani, wasn't it?

She paused on the porch, and he waited for a moment for her to go inside before he remembered she *couldn't* go inside.

Because he had the only key.

Dumbass.

Stifling a sigh, he unlocked the door and held it for her to walk through.

Her quiet studying continued as she stepped into the hallway, as she glanced at the pictures he had lining the wall on either side. He saw her lips curve, her hand lift to point at one of his mom's favorite photos—him amongst a giant stack of books.

"It's come to you naturally then," she said softly.

He chuckled. "That it does. Both of my parents are giant nerds."

"You saw my stack of books. What does that make me?"

"A nerd." He tugged a lock of her hair. "But an adorable one with obscenely sexy toes."

She froze. "What do you mean?"

"I *mean*," he said, "that your toes are sexy."

Dani spun for the door.

"What are you doing?" He placed his hand on the panel before she could open it.

"You've apparently got a foot fetish," she said, "and sorry, but that's a step too far for me."

"I don't have a foot fetish," he said, stepping close. "What I do have is a *Dani* fetish, and that includes sexy dresses and toes and turquoise glasses."

Her brows dragged together. "You like my glasses?"

"And your feet." He leaned against the door, his shoulder against the wood, his chest facing her side. It was convenient because he was able to study her *and* prevent her escape. Muha-haha. "Though, not in a creepy way. Now, going back to the glasses. I haven't seen you wear them before."

A blip of something—no, of *pain*—in her eyes. "No, I . . . um . . . wear contacts at work." A shrug. "After the game last night—" She shook her head, stopped talking, and he waited a few moments for her to finish the thought. When she didn't, he pushed away from the door, took her hand.

"What happened after the game last night?" he asked, drawing her down the hall.

"Nothing," she said, dropping her chin to her chest and studying the woodgrain of the floor. "I fell asleep with my contacts in. That's bad, and my eyes hurt this morning, so I wore my glasses today."

He studied her face, the tendrils of pain clinging to the edges of her expression. "No," he said. "No, that's not it."

Her brows raised. Her hand slipped from his.

He amended. "Or, at least, that's not *only* it."

"I thought we were getting to know each other over food shopping," she said, turning back, her eyes drifting over the pictures again before she reached the opening to his kitchen. "This isn't the grocery store. Your bags in here?"

"No."

She spun to face him, lifted a brow.

"Want to elaborate?" he asked. "A pregame to the getting-to-know-you grocery talk?"

Her throat worked, panic in the depths of her amber and russet eyes.

"Or how about I just grab the bags?"

There.

He saw the exact moment she relaxed, her shoulders settling, her lips curving just the slightest bit. "You snoop," he told her, "I'll go out back and grab the bags."

"Out back . . ." he heard her say, but the words disappeared off into space when he slipped through the back door. His garage was detached and abutted the yard. Having been built later than the original house, it was plunked into the back corner of the lot. He didn't mind the short walk most days, though it sucked hauling shit into the house in the rain.

Luckily, this was California, and rain wasn't a common problem.

Still, at that moment, he quickly strolled across the yard, certain that she wouldn't just abandon him and his apparent foot fetish.

Why, one might ask?

He grinned.

Because he held her purse in his hand. Which conveniently held her car keys.

Another muahaha.

He strode to his car, grabbed the reusable bags from the trunk, and strolled back in time to peek through the back windows and witness Dani snooping, or maybe not something quite so obvious. Rather, she seemed to be slowly studying each corner of the space, as though it were an art exhibit and she needed to take in every inch.

He waited for her to make a circle, to return to facing the back door, and her reaction when she completed that turn, when she was staring at him through the glass, did *not* disappoint. Her lips parted, and he'd bet this cute little house that her cheeks would be hot. Behind those turquoise frames, her eyes widened, and she clamped a hand over her chest.

Ethan tugged open the door. "Whatcha doing?"

To her credit, she got over her surprise in a flash. Shrugging, her tone completely even and without a hint of embarrassment, she said, "Snooping."

"That usually involves opening and closing things," he said, moving to a bank of drawers and tugging out the top one. "Like that." He nodded at it. "This exhibit is my junk drawer, and there are many interesting things in here that tell you about the various parts of my psyche."

Her lips twitched, probably because he sounded like a dumbass.

But whatever, she wasn't running from the house, so that was a win in his book.

"Like what?" she asked, peering down into the drawer.

Okay, that he wasn't really sure of. It *was* his junk drawer, a place to dump his receipts, old keys, etc. His gaze drifted down, and also apparently a place to dump several candy bars and a manual for his car. He reached in, picked up one of the bars. "I like Snickers?" he asked.

More twitching of those lips. "That is not on Rebecca's meal plan."

Probably why they were shoved in the drawer in the first place. "How about receipts?" He snagged one at random. "Look, this says I spent twenty-two dollars and ninety-six cents on gas."

She giggled. "That is actually more telling than you probably suspect."

"Why's that?"

She snagged it, pointed at the total. "It means you're one of *them*."

"What do you mean by *them?*"

"Them being," she said, lips twitching, "one of those weirdos who fills up their car when it's only halfway empty."

He tilted his head to the side, and he studied her closely. "As opposed to what?"

She set the receipt down, closed the drawer. "As opposed to us normal folks who drive until we're on fumes and then begrudgingly hit up the gas station."

"That sounds stressful."

Amusement in those amber eyes. "I like to live dangerously." She laughed. "Okay, not so much. The truth is that I hate going to gas stations."

"Why?"

A shrug. "It just always seems like such a waste of time. The cheap places always have long lines, and then it takes forever to fill up your tank, but not long enough to be able to do anything productive like reading."

"Bookworm," he teased.

"Takes one to know one."

He laughed. "Also, not sure if you're aware, but you're obsessed with this concept of wasting."

She smiled up at him. "I like to be as frugal with my time as possible, is all."

Curiosity threaded through him like fibers weaving into a basket, coiling, wrapping around each, pulling taut. "And what does being frugal with your time consist of?"

Her gaze drifted to the ceiling as she considered the question. Then she glanced back down, her eyes meeting his, and it was as though he'd been struck by a cattle prod. Electricity flowed through his nerves, his muscles tightening, his body going stiff—okay, maybe that was just his cock.

"Keystrokes are the most important frugal use of my time," she said, "followed by doing my best to never drive during peak hours, thus wasting my free moments in traffic." She ticked off the items on her fingers. "Also, I never spend more than eight hours in bed, even if I can't sleep."

He'd circle back to that later—because there were many reasons to spend more than eight hours in bed, especially with a woman like Dani. Right now, he had to bite on something else she said. Lifting a brow, he asked, "Key . . . *strokes?*"

A chuckle bubbled up in her throat, and she sighed. "Seriously?"

He took her hand in his again, lacing their fingers together, tracing light patterns on the inside of her wrist. She shivered as he touched that sensitive skin, but she didn't pull away. In fact, she shifted a little closer. He sidled closer himself, until his body was a hairsbreadth from hers. Her skin smelled like strawberries, and he found himself drifting closer, wanting to taste it on his tongue.

Patience.

"So, you never laze in bed?"

She swallowed, and he traced the lines of her throat with his gaze. "No," she said. "I don't have any patience for it. Too much to do. Too many things in my brain that . . ." She trailed off.

"That what?"

"Too many things that only seem to come to the forefront of my mind when it's too quiet, when dark has taken over the world." She shook her head. "That sounds ridiculous, I know." A smile that didn't look right in the least. "Come on," she said, turning for the front door, "let's go get food."

"Sure," he said, keeping his tone deliberately light, wanting to tug her out of whatever had made her sad. He could tell she didn't trust him enough yet to share what had wounded her so deeply. Instead, he teased, "I'd be happy to go on a date with you."

She sputtered, spun back. "I—uh—"

"What's the matter? I'll be a cheap date when you're paying,

I promise." His lips curved. "Most of the time, I'm only allowed to eat vegetables."

Dani shook her head, eyes wide, and arms stuck straight out at her sides.

He walked to her, not stopping until his toes were millimeters from hers. "Dani?"

There was a bead of perspiration on her throat, sliding down beneath the neckline of her dress, down between a pair of some of the most gorgeous breasts he'd ever laid eyes on. He could see her pulse thrumming, just above her collarbone, a tiny fluttering of butterfly wings.

"I wasn't asking you out," she whispered.

"I know." He took a chance, bypassing the miniscule touches, the barely there brushes, and cupped her cheek. "I am," he said. "Asking you out. At some point in the future, when you're guaranteed to say, yes," he added when he saw the protest begin to gather on her face.

Her sigh coated his skin, and for a moment, she leaned into his hand, her body drifting close enough that the tips of her breasts whispered across his chest. "I don't know that I will," she breathed.

His hand flexed on her cheek. "I do," he said.

There was something between them. He felt it. *She* felt it.

The same *thing* that had prompted him to invade her car and go grocery shopping together. The same that had her lingering near him, her body leaning toward his. It was an invisible thread, slender and reedy, but it was the promise of something different than he'd ever experienced.

Something that had him pushing forward when he would have normally backed off.

Because Dani was different.

She drifted a little closer, her chest brushing his, those glorious breasts barely making contact. It was a fucking tease, that light contact, and the urge to yank her close was intense.

But instead of giving in to her, he shoved that down, stepped back, and asked, "Groceries?"

Her chest rose and fell, her cheek slipped from his hand, and . . . a trickle of ice slid down his spine.

Because eclipsing that thread was the refusal he saw in her eyes.

Fuck.

"Or if not groceries," he said quickly. "Then maybe—"

He froze when she touched him, her fingers combing lightly through his beard, sending prickles of sensation down his throat, his torso, unseen fingers wrapping around his cock and squeezing tight.

"It's soft," she whispered. "I expected it to be rough."

Ethan didn't dare move, not when she was touching him with such feather-like strokes, not when it felt so fucking good. Not when—

She stepped back.

"Groceries," she murmured.

He wanted to wind his fingers into those sleek brown curls, to haul her flush against him, and to kiss her until they were both reduced to ashes. To forget all about the need for oxygen and food and . . . whatever other things humans needed to survive.

But . . . groceries.

So, he stuck the bags under his arms and let Dani lead the way out the front door.

SEVEN

DANI

She stared at the bags of groceries on Ethan's arms, one after another hooked on his big arms like giant bracelets hanging from wrist to elbow.

"Mandy"—one of the Gold's trainers—"is going to kill me if you get hurt because you were carrying my groceries," she murmured.

"Mandy," he said, smiling up at her with that fucking gorgeous grin that never failed to turn her insides to jelly, "will understand that sometimes a man needs to take care of a woman—"

"How incredibly sexist of you," she said dryly.

And who knew that *she* could be dry? Well, not in the non-wet sense, because she spent the majority of her time in that non-wet manner (aside from Ethan's effects on her pussy . . . *ha*), but rather in a witty, sarcastic way. She was usually so worried about all the jumbled thoughts in her head getting mixed up and tangled, those lame, mismatched bits trying to escape and rendering her unable to form a sentence, let alone any banter or a droll comeback.

But with Ethan, it was different.

Somehow, all the voices in her head expounding on everything wrong with her, all the mistakes she'd made, the stupid things she'd said, the embarrassing stuff she'd done . . . quieted when she was with Ethan.

"—*he* cares about," he said, continuing his silliness about a man needing to take care of a woman he apparently cared about, "no matter if she's strong and capable enough to carry in her own groceries."

She crossed her arms. "And *your* groceries? Should I carry those in turn?"

"My groceries will survive my walk back to my place."

"You're going to *what?*"

"Walk," he said, pausing by the door to her condo and waiting while she unlocked the door and held it for him, after shifting the single paltry bag he'd "allowed" her to carry after she'd pitched a fit, in order to stick the key in the lock and open it.

Also, that was new.

The fit part.

That she somehow felt comfortable enough with Ethan that she could argue with him. Aside from her mom and dad and two sisters, she didn't argue with anyone. She kept her head down, tried not to draw attention to herself, and lived her life to the best of her ability.

No.

The last part was a lie.

She lived her life to the best of her ability to keep herself safe.

That was to say, she hid.

From nearly everyone and everything.

Long-term relationships? Hell, no.

Friendships? Few and far between. She considered herself

closest to Stephanie, or Fanny as she preferred to be called, who was the Gold's skating coach, but that was a new friendship, still fragile and building, and she wasn't sure she'd ever be able to open up enough to find the closeness a piece of her deep inside craved. Aside from Fanny, she'd even resisted being folded into the friend group of the Gold woman, until Mandy had physically dragged her to one of their girls' nights out.

She'd had a nice time, and the women were all awesome.

But it was already hard for her to get a word in edgewise in a normal conversation, let alone with a group of beautiful, successful, smart, and funny women who *weren't* shy.

Dani did better one-on-one, and she did even better when that one-on-one was with a person or people she knew—like her parents or her sisters.

It was easier to get a word in when she remembered that Toni had once puked all over the carpet because she'd eaten too many bowls of Cocoa Krispies, or that Loni (yes, her parents had a thing with names ending in I) had once nearly burned down the house because she wanted to teach her hamster to jump through a tiny flaming ring.

Also, let it be noted that no hamsters were harmed in the training of said trick.

The curtains in their living room, on the other hand, had been permanently scorched, and the paint—freshly done by their mom—hadn't fared much better.

She could easily talk when she remembered that her mom had once broken her big toe because she'd gotten so mad at the washing machine that she'd kicked the clear plastic circle on the front—not once, but three times. And she could tease her dad about his inability to start campfires, even when provided with accelerant, a lighter, and dry wood.

Because she had years of memories, the comfort of all that time, and the fact that they'd stuck by her when things went to absolute shit.

It was just the rest of the world she couldn't trust.

Maybe that made her pathetic, but she'd been burned deeply enough to not be willing to put her happiness and mental well-being on the line.

Better to live in the small, happy world she'd created.

But with Ethan—who had walked past her and into her tiny kitchen and was currently stacking the bags on the counter—she was tempted to make that world a little bigger. She wasn't . . . well, she wasn't exactly comfortable with him. *Definitely* not comfortable. Instead, she was—

What?

Uncomfortable? Yeah, sure.

But also intrigued by the gentle, quiet, tamed grizzly bear way he'd managed to draw her into conversation, entranced by his smile, the kindness in his eyes, utterly, hopelessly captivated by the pushy—and yet somehow still charming—way he'd hijacked her afternoon, coaxed her into shopping with him.

She couldn't remember the last time she'd relaxed enough with a person she hardly knew, let alone a *man* she didn't know well, to actually laugh with him.

But she'd laughed with him.

A lot.

While walking up and down the aisles of a grocery store.

And . . . she had liked it, liked laughing with Ethan, liked spending time with him, liked *him,* plain and simple.

Did she like him enough to want to expand her little bubble of safety?

Maybe . . .

Her heart twisted, convulsing rapidly, sweat sheening the back of her neck as she considered, as she wondered, as she *wanted*. But ultimately, her old habits were too ingrained.

No. She couldn't risk it.

Even if he was handsome and charming, pushy and as cuddly as a teddy bear, she couldn't just put everything she'd worked for on the line for one man, and most especially for a man she worked with.

That was . . . stupid.

And no, that wasn't disappointment coiling through her at her decision, sinking into her bones, making her hate that safety net she'd erected. It was sensible relief that she'd chosen to keep that barrier in place. It was. *Really*, it was. Sighing, she finally unstuck enough to move forward through the wide entrance to enter the kitchen, opening her mouth to tell Ethan that she'd drive him and his copious amounts of vegetables and plant-based proteins back to his house when she got out of her head enough to process what he was doing.

What. He. Was. *Doing*.

Her fridge was open, and he was stashing the groceries neatly inside. The junk food—more than normal, since she'd both panic-bought during the first half of their shopping extravaganza and then had thrown way more than she'd needed into her cart when he'd begun teasing her about killing herself with all that refined sugar.

Spite carbs, that was what she'd blown her grocery budget on.

But, she thought, eyeing the stash of cupcakes and chips and pretzels and cookies, the spite carbs were totally going to be worth it.

He had put away all those carbs—okay, well, he'd efficiently lined up all the boxes, bags, and trays of junk food—on her kitchen island, a veritable smorgasbord of delicious sugar and artificial flavorings.

"Dani?" he asked, turning from the fridge, a bag of apples (See? She didn't buy *only* spite carbs). "You okay?"

Her throat seized, a haze settling over her—a mix of terror, hope, being touched by the simple act, and then more fear, knowing this would only end one way, and desire. And still, all she wanted in that moment was to not care that she already knew how it would end.

She wanted to find the courage to see it out anyway.

All because a man put her groceries away.

She was fucked. Completely and utterly fucked. Because that bubble had expanded without her permission, had shot forward to encompass this man and . . . now circling back to the fact that. She. Was. *Fucked*.

So, no, she wasn't okay.

How could she possibly be okay?

She spun, hustled from the kitchen, moving—okay, *running* straight down the hall and out onto the tiny little patio that was beyond the back door. Her chest heaving, she leaned back against the cool wall and sank down into a crouch, gripping her hair.

She couldn't do this.

It was fucking reckless.

Playing Russian roulette with her heart, just offering it up for him to pull the trigger over and over again until the bullet would inevitably fly through the air and tear through the organ.

Like it had before.

Fingers on her wrists, gently but inexorably tugging them away from where they held her hair.

Ethan didn't say anything, but Dani's eyes were open, staring first at the ground, then at the toes of his boots peeking into her periphery. He didn't say anything, just waited. Probably for her to give him some explanation for why the sight of him putting away groceries had caused her to turn and run.

Disgust slid through her.

Hating that she was like this.

So freaking bad at life, at people, at . . . normal fucking human reactions.

"I'm not good at people."

The fingers on her wrists began moving, tracing slow, light

circles on her skin. It shouldn't be a sensitive spot, not when that area spent the majority of its time resting against a keyboard, but the gentle touches set her nerves firing, made goose bumps prickle and rise, the hairs on her nape lift.

"What do you mean, sweetheart?" It was a low, husky question, one said so carefully that it slid under her defenses, threaded its way right through the gaps in the mesh of her safety net.

She shook her head, tugged her wrists free of his hold.

Her skin tingled, even after his fingers slid off, a phantom imprint of his touch lingering long after he'd sat back onto his haunches and waited.

The silence stretched—a taut, uncomfortable thing— reminding her of trying to wrestle herself into a too-tight swimsuit in a dressing room, squirming and jumping, tugging and wiggling it up, until it finally engulfed her from shoulders to hips, squeezing tight on her lungs, her stomach. Nausea coursed through her, burned the back of her throat.

"For the record, I think you're doing just fine with people," he said.

Dani froze, then her gaze flew up to his. Laughter bubbled up inside her, escaping out through her nose in a semi-painful snort. She sank down further, her butt hitting the concrete of the patio, her head resting back against the house. "You're delusional if you could possibly think that I'm good with people."

"Just because you don't interact in the same way as others doesn't mean you're not good."

It took her a minute to puzzle that out.

Then her brows drew together, her head shook. "You really are delusional."

One half of his mouth quirked up, but his tone was easygoing as he sank down opposite her, matching her position on the concrete. Its coolness was seeping through the fabric of her dress, making her shiver, or maybe that was just because he rested his hand on her ankle.

"Okay?" he whispered.

Throat going dry, she thought about the contact, knew that she should say she wasn't okay with it, just out of principle. But . . . the truth was that his large, warm hand resting on the bare skin of her ankle felt nice.

More tendrils slipping in through the gaps in her net, winding their way around her insides, filling her with warm, fluffy cotton candy straight out of the machine. Sticky fingers, the puffed sugar melting rapidly on her tongue, its sweetness bleeding over her taste buds, sinking down into her stomach, and all of those dopamine receptors in her brain blazing happily to life.

"Dani?"

Still wrapped in that warm, fluffy dopamine feeling, she found herself nodding.

The other half of his mouth curved, joining the first. Then he stretched out, leaving his hand where it was, even as his legs bracketed hers.

Bare skin brushing hers, the rough velvet of hair-covered male legs making her shiver in the absolute best way.

"Cold?" he asked, eyes soft and curious.

Since she wasn't about to admit that she was ridiculously attracted to those legs, to the dark hair covering skin that was tanner than she'd expect for a man who spent the vast majority of his time indoors, she just simply said, "No." Then hurried to ask, "Do you spend a lot of time outdoors?"

His brows lifted, perfectly framing gray eyes that were such an interesting mix of the shade—steel-colored with faint streaks of blue, a charcoal outline around his pupil. He didn't comment on her staring, on her random question, just nodded and smiled again. "Yes, after freezing my ass off in an ice rink for most of the year, I really like soaking up the California sunshine." A beat. "Do you?"

Her teeth found her bottom lip, nibbling, a stupid fucking nervous habit that she hated, one she immediately pulled back on, releasing it as she shook her head. "You saw the pile of books I picked up from the library, what do you think?"

"I think," he said, his fingers flexing slightly on her ankle, sending heat curling through her, though he didn't move any closer, "that you are the type of woman who can do whatever you want, whether that's kicking ass behind the computer, hiking to the top of Mt. Shasta, sailing around the Bay, or just spending the night in the bath with a book and bottle of wine." He smiled. "And that slice of cold pizza."

She laughed, but it sounded off because shock had sliced its way through her at the words, at what this man thought she could do, what she might *like* to do. Was there ever a person, even her awesome family, who'd told her she could do everything? *No.* She was used to people putting her in a box, to hearing, "you're a nerd because you like to build computers and game the night away, so there's no way you'd want to scale a mountain or sail around a body of water." Maybe the bath, wine, and reading would fit into their preconceived notions, but the rest of it?

No.

Not so much.

And that wasn't even touching on the numerous microaggressions—and oftentimes the aggressions that *weren't* microsized—the real-life discrimination and hate that came from being a woman of color in this world.

Even if she put that aside and focused on her nerdy qualities, on the things she'd been bullied for, Dani had always figured the rest of world saw her as a woman they expected to have a trio of cats named Austen, Brontë, and Dickenson, and to have her *Harry Potter* house tattooed somewhere on her body. (Also, yes, she was a Hufflepuff and had a tiny badger inked on the arch of her foot, but her cat in high school had been named Nora, after the queen of romance, not the others. Neither of which were important to the topic at hand, except to say that she'd lived so long considering what the world thought of her, what box they tucked her neatly into, that it was both odd and refreshing to have a man seemingly allowing her the space to define herself).

It won't last.

Her inner voice was a major fucking buzz kill, even as she acknowledged that it was probably right.

There was a reason for her safety net.

A reason she'd decided to get really good at keeping her safety net intact.

Even aside from the bullying that came from being a girl interested in tech, and a Black girl at that, she'd been burned enough times by friends and love interests after high school to know that her inner buzz kill spoke the truth.

His interest wouldn't last. He would put expectations on her. He would try to make her fit into those, to act a certain way, would twist and change and . . . *hurt* her.

That was why this was so dangerous.

Why her longing, that bubble expanding, that safety net wanting to unravel . . . why all of them were so terrifying. Because she wanted to undo everything for Ethan. But what did he want in return?

The man hadn't paid her any notice for two years, and now, after a handful of conversations, a couple of touches, and a few hours together, she was ready to melt for him, to let him in.

If he really wanted her, why had it taken him so long to take notice of her?

Except . . . she wasn't exactly an open book, was she?

Keeping people well enough away from her was kind of Dani's superpower. Right up there with making things really freaking awkward.

Case in point? Now.

"I have a badger tattooed on my foot," she blurted.

His gaze dropped down, fingers sliding along her ankle. "Where—*ah*"—his finger swiped along the arch of her left foot —"I see it," he murmured. "He's cute." His hand stayed on her foot, brushing lightly over the inked animal. "So, you're a Hufflepuff?"

Swoon.

Fuck, this man was treacherous for her heart.

"What are you?" she asked.

His smile twined around her insides, squeezed tight. "You don't want to guess?"

She rolled her eyes. "I don't have to guess," she said. "Without a doubt, you're a Gryffindor."

That grin widened. "Nope."

Her brows rose, shock weaving through her for a second time. "You're not a Gryffindor."

A solemn shake of his head. "Nope."

Except . . . there was something on his face that prickled her instincts. "Oh my God," she said, sitting up. "You're messing with me." She tucked her knees under her, cupping his cheeks in her palms. "You're totally a Gryffindor."

His hands covered hers. "Yeah. I'm a regular lion."

"A grizzly bear," she murmured.

"What?"

"You're like a giant, cuddly bear, who—" His thumb traced lightly over her bottom lip when she stopped, breath sliding out.

"You're so beautiful," he whispered, his mouth coming close.

God, he was going to kiss her, and she wanted it so badly, and—

What if he's different?

He's not, she countered. *He can't be.*

She sat back and stood, his hands slipping from her face. "I should drive you home."

She wasn't going to look at him. She *couldn't*. Because she couldn't allow more seepage into her net, couldn't allow any additional melting or bubble-expanding. But for all her best intentions, her eyes were drawn back to his.

Protest in the gray depths had her steeling her spine.

He stood, took a step toward her. "I figured I'd call a Lyft," he said, near enough that she could feel the heat of his body. But he didn't touch her again, and she spent a moment processing the disappointment swelling in her like a balloon attached to a helium tank that wasn't shutting off.

Growing larger and larger.

At *her* for not being brave and opening herself up to new experiences. At him for making her want those new, dangerous life events.

Swelling, the latex growing dangerously thin.

He brushed a finger across her bottom lip, gray eyes searching hers. "Yeah, I'll call a Lyft."

Then he was gone.

And she found herself sinking back down onto the patio, listening for the front door to close behind him.

When it did, she tried to convince herself that the balloon inside her didn't *pop* in time to that soft *click*.

But all that convincing didn't make one bit of difference; regret flooded through her, sinking heavy through her limbs as the sun descended and she finally managed to push herself up from the patio, heading into the house and seeing . . . the pile of her books stacked neatly on her counter.

Junk food.

Books.

And . . . a bottle sitting on top of a note.

Thought of you when I saw this.

Hope you get to enjoy a bath tonight.
-E

Bubble bath.

She popped the top, inhaled.

Strawberries.

The same scent as the lotion she slathered on every morning because she absolutely loved the way it smelled.

And the same scent Ethan had noticed enough to buy the corresponding bubble bath.

Dani's eyes slid closed.

She wasn't disappointed. She wasn't. She *wasn't*.

Anyway, even if she was, she understood herself well enough to know she'd get over it.

EIGHT

ETHAN

The hit came out of nowhere, smashing him into the boards hard enough that all of the air squeezed out of his lungs, his shoulder colliding hard with the glass.

Everything went out of focus for a heartbeat, but then he was shoving the opposing player back, kicking the puck forward and out of his feet, getting it back on the blade of his stick and forcefully carrying it out of the zone.

They were on the penalty kill, down a goal late in the third, and their players were tired.

He needed to get the puck over that blue line, get it deep enough into the other zone that they could change for the second penalty kill unit—the next group of his teammates, who would try to kill off the other team's one-player advantage.

But they weren't going to make it easy on him as he bodily shoved himself forward.

A hard swipe of the fucker's—aka a player from the other team's—stick against his hands, sent a stinging pain crawling up his arms. He'd had much worse, though, so he didn't falter, successfully creeping up the final six inches and getting the puck out of the zone. Now, the other team had to all clear out, and they had a little breathing room. Enough at least for him to be able to glance up, to see Max streaking forward, looking not the least bit tired, even though he'd just worked his ass off in front of Brit's net.

Ethan banked the puck off the boards, tapping it around the player trying to intercept, unconsciously holding his breath until it was on Max's stick and his teammate was skating down the ice.

Then, even though his lungs were burning, he sprinted to the bench, allowing Coop to jump over the boards and join the rush. It was two-on-two, but then Blue joined in, exiting the box as the penalty ran out, and the Ducks made a bad change, and in a second, the Gold had numbers with their opponents scrambling to get back into their end of the ice.

A pass skipped over Blue's stick was scooped up by Coop, who made a move that was all kinds of illegal (in a strictly that-was-fucking-amazing and not that it-was-against-the-rules-of-the-game way). He crashed the net, faked a shot, and passed it back door to Blue, who didn't miss a beat as he slammed it home.

The crowd erupted, the walls of the Gold Mine seeming to vibrate with the roars of pride and happiness (and occasional boos from the few Ducks fans in the stands), and for a moment, Ethan wasn't present in the game.

He was wondering if Dani was able to hear the cheering deep in the bowels of the arena, where her office was located, if she'd seen the play, seen him working hard.

Pathetic.

Certainly.

But maybe if he couldn't win her over by hijacking her afternoon of reading and librarying, then maybe he could impress her with hockey skills.

She liked the sport.

Right?

He supposed she had to, given how much of it she watched.

Which brought him back to hoping she'd seen it, even though he knew that she was probably busily reviewing angles in case the goal was challenged, labeling different portions of the video feed for review later. He also knew that sometimes she ran behind the actual game play, using the commercial breaks to tag all the various things the coaches wanted earmarked so they could be pulled and stitched together after the game or in between periods.

Still, his ego wanting to be boosted aside, Ethan knew Dani was working her ass off right at the moment, so he pushed all thoughts of stroking (sweet Christ, why was he always thinking about stroking with that woman?) aside and glanced down at the screen placed beneath plexiglass below the bench, the goal replaying over and over again from various angles.

He watched Coop's move again—fuck that was sick—and then was surprised, his eyes drawn from the screen when Bernard, their head coach, tapped him on the shoulder with the rolled-up sheaf of papers he always carried when coaching. Considering he'd never seen Bernard look at them, Ethan thought it was the older man's version of a fidget spinner. Not that he'd ever voice that thought aloud. Players didn't rock the boat with their head coaches.

Or at least not players who wanted to actually get a decent amount of ice time.

He met his coach's gaze, forced away thoughts of fidget spinners.

Bernard nodded approvingly. "That was you." Another tap, and then he was back focusing on the rest of the team, talking with the ref, saying something into Calle's—their assistant coach, who had a killer mind for offense (and also Coop's wife)—ear before focusing back on the ice.

Which was what Ethan should be doing.

Except, now he wasn't just wondering if Dani had noticed his role in the play, but whether she'd caught Bernard giving him props—something that was rare with their typically quiet coach and something that had his post-goal grin widening.

Probably not.

She had a million things going on at once.

But when he happened to notice the camera on him, spotting part of his face on the monitors beneath his feet, he lifted his head, stared directly into that lens and winked.

Hopefully, it was so fast that no one but Dani would have seen—he doubted this but was prepared to take any teasing tossed his way, regardless—

The ref blew his whistle.

Ethan focused on the ice.

The puck dropped.

The game went on.

And all thoughts of winks disappeared, but the notion that Dani might be watching stayed in the back of his mind, had him skating harder for those final few minutes, had him working his ass off as they wound down and the play moved into overtime. It had him positioning himself in the right place at the right time when he took his turn, accepting a pass . . . and stuffing it past the goalie.

Then as the horn blared and the crowd cheered, as his teammates surrounded him for the requisite hug, her presence stayed there.

Maybe she hadn't seen the wink.

But hopefully, she had seen the goal.

NINE

DANI

A wink.

God, it should have been dorky as all hell.

But instead, she'd nearly swallowed her tongue, had almost gasped out loud, both somehow at the same time, which would have been critically embarrassing considering Jess was in the room with her.

She could hear how the conversation would go in her head.

Why are you choking on your gasps, oh boss of mine?

Because I'm a dumbass, who nearly swooned over a wink.

Of course, Jess would never call her *oh boss of mine*, but that was far from the point.

The point being, of course, that Ethan had winked.

At her.

And she'd gotten all fluttery inside.

"Fucking hell," she whispered.

Sliding, sliding down that slope, the rope of her safety net fraying more by the second.

"I know," Jess said, her eyes on the screen. "That move was incredible."

"Yes." She focused back on her job, filing the wink to deal with later, and then added, "Coop has great hands."

Jess grinned over her shoulder. "Too bad he's madly in love with Calle, because those hands"—she clasped her fingers together, air-kissed them, a la chef style—"though Ethan isn't too bad. I wouldn't mind feeling that beard between my thighs."

This time, Dani did choke on her gasp, coughing as she attempted to capture the continuing play. "That's"—*cough*—"not"—*cough*—"very"—*cough*—"professional."

Jess grinned. "I forgot we did that here."

Dani snorted. "You know I'm not mad, it's just . . ."

"Shitty and reductive?"

A shrug. "Maybe."

"Probably." She tossed another smile over her shoulder. "I'll be on my best behavior from here on out."

Another snort, mostly because Jess was never on her best behavior, and that was part of the reason it was so fun to spend hours in the booth with her. "You forget I know you."

"You forget . . ." She scowled. "You're right."

Dani laughed.

Then they both got back to work, playing catch up at times as they broke each play down into tiny bite-sized pieces to be consumed later. But by the end of the game—and after a really nice goal from Ethan—the Gold had won, and they were packing up.

"Nice work," she told Jess, as her assistant shrugged into her coat.

Jess nodded. "It'll still be nice to get an actual intern to help us with the busy work, but we've got a good system down."

"Agree completely," she said, running the clips through a backup program. "But I'm back to the drawing board on that after our last debacle."

"We'll be good until it's sorted."

And with that, they hashed out a few details for the next game—an away one—before Jess slipped out into the hall.

Dani, meanwhile, waited for the backup program to run, even though she didn't strictly need to, since it was all automated. But she wasn't quite ready to head out into the hall, on potential collision courses with men who winked at her.

At *her*.

Because it *had* been for her, right?

"I mean," she whispered, swiveling in her chair, running her fingers over the keyboard, and really wishing she hadn't already eaten her one box per day limit of Hot Tamales during the game. "We spent all day together yesterday. He said he wanted to date me. Who else could it have been for, if not me?"

"It was for you."

Her breath caught, and she swiveled in her chair. Ethan stood in the open doorway, freshly showered and looking all too tempting.

"What are you doing?" she asked, when he stepped inside and closed the wooden panel behind him.

"If it's my dorky ass wink that you're referring to, that is." He smiled, and her brain melted. Just like that.

"Ethan," she murmured.

He sat in Jess's chair, wheeled it close. "Do you have any video for me?"

"I—um—" She sucked in a breath, released it slowly. "I don't have any video for you. Jess took care of that tonight."

"Good." He rolled closer until his knees were on either side of hers. "You okay?"

She swallowed. "Why wouldn't I be?"

"You were upset yesterday," he murmured.

No, she had been overwhelmed yesterday, frustrated at herself, scared that she liked this man so much.

That was the painful and unhappy truth.

She was the problem, not him.

"I wasn't upset at you."

He slid a little closer. "I know."

And . . . silence.

Good times. Happy times. Fucking awkward times.

"I'm not going to ask you out again," he began, causing her eyes to fly up from the pale pink she'd painted on her fingernails, matching the color he'd mentioned liking on her so-called cute toes. He wasn't going to ask her out? But what if she wanted him to?

Wanted him to?

Fucking hell.

She needed to get her head in shape before she even began considering whether or not she wanted the man to ask her, and how she might answer him, how fucking awkward she would be on a date if she *did* happen to agree to go with him.

God, because if she agreed to go out with him, then she would have to consider what she wore, what she said, what she—

"Would you kiss me?"

His gray eyes widened, the pink tip of his tongue darted out and tasted his bottom lip. "Dani?"

She shoved her chair back, stood, and moved to the door, intending to yank it open, to create an escape route—although her fuzzy brain wasn't telling her if it was an escape route for him or for herself—but then Ethan was there. Right there, pressing her front into the wood, his chest and torso hot and hard where it brushed her spine.

"Do you want me to kiss you, sweetheart?" he breathed into her ear, the bristles of his beard running over her jaw, making her shiver.

"I—I didn't mean now."

"No?" He rested his hand near her head, his hips resting heavier against hers.

"N-no," she murmured. "I meant on a date."

He inhaled sharply, body going still. "Yes, baby, I'd most definitely try to get a kiss, if you agreed to go out with me." The words were hot and damp, reminding her of other parts of her body that were hot and damp, reminding her of parts of *his* body that could play nice with those hot and damp parts of hers.

His lips brushed lightly over her skin, and then she didn't have to imagine what the prickles of his beard would feel like.

Glorious, was the answer.

The stubble had gooseflesh rising on her nape, had her hips arching back and pressing against the hard jut of his erection.

"Fuck, Dani," he murmured, that beard sliding lower, his lips trailing along her throat. "You are so fucking sexy."

"I—" She didn't know what she was planning on saying, probably something mood-killing about how she wasn't sexy, how she was too fat and frumpy and too fucking shy to be sexy.

But then he . . . sucked.

His lips pursed on her skin, sucked lightly, and Dani could have sworn that she melted—just turned right into an ice cream encountering the mid-summer sun, turning into a puddle as it dripped down its cone.

"Will you go out with me now?" he murmured.

Her hands clenched, and for a moment she didn't process that she'd reached behind her, was grasping onto his neck and shoulder, her breasts lifted, pleading for his attention, her fingers of one hand plunging into his hair, those on the other digging into the hard muscle of his deltoid.

"I—"

His hips were flush to her ass, his cock hard, and she grew even wetter as his hand trailed up her side, stopped just beneath where she wanted it, fingers running lightly over the bottom edge of her bra.

He nipped at the spot where her shoulder met her throat, and she jumped, spinning in his hold, wanting to see his face, needing to deduce what was in his expression. In the blink of an eye, the move had her against him, had her front pressed to his front, and fuck having an up close and personal view (and touch) of Ethan Korhonen was a damned good thing.

"Is that a yes—"

A knock interrupted his question.

"Ignore it," he whispered, his fingers tugging the collar of her shirt to the side, his lips and tongue and beard driving her slowly insane.

"Dani?" A voice called.

Except, it wasn't just *a* voice. It was Fanny.

Nosy, pushy Fanny.

Ethan cursed, pushed off her, plunking into a chair and somehow able to look cool, calm, and collected, even though she was still that cone full of melted ice cream, liquid leaking out of her and turning into a puddle.

Another knock.

Ethan pushed out of the chair, took Dani's hand and led her to her seat, pressing her down into it. "It's unlocked," he called, picking up a tablet and appearing in an instant as though he hadn't just been practicing giving her hickeys on her neck.

The handle turned, and Fanny came in, her gaze alighting on Ethan and then Dani, brows raising into sharp little rainbows on her forehead. "Am I interrupting?"

Ethan stood. "Nope," he said, voice calm and friendly. "I'm just returning this." He held the tablet out to her, his expression relaxed, though when his gaze met Dani's, his eyes held a heat.

One that she knew was mirrored in her own.

Then he was gone, and she was trying to convince herself that she wasn't disappointed she hadn't gotten to answer him, hadn't felt that stubble on her lips.

Nope.

Not disappointed.

Relieved.

That was what the sharp, jabbing pain in her heart felt like.

Relief.

Yup.

Yup.

Fanny sat in the chair Ethan had just vacated, and Dani felt a bolt of annoyance that her friend was there instead of the man she was lusting after. But then Fanny began expounding on her latest exploits as a thirty-something woman trying to find a man who wasn't a total freaking loser and . . . seriously, she could relate.

Except . . . Ethan wasn't a loser.

So, yeah, she was disappointed and annoyed—at herself.

Stifling a sigh, she tuned into Fanny's words, knew that she owed it to her one friend to pay attention.

But it was a struggle.

Because she couldn't help but feel that she was utterly, royally fucked to the moon and back.

But it'll be a fun, fun ride, her inner daredevil—the one that was usually stifled by her anxiety, her fear—said.

Until it's not, the sane part of her countered. *Until it's not.*

TEN

ETHAN

I t was almost time to get on the ice.

It was their last match at the Gold Mine before a six-game road stretch. Not that Ethan minded the trip. He wasn't leaving his family behind or a significant other. Actually, the whole trip was a net positive for him because his parents were coming to the game in Baltimore, and he was excited that he'd be able to hang with them for a day. Usually, the team only played their Eastern Conference opponents twice during a season, so he was glad his parents could make it out for one of the match-ups.

Not that he was like a little kid desperate for them to come and watch.

Rather . . . he was like a little kid excited to show off his new toy—and that toy was *not* Dani (she'd be fucking terrified if it was, though he couldn't deny he hoped to at some point get her comfortable enough to be folded into the Korhonen crew). Instead, his excitement was because he was with a team who valued him, who gave him ice time and the opportunity to play, and his parents would see that. It didn't matter how many games they'd already come to over the course of his career (and they made it to a half-dozen a year), Ethan still got a thrill from them watching him play in a *Gold* game.

They weren't coming to watch him sit on the bench like teams past.

They'd see him living his dream, on the ice, hopefully making a positive difference for the team.

They'd see him doing something productive, something *important*. Though not as important as their jobs, their teaching and research, at least when he was on the ice and not warming the bench, he was actually doing something that came close to the value they brought.

Which was why as much as he wanted to get his degree, as much as he knew that he was smart and capable of getting *that* degree, he'd always had a hard time reconciling what he did with what his parents did. They loved him, he'd never doubted that. It was just . . . sometimes being the jock son of two renowned professors made him feel like he was a pair of sneakers amongst a whole row of expensive high heels.

Couldn't measure up.

Didn't measure up.

Wouldn't *ever* measure up.

Smothering that feeling, shoving it deep down where it managed to live most of the time, he slammed his car door shut and started for the arena, but then his nape prickled, and he slowed, turning back toward a row of cars on the far end of the lot.

Because his inner Dani detector was ringing.

He walked over to her, watching for a moment as she wrestled with a series of bags in her trunk. Then he moved closer, some part of him pleased when she froze and rotated to face him. No surprise on her face, just expectation. "Ethan," she murmured, her eyes meeting his and flitting away.

He'd had his mouth and hands on her, knew how silken her

skin was, knew that she tasted of strawberries and cream. "Let me get those for you."

"Oh, no—"

Ignoring her, he hefted the totes, surprised to find they were so heavy. "What's in these?" he joked lamely. "Bricks?"

"Actually," she said, trailing off, her lips quirking up.

"Wh—" He peeked inside one of the bags, knowing it was rude but doing it anyway, and saw that while there weren't bricks within the sturdy canvas, there *were* rocks. Lots and lots of rocks.

She opened the one light bag he hadn't managed to wrestle away from her, showing him that inside were a few bottles of paint, along with some brushes. "PR-Rebecca had a doctor's appointment, so I offered to pick up the supplies for the newest Miner's Club activity.

Miner's Club was a group for any kid thirteen and under who was a Gold fan, and the PR and Community Outreach teams worked together to have fun crafts and activities in the concourse before puck drop for every home game. The kids loved it, and they especially loved that a lot of the projects they worked on ended up in the community.

Case in point, Dani saying, "They're painting rocks that will line the walkway of the new senior center."

"Make sure to slip in a few Gold logo rocks," he said lightly.

"You have any doubt that PR-Rebecca doesn't already have that planned out?"

He laughed, waited while she closed the trunk and locked her car. "Do I look like an idiot?" A grin. "I'd never doubt PR-Rebecca."

Dani stopped, eyes locking onto his. "No," she said. "You don't look like an idiot, you look like—"

She pressed her lips together.

He was dying for her to finish that statement, but a muscle in her jaw was clenching, her gaze deliberately turned away.

"What are you going to paint on your rock?"

Her fingers played with the strap on the bag and as they approached the door to the arena, he thought she wouldn't answer. But then she did, her voice quiet but steady. "What makes you think I haven't already painted some?" She reached into one of the bags, pulled out a rock about the size of her palm. "Here," she said, holding it up. "This one is my favorite."

The pale gray stone had been painted a bright white, several turquoise and blue flowers covering its front and back.

It reminded him of her dress from the library, the gleaming umber skin, the bright pink of her toes, the way it had felt to touch her, even if it had just been on her ankle.

He wanted it.

Wanted to take it from her hand and shove it in his pocket and to never, ever give it back.

But . . . he wasn't about to steal from senior citizens.

"There. You see?" she asked, her hand closing around the rock and tugging the door open. "I did a mediocre job throwing a few examples together so that Rebecca wouldn't have to." A smile as she waited for him to pass her. "I get my gold—no pun intended—star for the day."

"I didn't think techies liked arts and crafts time."

"Are you kidding?" she exclaimed. "We love arts and crafts time, or at least this techie does." A shrug. "Anyway, it was nice to do something that wasn't screen-related, at least for a little bit."

"It's beautiful," he told her truthfully.

Her stare came to his, held. "I don't know about beautiful," she said. "But I like drawing anyway."

"*You're* beautiful." Despite the bags, he managed to brush her fingers with his.

"Eth—"

He stepped closer, ignoring the fact they were standing in the doorway, blocking the entrance that any number of people needed to use, a doorway in which any number of those people could stumble upon them, all of whom would certainly spread the news about how they'd seen him mooning over Dani right where anyone could see.

But he found he didn't care.

Not with the scent of strawberries on her skin wafting up to tease his nose. Not with her eyes on his. Not with her adorable nose and kissable lips and the heat of her body very close to his.

The only thing he *didn't* care for was that his hands were full.

He couldn't touch her properly, couldn't tug her close, couldn't stroke them over her body, couldn't—

"What are we talking about?" Max.

Ethan held back a groan, shifting forward so he was out of the doorway, even as Dani all but jumped out of her skin in order to dart out of Max's path. "We're just delivering supplies for PR-Rebecca's Miner's Club project," he said calmly before she could sprint down the hall. "She's the brain. I'm the brawn."

Max chuckled, patted him on the arm. "Every once in a while, you can be amusing."

"And you try so hard but never actually succeed at it."

Dani chuckled.

Max clamped his hand over his chest. "I'm wounded."

"You'd have to have a heart for that," Ethan grumbled.

"Oof," Max said. "I'm doubly wounded."

"Liar."

"True." A beat. "Except about the heart stuff. Mine is huge, some might even say big and juicy, like *someone's*"—he took advantage of Ethan's full hands to scrub one of his over the top of Ethan's head and mess up his hair—"big, ole juicy brain."

Ethan managed to whack him in the kidney with one of the bags, which he considered a successful response to all the big and juicy stuff.

"Oof," Max groaned, hand pressing against his back. "You wound me."

"I *can* wound you," Ethan muttered.

"Children," Mandy warned. "What are you arguing about?"

"Ethan's trying to hurt himself," Max whined, "by carrying heavy stuff before game time."

Mandy glanced at the bags then at Dani, who at that moment stopped trying to melt into the wall and instead jumped into action by trying to snag the load from him. He held onto the bags, ignoring her efforts even as Mandy snorted. "Seriously?" the trainer asked. "*That's* what you're coming at me with?" She tapped her finger to her chin. "I think it's a thigh massage for you."

Max paled, and Ethan didn't blame the man. For one, Mandy's thigh massages were strictly for medical purposes and weren't what most of the populace would consider relaxing. Rather, they were beyond firm, beyond deep tissue, and more than a little painful—she called them physical therapy with a purpose, and that purpose seemed to be torturing. For another, the person who actually gave them—the team's masseuse, Darby —was tiny but with freakishly strong hands.

Hence the talk of torturing.

At that moment, however, Mandy was doing less torturing and more snooping. She moved toward him, peeked into the bags. "Oh, is this for the rock activity?" She released them, walking next to him as they continued down the hall. "Madeline"—her daughter—"is all about the need to get paint *everywhere.*"

Dani's throat worked, but Ethan didn't rush her—and to their credit, neither did Mandy or Max—each just waited as they strode through the hallways winding through the underbelly of the arena. "I put together a bag for the team kids to be taken up to the Family Suite," Dani eventually said, gaze flicking to his, then to Mandy's. "It's the one with the otter on the front."

Ethan's heart squeezed.

Lovely woman.

"Aw," Mandy said. "You're amazing. They're going to love that."

A shrug. "I know it's a little hard for the team kids to get upstairs sometimes, especially when they don't want to take away from anyone else's experience."

That was true.

It sometimes put the players' kids in an awkward situation, wanting to participate in the fun but not wanting to be seen as taking something away from the other kids.

"Anyway, I thought they'd enjoy it, so I figured I'd make it easy for them to participate," she finished.

"You're sweet," Mandy said, reaching across Ethan and squeezing her hand. "Do you want to take the bag up yourself?" Dani's feet faltered, and with Mandy's arm still extended in front of him, he was nearly clotheslined. Luckily, he stopped just in time, bags swinging forward and back.

"No," she whispered. "I—I—" A breath as she fumbled. "No, I've got stuff . . ."

"I can bring it up and give it to the babysitter who's in charge tonight?" Mandy asked when Dani trailed off. "Would that be easier?"

Gentle had crept into Mandy's tone, and he watched as it flowed through the air, as Dani processed it, her shoulders going stiff, her chin lifting. "No," she said, "I can take it."

"Are you sure?"

That chin rose further, and Ethan could have sworn that he heard her teeth clack together. "I'm sure."

Mandy nodded, pulled her hand back, and they began peeling off—Max into the gym for a pregame workout, Mandy into the training suite.

"Where do we need to take this?" he asked once they were alone.

"PR-Rebecca's office." A clipped statement. "Then the otter bag upstairs."

"Do you want me—"

"I *said*, I was going to take it up."

He stepped in front of her, forcing her to stop. "I was going to ask if you wanted to take the otter bag up while I dropped the other stuff off to Rebecca."

She skittered to a stop right in front of him, and he jerked to a halt, the bags colliding first against his body then against hers. "Oof," he muttered as rocks jabbed into his hip.

Dani winced. "Sorry," she whispered.

"No, I'm sorry. You okay?"

She shook her head. "I'm a mess."

"Because of me or the rocks?"

More halting, more shaking off her head. "Because . . ." A sigh. "Of me."

He studied her face, not liking the tinge of misery creeping into the edges of her eyes, clouding the amber and russet with cool steel, pulling those plush lips flat. "Well, if it counts for anything, I think you're a gorgeous mess."

She glanced down at herself, made a face. "I'm in jeans, a baggy fleece, and no makeup."

He set the bags down, tapped her temple. "I meant in here."

Laughter bubbled up in her throat, burst out from those kissable lips. "How in God's name could you possibly think that I'm beautiful in my head?" She threw up her free hand, the bag on her wrist keeping her other at her side. "That mess I'm talking about is *in* my head. I'm so screwed up from stuff I should be over that it's not even funny."

ELEVEN

DANI

One second, she was standing in the hall, readying to spill her guts to Ethan, and the next, the bags were on the floor, including the one hanging on her wrist. Before she could even suck in another breath, she found herself with her spine pressed to the cool wall, Ethan to her front.

And it was glorious.

It reminded her of the almost-kiss.

Reminded her of his mouth on her throat, his hands on her body.

"You don't have to justify the way you feel to anyone. Your past, painful or not, is what makes you Dani." His head dropped. "And from what I know of Dani, you're pretty fucking special."

Was it possible for her heart to beat its way out of her chest? Because with his silken voice in her ear, with the gruff *pretty fucking special* reverberating through her body like a ping pong ball zipping from rib to rib, it felt on the verge of doing so. Three words and she was ready to spill her guts—

No.

She'd been ready to spill her guts before.

Now, she was ready to let him in, to allow that safety net to peel back and take up trapeze as a hobby.

And *that* had her heart pounding for a whole other reason.

"I'm just Dani," she whispered.

"I know," he murmured, cupping her cheek, brushing his thumb over her bottom lip. "*Just Dani*, I really want to kiss you right now."

Her inhale was a sharp stake driving into the ground, or maybe the gasp one takes right before letting go of the trapeze bar and leaping to the next. "I'm—"

Voices trailed down the hall, echoing through the mostly concrete space, snapping her out of her Ethan haze—and seriously, the man was fucking dangerous to her mental aptitude.

He didn't move, just leaned his hips a little heavier against her, and she felt his erection, hard and unyielding and so fucking tempting, pressing into her stomach, before his mouth dipped down and and he whispered roughly in her ear, "Tell me you're dying to have my mouth on yours, sweetheart. Tell me that you're wet, that you're aching for me as much as I'm aching for you."

Her eyes flew up, caught the storm in his, his desire lightning strikes through the deep gray. "Ethan," she breathed.

Because . . .

Yes, to *all* that.

The need, the aching . . . the wet.

She wanted him more than she'd ever wanted anyone, and that was less about her and more about the invisible, persistent thread that connected them, a spool that wound tighter and tighter until—

His hand clenched on her hip.

His mouth came closer. "Do you want me?"

"Yes," she murmured and watched his features tighten, his eyes spark, his lips move—

The voices drew nearer.

"Fuck," he cursed and shoved back, bending to snatch the bags up just as Blue and Coop came around the corner. Brows lifted, probably because she was still against the wall, her chest heaving, hand pressed over her heart. "Here." He shoved two bags at Coop, another two at Blue. "Bring these to PR-Rebecca's office."

Blue opened his mouth.

Ethan pointed at him. "Not today, kid."

"You realize that we're the same age, right?"

"I'm older," Ethan grunted.

"Barely," Blue countered, but then he shut up, hefted the bags, and turned around, heading back where he'd come from.

Coop hesitated, a bag in each hand, eyes on Dani's.

She nodded.

One half of his mouth turned up.

And then he, too, headed for Rebecca's office, the bags clutched in huge, capable hands. Ethan slipped the otter one around her wrist, patted her hip, gaze still scorching, still making her ache to have his lips on hers. "Take these upstairs before we get caught making out in the hall like teenagers."

She wrapped her fingers around the strap and nodded, unabashedly watching him grab the final two bags, his strong, powerful thighs stretching the fabric of his slacks, his ass perfectly accented against the thin gray fabric.

She'd said it before, and she'd say it a hundred times more.

Hockey players had the best asses.

He turned, suddenly very close again, his voice the best kind of husky, his beard brushing her jaw, teasing her skin, need coiling inside her like a taut hose refusing to stay in place. Instead, it kept bursting forward, causing her fingers to tingle, her breath to catch, her thighs to clench.

His lips pressed . . . to her forehead. "I'll see you after the game?"

A shuddering breath, her bones threatening to melt.

"Dani?" he asked when she just stared.

She managed a nod.

That got her a sexy smile before he turned and headed down the hall, giving her another glimpse of his gorgeous ass as he went.

She was seeing him after the game.

Squee!

Shit.

But . . . *squee!*

Also, best. Asses. Ever.

Also, she bit the inside of her lip, watched as he turned the corner, hoping he liked what she'd put in his pocket.

———

She was riding high from the near kiss in the hall, the memories that normally made her cling tight to her safety net easing, fading into the background where they belonged. So much so that the anxiety that usually gripped her when dealing with people hadn't swarmed up and overwhelmed her as she'd walked into the Family Suite.

Kids and wives, fiancés and girlfriends filled the room with a kind of happy cacophony.

"Dani!" Sara called as the door closed behind her. "It's so good to see you!"

Sara was married to Mike Stewart and was close to Brit and PR-Rebecca. Dani had met her on more than one occasion, and the former figure skater was a genuinely nice person.

Today, Sara set down her pencil and sketchpad (she was also a talented artist) and crossed over to Dani, taking her hands. "How are you?"

Warm.

Sara was just really nice and warm.

"I'm good," she said. "I just brought some craft supplies from the Miner's Club for the kiddos."

A squeeze of her hands. "You're so sweet." Sara's smile had garnered many a sponsorship. "Do you want me to get it set up so you can go get ready for the game? I'm sure you have better things to do than wrangling team kiddos."

"Oh, um, sure," Dani said, relinquishing the bag, a sliver of disappointment sliding through her. She'd thought to hang out a little bit. She wasn't needed downstairs quite yet, and kids were always easy. Honest to a fault, but mostly a judgment-free zone.

Mostly judgment free because the last time she'd been up here, Aiden—Blue and Anna's son—had told Dani that she needed to relax her face, otherwise she'd get wrinkles.

Kids.

Back to the whole honest to a fault thing.

Sara stopped, eyes gentle. She was intuitive and probably reading too much into that tiny bit of displeasure Dani felt. "Or you can stay and—"

"It's fine." Dani smiled. "I really should get ready for the game."

And great, now there was regret in Sara's eyes.

God, why did she have to be so bad with people?

"Or maybe I could stay for a little?" she asked. "That way I can help you get them over their initial excitement."

Sara smiled again, the regret softening into amusement. "I'm sure you can picture me covered with approximately a hundred palm prints."

Dani's lips twitched. "Maybe."

Sara linked her arm with Dani's. "Come on, we'll use the old table." Thus called because it *was* old, but also because it was stained from years of similar craft projects, crayon marks, and matchbox cars driving over its deep oak finish. "Oh! And I want to introduce you to someone. Roxanne!" She waved her hand, and a slender blond spun to reveal a startlingly beautiful face. Her hair was styled to perfection, soft waves cascading down narrow shoulders, stopping just before gently curved hips. "Come here. I want you to meet Dani. She's the video coach for the team."

Roxanne's hand felt like actual velvet as it brushed Dani's, and she noticed that even Roxanne's nails were perfectly shaped, her nude nail polish impeccable.

They matched the rest of her outfit—crisp jeans with red flats, a shimmery beige and peach floral blouse. She was beautiful and feminine and effortlessly coiffed in a way that Dani knew she never would achieve.

"Hi, Dani," Roxanne said. "It's so nice to meet you. I was actually reading an article about video coaches last week. I didn't realize how much went into it."

"Oh, it's just a job."

Roxanne's brows rose, and Dani realized what that sounded like.

"I mean, I—" She sucked in a breath. "It has good and bad parts, you know. But I really do love it."

"I hear that," Roxanne said with a laugh.

This should have been the point in the conversation where awkward silence descended, but instead, Roxanne asked Dani a few easy questions, mostly about work, which was lucky for the other woman since Dani was most comfortable when talking about programs and editing equipment. Well, lucky was relative, she supposed. Lucky in this case meaning there wasn't awkward silence, but not so lucky as to not have to listen to Dani prattle on.

But during the few minutes they spoke, Roxanne didn't give one indication that she was bored to tears and desperate to escape.

Instead, she asked several intuitive questions.

"I'm a bit of a computer geek," Roxanne said when Dani looked at her with surprise. "I've been spending my spare time building a P.C." God, even her blush was fucking adorable, tiny pink swathes on each cheekbone, as was her self-conscious chuckle. "No wonder I'm single, huh?"

She turned when Aiden ran up to her, wrapped his arms around her waist. "Roxy!"

"Hey, little one," she said, crouching and beginning to speak to him quietly.

"Roxanne works at the gallery," Sara whispered into Dani's ear as they talked. "I'm going to—*oof!*" Madeline darted over and began begging to see what was in the bag. "Just a second, honey," she told Mandy's daughter. "Yes, it's a craft project that Dani brought."

"Crafts!" Madeline squealed.

Mandy had trailed her daughter across the room, snagging the tote from Sara and laughing. "Yeah, baby." She held up the bag. "The supplies are in here. We just have to go to the old table and get everything set up."

"I've got it," Roxanne said, standing when Aiden ran off again. "I can get things set up so you two can enjoy your chat."

"I—" Dani began.

But without any trace of awkward, Roxanne took Madeline's hand and led her to the table, easily getting everything spread out, even as more kiddos found their way into the supplies. In even movements, her musical voice trailing across the room, her smile bright as the lights inside the arena, she got each kid setup with a plate, a rock, brushes, and paint and didn't even get a speck on her.

Effortless. Again.

So freaking much that Dani should hate her, strictly on principle.

But she couldn't.

Because Roxanne seemed like a really nice person.

"I'll catch you guys later," Mandy said, moving to help Roxanne when a few of the boys thought it was a good idea to chase each other with paintbrushes . . . loaded full of paint.

"I'm going to set her up with Ethan," Sara said quietly.

Scratch that.

She hated Roxanne. She was the worst with her flawless hair and body and smile and no awkward in sight and—

"Isn't she just perfect for him?" Sara said. "I know he's a little scruffy, but he cleans up nice, and they're both just so nice. I can already picture tiny little blond babies with Ethan's gray eyes. They'll be adorable."

Dani's heart twisted and filled with lead, growing heavy, sinking to the bottom of the ocean.

Ocean of despair that was.

The past was weighty, intense, reaching up and sinking its talons deep, reminding her of everything that was wrong with her.

And everything that was right with Roxanne, a woman she hardly knew, and yet a woman she knew would be—

"Dani?"

Perfect.

Beautiful and flawless and *perfect* for Ethan.

The pressure on the seabed compressed her heart, squeezing it on all sides, squashing the organ, forcing out the hope she'd stashed there after her conversation with Ethan.

Wisps flitting away into dark water.

Her heart crumpled smaller and smaller, until she felt nothing.

Nothing except for pain and the urge to clutch her safety net closed.

This was why she didn't let people in.

Because Roxanne was lovely and perfect for Ethan, so much more than Dani could ever hope to be, and her only consolation was that if it hurt this much after a couple of conversations and a near kiss, then she was lucky to have been reminded of it now and not when she was in deeper and—

Fingers on her arm. "Dani?" Sara asked. "Are you okay?"

She shook herself. "S-sorry," she said hurriedly. "I just remembered that I needed to meet with Jess before the game." She edged away from Sara before the other woman could see how deeply the thought of Ethan with anyone else hurt. That was a ridiculous thought. He'd asked her out on one date, and she hadn't even agreed to that much.

He was much better off with a woman like Roxanne than her.

That was just reality.

And if she was in the way, she would deny Ethan his chance at perfect.

She couldn't do that. She . . . *fuck*, but she liked him too much to do that.

Perhaps, if her misery wasn't so heavy and forbidding, perhaps if she wasn't already on that seabed, water and pressure on all sides crushing her, she might have been able to recognize that Ethan could choose to be with who he liked.

Perhaps, if Roxanne just wasn't so freaking perfect, Dani might have seen past the wretchedness that had swept up and was smothering her.

But Roxanne *was* perfect and lovely.

And Dani wasn't good at shrugging off her insecurities.

"I should go," she said.

"Are you sure you're okay?" Sara asked.

A smile, one that felt and probably looked forced. "Just peachy."

Sara's expression darkened. "Are—"

Desperate times called for desperate measures. She patted her pocket, pulled out her cell and glanced at the screen. "Oh, that's Jess, I'd better run."

Sara opened her mouth, protest all over her expression, but

Dani put words to action and hustled out the door of the Family Suite. Her face felt hot, and her pulse scattered. God, her lungs weren't working. She couldn't pull in enough air, couldn't breathe.

She jabbed at the elevator button and managed to suck in just enough oxygen to stumble down the hall and into her office.

Then she closed the door, threw the lock, and sank into her chair, thinking how lucky she was to have had this close call.

Otherwise, she might have really gotten hurt.

Yup, she was really lucky.

"Definitely lucky," she whispered.

And if there were tears streaking down her cheeks, then she was just going to ignore them.

God knew, it wasn't the first time.

Twelve

ETHAN

I t took until he got into the locker room and sat down at his cubby before he felt it.

It being Dani's rock, he realized as he reached into his pocket and pulled out the hard object that was jabbing him in the thigh.

Sparks skating down his spine, tiny fireflies floating in his blood as he stroked a finger over the smoothly painted surface. Turquoise flowers and pink toes, glasses sliding down a nose, soft fingers on his jaw.

Want tearing him up inside, need stitching him back together.

God, he was in deep for that woman.

Noise gathered at the door, Coop and Max chatting as they came in, their gazes coming immediately to him, and he knew the gossip train was fully boarded and awaiting departure to its next destination.

As quickly—and slyly—as he could, he stashed the rock in his backpack and set about getting ready for the game.

A quick workout, stretching, copious amounts of foam-rolling, and then finally, at the last possible minute (a fact that used to drive his coaches to worry) getting dressed. But there was a method to his madness. He only got his gear on when he was in the right frame of mind.

Game time.

Or, he thought with an inner snort, *was it game* mind?

Decisions, decisions.

"Someone looks happy," Max said, sitting next to him, literally rocking the boat (bench) with his nosy enthusiasm. "I'm guessing this has to do with a certain shy female, who was looking at you like you're wielding Mjölnir."

Ethan waited for there to be more information in that sentence. When it didn't come, he said, "I think you underestimate my nerdiness."

"Right," Max said. "You're the career student who hasn't had the chance to learn all the important things." A beat. "Like Marvel."

Tugging on his T-shirt, he raised his brows.

"As in one certain blond-haired hero."

More brow-raising.

"As in Thor."

"Ah," he said, loving the irritation and disbelief creeping onto Max's face right now, as if he couldn't believe that someone hadn't heard of Thor and the movies. Ethan knew of both, had watched them, actually, since he did occasionally do something that wasn't book-related, but it was about fucking time that Max got a taste of his own brand of humor (that being mostly annoying and only somewhat funny). "We're talking about Norse mythology now."

Max choked for a moment then recovered. "We're talking about summoning lightning bolts from the sky, kicking ass with a giant hammer, and—" He stopped, probably because Ethan had little to no poker face. "You're fucking with me."

"'Bout time someone does."

Brit.

He glanced up.

She winked. "You boys running with me today?"

"God, no," Ethan said. "I want to have legs for the game."

Brit's pre- and post-game workouts were famous . . . or perhaps infamous was more accurate. She was fast, could run like hell, and no matter how hard Ethan pushed during the workout or trained beforehand, he never could catch up with her. The woman was like liquid lightning, graceful and effortless as she all but flew up and down the steps lining the arena.

"Baby," she grumbled. "Max?"

"Ditto what the Big, Juicy Brain said. Legs. Game. Don't wanna die."

She frowned, sighed heavily. "I miss Stefan. He always ran with me."

"Run with your boyfriend on your own time," Max grumbled. "God knows the man must be glutton for punishment, considering he's the only one who ever comes close to catching you."

Brit blew on her knuckles, buffed them on her shoulder. "That's how he put a ring on it."

Max snorted.

Ethan grinned, just as Coop and Blue strolled up, workout gear on. Those two, apparently, were gluttons for punishment.

"Ready?" Coop asked.

"These two"—Brit waved a hand at the pair—"are real men." Her voice rose. "Just in case anyone was looking for them." Boos and hisses abounded, along with a few rolled-up socks tossed in her direction. Which she caught effortlessly because she had that killer glove hand. "Later, losers," she called, throwing them back.

Ethan grinned, shook his head, and got ready for the game.

His way.

Though he found himself adding one new ritual.

Brushing his thumb over the rock Dani had painted and remembering the feel of strawberry-scented skin.

Yeah, life was good.

———

The game went great.

One of those perfect matchups where the system worked, bounces went their way, and they won handily in front of a kick-ass home crowd.

He'd skated hard, done his job, coming off the ice on a high that would take several hours to come down from.

Of course, he had one thought of how he'd like to come down.

Or . . . with whom, anyway.

Maybe he could tempt Dani into a milkshake from the Dairy. He wouldn't call it a date . . . just an exchange of milk-based fluids? He froze, hands in his hair, shampoo running down his back. Yeah, no, he wouldn't sell it that way. Instead, he'd call it . . . a chance to discuss the positive qualities of rock-painting in correlation to reduced stress and increased satisfaction? This time he snorted because that, too, was horrible.

How about just going for milkshakes in a no pressure, no expectation, no—

Just milkshakes.

Keep it simple.

Satisfied with that, Ethan knew he'd even slum it with a frozen yogurt variety (on the diet plan), if it meant that he could chisel out some time with Dani.

She was shy, nervous around people in general, but some-times she relaxed with him, and seeing that smile, hearing her talk without being self-conscious . . . well, the glimpses he'd gotten of that side of her made him feel like a fucking superhero.

Not to mention the little moan she'd given, rasping up from the back of her throat, sliding through the air and caressing his skin like velvet.

That made him feel like a superhero who was desperate to kiss every inch of her.

And then to plunge deep inside, to get his hands on that lush ass, to hold her close and bring them both up to and over the edge again and again and again.

But first, he'd start with milkshakes.

Because if he continued down this train of thinking, he'd end up giving himself a boner. In the locker room. With no shortage of teammates to tease him for eternity about it.

Shuddering, he pushed the thoughts from his mind and took his time through his post-game routine, knowing that Dani would have plenty of work to keep her busy in the meantime, then he dressed and slipped out into the hall, finding himself— look at that—in front of her office.

The door was open, Jess, her assistant, was shrugging into her jacket and gathering up her purse.

Their voices—one laced with humor and plenty of volume (Jess) and the other softer, more melodic (Dani)—tangled in the air, weaving together into a pleasant series of techie terms and players' names. Then Jess called out a goodbye and slipped into the hall, nearly stumbling into him.

"Oh," she murmured. "I'm sorry, I—"

"It's okay," he said. "My fault."

She looked up at him, and he struggled to keep his focus on her, his gaze already drifting to the office, to Dani.

"Go easy on her," Jess whispered. "She's had a rough day of it."

He frowned, wondered what that meant. Dani had been smiling when he'd left her, and not a fake one either, the beautiful, genuine smile he was just starting to learn. So, what had happened in the last few hours?

Nodding as he puzzled that out, he waited until Jess had disappeared around the corner before knocking lightly on the doorjamb.

Striking brown eyes on his.

Eyes that filled with happiness for one glorious heartbeat before they went cold.

And God, cold was such a fucking lame word to describe the ice that overlaid Dani's gaze, that shut down her expression, that had her shoulders curving forward and down, just slightly.

Just enough that he knew something bad had happened.

A vice clenching around his heart, frost prickling through his veins sharp enough to make his fingertips ache, he stepped inside, closing—and locking—the door, for good measure. "What happened?" he asked without preamble.

She became a statue.

Like one of those iron ones outside the library, a still life in repose, a granite formed into an amalgamation of life. But the statues didn't have her pain.

Pain that was sharp enough to wound.

"What is it?" he asked, crossing over to her. "Is someone hurt?"

In an instant her face changed, going completely blank, shoulders straightening, chin tilting up. She would have appeared . . . well, not completely at ease so much as neutral and unaffected—if he hadn't seen her in agony just seconds before.

"Nope." The P made a popping sound, and he was processing that serrated noise as she turned back to her computer, effectively giving him the cold shoulder.

"Dani?"

"You should go."

He gripped the back of her chair, spun it to face him. "What's going on, sweetheart?"

Silence, those russet and amber eyes on his then away then on his again. "I'm not going to date you."

Well, fuck, there went milkshake night.

He crouched down, hesitated for a second, then placed his hands on her jean-covered knees. "I'm going to ask one more time. What happened?"

The barest hint of ice retreated.

"Nothing's happened," she said. "The cost-benefit ratio of having a relationship with someone I work with is too great. I'm not doing it."

The cost-benefit ratio?

Seriously?

His fingers tightened. "Dani."

She stood, and he rocked back to his heels for a brief moment before he regained his balance and found his feet. "Look, you're fun to talk to. You even make me laugh every once in a while. But I'm not the person for you, and I never will be." She opened the door. "Now, go."

That was utter horseshit. She was herself, and that was enough for him. He opened his mouth to tell her just that.

"Th—"

Fanny walked up. "Dani, you ready to go—" She stopped, realizing several moments too late that the office wasn't empty. Her gaze moved from him to Dani. "Or I could just come back . . . *later?*"

"No," Dani said sharply. "Ethan was just leaving."

He met her eyes for a heartbeat, but it was long enough for him to recognize that he needed to regroup. In that moment, he wasn't going to be able to convince her of anything, least of all to tell him what was really going on. Fucking hell, what had happened?

Fanny's brows were lifted, but she slid back a pace, as though she were going to be the one leaving.

He glanced at Dani. "We'll talk later."

"No," she said, with a streak of fierce determination. "We won't."

His temper spiked, something that Ethan usually controlled, and for an instant, he considered hauling Dani against his chest and giving her the kiss he should have laid on her earlier. It would be good, he knew that.

He'd actually taken a step toward her before he realized what he was doing and stopped, clenching his hands into fists and shoving them down to his sides. He could kiss her, could make her like it.

But . . . fucking hell, he also knew that she deserved their first kiss to be something of passion and need rather than anger.

Fanny's voice intruded on that haze of fury. "I'll just—"

"No," he snapped then forced himself to soften his tone. "I'm sorry," he said. "I'm gone. Enjoy your . . ." His eyes drifted to Dani, to the muscle clenching in her jaw, her knuckles pressed in sharp relief against her skin. For as much as she wasn't talking, he knew this was about something deep, deeper than he could get out of her in just a few moments. He needed to regroup. ". . . evening."

And then with one more look at the woman who'd shyly woven her way into his heart, he turned and walked away.

Thirteen

Dani

"Want to tell me what that was about?" Fanny asked.

Hell fucking no.

She wasn't going to tell *anyone* about what had happened in the Family Suite. Not because she felt ashamed of the way she'd reacted—which, okay, yes, she *did* feel ashamed because she hated that she was still a person who didn't value herself. She should be like the other women of the Gold—strong and confident and woke and . . . lots of other things. Equality for all, including the shy, dorky girls. Confidence for days.

She should have just told Sara that she wasn't going to set Roxanne up with Ethan.

Because he was hers.

Except . . . he *wasn't* hers.

And why would he want to be with someone like her?

"Ugh," she groaned, plunking her head onto her desk and then *thunking* it several times for good measure. "I." *Thump.*

"Don't." *Thump.* "Know." *Thump.* "What." *Thump.* "I'm." *Thump.* "Doing." *Thump*—

Or it would have been another thump, if Fanny hadn't caught her shoulder and tugged her up.

"The team needs that brain," she said.

Misery coursed through Dani. "I—um—I—"

"Easy on the wheels zipping around in there"—a tap to Dani's temple—"I swear, smoke's gonna start pouring out of your ears pretty soon."

She shut her eyes. "I'm a mess, Fanny. I can't even agree to go on one date without freaking out."

Her friend squeezed her shoulder. "Let's go get a drink."

Dani's lids peeled back. "You're not going to pump me for information?"

Fanny straightened, leaned a hip against her desk. "Honestly?" A pause, gaze on her until she nodded. "You don't look like you can handle an inquisition, bub. Let's just get ourselves good and drunk, eat too many carbs, and then you can figure it out tomorrow, okay?"

Surprise and relief warred with that ever-present anxiety and self-doubt. "You'd do that?"

People weren't nice to her—

Except, she couldn't use that excuse anymore, could she?

Because without thinking hard, she could come up with a list that was plenty long of people who were nice to her, people who cared—and they weren't just her family, not any longer.

She had Fanny and Jess. Sara and Brit and both Rebeccas and—

The point was that she was living her life like it was the past, instead of realizing she was a thirty-year-old woman who wasn't on the receiving end of a bunch of mean-ass kids.

And it was high time she stopped giving that past power.

"Dani?" A shake of her shoulder. "Booze. Carbs. Sleep. Okay?"

Since that was better than living in her own head, letting it twist around her like barbed wire, hurting whether she moved or not, but doubly so when she moved, Dani pushed up from her seat and nodded. "That sounds good."

Fanny smiled, laced her arm with Dani's. "Great. I'll drive."

"But—"

"We'll have a slumber party at my place, but we'll stop by yours first, get your stuff packed for the road trip. That way in the morning, we can grab brekkie at Molly's and come straight here to hop on the bus."

Dani's brows drew together because there was a lot to process in that. Starting with, "But you don't travel with the team."

"I'm hitching a ride," she said. "My family is coming to the game in Chicago, and then we're road-tripping it for a week."

"That sounds fun."

"You haven't driven with my mother." A grin. "I'll be lucky to come back in one piece."

Dani found herself laughing.

Somehow, after she'd spent the last hours in a perpetual cycle of self-flagellation, she was laughing and walking arm-in-arm with her friend, and the bottom wasn't falling out of the world, and . . . she was beginning to wonder if she hadn't been the least bit hasty with Ethan.

Cue more internal whipping.

"Dani? Is there a reason you look like you've swallowed a lemon?"

"I'm . . ." She sighed. "My head is a mess."

"And here I've promised to not give you an inquisition."

Dani snorted. "You'd take advantage of a woman on the edge?"

"Hell yes, I would." A beat, a squeeze of her arm. "But I won't because I promised."

"A woman who sticks by her word."

"Yeah." Fanny nudged Dani with her elbow. "Kind of like my friend."

"I haven't had that many friends," she whispered, the words slipping off her tongue uninvited.

Fanny tugged her to a stop. "And why's that, do you think?"

"Because I'm . . ."

A nerd, shy, self-conscious . . . not worthy.

The last crept through her mind like insidious ivy crawling up the trunk of a tree. She waited, expecting the pang that usually accompanied the thought, the cold frost that followed, creeping in through the fronts of her sneakers, soaking into her socks, chilling her toes.

But the pang, the iciness didn't come.

Instead, something red-hot flared in its place, and suddenly, her brain went clear. She wasn't what they had said.

And why, why had it taken her so long to see?

"I was . . . well, for a long time I've made myself small."

Fanny's expression gentled. "Why, babe? When you're so fucking big and bright?"

"Because I'm an idiot?"

A shake of her head, brown locks flailing behind her. "Nope. That's one thing you're not."

A sigh. "Because I'm scared?"

Fanny tapped her nose. "Ding. Ding. Give the girl a prize."

Laughter floated up, like a balloon drifting toward the sky, escaping her lips in a quiet puff of sound. "I thought you said no inquisitions?"

"Well, you gave me a freebie, what's a girl supposed to do?"

"I—"

The question was what was *she* supposed to do? Because seriously, what the fuck was she doing? She needed to find Ethan and explain, to tell him . . . *something* that would come to her, knowing coming to fruition as she went after him.

It was bad. She needed to—

"Hang on." She tugged her arm free, started down the hall. "I need to—"

"Hey!"

She stopped, turned around.

Fanny's mouth was tipped up at the corners. "Should I wait?"

Nerves bubbled into the space laughter had just occupied. But . . . fuck . . . hadn't she been scared long enough?

Yes. *Yes.*

"No," she told Fanny. "Don't wait."

"Carbs and booze another night!"

She nodded in agreement . . . and then she ran in a very undignified manner toward the parking lot.

When she burst out through the door, the air was cold, spreading across her face, tightening her skin, drying out her lips —or maybe that was nerves. Because the urge to spin back around and run inside to find Fanny for the booze with a side of carbs was intense.

Grew even more intense when she found Ethan standing there, his gaze on the ground, his hands fisted at his sides.

Turn tail.

Run.

Hide.

Her spine prickled, her foot slid back.

And then his stare drifted up, collided with hers.

She couldn't miss the hurt in his eyes, the misery, the despair. The trifecta of emotions was a literal gut punch, and her foot stopped its motion. Then moved forward to join the other.

Her throat seized.

Words exploded.

"Sara brought a beautiful woman named Roxanne to set you up with, and I freaked out. I thought that I couldn't possibly measure up and shouldn't get in the way of someone who clearly fit you better than me."

His face turned . . . scary. That was the only way she could think to describe it, but instead of stoppering the words up, it only made them come faster.

"And I've always been quiet. My family is great, but they're all big personalities, and it was just easier to blend into the background, to sit back and enjoy the show. I wasn't ever the type of girl who'd battle to be in the front. I was just happy with what I had."

A fierce expression.

Gentle fingers lifting to grasp hers, his thumb brushing the inside of her wrist, tracing light circles on her skin.

And she found that the rest of it wasn't so hard.

"Then I reached for more," she whispered. "Then I dared to want something big and beautiful, and . . . the universe slapped me back." Her eyes closed, and those fingers gripped tighter, tugging her away from the door, slipping an arm around her waist and bringing her body flush against the side of his.

Warm and strong, one hand wiping away the tears she hadn't even known escaped, then drawing her even closer as voices came close.

"You coming, Eth?" Brit called from somewhere nearby.

Ethan shifted her, shielding her body with his, and she felt a piece of her heart chip away, slip right through the holes in her safety net and drift over to him, to his palm, to those gentle circles on her skin. "Another time," he called.

"Okay. But just so you know," she called back, "I'm pretending I don't see Dani with you."

"Stay in your lane, Brit."

"That's for race car drivers."

A sigh. "Then between the pipes."

"That I can do," she hollered. "See ya."

Then she was gone, and Dani was alone with Ethan again, only this time they weren't standing in the shadows next to the arena, they were moving.

Or maybe they'd been moving the whole time.

Because by the time she processed they were walking, Ethan was beeping the locks on his car, opening the door. "Sit," he murmured, plunking her into the passenger's seat and reaching over her to buckle her belt.

Then he crossed around the front of the car, got in, and drove out of the parking lot.

He didn't speak as he drove, navigating the bright lights of the waterfront, the semi-quiet streets. There were always a few people out in a city like San Francisco, but this late, it was a muted hum of activities, the traffic gone, most people tucked safely into their beds. She turned to look out at the water, wanting to explain more, wanting to apologize, to find something to make him understand.

Ethan reached out and squeezed her knee. "It's okay."

"That I freaked out or I can't find the words to explain?"

Another squeeze. "Both. You don't owe me anything, sweetheart. Explanation or words or otherwise."

"But . . ."

When she trailed off, words lost again, he didn't get impatient, just waited.

"I want to give it to you."

His fingers convulsed.

She sucked in a breath.

He turned into a parking lot, the lights twinkling at regular intervals, the water of the Bay in the distance. It was a clear night, the moon shining down on the waves and their crests, turning them shades of black and gray and silver. But the beauty of that undulating mix of salt and water couldn't hold her attention.

Not when every cell in her body was focused on the man next to her.

Not when he said, "I only want what you're willing to give."

And that unlocked the rest of it.

"I fell for the popular boy in high school." The memories threatened to swell up, to overwhelm her, but she shoved them down. "The long and short is that I was the baby in my family, the quiet one, the protected one, and I fell for a boy who didn't believe in protecting me in any sense. I was too weak or infatuated or *stupid* to recognize what was happening, and by the time I did, I was pregnant."

Ethan sucked in a breath.

"It's stupid, really," she said, hating the sharp slice of pain, the way this truth made her want to curl up and go quiet, to lock the hurt down. "I figured we'd get married, and everything would be perfect. I'd somehow have the fairy tale ending."

Her heart thudded.

Her palms were sweaty.

Her throat was tight.

But Ethan didn't rush her.

And she found that her heart slowed, her throat loosened, and the moisture on her palms dried.

"He just . . . pretended I didn't exist." A breath. "I told him I was pregnant, and he just dropped me off at my house, and then at school the next day, he ignored me completely. It wasn't even hours before he was with the most popular girl in school." A tall, slender blond, much like Roxanne. Except, she'd been snake-mean where Roxanne seemed nice.

"I was a teenager. I was emotional and heartbroken and hurt and—" A shake of her head. "And I tried to talk to him, but he was . . . well, cruel. So, then I knew I couldn't rely on him, couldn't expect a happy ending from him, so I thought the baby and I would make our own." Her eyes burned at the memory. "But I lost the baby, and I got really sick."

His fingers were like a vise on her leg, but instead of hurting, they grounded her, helped her finish the story.

"My parents hadn't known until I started bleeding, until it was bad, and they needed to call an ambulance." She shook her head, a thousand little slices of agony crisscrossing through her insides. "I was in the hospital for a while, and after I recovered, my family . . . they gave me a pass. I homeschooled for the rest of the school year, and we moved the next. New school. Fresh start for my senior year," she said with a sigh. "But I was different, smaller. Quieter. No happy ending. No fairy tale. No prince. No boyfriend."

Dani shuddered out a breath.

There it was. Her whole sad sob story.

One no one knew except her family.

But . . . shouldn't this feel better? To get everything off her chest? Cutting the bindings, releasing their hold on her?

Instead, the past was like a mace inside her, spikes jabbing at her from all sides, her spine as rigid and stiff as a piece of wood. God this *hurt*, and she wanted to crawl back into herself, to cover the pain, the spikes, wrap up and bury the splinters from that wood.

She wanted to be small again.

She wanted to not *feel* again.

No sooner had that thought crossed her mind before Ethan moved.

The car jerked as he shoved his seat back and then in the next instant, her seat belt was unlatched and she was hauled over the console, plunked into his lap with his warm, strong arms wrapped tight around her.

"I'm sorry."

Just two words but filled with empathy instead of pity for the first time. Her family had been sympathetic, sure, but they'd largely been pitying. Poor Dani. Poor, naïve, unworldly Dani.

It was different with Ethan, however.

No pity.

No pat on the head.

Just warm arms and a steady heartbeat against her ear when he brought her even closer.

"I should be over this by now." She found the words she'd thought to herself a million times before allowing them to slip out, and his arms grew tighter. "I was a teenager, and it was puppy love, and—"

"You were hurt and lost a dream. That doesn't just go away." A soft hand on her back, rubbing lightly. "That changes a person. Irrevocably."

"And what about your dreams?" she whispered, lifting up, her eyes meeting his. "Which ones have you lost?"

A shadow of pain across his face, and guilt swarmed her.

"I'm sorry," she whispered. "I didn't mean. I—"

"It's okay," he said, just as quietly. "I lost a friend. First year in the league. He was struck and killed by a drunk driver."

"Oh, Ethan." She covered his jaw with her palm. "I'm so sorry."

She half-expected him to say something along the lines of life happens or shit gets real or bad things sometimes happen to good people, or one of a myriad of other platitudes people pitch to each other when they don't know what to say or how to react.

Instead, he covered her hand with his own, his gaze on hers. "Thank you."

The moment stretched, growing taut, expectation coursing through the air, and then his lips brushed her forehead, her cheek, her jaw . . . her lips.

It was sparks, not like she'd expected after the hall, after the door.

Rather, it was sunshine on the tip of her nose on a summer's day, heat caressing her collarbones, her shoulders, drifting down to her fingers.

Gentle and so fucking sweet that it made her eyes prickle.

Then his tongue touched the seam of her mouth. Her lips parted, and that warmth exploded into heat. His beard was roughened velvet against her skin, the most intoxicating abrasion of her life, and his tongue, when it stroked along hers, was a sleek, hot dart driving pleasure to follow in the wake of that heat. Her fingers wove into his hair, the soft locks like silk on her palms, needing him even nearer.

Even as the thought entered her mind, Ethan's hands were on her waist, pulling her closer, his cock hard against her center, sparking through her nerves, sending pleasure coursing through her, despite the layers between them.

One hand slid up her side, and she groaned as those sparks spread, coalescing into a kind of need she'd never felt before.

And just as it was getting *really* good, just as it was burning so fucking incredibly and she found herself almost completely undone, Ethan pulled back.

"You are so fucking strong."

The rest of her heart shattered into a million pieces, those shards floating through the air and reforming . . . to encompass him.

She stretched up and kissed him again.

FOURTEEN

ETHAN

He was hard and aching, furious and in agony that Dani had been hurt, and he couldn't do a damned thing about it.

But nothing eclipsed the feeling of the key turning in the lock, of the sudden pop of a door opening, of right.

This was right.

This was *everything*.

She pushed at his chest, tearing her mouth from his. He almost expected her to draw back, to retreat, but instead she stayed close, her forehead resting on his, her palm on his shoulder.

A tear dropped onto his shirt.

Shit.

"Did I—?"

She pressed her finger to his mouth. "Why is it so easy with you?"

"Because this is right."

Her lips parted, her breath hitching, and he shifted, leaning forward to kiss her again, needing to kiss her.

It was a directive written into his DNA.

She slid her tongue into his mouth, tangling it with his. Desire pooled in his stomach, pressing his cock even more firmly against the zipper of his slacks. He really fucking hated himself for not having taken her directly back to his house. If he had, they wouldn't be having this conversation in a car, wouldn't be crammed in between the seat and the steering wheel, when it really would have been much better if they'd been horizontal—

"Why," she asked, pulling back again, her hand resting on his chest, probably feeling the way it was pounding haphazard and totally out of control, "do you taste so fucking good?"

He groaned, rested his palm on her nape. "Because this is right," he said again.

And as much as he wanted to kiss her again, to get lost in her taste and the feel of her body, he gently set her away from him, sliding her over into her own seat, sucking in a breath when she shakily pressed her fingers to her lips.

He wanted to kiss her again, to have her back in his arms.

But they were in an empty parking lot in the city, and it was after midnight, and he needed to keep her safe.

"Can I drive you home?"

Glazed eyes met his.

"I'll pick you up in the morning, and we can have breakfast."

"Or," she whispered, "maybe you could stay?"

His cock somehow grew harder, and he nearly reached over the console and grabbed her again. Instead, however, he cupped her cheek, told her the truth. "I want that," he whispered. "I've fantasized about that in six thousand different ways, but . . ." He trailed off at the disappointment on her face, and for a moment he wondered why he was being a Cub Scout, but then the answer was easy. She was important. She *meant* something. So, that's why he'd drive her home, kiss her goodnight on the porch, and continue winning her trust.

Her face evened out, the warmth tucked back into cool. "You have the game tomorrow. You'll need your rest."

"No." He turned on the car, navigated out of the lot. "I don't give a shit about rest. I give a shit about you, and I don't want you to do something that you might—" He couldn't force out the word regret. "I don't want to move too fast. I like you, Dani, more than I probably should, considering I've been fantasizing about you longer than I've actually spoken to you."

He heard her inhale.

"So, I'm going to drive you home where I'm going to make out with you on your front porch, and then I'm going to see your sweet ass in the morning, so I can buy you a breakfast I can drool over but can't actually eat myself." He glanced over, saw her lips quirk then looked back at the road. "I'll choke down my oatmeal and fruit, my single allotted cup of coffee, and then I'll drive us to the rink where we'll get on a plane, and know what?"

"What?"

He winked at her. "I promise to save the seat next to me."

She laughed.

"Now," he said, getting onto the freeway and heading south. "Tell me, how far have you gotten through that stack of books from the library?"

Silence.

Then she laughed. "How far do you think?"

He met her eyes for a heartbeat before returning his focus in front of him. "Pretty damned far, I think."

"You'd be right."

Another glance. "Will you tell me about your favorite?"

"Favorite book? Or favorite from that stack?"

"What? Do I look stupid? Favorite from the stack," he teased. "It's impossible for a true bookworm to choose her favorite."

"Spoken by a true bookworm?"

"My favorite that I've read recently was a list-topping thriller. Even though it was a bit formulaic, it was a nice reprieve from scientific papers." A beat, another brief look toward her. "Now, show me yours."

Laughter filled the car, and it was the best fucking thing he'd heard in a long time.

They talked about books as he drove.

Then he got his kiss. Well, *kisses*.

And then he went back to his place, jerked off because he had the erection to end all erections, and even as he slept, his mind was only on one thing.

Dani.

The taste of her. The feel of her. The sound of her laughter filling the air.

———

"And then Blue tried to steal Max's figurines," Dani said, "but Anna found out, and she thought it was stupid as hell and was really, *really* done with them pranking each other, so instead she stole Blue's lucky socks."

He scooped up a bite of his oatmeal. "Okay, so this is the part I've heard. Or at least the part that had Blue tearing apart the locker room looking for those damned socks."

Dani laughed. "Poor guy."

A shrug, his lips twitching. "He was in full meltdown mode. You don't get between hockey players and their good luck charms."

"Well, from what I heard, no harm was done, and Max *and* Blue figured it out."

"They certainly did." A beat, his lips twitching. "Eventually."

Because with a little help from Angie, Anna had also stolen

Max's special lucky figurine he had to stroke before every game —which sounded grosser than it was in actuality—then had left a ransom note for both the socks and the figurine, forcing Max and Blue to work together to rescue those good luck charms.

"So, the socks and figurine were found," Dani said, scooping up a bite of what looked to be a truly delicious waffle. "And the prank war was over."

"And we all breathed a sigh of relief in the locker room."

A giggle as she ate more of her waffle. "How long did it take for the dubious duo to find them?"

"Too close to game time, as far as Bernard was concerned." Ethan chuckled. "Far too soon, as far as the guys in the room went."

"That's a shame."

"Eh." He scraped the last bit of his oatmeal up. "It was a fantastic prank on Anna and Angie's parts."

"Angie told me Max made her sleep on the couch."

Ethan choked.

Dani giggled again. "But that she woke up in Max's arms."

Ethan set his spoon down, smiled. That sounded much more like his friend and teammate. "Those women keep their men on their toes."

"Still want to date me?" Amber and russet eyes glimmered with mirth, but there was also a layer of insecurity beneath.

"I'm looking forward to tiptoeing all over the place."

Her expression shifted, warmed. "Last chance."

He reached across the table, took her hand. "Scared?"

"Fucking terrified." Her shoulders rose and fell on an exhale. "But I'm also ready to finally live my life."

His fingers twitched. "What should we do first?"

"First, we should pay the bill." A smile. "Then we should get our butts to the rink so we don't miss the bus."

He glanced at his watch then reached to pull out his wallet. "I'm loving this whole dating thing already."

"Then you're going to love that I already paid the bill, so we can just go straight out to your car."

"What?" His brows drew together, his hand still half in his pocket, since he'd been in the process of pulling out his wallet. "What do you mean—" But his question was cut off when Dani sat down next to him, tugging his hand out of the opening, shoving his wallet back inside.

"I said, I got it." Her fingers lightly brushed his. "Which means you still owe me a date."

Joy swirled through him, a tiny tornado growing in intensity with each second he spent in the presence of this woman. "I'll take that deal," he said, sliding his hand up her arm, lightly gripping the side of her neck. "Because it means more time with you."

"I like you, Ethan Korhonen."

"Well, right back at you, Dani Eastbrooke."

He brushed his lips over hers.

She turned the kiss into something that had his heart pounding, his cock going to granite.

Then she stood, took his hand, and he knew he was in for a hell of a ride.

FIFTEEN

DANI

She was sitting up front by Fanny; the man who made every cell in her body sit up and pay attention was several rows back.

She'd been intending to sit by him, but then Max had gotten ahold of Ethan, and Fanny had come to carry out her aforementioned interrogation, and . . . next thing she knew, she was in her normal row on the bus, her friend chatting her ear off as the vehicle got loaded.

Brit walked by, winking when she caught Dani's gaze as she made her way to the back of the bus.

Seniority ruled when it came to seat position.

Coaches up front, then support staff, then rookies on back to the senior citizens.

Dani wondered what Brit might say if the goalie knew that Dani mentally referred to her, Blane, and Max as the senior citizens.

They *were* the oldest players.

But the lithe, strong Brit wouldn't be happy.

Still, Dani filed it away for use at a future date—maybe during one of those times where she was hanging with the women of the Gold and worked up the courage to actually say something.

If she were living her life for real now, she'd need a few teasing statements stowed away and ready to roll.

"What are you smiling about?"

She blinked, glanced up to see that Fanny had vacated her seat, and it was suddenly occupied by a man who took up much more space than her tiny figure-skating friend. "I was categorizing Brit as a senior citizen."

He froze. His face an expression in shock.

And then he burst out laughing, drawing the notice of pretty much everyone on the bus. They were probably wondering what the heck quiet, shy Dani could be saying to make a man like Ethan laugh so riotously.

But for the first time ever in her life, Dani didn't care what anyone else was thinking.

She only cared what Ethan was thinking, and she supposed, what *she* was thinking. And the thoughts floating through her mind were light, happy ones, cautious optimism and a need to know everything about this man. His family, his parents, every sad and positive story of his life.

She wanted to know his favorite color and food and—

"Why's there smoke coming out of your ears?"

"What's your favorite color?"

He straightened, lips parting and then curving. "It's like that, huh?"

"It's a perfectly acceptable first date question."

"We're on a date?"

Her sigh was disgruntled, and she swatted at his chest. "We're going to be at some point. Well, if you stop being such a pain in my ass, that is."

He grinned, his gray eyes dancing, and she nudged him with her elbow. Which just had him snagging her arm, tucking it against him . . . tugging *her* against him. Her breath caught, desire swirling through her, and she was quite desperate to taste him again.

His hand came to her cheek, his thumb brushing along her bottom lip. He groaned. "Don't look at me like that."

She would give almost anything right then to be able to kiss him like she had on her porch the night before, like her body was an extension of his and if she just kept sipping at his mouth, the rest of the world could go on without them.

"Not helping," he murmured, that thumb still running back and forth.

"You came up to sit by me."

"I like you," he said. "I like to sit by people I like."

"That's a lot of likes."

He tapped her nose. "Sass. I like that, too."

She laughed, shook her head, leaning back enough so she could focus. "Well then, just answer the question already. I want to know *all* the little things."

"*All* the little things?"

"Leave the comedy to Max."

"Fuck."

She froze at the suddenly gruff tone. "What?"

"I really fucking like you, Eastbrooke."

This whole conversation, paired with his body next to hers, was threatening to turn her into a pile of mush. Which meant that she needed to pull herself together. Otherwise there would just be a pile of Gold emblazoned clothing on the floor sitting in a Dani puddle. "All right. All right," she said. "Enough of that." She waved a hand. "I'm ordering you to answer my first date question."

He paused. "I think I like taking orders from you."

"*I* think I can't give you the kind of orders I really want, so you need to behave yourself for the duration of the ride to the airport."

Warm fingers laced through hers, a rough palm engulfing her hand, tendrils of heat curling up her arm, sliding through her middle, and his eyes were filled with liquid lightning when they came to hers and held, the air between them crackling. "Raincheck on the orders, love."

Her lips parted, her lungs shuddering. "Be good."

"As long as you promise to stroke me at some point in the future."

The heat was no longer a curl. It was an inferno, a forest fire, a volcano exploding within her. She swallowed hard. "Ethan," she whispered.

"Raincheck, sweetheart."

"Your fault," she murmured.

His smile was sexy and scorching and just the right kind of wicked. "Definitely my fault." Then he straightened, pulling slightly away from her, the fog of his nearness dissipating, allowing her to at least put a few thoughts together.

"Favorite color. STAT."

"Blue," he stated without preamble. Then paused, said, "Actually, no. Not just blue. Turquoise."

And out of his pocket, he produced the stone she'd slipped him the night before.

Her heart was a kitten in her chest, batting a ball of yarn around inside her torso, twisting this way and that.

"Yours?" he murmured, sliding closer as Coop made his way down the aisle. Calle had slid into the row in front of them, and Dani didn't miss the look she tossed their way.

Gossip would be flying.

Or *was* flying already.

She could feel the gazes on them.

A tug of her hair as the bus started moving forward. She blinked, reprocessed the conversation. "Yellow," she whispered.

"Why?" he asked.

"Why?" she repeated.

"Yeah." His thigh pressed to hers. "Why is yellow your favorite color?"

"It's bright." A shrug. "Like sunshine and warm sand and pineapple juice."

He leaned close, his lips coming to her ear. "Did you just call warm sand yellow?"

She was focused on Ethan, on his lips brushing the lobe of her ear, on the goose bumps his warm breath raised on her skin, on the heat from his body, so his words didn't immediately process.

Then they did.

Straightening, she looked down her nose at him. "Really?"

He leaned in, nipped her bottom lip. "Really. It's a travesty. Clearly, sand is beige, not yellow."

"You have permission to smack him," Calle said, glancing over her shoulder with a smirk. "No man should be that at ease when he's trying to win over a woman he likes."

Ethan bent in again. "For the record, I'm not at *ease*." His eyes flicked down, drawing hers to follow, to see that he was hard in his slacks.

"Oh," she murmured, biting her lip.

"But I *am* trying to win over the woman I like," he said. "Now, it's my turn to ask some First Date questions, okay?"

Her heart stuttered, that kitty with its ball of yarn making a reappearance, as the bus pulled onto the freeway, as Ethan began peppering her with more First Date questions. Which she was fine with answering, so long as she was able to get his answers in return. She nodded, whispered, "Okay."

He smiled.

She smiled.

And by the time they got on the plane, she'd learned his favorite TV show, food, place he'd traveled, animal, and superhero movie—*The Office,* steak, New Zealand, lion, and *Captain America: Civil War.* She'd approved of all his choices, aside from the steak, as clearly a Caesar salad was the best food on the planet, and while she liked all the Marvel movies, her favorite supe flick was *Wonder Woman* (the first, clearly . . . because that thigh jiggle and Chris Pine and former princesses being badass warrior queens).

They kept talking as they pulled their respective supplies out —laptop for her, pens, notebooks, and reference materials for him—and then, somehow, effortlessly they fell into silence, working side-by-side without a weird transition of quiet. The conversation just stilled, they both worked until they got drowsy —or at least, she did, closing her laptop after a few hours because planes always made her sleepy.

And then Ethan did an amazing thing.

Without a word, or even seeming to look at her, he lifted the armrest, wrapped an arm around her, and then coaxed her to lie down in his lap, her head on his thigh, her shoulder pressed to his leg, his fingers stroking lightly through her hair.

Her eyes slid closed.

The rumble of the engines coaxed her under.

She was out in moments.

Sixteen

ETHAN

"Hey," he murmured.

For once, Dani didn't jump.

She just spun in her chair and stood, crossing over to him with a smile that made him feel as though he could lasso the sun. "That was some move tonight, Korhonen."

He wrapped his arms around her waist. "Want to come somewhere with me?"

They were off the next day and would fly out the following evening. Tonight, however, they were in Denver, it was beautiful, and he had the need to take Dani on their first official date.

She smiled. "Yeah, I do." She spun, packed up her equipment and shoved it into her backpack, which she swung up onto her shoulder.

Which he promptly snagged back down her shoulder and then lifted up onto his.

"You just played," she began. "You're tired—"

"I'm a man."

Her brows lifted. "And that means what exactly? That I can't carry my own bags?"

"Sass." He tapped her nose. "No," he said. "It just means that you don't need to, whether they're filled with rocks and paint or computer equipment."

"And what can I do with my *womanly*, delicate arms?"

God, that arch tone brought forth his naughty librarian fantasies.

"Wait," she said, interrupting him before he could answer that, which was probably for the best because he didn't have a good answer for her question anyway.

However, when she continued talking, he realized he was in even more trouble.

"Why are you blushing?" She snagged his hand when he tried to turn for the door. "What's with the red cheeks, Korhonen?"

Dani in a short skirt and knee-highs, telling him she'd check the reference stack for him, that was the cause for his red cheeks.

Also because in his fantasy, that reference stack would be on the bottom shelf.

Bending over, a glimpse of a lush ass. He'd hop the counter, lift her skirt, and—he cursed under his breath when his cock went hard.

Romance, not fucking.

Romance.

Not *fucking*.

He swallowed hard. "Just a post-game flush," he said.

Her brows went up, and he knew she didn't buy that for one second.

Which was why he slid his arm around her waist, tugged her against him, and kissed her. It wasn't gentle or careful. It was a touch borne of need and fantasy, of that moment of dreaming about something for so long, thinking it would never come, even while wishing so fucking desperately that it would.

Sensation roiling through his skin, sparking down from lips to toes. She tasted sweet and spicy, as though she'd just had a stick of cinnamon gum but coated her lips in frosting.

Strawberry frosting.

Her tongue dipped into his mouth, fanning the flames of that spice, draping it across his taste buds, boiling the cytoplasm in his cells, heating his DNA and changing it, transforming it, *morphing* it into something that didn't just exist to perpetuate his own survival, not any longer. Instead, it existed for her, for Dani, for this intoxicating, lovely woman who was quiet, but not with him. Who held her painful memories tight, but shared so he could understand. Who didn't let very many people in, but had let him in.

Her nape was soft against his palm, her curls bouncing when she came closer, when she tilted her head back, tickling the skin of his hand, and the quiet moan, the rasp of his name transmitting from her mouth to his had him fighting the urge to strip her naked and kiss every inch of her.

Work.

They were at work.

Slowly, he wrestled with his control, first finding a slender thread buried deep, gradually drawing it forth, coiling it as he struggled to find another, and then another. Until he had a good-sized chunk of it, until he was able to slow the kiss, to lift his mouth.

His hands . . . he hadn't yet found the control to remove them from her body.

But she didn't seem to mind, not with every lush inch of her pressed to his front—which wasn't exactly helping him in his quest to remove his hands. Still, the way she stared up at him, pupils dilated, lips swollen, and he wasn't in any hurry to summon up any more control.

Dani, however, seemed to have held on to more brain function than he had.

Because the first thing out of those kissable lips was, "Why were you blushing, baby?"

Maybe it was the baby.

Perhaps it was that he'd suddenly become a living, breathing bag of blood existing only for this woman.

Or possibly his filter had been erased at the same time that the spice of cinnamon had hit his tongue.

But whatever the reason, Ethan found himself telling her the truth.

"I have a library fantasy."

Her chin jerked, eyes going wide. "Care to elaborate?"

His brain started working, right about the time she rose on tiptoe and her mouth came to his, searing him with a blazing kiss that made his legs tremble as though Fanny had just put his ass through the worst sort of drills on the ice.

"Ethan?" she asked when she dropped back down.

"Yeah?"

"What's the fantasy?"

And hell, if it got her close to him, had her body flush to his, her mouth on his then he'd tell her every last fantasy he'd harbored over the months and years.

"You in a short skirt and knee-highs, bending over the reference stack while I fuck you from behind."

She froze.

Fuck.

Too strong. Too fast. Too much.

He'd just gotten her used to him sitting next to her on the bus and plane, had finally secured a date. He wasn't supposed to skip over the rest of the first-date-getting-to-know-you stuff and dive straight into role play and fantasies.

"I—"

Her thumb brushed over his bottom lip. "Would I wear my glasses?"

His cock twitched, a groan tumbling out of his mouth.

She smiled, no sign of shy. Only a confident, smart, sexy as fuck woman standing plastered against him. "I'm reading that as a yes."

He bent his head, desperate for just one more brief taste of that spicy and sweet.

"Yes," he said, when he managed to pull back. "You'd wear the fucking glasses, sweetheart."

Her eyes were glazed, but her smile was fucking gorgeous. "Okay, then."

"Okay," he murmured, his hand shifting to cup the side of her neck, the other clenched on the sumptuous curve of her hip. He stared into her eyes, at her face, tracing every millimeter, committing the faint scar crisscrossing her left brow to memory, making a mental note to ask her at some later point where she'd gotten it. Ethan wanted to know everything about her. Her eyelashes were so long, nearly touching the skin of her cheekbones, her top lip plump, fading from almost maroon to a lighter mauve as it dipped inward. Her earlobes were attached and pierced, though he'd never seen her wear earrings and made another mental note to find out if, like her glasses, she just didn't wear them to work, or if she didn't wear them at all.

"Ethan?" she asked what could have easily been centuries later.

He couldn't be counted on to keep track of meaningless things like time when he held this woman.

"Yeah?"

"Weren't you going to take me somewhere?"

He blinked, mentally shook himself.

And then he found the control to release her, to lace their fingers together. "Yeah, I am."

———

"Is this a kidnapping?" Dani asked as he tucked her into the car he'd managed to borrow from a buddy. Ethan had planned ahead, had his friend leave the small SUV at the arena, and would be doing Tim "a favor" by returning it to the amphitheater so Tim would have it when he got off his shift that ended—

Ethan's eyes flicked to the dash.

Twenty minutes ago.

Meh, Tim was a good guy. They'd played in college together, and Tim had gone on to managing bands, and eventually when he'd had a family, managing venues, including this one outside of Denver.

So now, Ethan's friend had a municipal job (the city technically maintained the amphitheater) with good benefits and a pension, a wife and three kids, and a soft spot for a man (Ethan) trying to win the heart of an incredible woman. Oh, along with the clearance to let visitors into the park after hours for a romantic date.

Keys. Romance. Check. Check.

And in return, Ethan had scored Tim and his family tickets to the Red Wings versus Avs game. Good seats, too. Club level, just two rows behind the glass.

He could have gotten better for a Gold game, but—gasp—Tim's favorite team was not the one that Ethan was currently playing on.

So much for friendship, huh?

Fingers on his cheek startled him, and he realized he'd been quiet as he navigated his way to the freeway. Starting the date off right by ignoring the woman he was supposed to be wooing. Way to go.

"I like when you smile," Dani whispered. "It's like a surprise hidden in your beard, only revealed if someone looks close enough."

He captured her wrist, pressed a kiss to her palm. "The first time you smiled at *me*, I almost ran into a pole."

"What?"

"I'd been trying to get you to notice me for months, to really look at me." He laughed. "But it seemed like you were completely indifferent, even though I was burning up for you. You're quiet, but I always felt like there was so much more going on in your head than the rest of the world could see—"

A snort. "Yeah. Like crippling social anxiety."

"I like you, just the way you are." Another kiss to her palm before he placed her hand down on his thigh. "Anyway, back to my pining. Max was teasing you like he teases everyone, and then suddenly you came back with some quip about his game and how your character 'had significantly more melee than his pathetic excuse for a paladin,' and Max froze, his face warring between shock and horror. I laughed, because I'm a cruel asshole, and then you glanced up, gave me a full look at those gorgeous eyes for the first time, and I . . ."

"What?"

Fell for her. Right then and there.

Vowed that he'd win her over, would own her heart.

Because she owned his.

But that was too much too soon. So, he needed to temper it back, return to first date vibes.

"I knew that I had to get to know the woman who decimated Max's video game prowess."

She chuckled. "Do you want to know something?"

He wanted to know *everything*.

But first date, and all that. Yadda, yadda, yadda.

Which was why he just nodded instead.

"The truth is that I didn't even play that game. I was just really freaking tired of hearing him blabber on about it." A shrug. "Luckily, I knew enough about it that I was able to fool him."

Amusement was a coiled spring, one that unloaded, laughter bursting out of him as he took the exit that would take them off the highway and up toward the twisting road leading to the amphitheater. "You're devious."

"I couldn't believe he fell for it." Ethan saw one shoulder lift and fall out of the corner of his eye. "I actually felt guilty about it and wanted to tell him the truth."

Her palm on his leg squeezed. "Why didn't you?"

She was quiet for long enough that he expected her not to answer him. "Because of the way you looked at me."

He'd just turned into the driveway, saw Tim standing by the gate, and braked. "How did I look at you?"

"Like you saw me."

SEVENTEEN

"Like you see me."

The words had burst out of her in an unconscious blurt.

The truth.

But still, something that revealed too much.

Except . . . did it *truly* reveal too much? Ethan had been pretty fucking clear about how he felt about her, more now that she could recognize since she'd decided to yank the blinders off, grasp onto the attraction, the mutual like, and to take a leap of faith.

She'd spent so long being dissatisfied and lonely and sad.

Enough was finally enough.

She needed to buck up . . . or accept the loneliness.

And since that bitter isolation had grown to be a heavier burden, a tighter corset, squeezing the life from her more by the year, she'd bucked up.

Which meant she would have to accept that the whole

bucking up process meant that she would be saying revealing things such as *like you see me*.

What she wasn't prepared for was his reaction to it.

The way the car slid to an abrupt stop, the emotion in his eyes when he snagged her hand from his thigh and brought it to his chest, resting it over the spot where his heart pounded below —a rapid *thrum-thrum* that matched her own pulse.

"I see you, sweetheart," he murmured. "And it's the prettiest fucking thing I've ever had the privilege to lay eyes on."

Thrum-thrum.

Thrum-thrum.

Thrum—

Knock-knock.

She jumped, the seat belt tightening around her shoulder, heart pounding for a completely different reason. Ethan's lips formed a curse, and then he gently released her hand and turned to lower the window.

"Hey, Tim," he said, shaking hands with the man who'd approached the car. "Thanks for doing this."

"You sure you don't want me to hang around and drive you back?"

Ethan shook his head. "I've got it covered."

"All right then." He released Ethan's hand, tapped on the frame of the door, eyes coming to Dani, and his lips turning up. Even in the dim illumination from the moonlight, she could see he was a handsome man with thick, dark hair and a winning smile along with curiosity written all over his face. Though to his credit, he didn't probe, just nodded at her in hello and said, "Park up ahead." Another tap. "Everything's ready for you."

Then he stepped back, and Ethan drove forward, parking in the shadows next to something that appeared dark and forbidding—except if she squinted and turned her head to the side, she could see a few lights up at the top.

"Why do I feel like I should circle back to questioning you

about your kidnapping tactics?" she asked as Ethan came around and opened her door. "Is this where you take women who've pried out your deepest darkest fantasies as punishment?"

He ran a finger over her cheek. "That one fantasy is hardly the deepest and darkest one I have about you."

A little shiver of heat skated along her spine. "What other ones do you have?"

His hand found her waist, drew her close. "Why don't you tell me one of yours?" More heat, embers coalescing into tendrils, those threads growing and twining together into a thick, heavy rope.

Her cheeks were hot.

Her pussy was wet.

But that was beside the point.

Well, maybe, maybe not, because one point—a really important one—was that she wanted him. Badly. The other important point was that even with the desire burning within her, a perpetually burning flame that threatened to incinerate her, she wasn't sure if she could share any of her fantasies with this man.

They were too deeply entrenched, hidden behind walls she wasn't sure she could allow him to breach . . .

This was still too fresh and difficult to accept.

And . . . maybe she was just too shy.

The backs of his knuckles brushed her cheeks, drawing her focus to his face, to the clean lines cut by his beard, the silver cast of his skin from the moonlight, the flash of white teeth when he smiled gently at her. "Rain check?"

"Wh-what?" she sputtered.

"Rain check on whatever fantasy or fantasies are bouncing around that brain of yours."

His light tone had her smiling. "I'm neither agreeing nor disagreeing to this."

Another brush of those knuckles. "I think I can tempt it out of you."

"You could try."

Laughter, warm and heady, filled the night air as he tugged her up an incline. "I think I might know a way to succeed."

He was probably right. Hell, he *was* right. Ethan most definitely could find a way to tug the information out of her mind.

"Rain check," she murmured.

A husky chuckle. "Deal, sweetheart."

"Tell me about your parents?"

He nodded, shifting her closer, and Dani found herself resting her head on his chest. She was far too short for it to rest on his shoulder, but it felt nice to be nestled in the crook between arm and side, for the sound of his steady pulse to fill her eardrum, his voice rumbling through his body, vibrating against her as he answered her question.

"Mom's so fucking smart that sometimes I feel like I only understand half of what she's saying, especially when she's talking about something with regards to her work," he said, his voice filled with a warmth that she was coming to recognize.

Because she'd felt it directed at her.

"What does she do?"

"Russian literature and its intersection with early eighteenth-century American works."

Dani paused. "I only understood half of that."

He kissed the top of her head. "Join the club."

"And your dad?"

"He's also a professor. His specialty is higher mathematics. Think calculus but on steroids." A laugh. "I understand even less of his work. It has more letters and symbols than numbers."

"Sounds intense."

"It is." He smoothed back her hair. "And they ended up with a son who is an athlete. Two of the great brains of their time, and you've got me."

There was an interesting note in his tone, but it wasn't remarkable in a good way. Instead, it bristled along her skin, making her feel as though she'd been yanked backward through a hedge. It spoke to the insecurity inside her, called like to like, and . . . she fucking hated it.

She spun into him, halting him in his tracks, bringing their bodies flush against one another. They'd reached the top of the slope, and her eyes needed a moment to adjust, to see what was in his eyes.

More bristling.

"What's that?" she asked, waving a hand at his face.

"What's what?" he countered.

"That tone. That expression." She cupped his cheeks, made easier since she was at the top of the incline and he was a foot behind her, the angle aligning their faces. "Do you think for one second that your parents aren't proud of you? That you haven't done something fucking incredible?"

He turned his head, kissed her palm. "I just shoot a puck at a net and get in an occasional fight on the ice. It's nothing as important as the work they're doing," he said. "Nor even as important as yours. I'm a cog that can be replaced. An athlete with a shelf life, and that's just fact. They're discovering knowledge, helping others gain it. You're aiding in the running of this big machine, helping dozens, if not more people be successful and have jobs and make a living." He peeled her hands off, wove their fingers together. "Without me, they'd be fine. Without *you*, without others, they'd be lost."

There was a lot to unpack there.

Starting with the fact that she'd never quite been able to articulate anything close to what he'd just said, even though she had felt the same way too many fucking times over the course of her life.

But it was funny.

She'd found herself growing a lot over the last days, identifying the painful memories, understanding their hold on her, finding the courage to begin taking baby steps forward. And now hearing that same note of pain in Ethan's voice was like leaping backward, falling into a dark hole, hating that someone could feel that way about themselves.

And if she hated that *he* could feel that way, how had she lived for so freaking long feeling the same?

It was . . . enlightening.

Frustrating.

Infuriating.

Illuminating.

"You are a wonderful, smart, talented, lovely man. You are more than a cog in a machine. You're . . . Ethan, and I feel so lucky to know you."

His lips parted, a shuddering breath slipping out and coating her skin. "Dani," he murmured, his tone almost pained.

"You see," she whispered. "I was accosted outside my office by a man, who dropped my treasured tablets on the ground, and then again by him outside the library where he stole my books. And again in a hall where he stole my bags of rocks"—his mouth curved—"and that man, well . . . he's pretty fucking amazing. He gave me the courage to peek at the memories I'd locked down, to release them and their hold on me. It was terrifying, letting go of that safety net." She squeezed his hands. "But I found it wasn't so scary when I understood that he'd be patiently waiting to catch me."

Another of those breaths, stuttering and staccato, a big chest practically vibrating against her.

Then his hands wove into her hair, and he kissed her.

The man had a fucking glorious mouth, soft and plump, ringed by the short bristles of his beard. Rough and smooth, no caution in the way he held her, how he plundered her lips.

But eventually, they had to breathe, so she pulled back, reveling in the way he held her face in his calloused hands. "I told you that you could do anything that you put your mind to."

"I'm starting to believe that."

His forehead rested against hers for a heartbeat.

Then he took her hands again and tugged her forward. "Come on then. Our first date awaits."

He spun her around, tugged her around the edge of the building . . .

And quite simply, she fell in love.

A small, round table sat near an opening in a plain white railing, the gap showing a staircase leading down to a gorgeous stone amphitheater. "It's Red Rocks," she whispered, as he led her to the table. "I've always wanted to come here for a concert."

He tugged out her chair. "We'll have to come back for one."

When he pushed it in, lights turned on, shining up along the burnished rust-colored stone walls, soft music filling the space. It swept up those stairs like a thunderstorm, a low rumble that bounced along the rock, quivered through her abdomen, filling her with the gentle melody of one of her favorite pop songs.

"How did you know?" she whispered.

"I've seen you perk up when it comes on during warm-up."

"How?" she asked again.

She shouldn't even have been there, had been sneaking out because she was desperate to catch a glimpse of him while he'd skated. Instead, she should have been prepping for the game, not mooning over him.

He sat down across from her, took her hand. "How could I not?" A squeeze. "How could I not notice you?"

Dani melted into a puddle of goo.

Either that or she fell a little bit more in love with him.

Then he lifted the silver cover on the plate between them, and there was no doubt, she'd plummeted into love with this man.

Eighteen

Ethan

The Lyft deposited them outside the hotel lobby, and he felt a kind of peace he'd not experienced before as they walked inside and headed for the elevators.

He would have liked it better had they been going up to a room they shared, but for now, he rode the elevator to her floor, walked her to her door, and stole several more kisses.

She threaded her fingers into his belt loops, tugged him close. "Come inside."

Ah, a statement that could be taken so many ways.

Alas, they were still riding First Date vibes, so he said goodnight.

Then went down to his room, jerked off, and fell headlong into sleep.

———

The knock on his door in the morning was unwelcome, but he stumbled to the peephole, stared through it . . . and suddenly, it was a lot more welcome.

He pulled open the wooden panel. "Hey, sweetheart," he said, knowing his voice was raspy.

Her eyes went wide, and Ethan watched her throat work as she swallowed. "I—"

"You okay?"

Her gaze slid down, a heated, tangible thing that had him remembering he was only wearing boxer briefs. When her stare stayed down, he allowed his own gaze to drop, saw that he was sporting some intense morning wood, even more than normal considering the need for this woman that was a fire coursing through his veins.

"I—I'm—"

Warm hands on his chest.

Warm hands shoving him—not gently. He was so surprised, he stumbled back several paces, and then the door was slamming closed, and Dani was launching herself into his arms.

And her mouth was on his.

Flames bursting to life, coating his skin, burning him to ash.

A warm, curvy woman against him, her hands stroking every inch of him as she continued shoving him, forcing him to retreat . . . until the backs of his legs hit the bed.

He tumbled onto the mattress, his hands coming around her hips, drawing her over him, her thighs straddling his. "Ethan?" she murmured.

Her hands were on his skin, on his *naked* skin. Her pussy hot and damp even through his underwear and the black leggings she wore.

"Yeah?" he replied gruffly.

"Are you okay?" she whispered.

"No," he admitted. "I'm not okay."

She drifted closer. "What's the matter?"

"I'm trying to remember that we've only gone on one date," he said.

"And?" she asked, when he didn't say anything else.

"And I'm trying to remember that, so I don't strip you naked, flip us over, and get my mouth between those fucking gorgeous thighs of yours."

Her breath shuddered out. Then she inhaled sharply. "Ethan?" she asked again on the next exhale.

"Yeah?" he said again.

"Do you really want to do that?"

He moved, an abrupt action that he seemingly had no control over, snagging her hand, tugging it down until it rested against the hard jut of his erection currently tenting the front of his underwear. "I'm fucking desperate to do that," he said, groaning when her fingers convulsed. "But I also know that we're just starting to get to know each other and—"

His words faltered.

Because she reared back and yanked her shirt over her head. Then reached behind her, unhooked her bra . . .

And let it fall to the floor.

"Yes, please," she said.

"Y-yes"—he choked—"please?"

"Yes, I want you to take me, to strip me." A beat, her lips turning up. "Well, the *rest* of me, and—"

Words failed him, but luckily action didn't. He flipped them, slanted his mouth across hers, cutting her off, knowing that if she uttered another sexy request, he was very likely to come in his boxer briefs. Aware that if she kept talking, he was going to lose control and forget he didn't have a fucking condom. Because she was *topless* and her breast were . . . fucking incredible, so much more glorious than he'd imagined—and he'd imagined a whole hell of a lot.

It would be so easy for him to lose his underwear, to yank off her leggings, and then he could be plunging home and—

Her lips found his, and they rolled on the mattress, his body pressing into hers, hers pressing into his, until eventually he managed to flip her again, to sink his body over hers, and even with their bottoms between them, it was the best fucking sensation of his life.

He trailed his hand along her side, and she threw her head back, the lines of her throat taut, the tendons in sharp relief, the slope calling to his mouth, and he heeded that call, dragging his lips along her skin, inhaling the scent of strawberries, tasting that sweetness on his tongue.

She moaned, gripped his shoulders, her nails digging in slightly when he reached the part where her neck met the slender curve of her collarbone.

Pausing, he spoke against the delicate divot. "You like that?"

Her eyes slid down, met his, and he expected her to shy away, to pull back, to do . . . something that wasn't wrapping her legs around his waist, her hips undulating against him, her words and gaze steady when she murmured, "Yes, Ethan. I like that." Her hand drifted up, cupped his jaw. "I—I—" She faltered for just a moment, and then he watched determination firm the gentle lines of her face. "I like *you*."

His cock was hard, aching, but what he felt for this woman was more than just desire and need.

Or perhaps, it was need in a different way.

To just be with her. To understand all the little idiosyncrasies that made Dani *Dani*.

So much tenderness and curiosity and affection, and while he knew her in many ways already—he knew she was a woman a man kept, knew she was someone who he'd cut out his heart for —he also wanted to know all the little things about her. What made her laugh, what made her sad. The places she wanted to travel. The books that made her cry and long for more. He wanted to glean every tiny detail because she was utterly fascinating. And as much as he couldn't wait until he knew all those parts of her, he was also looking forward to the journey, to the slow, incremental learning.

Which probably couldn't happen if she was topless in his hotel bed, but . . .

She was topless. Beneath him. With only leggings and some underwear between them.

And she wanted his mouth on her.

So he'd know her that way before the rest of it.

"I like you, too," he murmured. "Probably more than I should." Given how short a time she'd been allowing him in to see the real Dani.

Her lips tipped up. "I don't think you're supposed to admit that to the woman you're on top of."

He bent, nipped at her bottom lip. "It's better than liking you less than I should."

Amusement had been glittering in her eyes, that mouth curved, but his words made her pause, just for a brief moment, the delight flattening out, turning the warmth in those irises cool, unfeeling.

Then she smiled again, wider this time, but it was missing all the warmth, all the delight from before.

"What is it?" he asked, knowing this was one of those things that time hadn't yet granted him the opportunity to learn.

She wrapped her arms around his shoulders, fingers gripping his hair. "Kiss me."

An order.

One he obliged, slanting his mouth across hers, absorbing the wonder of this woman and how she tasted, how she felt, how she made everything inside him realign in a completely different way. But even as he kissed her, he shifted them to the side, tugging her so she was cradled against his chest when they broke apart for air. He couldn't stop himself from running his hand up and down her spine, bit back a groan when she slipped her palm between them, trailing warm fingers along his abdomen.

"Why'd you stop?" she murmured.

"What did I say?" he asked. "That hurt you?"

"Nothing." She smiled again, pressed her mouth to his, kissing him deeply, until his lungs were straining for air, until his cock was aching, his fingers trembling, desire hazing his vision, turning the edges red. Until he was wondering why in the fuck he was pushing this, why he wasn't just getting back to the tumbling and kissing and licking every single inch of her part.

But . . . he needed to know why she'd gotten sad.

Because he didn't want to be the one who hurt her. Not *ever*.

"Dani," he whispered, tearing his lips from hers.

She sighed, closed her eyes. "Please, Ethan."

That *please* almost broke him. It was just . . . he had to do the right thing here, had to be himself, and he wasn't the type of guy who pretended to not know the truth, who dismissed it just because he had a boner, and it would be easier *not* to talk about it.

Did he want her? Fuck yes.

Did he want her pain between them when he had her? No.

He didn't want that coloring their interactions, her pleasure, their time together in each other's arms.

She meant more than a quick fuck.

She meant *everything*.

It was as simple as that.

He squeezed her shoulder. "Tell me, sweetheart."

Her chin dropped to her chest. "Why can't you just take advantage of the half-naked woman in your arms?"

He stroked a hand over her hair, told her the truth. "Because I don't want to take advantage of you. Ever." Fingers under her chin, drawing it up so that her gaze was on his. "And I want to know you. Even the sad pieces. The hurt and broken. Give them to me. Let me help you put them back together."

Lips parting, a shaking sigh coating his skin. She shifted

closer, her mouth a hairsbreadth from his. "You're not taking advantage of me."

He ran his thumb over her bottom lip. "I don't want to hurt you."

"You're not." But there it was again, the falter. The hint of pain.

"Yet," he said gently, cupping her cheek. "That's the part you're not saying, isn't it? I haven't hurt you *yet*."

She went still and then sighed again, caution edging into her expression. "Should I remind you that I'm still half-naked and waiting for you to do the whole kissing every inch of me part?"

"I want to," he said. *Fuck*, he wanted to.

"But . . ." she whispered after he didn't say anything else.

"But . . ."

He needed her to tell him every detail of her past? Fuck, that made him an even bigger asshole than spending the last minutes ignoring the lusciousness of her curves and the blatant invitation in her words, her eyes. She'd already shared so much, and besides that, she didn't owe him an explanation of her past, not even because she'd offered up her body, allowed him close, had gone on a date with him, had told him what had happened in high school.

The truth was that she didn't owe him anything. Period.

And frankly, he hadn't earned enough of her trust to expect anything.

He had to believe that they would get there, that he'd unlock her inner core with patience and perseverance. She'd already given him so much in the short time they'd been together. "But, nothing," he said gently. "I'll be here, ears available for when you're ready to tell me."

Still.

Dani could go so perfectly still. Like a beautiful statue rather than a living, breathing woman. Of course, she was a statue with a stare that bored into him. "You're beautiful," he whispered, brushing the backs of his knuckles over her throat.

She unfroze, her hands coming to his cheeks, a blip of pain trailing across her face. It was gone in an instant, and then her mouth was back on his.

"Charmer," she whispered.

"Truth," he whispered back.

NINETEEN

Truth.

He'd just whispered the word like it was the most obvious thing in the world.

Even though it wasn't true, couldn't be true.

Despite the progress she'd made, she knew she wasn't beautiful, and most of the time she certainly didn't feel beautiful on the inside or the out. She was just Dani, just a woman, who'd been so fucking lonely and scared and filled with shards of broken glass and twisted memories that she hadn't been living—

She was half-naked, and Ethan was holding her.

She'd gone on a date, had talked to him like a woman talked to a man, hadn't panicked—or not much anyway.

And perhaps it wouldn't seem like a lot to other people, perhaps it was the smallest baby step to the outside world. But to her . . .

She'd taken a giant leap forward.

So she was going to damned well go with that.

She brushed her tongue along the seam of his mouth,

dipping it inside when he parted his lips, tangling it with his. His groan sent tingles through her nerves, dipped down between her thighs.

He rolled them again, pressing her down into the mattress, his body heavy and hard. His hand slid down her side, cupping her hip, slipping beneath her leggings to take one globe of her ass in his rough palm. The hot brand had her gasping, her pelvis tilting, wanting him closer, even though he was wearing far too many clothes.

He was wearing one item of clothing.

It was still too many.

Speaking of which, she shoved down her leggings, their limbs tangling as she kicked them off her feet, as she shimmied her panties down behind them. And since his chest was right there, she took the opportunity to kiss it.

His skin tasted of sunshine and the gentle, cool breeze that gathered on one's skin just before the sun started to set.

Lower and lower.

Until his chest existed only for her gaze and mouth, until he halted her explorations before she could taste every inch of him like she desired. Capturing her hands in one of his, he brought them up to his mouth, kissed the back of them, dragged his teeth along the sensitive insides of her wrists.

She shivered, flexed against his grip. "I want to touch."

"And I don't want to come in my underwear," he countered, lips moving up her forearm, light kisses along the way until he made it to the inside of her elbow, and fuck her if that spot didn't seem to have a direct line connecting straight to her pussy.

A shudder wracked her frame before she could tease him about his threats of prematurity. "You could come *in* me," she said breathlessly, as he continued kissing up her arm and then down her chest, drifting closer and closer to the hard buds of her nipples.

He froze, groaned, dropping his forehead to her collarbone. "Killing me, sweetheart."

"I'm the naked one," she said.

"Exactly," he said. "And *I'm* the one without a condom. So, I'll say again"—his finger trailed down her chest—"killing. *Me*."

"Is that all?"

He sputtered, and her amusement was a joyful, buoyant thing, setting her heart fluttering, her lips twitching. "Is—"

She nudged him back, sliding from the bed.

Somehow, she didn't feel self-conscious striding over to her purse, where it had fallen when she'd gone all cavewoman by the door, unzipping it and pulling out her emergency toiletry kit. Probably because when she glanced over her shoulder, it was to see his hot gaze on her, desire evident on his face. No derision. No disgust.

Just wanton need.

And she suddenly wasn't shy.

It was like all the heavy, gaudy varnish on a piece of furniture was sanded off, the beautiful grain of the wood below finally visible.

She was . . . finally *herself*.

"You're doing makeup at a time like this?" Ethan asked, his tone light, making her realize that she'd been acting like a statue again, bag open in one hand, a tube of lipstick in the other.

She tossed the latter aside, clenched the bag in her hand. "It's your fault," she muttered, climbing onto the bed next to him.

He was lying there like a tasty morsel she wanted to taste every inch of.

" *What's* my fault?"

"You're too fucking attractive." More muttering, though this time it was accompanied by her rustling through the contents of her bag. "Too damned distracting."

"I'll circle back to your need for my sexy body in a moment."

He sat up, trailed his fingers along her shoulder. "For now, tell me what you're looking for."

"I'm ... looking ... for ... ah-ha!" Her fingers closed around the plastic square, she pulled it out with a flourish and held out the condom. "This!"

His lips turned up. His eyes went even hotter. "You're a fucking goddess."

More joy bubbling inside her. So much that her face actually hurt from smiling so wide. "This, I know," she said lightly, thinking that in this moment, in this bed, with this man, she really *could* be a goddess, could go after what she wanted and not be a fucking coward. "I'm—"

His mouth found hers for a kiss that stole her breath, had her melting down to the mattress, him coming on top of her.

"You taste like temptation," he murmured, kissing his way back down her chest. "And the woman who has captured my soul." Those words bounced around her chest, bringing pleasure in their wake. Love and need and desire all wound together, lifting her higher than she ever thought possible. His lips dragging over her skin as she basked in that, his heated, damp mouth a fraction of an inch from her nipple.

"I—" His head lowered. "Oh, God—"

She groaned, lost her train of thought for long minutes as he lavished her breasts with attention, before slowly drifting lower. Her hands found his hair, stalling his downward progress when she found a particularly sensitive spot.

He obliged her unspoken request, stroking and kissing, nipping and tracing the area beneath her ribs, delving into her belly button, using his tongue and lips to create patterns on her skin that had her nerves prickling, her temperature rising. Fingers and mouth along the curve of her stomach, over her hip bones, drifting down between her thighs, coaxing them apart and settling his shoulders between them.

And then he paused, hot breath on her pussy, hands beneath

her ass. "Yes?" he asked, his voice a rasp that made her nipples bead tightly, her toes curl against the mattress.

"Yes," she breathed.

"Thank fuck," he said, the curse against her labia, vibrating through her, gathering slick heat in her center, taking her dangerously close to an orgasm even before his tongue traced through her folds.

That single slide through her pussy was the best sensation of her life.

One that was quickly eclipsed by the next, and then the next, and then the *next*, desire pooling, need spiraling higher as he ground his mouth against her and set about wringing every drop of pleasure from her body. Her head fell back, her hips bucked against his lips, moans tumbling from her mouth one after another.

That beard . . .

Fuck, it was *everything*.

Sensitizing her nerve endings, ramping her pleasure. She gripped his head, held him tight, and just hung on for the ride.

And what an incredible ride it was. She was shooting through the sky like a rocket taking off. Not a gentle slope to that precipice. It was straight the fuck up, and her engines were firing on all fucking cylinders until . . .

Boom.

Explosion.

It began at her clit, his mouth latched tight, his tongue flicking rapidly against the bundle of nerves. Then that wave of pleasure spread like a tsunami, flowing through her folds, clenching tight against the finger he'd pushed deep, was curling up against her g-spot. Every muscle in her body went taut for one brief moment and then lax as bliss flowed through her.

"Fuck," she whispered, going limp against the mattress. "Fucking *hell*."

Ethan prowled up her body, gathered her into his arms, one

palm smoothing her hair back. "Fuck, is right," he murmured, his mouth moving to her ear, nipping lightly at the lobe, his words making her shiver. "Fucking hell, you're the sexiest woman I've ever been given the privilege to lay eyes on."

Gravel in his voice, whispering over her skin, fanning the fires between her thighs. She rolled them, pushing him back to the bed, leaning down and slanting her mouth across his.

The sleek dart of his tongue, the soft sting of his teeth against her bottom lip, his kiss was sustenance and torture. Her lungs screamed for oxygen, but she could get enough air by kissing her way across his chest, sucking it in through her nose as she laved the divot of his throat, used her teeth lightly at his nipples. His muscles grew harder with each inch of skin she paid homage to, until he felt as hard as granite beneath her.

She kissed her way down, lower and lower until . . .

"There you are, gorgeous," she murmured.

His cock was pressed against the front of his boxer briefs, its glistening head just barely poking out the top, and she gave in to the urge to taste that moisture, flicking her tongue out to lap up the salty drop.

The brackish flavor had barely hit her taste buds before she found herself on her back, Ethan on top of her. His color was high, his hair tumbled, his beard slightly askew, but it was the way he was looking at her that had her thighs clenching around his.

Slowly, his hand slid up her side, the rough calluses on his palm making her squirm, especially when he trailed it in, pausing right below her breast.

"Eth," she murmured, trying to shift so that it would move just a few inches higher.

He smiled, but there wasn't anything amused about it.

She felt like the seal swimming frantically for shore, a Great White circling beneath, readying to strike.

If his cock brought her as much pleasure as his mouth had

earlier, she was in very good hands . . . penises? Teeth? Tongue? Hands again? All of the above. *Ha.*

That desire tempered, his smile softening. "What?" he murmured, tracing the edge of her mouth with his thumb. She realized her amusement must have bled over into a smirk.

"I was thinking I was in good hands"—her gaze dropped—"or cocks."

That cock in question twitched against her. "As in plural?"

She swatted at him. "You know what I mean." Then arched a brow. "Unless you keeping your underwear on means you have something you need to tell me?"

He shoved his boxers down, his cock springing forth. "Nothing to fear on that front."

She clamped a hand to her chest, feigned swooning. "Well, thank God for that."

"Thank *God* for your tits and the way they jiggle when you do that."

"Thank God," she countered, loving his expression—the open need, the desperate desire sharpening the edges of his face —as she reached for his cock, stroking a finger over the velvety head. "For your single penis. Because I need it inside me."

He cursed, using far more creative language than she'd anticipated.

"Wow," she breathed.

His lips found a spot behind her ear, one so sensitive that she felt her pussy clench. "Wow, what?"

She turned her head, halted with her mouth a hairsbreadth from his. "I like it when you talk dirty to me." A hand sliding down his stomach. "Remember how you asked me if I always stroke things so carefully?" Her fingers wrapped around him, squeezed. "I promise, I do."

Another curse, Ethan letting his weight come down on top of her, trapping her hand between them. Not that she minded, especially considering she had it wrapped around his cock.

"I don't think you're shy at all," he murmured, lips finding her throat and sucking deeply.

"I don't feel sh-shy," she said, the fingers of her other hand drifting up his spine, slipping into the short locks, gripping tight. "With you, I feel like I can just be Dani."

Motionless.

He took a turn to play statue and froze on top of her.

For just a single heartbeat. Then his mouth was on hers, and she was being devoured again, that strong, powerful shark threatening to swallow her whole. His hands were on her ass, her hips, her breasts, cupping her cheek so he could kiss her deeper and harder and—

He pulled back, one hand flat on the bed next to her face, the other on her jaw. "That is the sexiest thing you could have ever said to me."

"Eth—"

Another kiss that stole her breath, only this time she was ready for the intense, demanding man on top of her. She kissed him back, glad when he lifted up enough so she could use her formerly trapped hand to fondle his cock. He groaned into her mouth, hips jerking forward.

"I should probably warn you that it's been a while," he said, another groan tumbling from his lips as she showed him how well she could stroke.

"Then get inside me and make it less of *a while*."

He swallowed. "Dani," he growled. "I'm trying to make this good for you."

"I don't need good"—not strictly true, but she needed this man inside her, and if his oral skills were any indication, she already *knew* it would be fan-fucking-tastic, so he didn't have anything to worry about—"I just need *you*."

"We don't have to rush," he said, and every syllable was strained.

But seriously, the man didn't look like he could spend all day like this, teasing and coaxing their pleasure higher and higher. He looked ready to explode. And she wanted that explosion inside her.

"Inside me," she whispered, aloud this time.

"Fuck, sweetheart," he gritted. Sweat gleamed on his forehead, his chin dropped to his chest, lungs sawing in and out. His palm fell from her cheek, dropping to the bed beside her head, the tendons and muscles on his forearms taut and pressing against skin.

Fuck, what was it about men's forearms that were so fucking sexy?

She rotated her head to the side, keeping her hand on the hard length of his erection, pumping up and down, but giving in to the urge that had filled her at the sight of his strength by sinking her teeth into the muscles, not firmly enough to hurt, but enough that she could taste the salt and spice of his skin, feel the power of those arms in her mouth.

He jerked, more curses tumbling from his mouth.

And a second later, her hand was tugged from his cock, and he was grabbing the condom she'd retrieved.

She wanted to roll it down the length of him, but he was too quick, tearing into the corner of the plastic square with his teeth, yanking the condom out, and covering his cock with it in the next moment.

Then he knelt between her thighs and paused with his erection . . . so . . . fucking . . . close.

"Are you su—"

She gripped his ass, tugging down while at the same time jerking up, and that first stretch of him filling her was the best pleasure-pain of her existence. It had been a long time for her, too, and no one had ever felt like Ethan. Wide and beyond hard, pressing deep, spreading her thighs wide as he stroked his way all . . . the . . . way . . . home.

"Fuck," she said on an exhale.

That was . . .

"Incredible," he murmured, dropping to his elbows, his mouth finding hers for a scorching kiss as he pumped deep and slow and steady. "You're so fucking beautiful," he said when their lips fell apart, when she arched back, her neck straining, pleasure coiling, her hips rising to meet his in a rhythm that was set to send her straight into her first-ever double orgasm.

"*Ethan*," she whispered when he hit something, some place really, *really* good. "Baby, I—"

His eyes locked onto hers, staring deeply, seeming to read into the urgency in her tone because he kept moving in that inexorable way, with firm, sure strokes, only they grew faster and harder, and she felt sweat bead on her skin, her lips tingle, her muscles grow tight as the ache inside her grew and expanded. Her breathing sped, that edge was right there, and then . . . he slipped a hand between them, lightly caressed that bundle of nerves at the apex of her thighs.

And . . .

She exploded.

Fuck, that was good.

But good grew as Ethan sped up, hips pistoning, thrusting deeper, a growl bubbling up in his throat, every time he bottomed out, her orgasm flared anew, fresh sparks of pleasure scattering through her, shooting stars of sensation until he groaned her name, thrust once, twice more, and—

Collapsed on top of her.

He was heavy, making it hard for her to breathe, but she didn't mind, actually liked the feel of him surrounding her, pressing her into the mattress. She loved the fact that he'd lost it so much that he was unaware, especially when he'd been careful the whole time with his strength. There was something so incredibly sexy in him not being in control.

"Sorry," he murmured, wrapping his arms around her and rolling them so she was sprawled across his chest.

She was feeling too relaxed to summon any words. Instead, she just nuzzled into his embrace, smiling when he tugged the blanket up and over them.

"You okay?" he murmured sometime later.

Her eyes were sliding closed, sleep threatening to take her under, and she must have managed some sort of reply because he chuckled as the blankets crept higher. Distantly, she was aware of the bed shifting, of Ethan walking to the bathroom to deal with the condom.

Then he was back, tugging her into his arms.

She stirred, feeling like she should summon the energy to say *something*.

"Sleep," he ordered, smoothing his hand up and down her spine.

"We should get up," she murmured.

"Sleep," he ordered again. "Just for a little while." His hand continued moving, and with that slow and steady rhythm, with his warm, hard body surrounding hers, that was an order she didn't mind obeying in the least.

Her eyes slid closed.

TWENTY

ETHAN

It was ten days later, they were in Baltimore for their twice-yearly matchup, and he was kissing Dani in the hall.

Where anyone might see.

But it was before the game, and she'd just agreed to go to a late dinner with his parents after the game.

From first date to casually dating to meeting his parents.

All in the span of less than two weeks.

So yeah, Ethan was feeling high on life.

Of course, it had taken him years to work up the courage to make that first move, years he was kicking himself doubly for, considering how good these couple of weeks had been.

From the library to this hall.

He loved spending time with Dani.

He just . . . plain loved Dani.

That wasn't a surprise. He'd been half in love with her from the moment he'd made her laugh at Max's expense all those months before. Now, he was firmly entranced, falling in deeper and deeper with every minute that passed, whether in her presence or not.

He loved making her laugh and smile. He fucking loved . . . fucking her. He'd gone out and invested in a giant box of condoms, and they managed to find themselves in one another's room most nights.

The sex was great.

But the rest of it was fantastic. How she forgot to be shy with him. How he could coax her to step out of her comfort zone if he kissed her just right. How she found the strength in herself to do the stepping without him. They filled their hours together with meals and movies, with learning all the little things.

So, fantastic was the minimum description he could muster.

And now, she was going to meet his parents.

It was going to be great. His mom would love her. His dad would clap him on the shoulder and beam and then later would whisper in his ear, asking him where in the fuck he'd found her because she was way too good for the likes of him.

Which was nothing more than the truth.

Dani was leaps and bounds above his level, so much more than he was worth and more than he deserved—

She pushed against his chest, lips swollen, chest heaving. "We need to get ready for the game."

That was true, but for the first time ever, he didn't want to play hockey. He wanted to skip on the game, to take this woman into a closet and make love with her, and then he wanted to introduce her to his parents.

Probably, he should reverse the order of things.

But the body wanted what the body wanted.

Which was why he tugged her close again.

"Ethan," she laughed.

"One more," he murmured. "Just one more."

"Oka—"

He cut her off with a kiss, held her tight until she pushed him away.

"Give a woman a chance to breathe."

"No, love," he said. "If you can breathe, then you can think, and pretty soon you'll start questioning why you're with a man like me."

Her face clouded. "Baby."

He hadn't meant it the way it sounded, and God knew he didn't suffer from a confidence problem. But once the sentiment was in the air, he couldn't deny that it was the truth—at least a little bit. Hell, even in his mental conversation with his parents, the same notion came up.

She was wonderful.

And he was damned lucky to have her.

"I'm being self-deprecating," he said. "That's all."

Her face gentled. "Well, don't tease like that. If I've made a promise to stop putting myself down, then you have to as well."

He ran his thumb back and forth along the inside of her wrist. "I can do that."

"Good." She swatted him on the ass. "Now go. Skate your butt off."

"Then you couldn't do *that*."

She grinned, knowing him losing his hockey butt was never at risk. It was a glorious side effect of the sport.

He released her, turned down the hall.

"Ethan?"

He spun back.

"Remember that I'm always watching."

Laughter bubbled in his chest.

She nibbled the corner of her mouth. "I didn't mean it like that."

Ethan had to steal one more kiss, to taste the chagrin on her lips. "I know," he murmured, nipping at her jaw. "I promise, I won't wink tonight."

He'd received no little amount of shit for his previous wink. Which meant that Dani had also received no little amount of shit for the same.

Same went for the ones he'd given her during every game since.

She groaned. "I hope that's true."

He bopped her on the nose. "It's not."

Another groan.

"See you after the game, love."

"Oh, God," she moaned. "I'm meeting your parents."

He kissed the fear off her lips. "They're going to love you," he promised.

"Go," she said, shoving him back. "Before I freak out even more."

"Leaving." A tug of her hair. "I'll try to get on some of those highlight reels." He patted her hip, turned away.

Quiet greeted him, all the way down the hall. Broken only when he nearly turned the corner.

Then she called, "See that you do."

He grinned, love for this woman filling him to the brim.

And Ethan found that when he hit the ice, he was still smiling.

———

Dani was a quiet statue at his back.

His mom and dad had taken turns hugging him and were now chattering his ear off.

"Honey, you played great," his mom said, "and then you did that . . . thing with the puck to get it up to . . . your teammate."

He laughed, squeezed her hand. She could wax poetic on

Russian literature, but she couldn't distinguish a forehand pass from a backhand, let alone discerning between players as they moved rapidly on the ice. "Thanks, Mom," he said.

It had been a great game. The system working, riding the high of a series of goals from up and down the lineup. He felt like he was actually contributing and not just in working away from the puck. Ethan was connecting passes, making good defensive plays—he'd had a fire under his ass, both because Dani was watching and because his parents were there.

Things had just clicked, so Ethan was riding a definite high when he'd met up with Dani outside her office and had taken her to meet his parents.

A high that was so intoxicating it was certainly the reason for him missing what he really should have seen. Something he didn't recognize until later. Until it was too late to fix.

Until everything had changed.

"And who's this?" his dad asked.

Ethan turned and slipped an arm around Dani's waist, tugging her forward. "This is Dani."

His mom grinned, her brown curls a cloud around her head. "Hi, Dani, I'm Constance, and this is my husband, Brian." She stuck out a hand for Dani to shake. "It's so lovely to meet you. I feel like Ethan has been telling me about you for years."

Dani's lips parted, wide eyes coming to his.

He brushed his thumb over her cheek. "Someone might say that I've been a bit obsessed with you."

"For years?" she breathed.

A nod.

"Wow." She shifted closer, murmured, "Me, too."

And they'd wasted how much time circling each other? God, he should have made his move much sooner.

But his regret was something that would have to wait.

"I-it's nice to meet you," Dani stammered, and he watched

her shake his mom's then his dad's hand. It was strange to hear the quiet voice, the shy taking over. She'd been so relaxed with him, so much *Dani* that he'd almost forgotten about the shy side of her.

He squeezed her waist. "Should we go to dinner?"

His dad nodded, eyes going from Dani to Ethan. "Yes, let's head out. We have reservations." He swept forward, wove his arm through Dani's, tugged her away from Ethan. "Is my son treating you well?"

"I—um—"

"Yes," his mom said, closing ranks on her other side. "Give me all the gory details. Has he brought you flowers? What about chocolates? Jewelry?"

"Those are all too cliché."

A scoff. "They may be cliché, but they're still beacons of romance."

"Cliché romance," he said, coming up behind them.

"Tell me, honey," his father murmured, "do I need to have a talk with my son about the merits of flowers and chocolates?"

Dani tossed a glance over her shoulder, fear in her expression.

He stepped forward, ready to move between them, to be a barrier between his parents and her discomfort, to shield her until she was prepared to speak.

But then her face changed, determination pushing out the fear.

"No," she murmured. "You don't have to have a talk with him."

"You sure?" his mom asked.

"I'm sure." Another glance, this one filled with warmth. "He bought me my favorite body wash." She leaned closer. "And then he planned a candlelight dinner for me at Red Rocks."

The first had drawn his mom's gaze to his, her brows arched fiercely. The second had made her face soften.

"That's my boy," she mouthed as his dad took over the conversation, saying something that had Dani laughing out loud, the lovely, ringing sound filling the hall.

And his heart.

And Ethan knew this was going to be the best night ever.

TWENTY-ONE

DANI

She'd thought she was doing well, thought she'd managed to get past her insecurities because she was meeting people who loved Ethan.

And because *she* loved Ethan.

Dinner had gone well.

She'd started off a little slow, a bit stuttering, but once she really started listening, Constance had reminded her of her own mom. A force to be reckoned with, whip smart and funny, with plenty of pushy thrown in.

Then they'd dropped her and Ethan off at the hotel.

Or the initial plan was dropping them off, because they'd ended up staying for a drink in the bar, and that one drink had turned into three.

Dani had peeled off to use the bathroom, a little buzzed, more than a little high on life. She'd done her business in the single stall, had washed her hands, reached for the doorknob.

And then she'd heard it.

Well, *them*.

Voices in the hall, undoing everything she'd spent the last few weeks building up.

She recognized Brian's voice even through the door. "You've got a good one there, Eth."

Footsteps coming closer, their words rising in volume.

"I know I do."

The doorknob jiggled, making Dani jump, her hand clamping to her chest. The footsteps moved on, voices dimming, but not enough for her to miss hearing, "I love her, Dad. So fucking much."

"Oh shit," she whispered.

Shit. Shit. *Shit.*

Her knees gave way, and she sank to the floor, her ass hitting the cold tile. She should be happy. Thrilled even. She was helplessly in love with Ethan, had been for a while, even if she was good at pretending she wasn't.

Except . . . he *loved* her.

Fuck.

Her throat seized, spots flashing behind her lids, and her lungs worked without actually drawing oxygen into her bloodstream.

He loved her.

Fucking hell.

That . . . that . . . Her fingers scrambled for the lock, flicking it open, yanking the door wide. She stumbled out . . . right into Ethan.

Oh, fuck.

She wasn't ready for this.

She couldn't do this right now. She needed to have a panic attack in peace, needed to get to her room, to shove down all the old emotions of unworthiness that had burst forth at his words. It was just . . . too much and—

A soft hand on her back, rubbing up and down. "In and out," Ethan murmured. "In and out. That's it. You've got this."

Eventually, the edges of black receded, and she came back into herself in the hall, Ethan having tucked her close, his body wrapped tightly around hers. "You can't love me," she whispered. "You can't, you just can't."

His face gentled. "Except I do. I love you, Dani. Of course, I'd expected to tell you in a romantic setting, without the side of toilet. But I do." He cupped her cheek. "I love you."

She shook her head.

"Yes, baby. I do."

Her pulse thundered in her veins, her heart twisting this way and that. She needed a moment. She needed to think, to freak out, and then to recenter. To tell this man she loved him too.

"I love you, Dani," he murmured.

She pushed against his chest until he released her, staggering to her feet, shoving the hair out of her face. "I need—" She sucked in a breath. "I just need some time to—"

He rose with her, hands coming to her shoulders, eyes bright. "You don't need time. You need to accept that I love you." He jostled her lightly, making her head shake. "You have to—"

Her lungs went tight again.

The black crept back in.

"Just a second," she breathed, slipping out of his hold. "Ethan, this is so much. Too much. I need to think. I need to—"

Come to terms with the fact that her entire life had shifted on its axis again.

She loved the man, loved him back so intensely, but she couldn't muster the words out of her mouth. Instead, she scrambled for air, her throat swelling, her muscles spasming.

He loved her.

She loved him.

And . . . she was going to fuck it up. Or he'd realize that he wanted something else, deserved something more. The image of Roxanne burst to life in her mind, and for all she'd worked to exorcise those demons, to embrace her self-worth, to remember that Ethan had pursued her, had showed her over and over again that he chose her . . . she just . . . well, she was just too fucking panicked for something like logic to be effective.

He took a step toward her.

She skittered back. "Stop."

Hurt edged into his expression. "Dani?"

"I can't." A sharp shake of her head. "I just . . . I can't." More time. Space to think. A moment to clear this out, to push back the panic and to come back into herself. Then she could find the words, tell this man—

"You don't love me?"

She shook her head again.

Ethan paled, and she watched in horror as his hand lifted, pressing to his chest, to the spot over his heart, as though the organ inside ached.

Pain splintered through her.

He staggered back.

She stepped forward, realizing that he'd thought the shake was in answer to his question. That wasn't what she'd intended, not at all. She'd just been trying to clear her head. To stop the fucking tornado in her mind.

"Ethan."

He'd been staring at his feet, but the sound of his name on her tongue had him looking up. "It's okay, Dani."

There was a note of resignation in his tone.

One that had the panic in her disappearing in an instant.

As though he'd expected this all along.

"That's not what I meant—"

He turned and disappeared down the hall.

Horror froze her in place for a long moment then she hurried after him. Because fuck the panic, fuck having to think.

She needed to tell Ethan she loved him.

But when she made it out to the bar, it was to find that

Ethan and his parents were gone. She spun in a circle, searching, and then caught a flash of him, walking toward the front doors of the hotel.

All but running through the lobby, she snagged his arm just before he would have pushed out.

"Ethan," she began.

Constance turned. "Oh, there you are, honey. Ethan said you'd gone up to bed." She stepped forward, pulled Dani into a hug. "I'm so glad to finally meet you. We'll come out to San Francisco soon."

"I—I'd like that," Dani murmured, her eyes on Ethan.

But he wouldn't look at her, just stared out the large plate glass windows.

Brian swept her into a hug the moment Constance released her. "He gives you any trouble, you just call me, and I'll get him in line."

"He won't," she murmured. "You raised a good man."

Ethan flinched, and she stepped out of Brian's arms, reached out to grab his hand. He backed away, moved to the doors so the sensor picked up his presence and the glass panels slid open.

Brian and Constance waved goodbye and walked out.

When Ethan went to follow, she gripped his elbow. "Wait, I didn't mean—"

"I'm going to walk them to their car." He slipped free. "Wait here."

"O-okay," she whispered.

His eyes searched hers for a long moment, and then he turned and walked out the doors.

She waited.

But he didn't come back.

And when, hours later, she knocked on the door to his room, he didn't answer.

Why, fucking why hadn't she just been able to say she loved him, too?

Twenty-Two

Ethan

They'd hopped on a plane for an early flight.

Meanwhile, he was a ball of misery.

But he was in the business of pretending he wasn't miserable, dodging Dani at the hotel, arriving at the plane mere seconds before they were supposed to take off, and deliberately choosing a seat far away from her.

All to bask in his misery . . . and his idiocy.

He'd fucked up royally. He'd pushed when he should have been patient, and because of that, he'd gotten an answer that stung like a motherfucker.

Dani liked him.

But she didn't feel the same way about him.

Not yet, anyway.

He yanked out his notebook, spreading out his papers and books next to him, determined to focus on his schoolwork, something he'd been neglecting of late, and hockey.

The team typically traveled to their road destinations right after their game, unless there were more than the usual two down days in between matches. It made for a killer type of red-eye, but it was safer than potentially hitting a delay that might make them late for a game.

Because there was nothing professional athletes hated more than being off their routine.

Arriving the day before a game, sometimes getting in a practice or an optional morning skate in, let them get acclimated to the time zone, the weather, to get enough rest and exercise, and to continue their aforementioned routine.

For Ethan, this included joining in on Brit's killer off-day workout and then spending an hour on the bike and another in either the hotel's hot tub or sauna or the arena's—if they happened to have the facilities for the away team. Not all did, including the one they'd be playing at the day after tomorrow—the final game of the road trip.

Which meant that he'd wake up in the morning, be tortured by Brit and company, and then head back to the hotel for food and hot tub time.

And all the while, he would be pretending that he hadn't fucked up with Dani, that he hadn't blown it, that he wasn't spending all his time trying to figure out a way to explain to her what had gone through his head, and trying to find the strength to not push, to be patient, to hope she'd eventually feel the same way as him—

"Fuck," he whispered, stretching back in his seat, the rumbling of the engines a pleasant drone that would normally make him sleepy. Most of the team was similarly coaxed, the adrenaline wearing down and the familiar sound luring them under. Brit was curled up in a seat across the aisle from him, Coop in the row behind her. If they abided by their routine, Calle would join him shortly, the two lovebirds, still sickeningly infatuated with each other. They'd probably fall asleep holding hands.

Ick.

Also, this just in, he was jealous.

Soft footsteps made him grip his pen tighter, writing faster in the notebook where he was jotting down ideas for one of his final papers. He just wanted to finish it, to get his thoughts on paper, and then he'd try to sleep for a bit.

Try to pretend he wasn't responsible for gouging out his own heart.

The footsteps slowed.

He wrote faster . . . until heat prickled on his nape. Until he glanced up and saw it was Dani.

No, he'd *known* it was her.

That sensation on his skin, the rightness in his chest, the heat arrowing straight for his cock. It was the built-in Dani Locator, and right now she had stopped by his seat. Their gazes collided, and he felt the impact of those gorgeous eyes in his heart, as if she had reached a hand between his ribs and squeezed it tight.

"Hey," he whispered.

Her mouth twitched, as though she'd been going for a smile, but then she seemed to catch herself, nodding and whispering, "Hi." She hesitated. "I . . . about last night. I didn't mean—"

"Say no more," he said. "It's fine."

"It's not fine—"

"Ethan."

They turned, saw that Bernard had come up. "Need a word."

"I—"

With one long look at him, Dani moved back up the aisle. He knew she'd be on her laptop, working until the plane landed, making sure that everything was ready for the team when they needed it. The equipment managers, the trainers, the video coaches—including Dani—were some of the hardest working people in the organization. Their jobs usually began before the players and ended long after them.

The equipment team washed and prepped gear and jerseys

for travel, made sure extra sticks, laces, tape, and more were available during the game. They were constantly drying gloves, making sure the players' skates were in good shape, their helmets weren't worn or damaged. Hockey, as a sport, required a shit ton of equipment, and that meant their job didn't stop. But the trainers were just as important. Their job being to keep the players healthy, to come up with workouts and rehab and conditioning plans in order to make sure everyone was skating at their best. Diet was one part. Injury treatment another. Building specific types of muscle strength was still one more. And they had to keep track of that for an entire roster. Not easy.

But as hard as they worked, he'd never seen anyone else pull the kinds of hours Dani did.

Part of the reason he loved and respected her was because she never missed a beat, was always impeccably prepared, a consummate professional. Even as shy as she was with most people, she got her shit done, and the team was the better for it.

In a word, she was amazing.

Multi-faceted. Smart. A hidden well of fire and spine. And pain. And fear. And so much fucking courage.

And he'd fucked up.

He'd pushed her beyond that bravery and into fear, and he'd never forgive himself for doing that. But now, he just needed to figure out how to get beyond that, to convince her to move beyond the scared and trust that he wouldn't hurt her, to believe him when he said he wouldn't push her again. But for all his wants and needs, how could he possibly expect that faith?

"We need to talk about the game tomorrow. I wanted to . . ."

Bernard kept talking, explaining a shift in the system, how he would be playing a bigger role, at least for the time being. Normally, that would have been the best fucking news ever, but today, he was too busy being miserable.

After a few minutes, Bernard moved up the aisle, sitting in his usual spot.

But Ethan's eyes didn't stay on his coach. Instead, they drifted to Dani. Because . . . she was his heart.

"You're staring."

He glanced to the left, away from the aisle that Dani had walked up, saw Fanny leaning against the seat opposite him, her generous mouth curved into a smile. Since she didn't normally fly with them on away games, he asked, "Just couldn't get enough of us?"

The tall, statuesque brunette glanced behind her, then propped herself on the arm of the empty seat next to him. Well, mostly empty since it currently held a stack of his schoolwork.

"Well, actually," she said, lips twitching, "now that you bring it up . . ."

He chuckled quietly. "Visiting family?"

A nod. "Well, I *had* been visiting. We took a road trip of our own, and now I'm with you guys until we fly back to San Francisco. But don't worry, I'll be working plenty. I've got a whole slew of new skating drills to torture you with."

He groaned good-naturedly.

Yes, he hated skating drills. Especially after a lifetime of doing them.

But old—bad—habits crept in quickly, and Fanny kept him straight.

"You love them," she said. Then she leaned in.

Aw, fuck. Here they went.

"Who ya looking at?" she asked casually.

"No one."

"Hmm." A beat. "So, why is Dani walking around with pain and indecision in her eyes?"

He didn't bite.

"Ah, a recalcitrant one." She tapped her chin. "How many ways to destroy your legs shall I use?"

"I fucked up."

"Ah," she said again. "So, I need to destroy you."

He groaned, rested his head in his hands.

She sighed, scooping up his papers and books then sitting down in the seat next to him.

"You know I had a system for that, right?" he muttered.

"I *know* you had a mess." She opened the tray table in front of her, began stacking and organizing the texts in a way that he knew would make sense—just based on her totally organized system of drills both on and off ice, plus keeping track of players' milestones and goals. Fanny was far better suited for balancing a career and degree than he was. "There, now," she said, straightening the stack and turning toward him. "All in order. Now tell me, Dani and you, what's up?"

He made a face. "I told you. I messed up."

"How?" She pointed at said face. "And how badly?"

"Badly." Her expression clouded, and deliberately he dropped his eyes back down to his notebook, ignoring the steady brown gaze trying to force the rest out of him. He'd dealt with Fanny enough on the ice to know that she was a fucking force to be reckoned with once she picked at the thread of something. On the ice for him, it had been his backward crossovers, specifically him not putting weight on the proper edge on his left foot. She'd pulled that out of nowhere, had picked and prodded and drilled the shit out of him until he'd fixed that bad habit. It had taken the entire fucking summer, but he'd managed, thanks to this woman's bulldog tendencies.

And now, she was focused on Dani. On him and Dani.

Things were off. He was moping. Dani was hurt, and Fanny had seen that pain. Which meant it wouldn't be long until the rest of the team would notice.

He'd be getting wooing advice from Kevin, who'd managed to snare PR-Rebecca. Gabe, who was the Gold's head trainer and with Nutritionist Rebecca and really good at asking for forgiveness, would give him a multitude of tips, all while prescribing uncomfortable TENS therapy and/or a pressure point massage as punishment for Ethan's wrongdoings. And Brit would be all over it, enlisting Max and Blue and Coop to enact revenge.

That wasn't even including Blane, Stefan—their former captain and Brit's hubby, Mike, Liam, and Logan.

They'd all have an opinion over his mistakes, would drag him over the coals with one breath, and with the next, they'd want to help him fix his fuck up.

It would be awful.

It would be fucking great.

Because they were family, and they cared.

Ethan just . . . he already had put enough pressure on his own shoulders to try to fix things with Dani. The full-court press of the entire team would probably work against him, make it even harder.

Either that or he was worried that she really didn't love him, wouldn't ever find her way there, and she was just looking for some fun, exploring her attraction to a semi-good-looking guy with a decent job, some smarts, and a nice body. Maybe she didn't actually like what was beneath the surface.

Maybe she didn't see the same future he did.

And perhaps that was the biggest mindfuck of all. Because he wasn't the type of man to back down from what he wanted.

The degree was difficult with his job and travel. He was making it happen. It might have taken longer than planned, but he'd done it. His parents didn't want him to help them when his father had been let go from his job a few years back. He'd paid off their house, refused to accept any repayment when they'd sold it after his parents had both gotten jobs at a different university. He wasn't the most talented guy in the league (not by a long shot). But he'd put his fucking head down and worked to make a place for himself on the special teams. He'd found a way to be valuable and content without trying to be a superstar—not that he had the skill for it.

And that wasn't self-deprecation.

It was reality.

So he was living the fucking dream, feeling fulfilled in his work, in his life . . . well, in most parts of his life.

Because he couldn't make Dani love him. No matter how much he wanted her to.

"Earth to Ethan," Fanny said lightly.

"I'm working," he muttered, squeezing his pen.

"Thinking about Dani. Thinking about how to fix your fuck up."

"Fanny," he warned.

"Ethan," she warned back.

He sighed. "I love her," he said. "But she doesn't love me." His voice dropped to a whisper. "And I can't make her. Even though I really want to."

Fanny's mouth fell open, but he had to give her credit; she recovered quickly. "Ethan, that's—"

"Don't."

"That woman has come alive since you've started dating. She likes you. She *loves* you." Fanny squeezed his hand. "She may not be ready to say it yet, but have no doubt that her heart beats for yours."

The pain in him lessoned, the edges of the gaping wound closing slowly. "I still need to find a way for her to forgive me for pushing."

She snorted. "You're a man. Men push."

"That doesn't make it—" He broke off when her lips twitched. "Hilarious. I should make you do skating drills."

"I'd kill your puny little skating drills." She narrowed her eyes, lips twitching again, and more of that painful, caused-by-his-own-hand wound closed. "Dani is a good person. She's clearly crazy about you. So just be patient but persistent, and"— she leaned in, voice dropping to a whisper—"for the record, she loves Hot Tamales."

"What if she doesn't love *me?*"

Fanny smacked him on the arm. Hard.

The woman was stronger than she appeared, but her tone was even more fierce. "You are a fucking catch, Ethan Korhonen, and if you don't believe that, look inside yourself and imagine how you'd feel if Dani thought that she wasn't worthy of your love."

His jaw clenched as reality struck home.

How could he expect Dani to see herself as he saw her—wonderful, beautiful inside and out, smart, funny, incredibly strong—if he continued to view himself as never quite measuring up?

She nudged him. "Exactly. So put that derision and self-doubt to bed once and for all, woman up, and love her with every bit of your soul."

Fanny was out of the seat and walking down the aisle before he could summon any words, the reality of her words hitting him hard enough to momentarily freeze his lungs.

Because he finally understood.

Self-deprecating took on a different tact when it was laced with self-loathing, when it was used as a joke, but one with a painful center. He stared down at the tray table, knowing that it had begun long ago when he'd overheard one of his father's colleagues telling another colleague that Ethan's parents must be "so disappointed" to not have an "intellectual child."

Because he'd played hockey.

Because he hadn't taken to piano or Math Club. He hadn't had the patience to want to join the debate team.

He loved learning, but only what he found interesting.

Because outside of that, he'd loved even more to *move*—to be on the ice, to feel the cool air on his face, the joy of a team-mate scoring or connecting a sweet pass, the terror when a player was streaking back toward their zone, the dip in his stomach when a goal went in their net, the tightness of his lungs, the burn of his quads when he worked his ass off during a shift.

And he'd never quite realized how much how he'd valued that as less.

It had been masked by humor, by self-decrepitation over the years. Yes, the team called him *Big, Juicy Brain*, but he'd never felt that way—and how could he? He knew he was nowhere near as smart as his parents, and he'd been okay with that.

Except . . . he hadn't.

Because beneath all that *okay* was a thorn pressing against the inside of his ribs, jabbing him every time he threatened to breathe too deeply, to look too closely.

For all the joking and pretending to be confident in his place and unaffected by the bullshit that others brought, deep down Ethan didn't feel like he was enough. When he peeled back the layers, studied what was beneath that veneer, *he didn't feel like enough*. It was a painful fucking truth, because he wanted to be what he appeared to be on the surface, self-assured, comfortable in his space.

He'd found that professionally, felt it like a second skin settling over him by finding his place on the Gold. But as he'd found that, it had masked the rest of the turmoil beneath.

Why his first reaction when Dani hadn't returned his declaration had been to assume that *of course* she couldn't love him back.

Why he'd stayed away, avoided her like hell because he'd *known* that she was going to cut him loose.

Why he'd been so wrapped up in his own head, his own certainty that he wouldn't be enough instead of moving forward with patience and understanding, with openness instead of silent misery.

And, most importantly, finally, *finally* understanding that he could never love Dani properly if he was always worried about being worthy of her heart. He had to believe he was worth it, not to just give her his in an effort to avoid looking beneath.

But *could* he?

As he wrestled with that, with understanding he needed to be able to accept her love so they could build something lasting, his cell—connected to the plane's WiFi—buzzed.

He tugged it from his pocket, saw a text from his mom.

Thanks for letting us crash your date with Dani. She's wonderful.

Yes, she was.

It's not crashing when you're invited. Thanks for coming to the game.

The "..." danced on his screen, and he waited for the message to appear. Waited what felt like an eternity since his mom was a slow texter. But as he did all that waiting, he found his own fingers moving, tapping out a question he didn't really process until it was sent. Until the "..." on his mom's side disappeared.

Do you ever wish you had a different son?

His throat seized, fingers flying again, wanting to explain that he'd meant intellectually, or with a different profession, or—

No.

And then his cell vibrated with an incoming call. From his mom. And fuck, he didn't want to have this conversation, didn't want to delve too deeply, not when the realizations already had him feeling raw.

"Hello?" he murmured, after putting his earpiece in.

"I know you're on the plane," his mom said, her voice an odd blend of fierce and gentle, "so I'll keep this brief. I love you. Just as you are." She paused for a brief moment then went on, "When I see you doing something you love, when I watch you interact with others, demonstrating warmth and kindness and empathy, you make me so fucking proud to be a mother. To be *your* mother. I look at you and feel like my heart is going to explode with pride."

He inhaled, but she kept talking.

"And I'm so sorry that I haven't made that clear, that I made you doubt, that I didn't—" Her voice cracked.

"Mom," he whispered.

She cleared her throat, voice going brisk. "And I know you're on the plane and aren't really supposed to talk on the phone, so I'm going to hang up now. But that doesn't mean that what I just said isn't true." A breath that rattled through the speaker of his earpiece. "And it doesn't mean that I'm not getting on a plane and coming out to San Francisco as soon as possible for us to talk about it in person, okay?"

"Mom," he whispered again.

"Okay?" she repeated.

"Okay," he said.

"I love you."

"I love you, too," he murmured before hanging up and sitting back, his heart pounding, eyes sliding closed. The words washed over him, settling inside, and he felt the wound in his heart start to stitch closed. It wouldn't go away with a few conversations, he knew that. But it was on the way, and he also knew that he'd continue to work on it.

Because he wanted to live without that spike jabbing at him. He wanted to be whole, so he could move forward.

With Dani.

He was *going* to move forward.

With Dani.

Determination washing over him, he glanced up the aisle and saw Fanny staring at him, concern on her face. He nodded, mouthed, "Thanks."

She smiled, nodded, mouthed back, "Family."

Another blip in his heart, more of that wound stitching closed. Because she was family, just as the team was, and he was finally understanding that his place in it was more than professional. It *was* family. Truly. Not just something that was said on the surface or a good sound bite. They saw his value, and he was doing them a disservice to not see the same.

Another understanding came on the heels of that one.

If he kept the team out of this, if he kept their family out of his attempt to win Dani, he'd miss out on *this*. On the family coming together, looking out for one another. He'd miss out on the little insights from some of the people who knew her best, on the advice from his friends who'd won their own happy endings, on the kick in the ass he needed when he was feeling defeated.

This didn't need to be a victory he earned on his own.

He could—and *should*—use every tool in his toolbox.

Flipping the page in his notebook, he began a list.

The first item was Hot Tamales, followed by the types of junk food she'd bought during their grocery shopping outing, during their time together over the last weeks. Luckily, he paid attention to everything that was Dani-related, so within a few minutes, he had a decent list. Or at least, he had enough information to *feed* her.

That was a start.

He spent a few more minutes not working on his term paper as he probably should be doing, but instead making a list of questions to ask Fanny, ideas of things to do to win Dani over, other people he needed to pump for information—Brit, for one, Max, for another (the two biggest gossips around), and Kevin, for a third (because Ethan probably needed to admit that clearly he wasn't the best at romance and again . . . more tools for his toolbox).

By the time he'd filled a couple of pages and his eyes were burning enough that he knew he should give it a rest, he decided that he'd done enough planning for the moment.

He closed the cover, capped his pen, began stacking books, and—

Froze.

Because Fanny hadn't just been organizing.

The woman had deposited a box of Hot Tamales on that tray table, hidden amongst the books like an Easter egg.

Burning eyes forgotten, he ran a finger along the edge, smiled.

And then he pulled out a piece of paper, wrote a note, and tucked both into his bag.

He'd arrange for a special delivery later.

Twenty-Three

Dani

It was an hour until game time, and she was feeling absolutely wretched.

Since that night in Baltimore, since the brief interaction on the plane, she hadn't seen Ethan.

He'd disappeared while she'd waited for her bag.

And when she'd found his room number, had finagled a key by begging, borrowing, and stealing, he hadn't come back to his room, even though she'd slept in his bed and had waited.

She'd bungled things.

Badly.

She needed to make them right.

Only, she didn't know how. And now, she was trying to find a way to make it all right. But how the hell was she supposed to make it all right if she couldn't even lay eyes on the man she loved?

Hell, twenty minutes ago, she'd even gone to the locker room, prepared to announce her love to the entire locker room if need be.

But she'd gotten to the door, found it was locked to everyone outside of the players, and had come back to prep for the game, her wretchedness rising by the second. How was she supposed to focus on her computer when she couldn't tell the blasted man that she was fucking in love with him?

Groaning, she rested her hands on her head, her elbows on her desk.

Knock. Knock.

She dropped her hands, glanced up, and saw Kevin lounging outside the door to the office she'd commandeered. A far cry from her plush space back at the Gold Mine, it nonetheless did the job.

"H-hey, Kev," she managed.

He smiled. "How's it going?"

Her lungs felt tight, small talk with the gorgeous, built man not easy, especially when it felt as though her heart had been pierced straight through. Still, he was one of the biggest teddy bears on the roster, so she got over her shy, her pain, and spun her chair to face him. "I'm good."

Ugh.

She was so *not* good.

"Dani?" Kevin asked, tone concerned.

Double ugh.

Now she was lost in fucking thought instead of focusing on the man in front of her. "Sorry," she said, pushing out of the chair and moving toward the door. "What can I do for you?"

"Nothing."

Her feet skittered to a stop. "Um . . ."

He held up a box. "I think this is for you."

Turquoise paper. A pretty silver bow.

She shook her head. "That can't be."

He turned it in her direction so she could see there was an envelope taped to the top of it, and sure enough, her name was scrawled on the top in large, blocky letters.

"I—" Another shake of her head.

Kevin crossed over to her, pressed the small box into her hands. It rattled quietly, as though there were lots of small, hard things inside. "Go easy on him," he said, once she'd wrapped her fingers around it. "The man's just starting to learn the art of romance."

"What—"

He winked, was gone a moment later, well before the faltering question made it past her lips.

Dani had been left alone in the quiet room when her watch buzzed. She glanced down to see it was her assistant, Jess, telling her she was ready and waiting for them to complete their pregame check. Jess stayed back in San Francisco on away games, their tag-teaming engulfing both coasts—or in this case, the Midwest and the West Coast.

She voice-texted back, asking for five minutes, able to hear that her tone was off, her words shaky, all because of a tiny, rattling box held in her hands, but beyond glad that the artificial intelligence wouldn't pick up on her anxiety when it transcribed her words.

Technology was her friend.

For the moment, she had five minutes.

Sucking in a breath, staring at the box, debating opening it, she stroked the shiny ribbon for a few moments (which only further served to remind her of her fuck up with Ethan) before curiosity got the better of her and she slipped the bow off then tugged the envelope free. The flap was open a moment later, her fingers pulling out the note inside. As she processed the words, her lips curved up into a smile, and she felt a giggle bubble up, mix with relief in her throat.

Sweetheart,
Wouldn't want your body to get low on all that refined
sugar.

-E

Then she ripped off the paper, her head shaking in disbelief at the contents of the rectangular-shaped box.

Hot Tamales.

Probably the single type of candy she loved that she hadn't actually bought with him on their trip to the grocery store and only because she had already ordered a giant stash, one that filled up nearly an entire shelf in her pantry. A stash she'd bemoaned to Fanny about forgetting to hit up before they'd gone on the road trip—stupid feelings making her forget the important things in life.

Refined sugar.

Cinnamon.

Ethan.

But the appearance of this yumminess meant that Ethan had mind-reading abilities, either that or he'd snooped in her cabinets.

Or . . . Fanny had spilled the contents of her bemoaning on the plane.

There was a knock on the door before she'd delved too deeply into that, into what else Ethan might have learned over the last few days. She swiveled in her chair.

Mandy, one of the team's trainers, stood there, warmth in her eyes and another box in her hands.

"This is for you," she said, crossing the room and setting it on the desk next to Dani. A squeeze of her shoulder, no further words, and Mandy was gone.

More turquoise paper.

Another silver bow.

No note on the outside, but she discovered that was because the note was inside the box, folded and placed in a small silver and turquoise-speckled bowl that had been painted with, "Dani's Candy."

She unfolded it with shaking fingers, read it, and was . . . touched and hopeful and charmed . . .

And still just a bit scared.

Okay, a whole lot scared.

But also, a whole lot relieved. Because Ethan wasn't avoiding her—or she supposed he *was* avoiding her, but he didn't hate her. Rather, he was being sweet and sending her notes, and . . . God, she loved him.

Her fingers trailed over the slanted letters of the note, the crisp handwriting.

For your sugar stash.
-E

She ran a finger around the smooth, glazed edge of the bowl, and then, very carefully, she opened the Hot Tamales and poured in the inch-long red cylinders.

As she suspected, the box filled it perfectly to the top.

"How?" she whispered. "Why?"

But there was no one around to answer her quiet questions, so she spent the next ten minutes on the phone with Jess, going through their checks, making sure all would run as smooth as possible while the game was running.

And during this time, she was interrupted by no less than three more players.

First Max, who handed her a brand-new pair of ridiculously pricey Bluetooth headphones she'd mentioned wanting to Ethan in passing once. Then Coop, who came bearing her favorite coffee. And finally, Blue, a giant smile on his face as he deposited a box that turned out to hold the softest, cuddliest hoodie ever.

Yes, she put it on.

Yes, she drank the coffee while it was hot.

Yes, she synced the headphones with her laptop.

And . . . yes, she fought off the urge to storm the locker room, to grab Ethan and kiss him senseless. Barely.

Knock-knock.

She glanced up, jerking her hand away from the bowl and the smooth edge she kept fondling to see Brit standing in the open doorway in her usual pregame workout gear, worn during her warmup of running through the arena. She also wore a knowing smile and held yet another small package in her hand.

Christ, at this rate, Dani wouldn't have any room in her luggage.

"What now?" she found herself snapping. Then immediately slapping her hand over her mouth. "Sorry," she mumbled, the word muffled. "I . . ."

"Long day?" Brit asked.

She dropped her hand. "You have no idea."

Brit's brown eyes twinkled. "I will neither confirm nor deny any ideas held."

Dani stuck her hand out. "Just give it to me, already. I don't want Ethan's mission to mess up your routine."

"Who said anything about Ethan?"

"*Brit,*" she warned.

The tall blond moved toward her. "I've never seen you growly," she teased. "If it's because of the aforementioned certain yummy, bearded man, then I say it's a good look on you."

"You have your own scruffy, bearded man," Dani muttered, lifting her hand.

One brow went up. "And so I should keep my hands off yours?"

Dani felt her cheeks warm. Thank God, her skin didn't reveal her blush. "I didn't say that."

The second brow joined the first. "It was implied."

"No, it wasn't."

Brit pointed at the monitors. "Should we go to the tape?"

"You're not funny." A beat. "No, go get ready to make all

sorts of pretty saves I'm going to chop up into awesome bite-sized replays."

"For the record, I like you with attitude." She squeezed Dani's shoulder, turned away.

"What about the bag?" Dani asked when Brit started to leave with it.

"Who said it was for you?" A teasing question, but before Dani could start sputtering, embarrassment flooding forward to take hold, Brit plunked the bag down. "Ethan's a good guy," she said. "Love him. It'll be good for you both."

Then she was gone, the door clicking closed behind her.

"I'm trying to love him," Dani muttered, tossing her hands up. "If only the damned man would stop avoiding me."

Twenty-Four

ETHAN

"She seemed like she wanted to murder me," Brit said, strolling into the locker room and plunking her ass onto the bench next to him. "I'm assuming you know what you're doing?"

"Mad is better than running screaming for the hills," he replied, picking up his skate and checking his laces, his edges.

Brit paused, head tilting from side to side as she considered that. "Okay, you may be smarter than I anticipated."

He punched her on the shoulder.

Not lightly, because she didn't appreciate her teammates going easy on her. But also not hard, because she was his goalie, and he needed those arms in fighting shape for the game.

She scowled. "*Ow*."

"Liar."

A beatific smile. "That's true." She clapped her hands together. "What was in my bag?"

He knew what she meant without needing her to clarify. He hadn't told any of his "assistants"—as Kevin had termed them when he'd asked his friend's advice for winning over Dani—what was in the packages, and thankfully they were nosy enough to just be happy about being part of the process, not needing to know every detail.

But Ethan had known that wouldn't last.

And sure enough, Brit had that look. The one that told him she wasn't going to let this drop, not until he gave her the dirty details.

He picked up the other skate, studied the edge, making Brit wait because he thought it was funny as hell that she was impatiently wiggling like a puppy on the bench next to him, curiosity threatening to make her burst.

Just before she got to that point, he set down the skate, turned to her, and said, "A bag."

Her brows formed a little V on her forehead. "That's cheating. I already know I gave her the bag."

He chuckled. "No, Brit. The present was a bag."

Her face screwed up. "Just to confirm, what was inside that cute turquoise bag was, in fact, another bag."

His lips twitched. "Yup."

"A fancy bag?"

He shook his head. "Nope."

More screwing up. "What kind of bag?"

"I don't know." He shrugged out of his shirt, slipped into the skintight one he wore under his gear. "One of those ones with the opening at the top and the straps."

"A tote bag?"

"Yup. That sounds right." He unbuttoned his pants, shoved them down, and pulled on his jock.

"You had me deliver a *tote bag*."

"Yup."

"Just a tote bag?" she asked. "Without gold straps, and it wasn't filled with diamonds or chocolate or anything, right?"

"No gold. No chocolate. No diamonds. Just a bag."

"Brit! Stop snooping, and get your ass in gear!" Max yelled from across the room.

She scowled, jabbed a finger in his direction. "I can't believe everyone else got to deliver cool things, and I gave her a lame tote bag."

"She needed something to hold all the cool things," he pointed out. "And also, the bag had a badger on it."

More V-deepening in her brow. "A badger?"

"Because she's fierce." He smiled, didn't share that it was also because she had a badger tattooed on her foot, just added, "Especially when cornered."

Brit's face smoothed out, shock in her eyes.

Then she nodded approvingly. "Yeah, Eth," she said, punching him on the shoulder, "I am *so* glad I'm helping you with this."

———

The game ended up in a shootout, one they'd lost, much to Brit's consternation.

But the season was long, and they were in the early days yet. They always wanted the two points, but they'd take one, and a game where they'd ultimately played well, followed their system, even though the bounces hadn't gone their way.

That happened sometimes.

The Hockey Gods weren't smiling down at them, or whatever.

Still, they weren't professional athletes because they liked losing. It stung like hell, especially in the close ones, but Ethan, at least, had gotten better at compartmentalizing it away. He'd have tape to watch, a practice or two to try and flush out those mistakes, and then they'd have another game in two night's time.

Play hard. Take the licks. Rework the negative. Highlight the positive.

And do it all over again.

Done.

In the meantime, though, he needed to hope that his parade of gifts had begun the process of winning Dani over, because he needed to see her, needed to talk to her, needed to fix this . . . with more words and fewer presents.

"Ethan!"

He glanced behind him, stopping on the threshold of the locker room.

Scarlett, PR-Rebecca's assistant, her hair as red as her name, hustled up, clutching an iPad in one hand, using her other to push up her glasses. Her blue eyes shone with worry.

"What's up?" he asked, stepping toward her.

"I fucked up," she whispered, darting a glance over her shoulder. "I am *so* getting fired. This is the first time I've been on my own, and Rebecca finally trusted me to pick up some of her slack, and I am so *totally* going to get fired." She groaned, and he figured she was approximately a millisecond from freaking out.

Which was why he just crouched a little bit, enough to meet her blue eyes, and asked, "What can I do to help?"

"You're late for a meet-and-greet," she hissed. "A meet-and-greet," she added in reply to what was no doubt a confused expression on his face, since he didn't have any fan interactions scheduled. He always received notice before, always had them cleared with him just in case . . . and *ah*, he realized, finally comprehending her miserable expression, *that* was her fuck up.

"You're going to tell Rebecca, aren't you?" she asked dejectedly.

He patted her shoulder. "Let's worry about the fans before we panic about Rebecca," he said. "Give me the specifics."

She rattled them off.

"Okay," he said, stripping off his jersey. "I've got this."

And truthfully, he didn't mind this kind of thing. He wasn't a big draw, so these interactions weren't frequent enough to be draining, and when they involved kids, like tonight's, they were extra special.

"You're definitely going to report me, aren't you?" she asked morosely, as they walked down the hall. "It's my fault. I didn't tell—"

His shoulder pads were driving him crazy, so he took those off next. "If you can get these to Richie"—the equipment manager—"then we'll call it even."

"That's not—"

"It's fine," he said, squeezing her hand. "I promise you, this is fine."

"You'll still tell Rebecca, won't you?"

Ethan paused, considered that. "I'll have to if she asks," he said truthfully. "But I don't see why she'd specifically ask about this. She'll ask if you did your job well. She'll want to know that you care about the team as much as she does." He squeezed her shoulder. "And my answer to both of those will be yes."

Relief slid through her expression.

"You good with the gear?" he asked, less because he needed her to take care of his shoulder pads and more because he felt like she needed something to do that wasn't worrying about stepping into PR-Rebecca's shoes.

"I'm good," she whispered.

"Thanks," he said, handing them to her, and then he moved toward the teeny, tiny little girl and her mom, crouching down to talk about his three favorite things: hockey, more hockey, and . . . YouTubers.

Grinning over the girl's—Catherine's—head, he saw her mom sigh and open her mouth, like she was going to interrupt, but he shook his head, letting her know it was all good, and then listened as Catherine explained what sounded like a very intense trick shot that had been performed by her favorite, yup, he'd guessed it, YouTuber. "Do you think you could do it?" she asked once she'd finished.

He solemnly shook his head. "No way."

Her face fell.

"But I bet you'll be able to do it before I can."

She smiled wide enough to light up the already bright hall then threw her arms around his neck. "You really think so?"

He nodded. "I know so. Also," he said, handing her the jersey he'd stripped off earlier. "This is for you."

Another huge smile that had his heart squeezing tight. "Really?"

"Really."

Catherine yanked it over her head, practically swimming in the fabric, but she was happy, her mom was happy, and he chatted with them for a few more minutes. It got harder to concentrate as those minutes passed because he felt *it*.

Or rather *her*.

As Catherine spoke, his nerves prickled, the skin on his nape prickled, awareness filling every cell. His inner Dani detector was on full alert, telling him she was near.

He wanted to break off the conversation, to track her down.

But he wouldn't.

Because this moment was one of the big ones, an important interaction, something that—even at risk of him sounding egotistical—but it might be something Catherine remembered forever.

So, he'd give the little girl his time, his patience.

His complete focus.

Also, this just in, apparently men *could* multitask—or at least his inner Dani detector could still work while he listened to Catherine chatter. He felt her watching him, sensed her staying in place.

And that gave him the strength to finish the conversation.

Eventually, though, Catherine yawned, and her mom bustled her away after he'd signed the jersey, thanking him. He scored one more hug and a super special fist bump before mom and daughter disappeared down the hall, Scarlett swooping in out of somewhere to show them the way.

Thankfully, that inner detector was still blazing strong.

He turned, his gaze immediately arrowing in on Dani.

Twenty-Five

"Why do you like to be called Fanny?" she asked her friend, who was lingering in her office waiting for the bus to the airport and the plane that would take them home.

"What's going on between you and Ethan?" Fanny countered, making Dani's mouth drop open and her finger slip as she nearly deleted the wrong video file. Quickly, she closed and saved everything, knowing she could finish the rest of her work on the plane, when she wasn't at risk of crashing her whole system.

"Nothing," she squeaked.

"Sure." Plump lips turned up. "You were all lovely-dovey for a few weeks, and now I'm surrounded by mopey Joes, but nothing is going on." She sank onto the edge of the desk. "Also, I go by Fanny because every other girl in school growing up was named Stephanie." A shrug. "Being Fanny helped me stand out from the fold. Plus, I had plenty of opportunities to practice my comebacks for someone comparing me to a butt and/or a vagina."

Dani shuddered. "That sounds horrible," she said.

"Life is horrible sometimes." Another shrug. "You might as well control the shitty parts as much as you're able."

"That's actually kind of deep."

"I can be deep," Fanny said. "Just like I know that you're in love with the man, and yet you're not in his arms making goo-goo eyes at him."

Dani groaned, covered her face with her hands. "I blew it," she said. "He announced he loved me, and I freaked out. Yes, I love him, too. I've loved him for ages, but by the time I found the words, he was all shut down, and now I keep trying to talk to him, but he's either hiding or avoiding me and . . ." She groaned again, banged her head on the table, and wailed, "I still haven't been able to tell him that I love him!"

"He can't avoid you forever," Fanny said, "you work together."

"Well, he's done a damned good job of it so far," she muttered, opening her laptop.

"It'll be okay," Fanny said.

"How?" Dani lifted her head. "I hurt him."

Fanny squeezed her shoulder. "He loves you, babe. *That's* how I know it'll be okay. Plus, you have this organization of perfectly matched soul mates to serve as an example of how everything will work out." Another squeeze. "It's almost sickening how many HEAs we have among the Gold. You two are in good company."

"I know, but . . ." Dani sighed, cut herself off, hating that even though she had so much love for Ethan, she was still worried it might all implode.

Fanny bumped her shoulder. "Self-reflection builds character, but too much can freeze you in quicksand." Brown eyes gentling. "There is always risk in life, always a chance it might go wrong. But courage goes to those who can grab on to their happy." A flash of a smile, before her face went serious. "Because when you love someone, when you stop being afraid and just go for it then . . ." She released a breath. "It's like that, as simple as breathing, but you finally feel like your lungs can work fully. You can be yourself without fear, without being so locked down that you're not open to new experiences. You can be . . . happy."

Dani ran her thumb lightly back and forth along the space bar on her laptop, not hard enough to depress the key, just enough to feel the warmed plastic slide along her skin. "You make it sound easy."

Fanny pressed her thumb down on the key. "It is easy. As easy as striking a key," she said, returning her hand to her lap, "and it's also the hardest thing you'll ever do."

"Is that what your experience was like with love?"

Fanny smiled sadly. "That's a story for another time, preferably when I've had an entire pitcher of daiquiris."

"I'm sorry, Fan." Her eyes went to the single space on the blank document, the cursor blinking to its right. "I'm sorry you were hurt."

"I'm not." She swallowed. "Now, I have it on good authority that a certain sexy, bearded forward is . . ." She named a location that wasn't too far away.

No fear.

Just rightness.

"Excuse me," Dani said, pushing up out of her chair and moving to the door. "I need to go to him . . ."

"Dani?" Fanny called just as her fingers wrapped around the cool metal of the doorknob.

She stopped.

"For the record, no one is allowed to tell you how to feel. Not even me and my pushy self," Fanny said with a smile. "And definitely not those asshole inner voices. Just . . . throw in some mental earplugs and listen to your heart. That will always give you the strength to make the right decision." Fanny went to the door, warm brown eyes staring into hers, turned the knob, and opened it wide. "You got this." A wink. "Plus, love and the power of the Gold are on your side."

Dani released a long, slow breath and nodded.

Fanny smiled approvingly. "It's just that easy, babe." A beat. "Now, go on and tell that man what he means to you."

Dani slipped into the hall, moving toward the place Fanny had mentioned, knowing there were a million other post-game things she *should* be doing, and number one of those was that she shouldn't be walking out of the office she used while at this arena. She should be labeling and splicing and loading content onto devices, emailing it out to players and coaches so they had it before they could even think about wanting it. But tonight, as she took that first step, as she strode down the hall and passed the tunnel that led to the arena, the cool air of the ice hitting her skin, she paused and watched the men and women walk across the rink, repairing it, prepping it for the next game.

And she found peace . . . and courage.

Ethan could run, but she'd find him.

He could avoid her, but she wouldn't stop showing Ethan she loved him.

So, yes, there was courage inside her.

Instead of pain and fear, anxiety and insecurity. Those sharp spikes that had lived inside her for so long, eased by Ethan but still hiding in the background, threatening, waiting, making it so she had to breathe carefully and move cautiously, lest she do either wrong and jab herself . . . they'd retreated, disappearing into the ether.

Permanently.

Because she loved Ethan.

She turned away from the rink, and with that simple thought on her mind, in a sort of perfect moment of symmetry, she spotted Ethan.

Dani watched as he, still in the bottom half of his gear, his strong chest and arms on display with a tight black undershirt, smiled and fist-bumped a little girl who was maybe seven, the Gold jersey she wore engulfing her from her neck nearly down to her toes. After they spoke for a few minutes, he gently reached for the little one, those hands giant on tiny shoulders as he spun her so he could use the marker her mom held out to sign his name.

That done, he handed the pen back, and they talked for a little while longer. But he didn't seem to be in any rush, even though he had to be tired, had to be wanting a shower and to get out of that wet gear.

Finally, he took some pictures, got a hug and another fist-bump, and waved at the mother and daughter as they disappeared down the hall.

Dani waited, hardly breathing, and the moment the daughter and her mom were gone, Ethan turned, his eyes coming unerringly to hers, as though it wouldn't have mattered if she possessed the ability to camouflage with her surroundings, he would have still known she was there.

Her lips parted on a silent exhale, her heart thumping against her ribs.

He walked toward her.

Clunk. Clunk. Clunk.

Then he was there, towering over her even more than normal with the extra inches gained from his skates, and her nose was filled with the scent of salt and spice and . . . Ethan.

"I'm sorry," she blurted.

His eyes gentled. "Sweetheart," he murmured, his hand wrapping around her wrist in one smooth move—as though it were an unconscious action, as though he'd greeted her that way for an eternity, with his slightly roughened fingertips running along the delicate skin there. "I'm the one who's sorry. I shouldn't have rushed you. I should have—"

Unbidden, her eyes burned, her throat working as she attempted to swallow the sob bubbling up in its depths.

She wanted this.

She wanted *him*.

"I love you, Ethan."

"Sweetheart," he said gently, his thumb drifting a little higher.

"I've been trying to find you all damned day, wanting to tell you that from the moment you left with your parents." She grabbed his shoulders, shook him lightly. "I was surprised, yes," she murmured. "And scared. And had a full-on panic attack." She inhaled sharply, released it slowly. "Truthfully, I am still a little scared because what I feel for you is so big, so intense, so much more than I'd ever hoped. But I love you, so fucking much."

Her eyes continued to burn, and in a heartbeat, she lost her battle with tears, one sliding down her cheek, a hot, liquid brand, then more streaking in their wake. "I thought I'd messed it up." She sniffed. "I thought I'd lost you, and for one second, I wanted to give up." She shook her head. "But I won't give you up, even if you keep trying to avoid me and push me away."

"I wasn't."

She blinked at the fierceness in his tone. "What?"

"I wasn't trying to push you away," he said, cupping her jaw. "I fucked up. I hurt you. I *scared* you. I needed to find a way to prove to you that I would wait." He rested his forehead to hers. "I needed to make it up to you. To—"

She yanked out of his hold.

"You stupid, stubborn man!"

His mouth fell open.

"That was a universally stupid thing to do!" she snapped, shoving away from him.

"You didn't like the gifts?"

She froze, spun back. "They were wonderful."

"So, why am I stupid?"

"Because you could have come back, and we could have

talked it out, and I didn't need the gifts. I was miserable and hurt, and I—I just needed you."

A warm chest pressed to her back, arms around her middle. "You're right. It would have been much simpler to talk. Though I wouldn't have gotten the whole team on my side, helping, wouldn't have learned you loved Hot Tamales. Wouldn't have gotten to shower you with the small gifts that are only a fraction of what you deserve."

"I didn't need—"

He spun her to face him. "But I did. I needed to give them to you, and I'm going to keep giving you everything you need in a thousand different ways."

"Eth—"

"I love you. I'm going to take care of you."

"I feel the same—"

His thumb brushed over her lips.

"But I didn't think I deserved you. I had this well inside me that said because I'm not as smart as my parents because I'm not the most talented player on the ice, that because . . . so many other things . . . I thought you couldn't want me. That I'd need to be more." His hand slid down, lightly gripped the side of her neck. "And for you, I *want* to be more."

"I don't want more. I just want *you*."

He shuddered, his chin resting on top of her head, his arms banding tight, drawing her against his chest. Probably, she should be disgusted to be wrapped in the sweaty embrace of a man who'd just spent the last three-plus hours working his ass off, but instead of that, she was just wrapped in everything that was this man—his scent, spice and salt, but not unappealing; his gentle touch, his arms slipping around her, holding her carefully; and his words, softly whispered in her ear, words of love and romance, ones she didn't fully process at first, except to under-stand that the tone was smooth and easy, and then she did, and more tears joined those on her cheek, her lungs breathing.

Because this man was wonderful.

Ethan ran his hand up and down her back, calming her, still murmuring gentle words, comforting her without telling her to stop crying.

Because she hated that, hated when someone told her to not cry.

And of course, he instinctively knew that, just continued to whisper that he "had her," and held her tight, stroked her gently until she'd gotten herself under control, until the tears no longer came, and the sobs quieted.

"Sorry," she whispered, wiping her eyes and cheek with the hem of her shirt, glad that what little makeup she wore was waterproof and so wouldn't end up with her fun, sparkling gold eye shadow smeared all over her face. "This was supposed to be a romantic moment, but now I snotted all over you."

"You never need to apologize for letting me hold you," he said, cupping her cheek, thumb drifting up and wiping away some moisture she had missed. "Snot or otherwise."

Inhaling and exhaling slowly, Dani shook her head. "I didn't mean to lose it. I—"

"Dani."

She was already forming the next reply in her mind, started to pull herself out of his arms. "I just. It's been a lot and I—"

His hand on her waist tightened, holding her against him. The one on her cheek stayed gentle. "Dani."

"And I—"

"*Dani*," he said. "I'm telling you this in the nicest possible way." A beat as she watched laughter trickle into his expression, his mouth softening, so fucking tempting that she wanted to rise on tiptoe and close the distance between their lips. "But please, just shut the fuck up."

Outrage down her spine.

A gasp of indignation on her tongue.

But he didn't stop talking, just continued to hold her stare as he said, "I love you." That thumb swept forward, traced over her bottom lip. "You've held my heart in your palm from the moment I first saw you stroke an iPad, from the second you laughed and let those amber eyes meet mine."

She wrinkled her nose. "They're just boring brown."

"Lies." He shook his head, hand sliding up, thumb now lightly drifting across the bottoms of her lashes. It tickled, but she didn't back away. "You have tones of mahogany and amber in there, tiny streaks of gold and russet. I swear," he said, tone going a little husky, "every single time that you let me see them, I find a different shade in them."

Her pulse skipped around in her veins, as though someone had somehow dumped Pop Rocks into them. "I like your eyes, too," she whispered.

He smiled, that lovely turn up of his lips Dani felt in the depths of her soul—sticky cotton candy on her fingertips, sweetness tingling on her tongue, warmth in her belly . . . desire pooling between her thighs.

"Dani?" he asked again, and God, she loved the way he said her name.

"Yeah?" she whispered.

"I'm going to kiss you now." A millisecond later, his mouth was on hers, his palm tilting her head back so their lips were perfectly aligned, his hand on her hip drawing her a little closer, until she could feel his shin guards pressing against her legs, the thick protective hockey pants he wore firm against her pelvis and stomach, his chest hard where it met hers, his muscles gloriously clad in just that thin, black material. Her nipples tightened, her womb clenching in her abdomen, her pussy growing damp.

His tongue flicked against her mouth, deftly parting her lips to drift inside her mouth, to tangle with hers.

She rose on tiptoe, drifting closer, her tongue and lips not shy but joining in the glorious dance with him. The world fell away. She forgot about his gear, about the cool air of the ice drifting down the tunnel—she was plenty warm in his arms anyway. She forgot all about the publicness of their position.

And she wouldn't care anyway.

Because the team was part of their love story.

And anyway, Ethan was the only thing she could process.

His body, hard. His touch, gentle. His ability to melt the very marrow of her bones, vast.

His kiss, marking the beginning of their happy ending.

His hand slipped from her cheek to skate along her jaw, to drift up into her hair, fingers tangling in the curls, and he kept his mouth on hers, kissing her until she was a bundled ball of nerves, *desperate* for more.

He nipped her bottom lip, kissed her deeper, hauled her closer.

She moaned, nipped him back, and murmured, "I love you."

He froze and for one instant, the kiss got somehow even hotter. Their bodies coming even closer together, her hands gripping his shoulders, his drifting down to cup her ass, but then as things were just getting *really* good . . .

He pulled back.

With a wince.

Horror and embarrassment flooded through her. Oh God, she'd . . . done something. Hurt him somehow. Shit. He'd taken a puck to the ribs during the game.

She must have hit it.

She jumped back, flinching when his fingers caught on her hair for a heartbeat. "I'm so sorry," she said, fumbling with the words, her hands wringing in front of her as she stood in that cool tunnel.

Ethan took her hands. "You're sorry for giving me the hottest kiss of my life? For returning my love? For making me the happiest I've ever been?"

Well, put it that way.

She was sucked into the thunderstorm of his eyes. "I'm sorry I hurt you."

"I love you, you ridiculous woman." He straightened, a slow breath slipping out of his lips. "But what could possibly make you think I was hurting?"

"I saw you wince."

Now a smile teased the edges of his mouth. "I don't suppose you noticed that I'm still half-dressed."

Dani blinked at the humor of his tone. "Um, yes, I *did* notice that."

"Well"—hint of pink tinged his cheeks—"there's not really a delicate way to say this except to confide in you that an erection in a cup isn't exactly conducive to comfort . . . or blood flow."

Formal words that took her a moment to process.

Then when they did . . . her mouth dropped open, and her gaze . . . well, it dropped south, arrowing in on the region covered by hockey pants and the aforementioned cup. "You're hard right now?"

He groaned, put a finger under her chin, tilting it back up. "Not helping, sweetheart," he murmured. "I've got to go back into that locker room, and I can't be swinging my hard dick around."

"But I like seeing you swing it around. I especially liked it when you—"

"Not cool, Dani," he murmured, pressing a kiss to her mouth, though his eyes sparked with humor. "I'm trying to not have a boner, and you're not helping my problem."

"I like your—"

"You're a menace," he growled.

A blip of pride wove through her.

No one had ever called her that before. "I love you."

"God." His breath whispered against her mouth. "I love it when you smile like that."

"Like what?"

"Heat on the edges, sweet in the center." He groaned again. "One more, and then I promise I'll shower before I take you back to the hotel room and show you how good I can swing my cock around."

"We're hopping on the plane after this."

"Fuck." A pause, dancing storm cloud eyes on hers. "Mile high club?"

She burst out laughing. "I can barely fit into the bathroom, let alone both of us."

A grin, a brush of his thumb. "I think we can do anything we put our minds to."

She nipped that thumb. "Even loving a stubborn, shy woman?"

"*Especially* loving a shy, stubborn, wonderful woman," he said. "Now, give me my one more."

Before she could agree to that sentiment—and for the record, she would have wholeheartedly agreed—but before she could tell him yes, before she could just flat out kiss him again, his lips were on hers, his tongue in her mouth. Both hands went to her ass, lifting her against him, narrowing the distance so he didn't have to bend so far, their height difference dramatic with him in his skates.

And . . . then she stopped thinking about the movements and height difference and slipped back into strictly feeling, soaking into the sensations his kisses evoked. The prickles of his beard on her skin, the slight tickle of it brushing along the underside of her nose. Desire licking along the underside of her skin, burning along the edges of her nerves.

"Fuck," he gasped, breaking away so quickly that she wobbled on her feet, might very well have toppled over if not for him catching her shoulders and righting her.

"Yes," she murmured.

He smiled. "Yes, what?"

"Yes, we can try for the Mile High Club."

Ethan burst out laughing, bending at the waist, coaxing laughter out of her until her cheeks hurt.

Until that happy ending was a living, breathing thing within her.

He tugged one of her unruly curls, smiled that special smile just for her. "You just try and get rid of me."

Her breath caught, and she almost launched herself right back into his arms, the temptation to taste him, to hold on to this lovely, buoyant, confident feeling so strong that she didn't want to chance not feeling it again.

But then Brit came around the corner, Fanny at her shoulder, and both women took in Dani's closeness to Ethan, his hand still on her shoulder, both of them flushed, their lips kiss swollen. In an instant, Brit grinned and clapped her hands together. Fanny smiled, nodding approvingly.

And knowing this was going to be fodder for the gossip train —and not giving a damn—she found herself turning toward Ethan, tugging his head down, and kissing him with every bit of joy and love she felt.

Then she pulled away, loving the red staining his cheeks, the dazed look in his eyes. His fingers were tight on her hips, his lips glistening from their kiss. She nudged him back, stepped away. "I'll see you on the plane."

And then she walked past Brit, knowing she was wearing a cat-ate-the-canary grin, and not giving a damn.

"He's mine," she announced, patting the goalie's shoulder. "My bearded, sexy man."

"Hear, hear," Brit said.

There was no reason to deny it, not when it was in her heart, her soul, not when there weren't any secrets with the team, with her *family*.

Her love for Ethan was forever.

EPILOGUE

PART ONE

ETHAN, SIX MONTHS LATER

He was being stared down by three gorgeous women with amber and russet eyes.

"What makes you think that you could possibly be good enough for my Dani?"

"I'm not," he admitted, picking up his glass of water and wishing that when he'd met Dani's mom and sisters, it hadn't been on a night when he needed to stick with the diet plan.

Because fuck, what he wouldn't give for a beer.

"Mama, *stop*," Dani said, sweeping into the room with a big platter of food. She set it on the coffee table then came over to perch on the arm of Ethan's chair. "I love Ethan, and he loves me, so stop doing the whole scary parent thing."

He covered her knee. "I don't think she's *doing* the scary parent thing. I think she *embodies* the whole parent thing."

Dani sighed.

Belle, her mother, smiled. Barely, just the corners of her lips turning up. "You'll do, Ethan. I think you'll just do." He relaxed marginally, and the smile flattened. "For now."

Dani sighed again. "Loni, can you please talk some sense into Mom?"

"Nope." She reached for the platter of cheese and bread and started scarfing both down in rapid succession. "Mom gets to be Scary Mom for all first boyfriend interactions." Loni glanced at him, winked. "But don't worry, she calms down after a while."

Toni was in the midst of filling another plate, though she passed it to her mother, then did the same for Dani and Ethan.

It contained all sorts of things he couldn't eat, but he smiled his thanks anyway.

"For the record, my mother never calms down," Toni said, once she'd made up her own plate.

Dani sighed for a third time.

He chuckled.

She swatted him. "Don't encourage them."

Setting their plates on the table, he tugged her off the arm of the chair, brought her close. "They remind me of you." He kissed the tip of her nose. "So, I'll always encourage them." A beat. "And you." Grabbing her plate again, he held it for her. "Now eat," he ordered.

"Ethan."

He lifted the plate. "Food."

"I'm not."

"*Food.*"

"I'm—"

"Will you just eat the fucking piece of cheese?" Loni burst out.

"Language!" Belle scolded.

But Ethan didn't give a shit about language. He'd gotten fed up with the orders and the plate *and* the cheese. He swapped their positions, dropped her into the chair, and knelt at her feet, tossing the aforementioned cheese onto the table.

That was when she finally noticed it, her eyes going wide, her mouth parting on a gasp. "Is that—?"

That being the diamond ring Toni had done him a solid by hiding.

"Dani," he murmured. "I love you"—he glanced behind him —"and your family—"

"You haven't met my dad yet—"

"He has, baby," Belle said. "He's met all of us. And Daddy approves."

Dani sucked in a breath, her eyes wide.

"I—" He froze, all the pretty words he'd had planned in his brain drifting off into nothing, leaving him with a fuzzy tongue and a desperation to hear this woman say yes. "I love you—"

"You said that already," Loni grumbled.

"Shh!" Toni whisper yelled.

Dani lifted a brow. "You seriously volunteered to include them in this?"

"They're your family," he said. "Our family, and I want us to —want *you* to have everything you've ever dreamed of."

"I have you," she murmured. "Which means I already have it."

Fuck, he loved her.

"Dani Eastbrooke, will you—"

"Yes, she will!" Loni burst in. "Now kiss her already so we can have more cheese."

"Loni Eastbrook, you will be the death of me," Belle began.

"God, seriously, I wonder if you were adopted," Toni muttered. "You're ruining a perfectly happy and romantic—"

Ethan tuned them out. "Will you marry me, sweetheart?"

She slipped out of the chair, knelt with him. "You sure you want to be part of that mess?" A nod over his shoulder, where the voices were rising in volume.

"I can't wait to be part of that mess."

Tears leaked out of the corners of her eyes. "Then, yes, baby. Yes, I'll marry you."

Then with a conversation—no, an argument about the

proper merits of really good cheese happening in the background, the voices increasing in volume, he slid the ring on her fourth finger.

And then he kissed her to the sound of a debate over ranch vs. blue cheese.

A glimpse of his happy ending.

And a damned perfect one at that.

————

FANNY

She glanced down at the text from Dani, the picture of the gleaming diamond ring on her finger, and smiled.

Yeah, Dani was one of the good ones, and she deserved the good that Ethan brought into her life.

She typed out an enthusiastic response then set her cell on the counter and blinked rapidly. She'd had that once. The diamond ring, the loving fiancé, the wonderful, joyous hope of a future.

But it had all been taken away.

As she'd tried on wedding dresses.

"Fate can be a real bitch sometimes," she muttered, going to the cabinet and retrieving a glass—a big glass—because she was most definitely happy for her friend, because she wasn't the kind of woman who wanted everyone else to be miserable just because her happy ending hadn't worked out.

Shit happened.

Unfortunately, a heap of that shit of life had landed on her shoulders.

She opened the fridge, pulled out the stopper on her bottle of wine, and then poured a generous splash into her glass.

And then remembering the diamond ring that had once sat on her own finger, she poured another long splash.

"Come on, Fan," she murmured. "You're going to change into pajamas, put on a face mask, and watch the *Saw* franchise until you forget all about failed romances and remember that you have a very fulfilling life."

She paused, considered that.

Then nodded once, proud of her very sound plan.

Bringing her wine with her, since it was the first step of necessary oblivion, she made her way upstairs and into her bedroom, slipping into pajamas even though it was barely five in the evening.

"Plan, Douglas," she muttered. "Stick with the plan."

Right.

Wine. Check. Pajamas. Check. Mask. Next on the agenda.

She reached for the very expensive jar, washed her face, smeared on the cream, and then she belted on her robe, grabbed her glass, and headed back downstairs, plugging a food order into her cell for the fattiest, greasiest carb load she could find.

In forty-five minutes, she was going to be at a great place.

Nearing a heart attack.

But all the happier for it.

"Movie," she whispered, cueing it up as she popped some popcorn—because if she was going for greasy and fatty, she needed that, too.

Pretty soon, she was on the couch, the slasher flick rolling, buttery fingers gripping her wine and feeling so much better for it. There was no thought of unhappy endings, no heartbreak and pain.

Just actors on a screen playing a part.

And a nice buzz floating through her brain.

She wouldn't think about the past, about Brandon—

The doorbell rang, just in the nick of time.

She paused the movie before jumping up and hurrying down the hall, her memories chasing her like the hounds of hell.

The food was early, thankfully, would take her mind further off everything that had happened.

Flicking the lock, she turned the handle, pulled open the door, expecting to see a delivery person with a bag in hand.

Instead, she saw . . .

She blinked.

Impossible.

The wine had gone to her head, because he could not be on her porch. She was hallucinating. The alcohol content of the pinot noir was higher than she'd expected. This was food, that was all—

"Brandon?" she whispered.

The figment of her imagination stepped forward, the shadows disappearing from his face.

"It's me, Fan."

Her lips parted, every cell inside her waiting for his next words.

"I remember," he murmured. "I remember *everything*."

Her buttery fingers spasmed, and she lost her hold on her wine.

Glass shattered.

Red splattered all over her bare feet.

"Oh, no," she whispered, her breath catching. "Not again."

CRASHED

GOLD HOCKEY #12

ONE

FANNY

Wine. Solitude.

The perfect duo.

Stephanie "Fanny" Douglas was well-used to both.

She'd been single for roughly . . . well, for roughly an eternity. (*Eternity,* in this case meaning, a decade). Which meant that she'd moved beyond lonely, beyond being concerned with how much wine she consumed in the evenings during the week —a bottle every other night—and on to enjoying the simple pleasures where she could.

Alone.

Just as she preferred.

Her cell buzzed, and she glanced down at the text from her friend, Dani, gasping when she saw the picture of the gleaming diamond ring on her finger. Then smiling. Because she'd helped Dani's boyfriend—fiancé now, she supposed—pick out the exquisite piece of jewelry.

Sparkling. Huge. *Perfect.*

Exactly as Dani warranted.

Because Dani was one of the good ones, and she deserved the good that Ethan brought into her life. Luckily, Ethan recognized the gift he'd been given when her shy, lovely friend had opened herself up to his love, and he treated her with care.

So, Fanny didn't have to kill him.

Off the ice, that was.

Off it, killing the built, six-foot-several inches, two-hundred-and-something-pound forward would be difficult for her five-foot-three, one-hundred-and-thirty-pound self. She was softer than her figure skating competition days—though she was still tough with a competitive streak that had never faded—but even more muscle wouldn't give her the ability to take down the professional hockey player.

But that was okay. Because if he hurt her friend, she could always kill him *on* the ice.

Fanny was the skating coach for the Gold—having made the jump from the Gold's AHL affiliate (minor league team) a few seasons before—and being part of a team that wasn't new, and had won the Cup twice now in their short tenure, meant they had the resources to hire people like her. She'd been running her own skating company before the Gold had brought her on to the payroll with the Rush, and while she still ran her business (clinics, private lessons for NHLers and other professional hockey players during the off-season, and other classes throughout the year for everyone from beginners to those hoping to make the big leagues), her main priority was picking apart the guys' skating skills and improving on everything from edge work to weight distribution.

She loved it.

The guys were awesome.

And being able to threaten them with extra skating drills meant that she was feared and revered in equal parts.

Exactly as she liked. *Muhaha.*

Her phone buzzed again—a collection of emojis that had Fanny grinning, and she typed out an enthusiastic response (with emojis a plenty), sent it, then set her cell on the counter, her smile fading, the joy she had for her friend dissipating like fog receding from over the Golden Gate. "Don't go there, Fanny," she murmured as she blinked rapidly, the memories pulling at the edges of her mind, threatening to claw her apart, to bring her back down into a place she'd barely survived the first time.

But it was hard *not* to go back there.

Years ago, she'd had what Dani now had. The fairy tale, the once upon a time. True love that had been tested and rebuilt stronger. A man who adored her. The diamond ring, the loving fiancé, the wonderful, effervescent hope for a future and a happily ever after.

But it *had* all been taken away. Seized for good, even though she'd fought so, *so* hard to keep hold of it.

Ripped from her as she'd tried on wedding dresses.

"Fate can be a real asshole sometimes," she muttered, moving to the counter and setting down her wineglass—her *big* wineglass. She was most definitely happy for her friend because she wasn't the kind of woman who wanted everyone else to be miserable just because her happy ending hadn't worked out.

Shit happened.

Unfortunately, a heap of that shit of life had landed on her shoulders. Twice.

She opened the fridge, pulled out the stopper on her bottle of wine, and poured a generous splash into her glass.

And then—remembering the lovely diamond ring that had once sat on her own finger—she poured another long splash.

"Come on, Fan," she murmured, knowing she was talking to herself, having an entire conversation with herself, in fact, and that wasn't good. But also knowing that it was a desperate bid to snap her out of her memories, so she was going with it. "You're going to change into pajamas," she continued, "put on a face mask, and watch the *Saw* franchise until you forget all about failed romances and remember that you have a very fulfilling life."

She paused, considered that.

Then nodded once, proud of her very sound plan.

Bringing her wine with her, since it was the first step of necessary oblivion (more wine first, gory horror flicks second), she made her way upstairs and into her bedroom, slipping into pajamas even though it was barely five in the evening.

Probably she should do something productive. Review tape of the guys, plan her next clinic, return emails from an inbox she never seemed to get ahead of nowadays.

But . . . she didn't want to.

"Plan, Douglas," she muttered. "Stick with the plan."

Right.

Wine. Check. Pajamas. Check. Face mask. Next on the agenda.

She washed her face, reached for the very expensive jar, smeared on the cream, and then she belted on her robe, grabbed her glass, and headed back downstairs, plugging a food order into her cell for the fattiest, greasiest carb load she could find.

In forty-five minutes, she was going to be at a great place.

Nearing a heart attack.

But all the happier for it.

"Movie," she whispered, cueing it up as she popped some popcorn—because if she was going for greasy and fatty, she needed that, too.

Pretty soon, she was on the couch, the slasher flick rolling, popcorn in her tummy, the buttery fingers of one hand gripping her wine, the other swiping fast and furious on TikTok while she giggled like a loon . . . and feeling so much better for it. There was no thought of unhappy endings, no heartbreak and pain.

Just actors on a screen playing a part. Just funny people

making her laugh spouting about things she'd never even considered.

Plus, a nice buzz floating through her brain, softening the edges of the past, until she could almost pretend that she hadn't *ever* had a diamond ring, or a fiancé, or a twice-broken heart. Just random dates from men who never lasted long, whose sole purpose was to keep the matchmakers of the Gold—because hockey players were the *worst* gossips and busybodies—at bay.

She wouldn't think about the past, about Brandon—

The doorbell rang, just in the nick of time, chasing his name, the memories from her mind.

Thank God for *that*.

She paused the movie before jumping up and hurrying down the hall toward the front door, wine in one hand, still clutching her phone in the other, while doing her best to ignore the reminders of *him* that were chasing her like the hounds of hell. At least her food had arrived early. Stuffing her face would take her mind further off everything that had happened.

Fumbling with her cell, she flicked the lock, turned the handle, and pulled open the door, expecting to see a delivery person with a bag in hand.

Instead, she saw . . .

She blinked.

But . . . that was impossible.

The wine had gone to her head, because *he* could not be on her porch. She was hallucinating. That was it. Or drunk because the alcohol content of the pinot noir was higher than she'd expected. This was food, the delivery from—her eyes darted to her cell—Melissa, and that was all. A.L.L. *All*.

"Hey, baby."

His voice was—God, it brushed along her nape, drifted down her spine, caressed her abdomen, reached inside her rib cage, and dug its claws into her heart, slicing deep.

"Brandon?" she whispered, all her denials of *him* flitting

away as the figment of her imagination stepped forward, the shadows disappearing from his face.

"It's me, Fan." He swiped a finger down her face and lifted it to his nose, inhaling deeply, the pale pink clay mixture staining his skin. "Still the same," he murmured, those claws digging deeper, goose bumps prickling to life on her arms, lifting the hairs there, causing her knees to tremble. "God, I missed this." A beat. "God, I missed *you.*"

Her lips parted, every cell inside her waiting for his next words, knowing they would change everything.

"I remember," he murmured. "I remember *everything.*"

Her buttery fingers spasmed, and she lost her hold on her wine.

The goblet fell to the porch. Glass shattered. Red splattered all over her bare feet. The shards glittered like malformed diamonds in the evening light.

"No," she whispered, her breath catching. "Oh, no. Not again."

The silence between them was terrible.

Almost as terrible as the clawed memories tearing into her, ripping everything open, making her *remember*—the diagnosis, the treatments, him being so sick, her at his side, the surgery, him looking at her blankly, not knowing her . . . and then the cancer coming back and going through that all over again.

Nausea twisted her stomach and she gagged, thinking for a moment the popcorn she'd consumed was going to make a reappearance.

She *couldn't.*

She couldn't go through that all again. She couldn't have this man be the most important thing in her life and then lose him.

Not when she'd been so thoroughly broken after the second time.

"Fanny," Brandon said, stepping toward her, cupping her jaw, and she gagged again. He'd touched her face, swiped off some of the mask, but she'd still been hoping he was some drunken apparition. She couldn't pretend, not when she felt his fingers, slightly roughened at the tips, stroking along her throat, gently encircling her wrist. "Look at me, baby," he said quietly. "Breathe. It's okay."

The soft command loosened the stranglehold on her abdomen, eased the queasiness.

She breathed.

She didn't lose the popcorn.

"There you go," he said, smoothing back her hair. "It's okay."

Fanny didn't think that would be the case, not in any way, shape, or form. But still, she found herself leaning into him and when that wasn't close enough, she started to step forward.

"No," he said, slightly sharp, nudging her back, and she realized she'd nearly trodden over the shards of glass.

Her throat worked, tried for words.

Failed to summon those words.

"I . . . um . . ."

Fanny blinked at the strange voice, saw the girl with the paper bag of food. Ah, *there* was Melissa.

"I have a delivery for Stephanie?"

"That's me," Fan managed, and Brandon stepped back, took the bag from the girl, and plunked it into Fanny's hands. "Thank you," he said, tone polite but dismissive.

"Are you okay?" Melissa asked, looking between the two of them, the broken glass on the porch. "Do you need me to . . ."

Fanny finally unfroze, mostly because Melissa was great.

She nodded at the girl, heart squeezing at the concern the other younger woman was displaying. Solidarity, and all that. "Thank you for asking," she said, releasing a slow breath. "But I'm really okay."

"You sure?"

Brandon stiffened as her eyes went from him to Fanny again. "I am."

Melissa nodded, disappearing back down the driveway. Fanny heard the soft *thunk* of a door closing, the faint rumble of an engine starting up. A moment later, it was quiet again.

"Can I come in?"

Her pieced-together heart pulsed—hope and old pain all twining together, but she didn't step back, didn't invite him in. Not yet. Not—

"You remember . . . me? Us?" she asked, staring up into his deep brown eyes, trying to discern the truth. Because the last time she'd seen him, his long-term memory had been affected by the surgery that had saved his life. He had looked at her like she was a stranger.

"I remember."

But for how long?

Because when she said she'd had her heart broken twice, she *meant* twice. First in their teens, when his memory had been affected—though it hadn't been as bad, and they'd managed to help him remember after just a week. Then in their twenties, a seizure and car accident revealing the tumor was back, and while the surgery had gotten rid of the cancer, it had also taken all of the love he'd had for her.

"How?" she breathed.

His gaze flicked beyond her. "Can I come in?"

Fanny's eyes slid closed. "Brandon," she whispered.

"I remember," he repeated.

"But for how long?" she said, out loud this time.

His inhale of breath was sharp, harsh amongst the quiet of the night, and she knew that he couldn't tell her. *No one* could promise he wouldn't get sick again, that she wouldn't be forgotten and broken and forced to pick up the pieces once more.

"Fan," he said, stepping toward her, the glass crunching under his shoes. "Can I come in? Please?"

She stumbled back a step, shook her head, her "No," more of a shaking exhale than an actual refusal.

He heard anyway.

And he stopped.

Because he was the kind of man who listened, who was respectful of boundaries. Who wouldn't force himself in where he wasn't welcome.

"Fan," he hissed, not moving, and the agony on his face had the claws inside her lashing out, striking deep enough to *hurt*.

Tears began falling, slipping out of the corners of her eyes. "No," she said again. Stronger this time.

Brandon didn't move.

She shut the door.

―――

Fanny opened the front door of her house in the early hours of the following morning, having barely slept. The greasy food left to go bad; the wine and glass allowed to stain and litter the concrete of her porch.

Memories had tormented her all night long, had made it impossible for her to not see Brandon when her lids slid closed.

On the ice, playing travel hockey.

On the sidelines, cheering her on as she competed at increasingly bigger competitions.

Brushing back her hair and kissing her—her first—after she'd won Nationals.

Missing an important final so that he could watch her compete for gold.

Flowers and gentle touches, a room full of candles and giving her a narrow silver bracelet before they'd both lost their virginity.

The headaches. Passing out. The diagnosis. The surgery. The treatment. The—

She closed her eyes, focused on breathing in and out, but that didn't exactly help. Not after last night, not after Brandon had stroked her gently and told her to, "Breathe," in that husky voice of his. Because then she was thinking of his lush curls, those deep brown eyes, his strong shoulders, and roughened fingertips. He was the same and yet completely different.

A man.

Not a boy in the beginnings of adulthood.

And thank God the glass had stopped her from launching herself into his arms. He was a good person. She was glad he'd gotten better and that he looked so fit and healthy.

But she wasn't going there again.

Speaking of glass, she stepped forward, bringing the broom and dustpan with her. Then froze, eyes scouring the porch.

The glass was gone, not even the smallest sliver glittering in the overhead lights.

And the wine had been cleaned up, only a faint stain on her doormat telling her the entire interaction hadn't been a figment of her imagination.

"Brandon," she whispered, knowing instantly that he'd cleaned it.

Either that, or the magical wine fairies.

Snorting and feeling a little better now that her sarcasm had made a comeback, Fanny turned for the house and made short work of stowing the broom and dustpan before heading back out to her car.

Coffee.

Carbs.

Skating.

Another trifecta that had gotten her through the last decade.

Luckily, there was a Molly's around the corner, so she'd be

able to obtain the first two easily enough, and the third was already on the agenda for the day.

She was running a power skating class that morning.

With seven-to-ten-year-olds. Heaven help her.

They'd be busy and talkative, and her head would be spinning by the time she was done, but she'd take the almost headache caused by her charges instead of the one that came from Brandon showing up on her front porch and making her *remember*.

"Carbs," she whispered. "Caffeine. STAT."

With that, she got into her car, hightailed it over to Molly's, managing to make it to the front door just as the Open sign flicked on, and snagging two apple cinnamon muffins—still warm and smelling absolutely delicious—along with a chocolate croissant—because when she said carbs, she *meant* carbs. Molly took one look at her and wordlessly made the large coffee Fanny had ordered an extra-large.

"Thanks," she said.

Molly just squeezed her hand before turning to help the next customer who'd come in.

Fanny stepped out onto the sidewalk, sucking down coffee and burning her mouth, but the caffeine rush was *so* worth it, and when she got to her car, she peeled back the wrapper of one of the muffins, consuming it so fast that she felt a bit like a snake. Just unhinge her jaw and let it slide down her throat.

"And now isn't *that* a pleasant thought?" she muttered, navigating out of the parking lot and onto the freeway, downing the other muffin without the least bit of guilt. She hadn't gotten her grease fest the night before. The least she owed herself was apple cinnamon deliciousness.

Along with chocolate croissant deliciousness.

Because that was also gone by the time she reached the rink.

Same as the coffee.

But at least she felt awake and somewhat better by the time

she had her feet in her skates, the laces tied, the cold air biting at her nose and cheeks.

Home. This had always been and always would be *home*.

Cones and spray paint. Her clipboard, gloves, and beanie. The ice broken up with barriers and . . . kids. Talking and laughing, stumbling their way onto the ice, falling and getting up and tumbling into each other with a casual perseverance that reminded her of herself when she'd been their age. Well, that and the fact that they were so much closer to the ice than she was.

It hurt less when they fell that shorter distance.

Not that she was all that much taller, even now.

But a coach had to have her excuses, didn't she? Especially when the twins skittered toward her, nearly taking her out in their exuberance to show her *all* the hockey checks they'd learned in the two weeks since she'd seen them.

Grinning, she gently shoved them back, those claws in her mind finally slipping free. She could breathe. She could laugh. She could . . . torture.

Muahaha.

Lifting her whistle to her lips, she blew a sharp trill to call the kids in.

And then she got down to torturing.

Two

BRANDON

His eyes felt gritty, and his finger still throbbed from the cut he'd gotten picking up the shards of glass from Fanny's porch.

But that wasn't what had kept him up the night before.

No, that was all Fanny.

Or at least, the expression on Fanny's face when she'd seen him, when he'd told her he remembered everything about them. Because it had been raw and hurt. *No.* She'd been anguished because *he'd* hurt her.

Too many times.

Cancer had taken too much from him. From *them*.

And still, he'd expected to walk up to her house, ring the bell, and for her to just fall into his arms.

Fucking idiot.

Sighing, he started for the front doors of Prestige Media Group, or PMG for short. He'd gotten a job here only recently, having made the switch from independent athlete representation to a firm. Not only did it pay better and the risks were lower

—especially when the established company was the premier sports agency in the business—but his clients now had access to better perks than he could secure on his own.

Including Kaydon Lewis.

The former number one pick had recently been traded to the Gold. A good pickup for them because Kaydon had talent, even though he'd been battling some lingering injuries and hadn't yet lived up to the hype of being the first-round selection in the draft.

That would be different this season.

Brandon had seen that in the few pre-season skates the team had organized.

Which was how he'd stumbled upon Fanny. He hadn't known she worked for the Gold, hadn't known anything other than she'd moved to California all those years ago when he hadn't understood how important she was to him.

When the fucking cancer had taken that from him.

But fate had given him something back. Fanny on the ice when he'd gone to watch Kaydon, to make sure he wasn't pushing his recovery.

Brandon had . . . well, he didn't know what in the fuck all he'd done aside from standing there, mouth agape as he'd spotted Fanny on the other side of the glass, her dark hair pulled back into a ponytail, a light blue headband standing out sharply against the brown locks, glittering earrings dancing in her earlobes, legs and ass encased in tight black leggings.

A woman now.

And even more beautiful.

So he'd become a statue, soaking in every detail of her—her smile, the confident way she approached the players and nudged them this way or that, touching a knee through a shin guard, a hip through hockey pants, a shoulder through pads. He'd hated that she had her hands on other men, even knowing it was ridiculous for any number of reasons, not the least of which was the fact that it was her job and perhaps, the biggest being that he had no fucking claim over her and hadn't for nearly a decade.

He'd shoved down the jealousy, and instead, he had *seen*.

That she was good, that the guys respected her. That she knew her shit, even for Kaydon, who was new to the roster. She'd helped him through favoring that right knee, had pulled him aside and worked with him individually for a while.

Then she'd gone back to the team, running them through several drills that had the giants on the ice moaning and groaning.

By the end, the guys had dragged themselves into the locker room, and she'd all but skipped her way down to the hall that led to the offices of the practice facility, her ponytail bouncing behind her as she disappeared.

Not once had she looked his way.

So, he'd done some sleuthing.

And he'd found out where she lived (thanks to the IP address registration for her website).

Then had shown up on her porch like an asshole, obviously interrupting her evening in and making her hurt all over again and . . .

Being an asshole.

Fuck.

"Why do you have a sour lemon face?" Olivia—a VP at Prestige—asked, and he realized he'd been glaring at the front door to the business but hadn't gone through it. "The sponsorship deal with Kaydon giving you problems? I can reach out to my rep."

"No," he said, forcing himself to snap out of it. "I just didn't get much sleep last night."

She eyed him for a long moment before shifting forward and opening the door, holding it wide for him to pass through ahead of her. The light breeze whipped her black hair around her face as she stepped closer and asked softly, "Are you feeling okay?"

They—Olivia and Devon, the owner of Prestige—knew about his history.

Brandon had felt the need to be straight with them before they'd hired him on. He needed time off occasionally for doctor's appointments and checkups and though, up to this point, his scans had all come back clean, Brandon knew that might not always be the case.

And he didn't want to hide that.

"I'm good," he said. "Just a shitty night's sleep."

She nodded, studying his face for one more moment before turning toward the parking lot. "Let me know if that changes."

Now was his turn to do that.

At least to start nodding.

Because just as he'd started to incline his head, Devon Scott stormed up to the building, the former hockey player's body encased in an expensive suit, though the tie was loose around his neck and there appeared a be a Cheerio stuck to the collar of the crisp white shirt. "You will *not* believe what Becca did," he announced without any preamble.

Olivia whipped around, her eyes gleeful—she loved to gossip —as she clapped her hands together. "I thought you were going to stay home after lunch?"

"I *went* home—"

"And were apparently attacked by Cheerios?" she asked, brushing the collar of his shirt and tightening his tie.

Brandon bit back a chuckle.

Devon's face softened, the love he had for his toddler son evident. "Jasper was a little . . ."

"Don't talk bad about my godson," Olivia warned, lips tipping up at the corners. "He's a perfect angel, just like his Auntie Olivia."

This time Brandon couldn't hold back the chuckle, earning him a glare from Olivia and a smile in male solidarity from Devon. "What did Becca do?" he asked, trying to get Olivia's piercing blue eyes off him and back onto Dev, who was clearly more adept at handling her laser focus, if only because the other man had known her longer.

Devon sighed and thrust a hand through his hair. "You won't believe it."

Olivia grinned. "She made you sleep on the couch again because you snore?"

Dev scowled. "No."

"Hmm." Olivia tapped a finger to her chin. "Then are you mad because she had barely agreed to work for Prestige again before getting pregnant, having Jasper, and then decided not to come back and work for us—for *me*—again?"

"What?" A sharp shake of his head. "*No*," Dev said. "I'm fine with her working or not. I liked her here, even when she was working with you. It's just . . ." He trailed off, eyes going unfocused.

Olivia patted him on the shoulder. "That Bex cut you off from sex because you have an obsession with desktop fucking fantasies?"

"What?" Dev shook his head, his scowl deepening, though there might have been the slightest bit of red on his cheeks. "Where do you get these things?"

Olivia tapped her temple. "From the gloriousness of this giant brain." A beat. "And also because I'm friends with your wife."

Brandon snorted.

Dev continued shaking his head, kept scowling as he said, "Becca signed me up to be raffled off." He tossed up his hands. "I'm a prize for the Miner's Club charity event."

The Miner's Club was the Gold's charity, focused on providing sports opportunities for kids in the Bay Area, along with donating school supplies and funding after school activities for kids who either couldn't afford them or who didn't have safe places to be once the school day was done.

"That doesn't sound so bad," Olivia said. "I know a lot of men would like to be considered a prize."

"Would Cole"—Olivia's husband—"like being a prize?"

"Well," she said, waving a hand, "one could say he already is one. Both figuratively *and* literally."

"He's being raffled off, too?"

A nod.

Dev's scowl came back in full force, as though learning that piece of information meant that any hope of getting out of the event had now been dashed.

Olivia went on, "He's taking one winner up to the ranch for the day." Cole's ranch was another children's charity, introducing kids to the outdoors—hiking, swimming, horseback riding. All things that might not be readily available to children who lived in the city.

"The ranch." Dev made a face. "I'm a *date!*"

Brandon's brows lifted.

"So?" Olivia asked.

"*So?*" Dev's nostrils flared. "My own wife is setting me up on a date!"

Brandon's phone buzzed, a reminder that he needed to get moving.

"Oh Lord," Olivia sighed, threading her arm through Dev's. She met Brandon's eyes, him checking his phone apparently not having escaped her notice. "Run off while you can, young Jedi. I've got this one." She started to lead him back to his car. "Becca knows that you'll be a good prize. You'll raise lots of money and . . ."

Their voices began to fade, and Brandon found himself smiling.

Then he found himself trailing after them and offering, "Let Becca know that I'm happy to help out, too?"

Dev's eyes widened. "To take my place?"

Brandon shuddered. The only one he wanted to go on a date

with was Fanny, and only if that meant he wasn't going to hurt her. The idea of entertaining some random man or woman for the evening, having to make small talk all while being uncertain of their expectations . . .

Well, he was hard-pressed to stifle his shudder for a second time.

"I . . . um..."

Olivia frantically shook her head, mouthing, "Don't do it."

"No," he said, "I was actually thinking that I could help in some other way."

Dev's shoulders fell. "Right." A beat. "Cool, thanks. I'll tell her."

Olivia patted his arm. "Your wife loves you. The date is a good thing. And if it really bothers you, just tell Becca you don't want to do it."

"You know I can't do that," he said. "The baby—" A sharp shake. "I don't want to stress her out and have something happen . . ."

Becca and Dev had struggled with infertility over the years, and Brandon knew she was only a few months along with their second baby. That alone nearly had him rescinding his refusal to take Dev's place. Olivia, apparently, knew that. She shook her head at him and made a shooing motion. "Go," she mouthed. "He's fine."

Hesitating for another moment, at least until his phone buzzed again, the reminder telling him he really *did* need to go otherwise he'd be late, Brandon slipped away and retreated to his car.

And drove away just as Olivia folded Devon into his, the other man still scowling.

But at least he was sans Cheerios.

———

He closed his eyes and held still as the noise rattled through the space around him.

Loud enough to make his ears ring and his jaw clench.

It was his yearly scan, and one would think he'd gotten used to the sound and claustrophobically small space by now, but he still hated MRIs with a passion, and just being in the narrow tube had sweat breaking out on his nape.

Slow, even breaths.

Not moving unless he wanted to repeat the whole damned thing.

Which, for the record, he didn't.

But being trapped in a white tube, magnets zipping all around him, was not his favorite place to be. Being still and quiet with no other distractions *also* wasn't his favorite place to be. That allowed him far too much time to think.

To remember.

When fuck, this whole shitty scenario began because he *couldn't* remember.

And now, he could only think of the bad things. Of the buzzing sound that had replaced words when he'd sat in that doctor's office and heard he had cancer the first time. His parents had been there then, still alive, and Fanny had been, too, her fingers finding his and holding tight when he'd received the news.

Her fingers had found his so many times over the years.

Just before he'd gone under for surgery the first time.

When he'd awoken and not remembered who she was, even though it was only for a week the first time. She'd still come every day, still held his hand.

She'd skipped school, snuck out from her house, stopped skating until he'd remembered and had forced her to return to the rink, to her training.

But even with school, with her skating, he'd never doubted that she was there for him.

Their friendship, begun at the rink, had grown into young love, and after he'd gotten better, they'd shared their first kiss, their first time making love, they'd spent every single day together, including him traveling to watch her bring home a silver medal on the world's stage. Then he'd gone to college while she'd performed on the pro tour circuit, and though the distance had been brutal, she'd been wrapping up her commitment, and he'd just graduated when he proposed.

She'd planned—*they'd* planned—everything. The venue. The food. Their honeymoon.

She'd tried on dresses, dresses he'd never gotten the opportunity to see her in.

They'd tasted cakes and couldn't wait to lay out on the beach together as newlyweds.

And then it had all gone to shit.

He'd made it all go to shit.

His eyes stung, throat burning, and he knew that he was seconds away from losing his shit in this fucking tube, the goddamn buzzing scratching over his skin. It was too small, too loud, too much stimulus for his overwrought brain.

He needed to get up, to get out, to—

His fingers twitched then his toes, and he clenched his jaw.

Don't move.

Don't move.

Don't—

Fuck it, he was going to move. He had to get out of here, had to—

The whirring stopped. "Mr. Cunningham?" the radiology tech's voice rolled through the small space. "Are you all right? Your heart rate has accelerated."

Fuck. *Fuck.*

He forced a deep breath, released it slowly. "Sorry," he rasped. "I must have dozed off there for a bit. Nightmare."

The tech laughed, and Brandon's throat burned. The prickling feeling didn't dissipate, but he forced his breathing to slow, to steady.

"I feel your pain," the tech said. "Good news is we're almost done here."

"Okay, thanks," he managed to squeeze out, even though the words were hardly decipherable.

The whirring picked up again, the tech didn't say anything else.

And Brandon slammed his eyes shut, pretending that he was anywhere but there.

THREE

FANNY

She was right about her head spinning by the time she got the kids off the ice, much later that afternoon.

Exhaustion had crept into every inch of her, and her toes were absolutely freezing . . . along with her fingers and her legs and her nose and her arms and—well, every part of her was frozen. She was ready to call it a day, probably should have called it a day about three classes ago. But her coach that typically did the afternoon lessons had looked a little peaky, so Fanny had sent her home.

She didn't mind . . . except for the whole freezing part.

She'd warm up. Eventually. And the exhaustion would help her sleep.

Plus, before she hit her bed, she'd have her wine and horror flick and carbs, take two.

After skating to the far side of the ice to snag the last cone—there always seemed to be one left behind—Fanny made her way off the rink. A perky, adorable redhead was waiting for her at the door to the ice, practically bouncing on her toes. She waved, nearly dislodged her glasses, and then immediately pushed them back up her nose. "Hey!" she called.

"Hi, Scarlett," Fanny called back, biting the inside of her cheek to hold in her smile.

"I wanted to talk to you."

"No kidding?" she asked dryly, coming to a stop before her.

Scarlett, the assistant publicist for the Gold, swatted her arm then backed up so Fanny could get off the ice, move to the bench, and pick up her skating bag. She rolled it toward the front of the rink, pushing through the doors that led into the warmer lobby area—thank God for that.

Step one of unfreezing.

Step two?

Resting her tired tootsies by sitting on the bench as she unlaced her skates. Scarlett plunked down next to her, talking a mile a minute. ". . . and so the raffle is going to be the big fundraising initiative for the year, and we need to raise enough to fund all the big projects, and our agenda this year is *huge*, and that's a lot of responsibility, and Rebecca wants me to—"

"Scar," Fanny interrupted, smiling at her friend. "You can save the hard sale for someone else." She bumped Scarlett's shoulder with her own. "I'm happy to help. Just tell me what you need me to do."

Scarlett beamed. "Can you donate some private lessons?"

Fan dried the blade of her skate, slapped on the guard, and tucked it into her bag. "Of course, I'll donate some. How many? Five?"

"Five would be awesome!" Scar's smile went somehow wider.

Fanny took off her other skate, dried it, and put it away as Scarlett kept talking about the raffle—Devon Scott—retired player and former member of the Sexiest Player of the Month club—would take a fan to dinner, Stefan Barie—their former captain—had offered a seat next to his for a home Gold game,

Char Harris—the Gold's GM—was making herself available as a mentor. And all of that goodness would be followed by a silent auction with more items like tickets to Disneyland and wine tours of the North Bay. "Wouldn't my prize fit in better with those?" she asked when Scar finally took a breath.

Private lessons from a skating teacher hardly compared to the goodness of the others.

Her friend shook her head. "Um, no. A silver medalist giving free private lessons is a big prize."

"Except they can"—she swept her hand toward ice—"just come to the rink and sign up for a class."

Scar shrugged. "I'll give you that much, except that you don't teach too often anymore."

Not true exactly.

She did teach, but rarely instructed adults outside of the Gold roster. Maybe that was the draw?

Whatever the reason, Scar was emphasizing her silver medal and the private nature of the lessons—which was starting to sound a little more call girl and a little less instructor—and Fanny's strong suit wasn't selling people or spinning publicity or creating a great charity event. It was skating.

So, she let Scarlett run the show.

"Okay," she said during another pause in the one-sided conversation. "I'll do whatever you want."

Scar clapped her hands together. "I love it when people say that!"

Fanny snorted as she rolled her shoulders and stood. "I bet you do." She stifled a yawn. "Well, I should head home. I'm exhausted."

"Kids." Scarlett made a face.

And exes, she thought, struggling to keep her own expression neutral.

"But that's no excuse," Scar said. "Because you're not going home. You promised to go to dinner with Dani, Ethan, and me, and you're not flaking out this time, not just because of some kids."

"So says the woman who hardly has to deal with kids."

"So says the woman who is helping to run a charity *for* kids," Scar countered.

"*For* doesn't mean dealing with." Fanny chuckled at the expression of consternation on her friend's face. "But I really am tired. Do you mind if I flake?"

More consternation.

Crossed arms and a pouty bottom lip.

"No," Scar muttered, though that was very much a *yes*.

Fanny was immune to pouting. She'd had kids throw pretty much everything at her over the years—and that went for men and players, too. Because kids weren't the only ones with temper tantrums, though typically the ones she dealt with from the Gold were in jest.

Still, Scar's pouting in that moment had her reconsidering.

Not because of the stuck-out lip, but because of the prickling in Fanny's brain, the sudden knowledge that if she went home to her quiet house, to her cleaned-up front porch, to her wine and movie, that she wouldn't be able to keep her mind off Brandon. No matter how much popcorn she crammed down her throat. No matter how many carbs she consumed.

Maybe going to dinner would be better than being alone.

Scar's lip slid out a little further.

Maybe not.

Scar dropped her arms and pulled out the big guns. "We're going to Bobby's," she cajoled. "Mozzarella sticks, tacos, that weird panty-named drink that you love."

"A Panty Dropper?" Fanny sputtered. "I got that as a joke *one* time."

Scarlett nudged her with her elbow. "Well, maybe it's time for a second?"

It was the eyebrow waggle that did it. That and the fact that exhaustion meant she didn't have a lot of fight left in her.

Lie.

But sometimes a girl needed to lie to herself.

Plus, there were tacos on the menu.

"I know that face," Scar said. "It's the coming to Bobby's face."

Now she wanted to lie and say no all over again, just to wipe the smug expression off *Scarlett's* face. But . . . tacos and maybe she would go crazy and order a Panty Dropper, just to watch Dani blush all over again.

"Am I wrong?" Scar said when all Fanny did was glare at her.

"You're not wrong," Fanny said, ignoring the gleeful squeal as she grabbed the handle of her skate bag and started to roll it out of the lobby. Her car was parked out front, and when she got to the lot, she saw that Scar had taken the space right next to hers. "I'm surprised that you didn't block me in before I agreed to come with you."

Scar winked. "I had confidence in my skills of persuasion."

Laughing, Fanny just shook her head as she stuffed her bag in the trunk. "Want a ride?"

A nod from the girl with sparkling blue eyes. "You know how much I hate driving."

That her friend did. Not only did she hate it, but she was also terrible at it, having gotten into a number of smaller fender benders over the year or so she'd known Scarlett.

Mock-sighing, she hitched a thumb toward the passenger's side. "Get in, Trouble."

Scar frowned. "I don't *try* to be trouble, you know that, right?"

"Right," Fanny said, agreeing both because it was the truth —Scar didn't appear to seek out trouble, even *if* trouble seemed to follow in her wake everywhere she went (hell, it was a miracle Scar had parked next to her and Fan's car had remained unscathed)—but also agreeing because she really was hungry, and those tacos were calling her name.

Mmm.

Carne asada.

Maybe that was better than wine and solitude and slasher flicks.

She opened the door and sat down in the driver's seat, opening her mouth to ask Scarlett how work was going.

But she didn't get one word out before Scar blurted, "My brother's moving to town, and I want to give him your number. His name is Charlie, and he has pretty blue eyes, a great smile, and a stable job. Plus, he's got the perfect amount of squish."

Fanny's brows lifted, but she didn't get the chance to ask the question on the tip of her tongue (namely asking what was the perfect amount of squish) before Scar kept talking.

"He's huggable and good-looking and funny. Plus, he's single. He's the perfect Fanny material."

She'd hope so—the single part, anyway—if Scar was trying to set them up.

"I'm not really—"

She picked up Fanny's phone, plugging in the code to unlock the screen, and for a moment, Fanny regretted having shared the set of numbers that last time they'd ridden together. Then it had been to access a playlist; tonight it was to plug in Charlie's information.

Or at least, that was what Fanny assumed by Scar setting the cell back into the cupholder and leaning back in her seat. "There. Now you can call him and you two can meet up and you'll fall in love and then you'll have to be my sister and put up with me."

Heaven help her.

But she caught a glance of Scarlett's sparkling eyes, the utter joy and life and . . . found Scar's enthusiasm contagious.

At least enough to smile and say, "I don't know about the love part."

"But you'll call him?"

Fanny pressed her lips together to stifle the chuckle. Persistent meet trouble.

And Scar hadn't even pulled out the pout this time.

She drove out of the lot, navigated to the freeway, and found herself agreeing. "Yeah, Scar, I'll call him."

———

"And *that's* when Dani started blushing and swatting me, trying to shut me up," Scarlett said. "But I wouldn't be deterred. Madeline"—Blane, a defenseman, and Mandy's, the trainer for the Gold, oldest kiddo—"deserved that Tickle-Me Elmo, and I was going to die on that field to get it."

"And by *field,* Scar means the long, white aisles of Target," Dani said dryly.

Ethan was grinning, his arm around Dani's shoulders, his hand rubbing up and down her arm.

She'd had that.

She missed that.

Missed *Brandon.*

Swallowing hard, she took another long swallow of her Panty Dropper—her third? Fourth? *Fifth?* Honestly, she'd lost count, hadn't realized how hard it would hit her to see the diamond ring, the happiness on her friend's face, the obvious love between her and Ethan.

It wasn't like she hadn't seen them all lovey-dovey before. Of course, she had. Hell, she'd pushed them together, had helped Ethan select the ring.

But . . . Brandon.

She was raw and exhausted and . . . drunk.

So, she had that going for her.

Cool.

The server came around, refilling drinks. "You want another?" she asked Fanny.

The room was starting to spin at the edges, but Dani and Ethan were still in focus, so she nodded. Irresponsible? Yes. But Scar, who was drinking water, could drive her home—and hopefully not wreck her car in the process.

Solid plan.

Yes, that was the Panty Droppers talking.

She lifted her glass, and oh look, it was good she'd ordered another because it was empty. Still, she sucked down a few more drops, mostly the dredges of melted ice. When she plunked the glass back down on the table, her gaze caught on Ethan's.

And because he was still in focus even though hardly anything else was, she saw the concern on his face.

Fuck.

Scarlett was still talking, but he leaned closer to her and asked softly, "You okay?"

She slapped on her award-winning smile. The one that she'd once used with sponsors. The one that had given her enough cash to have a decent retirement savings *and* to start her business. "Just tired. Kids are monsters," she added with a chuckle that sounded forced, even to her own ears, when the concern didn't go away.

Scarlett chimed in. "Fanny was on the ice *all* day."

"And I couldn't even torture them by making them do ladder drills."

Ethan winced. "I hate ladder drills."

She smiled widely. "I like what they do to your endurance."

A grin. A shake of his head.

"Plus, you really hate the Umbrella." A drill she'd come up with that involved cones and a copious amount of edge work.

And one that Ethan, who struggled with using his outside edge on the right side effectively, really *really* hated.

Case in point, he shuddered. "I do," he muttered. "I do."

"You should make him do it anyway," Dani said with a smirk that was very un-Dani-like.

Fanny lifted her brows. "Torturing him not one day after the man gave you a giant ring?"

"Yup." The smirk widened.

Ethan clamped a hand to his chest, over his heart. "You wound me."

Dani snagged that hand, kissed the back of it. "I kid. I kid. You know I love you, and I only approve of Fanny's torturing because I get to reap the benefits of it on your body."

Scarlett cackled.

Fanny grinned, pretended to make a tick on her mental checklist. "Umbrella. Check. Ladders. Check."

Ethan groaned.

"Think of it like medicine, baby." Dani patted his cheek. "It's good for you."

Another groan.

They kept teasing Ethan, and he was a good sport about it. And she was glad she'd come, even despite the happiness radiating from the happy couple across the table making her teeth ache. They deserved that happy, and . . . she did, too.

For the first time in a long time, she thought that she did, too.

And—oh look, right on the tail of that uncomfortable thought, the one that had her throat squeezing tight, bile churning in her gut—her glass was empty again.

She signaled to the waitress for another.

"You're driving," she told Scarlett when her friend took a breath and Dani started teasing Ethan about how he'd cried at the movie they'd watched the previous weekend.

Scarlett glanced from the glass to Fanny's face. "You're not okay," she said.

Fanny sipped again. "No," she admitted. "But I'll get there." A beat. "I always do."

———

Later that night, Ethan took pity on Fanny (and her car and the risk Scar's driving might bring to it), and drove them back to the rink. They stopped long enough to drop Scarlett off at her sedan before heading to Fan's house.

Fanny was less drunk and more buzzed, even after having finished that last drink, mostly because Ethan had ordered another plate of mozzarella sticks and everyone knew that greasy cheese soaked up alcohol. Right. Stifling an inner snort as Ethan swung the car out of the parking lot, she knew that last couple of drinks were a mistake. Mostly because she was nowhere near sober enough to drive.

And because her drinking too much, her losing control was unusual, she knew that she had sparked Ethan's protective tendencies.

He wasn't her man, but she was Dani's friend and part of the Gold, and that meant she wouldn't put it past him to pull out his caveman proclivities, trying to ferret out what was wrong and then invariably solve whatever problem he discovered.

It would be sweet.

But unnecessary.

So, she headed him off before he could get that far.

"Dani told me that you're thinking about getting another master's degree?" She nudged his arm. "What? Need to prove you're the smartest one on the team all over again?"

A smile in her direction, though she knew that if it were light out, she would probably see his cheeks were slightly flushed, despite his cocky words that followed. "There's no need to prove that I'm the smartest one." A beat. "I already know I am."

She snorted, this time aloud. But she asked him about his studies, despite the arrogance.

One, because she was interested. Two, because talking about

it would hopefully distract him from any concern she might have triggered.

He started telling her about his latest round of courses, and he had a soft, rumbling voice.

It was pleasant and warm and with the streetlights whizzing by outside the car windows, the soft hum of the engine, she found her lids growing heavy, her brain slowing down, her muscles growing slack.

Black slid up and slowly, inexorably dragged her under.

Four

Brandon

He was sitting on the porch, outside a dark house.

Outside Fanny's dark house.

There was no movie noise this time. Nor was every light flicked on, illuminating the ground floor like it had been when he'd come last night.

It was quiet and still.

Where was she?

He knew it was wrong for him to be there, especially after her reaction the previous evening, but he'd gone home after his appointment, had sat in his own quiet and still condo, and had found it impossible to stay there.

The walls were closing in.

He'd gotten in his car, and he'd driven off, intending to just circle the block or the neighborhood in order to clear his head.

But invariably, he'd found himself on her street.

In front of her house.

On her porch.

And now . . . watching her walk up the path toward him in the arms of another man.

If he'd been in the right frame of mind, he would have recognized that man as a player for the Gold—Ethan something—who was madly in love with his girlfriend, now fiancé. If he'd been in the right frame of mind, he would have noticed that the hold was more steadying and not sexual.

But he wasn't in the right frame of mind.

And Fanny—*his* Fanny—was in the arms of someone who wasn't him.

He rose from the porch and stalked toward them. Fucking stupid that was, the man towered over him, was huge and built and could turn his puny ass at five-foot-eleven, with a runner's body (reason one why he never would have made it to the NHL, even though he had loved playing) instead of that of a freaking hockey player, into pulp. But he'd already established that he wasn't thinking.

"What the fuck are you doing?" he snapped.

Fanny's head shot up, surprised eyes meeting his, but the man with her reacted faster, tucking her behind him and stepping toward Brandon. "Back up."

Two words, icy cold as another car pulled up.

Another person—a woman this time—walked up the sidewalk. "Ethan?" she asked.

"Get back in the car, baby," Ethan said, "and take Fanny with you." He never took his eyes off Brandon. "I'd suggest that you leave. Immediately."

The woman who'd paused next to Fanny, took her arm. "Come on."

Fanny didn't move, just stared at him.

And Brandon, even though it was stupid to not be keeping an eye on the man, who was a freaking giant and who could destroy him, found he couldn't stop watching Fanny, couldn't stop himself from pleading with her with his gaze.

He just wanted to talk with her.

A hand on his shoulder, shaking him roughly. "Get in your car and go."

The woman had stopped trying to drag Fanny down the path and now stood between her man and Fanny, another layer of protection.

"Fan," he breathed. "Please. I just want to talk to you."

She inhaled sharply, dropping her chin to her chest. But she didn't reply.

"She doesn't want to talk to you. Go home," Ethan said. "Stay away. She'll call you if she wants—"

Brandon took a step forward. "I need—"

"I don't give a fuck what you need," Ethan growled. "It's past midnight. She doesn't want you here, and—"

"It's okay," Fanny said softly.

His heart thudded hard against his ribs, hope blossoming in his bloodstream.

The behemoth in front of him glanced back over his shoulder. "Fanny?"

"It's okay," she repeated. "He's safe—" A shake of her head. "He won't hurt me, and . . ." A sigh. "We do need to talk."

"You don't have to talk tonight," the woman said.

And was right.

It *was* after midnight, and he could see the dark circles under Fanny's eyes, even when the moonlight was the only illumination. He should go, should reach out at a more appropriate time and—

"I want to get it over with."

A sharp slice of pain across his middle had Brandon rocking back on his heels.

He deserved that. God, he deserved it.

The woman linked arms with Fanny. "Okay then, we'll stay and—"

"No." Fanny shook her head. "I've got this. You and Ethan

should go." She dropped her arms, stepped toward Ethan, and kissed his cheek. "Thanks for having my back and for driving me home. But I'm okay."

"Sure?" he asked softly enough that it barely reached Brandon's ears.

"Sure."

"We'll talk about this tomorrow," the woman said.

"I know, Dani," Fanny murmured on another exhale, this one slow and shuddering and with far too much defeat in the words to suit him.

"You'll text me when he leaves?" Dani asked. "No matter the hour?"

"Yes." More defeat. More resignation.

Brandon almost relented then, not wanting to hurt her anymore.

But then the couple was leaving, and Fanny was brushing by him, telling him, "Come on," as she walked up onto the porch. "You know," she said after she'd unlocked the door and walked inside, leaving it open for him to follow, "I never tolerated the caveman jealousy bullshit when we were together, and I certainly won't tolerate it today as a grown woman who's in charge of her own life."

He sucked in a breath. "Fan."

She flicked on a light and turned toward him, brown eyes flashing. "You wanted to talk," she said. "So, we'll talk."

But she didn't start talking at that moment. Instead, she spun on her heel and strode from the hall, into a room he saw was the kitchen as she moved to the fridge and pulled out a bottle of wine.

His mouth moved before his brain. "Haven't you had enough?"

Dumbass.

Yes, in the light of the kitchen, he could see the dark circles that were only hinted at outside, but he'd also seen the flush on her cheeks, the slight glassiness of her eyes. She'd been drinking. That was why Ethan had driven her home then.

And he'd reacted . . . like an ass. Twice over.

Fuck.

She glared at him but didn't comment on his inane question. Just went to a cupboard and pulled down a glass, pouring a healthy amount of wine into the container. And didn't offer him any. Rightly so, of course. Then took a long swallow, squared her shoulders, and asked, "What do you want to discuss?"

Her tone made him feel like they were in a business meeting.

Or two strangers on the street talking about the weather.

Impersonal. A little cold.

Could he blame her? Fuck, no. He absolutely couldn't.

But also, he didn't really know where to start. They had so much history, and it was all twisted and tangled, barbed with thorns. He found himself saying the only thing that came to his mind. "I'm sorry," he whispered. "So damned sorry."

Silence.

Charged and thick enough that it threatened to choke him.

But it didn't choke Fanny. Instead, it seemed to unfreeze her. She put down her glass and crossed to him, her face gentling. "It's not your fault."

He startled when her fingers found his, when her eyes came up and locked with his own.

"I should be the one apologizing," she said. "I'm . . ." She trailed off, her gaze drifting over his shoulder. "It hurt a lot to lose you that way, but it was just a terrible situation. You didn't mean to hurt me. Life just . . . happened, and having you show up brought it all back."

He turned his palm over, laced their fingers together. "I'm the one being an asshole. I showed up on your porch without warning. I just . . . I remembered, and I wanted to find you immediately, but I didn't know how to find you. I just knew you'd come to California." He cleared his throat. "So when I did see you, when I found out where you lived, I couldn't stop myself from coming."

"How long?" she whispered. "How long ago did you remember?"

"I—" Brandon shook his head. "Almost a year ago. My . . ." He paused, not wanting to bring up the woman he'd fallen for before he'd remembered Fanny.

But she was too smart, too intuitive to not miss his hesitation.

"Angela, right?" Fanny murmured. "Her name is Angela. I —" She cleared her throat. "I heard you two got married. What happened?"

"We were together for five years before we got divorced. She's . . . she was too good for me, and even if I didn't know you on the surface, something beneath knew she wasn't you." He squeezed her hand. "She's remarried now and has a daughter, along with one on the way."

"Oh."

The silence fell again, only this time it didn't unstick her. Instead, she went still, her eyes unfocused and her mind very far away.

"I'm sorry," he said again.

"I've never been mad at you—" A shake of her head. "No, I'm not going to lie. I was hurt and then mad, and it was easier to hold on to the mad. Because holding on to my anger meant it was easier for me to make it your fault that you didn't love me enough rather than some shitty thing that just happened that neither of us could control." She blinked, and her eyes focused on his. "It made you the bad guy, and that was much easier to accept than me thinking . . ."

"Thinking what?" he asked when long moments went by without her finishing.

"That it was my fault," she whispered. "That there was

something wrong with me, and that was why you didn't remember."

His heart twisted, rage and agony winding its way down his spine, making his free hand clench, his fingers twitch where they were intertwined with hers. He clamped down on the urge to clench there, too. Because it would hurt her.

Because it would hurt her *more*.

Instead, he inhaled slowly through his nose, exhaled just as gradually.

Then he unclenched his free hand, gently tipped her chin up so her eyes could meet his, and said, "Nothing is wrong with you."

Her throat worked on a painful-looking swallow. "Then why didn't you remember?"

Soft, soft words that he could barely hear.

But words that made his heart twist again, had fiery regret burning through his lips. This situation had been so fucked, so *absolutely* fucked, and there hadn't been anything either of them could do. "I don't know, sweetheart," he breathed, sliding his fingers to her hair and gently tugging her against him. "But I'm so, so sorry I didn't."

"I know," she whispered, as she came to him, as her body pressed to his.

It was . . . everything he'd remembered. The feel of her in his arms. The smell of her hair. The way she hugged him tightly and just . . . *fit*.

Right.

They were right.

He smoothed his hand down her hair, committing this moment to memory, wanting to burn it into the marrow of his bones, every neuron in his brain. "Can you ever forgive me?" he asked.

She squeezed his waist. "I forgave you a long time ago."

The next question was just *there*—bubbling up his throat,

dancing on the tip of his tongue, ready to give voice to everything he'd dreamed about since all those memories of them had come crashing down.

But before he could ask it, before he could ask her to give him another chance, she spoke.

And what she said sent all of his hope crashing down.

"I forgave you," she murmured. "But I can't do this again." A shuddering breath. "I'm sorry, but I just . . . *can't*."

———

He didn't know how he made it home.

He didn't know how he even left that kitchen.

Only that when Fanny had stared up at him, her eyes glistening with tears, her face drawn in sharp relief from the old pain, he'd known he couldn't argue.

He'd had to go, to leave her be.

Cursing, he pulled into his driveway and started to move into the garage, but a large box on his porch caught his eye. That hadn't been there when he'd left. Throwing his car into park, he got out and headed up the walkway.

It was huge.

The box, along with his disappointment.

And his understanding.

Which was the worst part. Because he got why Fanny couldn't take another chance on him, on them. He'd had a fulfilling relationship with Angela, while she'd been left alone, heartbroken, moving several states away from everything she'd ever known.

She'd had to start over.

He'd been in love with another woman.

Maybe he'd been kidding himself in thinking they could overcome the past. No, he *had* been kidding himself.

He hadn't been hurt.

Fanny couldn't just flip the switch and forget all of that.

"Fuck," he muttered, moving over to the box, and seeing the return label on the top of it had guilt scalding through him, all over again.

Angela.

It was from Angela.

His eyes slid closed, and he sighed.

Then he stepped back, returned to his car, and pulled into the garage, closing the door behind him. He moved into the house, flicking on lights as he walked through, making his way to the front door. Part of him wanted to leave the box on the porch and hope that someone would steal it. The rest of him knew he needed to know what was inside.

That was the piece prompting him to drag the box over the threshold.

And also the one that had him cutting through the tape and pulling open the flaps.

His breath caught at the note on top.

Somehow this came with me during the move. I thought you might need to see it. I'm so sorry I didn't realize what it was sooner.
—A

He removed the packing paper and froze, his fingers finding the soft blue fabric covering the album. She'd made this. *Fanny* had made this. The first time he'd lost his memory. She'd brought it to the hospital, and he'd flipped through it, and slowly, he'd begun to remember.

Fuck, why did the tumor have to be where it was?

Why couldn't he have lost something else? *Someone* else?

He could have lived without the memories of his teen years, his college years, if only he'd been able to keep those of Fanny. But instead, the tumor, the surgery to remove it, had obliterated them all, and even though he'd eventually remembered, first college, then high school, he hadn't regained the blank space that belonged to Fanny. Not until last year.

Would this box have made things different?

He pulled out the album, flipping through the pages, seeing the pictures of them. At prom. In the local pool with their damp arms wrapped around each other. Him holding her close, the tip of her nose pink from being in the rink for hours on end.

So many good times.

So much erased.

He set the album aside, saw the second one beneath, and knew his mom must have packed this up before he'd left the rehab facility, after he'd fallen for Angela, after Fanny had stopped coming around. Probably, she'd wanted to protect him, but part of him wondered what would have happened if he'd had access to this. Would he have remembered sooner?

The second album was filled with pictures of them as well, but it also had tickets and programs, from when he'd flown to watch her compete for gold, museum and movie receipts from their travels, a stub from sitting in the front row and watching her perform during the pro circuit. All interspersed with photographs, with memories.

With Fanny and their love and—

He closed the album and set it aside, seeing that the rest of the belongings weren't nearly as soul-crushing.

A few hockey trophies and medals, from before he'd been sick, before he'd quit playing. An old poster of a Lamborghini, one of some supermodel he couldn't remember the name of— and not from the brain cancer or the surgery, but just because that type of female hadn't interested him in a long time.

Not when he remembered Fanny.

The rest of the world ceased to exist when she was around.

He started to stack the trophies and medals back in the box, intending to throw them and the rest of the junk away, when he saw what he'd missed at first glance.

A small clay frame.

Fanny had made it when they'd first become best friends.

Before he'd fallen in love with her.

Though, he knew it was probably what had first sent him from that path of friendship on to one that led to love.

"God," he whispered, running his fingers along the sparkling pink and purple clay swirls. He'd known when she'd given it to him—her at thirteen, him so much older (at least to his teenage mind) at fifteen—that he should hate it on sight or be embarrassed. He'd been pretending to be a tough guy then. Into hockey and video games and girls, not pink and purple glittering swirls. But he'd loved this damn frame.

Because she'd made it for them.

Because of the picture she'd had printed and placed inside.

They'd been playing around on the ice, one of the few times that happened because Fanny skating was serious business, and she didn't waste her precious ice time.

But that day, her coach had gotten a phone call and his team, which had been practicing on the other rink, had ended their session early. He'd walked by the ice and had started teasing her —as one did when they were a fifteen-year-old boy who liked a girl but didn't know what to do with those feelings. And she'd challenged him to a contest.

A skating contest.

He'd laughed, dismissed it.

She'd taunted, convinced him.

Then had proceeded to destroy his ass with a series of techniques that had him stumbling more often than staying upright, even without using those that required a toe-pick—something his skates didn't have.

He'd refused to concede.

Her tasks had become increasingly more difficult.

And then . . . she had caught him when he would have fallen. For a second, anyway, because even back then, he'd outweighed her significantly. They'd teetered on their blades, wobbling, then had collapsed to the ice where they'd sat there in stunned silence for one long moment before laughter erupted.

Her coach had snapped the picture.

He loved it. Then and now.

Their arms around each other. Smiles huge, faces turned toward one another as though they'd shared the best joke either of them had ever heard.

Even though his ass had been bruised the next day.

Because they became inseparable after that moment.

One interaction, one taunt, one smile, and his whole life had changed.

But wasn't that life? A series of small moments, each having a huge impact. A few minutes of teasing that had brought Fanny into his orbit. Several more in a doctor's office that brought them closer despite the struggles. The sound of crunching metal, of smashing glass to take it all away.

He carefully set the frame on the table, but it tipped over, and something fell off the back. He snagged it, eyes searching its surface in order to make sure it hadn't broken, then turned his attention to what had fallen from the back. It was a notebook he'd never seen before, and when he opened the cover and saw his mom's handwriting, his heart ached.

He turned the pages, getting lost in her words, in the things she'd written, and missing her all over again.

Sighing, he shut the notebook and carefully went through the rest of the box, making sure he didn't miss anything else that was important then dumped the trophies and medals back inside. He didn't need the reminders of his mediocre efforts on the ice, nor of what he'd never been able to go back to afterward.

Then he carefully slid the albums onto his bookshelf,

making sure they would be out of the direct sunlight, that they wouldn't fall.

Yes, they'd stayed cooped up in this box for who knew how long, and yes, they'd made it across several states from his mom's place to the one he'd shared with Angela to Angela's *new* place to here. But though the belongings had been boxed up and thrust around, left unprotected, that didn't mean he couldn't treat them with care now.

And yes, maybe he knew that he was talking about Fanny now, and not the albums.

Both were still precious.

As was the frame, which he picked up and brought with him upstairs, staying by his side as he brushed his teeth and shoved his dirty clothes in the hamper. He held on to it as he crossed to his bed and slid beneath the covers, tugging them up and over him.

Only then did he release the frame, carefully propping it on his nightstand, staring at their happy faces as he let sleep sweep up and take him under, promising himself, the universe, fate, and whatever god, gods, or goddesses were out there that he'd bring that light back into Fanny's life again.

Even if it was the last thing he did.

FIVE

"Now again, but on the inside edge."

Groans abounded.

Laughing, she rubbed her hands together gleefully, channeling her inner villain, before waving the guys off to get started on the drills. Her time with the team in group settings like this would be winding down as the Gold focused more on hockey than on exploiting fundamentals, even if skating was probably the most important fundamental out there.

Stupid hockey players thought things like stick handling and shooting were important.

Meh.

If they couldn't skate, they couldn't play.

At least, that's what she liked to tell herself.

It inflated her grand sense of self and gave her a nice ego stroking at the same time. Win-win. At least for her.

Grinning, she skated up to Kaydon before he could take off with his group, indicating the boards with a tilt of her head.

He followed her over.

"You're favoring your knee again," she said quietly.

Caramel eyes met hers, a muscle in Kaydon's brutally defined jaw clenched. But he didn't say anything.

"Want to tell me why?" she asked.

His nostrils flared. "It's fine."

She slanted a glance over her shoulder, saw that the guys were progressing with the drill rapidly, and knew that if she wanted to keep this private and between her and Kay, then she'd need to have the discussion quickly. "It's not fine," she told him, "and if you don't want me to pull rank, you're going to tell me what's going on with your knee."

His eyes narrowed. His shoulders rose and fell on a breath. "I pushed it during my workout yesterday. Nothing is injured. It's just sore."

Fanny studied him closely. "Hit the showers. Check in with Mandy before you leave. Then come and see me the day after tomorrow. We'll work through the sore properly."

He opened his mouth.

"Kay," she said, placing a hand on his—or over his glove, anyway, "you're on the Gold, now. That means that you're not just a player or an asset. You're part of our family, and we take care of our family." She patted lightly. "It won't help anyone, least of all you, if you push your recovery so much that you can't play. We want you with us, but we don't want you to kill yourself getting there."

His lips pressed flat. "Right."

She'd heard rumors of the team he'd played with before, the drama and bullshit in the locker room, between the board and the players, the way everyone had turned on each other. Kay was new here, and she understood that he wouldn't necessarily believe the fluffy-puppy-dog-everything-is-rainbows approach that the Gold organization took. She hadn't at first. Until she'd legitimately seen that management cared for the players and made decisions based on their well-being and not how much they could squeeze out of them.

It would take Kaydon time to believe that.

But she wasn't going to let him fuck up his recovery until then.

"Do I need to pull rank?" she asked archly, when he didn't respond. "Either that or I can add some Elephants"—his most hated drill—"when you meet me."

Finally, his eyes seemed to melt, to soften, and one side of his lush mouth tipped up. "Ethan is right. You really are a monster in a tiny, sparkly package."

She grinned, swept a hand over the—yes, *sparkly*—logo on the custom shirt Brit had made for her. It went with her earrings (glittery pineapples today) and the bedazzled gloves that she wore. A woman had to take her happiness where she could find it, and sometimes that meant sparkles. Other times it meant wine and horror movies. Po-tay-toe. Po-tah-toe. She watched the guys finishing up and skating over to her one by one, knowing they could hear her. "It's good you know my inner colors. It'll save me the trouble of breaking your spirit later."

Kaydon scowled, though his eyes were dancing. "Like taming a horse?"

She considered that. "Or convincing a scared little kitten to come out from beneath the couch so I can pet him."

Silence.

Then the guys started busting up. Even Kay shook his head and smiled.

"So, Kitten," she teased. "You going to follow my orders?"

Max nudged Coop, who grinned and nudged Blane, who started to nudge Brit, but she sidled away, hissing, "Yeah, I heard. I don't need the elbow."

"Heard what?" Ethan asked.

"Kitten," Logan said, shoving back a hunk of brown hair that had slipped beneath his helmet.

Ethan's smile was slow and sexy and predatory. "Kitten," he agreed.

Fanny winced, glanced up at Kay. "Sorry?" Her voice pitched up on the end, making it more question than statement, and her apology was further ruined when she couldn't stop the laughter from bubbling up her throat.

"Monster," he repeated. But his lips were twitching, and he nudged her hip with his. "See you in two days?"

She nodded.

Kay headed for the door that led off the ice.

"Bye, Kitten," Max called.

The guys cackled.

Fanny winced again, though she couldn't stop her laughter again when Kaydon flipped them all off, his fingers looking like giant . . . marshmallows? No, that wasn't right. But anyway, it looked a little strange to be receiving the bird that was wrapped up in a bulky hockey glove.

"All right, you punks," she told them. "Because of you torturing poor Kaydon, I'm going to torture you all." She gave them a beatific smile in response to their moaning.

"You came up with the name," Max muttered.

"Just because we're going to keep using it," Coop added.

"Doesn't mean you need to torture us," Blane finished.

"Torture away!" Brit said.

The guys had been nodding in agreement. Until Brit.

Then they scowled. And Fanny rubbed her hands together again. "Okay, here's my proposition. I either give you all one more drill or . . ." She deliberately trailed off, almost laughing again when they all leaned in. "Or," she said again, even slower, "Brit takes you on a run."

"Run!" Brit shouted.

"Skate," everyone else yelled. Mainly because no matter how much they complained about Fanny's "torture," Brit taking them all on a run was the worst form of punishment they could imagine.

"Hmm." Fanny tapped a finger to her lips. "I think I heard run."

Ethan narrowed his eyes.

She grinned.

"All right. Fine. Umbrella. Three times on both feet"—Ethan slumped and Brit pouted—"and then our last group session of the preseason will be complete."

Whoops went up.

"Rude," she teased. "Maybe I need to schedule extra one-on-ones?"

Coop tugged her ponytail as he skated by. "You are small and shiny but equally as feisty."

"And mighty," Max added.

"And evil." Ethan.

"That doesn't rhyme," Max grumbled.

"Then evil-y," Ethan said. "Better?"

Max nodded. "Yup."

Shaking her head, Fanny skated to the boards, blew her whistle, and then focused her attention on the guys as they moved through the drill, making note on her clipboard of a few things some of the guys had to work on. But they were looking pretty damned good.

Not to pat herself on the back.

But . . . she patted herself on the back.

This was going to be a good season. She could feel it in her sparkly, evil bones.

————

The guys had cleared the ice, snagging the cones and tires she'd used during the session.

They were neater than the kids.

Or perhaps, better trained.

Or perhaps not, she realized just before she stepped off the rink, spying a small tire that had been left behind in the shuffle. Smothering a grin, she skated to the corner, scooped it up, and moved to the opposite side of the ice, where there was a storage unit for equipment.

She'd just tossed the tire inside when her nape prickled.

She looked up, and it was like some inner detector knew who it was and where *he* was. Where Brandon was.

By her skate bag.

Probably because he knew she would be trapped, would have to take off her skates at some point. She couldn't exactly drive home in them now, could she? Plus, she'd fuck up her edges.

He shifted from foot to foot, clearly uncomfortable.

The feeling was mutual.

But he didn't move away, even as she girded her loins and walked over to him. "Brandon," she said, proud that her voice was neutral. She'd meant what she'd told him the night before. She had forgiven him long ago, but that forgiveness didn't mean they could go back.

She couldn't welcome him back into her life. Couldn't risk it.

"Hey, Fan," he said softly, his voice sliding over her skin and making her shiver.

No. That was the cold air of the rink making her shiver. Not Brandon, nor his slightly raspy, all-too-sexy voice.

"I—" She broke off, cleared her throat. "What are you doing here?"

He held up a manila envelope. "Just had some paperwork for Kaydon."

Her brows drew together. "For Kay? Why?"

Brandon's brown eyes were warm on hers. "I'm his agent."

Surprise trickled through her, and yet she knew that it wasn't warranted. He'd gone to school for sports management, teasing that she would be his first client. Those plans had been derailed by the discovery of his cancer returning and his surgery, but of course, he'd found his way back to it.

And to me, her mind whispered.

Swallowing hard against the panic, and maybe the slightest bit of longing that thought invoked, she smiled. "That's great," she said, reaching out and squeezing his arm before she could stop herself. Sparks shot up her fingers, warmth coiling in her abdomen. "I'm so happy for you. Do you work for Prestige then?" she asked, knowing they represented a good chunk of the Gold roster.

Brandon nodded. "I brought my clients over and joined with them when I moved out here."

Speaking of which . . . why *had* he moved out here?

Was it for her? Or some other reason. Or—

"I didn't," he said quietly. "If I'd known where you were involved with the Gold, I would have come for sure. But I didn't."

Fanny's lungs seized. He would have come?

"Right after Kaydon was picked up by the Gold, I ended up running into Devon Scott at a conference. He wined and dined me"—a grin—"and convinced me to move over to Prestige. Luckily, my clients all saw it as a net benefit, so I'm pretty much doing the same thing I was before, just in a nicer office and in a better climate."

Her lips twitched. "No more snowy winters."

"Exactly."

Quiet descended, or at least it descended between them. The rink around them was noisy. The sound of the Zamboni cutting the ice echoing through the space, along with that of the kids who'd gathered on the opposite side, who were getting ready for practice. God, she loved this space. The noise, the smell, the cool air. Lucky for her, she supposed, considering she spent the majority of her time here, either with the guys or with her classes and clinics.

His eyes flicked over her shoulder, and she bit her lip. "I should let you go. Kaydon should be in the training suite—"

"Is he okay?" Brandon asked, concern whipping across his face.

"He's fine." She squeezed his hand again. "I noticed he was favoring that knee again, and he told me he just overdid it at a workout. I strong-armed"—a shrug when he glanced up at her—"or well, I *strongly encouraged* him to see Mandy."

"I'd wondered why he headed off early."

"You watched the session?"

He rocked back on his heels, studying her face, something flashing across his eyes that she couldn't decipher. "You're really good with them."

She inhaled, warmth blossoming in her stomach, spreading out to her fingertips. "They're good guys."

A nod.

More quiet.

Then he reached for her.

And for a moment, she didn't know what she wanted—to lean in and let him touch, to skitter back and run like her hair was on fire, to . . .

He held up a notebook.

Oh. *Oh.* He wasn't reaching for her. He was . . . trying to give her something.

Right.

"My mom," he said, and she immediately stepped back. That hurt, too. Because Brandon's mom had been wonderful. Sweet and funny and loving. Fanny's own parents were fine, albeit more than a little detached. She knew that they cared about her, but her parents were also very into their own lives. Her mom had a busy career, even now that she'd reached retirement age, and her dad had always been more interested in building his cars than her.

Skating and glittering skating outfits, new laces and music for routines hadn't appealed to him.

Nor to her mom.

They'd thrown money at Fanny's hobby, and that had been more than lots of other people had, so Fan knew she was lucky. It was just . . . she had traveled more with Sandy, her coach, than her own parents.

Until she'd gotten together with Brandon.

Then his parents had come to every competition they could, sitting beside Brandon in the stands. She'd had a support system she hadn't ever expected to have, and she really missed Grace. And Jeff. Brandon's dad had been a good guy, too.

She remembered one time when he'd helped Sandy track down permission to a piece of music so Fanny could use it for her long program.

Her own parents would have just told her—*had* just told her —to pick another song.

So the hole after losing Brandon had been big and threefold. It hadn't felt right to keep in contact when he was trying to build a life with Angela. And, if she was being truthful, it would have been too painful to talk with them, knowing that Brandon was a subject they couldn't broach.

Or at least, couldn't broach without it hurting too damned much.

"My mom," he said again, not moving toward her, but still holding up the little black book, "wrote in this. I think she meant for you to have it."

"Brandon," Fanny began. "I can't. That belongs to you." She swallowed. "You should keep it, especially—"

"I want you to take it. You should—"

"All good, Fanny?"

Jumping, she glanced over to see that Dani had walked up, suspicion drawing the lines of her face into sharp relief.

"I'm good," she said and straightened her shoulders, lifting her chin, her tone going almost brusquely professional. "This is Brandon, my ex. It turns out he's Kaydon's agent and is working for Prestige Media Group."

Dani's brows climbed up her face. "Hi, Brandon." Her tone was icy.

"It's nice to meet you, Dani. I'd like to apologize for my behavior last night." His gaze came to Fanny's, voice gentling and eliminating all that brusque professional distance in a heartbeat. "To you, as well. I was out of line showing up like that."

She nodded. "It's okay."

Dani huffed and narrowed her eyes, none of the shy woman who'd she'd been before Ethan. There was fire in her that was no longer banked, and it was fucking fabulous to see. "It's not okay," she snapped. "You don't just show up being all combative. You call first, and if Fanny wants to see you, then you come." More eye narrowing, this time accompanied by some poking in the chest—Brandon's chest. "And you definitely leave the asshole attitude at home."

Fanny clasped her friend's hand, tugged her back, fighting a smile.

Because this was her shy, uncomfortable in social situations friend. This was *Dani* who was so damned quiet and jumpy until Ethan, until . . . herself. Because her transformation wasn't all because of another person. It was from Dani herself. She'd fought hard to get beyond her insecurities, had embraced the wealth of strength inside her heart and soul.

Ethan had just been the whipped cream and cherry—or perhaps, the push to take that first step.

"I promise I will leave the asshole at home," Brandon said, and though his tone was even, his eyes had mirth creeping in on their edges.

It didn't escape Fanny's notice that he hadn't promised to stay away or call first.

Just to leave the asshole at home.

Hmm.

"Good." Dani turned to Fanny. "Can I talk to you privately?"

"I—" Her gaze flicked to Brandon's.

"Go ahead," he said. "I need to go speak to Kay, anyway." He sucked in a breath, released it. "I'll . . . see you around sometime."

He turned away, and Dani drew her to the side. "Seriously, are you okay? Why is he here, and . . ." She began peppering Fanny with questions.

Questions which she deflected.

With promises to confess all soon.

Thankfully, that was enough to satisfy her friend for the moment, so the topic turned to the charity raffle and everything that was going to go into it. There were a lot of moving parts, and it would be a good event, but it was also big and complicated, so by the time she said goodbye to Dani and sat down to take off her skates, a fair amount of time had passed.

Enough time, she realized as she unzipped her skating bag, for Brandon to have performed a little bit of mischief.

The notebook was tucked inside.

The man was nowhere to be seen.

But the mischief was better than the asshole.

And Fanny had learned to take her victories where she could find them.

Six

BRANDON

A knock on the door signaled the harbinger of darkness.

Well, either that or just his doctor.

Dr. Lyon was his new oncologist. He might have stayed with his previous one, even after having moved a couple of states away, but Dr. Philips had retired and had recommended Dr. Lyon, whose practice was conveniently located only a couple of miles away from Prestige's office.

Dr. Lyon was a petite brunette with a penchant for chunky necklaces and slacks paired with brightly patterned blouses.

After the perfunctory knock, she opened the door and stepped inside, closing it behind her with one hand, the other clasping a tablet. She glanced up, smiled. "It's nice to see you again, Brandon. How have you been feeling? Any changes?"

Always, his gut clenched when beginning this line of inquiry, even though he'd been feeling fine, even though nothing had changed, at least nothing that he could pinpoint anyway.

And that, the fear that something might be growing, but he couldn't feel it, never went away.

"No," he said. "No headaches or dizziness or nausea."

"Any more memories coming back?" They'd discussed the final return during their initial consultation when Brandon had first moved to California.

He shook his head.

"Anything lost?" she asked then pressed her lips flat. "Or rather, has anyone around you mentioned anything you can't remember?"

"No."

His memory hadn't been like that. The cancer itself had caused seizures and headaches, but it was always the treatment, the surgery that had been even more devastating, scooping out parts of him . . . or damaging them, anyway, leaving those pieces to heal so fucking slowly.

"Good. Good." She sank onto the edge of her desk and set the tablet in a holder, nodding at a large monitor on the wall as she plugged in a cord. "Your MRI has been viewed by the radiologist—"

His stomach twisted.

"—and everything is clear. There's absolutely nothing on the scans that indicate any return of cancer in your brain or anywhere else in your body."

He released a breath and was finally able to spare a thought for wondering why she'd asked him into her office. Usually, he just received a phone call with his results, and while part of him had been hoping it was just because this was his first checkup with Dr. Lyon, deep down he'd been worried they had found something.

And what that might mean.

"You have ten years of clear scans. Ten years free of cancer." She reached for his hand and squeezed it lightly. "In my medical opinion, I would consider you cured." Straightening, she smiled slightly as she pulled her hand back. "I wanted to make sure you understood that. You're healthy and young. You can have a full life." Her voice softened. "In case the specter of the cancer returning has been hanging over you."

How could it not?

But he appreciated what she was doing. What she was saying.

"Thank you."

"There's no reason for you to think the cancer will come back," she went on. "We'll continue with our yearly scans, because I think that will give you some further peace of mind"—she paused and glanced at him, so he nodded—"but I want you going out there and living your life without worrying about it. That worry will be my job. Let me shoulder that burden. You just . . . live."

He swallowed hard, his eyes shining.

Maybe it was presumptuous of her, because he didn't ever think the worry would one hundred percent go away, but it lightened something inside of him to hear those words, loosened some tension he hadn't even registered carrying.

Because it had been there for so long.

"Thank you," he said.

She squeezed his hand and straightened again. "You reach out to me at any time with any concerns, any changes no matter how small," she said. "But push me and this office and the scans out of your mind." She laughed. "Pretend I'm the boring mismatched sock, the one you forget about but never throw away."

He chuckled.

She grinned. "There, but forgotten is what I prefer. Or at least that's what I tell my single self." A wink.

Now he was laughing. In a doctor's office. Something he hadn't thought was possible, and Dr. Lyon joined in, too, her tinkling laughter drifting through the air, punctuating the conversation as she made sure he didn't have any other concerns or matters to discuss. Then she made her way to the door, smiling and waving before slipping out into the hall, and Brandon thought that if he wasn't hopelessly in love with Fanny, single Dr. Lyon would have been exactly the type of woman he could fall for.

But he was in love with Fanny.

Since that moment on the ice, *her* laughter coating his skin, *her* smile lighting up his soul nearly two decades before.

And now, he was deemed cured.

Now he had something he could give her, some reassurances where there hadn't been any before.

Now he could promise to be there and mean it, to not forget her, to be there for her exactly as she deserved.

Now he could finally give her everything.

He was grinning as he strode out of that doctor's office.

Hope.

That was what Dr. Lyon had given him.

And it felt damned good.

———

He tossed and turned, even despite going back to the office after his appointment and working on several contract offers, staying well past nine when the cleaning crew had come in.

The sound of the vacuum running had chased him from behind his desk, knowing he wouldn't be able to concentrate.

Not so much because of the noise.

But because the bubble of his concentration had been broken, and his thoughts had begun swirling about what the doctor had told him, and around Fanny and if he should tell her (how could he *not* tell her?). Wondering if it might make a difference because he understood that she needed to protect herself from being hurt again, and if he *did* tell her, how he could ask her to take a risk.

He wasn't the one who'd been devastated.

Sure he'd been sick, but he'd found love and happiness.

And Fanny . . . had been forgotten.

Sighing, he tossed back the blankets and went out the sliding glass door in his bedroom. It led to the back yard, darkened and full of shadows, the moonlight diffused by the thick covering of fog. The air was cool enough to have goose bumps prickling on his skin, but he didn't put on any clothes or shoes as he moved across the porch and leaned on the railing, staring up at the sky.

The fog curled and shifted as it trailed over him, giving occasional glimpses of the black sky, the twinkling stars, the nearly-full moon.

He had a decision to make.

No. He was kidding himself by thinking that. He'd made the decision already, the moment he'd first seen Fanny again, had watched her work her magic on the ice.

He wanted to rekindle things with her.

He wanted to build a life with Fanny.

He wanted to give her the white dress, the fantasy of happily ever after.

But what if she didn't want that? She'd told him that she'd forgiven him, made it perfectly clear that he was a risk she wasn't willing to take. Except, that was before Dr. Lyon had said he was cured. That would change things, right? That would make a difference and—

Maybe it wouldn't matter.

Because while Dr. Lyon had said she didn't think the cancer would come back, she also couldn't promise him with one hundred percent certainty that it wouldn't.

And maybe that wouldn't be enough for Fanny.

Rage whipped through him suddenly with a severity that sucked the breath out of him as his hands clenched into fists, as every muscle in his body went taut. "So what?" he snapped, well aware that he was talking to himself or the shadows or the fucking moon hiding behind the fog. "You're just going to give up? You're not going to fight for her?"

That was bullshit.

He'd almost died. Twice. He'd been through six rounds of chemo. Radiation. Had two major surgeries and the physical therapy.

And *now* was the moment he was going to give up?

"Seriously?" he muttered, banging his fist on the railing. "Now?"

Fuck that.

"Fuck *that*," he said out loud.

He had to fight for her. He'd survived. He remembered. He loved her.

Fuck, that *had* to be enough.

It had to.

His heart was pounding from confirming the decision, his hands still clenched, his muscles still tight, but just thinking that he was going to fight for her, just making that promise *to* fight for her had rightness settling over him like it was a second skin.

He'd never once given up on anything. Surviving. Getting healthy again. Finishing his degree. Starting his business. Even his marriage.

Angela had been the one to file the papers.

Not because he had been clueless to their problems or the fact that they'd grown apart and were heading in separate directions.

But because he *didn't* give up, and without remembering Fanny, he would have continued fighting for her. If he had remembered when he'd been with Angela, that would have brought a whole set of different complications. But he hadn't, so he didn't need to think himself in circles worrying about it. The point was, he'd fought for Angela and while he still loved his ex-wife (albeit that love was strictly platonic now and had been for years), that love paled in comparison to what he felt for Fanny.

The first woman to own his heart and soul.

The woman who still held it today.

How could he give up on her?

"I can't," he said, head tilted up to the sky.

It was as simple as that.

No matter the hurdles they still had to overcome.

He wouldn't give up on Fanny, wouldn't give up on their future, wouldn't give up on trying to build something unbreakable between them, on filling in the holes his illness had carved, on erasing the sadness in her eyes, her soul, her heart.

A few steps brought him back inside, a few more to his closet where he tugged on a pair of jeans and a shirt, pulled on socks and shoes before walking from the bedroom.

Past the pink and purple frame.

Down the stairs and to the garage.

He needed to see her car in her driveway, needed to make sure that she was home and safe.

He needed to see her house, even if he couldn't see *her*.

Because he wouldn't bang on her door, wouldn't barge into her house. He was going to win her over as she deserved—slowly and gently and with plenty of love and care. As promised, he'd leave the asshole at home.

He'd just get a glimpse of her car, her house, maybe even Fanny herself.

Then he'd come back home and plan.

SEVEN

FANNY

"What do you think of this one?" Scarlett asked, spinning in a circle, the emerald skirt flaring out.

"It's gorgeous," Fanny said, standing up from the chair she'd been waiting in and rubbing the material between thumb and forefinger. It was silky and cool and the perfect color to match the creaminess of Scarlett's skin, to highlight the deep red of her hair. "You're going to knock him dead."

Scar winced. "Let's not use that turn of phrase."

"Why not?" she asked, reaching up and straightening the straps. "You're beautiful in it," she said, glancing into the mirror and meeting her friend's eyes.

"Thank you." Scar reached up and covered Fanny's hand. "But no knocking them dead. We don't need to tempt fate, not when it comes to me and my thundercloud of trouble. You give voice to it, and it might happen, and"—she made a face—"I might not get laid."

Fanny laughed, smoothing the material of the straps before

stepping back. "Well, we definitely don't want to get in the way of you and several delicious orgasms."

"No, we don't."

She mimed zipping her lips shut. "Your secret is safe with me."

"Not sure it's a secret," Scar murmured, reaching down and checking the price tag, a frown dragging her red brows together. "Disaster follows in my wake, even without me trying."

"It wasn't your fault that the stick rack collapsed."

They were shopping for Scar's date, partly because Scar *had* a date and partly because Scar had needed a little retail therapy after an eventful day at the rink. They'd been shooting some publicity photos for the website and social media when trouble had struck.

At least, that was what Scar believed.

Brit had assured Fanny that Scarlett hadn't been anywhere near the equipment when the rack had fallen apart, scattering sticks every which way and making everyone in the vicinity jump, but Scar was convinced it was her bad juju and that it boded poorly for her date and maybe her future with the Gold.

Nonsense.

Because not only was Scar great at her job, but any man would be lucky to be dating her friend.

So when Fanny had gotten off the ice and seen her friend with a forced smile, she'd endeavored to find out what had happened, then to make it her mission to make her feel better.

A new dress was the first part of that.

Next would be shoes and undies.

And yes, she understood that it was ridiculous for her to call them undies. But *c'est la vie* and all that.

The point was that she was going to help Scar feel good, take her mind off the so-called bad juju and trouble that followed in her wake, and then she'd point her in the direction of her date and hope that she got some orgasms.

Oh, and maybe some fun and good conversation and a man who saw Scar for the lovely person she was.

That, too.

"It was my fault," Scar muttered. "I bumped into it when I first went into the room to get everything set up this morning and it—"

"And it decided to randomly fall apart hours later?" Fanny asked. "After many other people used it throughout the day?"

Scar ran her hands over the skirt and made a face at her in the mirror. "Fine. Be logical, why don't you?"

Fanny smiled. "I will." A beat. "Are you getting the dress?"

Scar tilted her head from side to side, the red waves of her hair sliding from shoulder to shoulder. "Yes," she said with a decisive nod. "I like it and even though it is way too much money for a freaking scrap of fabric"—this was true, the dress revealed more skin than it covered—"it's sexy and looks amazing on me, and that's good enough for me."

"As it should be." Fan nodded to the curtain. "Get changed. Let's get some stuff to go with that fabulous dress."

"Lace things?" Scar asked.

"If that's what you want," Fanny replied, hiding a smile, glad that her friend was finally getting on board with her plan.

"And shoes?"

"Duh."

Scar grinned. "What about you?" she asked as she slipped back behind the curtain to take off the dress. "Are you going to buy any lacy things for that ex of yours?"

Fanny's throat spasmed for a moment before she managed to get a reply out. Of course Dani had dished about Brandon . . . to *everyone*. The Gold gossip train was notorious and efficient, as thus Fanny had been getting questions about "the ex" from everyone—players to support staff to the front office—that entire day. But not from Scar, apparently, who had just been waiting for her moment to pounce.

"I think you already answered your own question," she muttered. "He's my ex for a reason. No lace for him."

Scar poked her head out from behind the curtain, her brows lifted.

"What?" Fanny asked.

"Nothing." Scar disappeared again, the curtain fluttering. She reappeared a moment later, the dress back on the hanger and all the others she'd tried on before the emerald one in her other hand.

Fan moved forward and took the rejects. "Let's go to shoes first." She hung them on the rack of go-backs, started for the exit of the dressing rooms. "I think I saw a pair that will look perfect—"

"Who is Brandon, really?" Scar asked, catching her arm. "Because he doesn't look at you like you're an ex."

"How does he look at me?"

"Like you're something he's desperate for." She clicked her teeth together, nom-style. "Like he wants to eat you up."

Franny inhaled sharply, shook her head. "I-I can't. It's—"

"Complicated?" Scarlett asked, tugging her toward the displays of shoes. "Everything that's really good in life is complicated."

"This is really complicated, Scar. Not just normal complicated."

"Why?"

This wasn't really a conversation she wanted to have in the middle of a department store. Okay, fine. This wasn't a story she wanted to share *ever*. But also . . . she *wanted* to talk about it. She wanted it off her chest, for the pain and longing to stop eating at her. She wanted her friend to understand, wanted *someone* to understand.

So, as they wandered through high heels, she told Scarlett everything about Brandon—how their friendship began at thirteen and fifteen, him becoming her first love when she'd turned fourteen and he'd been sixteen, the cancer, and that horrible week of him not recognizing her, not remembering. She told her friend how amazing it had been when he'd gone into remission, how his family had become hers and supported her during her skating career, how they'd made long distance work despite it not working for so many others. Her voice shook when she told her about the seizure when he'd been driving and how they'd discovered the cancer had come back, the surgery, him waking up and not knowing her.

"I tried for months," she whispered. "I tried everything. I brought out albums of us, made new ones with all of the things we did together, hoping that he would see something and it would spark his memories. I made playlists and brought him on field trips to our favorite places. I baked for him. I put on our favorite movies and TV shows." Her eyes burned. "I spent months and *months* doing that, along with accompanying him to his physical therapy, his checkups. I spent hours with him, all while loving him desperately, and he only looked at me like I was an acquaintance or a new friend he barely tolerated because I was so close to his parents." A sigh. "It never grew into anything, and I could have handled him not remembering me, could have put all my new energy into building a new future together, but . . . he didn't love me." She sniffed and wiped a tear that threatened to leak from the corner of her eye. "And then I watched him fall for his infusion nurse. I saw him light up for her every single time he went in for treatment, when they happened to run into each other when he was there for a different appointment. There was chemistry and potential, and I saw what it did to him to pretend those feelings weren't there."

"Oh, Fan."

Swallowing hard, she kept her focus on her hands. "Because even though he didn't love me like I loved him, he was still a nice guy and didn't want to hurt my feelings." She closed her eyes. "I waited six months. And then I rejoined the pro tour." She'd still held out hope that he would remember. That she would come home to visit her parents, and magically he'd know her and declare his undying love. "A little while after that, I saw a picture of them together on Instagram, and I knew that I needed to let him go." She sighed. "So, I did."

Scar was quiet, but only for a moment. Then she was wrapping her arms around Fanny, holding her tight, and saying, "I'm so sorry, babe. I'm so, so sorry."

She smiled, shook her head. "It was a shitty situation, but I'm fine—"

"No." Scar pulled back, gripping the tops of her arms, and she was going to wrinkle her dress if she kept that up. "Don't you dare minimize what happened to you, to *both* of you. Yes, it was shitty. Yes, neither of you could control it. No, you don't get to tuck your pain away into some deep, dark hole inside you while putting on a mask, pretending to be okay. You don't have to pretend with me. You don't have to be okay."

Fanny's heart thudded, her eyes burned like a motherfucker.

Scarlett was . . . well, she was right.

And incredible. There was that, too.

"You're going to make me cry for real if you keep being so wonderful."

"Don't worry, it won't last."

That had Fanny snorting out a laugh, albeit a watery one. "Come on," she said, linking her arm with her friend's. "Let's go spend some money."

———

"You should give him a chance," Scar said a little while later, as they walked through the selection of shoes again. They'd already each found a pair and then had moved onto lingerie. Now they'd been ensnared by all the pretties again, and Fanny had been contemplating the need for another pair of strappy sandals.

For the record, she was well aware that she didn't need the sandals.

Want, on the other hand?

The want was real.

Fanny's feet slid to a stop, and she gaped up at Scarlett. After all she'd told her friend, Scar was just going to throw that out there like that? It wasn't for casual conversation, especially now that she knew the history. Plus, they'd been talking about going to Molly's after this, and friends didn't throw friends curveballs when it came to drooling over or consuming carbs.

It was as simple as that.

"You know why I can't," she said.

"I know why you *haven't*," Scar countered.

"Plus, I don't even feel that way about him anymore," Fanny counter-countered, knowing it was a lie, but sticking by it anyway. Sometimes a girl had to lie to herself, and that was okay in her book.

But not, apparently, in *Scarlett's* book.

Her friend tossed her red locks over her shoulders, fixed Fanny with a look, and declared, "Bullshit."

"Hey, that's not—"

Scar held her in place with a piercing blue stare.

Fanny narrowed her eyes right back. "You've spent both interactions with him either telling him off, glaring at him, or staring at him longingly, with your face having gone soft." She said the last like it was a direct quote.

And it probably was.

Fucking Dani, spilling everything. "Yeah, so?"

"So?" Fanny asked incredulously. "So, you're supposed to be on my side. He's the bad guy in this—"

Scar lifted a brow. "To which I would have to say, that's more bullshit." A beat. "Also, which you know."

Okay, that *was* bullshit.

Scar smiled, probably knowing she'd won. The bitch.

She glared. If only Fanny didn't love her so much, she'd . . . do *something*.

Scarlett ran a finger over a pump. "Plus, I can't be the only one to get all the orgasms. He's hot, Fan. Those chocolate eyes—a woman could get lost in eyes like that. And not to mention the curls. Hell, I'm going on a date and spent the last couple of days thinking he was evil incarnate until Dani dished, but that still didn't stop me from imagining plunging my fingers into those curls and holding on tight while he—"

Fanny groaned, let her head fall back, not about to admit to all the times *she'd* lost herself in Brandon's eyes, nor how soft his curls had been against her bare skin, or how easy it had been to grip them when he'd positioned himself between her thighs.

He was probably even better than Scar could imagine.

And she'd bet her friend could imagine a lot.

And all her touching and getting lost in Brandon's eyes had been when she was barely an adult, both of them barely out of their teen years. He'd been all gangly muscles and still growing into himself. Nothing like what he was like now—the lines of his jaw fiercely defined and coated in a few days' worth of stubble, pecs she could grab on to, biceps that stretched the sleeves of his shirt, thighs and an ass that competed with the guys' on the Gold, and everyone knew that professional hockey players had the *best* thighs and asses. He was leaner than the guys but still fucking yummy.

This was a dangerous line of thinking, she knew, as her gaze moved to the fluorescent lights on the ceiling, and she sucked in a breath.

"He's hot, and you know it."

Her gaze flew down, met Scarlett's, and Fanny found herself cracking up when her friend waggled her brows and mimed something obscene and definitely not department store appropriate.

This conversation should hurt, especially after everything

she'd told Scar, but instead, Fanny felt lighter, as though it were finally okay to have a normal conversation about Brandon. To be attracted to all his pretty, yummy muscles. To maybe even joke about him, or if not joke, then to at least withstand a little bit of teasing when it came to him and their interactions. It was that lightness that prompted her to say, "Oh, God, here we go. You didn't even like him two days ago."

"I have faith that he'll table the asshole."

Fanny snorted. "Because Dani bullied him into it?"

"No. Because Dani says he looks at you right."

Her lungs froze on a sharp inhale.

"Plus, he's not what I thought, and you know why," Scar went on, snagging her arm and jostling her slightly as she dragged her away from the pair of sandals Fanny definitely didn't need. "This would be different if you were over him or if it was obvious that you didn't feel anything for him or if he didn't look at you like you hung the moon and the sun and all the stars in the sky."

Fanny sucked in more air, liking that last part far too much for her mental well-being.

Scar squeezed her arm. "I'm not trying to push—"

"You're not?" Fanny said dryly.

"No." A shrug. "Well, okay, yes, I am." Scarlett grinned. "Because I can see on your face, your feelings are still there. You're not over him, even if you want to be, and I think . . ." She trailed off, nibbled on the corner of her mouth.

"What?" Fanny found herself asking.

"I think you're still in love with him."

Fanny stumbled back a step, shaking her head. "No, that's not—"

"Shit." Scar squeezed her arm again, drawing her to another table of shoes. "Just forget I said that. You're not ready and—"

Panic gripped Fanny, and she whipped around, picking up a

random heel. "Look at this one. It'll be perfect with a dress, and you can even wear them with jeans or a—"

"Fanny."

"Or slacks. You could wear them with slacks!"

"*Fanny.*"

The sharp tone had her freezing, the heel in her hand.

"Ignore me," Scarlett murmured. "You're not ready."

Fat lot of good that did her with the words already swirling around her mind. Her emotions churned through her—the past and the memories and the growing glimmer of hope that was pushing her to track down Brandon, to tease out all the rest of her feelings, to take a step that would have her plummeting over the edge for him a third time.

Part of her wanted him. Part of her would *always* want him. Fuck.

"Fanny."

She glanced up at Scar, her pulse pounding in her veins, her throat tight and dry and—

"It'll be okay."

"I'm not so sure."

"Trust me." A beat. "And then ignore me."

Fanny shook her head. "Am I supposed to do both at the same time?"

"I believe I gave you an order for how to execute those two things already."

She glared, but at least her heart was slowing down, and she didn't feel at risk of passing out—at least for the moment.

"See?" Scarlett said, her lips turning up. "You're doing it already."

"What? The trusting or the ignoring?"

"Either." A grin. "Both." She plucked the heel Fanny didn't even realize she was still holding out of Fanny's hand and declared, "I like these. Let's both try them on."

Fanny swallowed hard, released a shaking breath, whispered, "I don't think I can."

"The shoes or Brandon?" Scar asked gently.

Fanny just looked at her.

Scar smiled kindly, nudged Fanny's shoulder with her own. "You don't have to decide today."

It felt that way, felt like Fanny needed to drop everything and figure out what to do with Brandon. But Scarlett was right. It was too much too soon, and she wasn't ready. "I—" she began, wanting to say something touching or emotional, or to at least express how much Scarlett's understanding meant to her.

But the words wouldn't come.

Luckily for Fanny, Scar heard them anyway.

"I know," she whispered. Then her chin came up, her volume increased, and she said, "Now, let's go ask the salesperson for our sizes. We both absolutely *need* these shoes."

———

She'd put away her new shoes—two pairs, the heels she and Scarlett had both tried on *and* the strappy sandals that she hadn't been able to get out of her head.

Funny how that kept going around, huh?

But she wasn't thinking about that, nor about Brandon or the notebook that was sitting on the kitchen island, burning a hole in the granite (figuratively, not literally, otherwise she would have much bigger problems in her life than an ex-fiancé with a memory problem).

And look.

She was joking in her own mind.

That was good, right?

That had to mean she was right to talk to Scarlett about Brandon and everything that went down, rather than continue to bottle it all up and pretend it hadn't happened. It was on the surface and exposed and—

Why that notebook was burning the proverbial hole.

Because she'd put away her purchases, had whipped up dinner—salad and leftover soup from Molly's, which Scarlett had treated her to after they spent their wad on shoes and lace (for *her*, not for Brandon, Fanny promised herself). Then she'd gone the whole popcorn, movie, wine route.

But that hadn't held her attention.

Every time she moved into the kitchen to refill her glass or get more popcorn or . . . hell, who was she kidding?

She kept going into the kitchen because she wanted to look in the damned notebook. It was time she admitted that and stopped lying to herself and . . . she wanted to know what Brandon's mom had intended her to have.

There. That was the truth.

No amount of fake blood and suspenseful music would change the truth.

She'd already torn open those barely scabbed-over wounds, had already told Scar everything, and plus, she'd forgiven Brandon long ago, was now nurturing the spark inside her that kept telling her to move forward.

And . . .

No more excuses.

She put down the wine glass, left the movie running in the background because the sound of the film was oddly comforting, and she moved to the island.

Releasing a shuddering breath, Fanny flipped open the cover.

The picture pasted to the inside had her breath shuddering all over again. It was of her and Brandon, both looking so damned young. He was in his hockey gear. She was in her skating leotard, earmuffs covering her ears, the fingertips of her gloves damp. Their arms were around each other. Their smiles huge.

God, she'd never stood a chance without him, had she?

He'd owned her heart, been that missing piece she hadn't even known she was lacking from the first moment he'd teased her when they were teenagers.

Sighing, she turned the page and began reading what appeared to be Grace's journal, or maybe it was more of a memory book. The entries were sporadic and only mentioned Brandon and his activities, and as she read about Brandon's hockey tournaments, the paper he got an A on in school, a memory sparked across Fanny's mind. She remembered seeing Grace writing in this, and her breath caught as she realized what the entries began to include.

Her.

Fanny was in these.

Grace had written about Brandon being infatuated with a girl. Then the first time she met Fanny and how much she had liked her.

Fan let her fingers drift across the words, wonder sliding through her. Grace had liked her.

Really liked her.

Okay, she'd known that, had felt that affection and love over the years, but there was something about actually seeing it in words, seeing it in something private. These were Grace's inner thoughts, and there wasn't any veneer of politeness.

And Grace had liked Fanny.

So that was big, and it had Fanny continuing to read, devouring the entries, the story of her and Brandon through Grace's eyes, and by the time she reached the end, she didn't know what to think.

Or maybe it was that she knew what to think, what she should be doing.

Who she should be running to.

But what she was too terrified to do.

"Fuck," she whispered as she read the last entry, the sadness Grace felt when Fanny had left for good.

I feel like I've lost a daughter. I'm so happy to have Brandon healthy and whole, happy that he's found someone to love . . . I just wish that someone could have been Fanny.

She closed the cover and stood, her heart pounding, her eyes stinging.

It was too much, too raw, too real.

Too close, when she'd spent so long trying to create distance between her past and present. Too open and out there when she'd worked so hard to rivet the lid on her past.

She turned for the front door without thinking, scooping up her keys, her skate bag.

She hurried outside, not caring that it was late and dark, and the rink would be closed.

Unlock her car. Her bag in the passenger's seat.

Her keys in the ignition.

Go.

Run.

Find a way to shove it all down again.

EIGHT

BRANDON

He pulled up to Fanny's house, still intending to just drive by.

Or maybe to pause at the curb and try to figure out how to make things right between them.

Or maybe to park next to her car and pretend he had a right to be there.

Or maybe—

To see Fanny run right out the front door and hightail it for her car. She didn't look around. She didn't notice his car at the curb. She didn't seem to notice anything as she all but ran down the walkway and tossed a bag into her passenger's seat and tore off out of the driveway.

As though the hounds of hell were chasing her.

It wasn't even a decision to follow her.

She drove away, and he immediately trailed her, his mind spinning, worry swirling through him. What had happened? Was she okay? Hurt?

His jaw was tight, fingers clenched on the steering wheel.

He was going to find out.

Her car hovered above the speed limit on the freeway for the couple of exits they were on it then did the same as she drove through the quiet streets, as she whipped into a familiar parking lot.

She stopped by the curb, and he watched as she got out, bag in hand, and unlocked the glass and steel doors, disappearing inside the darkened ice rink. Her skates must be in that bag, he knew now. Just as Brandon understood why she'd run out of her house, why she'd come here.

Fanny needed to out-skate her demons.

Which meant he should leave.

He knew he was going to stay anyway.

He parked behind her car, promising that he'd wait out here until she was done, would make sure she made it home safe.

He made it all of ten minutes before he got out of his car.

Fanny hadn't locked the door behind her.

He quietly slipped inside, making sure the glass and metal panel shut behind him, allowing his eyes to adjust to the dim lobby.

There were a few lights on in the rinks beyond—four in total —but he moved straight ahead, going to the sheet of ice he'd seen Fanny on both times he'd been here before. There was barely enough illumination to see the edges of the ice, the plastic boards surrounding it, topped by clear plexiglass.

And there certainly wasn't enough light to expose him where he stood just inside the second set of doors, shadows clinging to the walls, the bleachers filling up one side of the space.

But apparently, it was enough for Fanny to see, to do what she needed to do.

Her bag sat on the floor, open in front of that lowest bench of the bleachers, almost spotlit beneath one of the few lights that were on.

But that only drew his focus for a couple of seconds.

Because his eyes . . . they were drawn to the ice. To *Fanny* on the ice.

God, she still moved like a river, liquid and smooth and persistent. No barrier would stop her, but it wasn't brutal like a tidal wave, like the ocean swallowing up the coastline. She was the narrow stretch of a creek, flowing through rocks and trees, along the riverbed. Graceful and effortless and absolutely stunning.

There wasn't any music blaring over the speakers. There weren't any fans in the stands.

It was just her and the music in her heart, the joy in her soul.

He stood there, riveted in place, the only sound in the large space the crunch of her skate blades against the ice. She owned the rink, using every inch as she moved through a stretch of footwork he remembered her taking months to master. Only it was different at the end, as though she'd added to it and increased the difficulty of the movements. Then she picked up speed, skating around the edges, lining up for a takeoff. There was one less rotation than he'd seen the last time she'd performed, but the double axel was still impressive, as was the Lutz she entered into barely a heartbeat later.

But she didn't stop there.

She continued moving, flowing, and it was as though a decade had never passed.

She jumped again and again. Her skate blades glinted in the dim light.

Her chest heaved, and her hair was plastered to her forehead.

And then . . .

She stopped, her gaze arrowing toward him.

NINE

FANNY

She was in the middle of her routine, the one that had earned her a silver medal.

The one she'd tweaked and added to over the years. Taking out some of the more difficult jumps—because she wasn't in as good of shape as she'd been at seventeen and didn't like breaking her ass—but putting in some of the footwork she really enjoyed. That had become her specialty, mainly because she'd needed to be good enough to teach other people how to trust their edges, their balance, to correctly distribute their weight.

She'd spent hours and hours upping her game.

And tonight just flowed.

All of the tension and need and longing that had coalesced upon finishing reading that notebook flowed out of her as she skated to music she hadn't heard in more than a decade.

The last time she'd skated it with music, she'd been surrounded by thousands of people. Her parents had come, along with Brandon's, and they'd all been sitting together in the stands. But she'd only had eyes for him. For the boy she loved. The boy who knew every move in the program and would mouth them as she completed them.

Something she'd only discovered when a reporter had shown her video of Brandon doing it in the stands.

So fucking good.

He'd been so fucking good.

Was it any wonder that no one else had ever competed? How could they?

She'd had the perfect man, the perfect boyfriend and fiancé and . . . lost it.

Tears prickled at the edges of her eyes, but only for a second, because rage quickly followed, chasing them away. Rage at what she'd lost. Rage at herself for being scared of what might be between them now. Rage at Brandon for getting sick, for forgetting her even though she knew logically it wasn't his fault.

But logic wasn't ruling her right now.

The fury of the last ten years was.

She moved faster and faster, speeding through the footwork, then picking up speed as she circled the rink, prepping for a jump, a toe loop that was messy as hell because she was sucking wind, but she pushed on anyway, forcing herself into another double axel with her chest heaving.

She stumbled, hit the ice with one knee, her hands catching herself on the ice.

Dropping her head as she tried to control her breathing, she stayed in place, her one knee aching from the impact, her fingers burning as the cold soaked into her skin, her palms.

Her nape prickled, and her gaze jerked up.

She shouldn't be able to see him, not with the shadows, not with the dim light.

But some part of her knew he was there. *How* was he there?

He just was, moving out of the darkness, stepping toward the door of the rink, the loud metal *thunk* echoing through the quiet of the space as he opened it. As he waited.

And she couldn't stop herself from going through their old routine, the movements as natural as breathing. She pushed to her feet and skated to that open door, stopping in it, her chest still heaving, her fingers gripping the cold plastic of the boards.

Beautiful.

The man was so fucking beautiful. She wanted to stroke the stubble on his cheeks and jaw. She was desperate to see if he tasted the same. She wanted his strong arms to band around her. She wanted him to declare that he loved her and wanted her forever, even though Fanny knew that would terrify her.

So she stayed there, fingers aching from denying herself the need to touch.

His voice was barely above a whisper, his soft question familiar and part of that old routine. "Are you done?" And when she found herself shaking her head, Brandon just brushed his knuckles over her cheek then nudged her back slightly.

She turned.

The door closed.

And she went back to skating, starting that routine from the beginning, throwing every bit of skill she possessed into her movements, those long minutes of her, the ice, and Brandon. For herself, because she never felt freer than when she was skating, when she was pushing herself to the limit on the cold, hard surface, when she was moving in a way that spoke to her soul.

Only when her legs felt like they were going to fall off did she glance back up, half-expecting Brandon to be gone. But he was still standing there on the other side of the door, his gaze on her, his body statue still.

He opened the door when she came over again, not asking this time if she was done, only taking her hand when she stepped down onto the black mat that surrounded the rink, and like he used to, he nudged her to her skate bag sitting by the bottom row of the bleachers. Brandon knelt before her then undid her skates, and it was falling into another memory as he carefully dried the blades and covered them with her skate guards before putting them into her bag.

A moment later, he helped her slip her feet into her fuzzy boots before picking up her skate bag and then taking her hand again.

His fingers were warm and rough as they held on to hers, and they walked out of the rink together, the past and the present all twisted together as she locked up, before he walked her to her car.

They stopped, and her heart pounded as she stared up into his pretty face, wanting . . .

Too much.

Everything.

Nothing.

"You're beautiful," he murmured, releasing her hand to cup her cheek, and she couldn't stop herself from leaning into his palm, couldn't stop those words from soaking into her skin, her heart. "And you still move like liquid silk."

Her lips parted, and she rose on tiptoe, needing to be closer, desperate to taste him. "I read the notebook."

His eyes widened. "Yeah?"

She nodded. "Yeah."

"What did you think?" he asked gently.

What *did* she think? Too much, that was what. That was why she'd fled the quiet of her house, the tangled feelings pressing in on her. "I . . ."

His head dropped, his hot, damp breath on her skin.

"Fanny," he whispered.

She shuddered, leaned closer, pleasure coursing through her

when her breasts brushed against his chest. "I think we had a lot of good times," she murmured, her hand resting on his shoulder.

He ran his knuckles over her cheek. "I think we could have a lot more."

Inhaling, the air thickened, and time disappeared. It was just her and Brandon and the moonlight, the whisper of the breeze, the deep longing to go back to what they had before, to forget everything and just . . . touch her lips to his.

Closer, he moved.

Nearer, she leaned.

His mouth was right there. He smelled of mint and spice, of sandalwood and something musky that made her want to rub herself against him.

His breath mingled with hers. His hand slid down, cupped the side of her neck, and . . . he kissed her forehead.

Then. Stepped. Back.

Fanny's nostrils flared on a sharp inhale, but before she could say anything, before she could close the distance between them and get the kiss she wanted, he snagged her keys from her hand, unlocked her car, and guided her into the driver's seat. Head spinning from the sudden change of circumstances—from his arms to her car—she couldn't summon any words when he bent over her and set her bag on the passenger's seat, pausing only to buckle her seat belt before he straightened and stood.

"Drive safe, honey," he whispered.

He shut the door.

She blinked, hands finding the steering wheel and clenching the leather-covered circle tightly. Need was coiled tight in her stomach, damp heat had gathered between her thighs. She wanted him, wanted to open her door and go to him. To kiss him.

She fumbled for the handle, started to open the door.

Lights flared to life behind her.

Eyes flying to the rearview, she saw his silhouette, saw him sitting in his car, watched as he pulled away from the curb.

Her hand relaxed, dropping away from the handle, and no, that wasn't disappointment coursing through her. It wasn't. She glanced down and saw that her keys were in the cupholder; she picked them up with shaking fingers. A deep breath steadied her, tempered her need, her disappointment she was pretending wasn't disappointment still sitting heavy in her gut.

"Okay," she said on a long, slow sigh.

She turned on her car and drove away from the rink.

But that disappointment that wasn't disappointment faded when she noticed the headlights in her rearview again, when she watched Brandon's car pull behind her again, when he followed her all the way home.

When those headlights didn't disappear into the night until she was safe in her house.

Then there was no more disappointment, pretend or otherwise.

There was only the small kernel of hope.

———

By the next night, after not enough sleep, too many hours of clinics, and not one glimpse or call or text or barging onto her front porch of Brandon, that kernel of hope was very much at risk of disappearing.

She hadn't expected him to show at the rink.

For one, he didn't know her schedule, wouldn't know if she'd be teaching or not.

For another, the man had a job, and it wasn't like he could just drop everything to come seek her out.

But still, he hadn't texted, and he hadn't shown, and now it was ten at night and . . . nothing. Not one word or call or text. And yes, she was cognizant of the fact that he didn't have her number. But part of her wanted the man to work for it—or to keep working for it, anyway.

That he didn't?

That he didn't ring her doorbell during dinner or after it, even though she'd lingered downstairs for much longer than normal, pretending to watch a movie while really staring out the window, searching for any glimpse of a car pulling up to her house, threatened to extinguish that tiny flame of hope.

She tried for logic—it hadn't even been twenty-four hours, he didn't have her number, they were both up late the night before, amongst others—but it wasn't particularly successful.

And then her phone buzzed.

And the way her heart pounded as she reached for it was a damned good indication of how deep she was already in with him, despite her fighting the slide every inch of the way.

Her eyes flicked over the message, barely reading the words before she realized that it wasn't from Brandon.

Acute disappointment swept through her.

Strong enough that she dropped her phone on the bed and pushed out from beneath the covers, pacing to her window and staring out at the back yard, trying desperately to calm herself, to push down the feelings that threatened to overwhelm.

When she could breathe without it hurting, Fanny turned back to her phone and opened up the text.

Hi, Fanny. This is Charlie. I hope it's okay to text. Scarlett gave me your number.

So much for Scar thinking she was in—lalala—love with Brandon, or thinking Fan should give him another chance. Here she was, throwing her at her brother. She typed out a text to her friend.

You gave your brother my number?

A few minutes passed before her cell vibrated.

He's a good guy. Give him a chance.

"Give *who* a chance?" she muttered. "Brandon or Charlie?" Sighing, she tossed her phone down in disgust and paced away to the window again, staring out like the shadows might give her some answers . . . or like Brandon might appear out of them again, might watch her and hold her hand and this time, might kiss her somewhere that *wasn't* her forehead.

Her phone buzzed.

She couldn't stop herself from going over and reading the message.

Now I'm thinking I overstepped. Sorry about that. If you feel up to hanging out, hit me up sometime.

Damn.

Why did Charlie have to seem nice?

Why hadn't Brandon come over?

The second more than the first—and maybe later she would need to look into herself to truly understand her motivations and whether texting Charlie back and asking if he wanted to go to dinner the next night when she was so torn up with Brandon made her a giant asshole or not.

She was pretty certain it did.

But either way, she sent the message.

And when Charlie called her back instead of texting, she picked up the call. She talked and flirted and got to know him for almost an hour. Scar was right. He *was* nice. And funny. And he had a nice voice.

And none of the complications of Brandon.

So when she yawned as it neared midnight, and he apologized for keeping her up so late then asked if she really did want to grab dinner, she accepted the invitation. She even went so far as to suggest a place to meet since he was new to town.

She was going to give him a chance.

Charlie.

Not Brandon.

TEN

BRANDON

"I'm married, and my wife wants me to take another woman on a date," Devon snapped (again, since he didn't appear to be anywhere near ready to let it go) as he stormed into the conference room, bypassing the empty chair at the table and stomping to the coffee pot. As he poured himself a mug, Olivia glanced up from her phone and rolled her eyes.

Brandon smothered a smile.

It had been two days since he'd last seen Fanny. Well, fine. Technically it had only been one, if he counted that he'd trailed her home well past midnight the previous day. Not seeing her yesterday was hard as hell, but they'd made some progress at the rink, and he didn't want to push her too far.

I think we had a lot of good times.

She hadn't discounted what they had. Instead, she'd softened in his hold, had allowed him to touch her, to take care of her in one small way.

Progress.

But he knew he needed to play this carefully.

So, he hadn't gone over to her house last night, and he hadn't called her, even though he'd managed to get her number via Kaydon, who'd gotten it from someone in the Gold organization (which equaled Brandon being on the radar of the Gold and their gossiping hockey players, not that he cared). He'd gotten an in with Fanny, and he was going to do this slow and smart and steady. He would convince her to give him a chance, and he wasn't going to fuck it up by playing the bull in a china shop.

"A date!" Devon said again.

Olivia sighed. "I thought we were beyond this."

Devon scowled and stomped over, dropping into his chair and pouting. "I am. I'm doing it, even though I hate it." He sipped, plunked the mug onto the table.

"For the children," Olivia said, lips twitching, tone dry.

Dev narrowed his eyes. "Yes," he gritted. "I'm doing it for the children."

Olivia glanced at Brandon, which was really shit timing on his part because he was trying to hold it together, and seeing her blue eyes sparkling with mirth had him losing any hope of control. He burst out laughing, and Olivia joined in.

Devon glared at them. "You're both assholes."

"You love us," Olivia said, wiping her eyes. "You know it's true."

"I tolerate you."

"Love." She pushed out of her chair, pressed a kiss to his cheek, and swiped his coffee, sucking down a long sip. "As in, you love us both because we bring you excellent clients and negotiate kickass contracts."

"I hates you."

"Hates?" Brandon couldn't help but say.

Olivia started laughing again as she refilled his mug and plunked it back in front of Devon. "What, are you Gollum?"

Devon growled. "It's my precious," he muttered, snatching the mug.

"Which? The coffee or Becca?" Brandon asked.

Dev pointed a finger at him. "I don't like that you feel comfortable enough to give me shit already."

Brandon chuckled. "Bet you're kicking yourself for giving me that signing bonus, too."

"Fuck yeah, I am," Dev muttered. "But now I'm looking for a reason to fire you."

"And here I was going to offer to take your place," Brandon said. "If you could sell the organizers on Dinner with a Sports Agent instead of Dinner with the Sexiest Man of the Year."

"It was the Month. One *fucking* month, one *fucking* time."

"Your life is so tough," Olivia crooned. "Being a sexy hockey player." She pretended to swoon, the back of her hand going to her forehead. "Oh, the humanity."

Dev sighed. "I hates."

Olivia grinned. "I know."

Then Dev turned to Brandon. "You'd seriously do that?"

"After hearing you moan over this date for the past few days?" Brandon asked dryly. "Fuck, yes. Hell, I consider it a public service."

He glanced at Olivia. "Think you can convince my wife to make the switch?"

A smirk curved her lush mouth. "What'll you give me?"

Dev widened his eyes. "My undying love?"

"Pft." She waved a hand and leaned back in her chair, and Brandon could only smile as he watched her put her negotiating hat on. There was a reason she was at Prestige, and that was because she was damned good at squeezing perks out of contracts for her clients. "I'm thinking a trip to Aruba."

Dev snorted. "Like you'll get Cole off that farm of his."

One black brow lifted. "Who said I want him to go with me?"

Touché, Brandon thought, watching the two of them go back and forth as he smothered a smile.

"Two weeks at the resort you took Becca to."

Dev glared. "You trying to bankrupt me?"

A roll of her eyes. "If one trip would bankrupt you, we have bigger problems to discuss."

"Olivia," Dev warned.

She studied her nails. "Either that or you can talk to Bex yourself."

Dev was silent for a long moment. "No trip. What else?"

"Jewels."

He sniffed, shook his head. "Dude."

"I'm not a dude," she said sweetly. "Okay then, no trip, no jewels. My price is a new pair of heels."

Dev made a noise of outrage. "Those would be more expensive than a trip to fucking Aruba."

A shrug. "Do I need to remind you that you are in the position of disadvantage in this negotiation?"

"Baked goods?" Dev countered without acknowledging that true statement. He wouldn't give the point any credence because it would give Olivia even more power. And but seriously, Brandon felt as though he were attending a master class in negotiating.

"Ah, once that would have been golden," she said. "But alas for you, Cole gets Molly's to cater the ranch." A silken smile curving her fire engine red mouth as she waved a hand with all the regal demeanor of a queen. "But by all means, however, keep trying."

Devon's phone buzzed, and he muttered a curse. "Logan is here to sign the contract." He glared at Olivia. "Fine. Heels. Your choice. But only if you convince Becca to allow Brandon to take my place."

Olivia sighed as she slicked on a fresh layer of lipstick, even though the crimson color had looked perfect before she'd put on the newest coat, at least from what Brandon could tell. "It's not going to be easy."

Brandon could practically hear the bones of Devon's jaw clenching together. "Fine. *Two* pairs."

She smacked her lips together. "Three."

A vein pulsed in Dev's forehead before he nodded. "Three."

There was a knock at the door, and Olivia got up to answer it. On the way, she stopped and pressed a kiss to Dev's cheek, wiping off the red mark she'd left behind before moving to the door. "One pair," she said, smiling widely. "I can't help myself with negotiating, but I'm not going to drain my godchildren's college funds."

The tension left Devon's frame.

Brandon bit back another laugh.

Olivia opened the door and let Logan in.

And yeah, Brandon had just been lucky enough to witness that master class in negotiation.

Olivia was the shit.

———

He sipped the beer and wondered how quickly he could get out of there.

Not that he didn't like Ethan, Kaydon, and Logan. He did. The latter two were talented players and good guys, and Kay and he were close. But he especially liked Ethan after Brandon had apologized for the other night and explained in the most general terms possible what was going on with him and Fanny. Ethan had nodded his understanding then promised to disembowel him if he ever talked to Fanny like that again.

Brandon hadn't protested.

Mainly because if he did talk to her like that again, then he'd deserve the disemboweling.

But he liked that Fanny had people in her corner who'd protect her.

He liked that Ethan wouldn't stand in his way.

Because he'd decided to win her over. He wasn't desperate to try to earn forgiveness—he was lucky enough to have that—now he was going to weave his way back into Fanny's life and prove to her that he was worth whatever risk the future might bring.

Luckily, Ethan hadn't held a grudge—aside from the whole disemboweling threats—especially after Brandon had bought the first two rounds.

He was itching to get over to Fanny's, but he knew this time was important.

Not just to build the relationship with Kaydon as a client, but also because if he was going to build a full life with Fanny, that meant *he* needed to have a full life. He needed friends, and it wouldn't hurt if one of those friends happened to be the significant other of one of *her* friends. Maybe that was an Olivia-level move, but either way, he liked Ethan, would be happy to be friends with him.

Ethan's relationship with Fanny was just a side benefit.

Logan was a good guy, too. He'd been in the league for many years and had a whole wealth of interesting stories to go with it. He'd also been cool about taking Kaydon under his wing, having been through a similar injury early in his own career.

And fuck, did Brandon hate that Kaydon hadn't discussed the toxic environment at his last team with him.

Kay was a head-down-move-forward kind of guy, and though his work ethic had never faded, and he'd fought to push through the injury, though he did his level best to prove his mettle to the management at the to-remain-nameless team, none of those factors could fix a shitty work environment.

He'd been lucky to be released and luckier to be picked up by the Gold.

And not with a low-ball, insulting offer that he'd been given by other teams. With a fair bottom line and potential for growth if he really started rolling in the league.

Brandon had a feeling about this season.

He felt in his bones that the timing was right, and Kay had the right crew behind him, the right players with him. He knew, just *knew*, this would be Kaydon's year.

"So then Brit took off," Logan said. "But we were ready. Blane tackled her and stole her shoes, thinking that would slow her down."

Brandon grinned.

Kay leaned forward. "Did it?"

"No," Ethan said, shaking his head with a bemused smile. "She just ran barefoot and beat all of us anyway."

"And then we got in trouble from Mandy because Brit got a cut on the bottom of her foot."

Brandon started laughing. "The women stick together."

"The women," Logan said dryly, "like to stick it to us."

Ethan shrugged. "It's true."

"So, that's why you guys have given up . . ." Kaydon started asking, but Brandon stopped listening. Because the door to the bar had opened and a good-looking blond man had walked in.

Though that wasn't what had caught Brandon's focus.

No, every cell in his body shot to rigid attention at the woman walking in behind him. A brunette with curves he would know anywhere, with lips he needed to kiss, with eyes that were stunning, with a heart he needed to own.

He almost jumped off his stool, almost left the high-top table they'd occupied since coming to the brewery an hour before, but Kay laughed loudly at something, and that broke through the red haze coating his vision enough to think.

Think, Cunningham, he snapped to himself.

Maybe it was a business meeting.

They could totally just be here to discuss something with her business. He'd been researching it since the first time he'd seen her at the rink, knew it was growing, and there were quite a few organizations interested in partnering with her.

The door shut, and Fanny laughed as she trailed the blond man to the hostess stand.

Definitely a business meeting. Def—

They checked in and stepped to the side, probably waiting for their table, and the man slipped a hand around her waist as she leaned into him.

She let him touch her.

She. Let. Him. Touch. Her.

Touch. *Her*.

Not a business meeting. Not a *fucking* business meeting.

She was on a date.

Fuck *that*.

ELEVEN

FANNY

Charlie was great.

Good-looking. Funny. Attentive and sweet.

But . . . she didn't feel a modicum of attraction toward him. He was all those things she'd mentioned, but she didn't want to jump his bones. Hell, she'd take a slight urge to cuddle at this point.

Instead, every time he touched her, a light hand on her back, guiding her through a door, their fingers brushing when he pulled back her chair for her, she could only think of how it had felt when Brandon had touched her outside the rink. Or when his hand had pressed to her stomach, keeping her from stepping onto the glass on her porch that night.

Or his palm on her cheek.

Or—

"You okay?" Charlie asked.

She blinked, shook her head slightly. "Sorry, I zoned out there for a minute."

"I knew I shouldn't have started discussing the atomic

weight of sodium hydroxide." He made a face, though he couldn't hold it, his lips turning up at the edges, eyes dancing with humor, letting her know that he hadn't been testing her on her chemistry skills. "Told you I was out of practice with the whole dating scene." He tapped a finger to his mouth. "I know what will keep you riveted," he teased. "I can tell you all about my success on my track and field team in high school."

Laughter bubbled up in her chest as she reached over and squeezed his hand. "I'd be happy to hear of your accolades," she said. "Was it long jump?"

He flipped his hand over, lacing their fingers together.

They were warm and calloused and . . . nothing like Brandon's.

Fuck.

"Not long jump. I was a hundred meter guy," he said. "But I'm not the one who has a silver medal. What was *that* like?" he asked.

See? He was good.

Sharing about himself, but then able to return the favor, to encourage *her* to share. This man wouldn't stay single for long. She should jump in, grab on, and—

He wasn't Brandon.

"It's okay if you don't want to talk about it," he said, squeezing her fingers. "I'm sure you get sick of discussing it."

"No," she said, forcing herself to focus. It wasn't fair to Charlie. "It's hard to put into words." Her eyes slid closed, and she felt her mouth curve, able to transport herself right back to that moment. "I didn't fully achieve my goal of gold, but it still felt incredible to be on that podium. I remember the weight of the medal. I remember seeing my boy—" She stopped herself before she could say boyfriend or mentioned Brandon. "I remember seeing my *family*"—her true family, Jeff and Grace, even though they sat next to her biological parents—"in the stands, and the smiles they wore, how proud they looked. I remember seeing the flag being hoisted, the sound of the crowd and the music blaring through the arena. Russia's anthem." She opened her eyes and grinned at him. "It wasn't the Star-Spangled Banner, though it *was* still captivating."

Charlie squeezed her fingers.

And she found herself still talking, even though he'd been right, and she didn't like to talk about it. Even without the gold medal, she was proud of herself, proud of the work she'd put in. It was just . . . everything else that had come after had turned those memories into something that she buried rather than relished. She sighed. "But looking back now, it was like everything during that time was on fast-forward. Before the medal ceremony, everything was almost a blur with all the training and press and ice time and then competing. After, it was closing ceremonies—we were right near the end, and I didn't have much time to do anything besides focus on the competition—and more press and finally getting some sleep. So, when I was finally done and could actually let loose a bit, it was over."

"A whirlwind," Charlie said.

Her lips curved. "Precisely."

"Your parents must have been so proud of you," he said.

Ah. Well, that was almost as complicated of a topic as Brandon.

Both of which were way too complicated to get into a discussion about on a first date.

Which was why she simply said, "Yes."

Seeming to understand that was a touchy subject, he straightened slightly, still holding her hand. "Dessert? Or should I take you home so you can get some sleep?"

Her heart squeezed, and she knew—freaking *knew*—that if she weren't hung up on an annoying, curly-haired, handsome ex-fiancé, that he would be really good for her. He probably would be really good for her even with her still hung up on Brandon.

But he deserved someone without entanglements.

Someone better than her.

"Dessert," she said, wanting to pretend a little longer. "You pick." She tugged her hand back, started to push back her chair. "I need to use the bathroom."

"Is this a test?" Charlie asked lightly, standing when she did. Polite.

Probably *too* polite, considering who his sister was.

She shook her head. "How are you Scarlett's brother?"

"Why?" he asked, tucking a lock of hair behind her ear. "Because I have manners?"

"Precisely."

He grinned. "My mom taught us both. Scar ignored her."

"And you?"

His eyes, a deep blue, darkened enough to cause an answering echo in her middle, telling her that yeah, this man could be trouble, just like his sister. "I only put them to use for very special occasions."

Laughing and shaking her head, she stepped by him. "Order dessert, and if you pass, I might consider a second date."

Saluting, he sat back down and picked up the smaller dessert menu their server had left on the table not too long before. "Chocolate?" he asked, glancing up at her.

"Cheater."

"Or are you not a chocolate woman?"

Half her mouth turned up. "I'll never tell."

"Cheesecake?"

"Did you get in trouble in school for cheating?"

"No." A beat. "But only because I never got caught."

She giggled. Actually giggled. Then realized she was standing in the middle of the restaurant, blocking the walkway, and still not walking to the bathroom. Charlie was trouble all right. Just like his sister. Pointing a finger in his direction, she ordered, "Dessert."

And then she swept through the tables and into the hallway that led to the bathrooms.

Fanny was about to push into the single stall when a hand caught her arm and dragged her back against a hard, warm chest. "Charlie!" she gasped.

The fingers tightened.

The spicy male scent reached her nose.

And she knew, even before he spoke.

"Not Charlie," Brandon growled. He spun her, pinned her to the wall, his body pressing to hers, and it was . . . glorious. Everything she'd imagined, *more*. Because it was familiar and not, and the feel of him against her had a swath of heat rolling through her, hardening her nipples, bringing her thighs together, squeezing tight against the sudden burst of moisture drenching her panties as she arched against him.

"Brandon," she whispered.

"What the fuck are you doing on a date with another man?" he snapped.

She lifted her chin, anger pulsing, twining with her desire in some sort of fucked-up need for this man. She pushed at his chest. "Go away."

"Why?" he asked hotly, not moving, not even when she put all her force behind her shoves.

"Fuck you," she hissed, raging now.

He leaned heavier against her, causing her breathing to hitch. "Why are you with that asshole?"

"I can date who I want," she gritted out. "You don't have any right to—"

"Why?" he repeated.

And something snapped inside her. "Because you didn't come. Because I waited all day for you to call and show up, but you didn't. And I wanted you to." She shoved him hard, forcing him back a step. "Damn you, I wanted you to. I wanted . . . *you*."

His eyes widened. "Fanny," he breathed.

She started to clamp a hand over her mouth, unable to believe she'd said that. She was on a date with another man right now, and Charlie was great, and she didn't want to go back to the past. They couldn't ever be what they once were.

Right? *Right?*

But even as he stepped closer, she didn't push him away, she didn't leave that hall.

Even as his mouth lowered to hers, she didn't retreat.

She stretched up, lifted her chin . . . aligned their lips.

And kissed him.

Or maybe he kissed her. Or maybe—

Fuck if she didn't really care.

He parted her lips with a dart of his tongue, slipping it into her mouth and coaxing hers out to play. Sleek darts and shallow teases. His fingers sliding up along her side, her arm, her neck, before slipping back and weaving into her hair, tilting her head, and angling them.

It was new . . . and not.

It was familiar . . . and not.

It was . . . Brandon.

She moaned and wrapped her arms around his neck, bringing him closer, wanting his body flush against her, needing him close after he'd been far for so long. His other hand cupped her ass, brought her leg up. Without a moment of hesitation, she wrapped it around his waist, and then the other. His groan when he pressed her against the wall, their bodies perfectly aligned, the hard length of his cock insistent against the fabric of her underwear had her shivering, uncaring that anyone might walk down the hall and see them.

His fingers massaged her ass, his hips moved, grinding against her, and she was shockingly close to an orgasm in a matter of seconds.

"Bran," she gasped, when he pulled away and nipped at her

lips then bent to nip at her throat, the bared skin just above her breasts.

"So fucking beautiful," he whispered against her skin, tongue gliding along her flesh, along the seam of the deep V of her dress.

Down. Down. *Down.*

Until it felt like she'd fall, until it was only his hand and the pressure of his hips that kept her against that wall.

And then she wasn't thinking of falling.

Wasn't thinking of anything except the fact that his tongue was darting *in.* That it was slipping under the fabric of her dress and unerringly finding the hard tip of her nipple.

"No bra," he whispered, flicking his tongue there.

She moaned, and though a distant part of her understood this was insane, that she should push him away . . . the rest of her wanted Brandon too much to be thinking clearly.

She yanked the fabric to the side, and he didn't delay, just sucked her nipple deeply into his mouth and kept rocking against her. Sparks were shooting through her nerves, glittering pleasure was filling her veins, need and heat and moisture were gathering and coiling and . . .

Exploding.

Between her thighs, flooding the rest of body, a rapid surge that tightened every muscle and cell, one that flew through her with all the intensity of a lightning strike. And then it relaxed, her pleasure lapping at her, slowly receding, fading until it ebbed against her like gentle waves against a shore.

"Fuck, you're beautiful," he murmured, slowly tucking her back into her dress and kissing his way back up her throat until he reached her mouth.

He kissed her again, kissed her until she was reduced to ash, until she was reformed into someone completely different.

Only then did he slowly unhook her legs, placing her feet on the floor one by one, steadying her until she found her balance, his fingers and hold gentle now instead of whipping her into a frenzy of need.

"Beautiful," he said with another brush of his lips.

He straightened, stroked his thumb over her cheek.

"Get rid of him," he ordered.

And then he was gone.

Leaving her panting and alone in the hallway, wondering what in the fuck had just happened.

———

Kaydon looked toward the door to the rink, and she would have had to be blind to miss the longing in his eyes.

"All right," she muttered. "All right." She nodded to the exit. "Get out of here."

He didn't question her, just tossed out a wave and hauled ass to the door. "Thanks, Fanny," he called before taking off down the hall, "that was fun."

She grinned.

He didn't have to pretend it had been fun.

She knew it had been a combination of boring, small, repetitive movements he'd done a million times throughout the years and exhausting on-ice maneuvers that he'd never done before. He'd be sore tomorrow—and probably the night after—but it was the only way he would be able to properly relearn the muscle memory. At least to relearn it properly.

Because he'd had several seasons of skating through the pain.

Then another of jumping back onto the ice without proper rehab.

He had all sorts of shit to work through, and it was going to take some more time in order to get there.

Which was why she called, "See you next week!"

His groan echoed down the hallway.

She grinned, started to follow him, ready to get off the ice herself, but a voice called her name. Turning, she skated over to the little girl who'd been patiently waiting for the public skate to start. Opening the gate to let everyone on, she bent to hear the girl over the rush of kids jostling to get on. "Can I show you my axel?"

Fanny's heart squeezed. "I'd love to see it, Lily."

This was why she taught, and not just the big guys who thought puck handling was more important, but because it was a fucking joy to see skating through the eyes of kids. It was new and fresh and exciting. Especially in the littlest kids.

"Yay!" She snagged Fanny's hand and all but dragged her to the corner. "Stand here."

Fanny stood there.

Lily skated a few circles to warm up, then lined up her take-off, jumped, and . . . fell.

Closing the distance between them, she helped Lily up. "You were too far forward on your landing. Bend your knee a bit more to even out your weight, and that'll help for next time." She demonstrated. "Ready to try again?"

Lily nodded, determination on her face as she moved to have another go.

Then she jumped but rotated too early. She landed it, but barely, her hand pushing off the ice, so she didn't tumble.

Not that Lily cared. She spun toward Fanny and pumped her hands in the air. "I did it!"

"You did!" Fanny smiled, hugging her back when the girl threw her arms around Fan's waist. "Great job," she said.

"Someday I want to be able to do a triple."

"Someday," she said, tugging the end of her ponytail, "you'll be able to."

"You think so?"

"I believe in you."

Lily tossed a huge smile in her direction then went off to continue practicing.

Fanny started toward the exit for a second, only to be waylaid again. She saw some crossovers, a girl take her first strides without the aid of a bucket to hold her up, and then some snow angels. None of which she was getting paid to see. But that was okay. Because kids.

She really loved them.

Eventually, she managed to get off the ice and move toward the bench just inside the hall where her bag was stowed.

She had one skate off when she felt it.

The tendril of heat sliding down her nape.

Her eyes shot up, and there he was.

Striding up to her as though he hadn't made her come by dry-humping her in a public hallway, and then had left her, knees shaking, lips swollen, hair a fucking mess. She barely remembered stumbling into the stall and trying to put herself to rights, knowing that she looked like she'd been ravished. *Feeling* like she had been ravished . . . even while part of her wished that he'd torn her panties off, unzipped, and—

Fuck.

She'd eventually managed to peel herself out of the bathroom, looking somewhat put together, to find that Charlie had not only passed her dessert test, but fucking aced it. He'd ordered both chocolate cake *and* cheesecake, and not only that, while she'd been unleashing her dry-humping she-demon in the hall, he'd worried that she wasn't feeling well, so had asked the server to box them up.

Then had sent both home with her.

Then had followed her home, since they'd met at the brewery.

Then had walked her to the porch and kissed her on the cheek.

Then had fucking texted her to make sure she was feeling better the next morning.

The fuck?

Seriously. The man was wonderful.

And she was . . . orgasming courtesy of her ex, drooling over said ex, *dreaming* of him, and—

She was an asshole.

But she didn't have time to ponder the full extent of her assholeness before Brandon was crouching next to her and reaching for her skates.

"Don't," she hissed, jerking her feet away.

He lifted his hands, stayed crouched, but his face was gentle when he said, "Are you okay?"

Leveling a glare at him was her only answer before bending to unlace her skates and tug them off. She dried the blade, stashed them away, slipped her tired feet into her fuzzy boots, and stood before striding down the hall. Her car was parked out front and though this exit would put her farther from it, she was willing and able to take all escape routes.

"Fan," he said. "I should—"

She whipped toward him, narrowed her eyes. "If you're going to apologize, don't bother."

His brows lifted.

"I was just as much a part of that as you were."

He relaxed. She saw the tension bleed from his shoulders.

"But it was still wrong."

That tension snuck back in, tightening his jaw, flattening his lips. "It didn't feel wrong to me." He stepped closer, his lips finding her ear. "I came in my hand twice last night thinking about how fucking sexy you were wrapped around me."

Was there any oxygen left in the hallway?

Or had this man just stolen it all?

He'd never talked like that before, his husky voice, the sleek, muscled lines of his body so close to hers, bringing her right back to the previous night. She wanted him. She was two seconds away from jumping into his arms and wrapping her legs around him again, only this time with his cock *inside* her instead of against her. "Brandon," she breathed, shivering when he ran one rough fingertip down the side of her neck.

"What are you doing here?"

She jumped, probably looking guilty as hell.

Definitely *feeling* guilty as hell.

Her head jerked down the hall, seeing Kaydon walking toward her, though his eyes were on Brandon, and belatedly she remembered that it would be strange for Brandon to be here. Agents didn't just show up at practices, let alone show up twice in a week.

Brandon straightened slightly, and she watched him as he tucked the heat away, his expression going casual as he held up a folder she had completely missed.

Was he a fucking magician?

Where had he been keeping that?

"I had the signed contract from yesterday."

Kaydon studied Brandon for a long moment before he lifted a brow. "You couldn't email me?"

"I—"

Maybe it was cowardice. Maybe it was smart. Maybe . . . she just wanted to see what lengths Brandon would go to in order to follow her, to talk with her.

Would he chase her down? Catch her arm again?

So maybe it was another test, only instead of dessert, this time it was . . .

To see if he was interested? No. To see if he would forget her.

Or maybe it was all of that, twisted and tangled together along with the fear of letting him in again, but either way, when Kay asked Brandon to see the contract and then began asking questions, Fanny snagged her skate bag and hauled ass to the exit.

TWELVE

BRANDON

"I don't think she wants to talk to you," Kay said, closing the folder the moment Fanny was out of sight and fixing Brandon with an intense stare.

He turned to follow her.

Kaydon grabbed his arm, stalling him. "What are you doing, man?"

"Mind your own business." Brandon tried to shrug off his hand.

The fucker just held on. Damn hockey players and their giant hands. "Dude," Kay snapped, shaking him slightly. "What are you *doing?*"

"She's mine," Brandon hissed, finally managing to break Kaydon's grip. He started walking after her.

"Doesn't seem like she wants to be."

That had him stopping and turning around. "She's just scared because—"

Fuck. It was too complicated a conversation to have in this moment, especially when Kay didn't know any of their history.

"Scared why?" Kaydon's voice was deadly, his expression doubly so, and Brandon had the notion that he was seeing what the other man's face might look like just before he mowed down an opponent on the ice. "What did you do?" His words grew even icier. "Did you hurt her?"

Brandon bit back a curse.

"Not like you're thinking," he said, and when Kaydon grabbed his shoulder, fingers digging in fiercely, Brandon knew that even though Kay was new to the Gold, Fanny had already earned his respect. Just as he knew Kaydon would throw down to protect her—and not just because she was a member of the Gold, but because Kay had seen the woman Fanny was, seen how much love and care she deserved.

Which was why he took thirty seconds to lay it out for him.

Kaydon already knew about the cancer. When Kay's mom had been diagnosed a couple of years ago, they'd talked it out, and Brandon had shared his own experience, but Kay didn't know about Fanny and everything that had gone down.

So, Brandon told him in those thirty seconds, understanding full well that the tale might end up on the Gold's gossip train, that the team might intervene, and the intervention might not be in his favor.

He wasn't a safe choice.

But given a chance, he would love Fanny with every fiber of his being. He would love her until he was in the ground, or until that love was forcibly taken away from him. Brandon couldn't make guarantees. Fuck knew, he'd lived enough life to understand that, but he also knew that he wouldn't let her go without a fight.

To do that, Kaydon needed to understand.

And maybe the rest of the team needed to understand that as well.

"Fuck," Kay breathed when Brandon finished his short,

sharp explanation. "That's a fucking mess, man. You still love her?"

"I do," Brandon said, starting to move past Kaydon. He was probably already too late. Fan had probably already drifted off. "And she still feels something for me. So, I'm not letting her go. I'm going to fight for her and—"

"And if she doesn't want that?"

Brandon stopped.

"Will you let her go?"

Brandon dropped his head, staring at his feet, knowing the answer and knowing it probably wasn't the one Kaydon wanted to hear. If Fanny wanted him to move on, to let go, he honestly wasn't sure he could respect that wish. He thought that he might fight for her until he didn't have breath in his lungs.

"Make damned sure that you understand what's in your heart before you make your way back into hers."

Brandon sighed. "Not going to warn me off?"

Kaydon's mouth turned up. "I think you already understand how well-liked Fanny is with the guys. You'll have enough people to warn you off when they realize who you're after." He clapped Brandon on the shoulder and pointed back toward the rink. "You might have a chance to catch her if you go out that way. She usually parks out front."

With a nod of thanks, Brandon left Kaydon in the hall, holding the contract he'd printed out and hand-delivered for no reason other than Kay had mentioned his session with Fanny at dinner last night.

Then he exited the rink, knowing that a battle was forthcoming.

And looking forward to every damned minute of it.

———

She was just getting into her car.

He sped up, saw the redhead who'd been talking to her slant a curious gaze in his direction, and then a smug smile, but he didn't stop to analyze either.

Instead, he snagged the car door before Fanny could close it.

"Hey," he said, casually, standing in the open frame.

Her hand was still on the door, her arm outstretched, her fingers wrapped around the smooth metal handle. His greeting had her sighing and then glancing up at him, her brow lifted. "Really?"

"Hi, baby," he murmured, crouching down and running his fingers lightly up her arm. "Is that better?"

She shivered, snatched her arm back. "No."

Amusement coiled through him, but he was starting to understand that her snapping at him was a good thing. It meant that she felt something, and even if that something at the moment was being annoyed with him, then he'd take it. Annoyance was better than distance. And it sure as shit was better than not feeling *anything* for him.

"You here to talk to me about your masturbation habits again?" she gritted out.

Shock had him freezing.

But then the moment of surprise rapidly transformed into pleasure. He grinned slowly. "You want me to tell you about them?" he murmured, leaning close, not missing how she inhaled sharply, how her hands clenched into fists, her knuckles standing out sharply against her skin. "I don't mind."

She exhaled, slow and steady, but her seemingly calm breathing was belied by the fact that her cheeks had gone rosy, her irises dilated. "Well, I do," she muttered.

"No"—a tug of her ponytail—"you don't." He smothered a grin. "Want me to tell you how I was so turned on that it barely took me three strokes to come?" he said, loving that her cheeks flushed further. "Or that it didn't even take the edge off, not when I could still taste you on my tongue, could imagine what your slick heat would feel like around me. So"—he leaned closer, not bothering to hide his smile when she shivered—"as soon as I came, I had to jerk off again."

"That's disgusting."

Her voice was so breathless that he knew she thought that was anything *but* disgusting.

"Liar," he murmured, so close now that his lips brushed her earlobe, that he couldn't resist nipping the delicate dangling bit of flesh.

She moaned.

"Did you make yourself come?"

"Wh-what?"

"After what I did to you in the restaurant, did you go home and make yourself come?"

"I—" She shook her head. He hadn't moved back, so her hair caught the stubble on his jaw, her scent filled his nose. "No, of course not."

"Liar," he murmured again and had the pleasure of seeing her cheeks go fire engine red.

"Brandon," she whispered.

"Yeah?"

Her eyes sparked as her hand found his chest, shoved him back so he landed on the warm pavement.

"You're an asshole."

She slammed the door, nearly clocking him in the head. The *click* of the lock engaging had him jumping to his feet.

"You can run," he said, knowing it probably wasn't loud enough for her to hear.

But she could read his lips, apparently.

Just like he could read hers.

Because he watched her mouth move, watched it form the words, "I'm not running."

So, for a third time, he said, "Liar."

Then she revved her engine and took off.

For some reason, he was grinning when she nearly mowed him over.

Maybe he loved to live dangerously.

Maybe he just loved her.

Thirteen

Fanny

Fury was her companion the whole way home.

Through the traffic.

Through the stop for gas.

Through pulling into her driveway and going inside, accompanying her as she ate dinner, as she finished off her bottle of wine.

How dare he?

Seriously, how fucking *dare* he?

She should have run his ass over in the parking lot. Things would have been so much simpler and—

Her phone rang.

Sighing, she moved to the counter and picked it up, and no —*fucking no!*—that wasn't disappointment sliding through her when the caller ID showed that it was Charlie calling her and not Brandon with more surprising sexy talk that he'd learned somewhere along the way.

Because he sure as shit hadn't had it when they'd been together.

Which meant that he'd learned it somewhere that wasn't with her. Which meant that he might have learned it from Angela.

That painful thought had her picking up the phone.

"Hey, beautiful," Charlie said, his warm voice making the fury that had gripped her for the last hour dissipate.

"Hey," she said, smiling as she leaned back against the counter.

"You feeling better?"

Ah. There was the pang of guilt.

She deserved it after her shenanigans in the hall. Or maybe, Brandon did. He was the instigator—and yes, she knew she'd been an active participant. Damn. She really *should* have run over the fucker.

"Fanny?" Charlie asked. "You there?"

"Yes." She straightened as though he could see her, as though she were on her best behavior and not thinking about Brandon and running him over . . . nor about how delicious his sexy talk had been. Shivering, she forced herself to focus. "I'm sorry. I'm here, and I'm feeling better. Thanks for asking."

"If this is a bad time, I can let you go."

More guilt.

Fuck.

"It's not."

"So, it's not a bad time, and you're feeling better." Charlie's words were light. "Then it must be that you're immune to my patented charm."

She laughed. "Yes, it's that exactly."

"Damn."

"Thanks for dinner last night," she told him. "I had a really nice time."

"I'm glad. I did, too. Now, stop with the niceties and give me all the gossip about my sister. What kind of trouble is Scar causing?"

"Your sister is an angel."

"And now I know what your voice sounds like when you're lying."

Her amusement boiled over, and she found herself giggling —actually *giggling*. Like a little girl. *Again*. Charlie was just so . . . Charlie. A bright ray of sunshine in her life. "You're just as bad as she is."

"Oh really?" he teased. "Tell me more."

"How dare you, good sir?" she countered. "I'd never betray my friends."

"Hmm. So, you're one of *those*."

She picked up her glass of wine. "Those?"

"One of those rule-followers."

"You got me," she said dryly.

"Don't worry, Scar and I will fix that for you." A beat. "Did Scarlett ever tell you about the time she tried to push me out a second-story window?"

Fanny found herself laughing again. "What? No."

"I was two. She was three, and she hated that all my cuteness usurped hers. So, she . . ."

And then he spun a wild tale about a three-year-old Scar somehow plotting murder because he'd gotten more hugs from their grandmother than she had that day. She called him on his bullshit, and he readily admitted that it was just that—*bullshit*— before telling her that it was a bizarre and terrible accident, but that luckily he hadn't been seriously hurt.

As she listened to him, she had the notion that this is what it could be like with Charlie. He would make her laugh, and their conversations wouldn't be filled with tension and the painful past, with guilt and wishing things would have turned out differently.

They would just be light and fresh and . . . easy.

They talked for a long time, and all the while it was tempting, *so* tempting to continue to lean into the feeling he created within her, to pretend that Brandon didn't exist, and that she could be this woman, be the person she was with Charlie—whole, light, carefree—all the time.

But she couldn't ignore Brandon, couldn't pretend he didn't exist.

And she knew that she wouldn't ever be able to be fully present with Charlie, not in the way he deserved.

Which was why when he asked her out to dinner the following night, her answer was, "I can't."

Silence.

It wasn't fair to him, for her to be hung up on another man. He deserved more, so much more than she could give him.

"Ah," he said quietly, sober for the first time since they'd first begun talking. "Is it because of Scarlett? I promise I would never get in between your friendship."

"It's—" She broke off before she blabbed her entire sob story. "It's not about Scar," she said.

"I see."

"It's not you, it's . . . damn"—she sighed and shook her head —"I don't mean it like that. I'm just not in the right mental headspace for a relationship. There's someone from my past, and it's complicated, and I can't be with anyone while it's still so unsettled."

"I understand," he said gently. "No hard feelings."

"Would you—" Cutting herself off before she could ask. It wasn't fair.

"Would I what?"

Another shake of her head, even though he couldn't see her.

"Fanny," he ordered. "Just ask."

She winced then blurted, "Would you want to be friends?" God, that sounded stupid and juvenile, and she wanted to grab the words out of the air and shove them back into her mouth.

Silence for a heartbeat too long, then, "Of course, I would."

"You don't have to—"

"You're a cool chick, Fanny. Gorgeous, funny, and talented," he said, and she felt her cheeks heat. "So, even if you're not interested in me, I'd love to be friends." A chuckle. "Plus, if I can keep you nearby, I might get a second crack at dating you."

Laughter had her shaking her head. "You're—"

"Unbelievable in the best way possible?"

"That wasn't exactly what I was thinking."

Unfazed, he said, "Let's go to dinner. As friends," he added when she began to protest.

"As friends," she agreed.

"Perfect. That means I still have a shot to squeeze out more dirt from you about Scarlett."

———

By the time she got off the phone with Charlie, she was pleasantly buzzed.

They'd chatted and joked, and he'd given her several good blackmail stories about Scarlett that had Fan nearly in tears and looking forward to her newfound friendship.

Charlie was good people.

Eventually, though, she'd yawned, and Charlie had told her he'd see her in a few days at the charity raffle then had ordered her to get to sleep.

She was tired but not sleepy, so she went to the kitchen for more wine, topping off her glass and parking her ass on the couch. There was a new horror show she wanted to jump into, and tonight seemed as good a time as any to start.

The knock came when she was fully immersed in the show and at a particularly tense moment.

She jumped, nearly upending her wine, her heart pounding like a motherfucker.

"Shit," she gasped, clamping her free hand over her chest then glaring toward the front door.

The knock came again.

Probably, someone trying to sell her something.

Well, good for that person. She wasn't getting her ass off the couch. Lifting the remote, she turned up the volume and kept watching.

Whoever was on the other side of the door didn't get the hint. They knocked again. Louder and longer. She sighed, glanced at the clock, and realized it was late. *Really* late. Of course, it wouldn't be someone selling something. This was a different kind of visit.

And considering the persistence, as the knocking continued, she had a suspicion who it was.

"Fuck," she muttered. So much for not getting off her couch. Sighing, she hit the button to pause her show and stood up, making it to the front door just as there was yet another knock, this one near-pounding, instead of the medium-level tapping from before.

She whipped open the door.

And sighed.

In annoyance, not in pleasure. Not because the man looked fucking delicious standing on her porch in a pair of low-slung jeans that looked as soft as butter along with a tight blue sweater. He was holding a large basket, and she could see an inch of taut, golden skin exposed by his sweater having risen up.

"Hi, beautiful," he murmured, and she snapped her eyes up to his. Away from the temptation of the shadows of squares she could just barely make out, away from that peekaboo of his flat abdomen.

"What are you doing here?"

"I have something for you."

She frowned, wondered exactly why the hell he'd show up on her porch bearing gifts after . . . "I nearly ran you over with my car," she blurted.

He grinned, the fool. "Maybe I like that."

"You've lost it," she muttered, backing up, intending to slam the door closed.

But the fucker stepped forward instead, striding over the threshold and into her house, saying, "Thanks, I *will* come in."

And for all that she talked and instructed for a living, Brandon barreling his way into her entryway had her sputtering. "I—I—"

He walked right by her, disappearing into the kitchen.

"I—"

A car drove by, the headlights flashing past her front yard, and Fanny realized that she was just standing there, staring at the empty hall, the open door. Blinking, she closed and locked the door then turned and followed Brandon.

He was unpacking the basket on her kitchen counter.

"What the hell are you doing?"

"Here," he said, thrusting the basket at her.

She scrambled to take it, the contents within rattling, and she glanced down to see they were all wrapped. Then repeated her question. "Seriously, what the hell are you doing?"

A smile, before he spun away and began searching through her cabinets until he located a vase, plunking a large arrangement of sunflowers into it after he'd filled it with water.

"Cooking you dinner."

"It's after nine."

He lifted a brow. "Have you eaten?"

No, she hadn't. She'd been on the phone through dinner with Charlie, and truthfully, she was never great at eating dinner. She never had been. Oftentimes, she got lost in some task or show, and then she forgot to eat.

Plus, it was nearly bedtime. It was never good to eat at bedtime.

She was more of a breakfast person, mostly because she sometimes got so busy on the ice that she forgot to eat lunch, too. But anyway, that was beside the point. Breakfast was the shit. Give her a donut or a muffin or a croissant, and she was a happy girl.

"Right," Brandon said, turning back to the bag and continuing to unload what looked to be way too much food for two people.

"Do you think I have a hollow leg?" she muttered.

"I'm hungry. You've always been the type of girl to eat," he said, pulling out a package of chicken breasts. "I'm guessing that hasn't changed. Plus, you're too thin."

Her mouth dropped open, her gaze sliding down her body and making her realize that she was still holding the basket. "I am *not!*" she snapped, tossing the basket on the island.

"You're thinner than when you were skating."

Jaw clenching, she said, "I don't have that extra muscle."

"Bullshit," he told her. "You're plenty strong. You just don't remember to eat, and you don't have someone to take care of you."

"I—"

He set down a head of lettuce and crossed to her. "This is me telling you I'm going to take care of you."

She inhaled. Sharply.

He was close. Really close.

Which meant her inhale had the disastrous effect of bringing her breasts flush against his chest. Worse. Her inhale had her nipples brushing against his chest, heat scorching down her spine, moisture flooding her pussy, and making her suck in another breath.

Which just made the cycle worse.

Breathe. Brush. Pleasure.

And not once did Brandon back off.

His hand came to her cheek, cupped it gently, lightly running his thumb over her lips. "You've spent too many years without someone to take care of you. I'm not letting any more time pass without doing that."

Her lips parted.

A breath shuddered out.

Brandon's eyes went hot, his thumb pressed slightly more firmly against her bottom lip. His head came down . . .

He straightened, nudged her back, and returned to making himself at home in her kitchen. "Open your presents," he said as he bent and pulled out a pan.

Fanny blinked.

A long, slow blink.

She turned back to the basket, which was indeed filled with presents.

Another blink, her gaze rotating to Brandon again.

Who was still there, now pulling a cutting board out and getting busy with the lettuce.

"Fan?"

He'd moved on to the chicken, using a different cutting board as he coated them in some seasoning he must have brought because she didn't have anything in her house aside from olive oil, salt, and pepper.

"Yeah?" she asked, watching him put some oil in the pan.

"Open the presents."

She nibbled at the corner of her mouth, hesitating, but then, ultimately, she reached into the basket and picked up the first wrapped package. For one, she loved presents. For another . . . she loved presents. Smiling, she carefully began peeling back the tape, slowly removing it so that she could savor the experience. She didn't receive presents. She hadn't shared her birthday with her friends, and her parents . . . well, celebrating that day wasn't on their agenda.

The Gold went all out on Christmas, but she always timed her vacation for then, making sure to be out of sight and mind for the celebrations.

Actually thinking about it now, the last time she'd received a present from anyone was when Grace had sent her a pair of cozy pajamas for Christmas before she'd passed away. The memory had her fingers faltering, the present resting on the counter as she blinked rapidly.

Fingers on her chin. "What is it?" Brandon asked gently.

She should have lied, pretended she was fine. But, for some reason, the words came anyway. "I miss your mom," she whispered.

He went quiet and still.

And then his arms slipped around her, tugged her close. "I know," he murmured. "I do, too."

He held her for a few moments and then stepped away, returning to the pan, putting in the chicken. As it sizzled, he went to the sink and washed up. She focused on the present as he turned to continue with whatever else he was making, and she finally made some progress on the paper, getting all the tape off and then slowly peeling it open.

"Oh," she breathed, touching the soft blue ombre scarf that reminded her of the bright cerulean, cloudless sky meeting the turquoise waves of the ocean.

"Do you like it?"

"It's beautiful," she said truthfully, running her finger over the delicate material. "I—" She broke off, unsure what she wanted to ask.

Okay, that was a lie.

She knew what she wanted to ask.

She was just too much of a coward to say it out loud.

Brandon wiped his hands on a towel, came over, and plucked another present from the basket. "Open this one next."

She didn't hesitate this time, just carefully pulled open the paper, revealing an expensive box of sea salt caramels. "How—"

He was there again, reaching into the basket, handing her an envelope.

Fanny didn't have the same compunction to save envelopes

that she had to save pretty wrapping paper, so she tore into it and tugged out the card.

I have ten years to make up for. This is just a start.

"I'd planned on making sure you didn't open that before I left," he murmured, tugging out the paper that she hadn't realized was taped inside the card and handing it to her. "But I decided I wanted to see your face when you do."

Frowning, she unfolded the printout and felt her mouth drop open.

It was a reservation to a winery north of them. The same winery they'd planned on getting married at.

She didn't know how she felt about that.

"It's for two," he said, moving to the pan and flipping the chicken. "But only if you want it to be. It can just as easily be for one." He glanced up, but she couldn't decipher his expression, not when she was so surprised, not when her mind was swirling. "I just thought that you might want to wipe the slate clean and start over. A fresh start. Something we can experience together and—"

She put her hand up.

He stopped talking.

Her mind continued spinning.

"Why?" she asked.

"Because I love you."

If she'd thought her mind was swirling before, then she had no notion of the idea. Because *now* her mind was swirling, spinning faster and faster until her head felt like it was going to ratchet right off her neck. Her emotions were all over the place—joy and fear, hope and terror, desire and longing. They were all twisted up, and yet, the one thing she couldn't stop from coming to the forefront of her mind, the *one* emotion that overshadowed all the others, was love.

She had never stopped loving this man.

But she couldn't say *that*. Just the thought of being that vulnerable to him had her throat constricting, her pulse pounding in her veins, sweat breaking out on her upper lips. Her fingers clenched on the paper, her gaze unseeing as she tried not to hyperventilate.

She didn't know how long she stood there, shock and panic roiling just beneath her skin, but the next thing she was aware of was warm fingers stroking down her arm, tugging the paper from her fingers, a gentle hand nudging her toward the counter where a plate of food now sat.

"Eat, honey," he said. "I'm sorry about the trip. That was too soon."

The vise on her lungs eased slightly. "Brandon," she said. "I don't think we can start over. I'm not sure a clean slate will ever be possible. There's just too much between us."

"Then we don't start over, we move forward."

She scoffed. "It's not that easy. I—" She faltered, not knowing what she wanted, whether she wanted to keep moving forward with Brandon, or to cut things off once and for all. To give in to the longing, or to shore up the walls around her and stay safe.

He cupped the side of her neck. "We don't have to do this tonight."

"But—"

"All of this will hold."

Her eyes flew to his. "I—" She shook her head, knew that she wouldn't come to any conclusions tonight. The answers weren't simple. They never would be, and . . . she sighed because he was right. All of this would hold. She could take some time to think, to sort out what she wanted to do, or time to admit to herself . . .

Not. Tonight.

"Right," she murmured.

He smiled, and it filled her stomach with butterflies. Then he lightly pressed on her shoulder, coaxing her onto the stool. "Food."

She sat.

He passed her a fork. She scooped up a bite.

"That's my girl," he murmured, kissing her temple and sitting down next to her. On her left side, because he was a leftie, and sitting there meant that he could lace their hands together and they could both still eat.

Fanny held her breath, wondering if he remembered.

But a heartbeat later, she wondered why part of her thought he hadn't.

Because his warm, rough fingers intertwined with hers . . . and then he asked her about the show that was paused on her TV.

They ate and held hands and talked about the show then talked about everything and nothing.

There wasn't any angst or stress or painful memories.

It was just the two of them.

And for the hour he stayed before kissing her on the forehead, before he wished her a soft, "Good night," and headed out the front door, Fan felt like she was fourteen again.

Fourteen and in love with Brandon Cunningham.

———

The first game of the season was in less than a week, and the hockey boys sure cleaned up nice.

She didn't often get to see them in their big kid clothes.

And it was a damned good view.

"You look nice."

Fanny jumped as Charlie came up next to her. The man had serious ninja skills, but that wasn't what had kept Fanny running around the entire afternoon, setting up tall tables for people to gather, talk, and eat (and drink because the more they drank, the more they would spend), hanging decorations, checking in with the caterers and the bartenders, fixing a strand of twinkly lights when they'd gone out. No, that was all Scar and her clipboard filled with never-ending tasks.

Fan had hauled planters of live plants from the truck outside into the large auditorium, had positioned and re-positioned them until Scar had been satisfied there were enough intimate corners to encourage conversation but not enough to be a hookup zone.

Hookups did not bring money to the charity.

There was a long list of things that didn't bring money to the charity, and Scar had told Fanny all of them.

When Scar had finally released her from setup duty, Fan all but ran into the bathroom to wash her sweaty face, slap on some deodorant and makeup, pull on her dress, slip into heels.

Now, with barely ten minutes before guests were supposed to show up, she'd tossed Scar a hundred dollars for her donation and finally felt like she had a moment to breathe and admire the space she'd had a hand in setting up before she had to man her station and serve up drinks.

All she could say was that Scarlett was a genius.

Charlie had been commandeered to hang sheer swathes of fabric along the walls—Fan had hung the twinkly lights behind, fussing with them until Scar had been happy. Combined with the tables and flowers and plants, not to mention, even *more* strands of lights, the entire space seemed otherworldly.

A fairy garden brought to life.

And if Scar had her way, there would be plenty of revelry, enough anyway to open those pocketbooks.

"You look nice yourself," she told Charlie, tearing her gaze away from the decor, from where the guys were strolling through the door and positioning themselves at the various tables, readying to schmooze and get that money.

It was true—the whole looking nice thing.

Charlie had done some changing of his own, swapping the jeans and tee for a sleek black suit, his crisp white shirt making his skin look tan and strokable. The fit was tight, showing off the lean strength of his shoulders and thighs.

He smiled at her perusal.

And she narrowed her eyes in return. He knew just how attractive he was.

Too bad she couldn't appreciate it fully. He was like a lovely piece of artwork, but he didn't set her blood on fire.

"What job does Scar have you doing?" she asked.

"Manning the silent auction," he said. "You?"

"Bartend—" Fan started to answer him, but then her skin began prickling, her gaze drawn back to the door.

To the *man* walking through the door.

Sweet baby Jesus, now *that* was a suit.

If she'd thought that Charlie's fit him like a glove then Brandon's . . . hell, he might as well be naked for how well it was tailored. She could see the outline of his thighs, his torso, his arms, his abs—

He turned to say something to Kaydon, and she nearly groaned at the way the material hugged his ass.

She loved his ass.

She had loved it when they were together, loved looking at it, or even grinning as she gave it a slight smack when he went by. Because he was hers and she could touch him whenever she wanted, but she had especially loved holding on to it when he plunged deep inside her, gripping him tight so he could grind against her clit and—

Fan blinked, forced her gaze away, definitely not feeling fourteen any longer.

No, she was feeling like a woman—*all* woman—and that woman wanted the man who'd bought her favorite treat—the sea salt caramels—her favorite flowers—the sunflowers. The man who gifted the beautiful scarf to remind her of the ocean and the peace she felt there. The man who'd cooked for her and whose body she could taste every inch of while stripping that sexy as hell suit off—

Charlie shifted next to her, breaking her sexual haze. "Ah."

"What?"

His gaze flickered from her face and deliberately slid to where Brandon had spotted them and was approaching, his expression falling decidedly on the side of displeased. A coil of heat slid through her as she remembered the hall, him telling her to get rid of Charlie. She wouldn't, of course. She liked Charlie and had spent enough time living her own life to ignore orders from a *man,* even if that man was Brandon. "*That's* the complicated ex."

Mouth dropping open, she tore her gaze from Brandon and turned to Charlie. "That's not—"

Charlie leveled a glance at her. "I thought we were friends now."

"We are."

"Then save that bullshit for someone else."

Her lips pressed flat, shoulders falling slightly, and she sighed, admitted. "Fine. He's the complication."

Before Brandon reached them, Scarlett came up, snagging his arm and dragging him to a halt as she jabbered his ear off. Brandon nodded, apparently listening. But his eyes were on Fanny . . . and Charlie, fury flaring across his face as he looked at the two of them standing close together.

"Damn, he's scary," Charlie muttered, grinning at her. "So, why is he complicated?"

Another sigh. "It's too *complicated* to get into."

"Promise to tell me over tequila shots and nachos?" he asked.

Shuddering, she said, "No tequila. Not ever."

"Rum?"

"With nachos?"

His smile didn't fade. "Obviously."

"Well, then," she said. "That I can do."

"Good." He tugged a lock of her hair. "I'll hold you to that." He started to step back then glanced over his shoulder, moved close, and bent so that his next words puffed against the shell of her ear. "For the record, given the way he looks at you and his obvious wish to murder me for being this close to you, I say get over *complicated* and throw the man a bone."

"I—"

"Because I think a man like that could give you a good one."

Her mouth fell open again, and hell, that was becoming a habit.

One that continued when he straightened, winked, said, "I'm bi, but even if I wasn't, I could appreciate the scenery." He kissed her cheek, her damn jaw having dropped open again, and disappeared.

It only took her a moment to realize why.

Brandon.

As in, Brandon was *there*, in front of her, his fury radiating off him, forcing the space to go taut, her skin to prickle, her pussy . . . to get wet.

Maybe it was wrong, but she really, *really* liked it when Brandon got all possessive.

It was a new side of him, and that newness had her thinking that a future might be possible, that they might be able to discover new things about each other, build something fresh and unmarred and . . . *them*.

He crossed his arms.

She found herself leaning close, not missing when his eyes dipped, dropping to the deep V of her dress, to the cleavage that was on full display—part because Scar had said it would help her with the whole selling booze and thus people getting drunker and spending more money thing, but also because Fanny liked herself, liked her body, and she didn't mind showing off the curves she had.

Even if Brandon thought she was too thin.

Her breasts brushed against his chest as she rose on tiptoe, her mouth coming very close to his, bypassing it at the last moment before she stretched farther and whispered in his ear, "You still think I'm too skinny?"

His breath shot out of him in a whoosh, his fingers came to her hips, but before he could get a good grip, she spun away and walked to her station, saying over her shoulder, "Oh, by the way, you look damned good in that suit."

And if there was a bit of sway in her hips as she did so, then . . . there was a bit of sway in her hips.

The man had opened the door.

He'd shown her the possibilities.

He'd made her wonder and hope that he'd be there to catch her if she fell.

Well, he'd better have his glove ready because she was thinking she might finally be ready to leap.

FOURTEEN

BRANDON

Holy hell, what had he unleashed?

It took every bit of self-control he possessed to not follow after her, to not chase her down, toss her over his shoulder, and find out if that little display of flirting meant what he hoped to fuck it did.

Was she going to give him a chance to win her back?

She slipped behind a bartending station, and he moved to it, not caring that Scarlett had ordered him to make the rounds.

He didn't give a fuck about the charity, not when Fanny was there. His gaze dipped when she bent to scoop up some ice, giving him a full view down her dress, one he enjoyed, but one that also made him want to tear off his jacket and wrap it around her so no one else could see her breasts encased in black silk.

Then she straightened and plunked a glass in front of him.

Brandon blinked. "A Manhattan?" he asked after lifting the drink to his lips and taking a sip.

"Is it still your favorite?"

His mouth curved. "Yeah, baby, it is." He reached over the

bar top and snagged her hand. "Does you talking to me mean that . . ."

"That I'm going to give us another chance?" she asked.

He nodded.

"No."

His heart sank.

"But it means I'm considering it." She slipped her hand away, turned to smile at a woman who came up for a drink. "Especially, if you keep dressing like that."

Hope bloomed in his chest.

She turned and helped the woman, whipping up drinks like she belonged behind the bar.

"How'd you get so good at slinging drinks?" he asked.

Fan measured off a shot of vodka and began mixing it with cranberry juice, pouring both into a martini glass and accepting the cash from the woman. She stuffed it into a jar and then turned back to him. "When the tour ended, I bartended before my skating business took off." A shrug. "It was fun, and I like talking to people. Plus, I learned how to mix a lot of drinks." She winked. "I'm really fun at parties."

"I know you are."

Just as he knew that *this* was the Fanny he remembered. Beautiful and bright and happy. But more settled, comfortable in her own skin, and able to strike a mean conversation.

All that press, and he supposed, also the bartending made it so she didn't skip a beat as more people made their way to the bar, and she started pulling glasses and pouring liquor nearly as fast and furious as her words came. She charmed and chatted and pretty soon, there was a line of customers at her station.

She glanced at him—a sly look out of the corner of her eye—and said, "You going to stand there staring all night? Or you going to get back here and help?"

More hope.

He drained his glass, slipped behind the bar, and pressed a

kiss to the side of her neck, loving that she didn't push him away, loving the scent of her, loving . . . *her*.

"Tell me what to do."

"You take care of wine and beer," she said, nodding at the bottles behind them. "I'll do the rest."

He nodded. "I can do that."

She smirked. "We'll see."

And then things really got going. Fan glanced up at the man in front of them and took his order—two red wines, one beer—and then the woman behind him—two cosmos, one beer, one white wine—and Brandon promptly felt himself begin to scramble.

That scrambling didn't stop.

The next hour was more of the same. He was sweating, his arms exhausted, his brain fried from having to take money and make change by the time the line tapered off and people had gone from their first to second to third round of drinks. There was still a trickle of attendees coming up to the bar, but they had thinned out, giving him a moment to breathe and also to go back to staring.

She was gorgeous.

And funny and smart and really fucking good at mixing drinks.

"Is there anything you can't do?"

She lifted a rack of glasses—one he took from her and set on the table behind them. "Thanks," she murmured. "And yes, there are loads of things I can't do, things I suck at."

He slipped his arm around her waist. "Lies."

For a moment, she leaned back against him. "Okay, you're right. I'm brilliant at everything I take up, and I definitely, *definitely* don't have a closet that's overloaded with old clothes and needs to be organized, or always forget to take my car in for an oil change, or really, really suck at cross-stitch."

Brandon ran his fingers through the soft waves tumbling down her shoulder. "Cross-stitch?"

"I wanted a hobby." A shrug. "Turns out, I'm only good at making knots."

He bent, kissed her cheek. "Want me to make *you* a drink?"

A wide smile, warm eyes on him, her body melting back against his. She smelled like roses and vanilla. She smelled like *home*. She *felt* like home, there in his arms. "Okay," she said, and he realized his mistake because his offer had her slipping out of his hold. But then she was looking at him expectantly and with challenge in her eyes.

"Well," he murmured, "I know you like wine."

"Pft. Going the easy way out?" she teased.

"But," he said, talking over her. "I have a feeling that you're a straightforward drink kind of girl." He glanced at her, but her face was unreadable. "Not tequila," he murmured, remembering the hangovers they'd both gotten the first time they'd experimented with alcohol. Her expression didn't change, but her eyes warmed. He picked up a bottle of rum, used the shot glass measuring thingy to pour her a drink. One part of rum, and the rest of the glass with Coke and ice.

He handed it to her, watched as she sipped.

"Well?" he asked when she set it down.

Her lips curved. "It's a decent rum and Coke."

"Decent?" He wrapped his arms around her. "Just *decent?*"

A shrug that brought her breasts against him. A shrug that someone might interpret as casual, except for the hard nipples against his chest, the heat in her eyes. "Just decent," she repeated, her lips curving up, and it wasn't the time or place for it, but her mouth was tipped up, and her smile was sexy and—

He had to kiss her.

So, he did.

And then felt that hope inside him cover him from head to toe when she didn't hesitate to kiss him back.

Scar had interrupted the kiss, pulling Brandon away so he couldn't distract her best bartender.

"And the raffle is getting ready to start," she said. "You'll need to pull your ticket so I can make the announcement."

He nodded, started toward the table holding the huge glass bowls, most of which were now overflowing with raffle tickets.

Scarlett caught his arm.

"Also, if you hurt my friend again, I will chop off your balls, freeze them in those giant ice cube holders, and then shatter them with a hammer."

Brandon's brows lifted. "You're violent."

"I know it's not your fault. But"—she patted his cheek—"balls, hammer, shattered into pieces." A smile. "Don't forget it."

He shuddered. "Don't worry, I won't."

She led him to the tables, pointed out his bowl, and then had him reach in and pull out a ticket without looking at it.

"Thank you," she sing-songed, snagging it from his fingers, before flitting off to the microphone and quieting the crowd as he made his way back toward Fanny. Scar hadn't threatened his balls if he distracted Fanny, so he was going to make the most of their evening.

He slid behind the bar, wrapped an arm around her waist, and started to bend over to resume their kiss when he heard his name over the speakers.

". . . For dinner with a successful sports agent, Brandon Cunningham, VP at Prestige Media Group—"

Fan swatted him. "You're a raffle prize?" she asked.

"It's a long story. I'm helping out a friend."

". . . Insights from one of the best in the business, and he'll even pay the tab." The crowd laughed. "Our first prize winner of the evening is . . . Stephanie Douglas!"

The crowd applauded.

Brandon went stiff, though not as stiff as Fan. He glanced down at her, took in the shock on her face, the clenched jaw, he said, "I'm guessing you didn't enter for my raffle prize."

Her eyes narrowed. "No."

"Who—"

He didn't have to finish the question. "Ah. Scarlett at work."

Fanny nodded brusquely.

His lips tipped up. "Good thing I'd already planned to take you to dinner. Two birds, one stone."

Her eyes flashed. "We're not going on a date."

His brows lifted. "We're not?"

She pushed out of his hold. "No, we're not. I can't. We can't—"

"We are *so* going on a date," he said, snagging her again. "Whether it's from Scarlett's intervention or of our own volition."

A huff. "I'm going to—"

"Kiss me. And then go on a date with me."

"That's not happening," she growled, swatting at his chest. "I can't believe Scar did that. She needs to pick another ticket. It's not fair. I didn't enter for the prize, and someone else is going to miss out, and—"

He slanted his lips over hers, kissed her until they were both breathless.

"Go on a date with me," he said. Or maybe begged.

Either way, it seemed to do the trick.

She softened. "Okay to the date, but no to the stealing a prize from someone who paid good money to be here and—"

"You're accepting it."

Brandon managed to tear his gaze from Fanny and glanced over at Scarlett.

"That's not fair—"

Scar reached out and snagged Fanny from Brandon's arms.

She dropped her hands onto Fanny's shoulders and shook her lightly. "Life has dealt you more than your fair share of unfair. You're accepting this. You're going on a date with Brandon, and you're going to have a good time."

"But someone else might want—"

Scarlett just crossed her arms and waited.

Fanny sighed. "You're not going to change your mind, are you?"

"No." Scar glared. "I don't care if you throw a fit. You're still going to do this. Not for me, for yourself. No more waffling and worrying, just *go* for it. Go for what you want."

"You're a terrible friend," Fan muttered.

"I love you, too," Scarlett said, completely undeterred by the muttering, "but you're *still* doing this."

Fanny's eyes drifted up to his, as though expecting to find an answer in them, but Brandon wasn't going to touch that with a ten-foot pole. This was between her and her friend. He'd already gotten his date. He couldn't give a shit about it being the raffle prize, or having to have another dinner with another prizewinner.

Sighing, reading his reluctance to dive in, she turned back to Scar. "What are you doing?"

Scarlett leaned in and spoke in her ear, saying something that Brandon couldn't hear. Whatever it was, it seemed to have the desired effect because Fanny's expression settled and softened. She pulled back, nodded, and then hugged Scar.

A moment later, Scarlett had drifted away, probably to cause more chaos somewhere else. Or well, not chaos, but to do whatever it took to get that money.

He sidled up to Fanny, slid an arm around her waist.

She didn't pull away and that, more than anything else, was the biggest victory of the night. There was a chance at a future with her.

"So," he murmured, running his fingers down her throat, "where should we go for our date tomorrow?"

"To—tomorrow?"

"Tomorrow," he repeated, nuzzling her throat.

He had this in, the door was nudged a little wider, and he wasn't going to give her the chance to slam it closed.

FIFTEEN

FANNY

She was exhausted.

It was the evening after the raffle, she'd hardly slept the night before, and only part of that was because of Scar's shenanigans the previous evening.

The rest was nerves.

She'd driven home and laid in bed and hadn't been able to sleep for hours.

It was so easy to be confident when all the yumminess of Brandon was in her vicinity, to lean into him when he slid an arm around her waist, to kiss him back when his lips found hers, but when he wasn't there and she was in her bed alone, under the covers, and all was quiet, the old doubts had decided to creep in.

What if he got sick again?

What if he *forgot* again?

What if she got her heart broken again?

What if—

The scenarios were endless . . . and terrifying.

She'd been up until the sun had begun to rise, unable to sleep until she'd finally given in and walked to the kitchen, grabbing the scarf Brandon had given her, wrapping the only piece of him she had in her possession around her, and that was what it had taken for her finally fall asleep.

Obviously, she'd slept the day away, thanking God it was Saturday and she had no clinics to teach and could laze in bed.

Now, she was still in her bedroom, having gorged herself on caramels while she was getting ready for her date. Probably, she should deliberately dress all frumpy, just because he'd been so presumptuous with the whole date-asking, taking advantage of her being so discombobulated to get her to agree, but she couldn't bring herself to do it. She wanted to bring her A-game.

She wanted his eyes to pop out of his head.

She wanted him to look at her with the tangle of heat and need that had danced across his dark brown eyes the night before.

So . . . she'd brought her A-game.

Sleek black stockings that stopped at mid-thigh. A lavender garter belt that she'd bought on a whim and never worn, the thin elastic bands making her shiver where they pressed into the skin on the front and back of her legs. Her bra was hardly more than a scrap of lace with absolutely no support. It looked pretty and the material brushed over her already sensitive nipples, causing desire to pool in her abdomen, moisture to flood her pussy.

The man wasn't even here yet, and she wanted him.

Desperately.

Her hands shook as she stepped into her dress and tugged up the zipper, thankful that it was under her arm, and she wasn't forced to contort herself to get it pulled up.

Then she was stepping into her stilettos, knowing her feet would be killing her in no time at all.

Worth it.

They made her legs look long and lean, and paired with her

gorgeous black dress with its plunging neckline, short hem, and barely-there back, she knew she looked good. Combined with the full face of makeup, fake lashes, and long, loose curls down her back, she felt ready to take on the world when the doorbell rang.

She hustled to her bedroom and brushed her teeth in record time, thankful that her lipstick was the smudge-free variety, then moved downstairs and to the door . . . just as the bell rang again.

"Impatient," she muttered, reaching to open it.

"Sorry," Brandon said the moment it swung wide. "I wasn't sure you'd heard the—holy fucking shit." His jaw dropped open —literally open—and damn, that felt great for a number of reasons. First, she wasn't the one with her mouth gaping open, ready to catch flies. For another, she got that tangle of heat and need. And lastly, his throat worked for a long moment before he spoke again, his voice all sexy rasp that slid over her exposed skin. "You are so fucking beautiful."

"Yeah?" she whispered.

"Yeah." He reached for her then stopped, as though he didn't know where he could touch her.

If he could touch her.

She helped him cross that hurdle by stepping forward, not stopping until her body was flush with his. He looked good, too. Great, actually. He was wearing another one of those suits, and it showcased his long, lean lines. Mouthwateringly so.

But then she was against him and could see nothing but the strong delineation of his jaw, the soft cushions of his lips, the deep brown of his eyes.

He had a scar to the right of his eyebrow, one she hadn't seen before, and she found herself reaching up and brushing her thumb over it. "What happened?" she whispered. He hadn't had it when they'd been together.

His hand came up and covered hers, the roughness of his fingertips making her lean more heavily against him.

"I *should* tell you I got into a bar fight," he murmured, his words ruffling her hair.

"Or stopped a little old lady from getting mugged?" She played along.

"Then saved a stray kitten from a tree?"

She nodded, shifting back enough to see his eyes, her lips curving upward when she saw the amusement dancing through those chocolate depths. "Exactly," she said, slowly sliding her fingers down his temple, his cheek, his jaw, his throat until her palm rested on his shoulder. "So, you clearly won the fight, saved the old lady, and rescued the kitten, and . . . ?"

"Ran into a cabinet I didn't close?" he chimed in.

Fanny froze. Then busted out laughing. "Seriously?" she asked through her guffaws.

"Unfortunately, yes." He pushed back a lock of hair that had fallen into her face. "But I got six stitches *and* a lesson in why I should close them."

"But the question is *do* you close them?"

A grin. "Yes, I learned that lesson, I promise."

"Glad to hear my head is safe."

He smiled down at her. "Should we go to dinner?"

Fan nodded, started to step out of his arms, then realized how much she hated the idea of not being held by him, even for just a couple of hours while they drove to the restaurant and ate. "Brandon?" she asked softly.

"Yeah, baby?" he asked, smoothing his hand over her hair.

"Do you want to go to dinner?"

His hand stopped, just for a moment, before weaving into her hair and gently tilting her head back. "Do *you* want to go to dinner?"

She shook her head.

"Thank fuck," he muttered.

Shock had her blinking at him as he backed her into the house and shut the door behind him. *Click* went the lock. Then his mouth was on hers. She gasped, and he took advantage, slipping his tongue inside and kissing her until she forgot about the fact that her feet were already pinching in her heels, that her lungs needed air, that her heart threatened to pound out of her chest.

When he broke away, her pulse was thundering in her veins, her breathing in rapid gusts.

"Why . . . thank . . . fuck?" she gasped.

He grinned, not even out of breath when she was feeling like she'd run a goddamn marathon. "Because I don't have to fight off all the other fuckers who would be looking at you tonight."

That had her straightening, her brows dragging together. "I hope you're not being serious."

He just kissed her again until her lungs threatened to burst, until she forgot what she'd been saying, until her outrage—and okay, a little bit of pleasure—at his possessiveness was a long lost thought.

"Do you want me to cook you dinner?" he asked when he'd released her lips.

It was so silken, so quiet that it took her a moment to process. "Um, what?"

"Are you hungry?"

She was hungry for sure. But dinner was the last thing on her mind. But wait, she needed to remember what had sparked her annoyance a moment before. What was it? Oh—

"You're not going to tell me how to dress," she said, jabbing a finger into his chest. He'd hadn't tried to before, but this was a different Brandon in a lot of ways—older, stronger, more intense —and she needed to set him straight right off the bat. If she wanted to run around San Francisco naked during Bay to Breakers, she damn well could. If she wanted to wear her sexy dress and not care who looked, then she damned well would.

"Of course not."

The matter-of-fact way he said it took the wind out of her

sails. She'd just been getting her mad on, and he responded with the correct answer.

"Oh," she said.

"But I'm not going to pretend that I don't have a claim."

That made her brows lift.

"Is that going to be a problem?" he asked.

Fanny should say it was going to be, just out of principal. She was a strong, independent woman. The only one with a claim over her was *her*. But . . . she couldn't lie and say a tiny part of her wasn't thrilled with Brandon wanting her to be his, so long as—

"Is it going to be a problem when I claim *you?*" she asked archly.

He froze, his eyes got all melty, and he stepped closer. "No." His mouth came to her ear, his tongue darting out to taste the lobe. "I'd be honored to be claimed by you."

Her breath caught.

But she was that strong, independent woman.

Which meant that even though his eyes were warm and his tongue made her shiver, she still knew what she wanted.

And that was Brandon.

Oh fuck.

This wasn't considering giving him a chance.

This was him having a direct path to her heart—her realizing he always had.

Pulse pounding, fear and hope, need and longing all twisted up inside her, she stepped back, spun away from him, moving as fast as she could down the hall and into the back yard.

"Fan?" He tried to catch her arm, but she dodged it, kept walking until the cool air was hitting her skin, the moon was bright overhead.

What was she doing?

She should run.

Except . . .

He'd shown up on her porch and shaken her peaceful life, rattling the branches and sending leaves scattering, shattering everything she'd thought was important into irreparable pieces.

"Fan."

She put her hand up, not looking at him. "Please, just . . ."

He paused. She could feel his heat near her, could smell his scent, could hear the quiet rasp of his breath as he held himself back.

She needed to think, to process and—

She also didn't.

Because when all that had been scattered had settled, the broken shards gathered—when she'd read the notebook with all of his mother's memories of them, when he'd surprised her with the basket of gifts, with the certificate to the winery, when he'd cooked for her and offered tonight, when he'd been so gentle with her while taking off her skates, when he'd followed her home, when she remembered the hundreds of other sweet and gentle ways he'd taken care of her before—Fanny knew that irreparable didn't mean forever broken.

She would never be the same.

Neither would he.

There were no guarantees. There never could be. Neither of them could tell the future.

The only thing she *did* know?

That she didn't want to waste any more time.

Maybe the cancer would always be a frightening monster in the back of her mind.

Maybe her heart would always be the teensiest bit broken.

Maybe she would always be worried it might be taken away.

But . . . she could get mowed over by a bus tomorrow. She could get sick and die. She could lose Brandon all over again. And maybe it was the sexy underwear or the heated way Brandon looked at her, inflating her confidence, making her reckless with the urge to jump into things with him with both stilettos, but she also knew the truth.

That she was already *in* with him.

No matter how hard she'd fought in the beginning, she'd been sliding down this slope.

So . . . it was time to let go.

To be with the man she'd never stopped loving, even when she'd been broken into pieces by that love.

Enough time had been lost.

She didn't need to squander any more.

And with that thought, the last remnants of indecision floated away like a balloon flying up into the sky.

"I'm not hungry for food," she murmured.

He straightened, tilted her head back, and stared into her eyes. "What are you hungry for, baby?"

A deep breath, shoving that fear down and locking it up.

Not forever.

Because she didn't want it bubbling back up again. She'd take it out. She'd deal with it. They would build something new, something untarnished by the past.

Something that would mean *everything* going forward.

So when he asked what she was hungry for, Fanny said the only thing she could,

"You."

No hesitation. Not anymore. She was done running and hiding. She was going to grab on to her life, on to this man, and she was going to *live.*

Sixteen

BRANDON

His heart swelled . . . along with his cock.

Every cell in his body told him to sweep her up into his arms and fuck her on the next available surface.

But—

He had to make sure.

He'd hurt her before.

He—

"Say something," she whispered, and he'd have to be blind to miss the insecurity creeping into her eyes.

"My doctor says I'm cured."

She rocked back on her heels, her chin jerking up, and that was most certainly the *something* she hadn't wanted him to say, the one thing that could most easily douse the flames of the arousal that had been burning between them from the moment she opened her front door.

"What?" she breathed. "I—"

He'd wanted to tell her, but he shouldn't be telling her in

this moment. Fuck. Talk about ruining everything, about shoving their past in her face when she'd just finally decided to take a step forward.

"How?" she asked before he could say something, *anything* else.

"I . . . my doctor says that because my scans have been clear for ten years that medically I'm considered cured." He sucked in a breath, released it slowly. "Dr. Lyon says in her professional opinion, she doesn't think it'll come back."

"That's—"

He braced himself.

But she didn't toss words at him. Instead, she threw herself at him. "That's amazing, babe," she said, wrapping her arms tightly around him. "I can't—that's the best news."

Absently, he hugged her back, inhaling her scent and imprinting it on his soul.

"What happened to Dr. Philips?" she asked a moment later.

"He retired and recommended Dr. Lyon. Conveniently, her practice is in San Francisco."

She leaned back, stared at him. "Is that why you came?"

"No." He cupped her cheeks. "I could lie and say it was about my job, my doctor. I might have even told myself that was the reason I accepted Devon's offer. But the truth is that even though I didn't know you were working for the Gold, I knew you were in California, and after I remembered everything, I knew I would take any chance to be closer to you, even if it was just in the same state."

Her lips parted.

She didn't pull away.

"I love you. I wanted to be near you, even when I didn't see how we could have a future. I just knew . . ."

"Magnets," she whispered.

"What?"

"We're a pair of magnets, always drawn together, no matter

what comes between us." Half her mouth tipped up. "Cheesy." A shrug. "But—"

"It's the truth," he murmured.

"Yeah."

She fell quiet, and Brandon released her face, gripped her shoulders, and tugged her a little closer, wrapping his arms around her. They stood there holding each other. For once, the past wasn't between them. It was just him and Fanny. She was against him, and he could stand there with her forever.

But then she shifted on her feet.

Slowly, he released her. "Should I cook you dinner now?" he asked lightly, wanting to take her mind off the conversation, off the bomb he'd dropped.

Her mouth tipped up. "Still not hungry for food."

He waited.

"I want you."

His cock twitched, but she shifted again, and he pushed his desire aside. "Am I hurting you?" he asked, dropping his hands and stepping back.

"No." She closed the distance between them. Shifted again, only this time with a wince.

"You winced."

"I did not."

He slanted a look at her, retreated a pace, worry starting to thread its way through his mind. "I saw you. Don't lie to me," he said. "Did I do something—"

"It's my shoes, Brandon. They're sexy, but they hurt like hell."

"Your shoes?" he asked dumbly, his gaze dropping to her feet.

"Yes, honey. They're tall, they're pointy, and they're—*ah!*"

He swept her up into his arms, started for the stairs.

"What are you doing?" she exclaimed, her hands coming to his shoulders and holding on tight.

"Feeding you," he said, bounding upstairs, pushing one door open and peeking inside to find an office. Then another to find a bathroom.

"Feeding—" She shook her head. "Bedroom is last door on the right."

"Thank fuck," he muttered, heading there and bypassing what felt like a hundred doors in front of him to check. It was two, two more to look beyond, but she'd saved him the trouble, so he moved straight to that last room on the right, pushed through the wooden panel, and took approximately one second to scan the space before heading directly to the bed and setting her on it. "Sexy shoes," he said softly, kneeling in front of her and pressing a kiss to her ankle. He tugged off the first heel, rubbed her foot, noticing the red marks visible even through the stocking she wore, and ordered, "You're never wearing these again."

"I am," she said. "Just next time, we'll do a lot less standing up and talking."

He grunted, yanking the other heel off and tossing it over his shoulder. "Fine," he grumbled, knowing that he wouldn't be able to say no to her. He bent and kissed the red marks, chuckling when she squirmed against his fingers slightly tickling the soles of her feet.

"Brandon?"

He was kissing his way up her calf, her knee, her thigh. "Hmm?"

"Will you come up here?"

"Yes." He just had a pit stop to make. He inched the short skirt of her dress up, exposing . . . a narrow strip of lavender elastic, and froze. "Fanny?" he asked after a moment, leaning in to kiss the small half circle of skin on the inside of her thigh.

"Mmm?" she asked, her legs spreading as much as they were able with the tight skirt holding them close.

"Are you wearing a garter belt?" He darted his tongue out, tasted her skin, and bit back a moan.

She smelled of roses and caramel, tasted sweet and floral, and when he allowed his eyes to flick up, to glance beneath her dress, he saw that her panties were soaked, so much so that the pale purple had become nearly translucent.

"Mmm-hmm," she said, her eyes closing.

"Why?"

"Because I like them." Her breath hissed out when he ran his tongue beneath the thin elastic, drawing it up, up, up—

Until—

He stood, yanked Fan to her feet, and took advantage of her surprise to locate the zipper—under her arm—he tugged it down, peeled the fabric away, and—

It was a miracle he even had any blood left in his body.

It felt like it was all in his dick.

Because he'd pulled back that black material, tugged it up and over her head, let it fall down to puddle on the floor, and . . .

She was the most beautiful thing he had ever seen.

Her breasts were encased in a lace bra that did absolutely nothing to hide her hardened nipples, and when he let his gaze lower over the curve of her stomach to see her hips covered in more lavender, and those black stockings . . .

"Fucking hell," he muttered.

"Off," Fanny ordered, reaching for the lapels of his jacket and shoving it down his arms, leaving him to wrestle with it as she started unbuttoning his shirt. They struggled with the material, and as they did so, he cursed his decision for the suit. He should have put on a T-shirt and jeans. It would have been much easier to take off.

But finally, he managed to sling his jacket across the room, and Fan finished with the shirt buttons while he stepped out of his shoes, and shoved down his pants, yanked off his socks.

Then he was just in his boxer briefs, and she was in her sexy, little outfit, and *then* he got back to doing what he wanted to do before.

He nudged her to sit on the edge of the bed and knelt between her thighs.

And he had *his* dinner.

Her panties were tugged to the side, those elastics unsnapped, and her legs spread wide. He used the flat of his tongue to lick her from bottom to top, once, twice, and when her hands flexed on the mattress, he arrowed in on her clit, sucking it deep as he slipped a finger inside.

It was new, and not.

It was familiar, and not.

His body remembered what to do, remembered what she liked, or *had* liked then, but she'd changed, and so had he. There was relearning to be done, things to discover, things to let go of, but it wasn't difficult, and it didn't take long before he'd homed in on what made her moan and writhe and eventually—when he crooked his finger just right, when he sucked her clit hard —scream.

"Brandon!"

Her fingers clenched his hair, her thighs clamped tight around him.

And then slowly, like a wave creeping up a shore, she relaxed, her shoulders slumping, hands releasing, legs spreading wide.

Desire a heavy beat in his heart, he tossed her back up on the bed, coming on top of her and taking her in his arms. He kissed her long and slow, until her relaxation turned into tension, until that tension turned into need, until that transformed into something more, into something that pushed him over the edge. He scrambled off the bed for his pants, reaching into the pocket and pulling out his wallet. He yanked out a condom, tore the package open with his teeth. A second later, he was rolling it down the hard length of his cock, climbing back on top of Fanny, spreading her thighs, and positioning himself between them. He paused, waiting until she looked at him, wanting to make sure she was ready for this, ready for him, ready for them to take this step.

Every cell in his body was screaming at him, every nerve was on fire, every muscle ached, and his control hung on a razor's edge.

Thrust home. Take them both over the edge. It would be so easy.

But this was Fanny.

This was the woman who held his heart. There was no way that he would allow himself to take advantage of her in any way, shape, or form.

He loved her.

If she didn't want this, he would stop.

Even if that meant he would be going home with blue balls.

But poised between her legs, his cock one inch from salvation, sweat dripping down his spine, every part of him tense and needy, he prayed she wouldn't turn him away.

"Fanny," he said, his voice a rasp, "look at me."

Her eyes were closed, her head tossed back on the pillow, sweat turning her skin a golden color in the dim lights of the bedroom. "Brandon," she begged, reaching for him, tugging at his shoulders, drawing him down toward her.

He was desperate to push home, desperate to feel her wrapped around him again.

But he wouldn't slide inside that slick heat, not until he saw she was ready.

"Fanny," he demanded again, "*look at me.*"

Her eyes peeled open; those deep brown irises met his. He saw his desperation mirrored in her own gaze, felt the need making her hands shake as she clung to his shoulders.

But he needed the words.

"Do you want this?" he asked, brushing her hair off her face. "Do you want me like this?"

Her nails dug into his skin, a sharp bite of pain that threatened to shatter his control, but he held on. He'd waited a decade for this, he could wait until she was ready.

"Brandon." Her fingers dug in a little harder. "Look at me," she demanded. "*Really* look at me. Have I given you any indication that I don't want this? I'm naked and beneath you. I'm wet. I'm needy."

"Baby," he began.

"I'm still shaking from my orgasm, my legs are spread, my pussy is aching for you. I want you inside me. I want you to fuck me until we both can't see straight. And then"—she cupped his face in her hands—"I want you to do it all over again. I want to remember you were between my legs when I'm skating tomorrow. I want to feel sore and wrung out and thoroughly used, and—"

His control snapped. He thrust home, bottoming out, feeling the liquid heat of her surround him.

She was tight. She was everything he remembered. She was so much more than he had ever hoped.

"And then I want to come home, and I want you to have missed me so much that you fuck me the moment I walk through the door," she said, her eyes blazing, her legs wrapping around him, her hips meeting his as he began to thrust. "I want everything. I want you in every room of my house. I want you in every room of yours. I want to make up for all the things that we missed out on. I want the sex. I want the fucking. I want you to make love to me." She moaned when he thrust a little deeper, arching against him. "And I want the rest of it, too. I want the dinners together. I want to wake up with you wrapped around me. I want to watch bad TV shows together. I want to look up from a class and see you sitting in the bleachers. I want you in my life no matter what the future brings. I just want you, Brandon."

"Fanny," he breathed, so touched that his eyes begin to burn.

He blinked back the tears but felt one escape anyway; Fanny reached up and wiped it away.

"I want it all, too," he told her. "We missed out on so much time together, and I don't want to waste any more. I love you, and I will love you for far longer than my body will be on this planet. I will love you like the wind caresses the shoreline, the mountains, the desert, and the sea. Always there, even though sometimes you can't see it. I will love you with every single piece of me, whole, broken, or somewhere in between. I will—"

She sat up, wrapped her arms around him, knocking him back to his knees. "*God*, I love you."

Brandon's heart seized.

"I won't love you like the wind," she said. "You'll see my love for you every single minute of the day. You'll know that I'm here, that I fell for you when I was fourteen and that I've never felt the same way about anyone else." Tears streaked down her cheeks. "I know I'm still broken. I know the pieces are duct-taped together and a bit dinged from life, from our past, from the hurt I held on to for so long." He kissed those salty streaks of moisture away, held her tight. "But they're all yours. They've always been yours, and they always will be."

He was the luckiest fucker on the planet.

"Now," she said, lying back and drawing him down on top of her again, "you're naked and inside me. I'm naked and wetter than I've ever been in my life. Please, *please* fuck me."

His throat burned. He knew he still had tears clinging to his lashes.

But his woman needed him to give her another orgasm, and frankly, he needed one, too.

It had been too fucking long.

So, he began to move, mixing the new and old, the learning and remembering, the knowing and discovering, and he found a rhythm that had her matching his movements, meeting his thrusts. She writhed beneath him, bucking as her fingers clung tight, her nails digging into his shoulders, her hips pressing to his, over and over and *over* again.

And then she fractured, her eyes slamming shut, tossing her head back, her body stilling as her pussy clenched tight around him.

He let the pulses tug him over the edge, stroking into her as his orgasm swelled up and sucked him under.

He came to, somehow on his side, Fanny tucked against him.

They didn't say anything for long moments, didn't speak as their breathing slowed, as the sweat cooled on their bodies, and he pulled the blankets up and over them.

She was so still and quiet, that she could have been asleep.

And yet, he knew she wasn't.

"I love you," she said softly, "just in case you thought it was in the heat of the moment."

Brandon's mouth turned up, and he kissed the top of her head. "Good," he murmured. "Now"—he let his voice raise in volume—"should I cook you dinner?"

Her laughter was the best sound on the planet.

He soaked it in . . . and then he went downstairs and cooked his woman dinner.

SEVENTEEN

"Oh, my God," she said. "Now they're *trying* to lose money."

"I know," Charlie said. "Isn't it great?"

She giggled like a loon, as she often did with this man. They'd grabbed drinks and food a couple of times since their dinner and now had a standing friend date on Wednesday nights. Scarlett was jealous and often crashed their time together, but seeing as she couldn't stand the terrible reality show they were currently bingeing, she'd skipped that night.

The reality show in question followed a bunch of sexy people who liked to bone with no strings attached but couldn't because doing so meant they would lose out on the grand prize at the end.

"I've said it once"—she picked up her wineglass—"and I'll say it again. If I were them, stuck at a luxury resort for several weeks, with all the free booze and drinks I could get, I'd be boning left and right."

Charlie cackled as he clinked his glass to hers. "Damn right, you would," he said, then pointed at the screen. "Oh no, here they go."

She smirked.

Because damn right, they did.

They went. They kissed and cuddled and lost a boatload of money. It was glorious.

Fan and Charlie kept up their commentary through one episode and into the next, during which Brandon came over to her place—with a key she'd given him because . . . not looking back. He took one look at both of them on the couch then the TV and shook his head. Then he picked up both of their glasses, went into the kitchen, and refilled them.

Things had been a little testy between him and Charlie at first—more from Brandon's side than Charlie's, since the latter didn't know about the Hallway Incident. But as she was learning about Charlie, he'd quickly disarmed Brandon, and now the two were casual friends.

She'd take it.

She liked Charlie, and things would have been really awkward if Brandon had gone all He-man protective alpha on her.

But then again, he wouldn't do that.

Because Brandon was Brandon.

He cared about her and what made her happy. Charlie being her reality TV show watching buddy made her happy. Along with the stories he told her while they were out to drinks or dinner, even though those drinks and dinner sometimes took Fan away from Brandon (sometimes Bran tagged along, and sometimes he didn't).

When she'd asked Brandon if he had an issue with her being friends with Charlie—not that she would stop, because it was her freaking life (though she could be friends in a way that made Bran more comfortable, if necessary)—he'd simply asked if

Charlie made her happy. She'd nodded. Then he'd smiled, kissed her cheek, and told her to have fun.

Though it should be noted that before she'd left, he'd pulled her close, kissed her within an inch of her life, then murmured in her ear, "No hallways."

The murmur was more order than not.

But anyway.

Now she and Charlie were close, and she got to see more of Scarlett when she wasn't traveling with the team, by benefit of her coming over to hang with Fan and her brother, a la two birds one stone.

Brandon plunked the glasses on the table just as she and Charlie squealed.

"They're not going to have anything left," Charlie exclaimed, picking up the glass and taking a large sip.

"No, they're not." She grinned at him and then sipped before turning to Brandon. "Thank you."

A tug of her hair before he disappeared back into the kitchen.

She was firmly in Reality Show Fog when he returned, a beer in hand, and slid next to her on the couch, his arm coming around her shoulders. He kissed her temple, and she snuggled in to watch, perfectly content in Brandon's arms.

It wasn't until later that she realized she'd fallen asleep.

The show was paused on the TV. She was tucked on the couch, a blanket around her, and when she turned her head, she could see Brandon and Charlie talking in the hall.

"Thanks for being cool with this," Charlie was saying quietly. "She's . . . incredible, but I want you to know that I wouldn't overstep, and neither would she. We just like hanging out, and she's made it clear that we're friends and nothing more."

Brandon nodded. "I know. I trust her." A beat. "Maybe not you, but I trust her."

Charlie smiled wolfishly. "I get it. A woman like that makes a man take notice, but I promise that I'll respect the boundaries she laid out. Friends. Nothing more."

Brandon nodded again, and if she hadn't had so much wine, and hadn't been up so early at clinics that morning, and wasn't so warm and cozy under the blankets on the couch, she would have gotten up and told the both of them what she thought about them discussing her like she wasn't in the room.

Or the next room, anyway.

But she was tired, and a little buzzed, and more than a little snuggly. So she didn't get up and tell them off. Instead, she let her eyes close again, burrowed into the couch, and drifted off.

She was exhausted and slightly drunk and cozy.

She still distantly heard Charlie leave and even more distantly felt Brandon pick her up off the couch and carry her upstairs, tucking her under the covers before slipping in beside her.

"How much money did they lose?" she murmured, burrowing into all of *his* snuggliness.

A beat, his fingers drifting through her hair. "All of it."

She smiled, pressed her lips to his throat, and was tugged completely under.

———

They had gone to the movies. They had stayed in and cooked dinner. Brandon had waited for her after clinics at the rink, and she stayed at his place.

They had spent ten years apart, and yet, over the last month, it felt like no time had passed at all.

And now, she was looking forward to using the gift certificate he had given her, only instead of using it by herself as she'd thought she might when she'd first opened that envelope, he was by her side.

As they walked through the space where she once dreamed her wedding would be held.

The sun was shining, the wind was floating through the vines. Brandon held her hand, and they both had taken on a quiet that was somehow both hopeful and tense, as though they were both expecting the past to come up, dig its claws into them, and drag them both under once again.

But as they flowed through the space, the sun still warm, the wind still gently blowing, Fanny found herself beginning to relax.

The past was just that. Past.

And she was done letting it have a hold on her.

So, she just kept taking steps forward, continued feeling the sun, continued feeling the wind, continued feeling Brandon holding her, and . . . she let go.

"I remember visiting this place," she murmured, holding Brandon's fingers a little tighter. "I remember thinking that we'd be so happy here. I remember thinking this would be the start of us. And in a way, it was."

Brandon turned to face her, his eyes full of old pain and she felt an answering echo in herself.

But that wasn't why she'd brought it up. That wasn't why he'd bought her the certificate for this place. They weren't trying to revisit old pain, to drive their fingers into the open wounds that were still healing. They weren't even trying to slap a Band-Aid on to those lesions, trying to stitch them up or cover them over.

Instead, they were trying to live.

Trying to face those hurts and move on.

"I was so convinced it was our turn to have our happiness," she whispered, "and I was broken when it didn't work out."

His jaw clenched and he dropped her hand, fisting both at his side. "I will never, fucking *ever*, forgive myself for hurting you that way. The first time was bad enough, but the second time, with Angela, with all those months you spent trying to get me to remember—"

"I will never regret fighting for you," she said, taking his hands and unfurling them. "Just like I would never, *ever* begrudge you your happiness, even though it didn't include me. Yes, I was broken. Yes, I had to start over. But I'm not broken today. I'm not living half a life. I have friends and a job. I have a career I love, and . . . I have you, which is the freaking icing on the cake, because I never thought we'd be here again." She smiled. "I never thought I'd be open to it, vulnerable to all I feel, if I'm being honest."

"Fan," he whispered, reaching up and swiping a hand over her cheek, capturing a tear on his thumb. "I don't want to hurt you—"

"I know," she said. "That's what always made it so hard before. You were still so damned nice, even when you didn't feel the same for me. Always polite, even though I was there *all* the time, and you had to want to get rid of the pesky girl who kept making you look at photo albums and listen to songs, hoping it would spark something." She slid a little closer. "But you not wanting to hurt me is also what makes that risk bearable today. I could lose you in an instant. I could die tomorrow and leave you. We have this one life, and I'm done living behind protective walls, just because I might not come out unscathed if I step beyond them."

He slipped his fingers into her hair, trailed them down her throat, playing with the strap of her dress, his rough callouses on the skin of her shoulder making her lips part on a sigh, her body shift even closer.

"What did I ever do to deserve you?" he murmured, bending his head and inhaling deeply, as though he wanted to imprint her scent on to his soul.

"You were you," she said. "And that's enough."

His head came up so quickly that she jumped, but she didn't

have a chance to do more than meet his blazing eyes before his fingers had wrapped around her wrist and he was tugging her forward.

"What—"

He scooped her up when she stumbled, pushing through the vines and walking unerringly in the opposite direction from the way they'd come.

"Brandon?" she asked.

He kept walking.

"What are you doing?"

His gaze met hers for a heartbeat, but that short beat of time was enough to have her thighs pressing together, desire a heavy wave of need flowing over her skin, taking the place of the sun, of the wind. "When we came here to scout wedding sights, I did some scouting of my own."

He pushed through a final row of vines, and she gasped at the sight in front of them.

A deep blue pond, grass—what would have been brown just a week ago, having turned green and lush from an unusual rainstorm just a few days before—surrounding its edges. Large, old growth oaks dotted the space, growing very close together near the water, as though they needed to soak in as much as they could—and they probably did, considering how often the area was in and out of droughts.

This place was California's version of a mirage, tall weeds with small, yellow flowers in the distance, the wind just strong enough to keep the bugs away, the pond looking even more blue from the sky reflected above.

Even the birdsong was mellow, just soft enough to create a beautiful background melody.

It was . . . peace.

It was perfect.

This was where she would like to get married. If she were choosing a spot as the woman she was now, not worrying about guest lists and a dance floor and a space for a DJ, *this* would be it.

She and Brandon. The sun shining overhead. Their future on the breeze, in the birdsong, in the warmth of the air.

But while she was reveling in the peace, in the fact that this man had known her so well then, knew her just as well now, Brandon had other ideas.

"I'd planned on stealing you away during the reception," he murmured, striding down the hill. "I'd planned on stashing a basket here"—he set her down gently, holding her while she found her balance, then reached between two of the trees to retrieve a wicker container—"and a blanket here." He reached up, and she saw what she'd missed before, the blue plaid material hanging from the branch. "I'd planned on starting our wedding night under the stars and the moonlight, with promises of bringing them both to you, if you only asked."

Love.

It could be a devastating feeling, could bring someone to their knees, destroy them and yank the foundation of their being out from beneath them.

Or it could be *this*.

Filling her up until she felt like she was floating, until the old cracks were sealed, until she was herself and . . . more.

"So, give it to me," she breathed, stepping toward him. "Give me every part of you, and *more*. Give me the moon and the sun and the stars in the sky and give me *you.*"

One second, he was standing there, the blanket in his arms, the basket at his feet.

The next *she* was in his arms, the blanket on the ground, his mouth descending. "It's already yours."

And then he kissed her.

It wasn't the frenzy of their first time, Fanny feeling like she was out of control, like she needed to have him *right* then. Oh yeah, she wanted him. Oh yeah, she was wet and aching. But this was more; this *meant* more. This was the beginning, their future. The sun, the moon, and the stars.

He laid her onto the blanket, his weight following her down.

"I love you so fucking much," he breathed in her ear, the hot words sliding over her skin, dipping down between her thighs. Then he shifted slightly, his front to her side as he dragged his mouth down her throat, along her collarbone, nudging the straps of her dress to the side, trapping her arms at her sides. A moment later, his hand was beneath her, sliding up her back and finding the tag of her zipper. He slid it down.

Naked skin exposed on a warm fall day.

He tugged the material of her dress down slowly, exposing the tops of her breasts. Lower still, catching on the tips of her hardened nipples.

Her lips parted on a breath, and she inhaled sharply, the pleasure arrowing straight for her pussy. She knew she was wet. God, she'd been plenty wet with Brandon over the last month, but in this moment, she didn't think she'd ever been wetter. She could actually feel the moisture of her arousal soaking through her underwear, dripping down her thighs, making her thighs slick as they slid across one another.

Hot breath on her skin, fingers flicking open her bra, parting the material.

Lips circling, descending, closing in, and then he was sucking her nipple deeply into his mouth, his groan rumbling through her flesh, her moan loud and mixing with his.

"Oh, God," she breathed, when he released her, drifting over to her other breast.

More sucking, more pleasure coiling, more damp heat between her legs.

"Bran," she urged, reaching up and grabbing his shoulders, trying to bring him more on top of her. He stayed at her side, his hands sliding up and down her body, his mouth on her breasts, and then inching slowly.

Only inching.

Slow. So *damned* slow.

When all she wanted was him *in* her.

But no matter how hard she pulled, he didn't speed up, didn't shift over her.

Instead, he continued with that inching, tugging her dress down, sweeping it off her legs. Her panties followed suit, and then she was naked beneath a huge oak tree, sprawled on a blanket, with Brandon worshiping her until she was a shaking, desperate heap of a woman.

He inched over her stomach, kissing along the smattering of freckles there, nipped her hips, and finally crawled over her, pressing her legs wide as he dipped his head and got to work.

Slow and steady, so fucking *slow*.

But good. Glorious even. Gentle licks, unhurried strokes. Every single one ratcheting her up, tightening every muscle, her desire a fire through her veins.

And then just as slowly, she came apart at the seams.

The pleasure slid outward, starting at her center, flooding her torso, her arms, her legs. It spread inexorably forward, shooting out her fingertips and toes, crawling up her neck, across her face, and she would be shocked to find that her hair wasn't on fire.

Maybe she might bother to check, if she could lift an arm.

Brandon stayed between her thighs, gentling her with those slow licks, the delicate circles, and when she expected him to get naked and climb on her, to thrust deep and fast and furious, he stayed slow and gentle, and incrementally ramped her arousal again, until her breaths came in rapid pulses, sweat coated her body. She'd lost her capacity for words, could only make pleading sounds.

But then—*finally*—he stripped off his clothes.

She wanted to worship him like he'd paid homage to her body, but she didn't have time or energy to bring voice to that request, before he was rising over her and sliding home anyway.

Unhurried strokes, reverent touches.

Crawling toward the precipice, not rushing, easing up and up and—

She almost didn't want it to come, wanted to stay like this with Brandon forever, and he seemed to feel the same, lingering on the edge for what seemed like an eternity. But eventually, they got too close, and her release almost surprised her, seeming to climb up the cliffside and drag her down, rather than her plummeting over the edge.

Nirvana in her blood.

The man whom she loved surrounding her, extending a hand to escort her back into reality, even as he found his own climax.

Her name was on his tongue, his body was heavy on top of hers.

But only for a moment.

Then he rolled them to their sides, their chests heaving, their limbs heavy and slick with sweat, and he ran his fingers lightly through her hair.

She summoned some sort of inhuman strength to open her mouth. "I—"

Her stomach growled.

Not just growled, but erupted, shattering the peace. Brandon propped himself up on his elbow, his hair a mess, his eyes warm and layered with humor. "Hungry?"

She didn't get a chance to reply before he tugged his T-shirt over her head, reached for the basket, and began plying her with food.

Her favorites, of course.

Because it was Brandon.

Because she knew he'd take care of her.

They sat on that blanket, next to the pond, watching the sun crawl across the sky, eating the food he'd stashed out here, talking about the past, the present, the future, and just . . . being together

It was perfect.

The absolute most perfect day of her life.

———

Later that week, after she'd been fed and pampered all weekend (and one might say, thoroughly fucked), they'd returned to their new reality.

But that reality was pretty damned great.

Because Brandon was in it.

Because she was finally allowing herself to live it.

"Want some?"

She blinked, knowing she had a sappy smile on her face, but it was impossible to stifle. Not when she was so damned happy. He'd come to the arena tonight, and though she was working, doing some in-game evaluations of the players, he'd seemed to make it his job to make sure she'd eaten enough calories to fuel both teams down there on the ice.

Taking care of her.

She scooped up a hand of buttery popcorn and mock glared at him. "Still think I'm too thin?" she asked before shoving it into her mouth.

He nuzzled her throat as he dropped into the seat next to her. "I'm an asshole."

"Yes," she teased. "An asshole who brings me food and scarves, and takes me on weekends away. Who gives me orgasms, *and* hooks me up with a seat in a fancy box so I can work, all while practically waiting on me hand and foot." She scooped up another handful. "Yup. You're a real asshole."

His lips twitched. "Glad we're in agreement." He leaned close and glanced down at her tablet. She had a notebook whose pages were scrawled with her shorthand, all color-coded. "What are you looking for?"

"Hmm?" She'd gotten lost in his eyes, in the stubble on the strong lines of his jaw.

He pointed to a column on the page. "I've been watching you take notes all game"—it was now final intermission between the second and third periods—"so, what are you tracking?"

She glanced from him to the page then back to him. "You really want to know?"

He lifted a brow but didn't deem to answer.

Probably, because it was a stupid question. Okay, it was *definitely* a stupid question. When had he ever given her any indication that he didn't want to know about her? (And no, she wasn't including during the lost memory years.)

"I use this for the video that Dani sends me," she said, nodding toward the tablet, "but most of that is done after the game because she and her assistants are too busy pulling stuff for the other coaches, and occasionally she's reviewing goals—making sure they're good, or deciding if the on-ice coaches should challenge one that was scored on the team."

"And the notebook?"

"I work with most of the guys in the offseason, tuning up where necessary, making sure their conditioning is solid and prepped for game play." Pride shimmied through her. She liked what she'd built, was happy with what she was doing. "That offseason time isn't just with the Gold. Other players from the league come and see me for private lessons. This"—she nodded at the notebook—"is my little black book. I keep track of the things we're working on, add any new bad habits that they might pick up, all in my patented shorthand."

He grinned. "Chicken scratch is more like it."

"Also that," she allowed. "So anyway, it just helps me stay on track, and though I have a program the team had created for me to track progress, I've found that my color-coded notebook works better for my brain."

"Tell me about the columns."

She kept glancing at him as she explained her system and the color coding, trying to gauge if he'd lost interest in what she was telling him. Typically, this was where people lost their fight in staying interested and their eyes glazed over.

But he was engaged and asked questions that told her he was paying attention.

Which made her feel . . .

Well, it had her leaning up and kissing him soundly on the lips. "I love you."

It made her love him even more.

He ran his thumb along her jaw. "So, tonight is just a check-in?"

"Sort of," she said. "You know I usually work with the whole team during the preseason"—he'd seen her at the practice facility—"but I keep track of guys like Kay, for instance. I want to make sure he's not skating in a way that might exacerbate his injury. And more than that, that he's not picking up bad habits throughout the season." She sighed and shook her head. "Though they do always seem to come back to the ice with them after every break. They're like that Whack-a-Mole game. The moment I fix one, there's another, and then when someone is traded or a rookie joins the roster, I have to evaluate them and then—"

She cut herself off.

"Anyway, that's most of it."

"Fan." He lifted a brow. "We doing this again?"

"I—" She sighed. "You're not bored." He shook his head, causing her heart to flutter. "Brandon?"

His fingers found hers, squeezed. "Yeah, baby?"

"Be patient with me," she said. "I've spent a decade locking down the part of me that wanted a romantic relationship with someone."

Another squeeze, but no hesitation when he said, "Always." He leaned close, brushed a kiss over her cheek. "I'll just have to keep reminding you."

"Will that reminding involve your tongue?"

A wicked smile. "Yes."

"Will it involve your cock?"

His chuckle ruffled her hair. "Yes, love."

"I'm okay with that."

They'd both started laughing when a cry rang out behind them. Used to the children of the Gold running around—screaming, tears, and joy all mixed together and sometimes impossible to tease apart—she set down her tablet and notebook and stood.

Becca—the wife of Brandon's boss, Devon—was holding their son, rocking back and forth, while the little boy cried.

"Sorry," she called. "It's this guy's bedtime."

Fanny was moving before she processed it, closing the distance between them and offering, "Want me to take him for a minute?"

Devon had been pulled out for a quick phone call, even though this was only supposed to be a working night for Fanny —or at least, that was how Brandon had sold the time in the box. She'd protested bringing her work to a situation that was supposed to be for fun, but . . . Brandon was convincing.

So, instead of being in the Gold box or bugging Dani in the video suite, she was here.

With Becca, who was looking exhausted and very pregnant and . . . well, she had two arms, didn't she? And she'd held more than her fair share of kiddos since her tenure with the team. The halls and family suite were practically crawling with them.

"Do you mind?" Becca asked. "I was just trying to pack up our stuff, but he hit the wall."

"I wouldn't have asked if I minded," she said, taking a page from Brandon's book—who she felt approach her shoulder, his fingers lightly grazing her nape, his chuckle in her hair.

"Well, then"—Becca passed Jasper over—"thank you."

The little boy was strongly in toddler mode, which meant that trying to hold him when he was tired and wanting to run around was like trying to wrestle a crocodile.

But Fan was older and stronger, and she'd wrestled more than a few kids off the ice in her day.

She took a little walk around the box with Jasper, pointing out all the exciting things, using her teacher voice that distracted kids who were scared or those who wanted anything but what she was asking them to do. By the time they were on their second circuit of the space, Jasper was less crocodile and more . . . angry panda?

Okay, she didn't know.

He wasn't actively crying or trying to launch out of her arms, at least.

"Do you want kids?" Becca asked quietly.

Fan blinked and rotated away from the painting that had the toddler's attention. Jasper caught sight of his mama and immediately wanted her, so Fanny passed him over. "Yes," she said, her throat going a little tight when Jasper cuddled close and held tight to his mommy's neck. "I've always wanted kids. Hopefully, I'll—"

The buzzer rang, signaling the teams coming out, the same time Dev came back into the suite after finishing his call.

Fanny hurried to extend her thanks and say her goodbyes before heading back to her chair and her notebook.

She slipped past Brandon, and his face was drawn, worry written into the lines around his eyes.

"Are you—?" She started to turn back, but that worry was gone, his normal smile in place, as he shook Devon's hand and said his own goodbyes.

She hesitated for a moment, wanting to make sure he was okay, but the whistle blew.

She needed to do her job.

One more look to make sure that he was all right, another to make sure his expression was back to normal.

Then she moved to her chair, telling herself that she'd imagined the look.

And that decision was catastrophic.

———

"Hey, would you mind sharing the picture they took of us at the winery?" she asked as Brandon unbuttoned the rest of his shirt.

He was hopping into the shower after having spent the day at a photo shoot with Kaydon.

That photo shoot had unexpectedly been moved to the beach after a pipe had burst at the first location, and his suit was not conducive to ocean air and sand. So, she'd met him here at his house instead of the restaurant so he could clean up.

She thought he looked good enough to eat, no cleaning necessary.

His hair was windblown, the tops of his cheeks slightly pink, and his lips were a little chapped.

Surfer Brandon . . . in a suit.

Ha.

But that was why he was showering. They had reservations at the fancy restaurant he had originally booked the night after the raffle, and Surfer Brandon wasn't the Brandon he wanted to be for dinner.

Shame for her.

Especially since he'd banned her from getting in the shower *with* him.

"Do you know what kind of favor I had to pull the first time to get this reservation?" he'd said, nudging her back when she drifted close and began unbuttoning his shirt. "Let alone the second?"

"No," she said, coming close again and wrapping her arms around his neck. "I don't care."

He smelled like the ocean and sunlight, and she wanted to eat him up.

Another nudge back. "I'm taking you to dinner."

Fanny pursed her lips as she stared at him. "Or you could just take *me?*"

He'd groaned and dropped his head. "You're killing me, baby." His lips were a hair's breadth away, and he kissed her until she'd become a lump of need and desire, and then had scooped her up into his arms and carried her to the bed.

She'd thought she won.

But he'd merely dropped her on his mattress and backed away, pausing only to toe off his shoes and socks and tug off his tie.

God, why was that so sexy?

Though not as sexy as him parting the fabric of his shirt, revealing smooth tan skin below as she watched, still on the bed. It was like her private strip show, and she had to say that she was kind of into it. Especially when he unbuttoned his slacks and stepped out of them and there was so much tempting skin on display that she almost forgot she'd asked him a question.

"Sure," he said, nodding to the dresser that took up most of the wall by the bathroom. "It's right here. The code is 1-9-2-2."

Aw.

Those were the dates of their birthdays.

He noticed her face, and his own expression softened. "Told you, I remembered."

"Want to come over and *show* me what you remembered?"

Laughter in his eyes. "You're incorrigible."

"And horny."

More laughter, though this time it was bubbling up his

throat and filling the air, and God, she loved that sound, loved that she could make him *make* that sound. Then he turned for the bathroom and she heard the lock *clicking* in place.

"You're not going to bring it to me?" she called.

"Nope." A beat. "Because if I do, we won't make it to dinner."

She pouted . . . for just a moment.

Then the shower came on, and she stopped her pouting, getting up and fussing with her dress—not the sexy black one from before, but a longer midnight blue one that hit just above the knee—in front of the mirror in Brandon's bedroom. She'd paired it with a pair of sexy heels that she could actually walk in and wouldn't be cursing if she had to stand in them for a fair amount of time.

And underneath . . . well, if Brandon knew what was beneath the silk, he wouldn't have been in that shower.

It was expensive.

It was skimpy.

It was sexy as hell.

Satisfied the bed toss hadn't messed up her hair or outfit, she headed to the dresser, snagged Brandon's phone, and then typed in 1-9-2-2. She'd text the pic to herself and then she would get it printed. She already had a plan to put it in the empty space by the entryway so that she could see it every time she came home.

It was a *great* picture, reminiscent of that one from nearly two decades before.

Their arms around each other, smiles on their mouths, laughter and love in their eyes, and the employee from the winery had taken it at the absolute perfect moment.

Probably because they'd spent the afternoon making love outside at the secluded pond, and she'd been half-delirious from orgasms. Either that or filled with shock that they'd somehow managed so much outside naked time without getting caught.

She started to pull up the photo as she moved to grab her

purse but tripped over the edge of the rug. Stumbling, his cell nearly flying from her hands, her fingers slipped on the screen, and she ended up jabbing the voicemail icon instead.

"Shit," she muttered, straightening herself—and the skirt of her dress—and tapping the screen to exit back to the photos section, but then her eyes caught on the text of the voicemail transcript she'd accidentally started playing.

This is Dr. Lyon. I have the results . . . Please give me a call right away. It's imperative we make some decisions . . .

Her fingers were frozen.

No, every part of her was frozen.

Results. Call. Imperative. Decisions.

Fuck. Was she losing him *already*?

She'd only just gotten him back and—her hands shook as she set the cell back on the dresser—and now—

Her eyes slid closed. She should . . .

Talk to him. Knock on the door, demand he let her in and ask that he explain how he'd gone from cured to results and imperative decisions.

But . . . she couldn't breathe.

Black was intruding on the edges of her vision, and she stumbled again, this time into the dresser. Her hand came in contact with cool wood, and then she wasn't thinking about talking. She was darting out of the bedroom, sprinting down the hall.

She was out the front door.

She was in her car.

She was driving. Far, far away.

EIGHTEEN

BRANDON

He showered in record time, not trusting Fan to stay in the bedroom.

He half expected her to pick the lock and join him.

But she hadn't.

And even though he really wanted to take her to the restaurant—she deserved so much, not the least of which was a nice meal at a fancy place, no matter how many favors he had to call in—he could admit that he felt a little disappointed.

Wet, slick Fanny would never be resistible.

Hell, it had nearly killed him to not climb into bed with her and to shower instead.

Sighing, he thrust a hand through his hair—which was as much styling as he did nowadays—and then wrapped his towel around his waist.

Then he unlocked the bathroom door and moved into the bedroom.

His cell was on his dresser, hers was next to it.

But Fan wasn't anywhere in sight.

"Baby?" he called, yanking open a drawer and stepping into his underwear. He'd expected to have to fend her off when he came out. But maybe she'd decided to give them both a break and go downstairs.

He tugged up a fresh pair of slacks then buttoned on a blue shirt that would match Fanny's gorgeous dress.

Shoes and socks. His phone in his pocket.

"Fan?" he called again. Maybe she'd taken a call.

No, dumbass, her phone was right next to his. He grabbed hers, too, stuck it in his pocket. Maybe she'd gone out back.

But she wasn't there either.

Nor was she on the couch, having fallen asleep.

Not in the kitchen or the other bathroom. Not in his office reading a book. Not . . . anywhere.

He opened the front door almost robotically, and his heart sank when he saw her car wasn't in the driveway.

Unlocking his phone, he went to call her, forgetting again for a moment that she didn't have her cell. It opened onto the message screen. Onto a new voicemail from . . . Dr. Lyon.

A sinking feeling settled into his stomach, tugging him down, *down.*

"Shit," he whispered, hitting play on the message.

This is Dr. Lyon. I have the results of the tests you asked me for. Please, give me a call right away. It's imperative we make some decisions regarding the status of the samples.

"Fuck!" he burst out after the message ended.

Because it didn't take a genius to figure out what Fan had heard, what conclusion she'd come to. Why she had suddenly disappeared.

Fury coursed through him.

He'd thought they were over this. That they were moving forward.

That they were done letting fear or the past take them down again.

And the *first* time he'd gotten a message about his health, the first *fucking* time, she'd run. What the fuck was that? Look, he got it. She'd been fucked over by the circumstances of his health almost more than he had. But this? This was fucking bullshit, and she needed to know it.

He sighed, trying to cool his temper, but it was nearing on impossible.

Why hadn't she just talked to him instead of disappearing?

Didn't she understand how fucked up that was?

But . . . trauma.

It didn't magically go away just because they were together. And the path to healing wasn't a straight one. Shit went down, things got fucked up, but the real mettle was being a person to fix things. He couldn't fix things before, couldn't make the cancer go away or the memories come back. But he sure as shit could fight for Fanny, could explain what the call was about, and stay, no matter how many times she pushed him away.

He closed the door, but only for as long as it took to grab his wallet and keys before heading back outside and getting in his car.

He knew where she would go.

So, he'd follow. He'd fight.

And then he would make her understand, shake some sense into her until she recognized that their lives were connected for-fucking-ever.

No matter where she ran.

And *then* maybe he'd kiss her.

Okay, he would *definitely* kiss her.

Especially if kissing was the most efficient avenue to get that sense into her.

NINETEEN

S he didn't realize where she was until her knees were frozen.

Literally.

Or they felt that way, anyway.

She was kneeling on the ice, just inside the door to the rink, some sense of self-preservation having kicked in so that her high-heeled self hadn't decided to start Bambi-ing on the ice without her skates.

Unprepared.

That wasn't like her.

She usually kept her skates in her trunk.

But she hadn't been planning on skating, not until Monday. She had *planned* an entire weekend of being in Brandon's bed, ordering food, watching movies, having copious amounts of orgasms, and not surfacing until they both had to get back to work.

She didn't know how she'd gotten to the practice facility or how there wasn't anyone on the ice. This evening slot would normally be a prime slot for public skating or a birthday party or someone might rent it. This was why her practice or head-clearing time came late at night or early in the morning, when no one else was around. But maybe she'd get lucky and could disappear and—

Brit skated onto the ice.

Or not. Because this was Brit's extra ice time. She remembered hearing Brit talk about getting Frankie—the goalie coach —and a few of the Gold players together for an hour so she could work on a couple of things.

And sure as hell, Kaydon, Blane, Coop, and Ethan skated out.

Fuck.

Brit started to head for the net, the guys for some pucks, and Fanny tried to slither toward the door, wanting to run far and away . . . but her fucking heels. And the dress. And—

She grabbed the boards, lifted a leg, and—

"Stop right there, Fanny Douglas!"

Brit's voice echoed through the empty rink, and Fanny found herself halting when she should have kept running.

Kept.

Running.

The words finally penetrated the panicked haze. Because, seriously, what the fuck was she doing? She hadn't even talked to Brandon. She hadn't even gotten an explanation. And even if that explanation was that he was sick, then what?

Was she going to run from him?

Was she going to be the woman who loved him and then just fucking left because he was sick?

Of course not.

"I need to get my shit together," she whispered. "We'll find our way back to each other, no matter what happens, no matter how long it takes. But"—her eyes slid closed—"I want this time. I want him for however long I can have him."

Skates crunching on the ice had her eyes opening just in time to see Brit coming over.

"Want to tell me what you're doing?" the goalie asked.

Fanny nibbled at her bottom lip. She liked Brit. A lot. But Brit was tough and amazing—hello, first female to play in the NHL outside of an exhibition game, the first female to earn a starting role, the first female to win a Cup (twice). She was a total BAMF, and there was no way she had ever done what Fanny just did.

Brit looked her problems in the eyes and then kicked them in the balls.

"Fanny?" Kaydon asked, skating up behind Brit; Ethan, Blane, and Coop, only a few moments behind. "Is everything okay? Are you hurt?"

Ethan's eyes sparked with fury. "Did *Brandon* hurt you?"

Blane's jaw clenched.

Coop's face stayed neutral, but she didn't miss the intense look in his brown eyes.

One word from her, and these men would have her back.

Hers.

And that, more than anything, snapped her back into herself. Because one word, and they would support her. *Her*. Because she was family. Because even if things went to hell with Brandon, even if he got sick, she would have *them*.

She wasn't alone anymore.

She didn't need to continue doing everything in her power to remain safe and lonely in her isolation.

"I fucked up," she whispered.

"What?" Brit asked.

"I fucked up," she said, louder, her eyes flying from Brit to Ethan, desperation clawing at her. "Oh my God. I saw the message, and I panicked, and I ran, and I . . . left him, and—shit" —she scrambled for her purse, seeing it on the two steps that led up onto the ice—"where's my phone?"

Brit dropped to the ice, her pads bumping into Fanny's leg.

Helmet tipped up on her head, she took the purse from Fanny's arm and reached into it.

Ethan slipped a hand under her arm. "Here," he said. "Come on and sit down." He helped her off the rink and sat her on the bottom bleacher.

Then Blane was there, taking off his jersey and slinging it over her head. "You're shivering," he said quietly.

Because she'd blown it and needed to call Brandon, and—

"It's not here," Brit said.

Ethan sat next to her, just as Coop returned with a blanket bearing the Gold logo, wrapping it around her shoulders. "What?" she exclaimed, jumping up and dislodging it. "It has to be there. I need to call Brandon and tell him what happened and ask him to—" She broke off, thrust her hands into her hair, tears burning her eyes. "I need to talk to him as soon as possible. I messed up, and—and I need to go. I should go. I—"

"No," Ethan said, gripping her arm when she would have launched herself to her feet.

"You're not going anywhere," Blane said. "Not like this. You need to take a couple of deep breaths and calm down."

"Calm down?" She threw her hands up, yanking out of Ethan's hold, moving for the doors, the blanket falling to the floor. "I can't calm down! I just torpedoed my chance with Brandon, and I promised I would be there and that I wouldn't let the past come back and haunt us." Tears began sliding down her cheeks. "And then the first time I saw something that might not be smooth sailing, I panicked and fucking ran off. Without my phone. Away from the man I love and—"

"Hey." This time it was Kaydon who caught her arm, and he tugged her to face him. "Listen to Blane. Take a deep breath"— she opened her mouth to protest, but he kept talking—"and I'll go get my phone. You can call him from it, okay? Tell him where you are so you can fix this."

Fix this.

Yes, that's what she needed to do. If she could just talk to him, then she could fix this.

"Okay, Fan?" Kaydon asked, his thumb wiping at the tears streaking down her cheeks and probably fucking up the makeup she'd painstakingly applied before she'd ruined everything. "Fan?"

She blinked, forgetting about the makeup, and nodded. "Okay," she whispered. "Thank you."

A nod, and then he was gone. Coop came up next to her, bundling her in the blanket again and leading her back to the bleachers, where he and Blane sandwiched her, their big, warm, bulky bodies comforting as they waited for Kaydon to come back.

"I'm so stupid," she muttered, her head in her hands. "I can't believe I ran."

Brit had knelt in front of her. "We all do stupid shit when we're in love." She dropped a hand on to Fanny's knee, squeezed lightly. "He loves you. It'll be okay."

"I wish I could be like you were with Stefan," she whispered.

Brit's relationship with Stefan had been in the public eye from the moment they started seeing each other, and Brit had never looked back. She'd grabbed on to her happiness and lived her life without fear drawing her down.

"What do you mean?" Brit asked.

"You were so brave. You knew you would be good together and just went for it," she said. "You didn't let anything or anyone get between you."

Brit's brows had lifted, and they were sky-high by the time Fanny finished speaking. She turned slightly to look at Blane.

Fanny turned, too, saw and felt him shrug. "It's not exactly common knowledge," he said.

Brit sat back on her heels. "Stefan and my relationship was a publicity stunt." Fanny's mouth dropped open. "At first," she added, "and then when it became real, I was terrified. Fucking *terrified* that I was going to do something to ruin it between us, that everything might go wrong, and I'd be hurt."

"You were?"

She nodded. "Love is fucking terrifying."

"Here, here," Blane said.

"Ball withering," Coop added.

Brit patted her knee. "But it's also the best thing that you can ever do."

Fanny thought about all the times she'd had with Brandon—the good, the bad, the tear-jerking, and the moments that had made her feel more complete and happier than she ever dreamed was possible. "Yes," she agreed, "it is."

Brit smiled at her, patted her knee again. "It'll be okay, Fan."

Fanny could only hope that was true.

Kay walked back over to them, extending his cell toward her. "Brandon's number is all cued up. Just hit the button, and you can call him."

Fanny started to take it.

"Or," Brit said, her gaze drifting to the left, "you could just talk to him in person."

Fanny's heart thudded once, hard against her ribs.

And then she followed Brit's stare to see Brandon striding through the doors.

"Oh shit," she breathed.

He looked furious.

"Want me to stay?" Brit asked.

"No," she murmured.

"We'll be close by if you need us," Ethan said, pushing up from the bench. He led the others back onto the ice just as Brandon reached her.

She stood, still clutching the blanket, opened her mouth. "I'm so—"

Brandon yanked her against him and kissed her.

She tried to push away from him.

Which was another mistake in the long line of mistakes she'd made that evening.

First, not talking to him. Then running like an idiot and leaving her phone. Now, trying to break a kiss that was clearly trying to show her that while he might be furious, he still liked her enough to kiss her.

"Bran—" she began when he eased up enough for her to form words.

It was formed against his lips, but she didn't even get his full name out before he was kissing her again, his fingers in her hair, his tongue in her mouth, and her body melting against his.

"You're not leaving," he eventually said, pulling back enough so that his words were formed against *her* lips.

"No," she agreed.

He kissed her again, deeper and longer until she could barely see straight. Then he took her hand and started dragging her toward the door, the blanket fluttering behind her like a cape.

She wanted to go home, to allow him to take her away from this.

But she knew that she needed to talk to him first.

"Wait," she began, yanking against his hold.

Brandon spun to face her. "No, Fan. I've been patient. I've understood that it's going to take you some time. I love you, and for a while I considered that it might be better to just let you live your life without the risk of me."

She gasped.

"But I decided that life is too fucking short to not go after what I want, and what I want is you. Forever. For as long as I'm able to have you." He touched her cheek. "And if you get scared again and run off, I'll find you because I know deep down in here"—his hand slid down, covered the spot just above her heart—"that you love me, too, that you want the future and—"

"I do."

She leaned in, pressed a finger to his lips when he tried to go on.

"I love you," she whispered. "I do, and I—I don't want to run. I know it was a mistake, know it was so freaking stupid. I should have just talked to you. I'm so sorry." She cupped his jaw. "But I won't do it again. I promise. I was going back. I was getting ready to call you." She dipped her head toward the rink, where Brit and company were probably soaking in every second so they could report back to the Gossip Train. "Kaydon had just given me his phone so I could call you and tell you how badly I fucked up. I panicked, and I didn't mean to come here and I wasn't thinking clearly, but when I realized what I did, how I reacted, I knew I'd messed up." A tear slipped from her eye. "I don't care if you're sick. I don't care if you forget me. I don't care if you fall in love with someone else." She swallowed hard. "If you don't remember, I'll make you fall in love *with me* again. I'm done running. You're worth better than that." She sucked in a breath, released it. "*I'm* worth more than that. I—"

He snagged her hand, kissed her palm. "Fan?"

She blinked, all the words she needed to say still swirling around in her mind, ready to tumble off her tongue. But they all got tangled in her throat, and all she could say was, "Yeah?"

"You'll *make* me love you?"

Her chin came up. "Yes."

"Babe," he murmured, and she couldn't read his face.

More words tumbled out. "I fucked up," she said. "I'm so sorry. I won't leave again. I promise I don't care if you're sick. I'll be there and—"

Soft hands on her face. "I'm not sick."

She blinked. "What? But the phone call—"

"Was from my doctor," he said gently, winding an arm around her waist and drawing her even closer. "She was following up because I asked her about the status of my sperm on ice."

"Uh—" Fanny was stunned into silence. "Um . . . what?"

He bent close, rubbed his nose against hers. "I banked it the first time I got treatment. I was told that I might not be able to have kids after the chemo." He kissed the tip of her nose and straightened to look into her eyes. "I saw you with Jasper, sweetheart. I heard you tell Becca that you want to have babies. I don't know if I can give them to you naturally, but I will try, and if not, we have the samples."

"But the message said it was really important that you make some decisions."

"She needs me to decide if I'm going to pay to relocate the samples out here, or if I'm going to keep them on ice back home."

"That's it?"

He smiled. "That's it."

"And I—" She broke off on a groan, pressing her hands to her face. "Oh, God."

Brandon was gentle when he peeled her fingers back, gentle when he brought her close, gentle as he held her against him. "You were coming back?"

She nodded. "I'm such an idiot."

"You were coming back," he said. "That's all that matters."

Her eyes prickled, and tears threatened to escape again. God, she was so stupid. "I'm so—"

"Fan?"

This time it wasn't Brandon saying her name. She turned to glance at Ethan. He'd come off the ice, or maybe hadn't been shepherded onto it in the first place. Not that Brit was going through her workout. Nope. She, Blane, Kaydon, and Coop were staring through the glass watching them.

Yup.

Gossip Train fodder.

"Yeah?" she whispered to Ethan. His face was soft, his tone even more so.

"You're not an idiot." He tugged her from Brandon's arms, wrapped his own around her, and bent to whisper in her ear, "You're not. Now, I know something of women who run when they're scared."

She leaned back.

He held her close and met her eyes. "*I* know what it's like to be scared and make mistakes. But I know that when you can let that go, you'll have something amazing."

Her lips parted. "You make it sound so simple."

"You've already made the decision to go for it," he said. "That's half the battle."

"I—"

Brit tapped her stick on the glass, and they all whirled to face her. "Go home and make it up to him!" she called. "Makeup sex is the best sex!"

Brandon snorted.

Ethan sighed.

Fanny found herself grinning for the first time since she'd come to the ice, and the guilt twining through her insides all but disappeared when she glanced at Brandon and saw that he was smiling, too. "What do you think, baby?" she asked. "Should we try our hand at makeup sex?"

Ethan snorted this time.

Brandon's smile widened.

Then he took her hand, hauled her away from Ethan, and kissed her senseless.

When she surfaced, Brit and the others were cheering. Brandon nuzzled her throat, nipped at her ear.

And then he took her home.

And Brit was right because makeup sex was the absolute best. It was made even better when paired with her sexy as hell underwear (which convinced Brandon that he didn't really care about the favors he'd had to call in to get the fancy dinner reservations that they'd missed . . . for a second time).

But what made it the best was Brandon holding her close afterward, stroking her hair, and saying, "Babies?"

She smiled and rolled to face him, knowing that while all the fear of losing him hadn't been erased and probably never would be, that she wasn't giving up. Shifting, she rested her hand on his chest, leaned down, and stared into those gorgeous deep brown eyes as she declared, "I can't *wait* to have babies with you."

"Fuck," he hissed.

Fan pulled back slightly, thinking she'd hurt him somehow. "What?"

His hand rested on her hip, tugged her back. "Just that *fuck, I love you.*"

"Goof," she teased, leaning close to kiss him, not caring when he pulled her to move fully over him so that she could straddle his hips.

That was right where she wanted to be.

The kiss broke. His mouth got to work, was joined by his fingers.

Pleasure began to coil, her pussy was drenched, need had her wanting to slide down and take him inside—

Wait a minute.

"Why condoms?"

Brandon's forehead was sheened with sweat, his cock was rock hard just millimeters from where she was desperate to have it. His eyes . . . well, his eyes said he didn't give two shits about her question, only that he get inside her and send them both into oblivion.

"What?" he rasped.

"Why have we been using condoms all this time if you can't have kids?"

He blinked. Once. Twice.

Then he flipped them, pressing her back down into the mattress. "I don't know if I'm definitely shooting blanks, baby. Figured it was better to be safe than sorry."

She smiled.

"Any more questions?" he asked against her skin, trailing his mouth down.

She bit her lip. "One."

A sigh, his mouth slowing to lave at her belly button. "Lay it on me."

She ran her fingers through those soft curls. "Will you come inside me?"

This time, his blink made her smile. But not for long because he recovered from his surprise quickly. He slid inside, wiping the smile from her face. She groaned, held on tight, and went along for the fucking glorious ride that Brandon gave her.

Stroking deep and hard, steadily driving them both up and over the edge.

It was glorious.

It was perfect.

And then when he rolled to the side and held her tight, whispering in her ear, "I really hope I'm not shooting blanks because that was fun, and I want to do it again," and they both burst out laughing, it somehow grew even more perfect.

Because Brandon was there.

Because she was finally living her life.

Because they had laughter and love . . . and the potential for him to not be shooting blanks.

P.E.R.F.E.C.T.

EPILOGUE

BRANDON

They were lying in bed, as had become their habit, talking about nothing, one of Fanny's movies on in the background.

They still hadn't made it to that fancy restaurant.

He couldn't give two shits.

Because he had Fan in his arms.

But it had been six months since that night when everything had threatened to fall apart but instead had all come together, and he figured it was time.

He slipped from the bed, pressing a kiss to Fanny's head when she asked where he was going. He'd just moved into her house that morning, and his boxes were stacked at the edge of the bedroom (and in plenty of other places), but what he needed was in the suitcase he'd stashed in the closet.

Deep down, beneath some other papers. He'd stumbled upon it when he'd cleaned out his filing cabinet.

Another notebook.

Only this time, it was one he'd written in.

One he'd started after his second surgery.

There were entries of being in the hospital and going through physical therapy, cataloging his recovery, jots of the things he remembered.

And drawings. Later, after she'd gone, there had been so many drawings.

All of one thing.

He brought it back to her, along with the folder he'd had put together for just this moment.

"What is it?" she asked, sitting up, the blankets tucked around her chest.

"This," he said, handing it to her.

Fanny froze, then slowly her eyes came back up to his. "What is this?"

"I think you know," he murmured, climbing on the bed and sitting down next to her.

Her gaze dropped, her fingers tracing over one of the pages, over the drawing of a house. Then flipping the page and seeing the same drawing, again and again and again. There were different details each time—outside a wraparound porch, a large back yard with a pond similar to the one they'd made love next to, a swing set, a winding path leading to above ground vegetable planters; and inside a large kitchen with a huge island, the upper cabinet doors made of glass, a laundry room, a huge sectional, a pantry door with frosted glass emblazoned with the word "Pantry."

Stone and warm wood. Granite and tile. Huge rugs and colorful throw cushions.

He'd drawn every angle inside and out.

Over and over again.

"How?" she breathed.

"I don't know."

This was the house that he and Fanny had dreamed about building. The one they'd discussed from the moment they knew they were going to be together forever. They'd discussed the kitchen on the phone when she'd been touring after her silver medal. They'd talked about furniture after he'd aced his finals. They'd planned the pond when he stayed up late to talk, her lying in his in bed after a tough practice. The pantry was during chemo when he couldn't keep anything down. The swing set after he'd finished with his PT.

It was the culmination of late nights and long conversations on the phone, of long, drugging kisses followed by whispering in each other's ears.

It was all of the small moments, the smiles and laughter, the quiet satisfaction after meals shared, the cool kiss of the night's air when they snuggled together in the back of his truck and stared up at the stars in the sky.

"When did you do this?" she whispered.

"After the surgery," he said, as she flipped another page, "and far after you left, all the way up until I remembered."

Her eyes were glassy with tears when she glanced up at him. Then she went back to studying the pages, slowly turning through each one until she reached the end of the notebook. "It's beautiful," she said gently.

It was.

Because it was their dream.

"So," he said, handing her the other thing he'd retrieved, the folder he'd put together, and taking the notebook. "I was kind of hoping that we might be able to live there."

Fanny frowned. "But it doesn't exist."

He opened the folder, showing her the sheaf of papers. Each packet had a listing of lots of land for sale in the area. Any of which could house their dream, could be the place where they built their future. "Pick," he murmured.

"Bran," she whispered, tears slipping free.

"I—*oof!*" He'd started to lean forward to wipe her cheeks,

but suddenly found himself sprawled back on the mattress, her arms around him.

"You wonderful, wonderful man."

Then she kissed him until he forgot about the papers, about the dream of the future, about everything except for the dream of now.

Of this woman, who'd found the courage to love him.

Of this time together, never promised, always precious.

Of this chance to build something new and never look back.

Only later—*much* later—did they go through the papers and narrow it down to two that they would visit in person.

Then he topped off Fanny's glass of wine, stole a handful of her buttery popcorn, and held her close as they watched a movie that was not full of blood and gore.

But instead, it was filled with love and a happy ending.

And Brandon thought that was pretty damned perfect.

P.E.R.F.E.C.T.

SCARLETT

Fanny all but sailed across the ice, pretty and graceful, and on a love-hazed cloud.

Scar's heart squeezed tight.

It would have been nice if she'd fallen for Charlie, but it was pretty damned great that she'd fallen for Brandon.

Who was working at a table in the corner of the rink, his laptop open, his earbuds in, papers spread out on the chair next to him. Even though he had a cushy corner office at Prestige Media Group, he preferred to bundle up and work where he could see the woman he loved.

A little girl was crying on the ice, but before Scar could make her somewhat shaky way over to her—they couldn't all be graceful silver medalist skaters—Fanny knelt and comforted the little girl, and in just a few seconds, they were both on their feet and back to class.

And Brandon was staring at his woman with warm eyes.

God.

She wanted that.

No. No, she didn't. She wanted to keep working. As assistant publicist for the Gold, her job was to manage the team's social media and do her best to keep the public loving them.

It wasn't hard.

The guys were great.

As great as Brandon was.

"Mrs. Scar."

She blinked, forcing her eyes away from Brandon and his obvious affection for Fanny, and looking down at the tiny boy at her knees. "Hey, Dominic. Everything okay?"

His bottom lip wobbled.

Oh shit.

"Hey, buddy," she said, clumsily getting to her knees. "Talk to me."

That lip kept wobbling and was now joined by tears.

Fuck.

"Candace said that I'm bad at skating."

All the kids were bad at skating. That's why she—equally as bad, or perhaps maybe marginally better, depending on who was judging—was helping out with class. She wasn't good enough at skating to help any other time.

Front and back.

Slow turns.

Doing her best to not eat shit.

And mostly she succeeded.

Unfortunately, she couldn't tell him they were all terrible.

"You're doing really good, buddy," she said. "You're just learning, and I know you'll be good in no time."

The tears were still there, but they were slowing. "Really?" he said, snot trailing under his nose.

"Really," she said, shuddering. She started to pull a packet of tissues out of her pocket, kept there for exactly this reason, but before she could get one out, someone else skated over.

Someone tall and handsome, who had her in a constant battle to keep her panties up and around her hips.

They just wanted to drop right off anytime Kaydon was around.

He had arms that made her drool, a strong jaw with a hint of stubble she wanted trailing over her skin, and lips that would pillow perfectly against hers.

If only they didn't work together.

She liked this job.

She *loved* this job.

Which meant she wanted to keep it.

And while the Gold were a treasure trove of couples working together and living out their happy endings, Scarlett didn't have that track record.

When she was in a relationship, things never went well.

And that unwell transitioned into her life, her job, her happiness.

She had terrible taste in men, and when those relationships ended, her shit got dive-bombed. She lost her job. She got kicked out of her apartments. She was dogged by debt collectors, or psycho ex-girlfriends she hadn't know existed (or were wives, in one case—and not the ex-variety—and the reason the man she'd been dating had become *her* ex), or mothers who were pissed that the wedding they'd been planning without Scar's permission (or their son's, for that matter) was off.

So, suffice to say, she was on a break from men.

It was work and friends and rebuilding her life.

No. Men.

But one look at Kaydon when he'd joined the team made her

want to reconsider her hiatus. But it was more than his glorious jaw and yummy stumble. He was nice and talented and was just a really decent guy.

Case in point?

Now.

Kaydon bent next to them, scooped up Dominic. He said something that made Dom laugh, and he didn't seem to care when Dom rubbed his snotty nose against Kay's shoulder.

His big hand came to the back of Dom's helmet, and then he took off with the little boy in his arms, zigging and zagging through the cones, avoiding the other kids effortlessly.

Dom laughed and held on and by the time they circled back, both man and boy had huge smiles on their faces.

A moment later, Dom's skates were on the ice, Kay holding him steady as he spoke quietly.

Scarlett couldn't make out the words, only could see Dom nod intently before he threw his arms around Kaydon's neck. And, oh sweet baby Jesus, her ovaries, because Kaydon didn't hesitate, just hugged him back and patted him lightly on the helmet before lightly pushing him forward so he could rejoin the other kids. Scar could barely resist the urge to clamp her hands to her heart and sigh, the longing to know him better was so intense.

Used to shoving that longing down—she'd done it for nearly an entire season—she pushed to her feet and continued to patrol the ice, making sure everyone was happy and tear-free and staying far, far away from Kaydon, lest he see that longing.

Eventually—thank God, for her ovaries—Fanny blew the whistle, and the classes were over.

Scar's feet ached, but she started cleaning up the ice, so Fan didn't have to, trying deliberately to *not* notice that Kaydon was picking up cones much more rapidly than she was.

And moving closer to her and her bumbling self.

"I can get this, you know?" he rumbled, skating past her, a pile of cones in his arms.

Much bigger than the pile she'd managed to collect.

"I know," she said.

Not that he could hear her.

He was already on the other side of her ice.

The rink had cleared out. The kids in the lobby, Brandon and Fanny in deep discussion over something at his makeshift workstation. Scar lumbered to the door to the ice, her cones the worst sort of Jenga tower, and managed to just barely climb up the step as Kaydon returned from stashing the supplies around the corner.

"Let me," he began.

She walked right by him.

"Okay," he muttered.

She ignored him. It was much better for her sanity.

But apparently today, he was done with her ignoring him. "What's your problem?" he asked, following her into the narrow hallway.

"I don't know what you're talking about," she said, gracelessly bending so she could place the cones on the stack.

She mostly succeeded.

Mostly because a few tumbled off and scattered on the ground. Stifling a curse, she knelt and started picking them up.

So did Kaydon.

Fucking hell. She was trying to be good.

"Scarlett."

Cones. *Cones!*

She set one on the stack, but because she wasn't paying attention, that setting resulting in knocking over, and the cones went everywhere.

Shit.

She reached for them, hands flailing, trying to shift around without slicing hers or Kaydon's—since he was too damned nice and still helping her—fingers off.

"*Scarlett.*"

A warning this time.

Glancing down, she realized exactly where she was reaching. His crotch. Well, for the cone that was less than an inch from his crotch.

She froze, but before she could pull back, his fingers encircled her wrist.

Warm and a little rough.

Her lips parted on an exhale, and she shivered.

"Scarlett," he said again, and this time his voice was like his fingers, warm and a little rough.

She wobbled. He shifted a little closer, smoothing a lock of her hair off her cheek. "Why don't you like me, Scar?"

Still processing all that warm and rough *and* him smoothing back her hair, it took her a second to process his question. But the moment she did, she unstuck, laughter bubbling up her throat and filling the air.

He let her laugh for a minute before his hand—the one not tracing light and lovely circles on her wrist—reached up and cupped her cheek. "I don't love being on the butt end of a joke, baby."

That stoppered up her guffawing.

His thumb moved, swiped at the skin beneath her eyes, and she realized that she'd been laughing so hard, she had tears on her cheeks.

"You're not a joke, Kaydon."

He was so far away from that it wasn't even funny. *She* was the joke. She was the one who was trying to be good.

She was the one who was going to fail.

Again.

Because she leaned forward, whispered before he could reply,

"It's not that I don't like you, Kay. It's that you are the sexiest man I've ever seen."

And then she kissed him.

———

Thank you for reading! I hope you loved meeting Brandon and Fanny! The next book in the Gold Hockey series is CYCLED. **No matter how hard Scarlett tried to be good— She always ended up being bad.**

READ CYCLED HERE NOW>

And if you enjoyed CRASHED, you'll love the sexy, sweet, and close-knit Breakers Hockey crew. The first book in the series, BROKEN, is now live!

The more she falls for Stefan, the more she risks her career... Don't miss the first Gold Hockey book. The over 400 five-star-reviewed BLOCKED is FREE!

"Off-the-charts hot, smexy scenes with one of the best book boyfriends I have come across!" —Amazon reviewer

DOWNLOAD BLOCKED FOR FREE >

I so appreciate your help in spreading the word about my books, including sharing with friends! Please leave a review on your favorite book site!

You can also join my Facebook group, the Fabinators, for exclusive giveaways and sneak peeks of future books.

SIGN UP FOR ELISE FABER'S NEWSLETTER HERE: https://www.elisefaber.com/newsletter

---

EXCERPT FROM BROKEN
Breakers Hockey, Book 1
Available now!
<u>READ BROKEN HERE NOW></u>

LUC

He was forty years old.

He was single.

He was happy that way.

Sighing, he lifted his beer to his lips and internally shook his head at himself. He wasn't happy. He was miserable and lonely. Oh, and he might as well add fucking pathetic to that tally.

Because the woman he was in love with was married.

To a perfectly nice man who loved her and cared for her and treated her like the fucking queen she was.

But that didn't help Luc or his loneliness problem.

So, he was drinking a beer, trying to forget the woman he'd fallen for two years before, only to find out she was married two weeks later. Lexi was with the legal team for the Baltimore Breakers, the NHL team he was the GM for. He'd fallen hard over her skills at contract negotiations, fallen harder when she'd proven to be whip-smart and hilarious in equal parts.

Then he'd run into her and her husband while grabbing a cup of coffee.

"Luc," she'd said, smiling up at him, its intensity punching him right in the gut, *"this is my husband, Caleb."*

Caleb?

What kind of name was that?

"Fucking hell," Luc muttered, taking another sip, hating the other man, and yet respecting him, because there was love there.

Deeply rooted love that spoke of a happy relationship.

He hated it.

Cue lonely, pathetic asshole.

Sighing, he stood up and turned toward his front door, reaching for the handle when he heard the screech of tires.

Spinning, he watched the car pull to a stop, the driver's door open, and Lexi tumble out.

He was running before he realized he'd moved, reaching her in seconds.

"What's the matter?" he asked, noting the tears, the reddened eyes, the mascara blackening the skin beneath her eyes. "Lexi, are you hurt?"

She nodded, threw herself into his arms.

"Where, honey?" he asked. "Where?"

Lexi tore herself away, and the pain in her gaze shredded his insides. "It's Caleb."

READ BROKEN HERE NOW>

―――――

Want a free bonus story? Hate missing Elise's new releases? Love contests, exclusive excerpts and giveaways?
Then signup for Elise's newsletter here!
https://www.elisefaber.com/newsletter

―――――

And join Elise's fan group, the Fabinators https://www.facebook.com/groups/fabinators for insider information, sneak peaks at new releases, and fun freebies! Hope to see you there!

GOLD HOCKEY SERIES

Gold Hockey

Did you miss any of the Gold Hockey books?
Find information about the full series here.
Or keep reading for a sneak peek into each of the books below!

Blocked
Gold Hockey Book #1
Get your copy at https://www.elisefaber.com/blocked

Brit

The first question Brit always got when people found out she played ice hockey was *"Do you have all of your teeth?"*

The second was *"Do you, you know, look at the guys in the locker room?"*

The first she could deal with easily—flash a smile of her full set of chompers, no gaps in sight. The second was more problematic. Especially since it was typically accompanied by a smug smile or a coy wink.

Of course she looked. *Everybody* looked once. Everyone

snuck a glance, made a judgment that was quickly filed away and shoved deep down into the recesses of their mind.

And she meant *way* down.

Because, dammit, she was there to play hockey, not assess her teammates' six packs. If she wanted to get her man candy fix, she could just go on social media. There were shirtless guys for days filling her feed.

But that wasn't the answer the media wanted.

Who cared about locker room dynamics? Who gave a damn whether or not she, as a typical heterosexual woman, found her fellow players attractive?

Yet for some inane reason, it *did* matter to people.

Brit wasn't stupid. The press wanted a story. A scandal. They were desperate for her to fall for one of her teammates—or better yet the captain from their rival team—and have an affair that was worthy of a romantic comedy.

She'd just gotten very good at keeping her love life—as nonexistent as it was—to herself, gotten very good at not reacting in any perceptible way to the insinuations.

So when the reporter asked her the same set of questions for the thousandth time in her twenty-six years, she grinned—showing off those teeth—and commented with a sweetly inno-cent "Could've sworn you were going to ask me about the coed showers." She waited for the room-at-large to laugh then said, "Next question, please."

–Get your copy at https://www.elisefaber.com/blocked

Backhand
Gold Hockey Book #2
Get your copy at https://www.elisefaber.com/backhand

SARA

"Sorry I messed up your sketch," he rumbled.

She nibbled on the side of her mouth, biting back a smile. "Sorry I stole your hand for so long."

He shrugged. "My mom's an artist. I get it."

Well, there went her battle with the smile. Her lips twitched and her teeth came out of hiding. If there was one thing that Sara had, it was her smile. It had been her trademark in her competition days.

Which were long over.

Her mouth flattened out, the grin slipping away. Time to go, time to forget, to move on, to rebuild. "Thanks," she said and extended a hand.

Then winced and dropped it when her ribs cried out in protest.

"You okay?" he asked, head tilting, eyes studying her.

"Fine." And out popped her new smile. The fake one. Careful of her aching side, she shrugged into her backpack. "I've got to go." She turned, ponytail flapping through the hair to land on her opposite shoulder.

"That—" He touched her arm. "Wait. I *know* I know you."

She froze. That was the second time he'd said that, and now they were getting into dangerous territory. Recognition meant . . . no. She couldn't.

There had been a time when *everyone* had known her. Her face on Wheaties boxes, her smile promoting toothpaste and credit cards alike.

That wasn't her life any longer.

"Thanks again. Bye." She started to hurry away.

"Wait." A hand dropped on to her shoulder, thwarting her escape, and she hissed in pain.

"Sorry," he said, but he didn't release her. Instead, he shifted his grip from her aching shoulder down to her elbow and when she didn't protest, he exerted gentle pressure until Sara was facing him again. "It's just that know I *know* you."

No. This wasn't happening.

"You're Sara Jetty."

Her body went tense.

Oh God. This was *so* happening.

"It's me." He touched his chest like she didn't know he was talking about himself, and even as she was finally recognizing the color of his eyes, the familiar curve of his lips and line of his jaw, he said the worst thing ever, "Mike Stewart."

Oh *shit*.

—Get your copy at https://www.elisefaber.com/backhand

Boarding
Gold Hockey Book #3
Get your copy at https://www.elisefaber.com/boarding

MANDY

Hockey players had the *best* asses.

No pancake bottoms, these men—and *women*—could fill out a pair of jeans. She wanted to squeeze it, to nibble it, bounce a dime—

Mandy dropped her chin to her chest, losing sight of the Sorting Hat cupcakes she'd been pondering.

Blane with his yummy ass had a unique way of distracting her.

No, it wasn't even distraction, per se. He had *always* been able to get under her skin.

And that was very, very bad for her.

"Ugh," she said, tossing her phone onto her desk and standing, knowing that she wouldn't be able to sit still now.

Nope, she needed about forty laps in the pool and a good hard fu—

Run, her mind blurted, almost yelling at the mental voice of her inner devil. *A good hard run.*

Unfortunately, the cajoling tone wasn't completely drowned out. *Some sexy horizontal time with Blane would be more fun—*

But the rest of the enticing words were lost as the roar of the crowd suddenly penetrated through the layers of concrete. Her stomach twisted. Mandy could tell, even before her eyes made it to the television, that it wasn't in celebration of a goal or a good hit either.

This was fury, a collective of outrage.

She was on her feet the moment she saw the prone form lying so still face down on the ice.

Her gut twisted when she spotted the curving line of a numeral two on the back of the player's jersey.

"Not him," she said and the words were familiar, a sentiment she had whispered, had *prayed* a thousand times before. She needed the camera angle to shift, for her to be able to see more clearly *who* was hurt. "Not him."

Then Dr. Carter was on the ice and the player moved slightly, rolling away from the camera, giving a full shot of his back and the matching twos adorning his jersey.

Fuck. Not him. Not Blane.

And that was when she saw the pool of blood.

—Get your copy at https://www.elisefaber.com/boarding

Benched

Gold Hockey Book #4

Get your copy at https://www.elisefaber.com/benched

MAX

He started up the car, listening and chiming in at the right places as Brayden talked all things video game.

But his mind was unfortunately stuck on the fact that women were not to be trusted.

He snorted. Brit—the Gold's goalie and the first female in the NHL—and Mandy—the team's head trainer—would smack him around for that sentiment, so he silently amended it to: *most* women were not to be trusted.

There. Better, see?

Somehow, he didn't think they'd see.

He parked in the school's lot, walked Brayden in, and received the appropriate amount of scorn from the secretary for being thirty minutes late to school, then bent to hug Brayden.

"I'll pick you up today," he said.

Brayden smiled and hugged him tightly. Then he whispered something in his ear that hit Max harder than a two-by-four to the temple.

"If you got me a new mom, we wouldn't be late for school."

"Wh-what?" Max stammered.

"Please, Dad? Can you?"

And with that mind fuck of an ask, Brayden gave him one more squeeze and pushed through the door to the playground, calling, "Love you!" over his shoulder.

Then he was gone, and Max was standing in the office of his son's school struggling to comprehend if he had actually just heard what he'd heard.

A new mom?

Fuck his life.

—Get your copy at https://www.elisefaber.com/benched

Breakaway

Gold Hockey Book #5

Get your copy at https://www.elisefaber.com/breakaway

BLUE

"Thanks for the ride."

"Try not to go out and get a fresh bimbo to ride tonight. I hear STIs on are the rise in the city."

Blue sighed, turned back to face her. "Really?"

She shrugged, smirk teasing the edges of her mouth, drawing his focus to the lushness of her lips. "Just watching out for Max's teammate."

He rolled his eyes. "Not hardly."

"Okay, how about I'm trying to prevent you from spreading STIs to the female populace."

"I'm clean, and I'm smart," he told her. "Condoms all the way."

"Ew."

Except there was something about the way she said it that made Blue stiffen and take notice. Because . . . he stared into her eyes, watched as the pale blue darkened to royal, saw her lips part, and her suck in a breath.

Holy shit.

"You're attracted to me."

Her jaw dropped. "No fucking way," she said, too quickly, pink dancing on the edges of her cheekbones. "You're delusional."

Blue got close.

Real close.

Anna licked her lips.

And fuck it all, he kissed that luscious mouth.

—Breakaway, https://www.elisefaber.com/breakaway

Breakout

Gold Hockey Book #6
Get your copy at https://www.elisefaber.com/breakout

PR-Rebecca

A fucking perfect hockey fairy tale.

Shaking her head, because she knew firsthand that fairy tales didn't exist outside of rom-coms and occasionally between alpha sports heroes and their chosen mates, Rebecca slipped through the corridor and stepped onto the Gold's bench.

Lots of dudes in suits—of both the boardroom *and* the hockey variety—were hugging.

On the ice. Near the goals. On the bench.

It was a proverbial hug-fest.

And she was the cynical bitch who couldn't enjoy the fact that the team she was with had just won the biggest hockey prize of them all.

"I knew you'd be like this."

Rebecca turned her focus from Brit, who was skating with the huge silver cup, to the man—no, to the *boy* because no matter how pretty and yummy he was, Kevin was still a decade younger than her—leaning oh so casually against the boards.

"Nice goal," she told him.

A shrug. "Blue made a nice pass."

And dammit, the fact that he wasn't an arrogant son of a bitch made her like him more.

She nodded at the cup. "You should go have your turn."

"I'll get mine," he said with another shrug.

She frowned, honestly confused. "You don't want—"

Suddenly he was in front of her on the bench, towering over her even though she was wearing her four-inch power heels. "You know what I want?"

Rebecca couldn't speak. Her breath had whooshed out of her in the presence of all that sweaty, hockey god-ness. Fuck he was pretty and gorgeous and . . . so fucking masculine that her thighs actually clenched together.

She wanted to climb him like a stripper pole.

"Do you?" he asked again when her words wouldn't come. "Want to know what I want?"

She nodded.

He bent, lips to her ear. "You, babe," he whispered. "I. Want. You."

Then he straightened and jumped back onto the ice, leaving her gaping after him like she had less than two brain cells in her skull.

The worst part?

She wanted him, too.

Had wanted him since the moment she'd laid eyes on the sexy as sin hockey god.

"Trouble," she murmured. "I'm in *so* much fucking trouble."

—Breakout, https://www.elisefaber.com/breakout

Checked
Gold Hockey Book #7
Get your copy at https://www.elisefaber.com/checked

"Rebecca."

She kept walking.

She might work with Gabe, but she sure as heck wasn't on speaking terms with him. He'd dismissed her work, ignored her contribution to the team. He'd made her feel small and unimportant and—

She kept walking.

"*Rebecca.*"

Not happening. Her car was in sight, thank fuck. She beeped the locks, reached for the handle.

He caught her arm.

"Baby—"

"I am *not* your baby, and you don't get to touch me." She ripped herself free, started muttering as she reached for the handle of her car again. "You don't even like me."

He stepped close, real close. Not touching her, not pushing the boundary she'd set, and yet he still got really freaking close. Her breath caught, her chin lifted, her pulse picked up. "That. Is. Where. You're. Wrong."

She froze.

"What?"

His mouth dropped to her ear, still not touching, but near enough that she could feel his hot breath.

"I like you, Rebecca. Too fucking much."

Then he turned and strode away.

—Checked, https://www.elisefaber.com/checked

Coasting
Gold Hockey Book #8
Get your copy at https://www.elisefaber.com/coasting

COOP

Without thinking, he caught her arm.

"You're not okay."

She shuddered to a stop when he touched her, not fighting the grip, chin dropping to her chest. "No," she said, "you're right. I'm not okay."

"Who was on the phone?" he asked gently.

Her jaw went tight. "My ex."

Fury blazed through him. "Did he hurt you?" he growled.

A shake of her head. "Not like you're thinking." She sucked in a breath. "He broke my heart."

Coop's own heart gave a twinge. "I'm sorry, Calle. That's—"

"Fucking stupid." Another tear joined the first, dripping down the pale skin of her cheek.

"It's not stupid to have loved someone," he said gently.

Her eyes went fierce. "It's incredibly stupid when the person who supposedly loves you right back doesn't give a damn that you're pregnant."

His jaw fell open. He knew it did.

But Calle? Even, gentle *Calle* had gotten knocked up and—

"Yup," she said, brushing by him. "See? Really *fucking* stupid."

And without another word, she disappeared into the rink.

—Coasting, https://www.elisefaber.com/coasting

Centered

Gold Hockey Book #9

Get your copy at https://www.elisefaber.com/centered

"Watch out!"

The warning came a second too late.

He'd already stepped off the curb, already put himself in range of the car that was blowing through the red light, tearing through the intersection, not giving a shit that there were pedestrians walking—

Well, of all the ways to go, at least this would be quick.

But just as the car came within an inch of him, Liam found himself jerked back onto the curb, his one-hundred-and-eighty-pound frame becoming unwieldy and clumsy.

Kind of like on the ice over the last few years.

That was his last thought before he found himself sprawled, ass first, on the San Franciscan sidewalk.

Gross.

"What. The. *Fuck?*" a female voice snapped.

The same female voice that had warned him.

"Do you have a fucking death wish?" she yelled, causing his eyes to snap open, making him look up at an angel . . . a foot tapping, arms crossed, seriously pissed, and seemingly way too small to have been able to haul his ass back onto the curb female.

Liam thought he just might have that death wish.

Especially if it meant he got to be rescued by a woman who looked like an angel. He opened his mouth to reply.

But apparently didn't work fast enough.

Because the woman, the beautiful, curvy female, made a disgusted noise and strode away from him.

He watched her go, watched that gorgeous ass stride down the sidewalk, and stop outside a storefront.

And suddenly, he thought that, hockey or not, he might just want to stay in San Francisco after all.

—Centered, https://www.elisefaber.com/centered

Charging
Gold Hockey Book #10
Get your copy at https://www.elisefaber.com/charging

"Your feet hurt."

Her brows drew together. "What?"

Logan nodded at her feet, clad in a lovely pair of heels that, while beautiful, were also the equivalent of bear traps—and if that wasn't the perfect metaphor for the man in front of her, she didn't know what was.

"Those heels hurt you." His head tilted to the side. "Why do you wear them?"

She scoffed. "None of your fucking business, Walker."

A smile—slow and hot and sliding like silk over her breasts, her stomach, between her legs. "I knew you'd say that."

"I—"

He held up a box she hadn't noticed, pushed it into her hands when she stepped back. "Open it," he said, voice dropping and joining that silk of his smile to dip between her legs. "If you think you can handle it."

And then he was gone, the door closing behind him, leaving her with a heavy ass bag packed with who knew what, aching feet, and a box in her hands.

A box given on a challenge.

A box he knew she'd open.

Because Charlotte Harris didn't give in or back down. She liked that even less than she liked losing.

So, she opened the lid.

And instantly knew she was in trouble.

—Charging, https://www.elisefaber.com/charging

Caged
Gold Hockey Book #11
Get your copy at https://www.elisefaber.com/caged

"Are you seeing anyone?"

Slowly, she spun back, eyes wide.

"That was my question," he said, when she stared at him in shock. "Dani?" he asked, when she just continued staring at him mutely. "Did I break you?"

A slow shake of her head.

He stepped a little closer, just near enough that she could feel the heat from his body. "No to the breaking you part, or no to the seeing anyone piece?" he murmured.

"The seeing anyone thing," she somehow managed to whisper, despite the fact that the question from a man like him to a woman like her was absolutely one hundred percent unfathomable.

Circling back to sad and single and—

He smiled.

And she actually felt her brain cells collide and fizzle into smoke. That smile was dangerous, could without a doubt, turn her stupid. *Really* stupid.

"Good," he murmured.

Swallowing hard, she nodded, cheeks on fire, and turned away again. "Right, I'll just—"

"Will you go out with me?"

Her fingers went limp. The tablets hit the ground.

This time, the *crunch* sounded much more ominous.

Or maybe that was just her heart.

—Caged, https://www.elisefaber.com/caged

Also by Elise Faber

Breakout

Checked

Coasting

Centered

Charging

Caged

Crashed

A Gold Christmas

Cycled

Caught

Cap

Breakers Hockey (all stand alone)

<u>Broken</u>

<u>Boldly</u>

<u>Breathless</u>

<u>Ballsy</u>

<u>Bewitched</u>

Love, Action, Camera (all stand alone)

Dotted Line

Action Shot

Close-Up

End Scene

Meet Cute

Love After Midnight (all stand alone)

Rum And Notes

Virgin Daiquiri

On The Rocks

Sex On The Seats

Life Sucks Series (all stand alone)

Train Wreck

Hot Mess

Dumpster Fire

Clusterf*@k

FUBAR (March 29,2022)

Roosevelt Ranch Series (all stand alone, series complete)

Disaster at Roosevelt Ranch

Heartbreak at Roosevelt Ranch

Collision at Roosevelt Ranch

Regret at Roosevelt Ranch

Desire at Roosevelt Ranch

Phoenix Series (read in order)

Phoenix Rising

Dark Phoenix

Phoenix Freed

Phoenix: Lex Tal Chronicles (rereleasing soon, stand alone, Phoenix world)

From Ashes

In Flames

To Smoke

ABOUT THE AUTHOR

USA Today bestselling author, Elise Faber, loves chocolate, Star Wars, Harry Potter, and hockey (the order depending on the day and how well her team -- the Sharks! -- are playing). She and her husband also play as much hockey as they can squeeze into their schedules, so much so that their typical date night is spent on the ice. Elise changes her hair color more often than some people change their socks, loves sparkly things, and is the mom to two exuberant boys. She lives in Northern California. Connect with her in her Facebook group, the Fabinators or find more information about her books at www.elisefaber.com.

facebook.com/elisefaberauthor

amazon.com/author/elisefaber

bookbub.com/profile/elise-faber

instagram.com/elisefaber

goodreads.com/elisefaber

pinterest.com/elisefaberwrite